A QUESTION OF POSSESSION a novel

John Fons

1/17/12

Gretchen & D.J.,
I hope you enjoy reading this
book as much as I enjoyed
writing it!

John

A Question of Possession is a work of historical fiction. Apart from the well-known actual people, events, and locales that figure in the story, all names, characters, places, and incidents are the products of the author's imagination or are used fictitiously. Any resemblance to real events or locales, or to persons - living or dead, is entirely coincidental.

Copyright 2011 by John Fons

All rights reserved.

LIBRARY OF CONGRESS CATALOGING-IN-PUBLICATION DATA

Fons, John

A Question of Possession / John Fons

1. Nazi Germany 2. Luftwaffe aircraft 3. Final Solution 4. Demonic Possession

2011963368

ISBN-13: 978-1468123104 (CreateSpace assigned)
ISBN-10: 1468123106

Book Design by Laura Granberry
Front cover photograph © John Fons
Author photograph © Michael Granberry

For Peter, Phyllis and Kathryn

CHAPTER 1

WHEN HE FIRST LEARNED OF HIS SON JACK'S extraordinary predicament – that he was possibly possessed by the spirit of a dead German officer: *Can such a thing really happen?* – Paul Johanson foresaw – just like anyone with an ounce of common sense could foresee – that things might turn out like this; that Jack might wind up in serious trouble. What Paul didn't know, and what he couldn't have possibly known at the time, was that Jack was already in serious trouble.

Paul had chosen not to share this information, the information that had led to his feeling of foreboding, with his wife, Nell. *Things being the way they are between us, telling Nell anything about Jack – especially revealing Jack's incredible condition – would surely lead to conflict and rancor. Besides, would Nell even believe me?*

It was a Saturday afternoon in September, 1952; and both Paul and Nell were at home. Paul had not consciously heard the telephone ringing – it sitting on the newel-post at the foot of the front stairs in the front hall, and him sitting on the back porch in a faux-rattan folding chair. Actually, it was the fact that the telephone had stopped ringing that had caught Paul's attention – like when the crickets stop chirping; that absence of noise that snaps you awake in the middle of a summer's night.

Whoever had been calling on the telephone did not concern Paul. His only concern was: *What has taken Nell so long to answer the telephone?* In fact, Nell had been reading a book in her upstairs bedroom with the door closed; just another one of her efforts to provide separation, to avoid having to engage in conversation with Paul which, more often than not, turned into bitter, acrimonious arguments – even over the most trivial of matters.

Upon hearing the ringing stop, and finally recognizing Nell's sweet voice reserved for talking with outsiders, Paul had been torn between listening to Nell's end of the conversation – probably with one of her D.A.R. old ladies – or to continue listening to the last few innings of a meaningless baseball game on the radio. The tone of Nell's voice – clearly less cheerful than the voice she would have used with someone she was trying to impress – captured Paul's attention; although he really didn't learn much from hearing Nell's terse replies to whoever it was on the other end of the telephone call.

Within moments after Paul heard Nell's business-like "Goodbye," she had appeared in the open kitchen door-way, her jaw set firmly, her eyes narrowed to slits; she was clearly upset. *What have I done now?* Before Paul could even begin to think about what he might have done to deserve such an angry gaze, Nell began relaying the contents of the telephone call.

"Do you have any idea what my bitch of a sister has done now?"

Paul instinctively knew that Nell was referring to her sister Rita – short for Henrietta. The two sisters had had a serious falling out several years ago; with Nell convinced that she was the innocent injured party. The crux of the spat, as Paul best remembered, was how Rita had criticized Nell on how she was raising her three sons. In reality, the animosity between the two sisters went much deeper, had a longer history, back to unresolved jealousy and rivalry. This animosity reached its culmination when their son, Jack, chose to live with his Aunt Rita. Nell's anger was directed primarily at Rita – "for stealing my boy Jack" – and then at Jack for his "disloyalty;" but also at Paul – for supporting, "indeed, for promoting" Jack's decision, and Rita's "theft." Nell had chosen to overlook the fact that it was her rejection of Jack – especially after the tragic accident – that had prompted Jack to choose to live with his Aunt Rita.

"No," replied Paul – for the moment relieved that it was not his head that was on the chopping block. "What has Rita done now?"

"That was the lady who runs the nursing home…informing me

that Rita has stopped coming to see Mother…has failed to pay the bill for August…and unless we pay the over-due amounts, and make new arrangements for future payments, they want us to take my mother out of their place. Rita didn't want to care for her, so why should I have to take care of that senile old lady?"

"Haven't they contacted Rita about it?" inquired Paul innocently.

"Of course they did…Why else do you think they've now called me," Nell retorted impatiently. "They said they've sent reminders by mail…that were never responded to…and they've tried to call Rita on the phone for days with no answer. Now they've been told by the phone company that the line to Fairways has been disconnected. It's just like the double-dealing bitch…she promises to do something… and then she fails to perform as promised…leaving me to pick up the pieces…and she's the one who has all of the money…while I have to scrape by."

"Now, Nell," interjected Paul, hoping to blunt Nell's growing anger, "aren't you being a little harsh…a little too quick to judgment when we don't yet know all of the facts?"

"That's right, take her side…just as you always have…I know enough right now to see that she is trying to stick me with Doddy."

"We don't know that for sure…That makes no sense…I think that there might be a more serious explanation…Maybe there has been a problem."

"What kind of a problem?"

"I don't have any idea what it might be," Paul lied. *It must have something to do with Jack, and with what Rita told me last fall in Kansas City; about Jack harboring the spirit of a dead German officer who could take control of Jack's body; and that she was now fearful that Jack might become a threat to her. But I'm certainly not going to tell Nell about that… Not now.*

"Well, right now, I'm more concerned about what we are going to do about Doddy…Well, don't just sit there Paul. We need to get going right now if we hope to get to the nursing home this afternoon… Mother must be frantic!"

"But, Nell…It's already after two o'clock…And it's a two-hour drive to Fulton…We've got to pack and lock up…And it will take me some time just to track down Mrs. Northwick, and get her permission to use the Ford. By that time it'll be too late today to get anything done at the nursing home today; and then we'll need to drive on to Fairways to see what might have happened to Jack and Rita."

"Utter nonsense! If we leave now we can be back this evening… And Mrs. Northwick won't even be the wiser that we used the company car…And I have no intention of going anywhere near Fairways…I could care less about those two…the worthless, lying bitch…that traitorous whelp."

Having observed where his "driving on to Fairways" suggestion had gotten him, Paul pursued a different tack: "I'd really feel better about going on this trip if I had Mrs. Northwick's permission to use the Ford…If anything should happen…"

"Okay, okay. Go ahead and call your boss…*you spineless, weak sister*… If you had done what I told you to do years ago, and demanded a raise from that old skin-flint, we could afford a car of our own again." Seeing the pained look on Paul's otherwise quite handsome face — caused by her last few words – Nell offered a small concession to her hen-pecked husband. "We'll go tomorrow morning…regardless of whether you have her permission…If anything happens, you'll just have to tell her it was an emergency, and that you had tried to call her."

DURING THIER SUNDAY morning's two-hour drive in the company Ford sedan to the nursing home in Fulton, a small college-town in central Missouri, silence prevailed; Paul drove and Nell fingered the rosary beads, her lips moving as she silently recited the Hail Marys.

There were several times when Paul was tempted to breach the subject of Fairways and, more to the point, what he knew about Jack, about his possession, and about Rita's concerns for her safety. He knew he had to tell her something, sometime, but he just couldn't come up with a way of saying what needed to be said without incurring Nell's wrath, without causing Nell to overreact; to cut off any further discussion, to forever forbid Paul from pursuing efforts to find and, if necessary, to save Jack and Rita.

As Paul had expected, Doddy was not frantic, not a bit; she was more rambling than lucid, barely able to understand even the simplest directions, clearly not able to recognize even her own daughter. Contrary to Nell's assertions that the nursing home was ready to throw the old lady out the front door, the manager and staff were most solicitous and flexible in setting up arrangements for Doddy's continued care; plans that would not break the Johanson's already slim budget. Once a plan was settled on, and Nell wrote the check for a portion of the back-due amount, and another for future care, they said their thanks and goodbyes; it was pointless to stay any longer with the non-responsive, comatose Doddy.

Returning to the company Ford sedan in the nursing home's parking lot, Paul recognized that it was "do or die," "now or never" time. Screwing up his courage, he said to Nell, who was standing on the other side of the sedan, extracting her sunglasses from her purse, "I really think we need to go on to Fairways…to check things out. I have a really bad feeling about what might have happened…that Jack and Rita are in serious danger."

"What makes you think I give a damn about what has happened, or might be happening to them? And what do you know about them that you haven't been telling me?"

Again screwing up his courage, Paul said, "Do remember my bowling trip to Kansas City last fall? Well, Jack and Rita were also in Kansas City that same weekend visiting with the Kaufman's, and I had lunch with Jack and Rita."

"So I suppose you just happened to run into them…And were the Jews – the Kaufman's – with them?"

Sensing that his attempt to persuade Nell to travel on to Fairways was about to go in the wrong direction, Paul plowed ahead with what he hoped would be his best selling point: "Rita had told me that she had uncontroverted evidence that Jack was sharing his body with the spirit of a German officer who was killed in '45, at the end of the War…that this spirit could take control of Jack's body…and that she had reasons to believe that this spirit might try to harm her in his efforts to return to Germany. She wanted me to speak with Jack...to impress upon him why he needed to be careful not to give the spirit any opportunity to take control...or to have access to any weapon or implement which he could use to overpower Rita."

"So you believed the bitch? You know that Rita actually believes that Jack might be crazy...Why else would she have taken him to that Menninger's mental clinic in Kansas...and had him seen by that Jew shrink...You know the guy who wrote that awful report...saying all those awful things about me...and you, too."

"Yes, I do... I also believe that Jack is possessed by this German guy. Look, I know how you feel about Rita and Jack, but I just think that it would be a grave mistake...something that we will regret for the rest of our lives...if we don't go to Fairways...and to not at least have explored what might have happened to Jack and Rita."

"If you think it is so important...if your conscience is bothering you...if it is because you love these two people so much...then go ahead...drive on to Fairways...But don't expect me to lift a finger to help you any further than this."

"Thank you...You won't regret doing this."

'FAIRWAYS', WHICH WAS the name of the farm located a short distance from the town of Greenville – basically a farming community which also had brick manufacturing plants that used a particular type of clay that was found and mined in the area. The countryside around Fairways consisted of rolling hills, with fields and pasture-lands, dotted with dense woods. The main-house which was set at the top of a hill, surrounded by towering elm trees, overlooked the fields, pastures, barns and other out-buildings situated on both sides of the graveled country road that came from town and led to other farms farther away from town.

Arriving at Fairways, Paul and Nell were immediately struck by the sight of the place. The usually immaculately kept fields, pastures and lawns surrounding the beautiful house were uncut, overgrown with weeds. Parking the company Ford sedan on the graveled spot in back of the house, they could see no sign of life, even the nearby chicken house was quiet, apparently empty; although groups of Hereford cattle could be seen grazing in the pastures some distance from the house.

Attempting to gain entrance to the house, Paul found that the doors – back, front and side – were locked. Peering in through accessible first-floor windows, Paul could see that the house had an unlived-in appearance. Checking the garage, hoping to find a spare house-key hanging on a hook somewhere, Paul noted that the spot usually occupied by Rita's big wood-sided Ford station wagon was empty; and he found no key.

Returning to the sedan, where Nell was leaning against a fender – her faced tilted up to catch the mid-day sun – Paul, with a perplexed look on his face, shrugged his shoulders, and said, "It's clear that no one is here…and from the little I could see through the windows, no one has been here for a while. None of this makes any sense to me… Its time that Jack should be back in school…They can't still be away on vacation, if that's where they might have gone to begin with."

"Well," said Nell, without even looking towards Paul, "did you see any signs of a struggle…anything to suggest that it was a hasty departure?"

"No…But that doesn't mean that everything is all right. I think we need to get into the house."

"And how are you planning to do that? Break a window?" inquired Nell sarcastically.

Ignoring her remark, Paul said, "Not knowing what we might find if we did get into the house, I'd prefer to have the police here when that happens."

"You chicken-shit…Besides, you aren't going to find anything suspicious in this locked-up house…Do really expect to find Jack and Rita in an upstairs bedroom…locked together in some death struggle? Or maybe Rita alone, her throat slashed…with the killer – presumably the dead German in Jack's body – having fled the scene…locking the doors behind him. And how did he get away…in the Ford station wagon? Jack is only thirteen…he can't even drive. And even if he could drive, he'd stick out like a sore-thumb trying to drive that big station wagon…And I can just see the gas station attendant's reaction when Jack tries to buy gas…And where would he go? No, if you find anything of importance in that house, I'll eat my…your…hat."

"You may be right about everything you've just pointed out," said Paul sheepishly, "but I am just convinced that there is something in this house that we are meant to find."

"I can't wait to see you try to convince the police to help you break into the house based on your premonitions…On what you've told me about a potentially possessed teenager and a dead German's spirit, you'll be lucky that they don't lock you up, sending you off for a psychiatric evaluation."

"Despite what you say, I'm going for the police. Are you coming with me?" Paul said with uncharacteristic confidence. *You can only push me so far, Nell…On this one I'm sure I've got it right.*

AT THE ADAMS county sheriff's office – located in Greenville, across the street from the courthouse square – Paul, carefully choosing his words and statements, explaining the circumstances of how they learned about Rita Kaufman's long absence from the farm, it's unkempt appearance, and the fact of Jack's absence from school, convinced the reluctant deputy to accompany him and Nell – who had come along after all, but said nothing – back to Fairways.

Within fifteen minutes of his arrival at Fairways, the deputy saw enough to agree that an examination of the house and its environs was warranted. Using a pick, the deputy was able to unlock and open the back-door. Upon entering the kitchen, the trio was immediately greeted with the strong, musty, stale odor of a closed-up house. Except for the unpleasant odor; which was traced to rotten produce in the kitchen pantry, plus the thin layer of dust covering any of the highly-polished flat surfaces, nothing else appeared out of the ordinary on the first-floor. A quick trip to the second-floor – where all of the bedrooms were located – revealed only minor clues that the inhabitants had left in a hurry; closets in disarray, open dresser drawers, clothing piled on the floor, toiletries cluttering the bathroom sink.

His policeman's interest now sufficiently aroused, the deputy commented that he thought that a systematic examination of the basement and of the out-buildings would be in order. As the deputy and Paul exited house to begin their further explorations, Paul expressed his feeling of vindication to Nell by giving her a wink and a tip of an imaginary hat – to which she responded by thumbing her nose at him.

While Paul and the deputy combed around outside, Nell took the opportunity to do some additional snooping of her own. *Maybe Paul's conviction that something bad has happened, and that we'll find some clues in the house, is correct after all.*

Once she had satisfied her curiosity on the first-floor – by opening drawers, looking through papers on the desk in the den, Nell mounted the front-hall stairs to the second-floor, headed directly towards Jack's room. She began with Jack's desk, where she found some recent brochures for western resorts and dude-ranches in the Rockies; suggesting a leisurely planned vacation, not a hasty, spur-of-the-moment exodus. *If, indeed, they had taken a trip out west, surely they would have returned by now; Jack would have been back in school. Besides, that wouldn't explain the unpaid bills, the cancelled utilities. And what about the unkempt appearance of Fairways...Rita would never let that happen. My God! I'm beginning to think like Paul.*

Now sufficiently convinced that something might be amiss, Nell – always intrigued by a good mystery story – riffled through the papers on Jack's desk and in its drawers. As she delved deeper into Jack's belongings, into the nooks and crannies adjoining his desk, and on the shelves in his closet, Nell stumbled upon dozens of cheap 'Big Chief' lined-writing tablets – the kind in which school-children did their lessons, practiced hand-writing. These tablets were piled helter-skelter, and in no apparent order; yet Nell was drawn to them. Thumbing through a few of the tablets, Nell quickly realized that they were filled with writings – mostly in pencil – the kind that one would find in a diary or a journal. But what intrigued her most was the fact that the tablets were not written all in the same hand, or all in the same style. It was as if two different persons had done the writing. *So, does this indicate that Jack is really possessed by the spirit of a dead German, or is*

Jack just suffering from a split personality? In any case, these are not ma-terials that I want Paul or the police know about – at least not until I have a chance to go through them. I suspect that if Jack is the author, then he will say some terrible things about me. I don't have time to read them here. I'll need to take them with me.

Loading all of the 'Big Chief' tablets that her search had revealed into an empty book-bag she found hanging on the back of Jack's desk chair, Nell gave the bedroom another look-around and, spotting noth-ing further of interest, returned downstairs. Making sure that Paul and the deputy were nowhere to be seen, Nell quickly exited the house – carrying the book-bag in a way that it would not attract attention – and dashed to the rear of the Ford sedan; where she opened the trunk, slipping the book-bag into the trunk, hopefully out of view.

When Paul and the deputy returned to the house, they found Nell sitting on the back-porch steps, working on her cuticles. "Did you two find anything of interest on your hunt," Nell asked smugly.

"Not really," Paul said. "Only further evidence that Rita and Jack left in a hurry…there are a lot of things in the barn that needed to be attended to that were left open, giving the good, and the bad, animals access to things they shouldn't have access to. Also, the lack of elec-tricity has left the cattle, the horses without well water."

"And I can't report that we found any signs of foul-play," the dep-uty chimed in.

"How about you," Paul asked, his question directed at Nell. "Or did you just spend your time doing your nails."

"Oh," replied Nell, "I did look around a bit, but I didn't find any-thing of interest." *You think you're so smart Paul. But you have outsmart-ed yourself. You knew things about Rita and Jack that you didn't see fit to share with me. Well, if you can hold back on me Paul, I am certainly not going to share what I found with you; even if what I have found holds the key to what has happened to Rita and Jack; even if it were to provide valu-able information possibly leading to their rescue.*

"Then let's get going," said Paul. "We have a two-hour trip ahead of us after we stop by the Sheriff's office to file a Missing Persons Re-port."

"That's my recommendation…although I can't guarantee it will produce any results…we really don't have any good leads right now…But it wouldn't hurt to get it on file," the Deputy said. "And it shouldn't take too long to fill out the report."

THE STAY AT the sheriff's office, filling out the Missing Persons Report was a lengthy process, taking much longer than the Deputy had indicated he thought it would take. When Paul and Nell arrived at the Sheriff's office, Nell made a great show of putting her purse in the trunk – for security purposes, of course – and having Paul lock the trunk; where it would stay until the company Ford sedan was parked in the garage behind the house in Saint Louis.

"We'll need some information about the folks you say are missing," stated the deputy as he inserted the missing persons form into his typewriter.

"Yes, of course," said Nell. "There is my son, Jack Johanson, and my sister, Rita…that's short for Henrietta…Kaufman."

"That's not quite correct," interjected Paul. "Remember, Nell, Jack is now Rita's son…His name now is Jack Kaufman…He was officially adopted by Rita."

"That's just a legal technicality…I should have never agreed with you to let that happen. In retrospect, what a horrible mistake that was," complained a sullen Nell.

"Hey, folks…I don't care what you two think…What's the kid's name?" the deputy stated, clearly irritated.

"Okay," Nell said. "There's the two of them…Rita Kaufman…and the boy, Jack Kaufman."

"Anyone else," asked the deputy.

"No." said Nell.

"I think there was someone else," Paul said somewhat reluctantly.

"What…What else haven't you told me?" Nell demanded. "This withholding of information from me is becoming quite tiresome"

"Well, I'm not really sure if she was still living with Rita and Jack… She was a displaced person…a Jewish refugee who Rita had sponsored. Her first name is Hannah...but I don't know her last name...I only met her once...just briefly in Kansas City."

"That ain't much help, Mister," groused the deputy. "You got any pictures...Any descriptions you can give me...For all of them, I mean?"

"No, but there may be some pictures of them back at Fairways," offered Paul.

And so it went on for the next twenty-minutes: Like two ancient fencing foes engaged in a grudge-match – Lunge, thrust, parry; lunge, thrust, parry.

THE SKY WAS getting dark by the time Paul and Nell departed the Adams County Sheriff's office in Greenville. Paul wanted to stop and get something to eat on the road – at one of the eateries the Ford sedan passed as they went through the many small towns en route to Saint Louis – but Nell demurred, even though neither of them had had anything to eat since an early breakfast. "We can eat at home... I'm sure that you can find something in the refrigerator to cook up for our dinner," proclaimed the ever-economizing Nell.

At home, while Paul puttered about in the kitchen preparing their make-shift dinner, Nell went back out to the garage, to the company Ford sedan, to "retrieve my purse," she explained when demanding the key to the trunk from Paul. But, as was her real purpose, she also retrieved the book-bag filled with the tantalizing tablets filled with mysterious writings. Entering the back door, quickly moving through the kitchen while Paul had his back turned working at the stove, Nell passed into the front hallway and up the front stairs to her bedroom; hopefully without attracting Paul's attention or curiosity.

"What was that all about," Paul asked when Nell returned downstairs to the kitchen.

"What do you mean," Nell responded, flashing Paul an innocent 'who, me?' look.

"Oh," replied Paul, "you know...your mad dash out and in the back door, then rushing through the kitchen and straight upstairs...like the devil was after you. Are you hiding something from me?"

"Of course not…What would make you say that?"

"Because you've never, in your life, gone out to the garage in the dark to get anything out of the trunk of a car…That's what you always have me do for you."

"I know…but you were busy…and I was afraid that if I didn't get my purse now…while I was thinking about it…I'd forget where I had put it…and would be scrambling around tomorrow morning trying to find it before I set out for work."

I'll bet she found something at Fairways, and she is hiding it from me… But I'll just wait a bit to see what she does with it.

OVER THE NEXT several evenings – after returning home from work and hurriedly eating the dinner prepared by Paul – Nell sifted through the writing tablets, trying to discern some semblance of order. The process was complicated because none of the tablets was dated; although she soon was able to identify, by the different handwriting, which writings were apparently authored by Jack, and which were apparently authored by another person – the real or imagined German named 'Fritz' – all of which gave her some idea of time-frames. The topics addressed in the writings also differed, so that was also of some help in organizing them into coherent, cohesive groupings. As Nell scanned through the tablets, she quickly came to the conclusion that the writings were beyond the ordinary; they were truly extraordinary – covering topics and matters of scope and depth far beyond the capabilities of a mere boy.

Just thinking about what these writings might contain, just contemplating the ramifications of what all this might mean, gave Nell a shiver of fright. *If these writings are true; if they are not the manifestations of a sick mind – then Jack may indeed be possessed by an evil spirit; he may be a lost soul!* With these thoughts, these concerns, these trepidations, in the forefront of her mind, Nell picked up the first 'Big Chief' tablet – simply labeled 'JACK' at the bottom of the red front-cover bearing the profile of the solemn Indian Chief – made the sign of the cross, folded over the cover, and began to read:

CHAPTER 2

BIG CHIEF TABLET ONE | JACK

My name is Jack. I am writing down what happened to me after Fritz, the spirit of the dead German soldier, came into my life, because that event made me different from everyone else. Maybe someday people will want to know why I was different, and I may need what I am now writing to help me remember and explain why. I have also asked Fritz to write down stuff about his life before he died; and about his time living with me as a spirit.

I don't remember many of the events and details of the day Fritz entered my body. Up until the blow to my head, it was probably like any other day. My Dad – Paul Johanson – probably woke me up that morning by yelling up from the kitchen either "Get up, Jack!" or maybe it was "Daylight in the swamp boys," something he often heard as a teenage lumberjack in Wisconsin's "north woods."

My older brother, David would already have left the double bed which he and I were then sharing; probably standing outside our only bathroom banging on the door yelling at my other brother, Chris to let him in. They were both in high school. Chris, being the oldest brother – close to 16 years old – had certain privileges not extended to David and me; like spending inordinate amounts of time doing whatever teenage boys do in the bathroom. I had to wait until they had both finished with the bathroom before I got my turn. If I couldn't hold my pee until then I was forced to race down two flights of stairs, to use the ancient toilet in our dark, smelly basement.

Being the nuisance "kid brother," life was never pleasant, and often it was downright risky; especially since both of my parents worked all day, and my older brothers hated babysitting me after school. I feared the times when both my brothers were at home, and I was alone with them. They would often tease me and torment me unmercifully – pining me down on my back, with their bony knees digging into my arms, giving me fifty "gill-burgers." Gill-burgers were one of my more painful torments, consisting of hitting my chest with fists with the middle knuckle extended.

Whenever I tried escaping these torments by locking myself in the bathroom, my sadistic brothers would light cigarettes, blowing the smoke under the door saying it was poisoned gas or pretending that the house was on fire. They knew that I could not escape by climbing out the second-floor bathroom window, and that I would ultimately unlock the door; once again falling for their ruse, listening in tears to their whoops of laughter. On other occasions I would try to escape my brothers' torments by crawling under a bed to get away from them; only to be driven out by threats of being hit with the leather belts they flicked at me while I cowered under the bed.

Once Chris and David even locked me in the kitchen pantry; where I remained imprisoned for hours. When they tried to release me from imprisonment, the door key broke off in the lock. After much cursing and failed efforts to unlock the door by other means, the lock was bypassed by pulling the pins out of the hinges and prying the door open from the hinged side. I was freed just moments before my parents got home; but I didn't dare tell my parents of this escapade.

Another time my brothers and their friends were playing "track and field" games in a vacant lot in another part of our neighborhood. I was designated as the "water boy" and sent off to fill a gallon glass jug from a water faucet on the outside of an adjacent apartment building. Being only four or five years old at the time, even the empty jug was too heavy and awkward for me to carry. When I had turned on the faucet, trying to hold the jug to the spigot, the jug filled with water, quickly becoming too heavy for me to hold on to it. The partially-filled jug shattered on the concrete sidewalk. Instantly, I knew I was in trouble, even though dropping the jug wasn't my fault.

Knowing what fate awaited me back at the "track and field" games, if I returned empty-handed, I ran away, back to our house, hoping to hide from my brothers. It wasn't too long before I heard my brothers coming up the alley to our house, where they called me out. I was petrified with fear, but I came out to them, trying to explain through stifled tears how I dropped the jug of water because it was too heavy for me to hold on to. Ignoring my efforts at explanation, Chris grabbed me, threw me over his shoulder, and started walking back down the alley to where they had been playing.

One of Chris' friends shouted, "Let's ship him to Siberia."

Several others picked up in cry. With the chant ringing in my ears the gang marched down the alley following Chris — with me over his shoulder trying not to cry — to the next cross street where there was a large postal box. At the box — which was equipped to handle large packages — one of the guys pulled down the lid and Chris started shoving me into it.

They were all still chanting, "Send him to Siberia."

At this point I burst into tears, yelling "No! No!"

To the sounds of laughter and shouts of "cry baby," Chris ended my physical torment by letting go of me and walking away from me. I was left there in humiliation and tears, hanging on the side of the mailbox. After I was sure they were out of sight, I scrambled down from the mailbox and ran home. My brothers and their friends kept teasing me about the 'Siberia' episode for weeks. Again, I was too scared to ever tell my parents about it, or to complain to them about how my brothers were treating me when they had me alone.

CHRIS WAS EXTREMELY bright and talented. Although he did well at school academically, he was often in trouble for break- ing the rules. He used to brag to David about his "stink-bombs" in chemistry class, or his Bunsen burner "flame thrower" in his high-school physics class. He was also always collecting things that didn't belong to him. Some things he claimed he "rescued," and some things he just stole. Much of his ill-gotten treasure he kept in his bedroom; where I loved going through his stuff when he wasn't around: There were arrow-heads, stone axes, a carbide miner's lantern, an army rifle clip with real bullets, different-style knives, and all types of other dangerous things. A lot of this stuff — which he didn't want our parents to see — he kept hidden in a bunker he excavated in a nearby vacant lot which he had under constant scrutiny; it could be seen from the upstairs back-porch of our house. He claimed that among his 'spoils' hidden in the lot was a dummy bomb used for bombing practice. I often spent time on the porch watching Chris and his friends playing in the vacant lot, hoping to see this "bomb."

David was less of a "collector" of stuff than Chris was. He was more interested in collecting friends — especially girl friends — than Chris was. David also ran with a different bunch of buddies, having a distinctly more conventional approach to life than my curious older brother. As a result, David just wasn't as interesting to me as Chris was. There wasn't any stuff of his that tempted me to go through his things as I did Chris' stuff — as easy as it would have been to do since David and I shared the same bedroom, as well as the same old four-poster double bed that had once been my parent's bed. They were now sleeping in twin beds, beds which David thought we should be sleeping in. When David complained to Chris about his having to sleep with me, Chris explained that our folks had no other choice — "They don't need another surprise." I didn't know at the time that he was referring to me; that I was the "surprise."

BY THE TIME I got up on that fateful day, Mom would have left for work; traveling by street car to a clerical job in a savings and loan company. After my brothers had gone out the back door to catch a street car headed in the opposite direction — headed for high school, I would have dressed myself; wearing the usual hand-me-down short pants and a used pull-over type shirt.

(Photos of me taken at the time — make me look like a war orphan.) When I finally came downstairs, Dad would still have been in the kitchen reading the morning paper; drinking a cup of coffee at the oilcloth covered kitchen table.

Waiting for me on the kitchen stove pilot-light would have been a bowl of almost room- temperature cereal; either oatmeal, Cream of Wheat or Ralston. In silence, Dad would have handed me the paper's funny pages, and then watched me struggle with eating the lumpy, cement-like cereal. When I finished eating what I could of the cereal, he would have put the bowl in the sink together with his empty coffee cup, washing them in cold water and putting them on the side to dry. He and I would have left the house at the same time, but headed in different directions; Dad driving the company car to the store at which he worked as the office manager, and I would walk the several blocks to the parish school where I was a first-grader.

I DON'T REMEMBER anything about school that day, but that's not surprising. I didn't particularly like first grade at the parish school. Most of my class-mates were older and bigger than I was, and they had been together since kindergarten. My mother had wanted me to attend kindergarten at the parish school the previous year so she could go to work. I remembered hearing my mother say that I had interfered with her being able to go back to work. Despite her desire and powers of persuasion, the principal and the pastor would not accept me for kindergarten because they said I was too young — less than five years old; so I went to kindergarten at the neighborhood public school instead. When I showed up for first grade at the parish school the following school-year, the kindergarten teacher came into the classroom and took me to her kindergarten classroom of five-year olds. I don't know what my mother did or said that evening when she charged into the priests' house to change the Monsignor's mind, but I was allowed to stay in first grade. I would have preferred to have stayed in kindergarten, but my preferences were never considered; it was what Mom wanted that counted.

It was made clear to me by the Mother Superior – who ran the parish school – and the nun – who was in charge of first-grade – that I was unwelcomed and unwanted, just like at home.

It was a very lonely time for me. Even though there were boys in first-grade that lived in my neighborhood who played together, I was not often invited to play with them. As a result, after school I was left to play alone at home, avoiding – as best I could - my big brothers who were supposed to be looking after me; hiding out in my own world of make-believe and 'let's pretend', using a hand-full of hand-me-down lead soldiers, a dime-store army tank, a cannon with a spring plunger that could shoot stuff out of its barrel, a die-cast P40 fighter aircraft, and my favorite toy – a highly-detailed, plastic model of the twin-tailed P38 fighter aircraft.

I DO REMEMBER that it was a day in early May, 1945, when I suffered the life-threatening, life-changing blow to my head. Chris and David were charged with my care that afternoon, taking me to the vacant lot to play at Chris' fort with their friends. I vaguely recall seeing two boys sitting on a large metal projectile – shaped like a bomb – attached to a long rope which hung from a limb of a very tall tree. I had been playing my own game of 'cowboys and Indians' among the huts that Chris and his friends had built out of old Christmas trees. When I came out of one hut – chasing one of my pretend Indians – running towards one of the other huts, I caught a glimpse of something large out of the corner of my right eye coming straight towards my head.

The next thing I remembered seeing was our living room ceiling spinning around above me. I was lying on the sofa on my back. I had no idea how long I had been there, how I got there, of what had happened, or why I was lying there – except that I had a terrible headache. I could feel a lump on the right side of my head, and I felt that my pants were wet. I shut my eyes to help stop the room from spinning. How long they were shut I don't know, but my next recollection is of opening my eyes, seeing a double-vision version of Dad standing over me with two figures — who might have been my brothers — standing behind him. It could have been minutes or it could have been hours later. It was still daylight. I heard voices and saw faces but I couldn't see the faces clearly or understand what the voices were saying.

Several more hours passed before I became aware of my surroundings, finding myself sitting in a chair in the kitchen. The radio — located on the radiator next to where I was sitting — was playing and a voice was saying, "The Germans have surrendered." I don't know whether it was the announcement or the room spinning, but I start throwing up on the kitchen floor. After that everything went blank again. Whether I woke up again that evening, or even if I was well enough to attend school the next day, was beyond my recollection. I believe I was seen by our family doctor the next afternoon, because that is what my mother told me; but I was never told by anyone what injuries I may have received — except for "a nasty bump on the head!" I didn't know it at the time, but that "nasty bump on the head" had changed my life forever!

IT WAS MONTHS, perhaps years, before the events leading up to that "nasty bump on the head" were explained to me. My brothers were reluctant to talk about what happened to me that afternoon. All they would ever tell me about the accident is that the "bomb" contraption upon which two of my brothers' friends were riding had hit me in the head as it was moving quickly through the air. I was knocked up into the air, landing on the ground several feet away from where I had been running when the "bomb" struck me. No one remembered seeing me in the path of the rope swing before it happened. I was left lying on the ground for perhaps a half-hour, lying motionless as if I was dead.

Chris told me that he, David, and their friends debated for some time on what to do with me. Eventually, Chris said he thought he detected me breathing, whereupon he picked me up and carried me home. When he and David got me home, they put me on the sofa in the living room, and called Dad at work.

During the time they waited for Dad to get home I remained un-conscious, motionless. Except for the time when I was sitting on a chair in the kitchen, throwing up, they thought I had remained unconscious until the next morning.

FOR THE NEXT several years, life around me went on, but not as usual. When Chris went away to college, David moved into his own room, and I got the big four-poster double bed to myself. David became a bigger social-butterfly — staying after school for cheerleader or theatre practice — and I became a latch-key kid with the house all to myself, at least until my parents came home from work. I loved the peace and quiet of being alone in the house after school; and I came to dread the evenings and week-ends when I had to deal with my parents' constant bickering and fighting, and my mother's unpredictable, but always difficult, moods. I tried to avoid Mom if I could. Let's be clear, I never called my mother Mom, or even Mommy to her face; I called her 'Mumby', because as a small boy, just learning to talk, I could only say 'Mumby'. Unfortunately, Mom thought that my calling her 'Mumby' was 'cute'; insisting that I call her 'Mumby' when addressing her. So if I inadvertently use 'Mumby'; you'll know of whom I am speaking, and why.

As capable as my brothers had been in making my life a living hell, they were not nearly as successful as Mom became. Even the physical abuse imposed on me by Chris and David was noth-ing compared to the physical and mental abuse Mom heaped on me on a regular basis. Besides the screaming and the whippings, it was her rejection of me that made my life miserable. I never re-member my mother showing me any love and affection, even as a small boy. Dad witnessed or at least knew about these abuses, but I never saw or heard him intercede on my behalf, and if he did, his efforts were ineffective. At least he hugged and kissed me and was generally kind and gentle towards me when Mom wasn't around.

I WANTED TO be liked and accepted by my classmates, but I had no skills in knowing how to make that happen. My athletic skills were also pathetic; I did not like to wrestle or engage in physical contact with the other boys because I was afraid of getting hurt. When teams were picked, I was usually the last to be picked, with good reason; I was skinny, weak, uncoordinated, and lacked any self confidence.

These handicaps also made me the perfect target for the school-yard bully. The bully's name was Bobby Malone. He was new to the school, and was an older, tougher, stronger boy always looking for a fight. Bobby was also clever; he never picked a fight in the school yard where he could be observed by the nuns who watched us like hawks. Instead, he would pick out his victim — a weak loner like me — and follow him home. Once he knew the prey's route home — living on a side street would be best — he would get to his point of attack and lay in wait. I knew Bobby wanted to beat me up.

In the school yard he told me, "You're a big sissy and I am going to hurt you."

I was scared. For days I avoided my usual way home, even hanging out with other kids who lived nearby on my walk home. This worked for a while, and I thought he had given up trying to fight me. And then one afternoon when I arrived at my house, there he was sitting on my front porch steps just waiting for me.

"Are you ready to fight me sissy? Or are you going to call for your mommy to come protect you?"

I knew there was no one there to protect me. In as strong a voice as I could muster up I said, "No. I don't want to fight you."

"Well fine," he responded, "I'll just wait here until you father gets home and I can tell him what a sissy his little boy is."

At this point I climbed the front steps going around him. I got to the front door and unlocked it. Bobby lunged at me, grabbed my arm and started pushing me into the house.

I screamed, "Let go of me! Get out of my house."

At this moment, my brother David, who was coming in the backdoor from high school, hearing my outcry, ran to the front door. He grabbed Bobby, and pushed him out the door.

"Let go of Jack and get out of here! I'd better not ever see you around here again! If I do I'll break both of your arms!"

Unfazed by David's threats, Bobby sneered, "You're little brother is just a sissy and needs to be taught a lesson!"

"And you're nothing but a bully," said David. "You're just lucky I don't call the police and report you for breaking into our house!"

At this, Bobby stormed down the steps yelling back over his shoulder at me, "I'll get you Jack Johanson, you just wait and see. You won't always have your big brother around to protect you."

I knew he was right. *What am I going to do now?* I thought nervously.

CHAPTER 3

BIG CHIEF TABLET TWO | FRITZ

At Jack's request, I am writing about my life before I died; and what impact I have had on Jack's life by my spirit living in Jack's body. Like Jack, I want to leave a record explaining to those people who might think that I am just a figment of Jack's imagination, that I am the 'real' spirit of a 'real' dead German officer. Unlike Jack, whose body I now share, I did in fact die in early May, 1945, somewhere in Bavaria. By all rights Jack's body should be mine alone. However, through a quirk of fate – or by the hand of God, Jack did not die when he received a death-dealing blow to his head, and his spirit – which was free of his body for just a moment – returned to his body at the very instant that my spirit gained entry into his body. As such, I am dependent entirely on Jack for my earthly existence, including my sight, my hearing, etc. While I continue to have my own thoughts, memories, feelings, etc., I am personally impacted by what Jack experiences and how he feels.

I am a German by birth and by choice. With all my heart and soul I love Germany; wanting nothing more than to spend the rest of my days in Germany. I was quite shocked, disappointed, and angry that I ended up in the body of a six year old American boy, let alone having to share his body. I was not expecting to have another chance on this earth. If I had, I would not want to happen what has happened to me. If I had a choice, I would have requested the sole possession of the body of a recently deceased German fellow of about my own age. Then I would have been able to carry on my life in Germany without major changes – like learning a new language. Even if the deceased German's body was situated with family and friends who were not to my liking, I could have adapted to those surroundings or moved elsewhere. With the turmoil and chaos existing in Germany at the time of my sudden death, it would not have been difficult for me to drift away in my inherited body to a different locale where I wouldn't be recognized.

But here I am stuck in Jack's body. There are many difficulties associated with sharing Jack's body, beyond the fact that he is a young boy. For as long as he remains a young boy there is no certainty that I am ever going to get back to Germany. To begin with, I spoke very little English, and Jack neither spoke nor understands any German. What Jack heard, what he said, and what he read was incomprehensible to me. I have been compelled by my new circumstances to learn English if I am to figure out what I was faced with in terms of what kind of life I had in front of me. Fortunately, Jack's youth has proved to be an advantage – at least insofar as to learning English. While Jack was reasonably proficient in speaking rudimentary English, he was just learning to read and write the language in school, and – by sharing his young body – I became able to comprehend the un-comprehensible English along with him.

FOR SEVERAL YEARS I lived on the periphery of Jack's consciousness; just learning English and observing what was going on in Jack's world. Although I could sense Jack's feelings, they really didn't mean anything to me because I had no reference point as to what drove his feelings. Until I could discern Jack's upbringing I was at a loss ascertaining just how Jack's character might affect my plans. Although I thought of Jack as just a means to an end, it ultimately came down to my own self-preservation. As much as I disliked the situation I found myself in, I needed Jack; and I needed him to be as tough, strong, brave, clever, and capable as I am. Though for this to happen, I had to take a personal interest in finding out everything I could about Jack; assessing what kind of person Jack was or was going to be.

What I discovered about Jack over the next several years – both through observation of his life-style and by exploring his memories – was that I was stuck in the body of a boy who – if significant changes in his development did not take place – was never going to grow up to be a real man. Jack was bright and creative; but he was also lazy, he was a liar, and – above all – he was a coward. It was clear to me, based on my experiences as a commander of fighting men daily facing death, that without some serious changes in Jack's persona – Jack was headed for a very troubled, dreadful life. This is not what I wanted to happen to Jack; for what happens to Jack impacts me. If Jack was to become the well-functioning adult that I needed him to be, then I would have to be the person who would make that happen; because no one else in his family appeared to care about Jack becoming a man.

If Jack was to be the vehicle to get me back to Germany, then Jack must be able to act on his own, and to act in a mature fashion. Only then would Jack be of any use to me in accomplishing my ultimate agenda; solving the mystery of my sudden, strange death – was it murder or was it an accident, and, in any event, who was to blame? There were circumstances and situations during the last days of Germany's collapse about which I needed to find closure. I also had family matters to attend to, including the safety of who was still alive.

How does one help another person to overcome years of incompetent upbringing and low self-esteem?

This was the task with which I immediately found myself confronted. My life experience and self-esteem were one-hundred and eighty degrees different from Jack's. I was blessed with good, loving, supportive parents, a happy home life, positive life situations, and supreme self-confidence.

How do I impart my own experiences to Jack in a way that brings about a life-changing transition in him?

These were my thoughts as I contemplated on how to rescue Jack. I began to catalogue all of those experiences that I thought made me the person that I think I am, and to determine which of these life experiences could in any way be used to help turn Jack around.

I CAN'T REMEMBER a time during my youth when I was not happy. I have to put it in those terms because I never really thought about whether I was happy or unhappy until now. As I think about it now, I was surrounded by familial love in a way that even if something bad happened to me, like a broken leg skiing, or the death of a favorite horse, or the failure to win a game or a school prize, or even the death of a close relative, I was never forced to bear the pain alone. At no time do I recall having to ask myself whether I was loved. Certainly, I have no recollection of being rejected by my parents or siblings.

Our house was always filled with joy and laughter, and not just at holidays or on birthdays. Each of my brothers and sisters, and there were two of each – with me in the middle, treated each other with respect, even though there were frequent opportunities for disputes and occasional fights, which was to be expected in a large, competitive family like ours. Besides, there was always someone around – a parent or an older sibling – to referee the more contentious problems.

My older sister, Marta – also known as the "Wise one" – could smell a problem developing between us boys: Wolfgang ("Wolfie"); me – Fritz ("Trouble"); and Ernst ("Toad"); and get it resolved quickly. As my nickname implies, I was the one that usually set a problem in motion, and the one who Marta would focus her concerns upon. She seldom had to involve our parents in these matters, as her word was law. If she had to involve either Poppa or Momma the resultant inquiry was likely to take the form of the Spanish Inquisition, with justice being delivered swiftly and painfully to the wrongdoer. Yet, as Christian believers, justice was more often than not tempered with a large dose of mercy.

I remember the time when I was ten, and my brothers and I – together known as "the Troika" – were picking apples in the orchard close to our house. It was a sunny, but cool, fall afternoon; a perfect day for picking the ripe apples hanging in abundance from the trees. Momma had promised us that our cook, Hilda, would bake her wonderful apple strudel for desert if we would gather a bushel of apples. It did not take long for the three of us to collect the requested bushel of apples. However, instead of taking the bushel basket of apples directly to the kitchen, I suggested that we pick some of the un-ripened apples and throw them at whatever happens to catch our fancy, be it animate or inanimate.

"Hey, Wolfie, I bet you can't hit Herr Muenster's rooster," I dared.

Wolfie, who was twelve years old, had a strong arm and was an accurate thrower, and I knew that I would probably lose the bet. But I didn't care about that. What I wanted was for him to kill our neighbor's prized rooster for waking me up too early in the mornings.

"Do it!" urged the Toad, who despised the rooster as much as I did.

The rooster was a beautiful bird with feathers of many colors, combined with bright, piercing eyes, and a large red comb which flopped to the side of his head as he moved about. When on the ground, he would strut about as if he were a great king. But his most notable feature was his crowing, which he exercised on a regular basis, especially early in the morning greeting the rising sun. Poppa told us that the rooster had a noble linage for his breed, and that this particular rooster had earned ribbons at local fairs.

Leaving the bushel basket behind and, as quietly as we could, we commenced our search for the rooster in the hopes of finding him on our property. Herr Muenster kept a ferocious bull on his land, and we were clearly forbidden to go onto his land. The rooster often came onto our property in search of bugs and other edibles. On that particular afternoon we observed him sitting on the fence separating our property from Herr Muenster's, facing away from us. Wolfie scanned the area around us – like a soldier on patrol – to see if anyone was observing us, and seeing no one, he switched the hard, green apple to the hand of his throwing arm, and hurled it at the rooster.

Wolfie's aim was good, but not precise; the apple struck the rooster a glancing blow on his right wing, knocking the bird to the ground on Herr Munster's side, where it began to make loud squawking noises and to run around flapping its good wing. Realizing that the dreadful bird had not suffered a fatal blow, we had to then capture the wounded bird before Herr Munster found it in that condition and began a search for the culprits. But, there was no way that we could capture the wounded bird without climbing the fence and going onto Herr Muenster's land. Who of the Troika was brave enough to enter the forbidden land, face the dangerous bull, grab the wounded, but lively, rooster, and make it back alive?

"It's my fault. I made a bad throw. I will go get the rooster," exclaimed Wolfie.

"No, it was my idea, so I'll go get it. Anyway, even if you had killed the bird, we still would have had to go onto Herr Muenster's property to retrieve it; so I'll do it. Anyway I don't see the bull."

"But the rooster is making so much noise, the bull is sure to notice it soon."

"I'm the smallest, and maybe the bull wouldn't see me if I went over the fence to get the rooster."

"How would you get back in time Toad if the bull did see you?"

"You could tie a rope around me, and if the bull sees me you could pull me back over the fence before he gets here."

"We don't have a rope here, and by the time we got one from the shed, it will be too late. We have to act quickly before the rooster gets too far away, or the bull or Herr Muenster hears all the squawking."

Considering the options, and weighing the risks, I started towards the fence. *Then it occurred to me, What if I can even catch the rooster without being seen by the bull or Herr Munster, and what if I can get back over the fence safely; what are we going to do with the wounded rooster? Even if we can restore it to health; where can we nurse it without being discovered? And if we kill it, Herr Munster will still want to know how it got killed. We are going to be in trouble whatever we do at this point.*

"We need to rethink this!" I said; explaining to my brothers my concerns about trying to retrieve the rooster.

"We should tell Poppa!" Wolfie suggested.

"We don't have any other choice."

We retrieved the bushel basket of apples and made our way back to the house. As we walked along, we talked about who should tell Poppa.

"It was my idea. It is my fault. I'll tell him."

"But I'm the oldest, and I should have known better than to act on one of your hare-brained dares. You really are Trouble."

"That's all the more reason why I should tell Poppa. I will take the blame. Let's just make sure that the Toad doesn't get blamed for any of this."

We entered the big house through the servants' entrance. As soon as the massive oak door opened, we inhaled the wonderful aroma of the meal being prepared by the cook. The heavy bushel basket of sweet-smelling apples slowed our passage into the large kitchen where Hilda was standing at the cook-stove ladling juices from the baking pan over the golden-brown pork roast.

"Where have you been so long getting these apples?" she asked. "I hope I have time to get Louisa to prepare them for me to make the strudel for dinner. Your papa won't be happy if it is not ready."

She placed the pork roast back into the oven, shaking her head, mumbling, "You boys!" We looked at each other, hoping that the Toad would not blurt out anything about our misadventure. There was no need to worry about the Toad talking out of turn, because our older sister Marta came prancing into the kitchen commenting in a sing-song tone,

"I saw what you were doing. Herr Muenster will be angry."

"Hush up, Marta!" I scolded. But it was in vain.

"And Poppa will be very upset. You know how he has warned you not to cause problems with Herr Muenster."

"What have you boys done today?" asked Hilda, who hearing parts of the conversation, quickly became interested in what Marta was saying. "Herr Muenster is not a neighbor you want to be angry with you. He is as dangerous as that bull he keeps."

"We know! We know," yelped Wolfie. "We were already planning to tell Poppa about what happened this evening."

"Please don't you tell him first" I pleaded. "Poppa needs to hear it from us; not you" I said, looking directly at Marta.

I dreaded even thinking about what Poppa would do if he thought we were trying to hide something from him. Poppa was a stickler for honesty and accepting responsibility. He expected it from those who worked for him; and from his family even more so. He placed great stock in the well-earned reputation of his centuries' old family name and title; taking extreme steps to avoid sullying that name and title – Kurt Baron von Bruckner. Nothing would be worse for Poppa than having his own flesh and blood undo all that he had done to achieve and protect his image; especially when Herr Otto Muenster might be the beneficiary of Poppa's downfall.

According to Poppa, Herr Muenster was more than just a neighbor; he was a powerful industrialist who, from humble beginnings, made his fortune during the Great War designing and manufacturing airplane propellers. He would like nothing more than to destroy Poppa who, to Herr Muenster's twisted way of thinking, represented all that was perceived to be evil and burdensome about German aristocracy.

Even though German aristocracy was abolished with the Kaiser's abdication at the end of the Great War, nobles – like a Duke – were permitted to continue using their titles. Poppa used his title only in family related matters; but never in everyday commercial activity, preferring instead to be addressed simply as "Herr von Bruckner." For reasons Poppa had not disclosed, he was convinced that Herr Muenster held a grudge against him, using the "empty title" label as justification for attacking Poppa's integrity. The "empty title" label was being applied by the nouveau rich to those Germans who used, or who were entitled to use, hereditary titles, believing that those titled persons held unearned privileges not available to the nouveau rich.

WE TOOK OUR dinner that evening in the wood-paneled dining room. While not a formal occasion, a meal served in the dining room required that the children be scrubbed and wear their better clothes, and that the servants be dressed in clean uniforms. Poppa, a devout Catholic, offered the blessing to begin the meal. The meal was presented in several courses, with much attention given to detail; what piece of silverware to use, where to place a used fork or spoon, etc. Despite the deference to etiquette and table manners, the banter among us was casual and lighthearted.

As the delicious-looking, delicious-smelling apple strudel was being served, I glanced at Wolfie, slightly nodding my head as a signal to him to broach the subject of Herr Muenster's wounded rooster. Apple strudel was one of Poppa's favorite pastries, certain to put him in a good mood after consuming the enormous slice placed in front of him.

"My God, Ursala, this strudel is outstanding!" exclaimed Poppa. "Please tell cook that she has outdone herself."

"I will," replied Momma. "But you may also want to thank the boys. Cook tells me that they picked apples for her this afternoon."

"Well, of course...Thank you, boys. It was very decent of you to lend a hand to cook so she could give us such a wonderful treat."

"Father," interrupted Wolfie, "Before you praise us too much, I think you better hear what happened this afternoon while we were picking the apples."

"Did you get hurt?" Poppa inquired, glancing at each one of us to see if he could observe any wounds or bruises.

"No," replied Wolfie, "Not us...but Herr Muenster's rooster had a close call when I hit him in the wing with an apple."

A dark cloud of concern quickly passed across Poppa's previously smiling, happy face. After a slight pause, Poppa's face brightened again. "I hope that whatever happened to that rooster, it is serious enough that I won't hear that noisy bird waking me so early in the morning. I truly detest that crowing, strutting rooster. He is waking me too early...every morning."

Poppa's blue eyes darkened with the color rising in his cheeks. "Besides, that damned rooster reminds me too much of his overbearing owner...Herr Muenster."

We all laughed loudly, except Momma. "Poppa" scolded Momma. "I don't think you should be talking about Herr Muenster that way. You will give the children the wrong impression about him."

Giving Momma a firm look, Poppa intoned, "Why don't you take the girls into the library, while I talk to the boys for a moment, or two."

"But Poppa," protested Marta. "I want to hear too. I saw what they did, and I can help you figure out how to punish them!"

"Marta. I'm sure you did, and I am sure you could...but I don't think I need your help. But you can help your mother with getting Maria ready for bed. Thank you."

Marta began to protest, but then having thought better of it said nothing. Tight-lipped and petulant, she stormed out of the dining room following Momma and Maria. We all knew that Marta was making a mistake in trying to get Poppa to change his mind; *I retain the painful memories of failed efforts.*

After Momma and the girls have left the room, Poppa, observing that the doors have been closed, stated, "Momma is correct. We must be careful about how we talk about Herr Otto Munster, or any other person. First, I don't believe in maligning others, regardless of how I might feel about them. Second, in Herr Muenster's case, he is becoming a force to be reckoned with. Finally, we don't need to have Herr Muenster as our enemy." Poppa paused, and then said, "Let me tell you boys why Otto Muenster is more than just a difficult neighbor with an annoying rooster. I, too, would like to see the end of that bird. However, I think we need to find some way to solve this dilemma. Nature could take care of the problem for us. There are plenty of predators out there – like foxes and weasels – who would find a wounded rooster easy prey. But we can't count on that happening." Poppa paused for a while, clearly thinking about what, and how much, to tell us. "We have a serious problem with Herr Muenster, and the solution to this problem needs to have a positive outcome for everybody."

"In 1914" he began, "When Germany was drawn into the conflict between Austria/Hungary and Serbia, I was offered a commission as an officer in the *Wermacht*. But because I had had flight training as a civilian, I was assigned to the fledgling Luftwaffe, first as an instructor, and then as a pilot. By the time I had married your mother, and you – Wolfie – were born, I was a Major, commanding a *Jagdeschwader* (Fighter wing) in France. I also had responsibility for aeronautical development and product procurement for new fighter aircraft.

"One of the innovations being worked on at the time was the mounting of the machine guns on the plane's fuselage right in front of the pilot so that he could better coordinate the aiming and firing of the guns. Previously, the machine gun was mounted on top of the wing above the pilot's head. Critical to placing the machine gun directly in front of the pilot – at his eye-level, was technology allowing the machine guns to fire their bullets through the aircraft's propeller, without shooting off the propeller. Our engineers developed a mechanism that synchronized the bullet firing mechanism with the rotation and speed of the propeller so that the bullets would pass precisely between the spinning propeller blades.

"Otto Muenster was in the business of designing and manufacturing airplane propellers. His design was adequate for the earlier model aircraft, but his design would not maintain the consistent rotation essential to synchronization with the bullets being fired by the machine gun mounted on the newer aircraft. The result was the loss of propellers, the loss of aircraft, the loss of valuable pilots, and the refusal of pilots to fly aircraft equipped with Muenster's propellers. As the officer responsible for product development and procurement, I advised Herr Muenster that the Luftwaffe would no longer purchase his propellers, but would purchase propellers from his competitors whose propellers were operating satisfactorily with the advanced firing system.

"Needless to say, Herr Muenster was furious. He came to see me in France, at the Western Front, where he yelled and screamed at me in his lowbrow German protesting to me that he had a perfectly good design, that I was wrong in blaming the crashes and deaths on his product, and that I was destroying his business. When I persisted in my position, Herr Muenster offered to make it worth my while monetarily if I would withdraw my objections to his product. I quickly and adamantly rejected his dirty bribe, threatening to throw him out of my office. Having failed to bring me over with a monetary bribe, Herr Muenster turned next to intimidation; threatening to go over my head, having me removed from my job if necessary.

"I subsequently learned from my superiors that Otto Muenster made quite a stink about my refusal to withdraw my order not to use any of his propellers with the planes utilizing the advanced firing system. There were even rumors that he offered bribes to members of the General Staff and tried to use political influence with some of the Kaiser's advisors and friends. To their credit, the General Staff stood by my order, especially when their pilots – especially their aces: like Baron von Richthofen, Ernst Udet, and Herman Goering – refused to fly any of the advanced aircraft equipped with a Munster propeller.

"Ultimately, finding no one who would submit to his bullying tactics,

Herr Muenster redesigned his propeller so that it would function with the advanced firing system. Thus, his propeller firm survived, his fortune may well have been expanded, and I made an enemy for life. Herr Muenster used part of his considerable fortune to purchase the estate next to ours. If he could have, he would also use some of his fortune to purchase a title; but with the demise of the monarchy, none were available. Even ancestral titles such as ours are no longer being used much in public. Yet people like Otto Muenster, who wanted the prestige associated with a title, let their envy of those who have titles drive them to distraction. The fact that I was never made a member of the General Staff may have been a blessing in disguise; how much more it would have caused Otto Muenster to dislike me."

Poppa paused in his soliloquy, hoping that the importance of what he had told us would sink in. After looking intently at each of us, he continued, "So now I think you can appreciate the delicacy of your dilemma. I say your dilemma because nothing would please Herr Muenster more than to get you in his clutches for maiming or killing his prized rooster. And…He would take great delight in embarrassing me through shaming you."

"Poppa" I interrupted. "Would it help the situation any if we were to buy a new rooster and take him to Herr Muenster; explain what happened, and throw ourselves on his mercy?"

"That would, of course, be the noble thing to do. It may be difficult to find such a prized rooster quickly. You may want instead to offer to pay Herr Muenster the amount of money necessary to purchase a replacement rooster. But let's wait until the morning to see whether we hear the rooster crow. Who knows, the rooster may not have been hurt as badly as you think, and he could be as good as new in the morning. If we don't hear him crow in the morning, then we can assume that he did not survive the night, and we can put your plan into effect. You had better hope that we hear that damn rooster crow at dawn! Even if he does, I still have to consider an appropriate punishment for your foolish adventure."

IT WAS A long night of tossing and turning waiting for daylight. *Will the damn rooster crow, or not?* I awoke before dawn, and leaving the confines of my bedroom, headed to Wolfie's room.

"Are you awake?" I inquired softly entering Wolfie's bedroom.

"What do you think? Of course I am...I've barely slept a moment all night!"

"Me neither. I've been praying for hours that we hear his crowing."

"That's funny. I've been praying that we don't."

"Why?"

"Well, because even if I broke his wing, he could still survive the night to crow his heart out this morning. And eventually Herr Muenster might find out that his rooster has been damaged and is no longer as valuable as he used to be. We are better off if he is dead! For Poppa's sake, at least we won't have to live with the uncertainty."

"You may be right. I hadn't thought about that. Well, it's in God's hands now. He'll know what's best."

We waited and waited. The sky turned brighter and brighter, but no rooster sounds reached our searching ears. More time passed. The sun finally cleared the trees in the east, but we still heard no sound of crowing. My stomach began to churn. "Oh, God," I silently prayed. *Poor Poppa! Poor us! We are not going to hear the rooster crow. Maybe St. Peter, after having denied Jesus in the Temple courtyard, had prayed for the same thing, but in vain.*

With long faces and little appetite we dressed and made our way downstairs to face Poppa at the sun-streaked breakfast table. He put down his newspaper as Wolfie and I entered the bright kitchen.

"At least I got to sleep until the alarm clock went off this morning. But, what got you two up?" he inquired sarcastically laughing at the sight of our glum faces.

CHAPTER 4

BIG CHIEF TABLET THREE | JACK

I went to bed that evening tossing and turning in the large four-poster bed, thinking about all that could happen to me the next day at school when I had to face the bully, Bobby Malone. Despite David's efforts to assure me that Bobby Malone would not bother me anymore, I imagined all kinds of dreadful, painful, humiliating encounters with him. *If only I could have the courage to face Bobby Malone, and to overcome my own fears.* I never felt so alone and scared.

Sleep finally came, but I don't know when. I woke up to Dad's calling to me to, "Get Up." I was unsure of where I was or what had happened to me. It took me several minutes to realize that I was in my own bed, in my own house, and that I had to go to school. Still, there was something more, something different. It was as if I had been carried back from a different place, a different time. Unlike the terror I had experienced going to sleep, I felt less alone, less vulnerable. I then recalled the very powerful, very vivid dream that I had just awakened from. It was as if I had been experiencing me through someone else's eyes; someone caring, someone wanting to help me deal with my lack of self-confidence.

In my dream I was lost in a deep forest of tall trees and endless undergrowth. I had no idea of how I got there, or for how long I had been there. My clothing consisted of short pants, a collarless shirt and sandals with no socks. Blackberry brambles and poison ivy surrounded me. There was no path, and it was getting darker and turning colder. There were no sounds in the forest of any kind; no birds chirping or squirrels barking, or any animals making scurrying sounds in the trees or on the forest floor. There was just the heavy, sweet forest smell mixed with the pungent smell of my own fear. I was paralyzed with fear. Even though I knew that I had to move on, trying to find a way out of this frightening place, I was unable to find the strength to take even one step in any direction.

Just as I found myself starting to cry I felt something cold and damp nuzzling my leg. I instinctively jumped backwards in fright, falling to the ground landing on my back. When I opened my eyes I was staring into the muzzle of a large grey wolf which had his front paws planted on my chest. But instead of panic, I felt a sense of peace; a sensation that grew more intense as the wolf began licking my face, making a low, soft guttural sound. I had hardly begun to appreciate what was happening to me when the wolf firmly grabbed the front of my shirt in his teeth and began to tug me gently onto my feet. As I became upright, the wolf opened his mouth and speaking in a low, non-threatening tone, said,

"Jack, my name is Fritz, and I will not hurt you. In fact, I am here to rescue you....But in return, I need your help."

In the next instance, Fritz the wolf and I were bathed in bright sunshine standing together at the edge of a rocky cliff looking out at an endless valley far below. It was a serene picture, in contrast to the bleak, frightening forest that I was talking to Fritz in just an instant ago. The valley was a blanket of green with trees and grass, and golden brown fields of grain, marked with the shadows from passing puffy white clouds. The air was clean and fresh, filled with the sounds of the farm animals from far below and the songs of the birds in the nearby trees. We stood together in silence for several minutes, drinking in the pleasant scene below.

"You're a wolf. How can you help me? And how can I help you?"

Sitting back on his haunches and looking up at me, the wolf

said in a very human, English-speaking voice, *"Jack, let me try to help you understand what is happening to you. I am not a wolf. I am the spirit of a dead German pilot sharing your ten year old body with you. This is as difficult for me to grapple with as it for you to understand. I was killed in Germany four years ago, and I entered your body on the day you were hit in the head.*

"During the last four years I have not revealed myself to you because I did not think we were ready to meet each other. You were not old enough to understand what I am now telling you, and I needed time to learn English – so I could talk to you. In many ways, I need you more than you need me. But you do need me to help you grow up and become a man. Only if, and hopefully when, you become a man can you act like a man, and begin to live a full, loving and productive life. And only then will you be able to help me solve my mystery and find release from this earthly prison. Always remember that as things unfold, that I mean you no harm. Indeed, I will do all that I can to help you, including what you can do to face up to Bobby and all the other bullies you will face in life."

"You know about Bobby Malone?" I asked.

"Of course, and I know much more about you; like how you have been mistreated by your mother and brothers, and how you have been abandoned by your otherwise well-intentioned father. I also know how lonely and vulnerable you feel. You need not feel that way. You are a good boy Jack. You just need some loving care and positive experiences which I think I can help you with."

I then found myself standing with Fritz – him now as a grown man in a *Luftwaffe* uniform. We were standing in a sun-drenched barn-yard beside a mud-splattered stone wall. There were sounds of engines nearby, and the voices of men – who are out of my field of vision – speaking a language which sounded to me as being the German I heard in war movies, but it could be another language, like Russian. There were sounds of clattering boxes being stacked on something wooden. Fritz was shouting something at these men. Then I heard the sound of a gunshot coming from behind us. Fritz crumpled to the ground beside me; blood oozing from darkening holes in the back of his uniform jacket. As Fritz laid there on the ground, I heard him mumble something that sounded like "P38." I started to look around to locate who had fired the shots.

At that very instant I was jerked awake hearing my father repeatedly calling my name, "Jack!" "Jack!"

———————

I SPENT MY quiet time over the next several days reliving my dream. *Was it just a dream? Is Fritz for real? Is he in fact sharing my body with me? Will I ever hear from him again, and how, and when? Is my life going to change if Fritz is real? I want Fritz to be real; I want him to be my friend. I sense, but I am not certain, that his presence has to remain a secret, especially from my family. I often wish that I had been adopted by my current parents; that my real parents would reappear and take me away from my current life from Hell. Fritz is my wish-come-true. Is he waiting for a signal from me; and what can it be? Or is all of this just the abnormal imagination of a sick mind? Am I going crazy?*

During my time of wondering about the reality of Fritz, I had several confrontations with Bobby Malone in the school yard. On each occasion I felt a moment of terror; wanting to run away from Bobby. Unlike how I reacted in the past, I now forced down my fear, my urge to flee. When I stood my ground, showing no sign of fear, Bobby did not approach me or issue threats or name-calling. Perhaps Bobby felt threatened by what David had said to him about going to the police or breaking his arms. Or maybe my reaction of defiance was enough to keep him from bullying me. If so, could I view this change as a result of what Fritz observed about me in my dream encounter? In any event, I felt better about myself.

Does Fritz also view my change of attitude with approval?

Despite my every effort to have Fritz contact me again, I did not "hear" from him prior to the end of the school year. I was quite disappointed, fearing that I would not hear from Fritz again, ever.

THEN I WAS off to spend the summer vacation with my Aunt Rita – really Aunt Henrietta, Mom's younger sister – who lived on a farm located several hours from Saint Louis – out in the rural portion of the state. This was an annual summer visit arranged by Mom once she concluded that my brothers could not be depended upon to look after me while she is away working at her job. The first of these summer-long visits took place the month after I received the "nasty bump on the head." I was too young at the time to understand why I was being sent away, or why I was being taken care of by Aunt Rita, a relative I hardly knew.

I had visited the farm, which was named "Fairways," on several occasions, but these visits, with part or all of my family, were just for the weekend. My grandmother, Doddy, also lived there with Aunt Rita, but she was old, losing her memory; spending most of her time walking around the house singing songs, or going "home" to visit her long-dead mother. Mom explained to me that Doddy was not well. She also told me that Aunt Rita was unmarried (another one of my mother's lies) and was not used to taking care of a young boy. I was advised by Mom to behave myself when I was with Aunt Rita; for if not, punishment would surely follow any misbehavior.

With this kind of negative preparation, I was frightened about staying at the farm alone with them. As it turned out, I had nothing to be afraid of. Aunt Rita was a wonderful contrast to Mom; showering me with love and affection. In the succeeding years, I looked forward to these visits with Aunt Rita. They were a welcomed relief from my ever increasing dreary existence at home.

CHAPTER 5

HAVING FINISHED THE QUICK DINNER PREPARED

by Paul, Nell climbed the stairs to the second-floor, and unlocked and entered her bedroom. She was anxious to resume reading from the stack of tablets she had pilfered from Jack's room at Fairways. Removing the book-bag containing the tablets from its hook in her closet, Nell extracted the entire collection of some thirty tablets, and going through them, selected from the carefully organized stack the next one to be read. Turning on the floor lamp and taking her seat in the comfortable upholstered chair, Nell began to read:

BIG CHIEF TABLET FOUR | FRITZ

When I was eighteen, Poppa enrolled me in the Technische Universi-tat Carolo-Wilhelmina zu Braunschweig – the oldest, most prestigious school of technology in Germany, where he hoped I would pursue a ca-reer in aeronautics. While attending the local gymnasium, I had shown an aptitude in science and mathematics; and passed the Abitur with flying colors. Even though Germany was prohibited by the Treaty of Versailles from having a military air force, there were private flying clubs, as well as aircraft design institutes being pursued on a civilian basis. I learned to fly aircraft as soon as Poppa discerned that I had an aptitude for op-erating airplanes. I was most excited to be able to fly and that I would be following in Poppa's footsteps in areonautics. It also meant that I would be going away to school where I would be on my own for the first time in my life.

There was considerable turmoil and unrest in Germany at the time I entered the Technological Institute, and it only worsened by the time I was in my third year of attendance. Many students were members of debating clubs representing a broad spectrum of political philosophies, including socialism, communism, bolshevism, monarchism, and fascism.

One of the more active and violent political parties was the *National Socialist* party which had its roots Bavaria. It was a minor party, but well-organized with uniforms and insignia that appealed to those German people who had a particular fear and dislike of the communists and Bolsheviks. Many of the industrialists were enamored with the *National Socialists'* attacks on the Versailles Treaty, especially its outlandish reparations requirements, and its restrictions on military rearmament. They also supported the *National Socialists'* for their rabid opposition to communism and Bolshevism. According to Poppa, one of the more prominent industrialists supporting the *National Socialists* was Otto Muenster who – as Poppa put it – "sees future profit and power flowing to him from his support of that party of degenerates." I frequently saw Herr Muenster's name mentioned in the newspapers as being close to the party's titular head, Adolf Hitler.

Because of his ties to the aviation industry, Otto Muenster was a frequent visitor to the Technological Institute where he sought to combine Nazi party promotion with industrial recruitment purposes. On one such occasion I received a personal invitation to attend a dinner Herr Muenster was hosting. I was curious as to the types of aviation-related employment Herr Muenster's firm might be offering, and attended the dinner on that basis. Needless to say I was also curious as to whether Herr Muenster would recall who I was and if he would tie me to the infamous dead rooster saga. The fact that I had received a personal invitation suggested that he did not. How wrong I was.

THE DINNER HOSTED by Herr Muenster was held in a wood-paneled private dining room on the second floor of an old restaurant frequented mainly by local businessmen and their out-of-town guests. The rows of dining tables ran the length of the room, perpendicular to the dais. This meant that the persons seated along the tables towards the front of the room had the best view of the dais, while those at the rear were clothed in darkness and anonymity.

It was at one of these rear seats that I wished to place myself. But it was not to be. There were place-cards on each table bearing the name of the person assigned to sit at that spot. As I worked my way up the one row of tables I did not spot my name until I had started back down the second row of tables. There it was: at the very first spot on the table located just to the right of the dais: *Fritz von Bruckner.* Others were now filing into the room, taking their seats. My first thought was to try to work my way back out of the room without creating a commotion or drawing undue attention to myself. But my way was blocked by a line of other attendees working their way up the table towards me. I was trapped.

As I was standing there behind my chair, I happened to glance at the place-card of the spot at my right: *Dietrich Muenster.* This seat remained empty for some time, while a long line of men took their seats along the table. At last, a tall, handsome young man, with short-cropped hair, about my age, made his way the length of the table, pausing along the way to greet friends warmly and to clasp the hands of others who spoke to him. When he reached the seat identified with the ominous place-card, my stomach sank. At first Dietrich Muenster ignored me as he waved to men who are still standing or who are seated at the opposite table. Upon sitting down, he looked up at me – as I was still standing behind my chair, frozen in place – with the darkest, most penetrating eyes, and with a supercilious smile said,

"You may sit down now. I am not the Kaiser, you know."

"From the way you were holding court with your admirers, I wasn't quite certain about that until you told me so" I replied to his cutting remark in a way that I hoped was disarming.

"Well aren't you the observant young aristocrat," he replied with a sneer. "My uncle Otto has told me a great deal about you, your brothers, and especially about your noble father, the Baron. Have you and your brothers killed any defenseless barnyard fowl lately? I think you will find this evening's speech to be very illuminating, if not particularly entertaining for you."

For the rest of the dinner I was ignored by Dietrich Muenster, and the other diners around me. I was left to deal alone with my fears and embarrassment.

Oh, Poppa, how naïve I was to think that anything good could have come from my attending this dinner. Had I asked you, you would have told me to stay away from anything having to do with Otto Muenster. What a fool I am! Now, I am going to be used by these vicious, evil men as a surrogate so that they can do to me what they cannot do to you directly. I know I must do all that I can to defend you and our noble name, but without making things any worse. It is going to be a most excruciating evening.

I barely touched my food as I thought about how I was going to be used during the speeches.

When the other guests had finished eating their meal, I waited anxiously as the waiters cleared the tables. There was a low murmur of many conversations in the room, which all came to an end when a man I recognized to be one of the professors at the *Institute* climbed onto the dais and made his way to the podium through a swirling cloud of smoke. The spot-lights, which had been dimmed during the meal, were increased in brightness, intensifying the effect of the smoky atmosphere.

"Good evening, fellow believers!" began the Professor, who paused until the tumultuous applause was reduced to a smattering of random non-descript cheers.

The Professor continued his introduction by extolling the many accomplishments of the featured speaker – Otto Muenster. Again there were more cheers from the audience. At this point a man stepped from behind one of the curtains at the side of the platform onto the dais to the sounds of recorded march music and deafening cheers and applause. I did not, at first, recognize the man: he looked far different from the Herr Munster who I had met over ten years ago. The Otto Muenster on the dais looked much heavier – almost portly – with white hair close-cut in a military-style, and a clean-shaven face. It was his intense blue eyes by which I finally recognized him. As he scanned the audience, row-by-row, his smile was broad and his eyes twinkled; that is, until he looked straight at me, and then his countenance changed dramatically – into a piercing scowl. It was the look that I remember from the day when Poppa, Wolfie and I took the replacement rooster to Herr Muenster's home over ten years earlier. It was a look that scared me as badly as it did back then.

———————

TO DESCRIBE THE results of our meeting with Herr Muenster ten years earlier as an unmitigated disaster would be putting it mildly. The meeting, which Poppa arranged through Herr Muenster's business manager Karl, took place in the private office Herr Muenster maintained above the stable at his farm. To call his estate a "farm," did it a great disservice: It was a palatial estate with a castle-like main residence constructed of stone and stucco walls, protected by a steep roof covered with multicolored slate shingles.

The chauffeur drove our big Mercedes up the drive, through the stone and stucco archway onto the cobblestone courtyard, parking the automobile in the area adjacent to stone steps which lead to the second-floor, where Herr Munster's office was located. An ornate doorway opened into a simple room with a highly-polished stone floor upon which were placed several plain-looking desks, tables and straight-back, wooden chairs. Karl, the business manager, was seated behind one of the desks, upon which sat a few papers and a telephone. Once we all filed into the room, Karl lifted the telephone handle from its cradle and, after waiting a minute or two, spoke in whispers to someone at the other end of the line. He replaced the telephone handle on its cradle and, in a sour voice, advised us to be seated.

After waiting for what seemed like forever, the telephone on Karl's desk rang just once. He immediately lifted the handle from its cradle, said nothing, and placed the handle back on its cradle. Karl stood and, in the same sour voice he used previously, announced that Herr Muenster would see us now.

Through dark-wood double doors, we were escorted into Herr Muenster's spacious, palatial office. Without any form of greeting, Herr Muenster, with a wave of his arm, directed us to the plain, armless wooden chairs placed directly in front of his ornate desk. His enormous, carved wooden desk was placed in the middle of this library-like room, directly beneath a skylight; Herr Muenster was sitting in a high-backed, red leather chair – his monocle glinting in the bright sunlight pouring in through the skylight. On the wall behind his desk was a life-size oil painting of Herr Muenster seated on a magnificent black Hanoverian stallion. In the over-done painting Herr Muenster was dressed in a dark-blue, military-style tunic – much like the one he was wearing that day, with light-tan jodhpurs, and highly polished black riding boots.

"You may sit!" growled Herr Muenster. It was more of a command than an offer. Before we could even comply with his directive, Otto Muenster started his attack: "I understand from Karl that you are here to try to re-place my wonderful 'Barbarosa' who your sons criminally assassinated! Karl has told me about how he found my beloved rooster torn to pieces by some animal – probably a fox. He also tells me that his wife, Helga, saw your sons throwing apples at 'Barbarosa' until they knocked him off of a fence, and then left him defenseless with a broken wing. Do you deny it?"

"Of course not," replied Poppa in a firm but civil voice. "That is why we are here. My sons want to apologize to you for their unacceptable behavior, and to set things right."

"The only thing that will set things right would be for your sons to suffer the same pain that I have suffered over the loss of my beloved 'Bar-barosa!'" bellowed Herr Muenster, ignoring Poppa's attempt at making this a civilized meeting. Now looking directly at Poppa, Muenster con-tinued in the same gruff voice, "Perhaps if you had been more diligent in punishing your sons rather than pampering them as you have, we would not be sitting here today."

I saw Poppa stiffen as if to rise to his feet, but he remained seated calmly saying, "I don't believe you have any knowledge of how I have raised my sons. But I can assure you that they have been raised to be gentle-men; the kind of young men who acknowledge when they have used bad judgment and seek to make amends, including restitution where neces-sary. By the same token, a true gentleman would accept such an apology and the offer of restitution in the same spirit in which it was given. But he certainly would not respond in a manner that intimates revenge or the exaction of punishment for punishment's sake!"

In response to Poppa's second effort at bringing a tone of civility to the situation, Herr Muenster's face turned beet-red, his eyes gave Poppa a hateful look; the one that I could not erase from my memory. "God damn you, and God damn your lecture on 'being a gentleman'. Your days of self-centered superiority are over. You and your aristocratic, gentle-manly types have brought the Fatherland to its knees. Rather than com-manding respect and bringing our weaker neighbors into Germany's or-bit, you have left the Fatherland to suffer economically and militarily at the hands of its ancient enemies."

At this point, red-faced Otto Muenster sprang to his feet, slammed his fist down onto his ornate desk, and demanded: "Get out of my office...get off of my property...and get out of my sight you arrogant bastard...And take your criminal sons and your poor-excuse for a replacement rooster with you. I'll take care of this matter in my own way, on my own terms, and in my own good time. You will deeply regret that you have once again trifled with my honor."

On our drive home, Poppa sat quietly in the spacious backseat of the Mercedes, with me on one side of him and Wolfie on the other.

"Poppa, what do you think will happen now?" I asked sheepishly.

Poppa stared straight ahead without responding.

"Do you think he will go to the police about this?" Wolfie asked ner-vously.

Again Poppa remained silent.

Not satisfied to leave things well-enough alone, I ask, "What did Herr Muenster mean about you trifling with his honor?"

Without raising his voice, but clearly indicating he did not want to talk any further about this matter, Poppa said, "There is more to this than the death of his damned rooster."

———————————

HAVING FORGOTTEN THE lesson of my earlier experience with Herr Muenster, I was not prepared for just how bad I would be used that eve-ning – in front of this audience – to suffer the vilification of my father and my class; all for the sake of Otto Munster glorifying the *National Socialist* party and his patron, Adolf Hitler.

I don't recall all that Otto Muenster said that evening as he excoriated me, my father and the German aristocrats we represented. His delivery was measured as he extolled the virtues of the *National Socialist* party and all that it stood for. His tone changed, however, when he introduced me to the audience by name, telling them about my pampered, delinquent youth, the "assassination" of his prized rooster at the hands of "aristocratic brigands," and how my father – the Baron – tried to buy his sons' way out of criminal prosecution. Herr Muenster then proceeded to attack the Baron as being a monarchist who despised businessmen – such as himself – as being beneath his aristocratic class.

"The Baron, his sons, and their ilk are out to destroy Germany and to turn its God-loving, God-fearing people over to the godless communists."

With this statement as the signal, Dietrich Muenster was on his feet, waving his arms urging the others in the audience to get to their feet in support of his now-beaming Uncle Otto. I remained seated as all of those men around me stood up, some pointing at me and laughing, while some shouted at me that I deserved a beating.

As if on cue, Otto Muenster urged the crowd to settle down, and when he achieved this goal, he told them that while I did indeed deserve a beating, "That is not the way the *National Socialist* party treats its opponents. We are the party of patriots, supporting the right of every citizen to have his opinion. We will, by our actions, in casting off the yoke of the Versailles Treaty, and turning out the communists and other radicals, bringing even those whose old world view is stifling our new world view to see the glory of a strong, vibrant Germany led by the *National Socialist* party and Adolf Hitler."

The damage – to the extent I could understand it – had been done. There was nothing I could do with this crowd, in these circumstances, to undo or mitigate what had been said about Poppa, his heritage, his image.

What can I tell Poppa about this evening? Is this just the beginning of the revenge Otto Muenster threatened us with ten years earlier?

All I knew for sure was that my family and I were now the targets of a very powerful, very evil man – Otto Muenster – and of his ruthless nephew – Dietrich Muenster.

How are we going to deal with such enemies as these?

CHAPTER 6

LOOKING AT HER WRIST-WATCH, NELL SAW THAT

it was still early; she had time to read another tablet before calling it a night. So far, she found that the tablets allegedly written by the spirit claiming to be Fritz to be consistent with what she knew of prewar German history. She also felt that the contents of the Fritz writings were certainly more advanced than she could expect to be produced by a young boy like Jack. Jack may well be possessed. Reaching down to the stack of tablets at the side of her easy-chair, Nell lifted the next tablet and began reading:

BIG CHIEF TABLET FIVE | JACK

It was summer vacation once again! My scheduled trips to visit Aunt Rita during summer vacation were always times of happy anticipation; being able to get away from my parents and my brothers, and to be with Aunt Rita. In the previous summers, Aunt Rita would drive into the city and bring me back to the farm; a trip of about three hours each way. However, this sum- mer – I was now ten years old – Dad had a business trip to a town close to the farm, which allowed him to take me to Aunt Rita, rather than Aunt Rita having to make the long round-trip to pick me up. Mom insisted – to my disappointment – that she travel with Dad and me.

The trip began on a Saturday morning in early June. We were traveling in a panel truck owned by Dad's employer; he was taking some furniture to a client of the firm's decorating services who lived in a town near Greenville. I was forced to sit on the floor among the furniture stacked in the cargo area of the small vehicle. An antique table and its two matching chairs were wrapped in padded blankets that smelt faintly of dust and fresh furniture polish. It was hot and stuffy sitting in the cargo area with the furniture.

In the windowless, semi-darkness of the cargo area I began to doze, thinking about all of the fun-things I hoped to be able to do when I got to the farm. I pictured Fairways, most of which was devoted to raising and feeding white-faced Hereford cattle. The rolling, tree-dotted land was divided into fenced pastures — for the cattle to graze, and fields — planted with corn and hay to supplement the cattle's winter grazing. There were several out-buildings: a large white barn with a windmill standing just outside the barn — bringing cold, fresh water to a concrete water-trough just inside the barn. The barn stood just across the graveled county road from the two and a half story house sitting atop a rise at the end of a long, white-gravel driveway. Surrounding the house were several elm shade-trees, and some white one-story buildings; including a chicken house; a combination feed-room/garage/horse stable; and small shed for the milking cow. The main house was a large, white-brick residence, with a walk-up attic. There was a full-length front porch and a matching second-floor balcony above it.

This was to be my home for the summer. It was a special place; a place filled with love and happiness, a place where I could roam and explore without restraints, a place where I could play at whatever I wanted, and a place where I could live without fear of criticism or complaint.

Suddenly, I was brought back to reality by a clanking sound — like the sound made by a large hammer hitting a steel anvil — coming from the engine compartment of the truck. In response, Dad steered the truck off to the side of the road, bringing it to a noisy stop. The loud noise continued until he turned off the engine.

"Oh, damn!" he said, stepping out of the vehicle.

Going to the front of the panel truck, Dad unlatched and opened the hood. After looking around under the hood, Dad climbed back in the truck saying, "I can't see anything wrong, but the engine shouldn't sound like it does. We'll need to have it looked at...preferably at the next service station we find down the road."

Dad restarted the engine and steered the truck back out onto the highway; with the clanking sound getting louder as Dad drove the truck slowly along the busy two-lane highway. Cars stuck behind the creeping panel truck honked their horns in frustration; passing on the left whenever they got the chance.

On the outskirts of a small town Dad steered the now loudly-clanking truck into a small filling station, and turned off the engine: There was instant, blessed silence. As the truck coasted slowly to a stop, I could see from my perch behind the passenger seat that the station consisted of two grimy, ancient gasoline pumps located under a sagging, peaked canopy attached to the front of a dilapidated building in need of repairs much beyond just a new paint-job. To the right of the dimly lit office – with its front-door propped open in the hope of catching any kind of passing breeze – were two open, but dark, service bays; one bay appeared to be empty, while the other bay was home to a rusting hulk of what looked to be a tow truck.

In front of the station, a man dressed in dirty, smudged grey overalls, removed his darkly-stained ball cap, showing his suntan line, and began scratching his head in puzzlement as to the source of the noise. He was leaning against one of the rickety wooden posts holding up the sagging canopy.

"I hear'd you comin down the highway for more'n a mile," he remarked to no one in particular. "You've either thrown a connectin rod or that motor's got a busted piston." Pausing to scratch his cheek, he added, "Either way, you got serious engine problems!"

Dad opened the driver-side door, hoisting himself out of the small truck into the hot sun. I could see the dark sweat-marks on the lower back and under the arms of his white shirt. Shading his eyes with his right hand, Dad asked the man,

"Are you the mechanic?"

"Yep." replied the man, after spitting a wad of brown goop.

"Can it be fixed?" inquired Dad in a hopeful voice.

"That deepens," the man responded skeptically.

"Depends on what?" queried Dad.

"Deepens on whether the block's been cracked or not."

"Can you determine if it's cracked?"

"I ain't sure, but I cain't look at it in any event until that engine cools off," the man responded impatiently.

"How long will that take?"

"Several hours, I suspect."

"Suppose the block is cracked. Then what?" asked Dad.

"Then probably, ya'll need a new engine."

Mom – who was wearing a white-cotton peasant blouse, a light blue flared skirt, and tortoise-shell frame dark glasses – had climbed out of the truck. As she walked towards the shade of the filing station's canopy she attempted to straighten her skirt and adjust her blouse. I followed her out of the truck by clambering over the back of the passenger seat, stumbling out of the truck onto the graveled driveway.

"Be careful, Jack," she admonished me as she saw me stumble. "You must be more careful! I don't want to have to wash your clothes the first thing I do when we get to the farm."

"Sorry, Mommy," I responded sheepishly in a whinny voice. *If you didn't want me to get these clothes dirty, why did you make me wear them? You knew I was going to be sitting in the back of the panel truck on old, dirty furniture blankets.*

Mom dismissed my apology with the wave of her hand; turning her attention to Dad and the mechanic. "Can you tell us whether any of the work you say needs to be done can be done today?" she asked, shading her face from the bright sunlight with her hand.

"Not hardly, ma'm." the mechanic replied politely, but flatly.

"Well, Paul, why are you making me stand out here in the hot sun, when we are not going to get out of here today, regardless of what this man tells us needs to be done. I hope you're not expecting me to spend much time in this filthy place?"

Well, we're at the mercy of this mechanic, and what is Dad supposed to do? Not wishing to hear any more, I turned away towards the garage with the intent of exploring the dingy, dirty filling station.

The tiny office was hot and stuffy; smelling strongly of melting grease, rancid oil, burnt rubber and an un-flushed toilet. Every shelf and flat surface was covered with grimy materials of one kind or another; materials that were quite appropriate for an auto repair place, but not for accommodating a person like my mother. There was no clean chair, or even a bench. The desk top was littered with darkly smudged papers, greasy sandwich wrappers, and assorted junk. The floor around the desk was littered with crumpled pieces of graying paper, and the decaying bodies of dead flies lying beneath the rolls of flypapers that were tacked to the ceiling in no particular pattern.

I figured that my mother would not dare step foot into this dreadful place; concluding that I was therefore free to roam and snoop around the office and the service bays as much as I wanted. As I started my search, I immediately sensed that there was something in this garage that I was supposed to see. After spending ten minutes in the cluttered office, thumbing through out-of-date auto parts catalogues and unfolding and refolding faded road maps, without finding anything of interest, I drifted into the service bays.

The light in the service bays was even poorer than in the office, and the sweet smell of lubricants, hydraulic fluids and tire repairs was even stronger. I fingered the equipment used to vulcanize the patch on a punctured inner tube; learning nothing about the magic of the process; managing only to get my fingers blackened. There was nothing in that bay that I could use to wipe my fingers clean – which I needed to do before facing my mother again. My search for a rag led me to cross over into the service bay where the ancient tow truck rested in a heap, the frontend facing into the garage. From the look of it, it was clearly "military surplus," in a severely decaying condition. Even in the semi-darkness of the service bay, I observed that the tow truck had seen a lot of use, but not recently; the boom was out-of-line, with cables and chains rusty and twisted. I prayed that our panel truck would not be towed anywhere by that heap.

As I passed between the front of the tow truck and a littered work bench standing against the back wall of the service bay, still in my search for a rag to wipe my still blackened fingers on, I spied, sitting just on the other side of the tow truck, sticking out from under a dirty canvas tarp, the front-end of a racing car. It was hard to tell much about the vehicle — being in the dark and under a tarp. Still, I could identify that it was a racing car because of the shape of the front, the lack of a bumper, and the bright, shiny red and yellow paint — just like in the pictures of the Indy racers that I had seen in car-type magazines. *My God! I have to see more of this car!*

I moved along the side of the car towards its back-end, to where I imagined the driver's compartment would be. On impulse, I picked up an edge of the tarp hoping to take a peek at the driver's compartment to observe all that might be in there; what the driver steered with, and what was on the instrument panel in front of him. No sooner had I raised the tarp to a point where I could get a good peek inside, when the overhead fluorescent lights came on and a voice firmly demanded, "What do you think you're doing here, son?"

I was momentarily shocked out of my wits, stammering, "I..., I...." as I stumbled backwards colliding with the side of the rusting tow truck.

The threatening voice was coming from where the service bay door stood open. I couldn't tell anything about the person standing there because of the bright sunlight silhouetting the form. At first I thought that it was probably the station mechanic with whom my father and mother had spoken to earlier. Once the silhouette stepped into the service bay, under the fluorescent lights, I could see that it was a different person; younger, taller and wearing coveralls that look as if they had been laundered recently. On his head he was wearing a pilot-style cap favored by airplane pilots, which was tipped back so that a shock of red hair stuck out from under the brim, with a pair of aviator-style sunglasses perched on top of his cap. I could see that he was smiling disarmingly; hopefully to calm my nerves.

"It's okay," he said, "I didn't mean to startle you so. We've had some break-ins around here recently, and I guess I'm just a little edgy about my race car. You're kind of young to be a car thief, aren't you?"

"No sir!" I stammered loudly; thinking maybe I should have

said, *"Yes, sir!"* "I just wanted to see where the driver sits," I continued nervously.   He laughed at that and began walking towards me.

"Have you ever seen a real race car before?" he asked in a gentle, teacher-like voice.

"No, sir," I replied softly. "But I've seen pictures of Indianapolis racers in magazines... Is this an Indy racer, sir?"

"No, young fella," he replied in a nasal tone – but not with quite the twang of the mechanic. "This isn't an Indy racer, though it may look like it to some people...Unlike the Indy racer, this beauty isn't designed to run on a race track in circles, like an Indy racer does. I'm building this vehicle to try to set the land speed record on a straight track...or a stretch of straight road...an abandoned air strip, or perhaps just on some flat open land – like a dry lakebed."

"My name is Buzz," he added, now standing directly in front of me offering me his hand to shake. "What's your name," he asked while shaking my hand.

"Jack. Jack Johanson." I replied.

"Well, 'curious' Jack Johanson, are you ready to take your peek at this marvelous machine?"

Some voice inside me urged, *"Yes, do it. You must learn all you can about this race car and about this man."* I made an affirmative nod of my head, turning back to the side of the race car to help Buzz remove the tarp.

"Just so you know, this vehicle is not a 'race car.' It does not 'race.' It is nothing more or less than a very powerful engine attached to four wheels. It does not have an official name. I just call her my *Speed Machine*."

We were just lifting the tarp off of the *Speed Machine* when I heard Mom's shrill voice calling,

"Jack! Jack! Where are you? Come to where I can see you! You dare not be getting your clothes dirty!"

I looked sheepishly at Buzz, calling back to Mom, "I'm in here!"

"Come to where I can see you!" she repeated, now angrily. "I am not very happy right now, and I don't want to have to come find you. We are trying to make arrangements to get the truck fixed and get out of this horrible place. I don't want to have to come find you, or you know what will happen to you!"

I dropped my edge of the tarp, looked again at Buzz, and walked out of the garage into the bright sunlight.

"My God!" she exclaimed sternly. "Just look at your filthy hands! How many times do I have to tell you not to get yourself dirty? You are a very disobedient boy! What am I going to do with you?" Mom stepped towards me with her arm lifted in the air, preparing to strike me with her hand.

"Step back from her," the voice inside me commanded. *"Don't let her hit you. Just move away from her and tell her you are 'sorry',* the voice continued. *"She will be all right. She just needs some space"* the voice assured me. Then the voice in my head added, *"But, you must see that machine."*

"I'm sorry Mommy," I mumbled softly, embarrassed to use the dreaded name, as I backed away from her.

As the voice predicted, she lowered her arm, saying, "The next time I call you, I want you to come running; and get your hands washed before you get that filth on your clothes!" She turned and walked away; and I headed back into the garage.

During my confrontation with Mom, Buzz had removed the tarp. Sitting in front of me was the most beautiful vehicle I had ever seen. It was sleek, low to the ground, and probably twice as long as the Indy racers I had seen in the magazines. The driver's compartment, with its tiny windshield, was located two-thirds of the way back from the front of the *Speed Machine*. The hood, which unlike a conventional automobile, opened from the side, folding up like a wing, was open, exposing the enormous engine. The machine was, as Buzz had said, just a motor on four wheels. The engine was at least eight feet long.

"Wow, what is that?" I asked, pointing at the engine.

"It's an airplane engine," responded Buzz. "It is an Allison V-12, liquid cooled engine. It is the starboard engine from a P-38L. When it was on the P-38 it was supercharged, which gave it more horsepower...but I haven't yet figured out whether I need to, or whether I can, add a supercharger to this motor."

"Did you fly the P-38 in the war?"

"No." he answered with a puzzled look. "But what do you know about the P-38?" he asked.

I couldn't believe what I was hearing and seeing. *Buzz has no idea of how long I have been in love with the P-38 Lightning, perhaps the greatest fighter aircraft in the Second World War – with its twin, super-charged engines, a single pod for the cockpit, its nose-mounted four .50 caliber machine guns and one 20mm cannon, and its unique tail assembly. I have several metal and plastic models of the airplane – most of them gifts, but one I shoplifted from a Woolworth's five and dime store. Although the war was over by the time I was old enough to know the differences in American fighter aircraft, I could identify the P-38 on sight; and I had the advantage of having two older brothers, especially Chris; both were into constructing model airplanes. But more importantly, I have recurring dreams – following my head injury in May, 1945 – which involve P-38s in vivid detail, along with other fighter aircraft which in my dreams I am unable to identify.*

I told Buzz most of what I knew about the P-38, skipping the embarrassing details – like the shoplifting and the dreams.

"You do have quite a background on the P-38 for a kid of your age," he observed.

"Can you start the engine?" I inquired hopefully.

"Not in here, and not until I can get some more aviation fuel" he replied.

"What's aviation fuel?" I asked.

"It's very high octane gasoline, much higher than the stuff people put in their cars or trucks...so there is none of what I need available at this garage," he said, with the shake of his head.

"Then, why do you keep the *Speed Machine* at this crummy old place?" I asked, trying to understand.

"Because it's the only place I can afford to keep it," he replied in a somewhat irritated tone.

"Be careful how you talk to this man," the voice inside me cautioned. *"If you want to know more about this engine, the P-38, and this man, you need to be very polite."*

"It's not that bad," I said. Making a sweeping motion with my arm, I added, "I guess there's plenty of room to work on the car in here when the tow truck is out of the way."

Why do I need to know more about Buzz? I silently asked the voice inside me; suddenly realizing that it was Fritz's voice! *I have been waiting for months to hear from Fritz, and now he is back.*

"Jack! Jack!" I heard a voice speaking to me. "Are you alright?" I then realized that I had been staring blankly into space.

"Yes... Yes," I stammered, trying to refocus on where I was. "I...I...I was just thinking about how great it would be just to sit in the *Speed Machine*," I lied, trying to cover up my mental withdrawal.

"Sure!" said Buzz quizzically. "Of course you can. Here, since there's no door, I'll help you climb in," he commented as he walked toward me — where I stood next to the cockpit — offering me his hand. "Maybe someday I can give you a real ride in the *Speed Machine*."

"This is so great!" I had no sooner placed my right leg and foot into the cockpit when I heard Mom again calling my name. My excitement was immediately dashed. I knew that she was preparing to leave, and I would not get my chance to experience the thrill I was envisioning. Back to reality! I screamed silently.

Immediately pulling myself out of the machine, I raced to the garage doorway where I could be seen by Mom. *I hope that was fast enough for her?* I checked — as best I could — my tee-shirt and shorts for any dirt or grease smudges. *I don't want a whipping; not here; not now; not ever again!* Thankfully, I didn't see any signs of dirt or oil. The real test, however, would be what Mom might observe, as I knew she would demand.

"Come over here, and stand in front of me!" Mom said, as I had anticipated. "Now turn around, so I can check your nice clothes for any soiling. We are going to go back to the city by bus while they repair the panel truck, and I don't want to be embarrassed by you having dirty clothes. It's bad enough that you smell like this horrible place, and that I will have to sit near you."

It suddenly hit me that we were not going to complete the trip to the farm and see Aunt Rita. Not only had my dream of sitting in the machine been interrupted, but now my hopes of escaping from Mom for the summer, and being with Aunt Rita, appeared to be dashed as well.

"Bite your tongue...and, for heaven's sake, don't start crying!" Fritz commanded.

Taking a deep breath, I did as the voice instructed.

"The panel truck needs repairs that this mechanic can't perform here," Mom continued after she completed her inspection of my clothes. "We have called a garage in the next town where there are facilities to perform the necessary repairs. This mechanic is going to tow the panel truck there as soon as his helper shows up. You and I will ride in the panel truck, and your father will ride in that filthy tow truck. I am told there is a Greyhound Bus station in the next town. We are going to take a bus back to the city. Then, when the truck is repaired, we will return, pick it up and drive on to the farm. It may be a week or two before the truck is repaired. We will leave most of our luggage in the truck, so we won't have much to carry on the bus."

By then the mechanic was backing the tow truck out of the garage. As decrepit as it looked, it started immediately, moving easily towards the panel truck. While the mechanic was attaching the tow truck's hooks and cables to the panel truck, Mom surprisingly said to me, "Why don't you run back and say 'Goodbye' to that fellow you were talking to. You looked as if you were having fun with him."

"Yes, I was!" I exclaimed over my shoulder as I ran towards the garage. I found Buzz as he was pulling the tarp back over the *Speed Machine.* I explained to him why I was leaving and where I was going; and about returning to here, and then going on to see my aunt at the farm. After thanking him for telling me about the machine, he asked me,

"Where's your aunt's farm?"

When I told Buzz that it was near Greenville, he said, "Sure, I know where that is. There are plenty of nice horse and cattle farms around there, and plenty of old, mining-family money. As a matter-of-fact, I get over there frequently to see some old war buddies...And there's one fellow I know you would like to meet; he flew P-38s in Europe and has some great stories to tell. Perhaps your aunt may know him. You might want to ask her...His name is Pete Roberts."

For unknown reasons, I felt my heart leap in my chest!

Fritz: *"Ach der lieber Gott!! I thought as I heard the name of the man who may hold the key to proving to Jack that I am who I say I am. It was such a shock to me that I knew that my reaction to his name – Pete Roberts – had to affect Jack physically. I also now knew that my presence in Jack was no mere whim of nature; this was an opportunity to close the book on a painful part of my life and to set me free. It was imperative that Jack meet this Pete Roberts. Hopefully, he is the man whose adventures were relevant to my search. I would only know if this is the right Pete Roberts when I hear his stories about his war experiences – and one story in particular. To prepare young Jack for this task, I will relate to him those portions of my life that he will need to have firmly in mind as he searches for the truth of my death."*

———————

NELL CLOSED THE tablet, placed it on the short stack of already-read tablets, and extinguished the floor lamp, choosing to sit in the dark, to assimilate what she had just read into the growing picture of what had been transpiring in Jack's life. She was not pleased with what Jack had written about her, treating her as the villain, contrasting her unfavorably with Rita. She could just imagine what was coming, what led Jack to forsake her in favor of Rita. She wondered what role Fritz played in the developing transfer of affections from birth-mother to aunt.

CHAPTER 7

WHEN NELL TOOK HER PLACE THE FOLLOWING
evening in her easy-chair, resuming her reading of the tablets, she was
thrilled to discover that the next tablet in the stack of tablets to be
reviewed appeared to be composed by Fritz' spirit, using Jack's hand as
the writing implement. She was impressed with what Fritz, his father,
in fact, what his whole family, had accomplished; of course, it didn't
hurt having important friends in high places. She was concerned,
however, with the growing enmity between the von Bruckners and the
villainous Muensters. *Could the Muenster family,* Nell thought, *be the
ones responsible for Fritz' untimely death?*

BIG CHIEF TABLET SIX | FRITZ

In 1932, I completed my studies at the Institute, and prepared to begin my
career in the aeronautics industry. I returned home to live with my family.
It was not a good time to be on one's own, searching for a job. Germany
was in the throes of economic, political and social unrest. Having survived the currency debacle of the early Weimar Republic – when the mark
became virtually worthless because of rampant inflation – Germany was
caught up in a world-wide depression. The Weimar Republic itself was
struggling to remain a democratic republic. Herr Otto Munster's National
Socialists – also known more commonly as the Nazis – were trying to
win control of the Reichstag, with Adolf Hitler as its leader. Although the
Nazis could never achieve a majority of the popular vote – and therefore
control of the Reichstag legitimately – through some highly irregular political maneuverings, they were trying to get Hitler named its Chancellor.
The well-documented Nazi political agenda included several elements
which were creating social issues, including its anti-Jewish policies.

On an afternoon soon after my return home, Poppa asked me to join
him at his firm's plant located adjacent to Berlin's Templehof airfield.
There were matters, he said, that we needed to talk about that could not

be discussed in detail at home. Momma was becoming seriously concerned with the direction of German politics and policies, especially whether Herr Hitler was leading Germany into another war. Each night at dinner she prayed for peace and for the welfare of the Jewish people who were coming under relentless attack by the Nazis. Poppa was afraid that some of the matters we needed to speak about might upset Momma.

Poppa's office, which was tucked in a corner of his Berlin aircraft factory, reflected his upper-class tastes and sense of style. Poppa's only accommodation to his status as owner of the firm, was a large brown leather sofa. The walls of the office were painted a light green, upon which hung a few family pictures and one of Momma's better attempts at oil painting.

A glass partition served as one wall of this office; allowing Poppa to view what was happening on the shop floor. The shop area, where aircraft parts were designed, manufactured and assembled, was neat, well-lighted and clean. The workers who were present in the shop on the day I met Poppa wore grey overalls and caps, and were utilizing metal lathes, hydraulic presses and grinding wheels to shape and perfect the high precision aircraft parts. Despite the noise coming from the shop, Poppa and I were able to converse without shouting and, more importantly, without being overheard. Poppa elected not to close the curtain over the glass partition.

I chose to sit in a corner of the sofa from where I could comfortably observe Poppa sitting in his "roll-about" armchair. Poppa ignited one of his favorite cigars – but I declined his offer of one. Minutes passed as Poppa went through the ritual of lighting and puffing on the cigar until he was satisfied that it would burn evenly. Putting the extinguished match into a large ashtray already filled with the consumed carcasses of other cigars, Poppa turned his chair to face me, asking me how long I planned to be living at home.

I attempted to explain to him that, as a result of the current economic and political problems, my hopes of launching a spectacular aeronautical career at this time were much diminished. I explained to him that my first avenue of pursuit was to seek employment with one of the larger aircraft manufacturing firms – like Fokker, Messerschmitt, or Heinkel. Alas, there were – as I had learned – no opportunities available there; both because of the poor economy, and because of the restrictions contained in the Versailles Treaty against building military aircraft.

I carefully pointed out to Poppa that his firm was not my first choice for employment because his business was crafting and supplying precision airframe parts for the bigger manufacturers; and I wanted a broader exposure to the aircraft manufacturing business. Poppa nodded his agreement. I also offered that while there were other large aircraft firms, most have the same, or other, drawbacks.

"Obviously," I threw into the conversation, "There are no opportunities for me with Otto Muenster's firm." Poppa, making an obscene gesture with his cigar, frowned. *Even if Herr Muenster was willing to hire me – which was highly unlikely – my father would disown me in a heartbeat. The memory of the way in which Herr Muenster had tried to humiliate me and discredit Poppa was too powerful and painful to ever fade.*

This thought caused me to remember the time four years ago when I told Poppa about what Herr Muenster had tried to do us at the dinner. "What a rotten, low-handed guttersnipe!" Poppa erupted as he turned livid, pounding his large fist down onto his desk top. "He may think he is making friends with the Nazis by attacking us and making political contributions to their cause, but he is sadly mistaken. They will simply use him and then cast him aside. His ambitions are only exceeded by his ego and his arrogance. I know there are high-ranking Nazis who thoroughly dislike and mistrust him. Herman Goering... my friend from the first war who saw first-hand the deaths of valiant pilots caused by Muenster's defective propellers ...just told me the other day that Herr Muenster is already trying to line up military contracts for when the Nazis take over the government and repudiate the Versailles Treaty. According to Goering, who is very close to Hitler, what Muenster wants is not going to happen."

That was the first time I learned that Poppa had contacts with people in the Nazi party. I was actually shocked at the thought of Poppa having anything to do with the Nazis. I knew he had been close to Goering during the Great War, and respected Goering as a bona fide war hero – having shot down twenty-five enemy planes, commanded the Richthofen Squadron, and won the most prestigious German military decorations: the Pour le Merit (popularly known as the Blue Max) and the Iron Cross First Class.

But more importantly, this respect was based upon Goering's support of Poppa when Poppa proved that Herr Muenster's propellers were killing German pilots. But that was then. To deal with Goering now did not seem to make sense. The Nazis were publicly opposed to the monarchy, the aristocrats, the officer-class, and the Catholic Church, all of which Poppa adamantly supported.

When Poppa heard criticisms of the nobility, he was quick to remind us of the fact that not only are we von Bruckners, but on Momma's side of the family, we are von Poppenhaus – who, in turn are related to the von Schulenburgs and the von Bismarks. It is was also no secret that Poppa was a staunch – but silent – monarchist; hoping that when President von Hidenburg dies, Crown Prince Rupert would be restored to the throne as a constitutional monarch like they had in England. After hearing my sad tale of how a job to my liking was not on the immediate horizon, Poppa spoke to me again about Herman Goering. Poppa was convinced that the Nazis were eventually going to gain control of the government, either constitutionally or not.

"No one," he opined, "Not the industrialists, the military, the Church are inclined to, or strong enough, to stop Hitler from becoming the Fuehrer of Germany." "In that event," he continued, "Goering, who is already the Minister President of the Reichstag, will likely become even more powerful and take on even more important duties. We need to make our plans based on what Herr Goering is able to achieve career-wise. Therefore, I want you to work with me until something opens up with the new government. Hopefully you can attach yourself with either the new *Luftwaffe* or with one of the large aeronautical manufacturing firms which will be getting government contracts to build military aircraft."

Once again, I was both shocked and puzzled by what I was hearing from Poppa. While it appeared to be sound advice, it looked to me that Poppa was willing to shake hands with the devil for the sake of some business or political advantage. I knew that my older brother Wolfgang was already working as an economist at the Reichsbank under the direction of Hjalmar Schacht, the President of the Reichsbank, a brilliant monetarist who saved Germany from sure bankruptcy during the early 1920s. While not a member of the Nazi party, Schacht was an outspoken supporter of

Hitler and had done much to bring the German industrialists into Hitler's orbit. Poppa worked hard to get Wolfgang an interview with Schacht, but it was Wolfgang's impressive school record that convinced Schacht to hire him. I was still not sure what Poppa was trying to accomplish in adapting his strong beliefs to accommodate the Nazis, but I had to trust him; and so I will work for him and wait.

As I started to rise from the sofa, thinking our conversation was over, Poppa touched my arm saying, "Please sit down again while I finish my cigar and we drink the snifters of Cognac which I have been saving for this occasion."

He rolled his chair to his desk, unlocked a drawer, and pulled out a bottle of what I knew to be a very fine Cognac. After pulling two large snifters from the same drawer and filling them, he rolled his chair towards me, handing me one. "Probst," he and I said in unison.

Upon completion of our toast, Poppa took a full sip, swallowed, cleared his throat, saying, "I suspect that you, like your mother, are puzzled by what I have proposed, especially about with whom I have suggested that you work and associate. Really, there is nothing sinister in what I am asking of you; quite to the contrary – this is what we must do to survive these next difficult years. Germany may be headed for serious trouble, even another war. Remember that we are first of all Germans, Germans who love the fatherland, and who want Germany to succeed economically, politically, socially and spiritually.

"Even if a majority of our fellow Germans have come under the spell of this Adolf Hitler – who may indeed be a madman or a devil, and make him our leader, we must do what we can to help Germany to survive and prosper. We can do so only if we are in government, industry or social institutions where we can exert pressure on the leaders, or the participants, to act reasonably and responsibly. That is why I have asked you to work with Goering, as I have asked Wolfgang to work with Schacht, and as I will ask Ernst to join the *Wehrmacht*; to work in jobs or to associate with people of influence with whom you may have very strong ethical and moral concerns."

At this, Poppa downed his Cognac, stubbed out his cigar, and exclaimed in loud voice, "God help us and save us!"

CHAPTER 8

BIG CHIEF TABLET SEVEN | JACK

Several weeks after the damaged panel truck engine had forced us to abandon our trip to the farm, Dad advised us at dinner that he had heard from the repair facility; and "the panel truck's engine has been rebuilt." We will, he said, "be taking a bus back to pick up the panel truck — and the stuff we left in it...and go on to the farm as originally planned." My heart leapt for joy when I heard the good news.

I will now get to spend what is left of my summer vacation with Aunt Rita.

Also, I will be set free from my overbearing mother and the clutches of my brother, David. Life at home — when I should have been staying at the farm — was not very pleasant. I was left in David's less-than-benevolent care during the weekdays when my folks were at work.

David was now seventeen; about to be a high school senior, full of himself, in love with a pretty, rich girl — Carol Ann (who our mother referred to as "little panties"). He was not at all pleased with having to look after his "stupid kid brother," when he could be spending his free-time with her or his friends. To me, David was just a tall, skinny guy, but to our mother, he was "handsome — in a young Jimmy Stewart sort of way."

David was always talking about Carol Ann, especially of the wonderful stuff her parents provided her with; a new Mercury convertible and access to their country club pool. As David described the country club, "it is a swanky place" — "it has lounge chairs with cushions, tables and umbrellas, free towels, diving boards, and black guys in jackets bringing you food and drinks just for asking."

"Jack, you just don't know how nice it would be if we had money — like Carol Ann's family. Her dad must be making a mint out of his funeral homes."

A funeral home must, I guess, be like a bowling alley. Dad said one time that the owner of the bowling alley where he usually bowls on Friday evenings was 'making a mint on the league bowling'.

"What's a mint?" I asked.

"It's just a lot of money. You know, like the U.S. government Mint prints tons of money...God, you're a stupid kid!"

Well, just another great conversation with my 'smarter than God' brother!" This unpleasant exchange ended any further discourse on the delights of being wealthy.

David's desire to have nothing further to do with me did not last long; it was overcome by an invitation he received by telephone from Carol Ann asking him to join her for a swim at her fabled country club pool. I was playing in the back yard with my toy soldiers under the shade of an ancient, twisted peach tree. "Hey jerk!" he shouted down at me from the back porch, "I've been invited to go swimming with Carol Ann, but I can't go unless I take you with me. So get in here and get ready to go... pronto!" he commanded.

My mind was suddenly in a whirl: *"Swimming? Swimming in a swimming pool?"* I had never been swimming before in a real swimming pool. *In fact, I have never been swimming anywhere before!*

"What am I supposed to wear?" I asked David as I walked into the kitchen.

"A swimming suit, you dummy!" was David's curt reply.

"But I don't think I have swimming suit."

"What do you mean you don't have a swimming suit? I thought everyone had a swimming suit." said David incredulously. "There must be something you can wear that will pass as a bathing suit.

Why don't you go look in the cedar chest on the third floor...You know, where Mom always puts all the old clothes we don't wear very often? Now get going! Carol Ann is picking us up in half an hour."

After running up two-flights of stairs to reach the cedar chest in the heat of the third-floor attic, and after much rummaging through the chest, I found a pair of dark-blue wool bathing trunks reeking of mothballs. The trunks looked old, but not moth-eaten. Holding them in front of my waist I thought they might fit me. I ran back down to my bedroom on the second floor, where I found David sitting impatiently on the side of the old four-poster double bed that he and I once shared. He was dressed casually, wearing a short-sleeve, blue shirt and khaki pants.

"Shit!" he exclaimed when he saw – and I guess smelled – the woolen trunks I was clutching in my hand. "Is that the best you could find?" he inquired. "Well, you had better try them on." I pulled down my short pants and began to pull the trunks up over my underwear.

"What are you doing, asshole" cried David in exasperation. "You don't wear a swimming suit over your underwear." It took me several seconds to get naked, and then several minutes of agonizing tugging to get the bathing trunks on my bean-pole body.

"Holy shit," exclaimed David. "You look like you just got out of a concentration camp with that milk-white, skinny-assed body of yours. Don't you ever get out in the sun? What are Carol Ann and the kids at the pool going to think about you? And those sorry-ass trunks – they must be at least a hundred years old. I doubt that no one but hillbillies wear old shit like that these days."

"Now take off those smelly old trunks, get washed up and get dressed in some clean clothes. You really need to take a bath – you are filthy...But since Mom won't let us have any hot water during the weekdays, I guess you are just going to have to wash with cold water in the bathroom sink. We'll get you a shower at the pool." As I washed up and got dressed, David lectured me on what to do, and what not to do, and what to say in front of Carol

Ann and his friends; in the car, at the pool, etc. He concluded his tirade with the threat; "If you do anything to embarrass me, I will kill you when we get home!"

I had barely finished getting into my rumpled clothes when I heard the sound of a car horn out on the street. David called to me from the foot of the stair-case, "Come on, Jack; let's go! And don't forget your stylish swimming trunks."

When I reached the open front door I saw a shiny new, crimson '49 Mercury convertible with the top down, sitting at the curb in front of our house. The car's radio was tuned to a top-ten music station, and Carol Ann — who was wearing fashionable horn-rimmed sunglasses and a bright blue scarf over her blonde pageboy hairdo — sat tapping her fingers on the steering wheel in time to Frankie Lane's *Mule Train*. Carol Ann turned her head towards us as we descended the front-porch steps. She gave David a big smile. When she observed me stumbling down the steps behind David, she gave me a more sisterly-like smile. *Well, at least she smiled at me. This just might be fun.*

David opened the passenger side door and, while making the briefest of introductions, hustled me into the backseat of the Mercury with a stern look and a less-than-gentle shove.

"What's that smell?" asked Carol Ann, not too pleasantly.

"It's just Jack's ancient swimming trunks that he fished out of the cedar chest," David said apologetically.

"Thank God we're in a convertible," laughed Carol Ann, looking back at me in the rear-view mirror, "Otherwise we could get asphyxiated on our way to the pool."

Carol Ann put the Mercury into first gear, pulling away from the curb swiftly and smoothly. I could tell immediately that she was a competent, confident driver; I pictured her piloting Buzz's *Speed Machine*. As Carol Ann drove the convertible along shady residential streets and busy boulevards into the suburbs, I tried to imagine what it would be like at the Country Club pool.

Splashing around in the pool, eating a sandwich, drinking some cola, enjoying the sun, sharing a laugh with Carol Ann! But wait a minute! I don't know how to swim. And if I can't swim, what will I do... and who will I play with? I know that David and

Carol Ann won't want to play with me or have me hang around with them and their friends. Suddenly my feeling of joyous anticipation turned into sour anxiety.

A sign announcing the country club appeared on my right; behind which were some buildings set among green hills and towering oak and elm trees. The main building – which I surmised was the club house – was a rambling, single story, white brick and stone building with a porch-like structure leading to the front entrance. Carol Ann drove past the club house, pulling into a graveled parking area across from a smaller building. The parking area was filled with sedans, convertibles and lots of station wagons.

Carol Ann and David walked hand-in-hand towards the pool house, which was joined to the club house by an ivy-draped covered walkway. The closer we got to the pool house the more I heard the sounds of happy children yelling and laughing. Trudging along several steps behind the giggling, happy couple, I was getting sadder and more anxious.

I don't want to be here, but I can't say anything to David about my anxiety.

David released his grip on Carol Ann's small hand when they reached the pool house doors, marked: "Men's and Ladies' Locker Rooms." I followed David reluctantly into the door labeled "Men's Locker Room." As soon as the locker room door closed behind us, David, after scanning the room and finding it empty, turned to face me, grabbing me by the shoulders; the color in his face rising to a shade of bright red.

"I just knew that this was going to be a big mistake!" He shouted as he shook me by the shoulders. "You are a dumb little jerk, and you say the stupidest things. Just shut up! Once we are out in the pool area, I don't want to see you, and I don't want to hear you! Do you understand me?"

I was now close to tears. David grabbed me by the neck, dragging me through the rows of lockers. He found an open locker, ordered me to strip off all my clothes. Naked, I was pushed down the row of lockers and into a large open showering area. It was all happening so quickly; I was in a total panic. David pushed me roughly into the shower, turned on the water, and, before I was even wet all over, pulled me from the shower, thrust a towel into my hands, told me to dry off. Back in the locker room, David ordered me to get into my trunks. Once again it was a struggle to get the smelly wool bathing trunks onto my damp body.

Already in his swimming suit, David grabbed me by the arm, dragged me out of the locker room into the sun-drenched pool area. I felt like a prisoner being ejected from his dungeon cell after years of living in the darkness: I was momentarily rendered sightless by the bright sunlight; squinting and shading my eyes with my hand. I began to hop around like an Indian doing a war dance in response to the stinging pain of the sun-baked concrete decking burning my feet. To add to my misery, my nose was assaulted by a laundry-bleach type smell, burning my nostrils and bringing tears to my eyes. *I thought that going swimming at this fabulous swimming pool was supposed to be fun! When will it become fun?*

"What's the matter, Jack?" Carol Ann asked upon seeing my obvious discomfort. "Is the chlorine stinging your eyes?"

"Sure, I guess so." I responded, happy that someone even noticed me.

Carol Ann approached me, putting her slim, sun-tanned arms around me giving me a tender hug. Her hair smelled of sweet shampoo, and her skin was oily smooth. I wanted that hug to last forever, but it didn't. Carol Ann let go of me, retreated a few steps, saying, "You'll get use to it...But, of course, the chlorine will sting your eyes if you open them in the water."

Seeing my alarmed look, she gently touched my arm, gave me a warm smile. "Don't worry, the stinging just lasts a second or two, and you'll be fine," she assured me. "Now, why don't you go get wet," she said, encouraging me along with a gentle push towards the pool. "David and I will come get you in a little while... And we'll have something to eat," she promised with another bright smile.

The sugary pep-talk from Carol Ann did little to diminish my panic. I didn't want to get in the pool. I didn't want to do anything but go back in the locker room and hide. With Carol Ann still watching me I realized that these were not options available to me. Taking a deep breath, I walked quickly to the edge of the pool, trying to find the shallow end. I observed an area where there were smaller kids frolicking in waist-deep water.

Carefully, I worked my way along the edge of the pool to where there were two or three broad steps leading down into the water. Once I descended the steps – slowly letting my legs get use to the temperature of the water – I began to edge along the side of the pool. I looked for David and Carol Ann, but I couldn't find them anywhere. The longer I was in the pool, the more I began to feel lost and abandoned; even in the midst of cheerful kids yelling, screaming and splashing water.

Then I heard the voice that has been silent for so long: *Don't be such a baby! You need to be a young man. Where is your sense of adventure? Just look around you. What a glorious opportunity you have to find out what you are made of.*

Is this Fritz, or am I going crazy with fear?

Now totally confused and disoriented, I pushed away from the wall into deeper water. The pool floor sloped downward ever so gradually towards the end of the pool with the diving boards. I observed for the first time just how long and how wide the pool really was. About two-thirds of the way to what I believed to be deeper water, there was a rope strung from one side of the pool to the other. In the water, on either side of the rope, there were droves of kids swimming around playfully.

On the far-side of the rope there were kids diving into the water from the diving boards or from the sides of the pool. The area where the kids were gathered around the rope appeared to me to be the perfect place for me to experience some adventure. Slowly I inched my way down the slopping pool floor towards the rope. There were kids – some of whom looked my age – diving from the sides of the pool – on both sides of the rope – chasing one another into and out of the water.

On a very tall chair facing the water, sat a suntanned, blond-haired young man watching the activities in the pool. He occasionally blew on the whistle that hung on a cord around his neck, yelling at kids who were apparently violating some rule he was there to enforce. I watched all of this exciting activity with great fascination. *Oh! If only I could be like these kids!*

Then it occurred to me: *I can be like them! All I have to do is dive into the water by the rope and start swimming with the other kids!* On the side of the pool where the guy with the whistle sat, there was a metal ladder. I inched my way along the side of the pool toward the metal ladder, clinging firmly to the edge of the pool. Upon reaching the ladder, I climbed out of the water.

For several minutes I just stood on the edge of the pool, dripping water onto the concrete deck, enjoying watching the boys and girls playing in the water. I watched how they dove into the water; rose to the surface; swung their arms and kicked their legs; moved about in the water. Some of the kids appeared smooth in their movements, while others made very ragged movements; but they all managed to stay on top of the water. I was convinced that I too could swim like them.

I stepped quickly to the edge of the pool, closed my eyes, took a deep breath, and launched myself headfirst into the water. Landing in the cold water chest first, knocked the breath out of me. No matter how hard I whirled my arms in wind-mill fashion, or kicked my legs like a frog, I failed to achieve anything remotely resembling swimming. With my head facing downward, my nose quickly filled with water, causing me to gasp for breath; but instead of drawing in desperately needed air, I wound up filling my throat and lungs with water. I felt myself going under, sinking. *My God! I'm drowning! I'm dying!*

FRITZ: *MEIN GOTT! the dumbkopf is drowning us! I have come too far with Jack to let this happen!* Immediately I attempted to communicate with Jack, urging him to move his arms and legs, but he was too panicked to hear me. Next, I tried forcing myself into his brain's motor functions in the hopes of getting him to reach for the surface where he might be seen; but my frantic effort at mind control also failed. Time was running out! Jack was drowning, dying. *What if Jack dies? What happens to me? Is it all over for me? What a cruel trick has been played on me if this is the end! Where is that damned lifeguard? Please, dear Gott, make someone find Jack, quickly!* In that instant, I felt some upward movement, towards the surface. Have my prayers been answered? As I began to mutter a prayer of thanks, I felt further movement as Jack was being heaved stomach-first onto the concrete decking. Someone began applying on-and-off pressure to Jack's back. In less than a minute of experiencing this pressure, Jack's body tensed as if throwing up or catching his breath. Jack coughed and sputtered. "Lie still," I heard someone say, *"You'll be okay!" Thank Gott! Thank Gott! Jack's alive, and so am I!*

This sensation of euphoria quickly passed; it is replaced by feelings *of gloom and dread — As surely as the hangover follows too much champagne. Jack's lack of self-confidence, his naivety, his childish judgment; all are leading to risky behavior. And my latest attempt to help Jack deal with these shortcomings — by urging 'manly behavior' — has turned into an unmitigated disaster! To be sure, I share much of the blame for Jack's latest fiasco. But what can I do to help Jack? Maybe I have expected too much from him? Jack is still so young; so, in time, he may be salvable. Perhaps if I just keep recounting to Jack my story, he will learn something positive from it, assimilating these lessons to his own predicament.*

CLOSING THE TABLET, Nell tried to imagine this event in Jack's life from a mother's perspective. Initially she felt anger that she had never been told, or even heard about, this near-tragedy. She also felt embarrassment at how immature Jack behaved — how incredibly naïve he was. Had she and Paul not given him the kind of attention, the breadth of experiences they had given Chris and David, that would have helped Jack grow up. *Maybe,* she thought, *this guy Fritz could help Jack mature. He certainly has all the right experiences. And besides, he helped save Jack's life. Let's hope that Fritz keeps being a positive influence on Jack.*

CHAPTER 9

BIG CHIEF TABLET EIGHT | FRITZ

Germany's last President of the Republic, Paul von Beneckendorf und von Hindenburg, died on August 2, 1934. According to Poppa, Hindenburg was the only political backstop against Adolf Hitler's usurpation of complete power over the fate of Germany and the German people. Herr Hitler – the former Austrian corporal who had risen from the gutters of Vienna – became Germany's Reich Chancellor, its Fuehrer, and, in time, would become its dictator. Under Hitler's unbridled leadership, Germany quickly repudiated the terms of the Versailles Treaty, and began the process of rebuilding its military strength.

The German military and the German industrialists – the only groups that could still successfully oppose Hitler – ignored all of the signs of impending disaster, throwing their considerable support to Hitler in order to gain the benefits and profits of rearmament. In terms of the dominant National Socialist Party, Hitler immediately consolidated his position by purging many of the party's earlier stalwarts, who Hitler now viewed to be either rivals or liabilities. As Poppa had predicted, his close friend from the Great War, Hermann Goering, was viewed by Hitler as his most important minister. Goering's star had risen very high in the Nazi party, giving him immense power within Hitler's inner circle. It was Goering who was primarily responsible for Germany's military rearmament, the Nazi party purge, and creation of the dreaded Gestapo.

Not surprisingly, after paying courtesy visits to General Goering, Poppa's firm was awarded some very lucrative government contracts for the design and fabrication of military aircraft parts; quite a coup for Poppa.

His old nemesis, Otto Muenster, had been reported to have the inside track to win these contracts because of his close ties to the Nazi Party, not because of his technical skills or manufacturing acumen. Poppa said that, "Herr Muenster does not have either." Upon the strong suggestion of Goering that further contracts may depend upon Poppa's commitment to the Fuehrer, Poppa held his nose, joined the Nazi Party; but in his latter words, "I never became a Nazi.".

Poppa demonstrated his new-found political clout by securing a position for me as a staff engineer and designer with Willi Messerschmitt's aircraft firm. This was supposed to be a temporary position; Poppa was intent on arranging for me to work with his old friend Ernst Udet as a civilian engineer at the Air Ministry. My brother Ernst had already been placed as an aide to navy Captain Konrad Patzig, the then head of the Abwehr (military intelligence). In the meantime, Wolfie, who was working with Dr. Schacht at the Reichsbank, became engaged to be married to the Countess, Louisa von Bachtelstein.

THESE CONSIDERABLE FAMILY achievements compelled Poppa and Momma to organize a celebratory dinner at the family estate. The guest list – anchored with family members – was impressive with notables from the government, industry, the arts and the military. Momma was in her element – preparing menus, hiring caterers and musicians, selecting music, wines and champagne, re-outfitting the staff, and turning the interior of the centuries-old baronial manor into a story-book setting.

The night of the party, I felt a special affection for the old manor; it reminded me of bygone Christmases, its festive lights, sounds and smells, and of my family gathered to celebrate in joyful merriment.

As I descended the great staircase into the resplendent, wood-paneled entry hall, Momma and Poppa were already greeting the first of the arriving guests. The servants were accepting top hats and capes from the men, and sleek fur coats from the women. Poppa was dressed in white tie and tails, and Momma wore a crimson silk gown that flattered her full figure. *This is going to be a very special evening indeed.*

I performed my duties in the reception line with Momma and Poppa for what seemed like hours; accepting congratulations and best wishes from family and friends. Most of these people were total strangers to me, and unlikely to ever see them again. Still, I basked in the warmth and sincerity of their praise. Beguiled by the smiles and comments of several attractive young women; one in particular caught my fancy. Before long, my eyes began to stray towards the other rooms in search of her; it was not hard to find her. She was tall, slender, with beautifully coiffed blond-hair. When my eyes fixed on the back of her lovely figure, she happened to turn to speak to someone nearby. Observing me looking at her, she smiled – a very lovely, inviting smile. In that instant I knew I must be with her. What began as a special evening for me was now turning into a night that I thought would be memorable.

As soon as it was polite to do so, I abandoned my place in the reception line to begin my search for this beautiful young lady. Frantically, I rummaged through my memory, searching through all the names thrust at me in the reception line, trying to visualize her name: *Was it Countess...or Duchess? Or was it just plain, Frauline?* What is her name? I was so struck by her beauty that I failed to focus on the name by which she had been announced. *I certainly can't speak to her without knowing her name.* Moving through the crowded rooms, one-by-one, I searched first for my older sister Marta. *Surely she would know the lovely lady's name.* Finding Marta in a group of her close friends, I beckoned her to join me so that we could speak privately. She smiled at me in a knowing way.

"I've been watching you for the last several minutes. Are you looking for me or are you on a mission?"

"Yes. Both!" I responded enthusiastically. "I need your help."

"Oh, then the mission is finding a lady, I suppose?" she inquired coyly.

"No!" I responded, somewhat hastily. "I have found the lady I was looking for, but I don't know her name. I must know her name before I can speak to her."

"Well, that depends," Marta said teasingly. "Can you describe her to me?"

"Of course," I replied without hesitation. "She is the most beautiful woman here tonight!"

"Oh, that doesn't help much...There are so many beautiful women here. You need to be more specific!" Marta said laughingly.

Frantically looking around the rooms, I spied the object of my desire, and tugging at Marta's arm while I pointed – discretely, I hoped – in the direction of my tall, blond-hair dream. "Her," I whispered, "Her!"

"The blond-hair lady?" asked Marta.

"Yes!" I replied, nodding affirmatively. "Her!"

"Hmm!" Marta mumbled in a guarded tone. "Yes, she is beautiful...But I don't think the Countess would you find you to be a particularly interesting catch. In fact, I believe she has someone else in her sights already."

I couldn't believe my ears. *What was Marta saying? The Countess smiled at me! There must be some kind of a mistake. Maybe she was looking at the wrong woman!*

"Are we talking about the same woman?" I asked fearfully.

"The tall blonde in the low-cut blue gown?" asked Marta quizzically.

"Yes." I responded apprehensively.

"Then, that is Countess Elisa von Fundel...And, from what I hear, she will soon be betrothed to Dietrich Muenster, who," Marta added "is someone I think you may have met before. He is Otto Muenster's nephew."

The dreaded, evil Muensters have struck me again! Suddenly, my special night had become a nightmare of enormous proportions.

"Don't despair, Fritz," Marta said. "The Countess has a reputation as a 'Heart-breaker'...And she will, in time, probably break Herr Muenster's heart too."

Well! Why not sooner rather than later?

As if reading my mind – as well as the set of my jaw, Marta cautioned, "I wouldn't do anything impetuous my dear brother. You, Poppa, and the family do not need to reignite hostilities with the Muensters, especially not now...We need to be accumulating well-placed friends, not antagonizing well-placed enemies."

Marta – the Wise One – has once again lived up to her well-earned nick-name.

For the rest of the evening I resisted urges to think about the Countess, or to find opportunities to join groups in which she held-forth with her beauty and charm. *The best way to avoid these thoughts and temptations is to keep busy meeting other, though maybe less attractive, women.*

There were many very charming, pretty young women with whom I then experienced pleasant, meaningful conversations; in some cases conversations which could lead to future dalliances and romance. But fanciful thoughts of flirtations with these young women paled in comparison to my fantasies involving the Countess. Damn the Muensters! *Why am I being haunted by these people? I can't let them destroy my happiness or my family. Is there anything I can do to exorcise the demons?*

Momma must have seen me deep in thought, sitting by myself on the stairway, avoiding contact with the guests. She meandered to the side of the staircase.

"Fritz. Is there anything wrong?" she inquired.

"No." I responded, unconvincingly.

"Well, you surely look unhappy, and we can't have that. Not tonight!"

Reaching for my hand, she announced, "Let's see if we can't fix things... I'd like to introduce you to some of my friends."

"But, don't I know all of your friends already?" I protested.

"Not the ones I want you to meet," she remarked.

We walked towards a group of women who appear to be younger than Momma. As we walked, Momma declared, "Marta has told me all about how interested you were in Countess von Fundel, and about how disappointed you were to learn about her interest in Herr Muenster. The Countess is a woman whose vanity exceeds the ability of any good man to meet its demands. I think Poppa and I have raised you to be a good man...one who loves God and who loves his fellow man. As attractive as the Countess appears to be, there is a side of her which is ugly and mean. You really don't need or want her in your life."

Puzzled by her condemnation of the Countess, I inquired, "Well, if the Countess is such an evil, heartless person, why did you invite her into our home to spoil this celebration for me?"

"She is the niece of one of Poppa's influential friends, General von Priester, who insisted on her accompanying him," Momma replied, somewhat unconvincingly. Sensing my disbelief, Momma continued, "Sometimes we have to make choices that are not consistent with our beliefs in order to achieve a more important result...just as we have accepted Herr Hitler as our Fuehrer in order to restore Germany's former glory ...a choice which I am afraid we may live to regret."

Just before we reach Momma's friends she whispered, "These ladies are dear friends, and represent the true spirit of Germanic womanhood... As I believe you will soon discover."

Momma's lady friends were grouped in a circle, each holding a flute of champagne or a glass of Riesling, chatting amiably; dressed fashionably in a variety of pastel-colored evening dresses. I expected these ladies to be of Momma's age, but upon closer scrutiny, some of these ladies looked young enough to be contemporaries of my older sister Marta.

"Ladies" Momma announced in a pleasant, but commanding tone, "I am sorry to interrupt your conversation, but I would like for you to have the opportunity to meet my son Fritz on a more casual basis...And for him, in turn, to meet you, my very best friends, while sharing a relaxing drink. Fritz, I am afraid, has spent too much of his youth in a boys' school, pursuing the serious aspects of learning a profession and pursuing a career. It is also clear to me that Fritz knows little of the more social graces."

Seeing me blush and looking for a way to escape from this group of smiling, laughing, charming ladies – who are much more attractive than I had first assumed, Momma quickly added, " There is no need to be alarmed or frightened Fritz...You may be under scrutiny but you will not be eaten alive. To the contrary, these lovely ladies are only interested in seeing that you are properly equipped to deal with the challenges presented to a handsome young man who may be in search of meaningful feminine companionship."

Observing – in a manner that is special to Momma – that I am still not convinced that I am not in any danger of embarrassment or humiliation by conversing with these ladies, Momma added, "Fritz, these are very special ladies...they are the widows and daughters of brave German officers who died on behalf of the Fatherland in the last war. They are condemned to live out their lives without the love and companionship of those men who made their lives worth living. These ladies represent the hundreds of thousands of women who have had their lives similarly wrenched apart through the horrors of war. Our family has been spared this agony through the grace of God. But as a young man who is about to embark on a career building...and flying...warplanes, you need to be aware that those warplanes will not only bring death and destruction to the combatants, they will also rip apart families, taking away from the women at home their husbands, fathers and loved ones. We women are the forgotten victims of war. So as you look for a woman to share your love and life with, keep in mind what future may lie in store for her."

I was shocked by what Momma had just said. The import of her statement crept over me like a dark cloud. *What could I say to these women that could possibly dispel the gloom in which I now viewed them? How could I ever assure them that I would never condemn any other woman to their same plight? Would I ever even consider making such an assurance? Why had Momma thrust this obligation on to me? And why impose it on me tonight; of all nights?*

My face grimacing with pain and frustration, Momma reached out, her gloved hand touching my face ever so slightly; pleaded softly, "Please don't fret my handsome son...this should be the concern of every person in this room tonight. Everyone here is involved...in one way or another... in the rearmament of Germany...which as sure as the Rhine flows into the North Sea, will lead us into another war."

With a look of grim determination, Momma continued, "And everyone celebrating our family's success here tonight may well look back years from now and see...but too late, I fear...the folly of what we have embarked upon with such high expectations."

Still struggling with the impact of this bomb-shell on my thoughts and emotions; struggling with whether to, or how to respond, I observed an attractive young lady detach herself from the others in Momma's flock. Dressed in a charming, but a not too stylish gown with a scooped neck displaying a hint of full breasts, she moved to stand in front of me.

"Herr von Bruckner," she addressed me with smiling eyes. "My name is Aneliese Reisling, but please call me Lisa. My father and my older brother were both killed in the last war. I loved them very much, and I was devastated by their deaths. It has taken me all this time to come the point where I am able to get on with my life. Please understand that I do not blame anyone for the death of my loved ones. Life can be full of terror and tragedy even when all attempts to prevent such from happening are to no avail. What I think your mother is trying to say is that each of must try to do the best we can to find a way to live our lives so as to foster peace rather than war. I know that war may be thrust upon us and that we must defend ourselves."

Then looking at me with her deep blue eyes, Lisa added, "I pray that the rearming of Germany is for such defensive purposes, and that you and other like-minded young men can keep it that way."

I was so struck by the intensity of Lisa's beautiful blue eyes that I failed to concentrate on what she was telling me. For all I knew, she could have been blaming me for the deaths of her father and brother. I needed to respond to her statements, but I was completely lost as to what I should say to her.

Miraculously, my sister, Marta – who had joined the group of women now surrounding me – spoke up, "I am sure that Fritz understands the obligation we all bear to avoid taking Germany into another war. Don't you, Fritz?"

Startled by Marta's voice, I suddenly realized what was occurring. I mumbled, "Oh, yes, Fraulien, of course." Despite the seriousness of the topic and the fervor of Lisa's pronouncement, the intensity of my statement caused light laughter to swirl through the group. It then occurred to me that these women were reacting to the lost look on my face; a look that displayed just how much I was captivated by Lisa. For the second time that evening, I succumbed to the considerable charms of an attractive woman.

Momma, as perceptive as ever, chimed in, saying to me, "Fritz. Why don't you and Lisa have some champagne and some food to eat? I am sure that you two have much to talk about." Lisa, not missing a beat, placed her white-gloved hand on my arm, leading me away from the group of now tittering women. As we walked away I overheard Marta whisper to Momma, "I think you may have solved two of your problems in one fell-swoop." *What is Marta talking about? What two problems? The remainder of the evening with Lisa was enlightening and wonderful. I want this awesome woman to be my wife.*

CHAPTER 10

HOPING TO CONTINUE HER READING ABOUT THE
intriguing Fritz, Nell was disappointed, when picking up the next tablet, to see that it was written by Jack. Having read Jack's last writing, where his problems at growing up were becoming unpleasant, Nell was afraid that the next writing would be just more of the same; maybe even more unpleasant.

BIG CHIEF TABLET NINE | JACK

My long interrupted trip to the farm, which had delayed my visit with Aunt Rita, was soon to take place; I was excited with anticipation. Even the rain storm that tracked our way to the farm added to the thrill of the trip, especially the reappearance of the sun over the towering clouds. For me it was an omen of good things to come. At first sight of the stately white house standing on the top of the sloping green lawn my heart leapt with joy. Wonderful memories of good times with Aunt Rita and Lady swirled through my mind.

But will Aunt Rita still hug me? Will Lady — the beautiful Irish Setter dog — still remember me and shower me with her wet kisses? Will there be new books to read and discuss with Aunt Rita? Will the food will be as delicious?

The moment the tires of the panel truck ground to a halt on the white gravel parking area at the back of the house, these thoughts dissipated as quickly as they had arisen. Aunt Rita's smiling, lovely face, and Lady doing her tail-wagging dance, was all I required. I quickly crawled out of the panel truck's cargo area, racing to Aunt Rita's waiting embrace and kisses. As Aunt Rita held me tightly in her arms, I felt Lady's excited nuzzling of my bare legs, and sensed Mom's displeasure at such overt signs of affection being squandered on me.

"Oh, Jack," said Aunt Rita. "Look how much you have grown, but you are still so skinny!" Hugging me close, she whispered in my ear, "I've missed you so much."

Turning to face Mom, Rita said, "It looks to me like you are still starving this poor boy. While I've got him here for the next two months, I'll put some meat on his bones and a smile on his face." With a smirk, Mom replied, "Take your pleasure while you can. Just remember Jack's still my child...and you spoil him at his peril!"

With a sudden sense of unease and uncertainty, I turned away from Mom and Aunt Rita and knelt down on the grass to pet Lady – who returned my attention with more affectionate licks. *What does all this mean?* I gazed around the farm trying to see if it measured up to how I remembered it.

Mom and Dad spent Saturday night at the farm. Hours after Mom had seen me off to bed in my own room, with Lady sleeping at the foot of the bed, I overheard Mom and Aunt Rita talking in the upstairs hall outside my bedroom door. *They must think I am asleep...but I am much too excited to sleep – like it is Christmas Eve.* Mom was setting out her instructions for how she expected Aunt Rita to deal with me while I am at the farm.

"Jack is to have a bath at least once a week, and he is to change his underwear... the ones I have packed for him...whenever you see that they are dirty. He is to brush his teeth daily, and he is not to have sweets. And one thing more, while Jack tries to be a good child, he sometimes fails to meet certain standards for acceptable behavior. You have my permission...indeed I encourage you – to punish Jack as needed. He respects discipline."

"And I am sure he does, Nell," Aunt Rita said sarcastically.

"You know nothing about raising a child. And stop trying to lure my boys away from me with your soft treatment and vulgar displays of affection. I know what you are trying to do with Jack. You weren't able to steal Chris or David away from me...so now you have set your sights on Jack. If I didn't have to leave him with you for the summer because I have to work...and you don't, thanks to your fortunate marriage...I would never let Jack get within fifty miles of you."

"Nell, you are a brutal, cold bitch! You may have given birth to your boys, but you have no clue as to how to be a mother, to rear a child properly. I concede that I have never had any children of my own, but common sense and innate motherly instincts tells me that children need love and affection. Yet, you have never shown any of your boys any love and affection.

"And now poor Jack – the surprise, the mistake, the burden – you want him to be a submissive, broken boy who is afraid of you, of his own shadow, of the world in general...just so you don't have to worry about him getting into trouble while you're away at work. I know that you wanted a girl, and were disappointed when you had a third son. I don't know that you hate him for not being the girl you so desperately wanted; but your cruel, loveless approach is turning Jack into a sissy, which is even worse. I don't know if I can undo most of the harm that you have already inflicted on Jack, or even prevent you from further damaging Jack, but as long as he is in my care, I intend to try to help him achieve some level of normality before it is too late...by showering him with love, affection, praise and respect. So unless you are prepared to take Jack back home with you in the morning, I intend to deliver a better, happier Jack to you at the end of the summer. Do we understand each other?"

After a long pause, I heard Mom say, "Yes, Jack will stay with you, but I must..."

Aunt Rita cut her off with, "No buts...No musts...No nothing! He either stays here on my terms or he goes home; that's it!"

Again there was a long period of silence, during which I wanted to cry out: *Please Aunt Rita, don't make Mommy take me home...I'll do anything you say...I'll be better than good...Just let me stay with you!*

Finally, I heard Mom say flatly, in an almost inaudible voice. "Okay...Jack stays." Then I heard footsteps walking away from my bedroom door...and a moment later heard another door slam shut. Poor Dad! Lucky me!

The goodbyes which were exchanged as Mom and Dad climbed into the panel truck lacked warmth and sincerity. As usual, there were no kisses or even a hug from Mom. Even Dad's attempt at a full kiss on my lips was rushed and awkward. I was reminded to write, and Aunt Rita assured that I would do so regularly. Dad honked the truck's horn and waved his hand over the top of the panel truck upon turning out of the driveway and onto the graveled road.

Aunt Rita, Lady and I watched from the top of the driveway in the shade of a towering elm tree as the panel truck wound its way along the gravel road — in and out of the trees and through the cuts — until it rattled across the old bridge, disappearing up the hill on the other side of the creek. Once my parents were out of sight, Aunt Rita came up to me and drew me into a loving embrace. Looking straight into my eyes she smiled and said, "Jack, I am so happy that I have you here with me. These next two months will, I hope, be the best in your life...and mine as well."

"Oh, yes!" I said, remembering how Aunt Rita stood up to Mom the night before.

"But for that to happen, young Jack, you must promise me two things. First, you must never tell anyone, especially your mother, what we say to each other. And second, you must always tell me the truth, no matter how hard or how embarrassing it might be. We are to have no secrets about anything. Whatever I ask you to tell me, or whatever you ask me, about anything, the answer must be truthful and honest. We must trust each other completely. Do you understand?"

"Oh, yes," I answered without hesitation.

"Before I tell you anything further about what I have planned for us...especially for you...I need you to tell me something. What you tell me will make a difference on those plans." Taking my face in both of her hands, and looking deep within my eyes, Aunt Rita inquired, "Did you hear any of the conversation that your mother and I had last evening in the upstairs hall?"

What do I say? What is the right answer? Was it wrong to hear what was said? Will she punish me if I say 'Yes'?

Then I heard the 'spirit's' voice: *"Tell her the truth. This may be the most important question you will ever answer. Trust me on this, just as she wants you to trust her."*

Lowering my eyes, I responded sheepishly, "Yes."

"I thought – at least I was hoping – that you heard us. Was what you heard painful?"

I nodded a 'Yes'.

"Do you hate me Jack for what I said to your mother?"

"Oh! No!" I answered emphatically.

"I am sure that a lot of what you heard was confusing to you. Do you want me to explain anything to you? Do you have any questions? Or do you want us just to talk about it? We need to get to the bottom of what you need, Jack, before we can begin to have a real loving relationship. You have to tell me what I can do to make you happy Jack.

"Just tell her that, based upon some of what you heard last night, you would like for her to treat you just as if you were in fact her son." Fritz said.

Oh, how long I had wished that I could be Aunt Rita's real son!

Overwhelmed with joy, I blurt out, "Please, Aunt Rita, just treat me like I really am your own son!"

The next thing I know, I was pulled into a bear-like embrace. As she rocked me back and forth, she kept saying, "Thank you, God! Thank you!" She bent down and uttered the words I had longed to hear, "I love you, my son Jack. I love you so much," my new mom said excitedly as she released me from her embrace.

I was filled with such a feeling of happiness; one I had not experienced before, ever. Without hesitation I threw my arms around her waist clinging tightly to her, not wanting to lose the marvelous feeling of joy. Again her arms enfolded me; then I felt her body start to shake. When I heard her sobbing, I instinctively pulled away thinking that I might be hurting her in some way.

"Are you all right?" I asked worriedly.

"Oh, yes, Jack, I'm just fine! We mothers tend to cry some-times when we are especially happy, just as I am right now." Wip-ing her eyes with one hand, she engulfed my hand with her free hand; and like a small-child with his mother, we walked hand-in-hand towards the house.

"I would like to take you to the country club for dinner tonight," she said as we enter the bright, cheerful kitchen. "However, the clothes you have on are awful; they will never do. Maybe a search through the clothes your mother packed for you will turn up something decent for you to wear to dinner. I want to show off my handsome young boy to my friends; so he needs to be dressed properly."

After rummaging through the tattered, old suitcase, crammed with hand-me-down, thread-bare clothes, Aunt Rita pulled out a few things which she proclaimed to be adequate.

"We really must get you some better-looking...more fashionable...boy's clothes. I'll take you into town tomorrow to shop for some. Won't that be fun?"

"Sure," I answered doubtfully. *How would I know whether it would be fun? I had never before gone shopping for new clothes. If it wasn't a hand-me-down, Mommy — and I have got to stop calling her that; just Mom — would buy what she wanted me to wear and tell me to wear it.*

Reading my mind, Aunt Rita said playfully, "I'll bet you have never even been clothes shopping before, have you? Remember Jack, tell the truth."

"No," I replied blushing.

"But do you think you will enjoy going shopping with me...if I promise not to hover over you?" she said with a wink.

"I don't know if I'll enjoy the shopping part, but I sure would like some new clothes. I'm so tired of being teased by the kids at school about what I am wearing, especially the really-old clothes with tears and holes in them. One time, one of the nuns marched me from the school yard, where I was playing with other kids, to the convent so she could patch the hole in the pants I was wearing. Everyone in the school yard could hear her loud comments on the age and poor quality of the clothes my mother dressed me in. Kids ran to the school yard fence to watch my walk of shame; I saw them smirking and smiling at my embarrassment."

Aunt Rita shook her head, making a sad face. "We're going to see to it that you are never shamed like that again...Damn your fu...u...Well, just damn your mother."

Despite the poor quality of the clothes Aunt Rita was forced to pick out for me, she declared that I was presentable; but she was not entirely at ease as she moved through the country club restaurant, from table to table with me in tow.   Still, her constant smile, and the many hugs she bestowed on me in the presence of her friends, convinced me that I was someone special. It turned out to be a wonderful evening; meeting her many charming friends, sharing a very delicious meal together. On the drive back to the farm, I revealed that this was the first time that I had ever eaten a meal in a "real" restaurant. Aunt Rita laughing at my confession, said, "Don't worry, Jack...I am sure that we will have many 'first-time's' together this summer!"

On days when Aunt Rita was too busy with her own projects, I found things to do on my own around the farm. One of Aunt Rita's projects was her frequent visits to a nearby nursing home where my grandmother, Doddy, resided. Doddy had a serious stroke several years ago, and now needed full time care. Thankfully, Aunt Rita took me to visit Doddy early in my stay; and for one visit only; it was an unpleasant "first-time." Doddy had no clue as to who I was. I understood that these visits to see Doddy were hard on Aunt Rita as well. Unlike my troubled relationship with my mother, Aunt Rita and Doddy appeared to have a very warm and loving relationship; as was evident from the many happy-face photographs of them together, which adorned the walls, desks and tables of the handsome house at Fairways.

Even on those summer days when it was too hot or too rainy to do things out-of-doors, Aunt Rita employed other entertaining activities. She introduced me to reading by having me read popular historical novels full of action and interesting characters...some of whom she insisted were distant relatives. Aunt Rita was a voracious reader; providing me with an unending source of books to read. Some books came from the shelves of Aunt Rita's own library in the den, and some books came from the local library in town. Reading books initiated Aunt Rita and me into long discussions about history, especially the colonial, revolutionary and civil wars.

ULTIMATELY, WE TALKED about World War II; leading us to discuss my Uncle Oliver, who I knew was in the Navy. According to Aunt Rita, Uncle Ollie was the commander of the naval airbase on the island of Guam in the Pacific Ocean soon after it had been recaptured from the Japanese in August, 1944.

Uncle Ollie and Aunt Rita had a particularly close relationship. Aunt Rita related to me in one of our late-evening, front-porch rocker talks that she and Uncle Ollie purchased Fairways when Doddy retired from her government job so that Doddy would have a nice place to live. Uncle Ollie persuaded Aunt Rita to move to the farm to be Doddy's companion. "I agreed to do it, both because Doddy did not need to be alone at her age, and because I needed something to occupy my time now that Jon, my husband, was dead."

I did not know until then that Aunt Rita had ever been married. I was sure that Mom told me that Aunt Rita was never married. Other than that, I couldn't remember hearing anything said to me about Aunt Rita's personal life. "I never knew you were married...Mom always said that you were never married."

Aunt Rita just laughed in a derisive manner, saying cheerlessly, "I'm not a bit surprised that your mother would tell you that...She did not approve of my marriage...and this lie is just her way of pretending it never happened."

After a considerable pause, Aunt Rita continued, "Jack, this is going to be one of those talks which I made you promise that it would be just between us. I was hoping that we could have this talk when you were a little older, but since you asked, and since I had promised you that I would always be truthful and honest with you, I am now going to tell you things about me which you probably have never heard before, but which you need to hear. This may take some time, so we may want to refresh our iced teas before I start."

We brought our freshened drinks back out on the now dark front-porch, settling back down into the comfortable rocking-chairs. Lady resumed her position at the top of the front porch steps, only lying down after she was certain that there were no threats lurking in the dark. Aunt Rita began her story, speaking

up louder for me to hear her over the din of the now fully awakened night-time insects.

"I'm not really sure where to begin this, or how disjointed it
may become, but...I think I'll tell you first about my marriage to
Dr. Jonathan Kaufman. I first met Jon when I was in my last year
of college at the University of Chicago. I was an art and music
major, and Jon was finishing medical school. We were introduced
by your Uncle Ollie who was attending officers' training school
at the Great Lakes Naval Station in Chicago. Ollie was already
a pilot, and he had met Jon in a saloon in some small village in
Columbia — that's in South America — when Ollie was carrying
the mail over the Andes Mountains in small, rickety, open cockpit
bi-planes. This was in the late 1920s. Jon was working in Bogota for the summer with his father, Dr. Stanley Kaufman, in his
father's medical clinic.

"Jon happened to be visiting at this out-of-the-way village
bringing medical supplies to his father from Bogota. Ollie had
dropped off the mail for the village and was spending the night.
According to Jon, Ollie got him drunk — which was not hard to
do in Jon's case — and then proceeded to give Jon his first airplane ride as a joke. But the joke was on Ollie. Ollie put Jon in
the front-passenger seat of the open-cockpit airplane. The plane
took off, climbing to several hundred feet above the ground; at
which point Ollie began to put the plane through some acrobatics involving rolling the plane over several times. In no time Jon
became violently ill throwing up leaning over the side of the aircraft. Because the passenger seat is in front of the pilot's cockpit, the wind stream blew the vomit back towards Ollie. Thank
God, Ollie was wearing goggles. We have laughed — just as you
are laughing now — every time that story is told, and it is told
frequently.

"Despite this inauspicious beginning, Ollie and Jon became
good friends. I don't know if they ever saw each other again
in South America, but Ollie told me they wrote to each other
frequently. I think they may have met one another a couple
of times before Ollie gave up flying those awful mail planes —
so many of Ollie's fellow pilots died in those death-traps — and

joined the Navy. Ollie and I dined together often while he was stationed at Great Lakes and before he went to the Pensacola Air Station in Florida to earn his pilots wings as a Navy officer. On several occasions, when Jon's schedule at the hospital permitted it — he joined us for diner. After Ollie left for Pensacola, Jon called me several times. We went out to dinner and, sometimes dancing. One thing led to another, and we started seeing each other seriously."

There was a long pause, and even though it was difficult to see Aunt Rita's face clearly in the dark, I could tell she was struggling with what to tell me next. Taking a deep breath and with some hesitancy in her voice, she said, "Jon and I were deeply and passionately in love. So much so that we planned to get married as soon as Jon finished his residency training. I had already received my degree and was working at an entry level job with the Chicago Symphony. Now, Jack, here comes the part of the story that may be difficult for you to understand. Rather than taking an apartment on my own, I moved in with Jon, although with his schedule at the hospital and mine with the symphony, we seldom were in the apartment at the same time. I knew that I had to tell Doddy where I was living...and of my plans to marry Jon, but I also knew that she would not approve. You see, Jon was Jewish...and I was a Catholic...an Irish Catholic.

"Doddy and your mother, but especially your mother, bear strong feelings against the Jews. From a religious standpoint, they hold a commonly-held Christian view that Jews were responsible for Jesus' crucifixion and death. As Nell says, 'They are Christ killers!' While this view is absolute nonsense and historically inaccurate, some Christians still believe it with gospel-like certainty. Many people also believe that the Jews are no better than Arabs, who, so they believe, are racially, ethnically, and religiously inferior to people like us — whose ancestors are white, Christian Europeans. Again, this is hogwash. It was just such sort of thinking on the part of European Protestants and Catholics that permitted Nazis Germany to exterminate millions of Jews, less than ten years ago."

Again Aunt Rita paused and took a deep breath. But before

she could continue, I asked, "If you don't feel that way about the Jews, why does my mother feel the way she does about the Jews?"

"Jack, that is a most intelligent question. I am not sure I know exactly why she thinks the way she does. You would have thought that she would have been conscious of what was happening to the Jews in Germany at that very time, and that she would have been more tolerant about the Jews. It may be that your mother was sent away to a convent school run by nuns, where the girls were subjected to overly-Catholic training...like, being a Catholic is the only way to get to heaven, and that the Jews were responsible for Christ's death. The local parochial schools... like you attend, and I attended...are usually not as rigorous about things like that. I guess I learned to be more tolerant towards other faiths than your mother.

"But," Aunt Rita continued, "Whatever the reason, I knew that Doddy and Nell were not going to approve of my marriage to Jon, under any circumstances. I also knew that Ollie, however, would not object. In fact, Ollie and I spent hours together before he left for Pensacola discussing my dilemma and what I should do about it. It was his sage advice to go ahead and marry Jon, and to tell them about it after the fact...which is exactly what I did.

"Of course, Jon was faced with similar parent problems. Although his parents would have preferred that Jon marry a good Jewish girl – and not a shiksa, which is what Jews call non-Jewish girls – they were more liberal-minded than some of their more conservative Jewish friend and relatives. Rather than raise questions within their Jewish community, after they met me and granted their approval for Jon to marry me, they suggested that we elope and get married by a justice of the peace.

"Jon and I were married by a judge in Chicago in June, 1933, right after Jon completed his residency in surgery; and just before he began to practice surgery with his uncle, Dr. Julius Kaufman, in Kansas City. We told Ollie of our marriage plans and of how we wanted him to be the best man. Ollie could not attend because he had just earned his wings and was being assigned to train new pilot recruits in the art of instrument landings. It took me several months after our marriage to send a letter to Doddy telling her of my marriage to Jonathon.

"At this time, the depression was just getting into full stride. Doddy had taken your folks and Chris and David into her home when your father lost his job. So when my letter to Doddy arrived at her home she, of course, shared it with your mother. I never received a response to my letter, and when I telephoned Doddy after several weeks of not hearing from her, it was your mother who answered the telephone. Nell's only words to me were, 'You have broken mother's heart...Don't you or that Jew ever darken our door!' and then she hung up. I was not surprised by Nell's invective, but I wasn't sure that she was really speaking for Doddy. Whenever I tried calling again, Nell would always answer the telephone; hanging up when she heard my voice. It was only after Jon was killed in late 1942, when a German artillery shell struck Jon's field hospital in Italy...and Ollie had told Doddy of his death...that I heard from her.

At this point in telling her story, Aunt Rita got up from her rocker and moved to the porch-rail. After facing out into the dark night for a long time, she removed something from her skirt pocket, bringing it up towards her face. I couldn't see much in the little light coming through the windows onto the porch, but I saw her shoulders shake, heard soft sobbing sounds. I started to get up to go to Aunt Rita, but the voice of 'the spirit' in me said, *"Leave her alone right now...Let her cry...She has held in her pain for so long, and she needs to let it go. Believe me, I know what it feels like...I know what she is going through!"* At first I thought Aunt Rita was crying because of what my mother had said and done, but then the voice added, *"She must have loved Jon so very, very much!"*

After what seemed to me to be an eternity — during which time Aunt Rita continued to cry — I felt a pain deep in my body. It was as if I, too, was sharing the loss of her husband, even though I hadn't even known him. Then it hit me; I was feeling Fritz, my 'spirit', grieving; I was experiencing his pain of loss; his loss of a loved one. In the next instant, I was on my feet walking towards Aunt Rita; as if propelled by magic. When I reached her,

I placed my cheek on her back, wrapping my arms around her waist, drawing her back into me in a tight embrace.

Immediately, some feeling or emotion coming from deep within me passed out of me and into Aunt Rita. She stiffened, trembled, relaxed. It was as if she felt the same sensation, only more intensely. She clasped her hands over mine, and leaning back against me, caused me to stumble backwards.

"Oh, dear," she exclaimed, trying to keep her balance. "Jack... I didn't realize it was you holding me...I thought it was a grown man." Regaining her balance, she released my hands, turning around to face me. "But, thank you so much for your...a...concern," she uttered with uncertainty. "It's as if you truly feel...and share...my grief and pain." Seeing the puzzled look on my face – even in the dim light – she added, "I hope I haven't frightened you."

THERE WAS NO more talking that evening. I feared that there would be no further talks about Aunt Rita's personal life for the remainder of my visit that summer. It was as if a door had been partially closed in our relationship. Even though we still shared fun times and loving looks, I came to sense that some of her carefree joy was missing. Sometimes I would catch Aunt Rita looking at me in a questioning way, but without saying anything to me.

At other times, when I was alone, either playing outside by myself, or when I was trying to go to sleep at night, I would dwell on what happened to us that evening; of how Fritz had – for a moment – taken control of my functions – both mental and physical. It was a frightening experience; the loss of control of my body and mind. *Will it happen again? Is there anything I can do to prevent it? Am I going crazy? Who would understand what was happening to me?* Never before had I felt so alone, or so helpless, as I did then! There were even times when the feelings would wake me up at night crying.

On one occasion, waking up crying, I sat up in bed to see where I was. In the light coming through the open bedroom door Aunt Rita was silhouetted, standing next to my bed. Instinctively, I reached my arms out to her; and she took me in her arms, sitting down on the edge of my bed. "Everything's okay," she crooned over and over, cradling me in her arms. I have no memory of how long it took me to stop crying, or to fall back to sleep. *Oh how good it feels to be held in Aunt Rita's tender embrace.*

When I awoke the following morning, I found both Aunt Rita and Lady curled up on top of the covers on my bed, with one of Aunt Rita's arms draped across the sheet covering my shoulders. I did not want to lose that moment...that feeling, but I had to go to the bathroom. Try as I might to sneak out of the bed without disturbing them, as soon as I moved towards the other side of the bed, Aunt Rita and Lady were aroused from their sleep. Aunt Rita looked at me warmly through red-rimmed eyes, but with a smile on her lips.

"Good morning, Jack" she grumbled groggily. "What can I fix you for breakfast?" she asked as I stumbled out of bed, heading towards the bathroom, with Lady trailing close behind.

"How about fried eggs and biscuits?" I replied cheerfully. *Maybe things will be all right again after all!*

———————

BY THE TIME the end of August arrived, I was — once again — busy being Aunt Rita's "handsome boy." In all the excitement of the last few remaining days I had almost forgotten about Buzz, the fellow with the racing car. On an afternoon when Aunt Rita and I were in town shopping for some new school clothes for me, I spotted Buzz climbing out of a ratty, old, war-surplus Jeep parked on the shady, tree-lined street in front of the county courthouse.

"That's Buzz!" I announced to Aunt Rita as she pulled the station wagon into an angle parking spot across the street from where the Jeep was parked. "He's the fellow who has the racing car I was telling you about," I exclaimed, quickly pushing open the door, jumping out of the station wagon, and waving my arms in

Buzz's direction, shouting frantically, "Buzz...Buzz!" Buzz looked towards the shouting, with a hand shading his eyes, but with no sign of recognition.

Then I heard Aunt Rita call out his name. "Oh, Buzz," she said with a warn note of familiarity in her voice. Buzz quickly turned in Aunt Rita's direction, giving her a broad smile of recognition. *Well, they obviously know each other!* Buzz sauntered across the street towards us. *My mission of meeting the P38 pilot, Pete Roberts, may not be as difficult as I thought it would be.*

"Mrs. Kaufman," Buzz said as he removed his well-worn pilot's cap with his left hand, wiping his right hand on his overalls before extending it towards Aunt Rita. Taking her hand in his, Buzz added, "It is so good to see you again. It's been a while since you've been over to Daddy's ranch. We've missed you."

"Well, thank you, Buzz...I, too, miss my visits to your folk's place. And, how are your mother and dad?" Aunt Rita asked with sincere interest.

"Who's your young friend?" Buzz inquired, looking at me with no sign of recognition.

"He's my nephew, Jack...I thought you knew him?" Aunt Rita replied with a puzzled look. "Jack claims he met you some time ago at the filling station where you keep a racing car."

Looking at me again with probing eyes, Buzz said, "Yes. There is something about you that looks familiar, but I really don't...." After pausing and looking at me more closely, he said, "Oh, sure...I know you! You're the kid who knows all about P38 airplanes...and has the bossy mother. When you said you were coming to your Aunt's place out here, I never made the connection with it being Mrs. Kaufman's place. We...my folks and me... we think the world of your aunt; she's a very special lady! And she has the prettiest farm around these parts."

"Jack," Aunt Rita replied with a warm laugh, "I want you to meet the greatest flatterer in these parts...Mr. Carlson...excuse me...Buzz Carlson."

"Pleased to meet you again, Jack...and just call me Buzz...like all my friends do."

As Buzz was shaking my hand, Aunt Rita asked, "Buzz, do

you have time to join Jack and me for a Coke at the Roxy Coffee Shop? I am sure that Jack is full of questions he'd like to ask you."

"I'd love to...but I've got to pick up some forms and stuff from the County Agent this afternoon...and I don't know how long that will take...I need them today 'cause Dad and me are heading to Canada in the morning to pick up a couple of prize bulls we're going to winter down here." Buzz added hurriedly, "But I'll be back in ten days or so...and maybe we can't get together then."

"That'll be too late...Jack's heading back home to the city next week."

"Oh, gosh...I'm sorry. If it was any other day than today...but I've really got to get going...I'm late as it is."

"Can I ask you just one question?" I inquired imploringly. When Buzz nodded his assent, I continued, "How can I find Mr. Roberts....Pete Roberts...The fellow you said flew the P38 in Europe...in the war...I need to talk with him?"

"I'm not sure. The last I heard of him, he had taken a job flying a plane for one of the pipelines out of Texas or Oklahoma... If I had the time I could find out, and maybe after I get back from Canada I'll find out, and pass the information on to your Aunt Rita...I gotta go," he stated, dashing across the street towards the courthouse.

"What was that about Pete Roberts?" Aunt Rita asked, turning away from the quickly departing Buzz. Walking towards the clothing store, she stated, "I've heard of him...and I may have met him at a cookout a couple of years ago...at the Carlson's I believe. What do you need to talk to him about?"

"Well, when Buzz told me that his racing car was powered by an engine from a P38, I explained to Buzz, how much I loved the P38 and of how I had read a lot about it. Buzz then told me that his friend, Mr. Roberts, had some interesting stories about flying P38s during the war that I needed to hear."

"I think that is very interesting...and quite nice of Buzz to let you know about Pete Roberts. I'll tell you what...next summer while you're here I'll invite Buzz and Pete Roberts out to the farm for the day...and you can talk with him to your heart's satisfaction."

———————

OH, THERE SHOULD never have been "a next summer." Had I known what that bitch Rita was doing to Jack, I'd have never let him spend another day at Fairways ever again. And I had trusted her to take care of my son. She took care of him all right, by turning him into "her handsome boy," Nell thought as she slammed the tablet down on the floor. She began to think that she could not stand to read another of Jack's writings, but realized that as hard as it was going to be, she had to get to the bottom of what happened to Jack.

CHAPTER 11

THE NEXT EVENING, AGAIN IN HER BEDROOM,

again overwhelmed by the number of Big Chief tablets yet to be read, Nell was relieved to find that the next tablet she picked from the stack was written by Fritz.

BIG CHIEF TABLET TEN | FRITZ

I was pleased, but still concerned, with what was happening with Jack! Although Jack has been spending his summer vacations with his Aunt Rita for several years, what I was seeing before through Jack's eyes and feeling with his feelings, was not what I was seeing and feeling that summer. Maybe for Jack, now being ten years old, made the difference; he was responding to her differently, or maybe his Aunt Rita was providing Jack with more love and attention than she had in the past. Whatever it was, I was beginning to believe that I can successfully complete my unfinished business in Germany.

From what I was seeing, this Aunt Rita had the intelligence, the energy, and the courage essential to an undertaking of the nature that I have been contemplating for Jack and me. Moreover, I was enjoying being around Aunt Rita; she is charming, attractive, witty and strong. I was particularly impressed with the fact that she had experienced deep, passionate love; and with how she dealt with the pain of losing a loved one. I realized that I really liked this brown-eyed, dark haired beauty who wears blue denim britches, riding boots and a man's work shirt when she goes out in public. I would like to know more about Aunt Rita; but to learn more about her Jack has to get her to talk more about her life experiences.

My more immediate concern though was still Jack. Although he had clearly made progress that summer with Aunt Rita's loving care, I was concerned about what was going to happen to him once he returned to his crippling home life? Will what he experienced that summer be enough for him withstand the debilitating effect of his overbearing mother and his ineffective – but loving – father? This was a gamble that I was not will-ing to take. Therefore, I clearly needed to play a bigger role in his physi-cal and mental growth. Now that I could gain control of his thoughts and emotions – at least to some extent – on a real-time basis, and not just through his dreams, I began to think that I might be able to bring about some important changes in Jack. But I needed to be careful in how I pro-ceeded with Jack; he was no longer just a boy. He was more conscious of my presence as well as perplexed by what was happening to him, as evidenced by his fear of my gaining control of his body and mind – as occurred in that awkward embrace of his Aunt Rita. Still, I must take ad-vantage of the times that Jack and I are away from Aunt Rita; preparing Jack – both mentally and emotionally – to tell Aunt Rita about me. Jack will have just one chance to bring Aunt Rita into my plans without caus-ing Aunt Rita to think he is insane or, worse...possessed by the devil!

MY FIRST ENCOUNTER with Reich Marshall Hermann Goering took place sometime in 1935. Poppa had at last secured a position for me with the Air Ministry, following two years as an engineer with Willie Messer-schmidt's aircraft firm. I was working as a minor functionary in the pro-curement division of the Air Ministry on Wilhelmstrasse in Berlin. Berlin is a short commute from my parents' home on the outskirts of Potsdam. I was still unmarried, living with my parents. I didn't want to get a place of my own until I knew whether I might need to relocate to another German city as part of my job.

It was also possible that I would be called up for compulsory military training of six-months or a year. With my background in flying airplanes with the civilian air corps, I hoped that I would receive my military training as a fighter-pilot with the currently clandestine *Luftwaffe*. Any such pilot training would take place at secret training sites in either Russia or Italy. As I was soon to learn, however, with the military – or for that matter, with any branch of government – any hoped-for assignment or stationing (even when specialized training or expertise would otherwise call for it) was unlikely to ever happen. I supposed, that based upon my educational training, as well as my experiences with aircraft and the flying of aircraft, the powers-to-be would determine that my immediate future would be linked to the development and procurement of military aircraft for the new *Luftwaffe*.

Within the Air Ministry there were a number of different divisions related to aircraft development and procurement, depending on the class or role of the aircraft involved. My assignment was with procurement of bomber aircraft which, as expected, was not my first choice of assignment. To me, bombers were like the slow, clunky freight trains; while the fighters were like the speedy, streamline passenger trains. My disappointment was somewhat assuaged by the fact that the *Luftwaffe's* primary concern at that time was in the design, development and manufacture of offensive weapons; and bombers – not fighter aircraft – were deemed to be offensive weapons. *But, aren't offensive weapons primarily used to take war to your enemies? Does this mean that Germany is preparing itself to wage a war, despite all the pronouncements of the Reich Chancellor Hitler to the contrary?*

General Erhard Milch – Inspector General of the *Luftwaffe* – head of the aircraft procurement staff announced a meeting with *Luftwaffe* Reichsminister Hermann Goering, to be conducted at the Air Ministry. No underlying information was given in the announcement as to the purpose of the meeting. Rumors, however, quickly circulated among the procurement staffs (there were several dozens of us at that time) that this was a 'come to Jesus' type meeting; the Reichsminister was expected to berate his staff for not assuring production of warplanes in accordance with his previously detailed timetables. Even at this early stage of the new Third Reich, orders from the high command – and especially from Reichsminister Goering – were not to be disregarded without sufficient reason. It was not to be a meeting that staff members would be looking forward to.

Although I had been on the bomber procurement staff for less than a year, I was intimately involved as a lead staffer in reviewing the design and manufacturing plans for a radically new bomber being examined for possible procurement by the *Luftwaffe*. The prototype was being assembled by the Junkers Aircraft facility, and was identified as the Ju-87. This aircraft was a "SturzKampfFlugzeug" (diving combat aircraft), or "Stuka" for short. This amazing, single-engine aircraft – designed to drop bombs – had characteristics more similar to a fighter aircraft than those of a traditional bomber.

The traditional multi-engine bomber generally delivers its payload of bombs – from a bomb bay containing from a few large bombs to many smaller bombs – depending on the size of the bomber – at a high altitude over an unseen target – from 5,000 to 10,000 meters. At these altitudes the bombs are subjected to many factors – like wind and evasive tactics – affecting the ability of the bombs to strike the target.

A dive bomber is a single-engine aircraft carrying two bombs – usually mounted under its wings. Its bombs are released at a very low altitude by the pilot aiming them directly at a specific target. This maneuver requires that the aircraft be placed into a steep dive at a high rate of speed directly down toward the target. The bombs are released during this dive as close to the target as is practical – at which point the pilot must put the dive bomber into a steep climb to a higher altitude, known as the 'pull-out'. These maneuvers place tremendous forces and stress on the aircraft's frame, wings, engine and propeller, especially in the pull-out.

For me, the Stuka was the perfect aircraft: It had the style of a fighter with none of the drawbacks of the bomber; providing me with a solution to my moral dilemma of working with an aircraft more intended to deal with battlefield situations than with an aircraft designed for bombing innocent civilians. It also provided me with a more versatile aircraft to which I could apply my design and engineering talents, and, hopefully someday, my piloting skills. Consequently, I pursued my staff procurement duties with great enthusiasm and dedication. I was familiar with even the smallest details of its design and capabilities.

Unlike many of my procurement staff cohorts, who viewed their work as a day-light desk-job, I spent long hours honing my design skills; spending a great deal of time visiting the Junker's facilities; examining and analyzing the Ju-87s construction and assembly processes. In the course of my many 'field visits' to the Junker facility in Dessau, I became acquainted with several of the key members of the technical design and engineering staffs, providing important input on a number of critical design issues. I even had the opportunity to make test-flights – once as its pilot – in an early version of the Ju-87, at the *Luftwaffe* test center at Rechlin.

The Stuka was still in its prototype stage, but I was so impressed by its flight characteristics and its durability, that I was in the process of preparing a formal Procurement Recommendation urging the *Luftwaffe* to acquire the Ju-87. I even furnished my superiors, including General Ernst Udet – Poppa's good friend from the war, and the principal proponent for the development of the Stuka – with draft copies of my assessment of the Ju-87, including my recommendation for its acquisition. When contemplating the upcoming staff meeting with the Reichsminister – who is also the *Luftwaffe's* Reichsmarschall – I felt quite comfortable that I would be able to address any questions about the details of the Ju-87, or about the support for my procurement recommendation.

On the morning of the scheduled meeting with Reichsminister Goering, I accepted Poppa's invitation to ride with him in the Mercedes from our home on the outskirts of Potsdam to his plant conveniently located adjacent to Berlin's Templehoff Airport – where many other aircraft fabricators and assemblers had their facilities. From there I rode the trolley to the Air Ministry building in the center of Berlin.

In the Mercedes, Poppa was unusually chatty; giving me his impressions of the rearmament of Germany, detailing the size and scope of the many job orders his plant was filling, and soliciting my opinion on whether all of this activity meant that the threat of war was imminent. He also asked me many questions about the Ju-87 aircraft, of its potential uses, and of the likelihood of its procurement. The tone of Poppa's questions and comments suggested that he had more than a passing familiarity with my work at the Air Ministry.

Dressed in my best dark-blue suit and conservative tie, I arrived at the air ministry earlier than usual that morning. Poppa had warned me that Reichsminister Goering was a "fancy dresser" and that he expected his underlings to also be well-dressed and well-groomed.

But would the Reichsminister even notice me in the spacious, but crowded meeting hall...especially if I manage to stake out a place behind a pillar or among some of the taller staffers?

At my cluttered desk – one of many desks – in the vast open work area to which staffers like me were assigned, I took the time to quickly review my recommendation; noting in particular the acquisition time-frames, which I knew would be most important to the Reichsminister should the opportunity arise. By ten hundred hours, I was ready to face the task.

The Air Ministry's main meeting hall was located on the ground floor, at the end of an ornate, wide passageway leading from the heavy bronze front doors of the building. The passageway has a highly polished marble floor, and its bas-relief ceiling was supported by stone columns. A large crowd of men dressed in suits – as well as a smattering of men in uniforms – made their way into the meeting hall through the single set of enormous oak paneled doors. Uniformed guards stood at the sides of the doors checking credentials of those entering the meeting hall.

Inside the meeting hall, there were several rows of chairs on either side of a main aisle facing a stage at the front of the dark-paneled, high ceilinged room. The long, dark drapes were drawn across the floor-to-ceiling windows lining both sides of the hall. With the drapes drawn, the room was brightly illuminated by ten or twelve crystal chandeliers. The stage at the front of the hall was decorated with a variety of military flags, banners and the ubiquitous Nazi swastika; all illuminated by banks of carefully aimed spotlights. In the center of the stage was a substantial podium; behind which were several well-spaced high-backed arm chairs, all of them empty.

By the time I made my way into the meeting hall, most of the hundred chairs on the floor were filled with higher ranked staffers and military officers. Younger staffers – like my self – were directed to stand at the rear, and along the sides, of the hall. I took my place along one of the side walls. There were a dozen, or so, dark-suited, well groomed young men standing on either side of the main aisle watching the dignitaries taking their seats. The front two rows of seats were still empty. The hall echoed with chatter; the air quickly became stuffy with the heat of the bright lights, the hundred or so bodies, and the clouds of tobacco smoke from cigarettes, cigars and pipes.

Standing there, absorbing the sights, sounds and smells of this setting, I was suddenly struck by the memory of my last encounter in a setting such as this...*The disastrous Nazi rally I attended in Braunschwieg when I was a student at the Institute...The rally in which Poppa and I were so viciously attacked by Herr Otto Muenster. A chill ran through my body, and my previous state of relaxation was replaced with a sense of dread and foreboding. Am I again being set up for a personal attack? Is there anything about my work on the Stuka project that should be cause for alarm? Have I made any decisions about the Ju-87 – changes in the design or manufacture – which might have offended Junkers, a supplier or a Nazi party official?*

And then I knew the source of my dread. The original prototype of the Ju-87 was equipped with a two-blade wooden propeller – perhaps the same type propeller manufactured by Herr Muenster that Poppa had condemned in the last war! In my recommendations, I had insisted that the Ju-87 must be equipped with a three-blade metal, variable pitch propeller, instead of the outdated wooden propeller. It was my opinion that the wooden propeller simply could not handle the stress of the dive and pullout! My opinion was borne out by my experience in flying the prototype Ju-87. Even though the dive I put the aircraft through was quite shallow, I experienced acceleration difficulties – almost to the point of stalling – during the pullout. Upon landing I examined the propeller, observing that it exhibited signs of stress fractures which would lead to disintegration. I did not know who supplied the propeller that I had condemned as dangerous; but if it was a Muenster-supplied propeller, then the family antagonist would surely have found someone to complain to, just as he did against Poppa in the last war

Was this to be a replay of that controversy? But Reichsminister Goering – who was a much-decorated pilot during the last war – sided with Poppa against Herr Muenster in that controversy...Would he side with Herr Muenster now, if asked to? Herr Muenster was well-known to be one of the many industrialists who supported the Nazi party financially. Was Herr Muenster also one of those industrialists who were rumored to provide Reichsminister Goering with secret funding as well?

Dreading another embarrassing moment at the hands of Herr Muenster, I pressed my body tightly into a space along the wall. I hoped to be shielded from view by the two gentlemen on either side of me who were standing slightly away from the wall to get a better view of the still-empty stage. Any thoughts of escape were destroyed by a loud shout of "Attention!" from someone in the rear of the hall; followed by a parade of *Luftwaffe* officers and dignitaries filing into the hall. It was difficult for me to see over the heads of the men who jumped to their feet on the command to rise. Only Generals Milch and Udet, and the Reichsminister ascended the steps onto the stage. The others in the parade must have peeled off to the right or the left as they reached the first two rows of empty chairs. I recognized the two generals; both because I worked for them, and because Poppa had photos of them from the last war in his office.

General Milch was short, stocky, in his early forties. In the last war he had commanded a fighter squadron, but was not himself a pilot. During the period after the war he founded and ran an airline. It was rumored that his father was a Jew, but Poppa said that Reichsminister Goering was not concerned about whether General Milch was in fact a Jew. Milch was placed in charge of the Reich's Aviation Ministry – known to us as simply the RLM – in 1933, answering only to the Reichsminister. General Milch's prime responsibility was armament production for the *Luftwaffe,* but most of the military aircraft procurement decisions were being made by the other general on the stage, Ernst Udet.

General Udet was even shorter than General Milch. Poppa said Udet was too short to be a military pilot. Not to be deterred, Udet took private flying lessons allowing him to join the Army Air Service. Even then he was relegated to the ranks of flying as an *Unteroffizier* (staff sergeant) in the artillery spotting unit. Based upon his flying skills and some heroics, Udet was then assigned to a fighter command. Ultimately commissioned as a *Leutnant,* Udet continued to flourish as a fighter pilot; eventually becoming the second most decorated pilot in the war, after Goering. Following the war, Udet built and raced airplanes, even going to Hollywood, California to be a stunt pilot in American movies. Although Udet and Goering were rivals during the war, Goering recognized Udet's abilities and brought him back into the military air service. It was General Udet's interest in dive bombers that gave me my opportunity to work on the Ju-87.

I also recognized the Reichsminister; whose corpulent frame, dressed resplendently in a light-blue *Luftwaffe* Reichsmarschall's uniform, was frequently displayed in flattering press photos. The two generals walked to their chairs, where they remained standing until the Reichsminister was settled, standing behind the podium. After the obligatory, "Sieg Heil!," Goering motioned for all who had seats to be seated.

"Gentlemen!" began the Reichsminister, "We have been handed a mandate by the Reichsfuhrer and the German people to rebuild the Luftwaffe into the most effective and feared air force in the world! It is our obligation to the Fuhrer, and our commitment to the safeguard of the Fatherland to see to it that this mandate is fulfilled in its entirety and as quickly as resources permit. And it is your duty – as agents of the Air Ministry – to oversee the design, the engineering, the fabrication, the manufacture, the assembly, and the timely delivery of the most technologically advanced aircraft the world has ever seen!"

Following lengthy applause and obligatory shouts of "Sieg Heil!," the Reichsminister continued, "With these obligations, commitments and duties clearly in mind, I am here to enlist each of you in a joint endeavor, of the Air Ministry procurement departments and the members of the aircraft industry, to work together – as if just one – to assure the prompt and appropriate allocation of resources – both of men and materials – to bring Germany back to its rightful place in air supremacy with all classes of aircraft to the defense of the Fatherland and its citizens."

The Reichsminister was interrupted with more applause and shouting. "This should," he continued, "be an easy undertaking: Germany is blessed with the brightest innovators, the most skilled designers and engineers...our craftsmen and workers are more productive and efficient than any others in the world...and our ability to find alternatives to any scarce resources is second-to-none!"

"Today, this Air Ministry building is filled with plans, designs, proposals, and the factories have available working prototypes of aircraft which, if in production, will return the German *Luftwaffe* to its previous glory! Unfortunately, however, the *Luftwaffe's* storeroom of state-of-the-art aircraft is bare...and we are here to see that each of you takes steps to change that situation immediately. There simply must be more production – and I mean real production – of technologically advanced warplanes! I don't expect each and every aircraft to be perfect before it goes into service; that would be a counter-productive requirement.

"What I want are aircraft that are safe, efficient and can beat anything else in the air. Even the best aircraft are sure to modified, refined and improved once our fine pilots put these aircraft through their paces. But this cannot and will not happen as long as the aircraft are just 'paper' airplanes. And this can't happen as long as prototype aircraft move incessantly from one prototype to the next prototype. No matter how exciting the prospects are for the ultimate success of an aircraft...the time comes when the beast must be put in the air and tested under actual, war-like conditions."

"For example, I am advised by members of the Air ministry that one of my highest priorities – a dive bomber – has been successfully flight-tested, but is still being treated only as a prototype, labeled: Not Ready for Production." *Oh my God! Here it comes!* "I don't know the details of the holdup, but I want the Stuka in production now! Not next year, but now...immediately! I expect that all who are responsible for its procurement and production...from Generals Milch and Udet and on down...to complete the procurement process...and have the orders for its production in my hands by the end of the day...tomorrow...or else!"

Whatever else the Reichsminister may have said after that, I heard only the pounding of my heart. I was then totally focused on what I still had left to do to meet the Reichsminister's deadline. *What am I doing standing here? I need to get back to my desk, completing the Procurement Recommendation. Fortunately, most of the work is complete, and I just need to finish up one or two loose ends. But if I try to walk out of here in the middle of Goering's speech, I am sure to be identified as the "bottleneck" to everyone who sees me leave, especially the Reichsminister. Still, I have little time to waste...It is simply a risk I have to take. Besides, I need to protect General Udet – who is ultimately responsible for this project – from incurring the Reichsminister's wrath.*

Throwing caution to the winds, I stepped away from the wall, started walking towards the now closed large double doors; where a platoon of uniformed SS troopers barred my path. *How do I get myself into these predicaments? Will the guards let me pass?* As the moment of truth arrived, there was only silence in the hall. The Reichsminister had stopped his speech, and everyone else in the hall had become eerily quiet.

With my eyes focused on the guards baring my exit – I heard a voice call out my name: "Herr von Bruckner! Won't you at least stay until I have finished my speech?" Turning to face the stage, I heard the Reichsminister add, "Have I perhaps said something that has offended you?" With a massive smile breaking across his broad face he chortled, "Or...maybe you have an airplane to catch?" Observing the Reichsminister's smile and comprehending his play on the words – "an airplane to catch," the audience commenced laughing; small laughter at first, swelling to a roaring convulsion. I, likewise, began to sense that the Reichsminister was making a friendly joke, but at my expense.

"No, Herr Reichsminister, I have already caught the aircraft which is the subject of your fancy and, with your permission, I was simply going to fetch it...Not the Stuka, but just the paperwork making you the proud owner of a whole flock of Stukas!...But I can wait until later if you would prefer."

The Reichsminister – as well as the entire audience – erupted again into peals of sustained laughter. When the laughter in the room subsided, Herr Goering, wiping away tears of laughter from his red face, spoke to me in a raised voice; "Your father would be proud of you...young von Bruckner...You have managed in one sentence to outdo even your father's well-known gift for employing misdirection when a situation to do so presents itself!"

After another pause to let the newest eruption of laughter to die down, he added, "By all means, go get your Stuka...We can't keep the aircraft waiting." Again, there was more laughter; over which Herr Goering shouted, "But... bring whatever you have to General Milch's office, not here!"

With a wave of his hand, he indicated to me, and to the guards, that I was free to exit the hall. I passed hurriedly through the now opened doors. As the doors shut behind me, I heard the Reichsminister announce to those still in the hall, "I wish that everyone would take my words so seriously!" *Was I set up? Did I handle it appropriately?*

Later that same afternoon, I was summoned to General Milch's top floor, corner office. Upon being ushered into the office by the General's aide, I immediately sensed an atmosphere unlike the one I felt earlier in the meeting hall. The two generals, Milch and Udet, as well as the Reichsminister – whose presence was a complete surprise to me – were sprawled casually in overstuffed chairs and the sofa – with their uniform tunics unbuttoned, basking in the late afternoon sun pouring in through the tall windows that graced the walls of the opulently furnished office. The Reichsminister was holding a half-full brandy glass in one hand and a large, partially-smoked cigar in the other. General Milch was staring out of the multi-paned windows. Only General Udet stood to greet me.

"Ah! Fritz," said General Udet as he gestured me towards one of the arm-chairs in front of the desk. "Thank you for joining us...I hope you had sufficient time to complete the paperwork...Oh! I see you have brought the Procurement Recommendation with you. Why don't you just put it there on the desk...We can look at it later."

"Yes!" echoed the Reichminister, as I took my seat. "I am most interested in learning exactly what you think of the Junker's Stuka...And if you can give me an estimate as to when the first of the production aircraft can be delivered to the *Luftwaffe*."

I moved from my chair towards the desk to retrieve the Recommendation. "Perhaps," I suggested, "the Reichsminister would care to look at my report...in which I cover all those details,"

"No!" responded the Reichsminister. "That's really not necessary...I have already seen the draft of the recommendation you recently shared with General Udet...What I want from you this afternoon is for you to tell me, in your own words, your personal assessment of the Ju-87. You see, Ernst has told me that you have already flown the Ju-87...and that you made some recommendations for changes...I should say improvements... to the aircraft based upon your own experience in flying the Stuka. You see, this is exactly what I was saying today...We have to get these aircraft into the hands of experienced pilots – like yourself – if we are ever to find out what it will take to make these aircraft winners."

I spent the next hour explaining to the Reichsminister and the two generals what I thought of the current version of the Ju-87 – the V4, and what I thought might be done to make it a better aircraft. The Reichsminister listened attentively to my explanations and recommendations. In-dicating that he had heard all that he needed to hear, the Reichsminister turned to General Udet and said, "Well, Ernst, I think we have our Stuka... What do you think?"

"I concur...And I want to thank Herr von Bruckner here for providing us with a clear, concise and convincing report..."

"Yes, of course," interrupted the Reichsminister. "By the way, von Bruckner," he continued, "General Udet...and others here at the Air Min-istry...speak highly of your work...both in what you accomplish and in the way that you go about it. Your exemplary work ethic is not unexpected... given who you are...and who your father is."

Turning towards General Milch, the Reichsminister continued, "Baron von Bruckner...this fine young man's father...furnished the Fatherland with exemplary service during the last war as a field colonel responsible for keeping us fly boys in technologically advanced...and safe...aircraft. The Baron is a fine man...one respected by one-and-all for his knowledge, dedication, and independent thinking. I hold the Baron in high esteem, and consider myself fortunate in having him as my friend."

Turning his gaze towards me, I could see in his eyes the respect he held for my father. He then asked me, "And Fritz, how is your father?"

"He is quite well," I replied. "Thank you...I will tell him that you have so graciously inquired about his well being Herr Reichsminister...He so often speaks highly of you and of your long friendship...and of the assistance you rendered on his behalf during the war."

"Ah, yes!" he acknowledged with a deep sigh. "The infamous Muen-ster propeller debacle...Your father's decision to reject that propeller saved a lot of pilots' lives...including...perhaps...my own. I am sure that all of you...especially you Ernst...have heard what Otto Muenster tried to do to have the Baron's decision over-ruled by the General Staff. There has been bad blood between your father and Herr Muenster ever since... Am I not correct, Fritz?"

I nodded my assent, the Reichsminister continued his thoughts. "And I understand that you wisely insisted that the wooden propeller proposed for use on the Ju-87 be replaced with a more advanced metal, variable-pitch propeller...The wooden propeller which you – like your father before you – have rejected, must not have been manufactured by Herr Muenster's firm...or I am quite sure that Herr Muenster would be raising holy hell to me about it by now," the Reichsminister said, shaking his head with a grim smile.

"In any event," the Reichsminister continued, "I have instructed General Milch to approve your Procurement Recommendation." After a pause he added, somewhat more seriously, "You may not know this, but Generalfeldmarschall von Richthofen has sent me a note indicating that the *Wermacht* has no interest in the Stuka, and is calling for ending the Stuka project. But based upon your recommendation that the Stuka will provide tremendous support for the ground-troops, General Udet has urged me to reject von Richthoven's instructions. I concur in Ernst's and your recommendation, and I am immediately ordering the manufacture of one-hundred of the Ju-87 Stukas."

As I started to rise, the Reichsminister motioned for me to remain seated. "I have also ordered General Milch to make some changes in your role here at the Air Ministry...These changes are necessitated by your performance on the Stuka project. I...like many others – as I have mentioned – have been impressed with your talents, and with your work ethic and enthusiasm. I have instructed General Udet to keep you assigned to the Stuka project until the *Luftwaffe* has received delivery of sufficient numbers of the Ju-87 that we can start the process of actual war-type experience. Only then can we determine whether the Stuka needs further refinements – both from your own experience and that of the other uniformed pilots."

Maybe it was my quite readily apparent facial expression of shock... caused by the Reichsminister's use of the phrase, "other uniformed pilots," that prompted General Milch to address me for the first time that afternoon. "A...a...a...the Reichsminister," he said haltingly, "has instructed me to provide you with a commission in the *Luftwaffe* with the rank of *Hauptmann*...With your experience as a pilot – even though most of it as a civilian pilot – and with the duties we are asking you to undertake on behalf of the Air Ministry – the Reichsminister, General Udet, and I believe you can better serve the Air Ministry, the *Luftwaffe*, the Fuhrer, and the Fatherland, by being a uniformed *Luftwaffe Hauptmann*. Certainly, your recommendations regarding the design and production of the aircraft under your supervision will be more highly regarded and adopted more quickly. You will continue to report directly to General Udet for the time being."

"Ultimately," interjected the Rechsminister, "I have plans for you to join my own *Luftwaffe* staff...After all, we must look after our friends... especially those who exhibit so much talent and promise..." After a brief pause – as if thinking what to do next to bring this meeting to a close – he added, "Perhaps you will be kind enough to take a glass of brandy with us to toast your meteoric rise in the *Luftwaffe's* ranks...Hauptman von Bruckner?"

"Jawohl, mein Reichsmarschall," I replied with the stress on the "marschall" to indicate that I understood my new status as one of Goering's officers.

"Good...You have made the transition from civilian to soldier very quickly...and smoothly," he said with a chuckle.

I was handed the glass of brandy, and to my surprise, the Reichsmarschall extricated his corpulent frame from the chair and, while buttoning his tunic with his left hand, raised the brandy glass in his other hand, saying with much enthusiasm, "To the Fuhrer, to the Fatherland, and to your continued devotion to the success of our *Luftwaffe*...Probst!" And then he added, "To your father...and my good friend...Kurt Baron von Bruckner!" We raised our brandy glasses in salute.

My head was so filled with thoughts of how dramatically my life had changed that I almost missed my trolley stop near Poppa's factory. *What has really happened to me...Is it as important a change in my life as I think it is...Why has it happened to me...Is this a good – or a bad thing – for me...What will Poppa – and Momma – and Lisa – think about my new career...Do I even care how they might feel...Do I even have a choice to say No...Does this mean that – like Poppa – I will have to become a member of the Nazi party...Where will all this lead?*

The trolley conductor, who had become accustomed to seeing me riding on his trolley, roused me from my thoughts in time to exit the trolley at my usual stop. It was just turning dark when I reached Poppa's plant on foot. The lights inside the building were burning brightly; through the windows I could see many people moving about inside the building. Entering the front door, I was instantly immersed into the high level of activity I had seen from the street; there were the sounds of metals being worked and shaped, the smell of paint, and the odors of lubricants, coming from the work area.

The older woman at the front desk – Frau Inga Schmidt, who had been a fixture in Poppa's office for years – nodded warmly as I passed through her domain into the narrow hall leading to Poppa's office adjacent to the work area. Atypically, Poppa's office door was closed. I knocked, but I did not receive a reply. Retracing my steps to the front area, I asked Frau Schmidt if Poppa was in his office.

"Yes," she replied politely, "But he has someone in there with him... Shall I interrupt him?"

"That depends on who is in there with him," I answered.

"I believe that it is Herr Steinberg."

As excited as I was to speak to Poppa about what had just happened to me, but knowing that Herr Asher Steinberg is Poppa's long-time chief designer, I declined Frau Schmidt's offer. Rather than waiting in one of unappealing wooden chairs that lined the front wall of Frau Schmidt's area, I proceeded down the hall-way in the opposite direction from Poppa's office, entering the large, brightly lighted space where a dozen or so designers, engineers and draftsmen worked at slant-top desks. Herr Steinberg's glass-partitioned office in the far corner was empty.

Herr Steinberg's assistant, Hans Uhlberg, upon seeing me enter the area, stepped down off of the stool at which he was seated, coming toward me with an intense look on his pale face. Motioning me to follow him, Hans walked hurriedly towards Herr Steinberg's vacant office. Once we were both inside the office, Hans closed the door. "Have you heard the news?" Hans asked solemnly. *This is not the kind of conversation I was hoping to have today.*

"What news? I just got here...and I haven't yet spoken with Poppa... He has Herr Steinberg in his office," I replied anxiously; adding, "What has happened? Can you tell me?"

"That's why Herr Steinberg is in your Poppa's office...The SS came to see your Poppa today...They have ordered him to fire Herr Steinberg...

because he is a Jew."

Poppa and Asher Steinberg are more than just boss and employee; they are close friends – almost like brothers, actually. I cannot imagine how Poppa could carry on his business without Asher Steinberg by his side.

"Is that what Poppa is doing now," I asked fearfully?

"I don't think so," was Han's uncertain reply.

"I am sure that firing Herr Steinberg is the last thing Poppa would want to do...But what else can Poppa do...Does he have a choice?" I asked incredulously.

"I am not sure what he can do about Herr Steinberg...but knowing your Poppa...and knowing how he feels about Herr Steinberg...I am sure he will think of something."

I hope so...I certainly hope so!

Out of the corner of my eye I saw Frau Schmidt motioning to me from the entry into the work space. I asked Hans to excuse me. Frau Schmidt turned away from me, walking in the direction of Poppa's office. Waving me towards Poppa's office she said, "He will see you now...but he is not in a good mood...I hope you are not bring him more bad news."

That depends...that may well depend on whether what I have to tell him positively impacts his thoughts on how to solve the Herr Steinberg problem.

I knocked on the still closed door. Upon hearing the familiar command, "Herein," I entered Poppa's office.

Poppa was standing with his back to the door, looking onto the work floor through the glass, floor-to ceiling partition, apparently watching the hustle and bustle of workers wearing grey coveralls. Seated on the large brown-leather sofa was Herr Steinberg, dressed in a white shirt and tie, but no jacket. He looked up at me as I entered the office. I could immediately tell from the look on his gaunt face that he was nervous and perturbed. His light blue eyes were rimmed with red as if he had been crying. It was hard to distinguish his short, salt and pepper goatee from his uncharacteristically pale, wrinkled face. He made no effort to rise, and I walked over to him, offering him my hand.

"I've heard from Hans as to what has happened...This is so terrible...I am so sorry!" I exclaimed gravely, clasping his hand. "There has to be something we can do," I said with more certainty than I felt.

"Of course we will!" Poppa exclaimed turning away from the partition, facing us.

I could immediately discern from the dour look on his face that he was not totally convinced of the outcome of any efforts to protect his great friend Asher.

"But before we get into that, tell us what happened to you today...Did things go well at the meeting with Herr Goering?"

I am not certain whether Poppa knows of which meeting with Herr Goring he is inquiring about. And what does it matter; both meetings were quite out of the ordinary. Do I dare tell Poppa everything in front of Herr Steinberg...or do I just tell Poppa now that it was 'fine' and save the rest of the story until a later time?

"Well," I began with trepidations, "I have had a most interesting, unexpected day...But in light of what has happened here...to Herr Steinberg... and to you...I am not sure you will want to hear all of the details...except that I have been...a...a...provided with a new career path...with far reaching consequences for me...for you...and for our family's relationship with the Reich. I am still trying to sort out all of what I was told...or maybe 'ordered' is the better choice of words...is expected of me." Here I stopped talking, waiting for directions from Poppa.

"Go on," Poppa said with eyes brimming with pleasant anticipation.

"General Milch," I continued, "was directed by Herr Goering to have me commissioned as a *Hauptmann* in the *Luftwaffe*, immediately. The Reichsmarschall also ordained that I am to continue overseeing the development, production, delivery and fine-tuning of the Ju-87 Stuka, reporting directly to General Udet. And I am being groomed ultimately to serve on Reichsmarschsall Goering's *Luftwaffe* staff."

"And." said Poppa, indicating that he wanted me to continue.

"Well, all of these developments appear to stem from your long-term, solid relationships with Goering, Milch and Udet; each of whom raised a toast in your behalf. Even the fact that they may have heard good reports of my work is clearly secondary to the fact that these men have tremendous respect for you. What happened to me today has very deep roots into the past...your past...And I suspect that none of this comes as a complete surprise to you."

"No...you are right...what happened is not a complete surprise," Poppa said proudly. "But not for the reasons you think," he continued. "First, and foremost, what happened today would never have happened if you had not demonstrated what a fine gentleman you are and what a grand Luftwaffe officer and pilot you will be. What you have accomplished to date has been judged by a higher standard than applies to most young men. That standard is the German Officer Corps standard. In many ways, then, I have been your greatest handicap; and you have overcome that handicap through your own talent, your own hard work and your own strength of character. To be sure, while it doesn't hurt to have friends in high places, you are to be congratulated. I am quite proud of you...as is Herr Steinberg, I am sure: Which is why what you have told us could be good news for Herr Steinberg."

Observing the perplexed look on my face, Poppa continued, "Reichsmarschall...or Reichsminister Goering – by whatever name you wish to address him in a given circumstance – may dislike the Jews, but he does not hate them or abuse them like some of the other Nazis. Indeed, as you know, he finds many Jews to be useful – either as sources of money or as sources of needed talent...such a General Milch. Everyone...including Goering himself...knows that General Milch's fathers – both real and putative; as well as his mother – have Jewish ancestors. It is alleged that when Goering was confronted with General Milch's Jewish roots, Goering simply brushed it aside by saying that, 'I decide who is a Jew'. Thus, it is my intention to seek Herr Goering's intercession on Herr Steinberg's behalf, if it comes to that. In the meantime, we are just going to ignore what the SS has told me to do."

––––––––––

OVER THE NEXT year, my professional life – except for my commission as *Hauptmann* – did not change that much. I continued my oversight responsibilities for the introduction of the Stuka into the *Luftflottens* ("air fleets") and to assure that modifications – based on real-life flying experiences (mine and others) – were carried out by Junkers. Thanks to the rigid flight test program undertaken during the prototype stage, the modifications to the production version of the Ju-87 were minor. The full production version – Ju-87A-1 – came about quickly, resulting in deliveries to the *Luftoffens* in early 1937.

Three of the Ju-87A-1s saw service in the Spanish Civil War; flown exclusively by German pilots. The Stuka proved to be extremely effective in destroying shipping and ground targets, vindicating General Udet's decision to reject Generalfeldmarschall von Richthofens order to stop development of the Stuka. The pilots in Spain found the production version of the Stuka to be rugged and easy to fly. Nevertheless, additional modifications were made to make it more effective, including a more powerful engine and a larger tail-fin.

In my personal life, there were many modifications and changes. As a new *Luftwaffe* officer, I was required to undergo officer training at the *Luftwaffe* training facility at Regensburg for four months. Upon my return to Berlin in the fall – at the conclusion of my training, I took an apartment in the Tiergarten area with another *Luftwaffe* officer who was also assigned to the Air Ministry. It was a two-bedroom, walk-up apartment on the third floor of an aging building on a narrow side-street. The only feature of this apartment that saved it from being classified totally as a tenement was its tall windows in the two front rooms; from which a glimpse of a tiny slice of the Tiergarten was seasonally available. On the weekends I usually escaped this hovel, spending quality time at my parent's estate in Potsdam.

Beyond the lure of the creature comforts available at my parent's home, the principal attraction for my weekly trips home was the opportunity to see and to spend time with Lisa. Ever since my fortuitous introduction to Lisa at the dinner party in my parent's home almost two-years earlier, Lisa and I remained in constant contact – either in person, by telephone, or by the Post. Our mothers played a major role in bringing us together as much as possible; through the sponsorship of parties, dinners, outings, picnics, and theatrical events. During these frequent, lengthy encounters, Lisa and I discovered that we had much in common. Inevitably, and to the great joy of our mothers, this mutual attraction had grown into a loving relationship.

Being the daughter of a widowed mother of modest means, Lisa provided a major portion of her own financial support. Trained in voice and piano, Lisa taught those subjects to young ladies, with or without talent or means. Her pupils generally adored Lisa for her warm smile, her endless patience, her infectious encouragement. I, too, thrived on these qualities, plus Lisa's beauty, and her incredible enthusiasm for life.

Not a day passes that I do not still thank God for placing Lisa in my life; even for the few years we had together as partners and parents. Oh how I yearn for Lisa's kisses and her warm embrace! My memories of Lisa and of our life together provide me with the only strength to continue my search for the truth of her and our son's loss; and the fuel to persevere in the ongoing quest for the source of my own untimely demise. As I have said before, it has not been easy, pleasant or encouraging to find myself locked in the body of a young boy with character and skills so foreign from my own, or from those of my lost son, young Kurt — who would be about Jack's age.

But, I am getting ahead of myself!

CHAPTER 12

BIG CHIEF TABLET ELEVEN | FRITZ

As much as Lisa and I tried to draw ourselves into our own cocoon, we could scarcely avoid the changes taking place in our beloved Germany. Perhaps, in this respect, we were naïve. Fortunately, our friends and my siblings were not looking at the world through rose-colored glasses, as we were. On many occasions, an evening's banter turned to discussing current events. Some of these discussions turned heated, but never ugly. For us, there was a sense of optimism. Except for what was happening to the Jews, especially our Jewish friends, we saw Germany's actions on the world's stage as a matter of national pride, and as the restoration of Germany's rightful place in European geopolitics.

In our view, the outrageous requirements placed on Germany by the Versailles Treaty were nothing short of punitive, and were designed for the sole purpose of rendering Germany a beggar nation. Hitler's repudiation of the Treaty was applauded by most Germans. Now Germany could grow as an economic and industrial power, with military rearmament being a minor part; or so we thought. None of us were thinking in terms of Germany going to war again. How could we when the horrors and depravations of the last war were so vividly engraved on the body and soul of the nation. Instead, our families and friends were focusing on only the good-side of Hitler's ambitious plans for Germany; we were too much enjoying the sweet fruits of Germany's economic strength and political power.

Not everyone shared this optimism that Germany's resurgence was a positive thing; with little risk of conflict. Hitler's destruction of the short-lived Weimar Republic, and his replacement of democratic principles imposed on Germany in the Treaty, in favor of his one-man rule were not – initially – viewed as a cause for alarm. Poppa, and most of his friends, was still hoping for a restoration of the monarchy. "Germans need a strong ruler; political-parties and majority-rule can lead only to rule by the ignorant."

But Poppa was no fan of Hitler, who he privately viewed as harboring dangerous ambitions for Germany that would bring it into serious conflict with the other world powers. Momma and my sisters, Marta and young Maria, as well as Lisa and her mother, also viewed Germany's prospects as a peace loving nation with skepticism and misgivings. Their concerns were driven by Germany's dark history of militarism, its age-old aggression towards its neighbors, and its intolerance towards the Jews. Marta had taken the time to wade through Hitler's *Mein Kampf*, which she found to be a troubling roadmap leading to Germany's ultimate destruction. "Hitler wants world domination and ethnic cleansing!" These were not sentiments that one would dare share with anyone except close family and trusted friends in private.

At a dinner party in late 1937, a party at Marta's spacious home to honor Lisa and my upcoming Christmas wedding, much of the dinner-table conversation revolved around the growing unease towards the *Fuehrer's* policies and the direction of his one-man rule. After an hour or so of jovial conversation over canapés and champagne, we were called to dinner. We had hardly finished taking our assigned seats at the elaborately decorated table, when Marta, interrupting the polite chatter, asked tipsily and without any apparent provocation, "Is there nothing that can be done to bring some sense of sanity to Herr Hitler's troubling policies and ambitions?"

"Marta! Be careful in what you say," cautioned older brother Wolfgang. "Unless you completely trust the servants, anything we say here tonight could be reported to the Gestapo. I need only remind you of what happened to my boss, Doctor Schacht. At one of his famous country-house weekends...which I had the good...or maybe bad...fortune to be in attendance, Doctor Schacht made some innocuous comment about the Fuehrer's failure to understand a very rudimentary economic concept.

This comment, as innocent as it may have been was reported by one of the servants to the Gestapo who then questioned everyone at the weekend who may have heard the comment. When Doctor Schacht was made aware of the questioning, he complained to Reichsminister Goering who, when he heard the nature of the perceived indiscretion, simply laughed and put an end to the matter. Doctor Schacht, however, was livid about the attack on his integrity. He also made a point of advising each of his upper-echelon employees to be on his guard. As he put it when he spoke to me about it, 'This is one of the perils of living in a police state'."

"Yes," Poppa interjected. "We are living in difficult times...No one is above suspicion...or immune from being interrogated for his or her views on any subject no matter how trivial or innocent it may appear to be. Being in high places...or even having powerful friends...is no guaranty of safety!"

"Well, if," began young Maria, in a barely audible whisper, "we are living in such a police state...like in Stalin's U.S.S.R...why do you (she paused to look at me and my brothers) continue to work at your government jobs...or (now looking directly at Poppa) provide the Nazis with military aircraft parts?"

"Enough!" said Poppa softly but gruffly. "This is neither the time, nor the place, to engage in such a conversation...We are here to celebrate Fritz and Lisa's upcoming wedding...not politics of any kind...We are, each one of us, good, obedient Germans. Our duty is to serve the Fatherland to the best of our ability...We want what the Fuehrer wants...and that is the best for each and every citizen of this great nation!"

I knew, and I hoped that everyone who heard what Poppa had just said knew, that Poppa sensed great danger, and he wanted to change the tone and direction of the conversation; and to convince any of the servants who may have overheard from the pantry or the kitchen what Maria had said, that the von Bruckners were not engaged in treasonous activity. In actuality, we were engaged in activities that could get us executed or sent to one of the many concentration camps that were springing up all over Germany.

Ever since Poppa's experience with Herr Steinberg, his Jewish chief engineer, Poppa's views about the direction of the Reich were changing.

He confided in me that, "I am afraid that I misread Herr Hitler...I now see what a dangerous man he is...but I don't think that the generals or the industrialists...who may have reached the same conclusion as I have...have either the desire or the guts to stop him...But if we don't stop him, I fear for the safety of every man, woman, and child within the Reich!"

Poppa did not think it was too late to do something about keeping Germany out of a war, but he believed that the window of opportunity was very small and was closing quickly. Without being specific as to what steps he was taking to rid Germany of Herr Hitler or to keep Germany out of a war, he asked each of us boys to do what he could to influence corrective change. It was imperative that whatever we did, "It has to be done in secret and without drawing attention or suspicion."

It was much later that I became aware of the extent of Poppa's involvement in clandestine attempts to affect a change in Germany's fate. As future events were to show, his efforts, our efforts, and the efforts of many other good Germans to change the course of history were to meet in complete failure. As will be seen, even the best of my few successful efforts had little impact on either ending or on achieving an early end to the war. Even the efforts of Momma, Marta, Maria, and my Lisa to stop the systematic elimination of the Jewish race were to be unsuccessful; although they had some success in helping many Jews escape the fate of the death camps.

Even before our Christmas wedding, I was hearing rumors at the Air Ministry that Herr Hitler was planning to bring German-speaking Austria into the Third Reich, with or without the consent of the Austrian government. To those of us with rearmament responsibilities, this meant that the German military and air forces would need sufficient arms and aircraft to bring Austria to its knees if a consensual takeover was unachievable. The secondary question that circulated the halls of the Air Ministry was what would France, England and Russia do if Austria resisted; would any of these countries come to Austria's defense, and was the fledgling German military strong enough to win a war against the vastly superior forces that France and England would bring to the field in a war over Austria? So it was that as I left on military leave in late 1937, for my wedding and honeymoon, the thrill and excitement of beginning a new life with my beautiful Lisa being undercut by the possibility war. After all, Lisa and I were going to travel to the Austrian Alps for our honeymoon holidays.

Much to my surprise, when I broached the subject of Germany's Austrian acquisition with Poppa and brother, Ernst, as we were secluded in Poppa's study on Christmas day, Poppa expressed a more positive attitude than I had expected. "This may be the very opportunity we need to give Herr Hitler the boot. I am sure that my good friend Chancellor von Schuschnigg will resist any overtures from Hitler for Austria to join the Third Reich. France and Britain will certainly defend Austria if it comes to that...And, certainly our generals know how unprepared our military forces are to fight, let alone, to defeat the more superior French and British forces. The generals must, therefore, stand up to Herr Hitler! And if they do, Hitler will lose face and the support of the German people, and he will be forced to resign."

"But, Poppa," Ernst interjected, "the scenario you just outlined depends on France and Germany coming to Chancellor von Schuschnigg's aid. And from what I am hearing from Admiral Canaris, my boss in the Abwehr (Intelligence Bureau), Herr Hitler thinks that while the British and French will put up a good front in opposition to his threats against Austria, in the end they will not fight for Austrian independence. According to the reports Canaris is getting from his agents in Britain and France, he thinks Hitler may be right; neither country has the stomach for another war in Europe; as they evidenced when our small military force marched into the Rhineland in '36. Remember, both France and Russia signed the Treaty of Locarno which guaranteed the Rhineland's independence, and yet they did nothing; even when our small military presence could have been blown to bits by the French army."

"Isn't there some way we can leak word to Britain and France that if they will stand up to Herr Hitler on Austria — if that happens — he will be forced to back down, and then we can get rid of Herr Hitler?" asked a down-cast Poppa.

THE WEDDING CEREMONY took place in the Potsdam Catholic Cathedral on the day after Christmas. It was a sunny, but cold day. All of the warmth that was needed was supplied by Lisa. Her beautiful, handmade wedding gown and her wonderful smile were radiant. I had passed on the option to wear my sky-blue *Luftwaffe* dress uniform in favor of the more traditional formal wear. Lisa's widowed mother insisted on a wedding reception that fit her style and budget. Momma, in turn, saw to it that we adhered to the budget, while at the same time providing much of the table linens and settings from her own pantry. The elegant simplicity suited Lisa and me just fine. "As far as I am concerned, we can hold it in a beer hall," I teasingly proclaimed to Lisa when she told me of her mother's plans. In actuality, the reception was held in one of our favorite country inns; dressed up of course with Momma's stuff, which paled in comparison to Lisa's beauty.

Despite what Poppa thought was taking place in Austria, our honeymoon trip revealed that little attention was being paid to the drama unfolding in Vienna. During our lunches at ski-chalets, and our candlelit dinners at the local restaurants, we observed how friendly and jovial the guests and the staff appeared to be. We noted the same light-hearted atmosphere on our day-long shopping trip in Innsbruck. It was as if there was no ongoing threat to Austria's independence or of an impending conflict; even though Austrian radio news broadcasts coming out of Vienna were filled with reports of the government's concern.

Although Poppa may have been right about how his friend Chancellor von Schuschnigg would react negatively to Hitler's designs on Austria, the populace in this part of Austria did not appear to be of the same mind as their leader; at least not yet. Perhaps threats of war were simply imaginary...or premature. At least my spirits were lifted as Lisa and I departed our love-nest and returned to Berlin. But a message from my commanding officer and mentor, General Udet, awaiting my arrival at the Air Ministry would change all of that, forever.

CHAPTER 13

BIG CHIEF TABLET TWELVE | JACK

Life back at home with my mother — who I refused to call "Mumby" or even "Mommy," but only as, "Mom"- was as unpleasant as ever. Initially it seemed worse, but that was just in comparison to my life with Aunt Rita at Fairways. Unlike in times past, I accepted my mother's harsh treatment and indifference towards my need for loving nurturing with less concern. I knew I was deeply loved by Aunt Rita to who I could turn to for affection and fulfillment. At times, I could tell that my mother was still rankled by the way in which Aunt Rita had stood up to her, and by Aunt Rita's refusal to treat me harshly. While nothing was said about my physical development and the new clothes I brought home with me, on more than one occasion I caught mother checking through my things. I had nothing to hide, and I was actually pleased to think that mother was jealous of my growing relationship with Aunt Rita.

There also was the growing relationship with Fritz, my bodymate — of which my mother had no knowledge and would, if I could help it, have no knowledge, ever — who was now providing me with meaningful guidance on my day-to-day challenges. The fact that this "spirit" was recounting historical events which I could, and did, verify from reading through my brothers' history books and articles about prewar Germany in periodicals, provided me with some measure of confidence that I was not going crazy. I was convinced that his presence was real, and not just an aberration of a sick mind.

At the same time, it occurred to me — just listening to the

story of his life – that this Fritz's character was – even as a spirit – much stronger than my character. This was not a stress-free relationship. *Will Fritz's robust spirit attempt to overwhelm my lightweight spirit and replace it with his own; thus effectively dispossessing me? I don't want that to happen! I want to be me, all of me! What can I do to keep my body, soul and intellect intact? I can't do it by myself; not yet. But, who can I turn to who can help me? Maybe Fritz will not try to dispossess me if he sees that I am trying to get stronger...or at least until I can get back to Aunt Rita...who will surely help me...as she already has helped me so much to be self-confident!'*

Shortly after having these troubling thoughts of 'dispossession' – or 'possession' depending on your point of view – Fritz communicated with me as I was drifting off to sleep one evening. The words he conveyed in the twilight of my consciousness were accompanied by the fuzzy vision of a dark-haired man in a light-blue military uniform. His voice was firm, but the words were softly spoken: *Jack, I mean you no harm...I have no intention of taking over either your mind or your body. You must understand that whatever I do it is intended to make you a stronger person, so that together we can bring a peaceful end to my need to share your body. I need your help... and we both need Aunt Rita's enthusiastic participation.*

———————

MOM HAD BEGUN to gather information about her ancestors. The dining room table – where we customarily ate only our Sunday morning breakfasts – was piled high with letters, papers and documents. There were also incomplete applications for membership in several organizations, about which I knew nothing. In the evenings after dinner she would sit in the dining room working on these papers. She also started receiving telephone calls after she got home from work from women with educated voices, lasting for hours. I didn't pay particular attention to what Mom said, but it soon became apparent that she was talking about what was on the dining table.

One afternoon after school, I took the opportunity — before Mom came home from work — to look at a few of the papers on the dining table. There were many sheets of paper with people's names, places, and dates of births, deaths, and weddings. One paper was an application with the title: "Daughters of the American Revolution." Another: "Colonial Dames." And a third: "United Daughters of the Confederacy." Mom had frequently talked about her father's family — the Douglases — being from Virginia, and of his ancestors having fought in the Revolutionary War and in the War Between the States. Until now, I had dismissed such statements as "just more of Mother's talk." *Maybe there was more than "just talk" to Mother's claims.* And, having been exposed by Fritz to his illustrious German family and ancestors through his stories, curiosity about my Mom's family history was now aroused.

"What are all those papers on the dining table?" I asked mother one evening as she pranced out of the kitchen with her china cup filled with freshly-brewed tea, leaving Dad behind to clean up the kitchen and to wash the diner dishes at the sink.

"Why should you care what they are!" was her quick response as she moved regally towards dining room table. "I hope you haven't been snooping through them!"

"No...I wasn't snooping." I replied as calmly as I could. "I was watering the plants on the window seat in the dining room as you instructed...and I saw the papers as I walked by the table."

"Well, what do you want to know?"

"It looked like those papers might be about the Douglas family...and I was hoping to learn more about my ancestors," I said with a look of genuine interest as I followed her into the dining room. Mom placed the tea cup and saucer delicately on the highly polished table, taking her seat in the Queen Anne arm chair at the far end of the table, searching out a sheet of paper from the pile of papers in front of her.

"I know I have spoken about my family on many occasions, but I guess you weren't interested or you were just not paying attention," she said sarcastically. "I suppose you're old enough now to learn something about your ancestors," she continued, but without much enthusiasm; motioning to me to sit in the chair to her left.

"What's the United Daughters of the Revolution?" I asked as I sat down on the designated seat.

"It is not the United Daughters of the Revolution," she responded impatiently. "It is the Daughters of the American Revolution...Then there are the United Daughters of the Confederacy...They are very different organizations. Many women qualify to belong to both groups...Like me," she said proudly.

"How do you qualify?"

"By having an ancestor who fought with the colonists in the American Revolution; or by having an ancestor who fought for the South in the War Between the States...In my case, I had a great grandfather – your great, great grandfather Hugh Douglas – who was a colonel in the Virginia militia, and fought with General Washington (she pronounced it 'Warshington') in the Revolution...And my grandfather, John Douglas, was a captain in the cavalry, and rode with General Lee in the Army of Northern Virginia in the War Between the States."

"But you said that your ancestor had to fight for the South... And your grandfather fought with the Army of Northern Virginia," I inquired with a puzzled look.

"Ha, ha, ha," she laughed. I mean she genuinely laughed – even with her eyes; something she rarely ever did in my presence. "I'll have to tell my friend Mildred what you just said...She'll find that humorous!" she giggled.

I really wasn't trying to be funny; certainly not around my mother. Seeing my perplexity, she added, "I can see your confusion...There are a number of names and terms about that particular war which frequently require some explanation...For example, some people – mainly Yankees, or people from the north – call the war, 'The Civil War,' while people from the South – also known as the Confederacy – call it the 'War Between the States'." You see, some thirteen southern states seceded from the United States of America and called themselves the United States of the Confederacy...Virginia was one of the Southern states...and your great grandfather John Douglas fought for the South...the Confederacy...so I can be a 'Daughter of the Confederacy'."

At this point, Mom took a sip of her tea and, upon replacing the cup on its saucer, glanced at her wrist watch. I could tell that Mom was debating with herself as to whether she wanted go on with this discussion at this time. Looking at me, she said, "Don't you have some homework you need to get done this evening?" I knew that she had decided the history lesson was over, and that I was being dismissed. Thank God! This is really boring; not like what Fritz is telling me. And, if I really want to know all about Mother's ancestors, I'll ask Aunt Rita...She'll know the same stuff, but she'll keep it simple.

––––––––––––

FRITZ WAS TRUE to his word. He gave me suggestions on how to improve my school-work, on how to make better friends with the other kids, and on how to build up myself physically. My biggest challenge was to make better friends. I am naturally bright and I love to read; and by applying myself in the classroom and by doing my homework religiously, my grades improved considerably. Developing my physical skills was more difficult, initially, due to my slender frame and lack of natural athletic abilities. Fritz had me write out a plan for a regime of daily strength exercises, like pushups, chin-ups, and running. I was puzzled by the fact that both of my older brothers were strong and athletic, but I never saw them do any training or exercises. Fritz said to just blame it on the genes – your brothers must, he concluded after hearing about my father's athletic prowess, have received my father's athletic genes.

My father is a tall, big-shouldered, handsome man who carries himself like an athlete. I always marvel at the size of his hands and the dexterity of his fingers. He often told us stories of his growing up on a farm, one of a dozen kids living in a one room log cabin. To help support his family he had been a lumberjack during the winters. During the summers, he worked as a camp counselor. During his spare-time he learned to play baseball, becoming an accomplished amateur ball player. There were even discussions of him becoming a professional baseball player, but that all ended when he wrenched his right-arm (his throwing arm) in a freak lumberjacking accident. He later taught himself to play golf and to bowl left-handed.

This left Fritz and me to tackling efforts to make better friends among my peers. Fritz observed that, lacking the more desirable athletic skills, my best hope of becoming an insider among the boys in schoolyard, would be to learn other boy-type skills, and to be able to handle myself bravely in the usual schoolyard fracas.

Jack, you must show these boys that you are courageous and self-confident, if you expect to earn their respect and admiration. If they don't respect you, then they won't like you...At best, they will just tolerate you. Even if you can't beat them, you have to show them a good fight; at whatever it is you are competing about. And you have to compete with honesty and with a smile on your face. And when you are not competing, you need to be a fun person; someone who is fun to be around no matter what the circumstances might be...That, in short, is what it means to be a friend."

In addition to making better friends with my schoolmates, I wanted to improve my relationships with Chris and David. Being their much-younger brother, Chris and David treated me with disdain; if they gave me any thought at all. To them I was a nuisance, a bother, a wimp. I recognized that there were times when my behavior was such that I deserved being treated by them as a pest. But even when I tried my hardest to stay out of their way, they seemed to go out of their way to make me feel inferior.

When I inquired of Fritz as to what he thought I needed to do to change my brothers' perception of me, he took a long time to respond; as if he was carefully formulating his response. *Sibling rivalry* was all that I heard, but I surely didn't know what it meant. Sensing my puzzlement he added: *'Sibling' means you and your brothers, and 'Rivalry' means that you and your brothers are competing with each other for your parents' love, affection, attention, even though you may not be conscious of doing so. It leads to jealousy, fighting, bick-*

*ering, teasing, and belittling; and it is almost impossible to cure. It hap-
pened in my family, among my brothers and me, and between my sisters;
though to a lesser degree...Sorry Jack, but you are just going to have to
live with how Chris and David think about you, and with how they treat
you.*

Although I didn't understand exactly what Fritz was impart-
ing to me — especially the stuff about competing for our parent's
love and affection; since there wasn't much to fight over in our
family — I did understand that I was doomed to be viewed by
my brothers' as their "bratty little brother," whether I was a brat
or not. This certainly simplified my relationship with my brothers; just stay out of their way, and be nice if contact could not
be avoided. Fritz did suggest that I try to find situations where
I could participate with my brothers in activities that they and I
might mutually enjoy.

As a follow up to my ongoing physical training program, Fritz
observed that I really should learn how to defend myself. He
thought that boxing might be a defensive skill that would give me
more self-confidence. At Fritz's urging I asked David if he could
help me learn to box. After initially refusing to have anything to
do with teaching me how to box, David surprised me one afternoon after school by bringing the old boxing gloves down to the
kitchen from the third-floor attic. He had a curious look as he
asked me if I was ready for a boxing lesson. After some weighing
of the potential risks, I said, "Yes...But only if you will fight me on
your knees."

"Sure, punk...I can even beat you also with one hand tied by
back," David crowed defiantly.

We lifted the kitchen table and moved it to one end of the
room, and stacked the chairs in front of the door leading out
onto the back porch. The old leathery-smelling boxing gloves
were like small maroon pillows which had to be laced with long
strings after the gloves were pulled on over the hands, one-by-
one. It is impossible to tie your own boxing gloves, so David
helped me pull my gloves on, and then tied mine before he put
his gloves on. Because my hands were now inside the boxing
gloves, David had to pull on his own gloves, leaving it for me to

wrap the lace strings around the base of his gloves, without tying the laces.

When David got down on his knees, his head was about even with mine, but his arms were still way-longer than mine. In a teaching mode, David held his gloves face-open in front of him so I could hit them with my gloves which felt heavy and awkward to me. David told me I had to jab at his right glove with my left hand, again and again, but to keep my right glove up in front of me to keep him from hitting my head or body with his left hand. This jabbing went on for a while. Occasionally David would jab at me, and the force of his punch would knock me backwards. Even being on his knees, David was able to move forward as I went backwards. He tired of just accepting my jabs, telling me to try hitting him with my right hand. When I threw right-hand punches David would simply brush them aside with his left hand, and then hit me with his right-hand in the chest and stomach. Not bothering to tell me that I needed to keep my left-hand up to protect myself, I was easy prey. David backed me into a corner where I couldn't move away from his punches.

Sensing my peril, Fritz directed me to: *Duck when David throws his next right-hand punch, and then step to your right and rise up swinging at David's head with a right-hand punch of your own.*

It took me a second or two before I figured out the rights from the lefts, but when I did I ducked, stepped right, and rose up throwing a right-handed punch, hitting David squarely on the left-side of his head, just in front of his ear. David immediately crumpled to the linoleum floor face-first. After what seemed to me to be an eternity standing there looking down at my prone brother, David managed to push himself back up on his knees, shaking his head.

"You little bastard," he cried angrily, "You sucker-punched me!"

"Sorry," was all I could think of to say as I stared at the red blotch spreading on the left side of David's face. But inside I felt so proud of myself...and Fritz, too. David and I took off the boxing gloves, moved the kitchen table and chairs back to where they belonged, and the boxing gloves disappeared back up into the attic — never, as far as I know, to be used again.

For the next several days, I stayed out of David's way. The red blotch on the left-side of David's face was slowly turning to grayish-blue. When Dad asked him, "What happened to your face?" David — avoiding eye contact with me — replied, "I ran into my closet door in the dark."

"You need to be more careful...Doors can be very dangerous in the dark," Dad said in a tone which suggested that he wasn't convinced of David's truthfulness.

I never let on that I knew the real reason.

———————

ONE GLORIOUSLY BEAUTIFUL Saturday afternoon in October, while I was playing step-ball in front of our house, I noticed that Dad and our good neighbor friend, Peter Wilson, were standing on the sidewalk in front of Mr. Wilson's house talking. Mr. Wilson was smoking one of his ever-present, pleasant-smelling cigars. I couldn't hear what they were saying, but Mr. Wilson kept gesturing with his cigar towards his shiny, dark-maroon, four-door 1939 Buick Special with oversized white-sidewall tires sitting at the curb.

We didn't own a car — the automobile at the curb in front of our house, a black, four-door 1946 Ford sedan, was owned by my Dad's employer. As the office manager, Dad brought the car home at night and on the weekends for safe-keeping. Having ridden in both automobiles, I liked the Buick best. Mr. Wilson doted on his Buick, keeping it in the garage behind his house at night, and washing and polishing it frequently. I thought it would be swell to have a fine automobile like that Buick.

At diner that evening, with Mom, David and I gathered around the oilcloth-covered kitchen table (my brother Chris was away at college), Dad told us that Mr. Wilson had ordered a new 1949 Buick Roadmaster four-door sedan with an automatic transmission. "He wants to know if we want to buy his '39 Buick."

"Why do we want to spend money on a car when we have the company car to drive when we need to go somewhere?" asked

Mom in a quarrelsome tone. "I take the streetcar to work...David takes the streetcar to school — and anywhere else he needs to go...You take the company car to and from work...Jack's too young to drive...and I don't know how to drive — and I don't want to learn how to drive...So the car will just sit in the garage, collecting dust."

"But Sweetheart," began Dad in response, using his most endearing tone — which earned knowing smirks from David and me. "Don't you see that there are times when we will need a car of our own? I can't use the company car for trips that you and I have talked about taking...David needs a car to go places with his friends — and he'll be in college next year...We need to take Jack to Fairways...we can't expect Aunt Rita to drive him back-and-forth each summer...and taking the train to there and back is very inconvenient (Dad had to swallow hard on that one — he loved to ride the train as much as I did)...Besides, Wilson only wants $500 for his Buick; and it's a "cream-puff. He tells me he can get more than that from the dealer as a trade-in."

"And where do you think you are going to get even $500."

"From our savings account," Dad explained imploringly.

"I don't think so," replied Mom emphatically. "That money is being put aside for college tuitions...And I have worked too hard to get that money to spend it on buying Peter Wilson's damned old Buick...Do you have any proof — other than Wilson's word — that the Buick is worth even $500?"

"No." responded Dad sheepishly. "But I have no reason not to believe what Wilson has told me...Why would he lie to us now; when he never lied to us in the past?" Seeing an opening, Dad added, "Didn't you buy that nice diamond ring from his jewelry store — using money from the savings account — without questioning his price...when he told you he was giving you a bargain?"

Sensing that the tide of this argument was shifting against her, Mom said, "Well let me think about it...How long do we have to let Wilson know if we want to buy the Buick?"

"Probably not too long...He is expecting delivery on the new Buick in the next couple of weeks."

Over the next several days I heard Mom and Dad discussing

the pros and cons of purchasing Mr. Wilson's ten-year old Buick. Many of these discussions were of a heated nature; based primarily upon need for our own automobile, and the cost of keeping an automobile in running condition. When the opportunities were present, David and I encouraged Dad to keep pushing Mom on buying the Buick. I was actually trying to help David, who was most in need of a having a family automobile — even a ten year old Buick — to drive instead of cadging rides from his friends. My interest in Mom and Dad buying the Buick was less practical than David's. This is one of the ways I hoped to get on David's good side after "blind-siding" him in our boxing match. Also, I just liked the looks of the Buick and the fragrant scent of cigar-smoke permeating its interior.

The fateful day arrived with Mom's decision still unresolved. Answering the ringing telephone, Mom said, "Hello...Oh, it's you... Is it that time...Let me get Paul." Holding her hand over the telephone's mouth-piece, she said in a loud stage-whisper, "It's Pete Wilson." Dad approached the telephone which sat atop the large wooden newel-post at the foot of the front-staircase. He turned to Mom, "What am I going to tell him?" After a long pause, Mom responded with an audible sigh, "I am doing this against my better judgment...Tell him okay...We'll buy the Buick." Mom handed the telephone receiver to Dad, who told Mr. Wilson the good news. David and I erupted into whoops of joyous laughter when Dad replaced the telephone receiver into its cradle.

"Well," Mom said in a raised voice, "I am glad you are so happy now!" "But just remember," she added in a somber tone as we quieted down, "You all pushed me into buying the Buick...I still think owning the Buick is a bad decision...And if anything bad happens because we own it, don't say I didn't tell you so!" *How will she feel if the Buick produces a life changing event?*

OUR FIRST ROAD trip in the Buick was a trip to Fairways at Thanksgiving. Aunt Rita called Mom long-distance on the telephone a few days beforehand, inviting us to spend Thanksgiving weekend with her and Uncle Ollie — who was on his way from

San Diego to Washington, D.C. When Mom told me of the up-coming trip, I was doubly excited; I was going to have my ride in the country in the Buick, and I was going to be with Aunt Rita.

The Buick departed for Fairways with a full car-load. The weather was rainy and cold, with a forecast for snow-flurries that night. The streets were crowded with cars, trucks and buses. The headlights of the vehicles and the traffic-lights at the inter-sections made red, white and green beads on the Buick's rain-splattered windows, which were showing signs of fogging up. The atmosphere inside the Buick was heavy with the smell of damp clothes, Mom's perfume, engine exhaust and the lingering smell of Mr. Wilson's cigars. Other than the noise of the defroster blower and the whine of the big tires on the wet pavement, the inside of the Buick was silent. *It is going to be a long two hours of riding.* It was made even longer that evening with many detours because of highway construction.

We were on the road for about an hour when Dad turned off of the main highway onto a narrower, less traveled, two-lane pavement. A few minutes later he observed, with some trepida-tion, "The rain is beginning to change to snow."

When I raised up from where I was dozing, slumped in the back seat, I saw the snowflakes swirling past the Buick's head-lights. This vision of snowflakes held my attention for a while – as seeing snowflakes always did – but I knew I had to keep silent. The flakes of snow began to accumulate on the windshield de-spite the efforts of the wipers to sweep them away. With each sweep of the wipers, the tension in the vehicle increased; Dad's hands were gripping the steering-wheel tightly. As expected, Mom silently mouthed the Our Fathers and the Hail Mary's as she fingered her rosary beads. Chris and David grew even more silent as they each peered out of the Buick's windows into the dark night. The big Buick, undaunted by the worsening weather, kept moving effortlessly along the whitening roadway.

"Paul, are we going to make it?" Mom inquired with alarm. "Or should we turn around?"

"I think it's too late for that...with the construction and the heavy traffic on Highway 40, driving in that direction would probably be worse than if we went on."

"Then let's keep going...But please drive more slowly!"

Even slowing down did not improve the tension inside the Buick, nor did it help the Buick's headlights discern the snow-covered pavement from the snow-covered shoulders and adjacent drainage ditches. Even gradual inclines and declines in the roadway became a cause for alarm. At times it was impossible to see turns in the road, even creeping along.

"Slow down," Mom cried out as the Buick went into a right-hand turn around a sloping bend in the roadway.

"I can't go any slower...the car is starting to lose traction as it is...If we go any slower we will get stuck in the snow."

When the Buick was half-way through a turn I felt the back-end of the vehicle slide to the left; Dad spun the steering-wheel in reaction to the sliding motion. At this point I remembered what Fritz had told me what he thought about the Buick: *This Buick is a nice automobile, Jack, with a powerful engine; but its center of gravity is too high – it is too tall and its wheel-base is too narrow – making it very difficult to handle on wet, slippery roads. In general, the Americans build good automobiles, but not well-engineered automobiles capable of high-speed driving. I have not seen any American automobiles as fine as the German automobiles, especially the pre-war automobiles – like the Mercedes. Now that was a well-engineered automobile, and a dream to drive – regardless of the road or the weather conditions. Then I heard Fritz add: See, I told you that the Buick is poorly engineered...But your Dad is doing a good job of driving in these conditions...But if this snow keeps falling this hard, the Buick will need some tire chains.*

Around the next turn in the road, a small town of not more than three or four blocks long came into view; with a flashing red light at its main intersection. Most of the houses on the way into town exhibited an accumulation of snow, illuminated by the light streaming from their frosted windows or from the occasional porch light. The few store fronts we passed were dark, but the lone, two pump filing station at the main intersection was invitingly lighted; an oasis in the snow.

"Shall I stop here and see if they have any tire chains?" inquired Dad sheepishly as he brought the snow-covered Buick to a gentle stop at the intersection. *Had Dad heard Fritz talking to me?*

"Won't they charge us an arm and a leg for them in this weather?" asked Mom defiantly.

"I don't think we have a choice...Do you really want to run the risk of getting stuck in the snow somewhere down the road...and having to spend the night in the car...and then pay for getting towed out in the morning on Thanksgiving day?" grumbled Dad as he pulled into the service station.

"You got here just in time," said the surprised-looking attendant, as he stumbled out of the station's front door, zipping up his heavy jacket. "We were just fixing to close up for the night...We ain't seen no vehicles for the last hour...since it began to snow... Where you folks headed to on a night like this?" Looking at the Buick's rear tires, the attendant observed, "I'll bet you're looking for some tire chains? Well you're lucky; normally we don't have a snowfall like this, this early in the season, and we got in a new shipment of tire-chains just the other day."

IT WAS WELL after 10:00 PM when the Buick– with its headlights proudly announcing its arrival through the still falling snow – at last climbed the driveway to Fairways, with its tires coming to a clanking stop on the snow-covered parking area at the rear of the house. The snow had continued falling hard and fast for the rest of the trip, and was several inches deep along most of the roads the Buick traveled in reaching Fairways. Without the "arm and leg" snow-chains – as Chris called them – we probably would have spent the night in a ditch somewhere along the way. Even with the tire-chains, and Dad's skillful driving, it was a harrowing experience.

"Well, we made it," Dad exclaimed with a note of relief as he trudged just behind me into the warm, brightly lit kitchen, with the first load of suitcases. "But I sure hope I never ever have to have another experience like the one we had this evening...There will be lots of stories to tell in the morning...All I want now is a stiff drink and a soft chair by the fireplace!"

"Of course," said Aunt Rita with a smile of relief, as she moved away from the sink drying her hands on the apron, removing it from around her waist. "We were so worried about you."

"If we hadn't found the tire chains at the filing station in Wright City, we wouldn't have made it...at least not tonight," Dad said as he put down the suitcase, struggling out of his snow-speckled overcoat.

"That was a bit of good luck," observed Uncle Ollie reaching out to help Dad remove his overcoat.

Mother was standing alone by the kitchen stove holding out her now gloveless hands over the empty stove-top, trying to catch some of the stove's remaining heat. Her face was marked with a frown. I couldn't tell for sure what has caused this frown, but I suspected it was because she had not been greeted as warmly as Dad had been by Aunt Rita and Uncle Ollie. Even my brothers, who had trailed Dad into the house with another load of stuff from the Buick, were greeted warmly and cheerfully by Aunt Rita and Uncle Ollie.

Aunt Rita greeted me with a warm smile and a quick wink when I had come in the back door; that was plenty enough for me, and a smart move by Aunt Rita in light of Mom's reaction to the greetings Dad had received. I knew that Mom and Aunt Rita had not yet mended the rift in their relationship; it had its origins in the verbal fisticuffs I overheard at the beginning of my stay with Aunt Rita this past summer. Aunt Rita remained quite adamant that Mom was too cruel and unloving towards me – and my brothers. I could tell from Mom's manner and tone of voice whenever Aunt Rita was mentioned in conversations following my stay with Aunt Rita; that Mom still did not approve of the manner in which Aunt Rita thought I should be raised. The fact that I constantly talked at home about all of the things Aunt Rita and I did during my stay with her probably did not soften Mom's feelings that Aunt Rita spoiled me and was trying to turn me away from her.

I turned away from the scene in the kitchen, following Lady into the main hall of the house, where we showered each other with pent-up affection that only happens between a boy and his dog. Lady had barked cheerfully and loudly when I crawled out of the Buick's backseat, jumping and prancing in the snow. In the mix of all the people and the general commotion of the transfer from the automobile to the house, Lady and I could only make fitful contact, until now. We warmly embraced; Lady licking, and me petting, as we rolled and tussled on the carpeted hallway floor. It was again just like it had been throughout my summer visit. Experiencing and sensing the love and affection of my two most favorite companions renewed my spirits; it also caused me to wish for it to be a permanent relationship.

THANKSGIVING MORNING ARRIVED with clear skies and a fairy-tale brightness that only occurs in the wake of a fresh snow-fall. Even with the fully-extended window shade and the tightly-drawn drapes, the east-facing bedroom I shared with Chris and David was engulfed with day light. Knowing better than to awaken my sleeping brothers I quietly slid from the roll-away bed, put on my slippers, and tip-toed to the closed bedroom door, which I quickly and quietly opened, exited and closed. Lady lay waiting expectantly for me with her tail wagging at the top of stair case. She stood to greet me and licked my face with great abandon as I leaned over to pet her, inhaling her distinctive, sleeping-dog odor.

We descended the stairs with cat-like stealth, crossing the hall that runs the center of the large house, and passed through the study with its fireplace still crackling with embers from last night's fire — filling the whole house with wood-smoke incense. Entering the front foyer with its large beveled-glass and dark wood-frame front door, I pulled aside the sheer curtains, impregnated with a sweet, rusty smell, and peered out the glass onto the snowy wonderland. Lady's and my breath made small fog circles on the frigid glass. As far as I could see, in every available direction, the landscape was painted entirely white; only occasionally interrupted with web-like black patterns and random green and brown splotches.

Just as I started to turn the big brass doorknob, for the purpose of letting Lady go outside and perform her morning ritual, Aunt Rita — who must have tip-toed into the foyer — startled me by saying in a soft voice behind me, "No...Not yet...Let's just drink it in for another moment or two before it's serenity is disturbed... by anything. It is so breathtaking...and it's a shame that it won't last like this."

Aunt Rita placed both of her arms around my neck and shoulders, pulling me back into her in a loving embrace. "I've missed you so much, Jack."

"Yes," I affirmed, squirming around to face her. "Your smile and wink told me as much."

"It's time to let Lady go do her duty," Aunt Rita said with a soft laugh and a gentle pat on my butt, bringing me back to reality. I turned away from Aunt Rita, opened the heavy front door, letting Lady dart outside. Aunt Rita and I stood together watching Lady bound across the snow-covered front porch and down the steps onto the sparkling white landscape.

"Why are you up?" I asked.

"It's Thanksgiving, and I have a big turkey to roast...and a big breakfast to cook to boot...Do you think you can give me a hand?"

"What can I do?" I inquired, uncertain of what she has in mind.

"Well besides keeping me company —since no one else, including your mother, has shown their face — I'll teach you how to make biscuits...It'll be fun!"

IT WAS GREAT fun! Just being alone with Aunt Rita was always fun, but that was special fun. I hoped that no one would come downstairs to interrupt our time alone; and I did everything I could to make the biscuits quietly. By the time the first tray of biscuits was placed in the oven, my pajama top was well-dusted with flour, as was my face and my arms — up to the elbows. Even the front of my uncombed hair showed evidence of the baking lesson. When I opened the back door in response to Lady's scratching, Lady failed to recognize my flour-altered appearance; she uttered a low growl and started backing away until my soft "Lady" triggered recognition. "You'd better get cleaned up before you scare away the other customers as well," Aunt Rita said laughingly.

Aunt Rita's unwelcomed prediction that "the snow would not last" came to pass quickly and with finality. The bright, fall sun and a warming southern breeze restored the landscape to its old, familiar green, tan and brown by the end of Thanksgiving Day. It was just as well; we had not packed for trudging around in the snow, and Aunt Rita did not own a real sled. The many steep, snow-covered slopes were enticing, but sitting on the business-end of a coal shovel as a sled, while wearing borrowed mucking boots, had its limitations; after a few valiant efforts at sledding, I found that holding a cup of hot chocolate while sitting in front of flaming logs in the fireplace, with a well-toweled Lady at my side, was the better place to be.

ON FRIDAY, WITH a bright sun and even warmer temperatures, the last vestiges of Wednesday night's surprise snowfall disappeared. The need for snow-chains was now just a bad memory; and Dad asked Chris and David to remove them from the Buick's rear tires. With some effort, and a few accompanying "damns" and "shits," the Buick was jacked-up off of the ground, the snow-chains were unhooked, slipped off of the tires, placed in their canvas bag, and stored in the Buick's spacious trunk. I watched this exercise with keen interest; it was not often that I had the opportunity to observe my brothers working together in a team effort.

Chris and David normally did little together, since their interests took them in quite different directions. As the effort to convince Mom — and Dad — to buy the Buick brought David and me closer together, so the ownership of the Buick was having a similar effect on Chris and David's relationship. Or, so I was thinking when I overheard Chris and David in our shared bedroom whispering about how unreasonable Mom's restrictions were on using the Buick, and about what pretext they could come up with to drive the Buick, with or without her permission. I thought about Dad's surreptitious, and all-too-brief, joy rides with the Buick; but elected to say nothing about Dad's escapades to my brothers – after all, a secret is a secret.

My brothers' opportunity to put their plan to drive the Buick into effect arrived that same afternoon.

"Jack," called my mother from the back porch. "We are all driving over to the nursing home in Fulton to see your grand-mother, so come in the house this minute and put on some of those nice clothes Aunt Rita bought for you," she commanded.

"Oh...do...I...have...to?" I replied in a whiny voice. I was playing with Lady in the feed room located in the combination garage and stable, where I hoped to find a rat for Lady to kill. I thought that what Lady and I were doing would be much more fun than driving forever to another town to see my demented grand-mother living in a place that smelled of pee and poop. Besides, Aunt Rita had taken me to see Doddy during my summer visit; Doddy didn't know who I was then, and probably wouldn't know me now either.

"Are Chris and David going too?" I inquired – more to set an excuse for escape than for gaining real information: If they weren't going, then I wasn't going to go either.

But my plan to use my brothers' escape from attendance at the nursing home into my own escape, never came to fruition. Each of my schemes and arguments fell on deaf ears. As I was being hustled into the backseat of Uncle Ollie's spacious, cream-colored, four-door Lincoln sedan, I observed Chris and David huddled together beside the Buick pointing and laughing at me. I could tell that they were engaged in trouble: Skullduggery was afoot!

The visit to see Doddy turned out to be more boring than I feared, but the ride to and from the nursing home was decid-edly more interesting, especially for Fritz. Dad sat in the front-passenger seat, and Uncle Ollie drove. I was sandwiched in the back-seat, with Mom on my right and Aunt Rita on my left. This was the first time that I had any exposure to Uncle Ollie. He was shorter and smaller than Dad; and he – like Mom – had adopted certain British affectations. Seeing my Mom and her brother together at such close quarters, hearing them speak, and observing their features, I was struck by how much my mother and Uncle Ollie resembled each other; both having light colored, thinning hair, a prominent forehead, sparkling blue eyes, a small nose, thin-lips and a strong chin. Overall, I considered them to be nice-looking people.

During the half-hour drive to the nursing home, Uncle Ollie surprised me by dominating the conversation. He spoke at length about his new Navy assignment, telling us how the Navy was converting most of its fighter planes from propeller aircraft to jet propulsion. Because of his extensive experience in both jet propulsion and aircraft operations, he was being promoted to Captain, and was being assigned as the head of flight operations on an aircraft carrier, "to perfect the technical aspects of carrier jet aircraft operations." He also described the Grumman "Panther" and the McDonnell "Banshee," which were "new jet-fighter aircraft especially designed to take-off and land on aircraft carriers."

I asked Uncle Ollie if the Navy ever flew the P-38 fighter aircraft off of aircraft carriers.

"No," replied Uncle Ollie. "Because of the P-38's twin-engine, twin-boom configuration, it is not suitable as a carrier-based aircraft."

I explained how I thought that the P-38 was the greatest fighter aircraft ever built.

Uncle Ollie just laughed, "Maybe in its day it was, but that was a long time ago in terms of aircraft development. Even the famous P-51 Mustang was obsolete as soon as the Germans got the Me-262 twin-engine jet fighter into production in late1943, or early 1944. There was no other aircraft that the Allies had that could match the Me-262 for speed and handling. Thank God Hitler wanted to convert it into a bomber...If the German Luftwaffe had had its way...using the Me-262 as an attack fighter against the Allied bombers...the course of the war...or at least the length of the war...might have been different. In any event,

the Me-262 might have been the best fighter aircraft in the war...
and, more importantly, it changed aircraft design forever, in very
significant ways."

At Fritz's prompting, I asked Uncle Ollie, "Did you ever fly the
Me-262?"

"No, I didn't. At the end of the war in Europe, when several
of the Me-262s were captured undamaged, I was running a Navy
air station on a Pacific island, still fighting the Japanese."

"Then, how do you know so much about the Me-262," I asked,
again at Fritz's prompting.

"After the war I was reassigned by the Navy to work with
the aircraft manufacturers — like Grumman and McDonnell — to
design and build the next generation of naval aircraft. Naturally, this required me to study jet propulsion and its adaptability
to carrier-based aircraft. I spent some time in England examining a Me-262, as well as reviewing captured design and production documents. I knew immediately that the twin-engine, on
the wing design of the Me-262 would make it inappropriate for
aircraft carrier based fighters; but there were many other features of the Me-262 which were quite technologically advanced,
and worth further study and refinement. As a matter of fact, the
McDonnell Banshee — which I had a hand in its development —
incorporates several of the German features. Perhaps you have
seen the Banshee, since the plant where they are being built...
and tested...is near Saint Louis?"

"I don't think I have actually seen a Banshee, but I have often
heard the sound of jet-engines which I think might be from a
Banshee. But I can never be sure what airplane it is since the jet
sound and the airplane are not always at the same place in the
sky."

"Yes," Uncle Ollie laughed. "You have observed one of the
principal features of jet-propelled aircraft...They can fly at or
faster than the speed of sound...By-the-way, how does a ten
year old boy like you know so much about fighter aircraft?"

"I don't know...except that I want to know all about things that
go fast...like locomotives, airplanes and racing-cars...and what
makes them work."

"That's amazing," observed Uncle Ollie. "I have the same interests, but I don't recall having them at such a young age..."

"That's because those things weren't around when you were Jack's age," chuckled Aunt Rita.

"Nevertheless," laughed Uncle Ollie. "I'm impressed with your grasp of these things, and I hope that we can continue our chat at another time."

I knew that Fritz wanted this conversation to continue, and for me to ask Uncle Ollie a thousand more questions about aircraft, especially the Me-262, like — *In your review of the captured German documents concerning the Me-262 did you ever come across the name "von Bruckner?"* — But I silently told him, *"Not now... It's not the right-time...I'm too young to be asking the types of questions you want answers to...Besides, I need to know more about why these questions are so important to you."*

When we arrived back at Fairways the Buick, with its tapered front hood and tear-drop, fender-mounted headlights — giving it a sad appearance — was standing on the graveled parking area, but not, to my eye, in the exact same spot that it had been at the time we left in Uncle Ollie's Lincoln. *Hopefully for Chris and David's sake, Mother does not have the same eagle-eye that I have.*

CHAPTER 14

BIG CHIEF TABLET THIRTEEN | JACK

My birthday fell on a Saturday in 1950. It was my eleventh birthday. Like my previous ten birthdays, I knew that I would receive only one or two presents; and they would be something Mom held back from Christmas — usually clothes or something cheap and unexciting. Such is the fate of boys born within a month of Christmas, with a mother who is decidedly practical. For the past several years that had been the pattern, and so I tried my very best not to get my hopes up for that birthday.

My birthday arrived with no plans for a birthday party with my friends; or even a party with my folks, as far as I knew. No one even wished me a Happy Birthday that morning; not even Dad who left for work early. All I knew for sure was that Mom had a D. A. R. meeting at some lady's house, and she expected Chris to drive her there and pick her up in the Buick. Dad would be at work until late afternoon as he always was on Saturdays.

Mom insisted that David and I ride along with her and Chris. Having the three of us go with her was very uncharacteristic. Chris and David were each capable of driving her to the meeting on his own, and I was then old enough stay at home on my own. I started thinking that maybe this was just a way of getting me away from the house while someone set up my surprise birthday party. Or maybe Chris and David were going to take me to a movie at one of the big downtown movie theatres — where the big Wurlitzer theatre pipe-organ would be played by a guy at a key-board that rose up out of the theatre floor — after they dropped Mom off at her meeting.

Mom informed us that her meeting would begin at 11:00 A.M., and would end at 3:00 P.M., and she expected us to pick her up at 3:00 P. M. sharp; "And no joy-riding! Do you understand me?"

For the several days just before my big Saturday, the weather was warmer than usual for mid-January. In fact, the day was sunny and quite spring-like, probably getting to be nearly 70 degrees.

On the trip to the meeting at the lady's home, Chris was charged with driving the Buick, and David sat in the front seat on the passenger side. Mom took her seat regally in the back directly behind David, who she expected to open the street-side back door and escort her out of the Buick when arriving at the lady's home. I, too, was sitting in the back seat, on the side away from mother.

The house to which we were headed with Mother was located in an older, upper-class neighborhood, with large, elegant stone or brick homes placed on large, terraced lots. Some homes had circular driveways, others had side porticoes, and others had series of steps leading from the street to spacious, covered front porches. The brown lawns were immaculately manicured and, even in the middle of January, there were well-trimmed boxwood hedges and shrubs.

We arrived at the attractive, three-story residence a few minutes early; too early for Mom, which required David, the 'footman', to remain in the Buick until she saw other guests arriving. During the wait, Mom fussed with her hair, checked her lipstick in the little compact mirror, and adjusted her gloves. "Now," she said very deliberately, and David performed his 'footman' duties. After she climbed out of the Buick she never looked back at us or said goodbye. Mom walked determinedly – her chin held high – up the front walk and the front steps towards the front porch.

Once Mom stepped her foot on the front porch, Chris shifted the Buick into first-gear, driving quickly away from the curb.

"Well, Chris, let's ditch the brat at home, and head out for some serious fun," exclaimed David as he leaned over the back of the front seat, taking a swat at me. I ducked under David's attempt at hitting me by falling backwards deep into the corner of the Buick's spacious rear-seat.

Having escaped David's attack, I rolled down the window and, with my head almost sticking out of the driver's side rear door, I breathed in the fresh air just like Lady did when Aunt Rita and I took her on drives in the country.

"You can't ditch me at home today," I protested. "It's my birthday!"

"How old are you squirt...eight? Nine?" inquired Chris catching my eye in the rear-view mirror.

"Eleven," I announced sullenly. "You're just being ignorant."

"Be careful smart-mouth, or we'll drop you off right here... and you can walk home."

"Sure...go ahead and try it...And I'll just have to tell Mom that you went joy riding in the Buick...Just like she told you not to do."

"You little jerk-off...Mumby's little snitch," said Chris defiantly as he pulled the Buick to the curb.

"Let's think about this Chris," said David. "You may be going back to college next week, but I'm stuck here with Mom and Jack...I don't need any trouble, especially about driving the Buick."

"Besides," I added. "I know that you took the Buick for a ride when we were at Fairways back at Thanksgiving...But I didn't say anything about it then."

"How did you know that...You're just guessing," snarled Chris.

"Try me," I replied with more confidence than I had reason to feel.

"Hey!" interrupted David, smilingly seeking a truce. "Let's just take Squirt with us...After all, it is his birthday. We can take him with us to Skeeter's Drive-In...and buy him a birthday hamburger and a chocolate milkshake...while we check out the girls. Who knows, having Jack with us may help us get the girls to talk with us...You know how gullible girls can be, especially when they see we are treating our sweet, young brother to a birthday meal." To add emphasis to his point, David reached out and tousled my hair in a brotherly fashion.

"Okay," groused Chris. "But, Jack, if I ever hear that you have said anything to Mother about driving the Buick without her permission...today...Thanksgiving...or ever...you'll pay dearly."

Maybe my efforts to get on David's good side are beginning to pay off...After all, he now knows that I did not say anything to Mom about the Thanksgiving joy-ride; even if he really thinks that I know anything about a Buick joy-ride at Thanksgiving. For the time-being, David and I have a mutual interest in keeping Mom out of our hair.

The parking lot at Skeeter's Drive In that Saturday was packed, as was the restaurant itself. The bill-of-fare in Skeeter's was primarily hamburgers, fries, cokes, and ice cream drinks. The greasy aroma of fried foods, mixed with the pungent smell of tobacco smoke was, at first, overpowering. Amiable, animated conversation competed with the noise of clattering dishes and the whirling, whining, hissing sounds emerging from the kitchen.

We stood around just inside Skeeter's waiting for a spot to sit. Chris and David waved at and spoke to several kids, but I recognized no one. Chris and David's friends, both the girls and the guys, were dressed casually, but in a clean-cut manner. After a bit we slid into a recently abandoned booth. I sat on the inside, with David on the aisle, facing towards the front door where we can observe the constant stream of kids entering and exiting Skeeter's.

Chris chose the opposite side of the booth so that he can – as he tells us with some enthusiasm – make eye-contact with an attractive, but provocatively dressed, bleach-blonde girl sitting in a booth at the back of our seating area. David was in constant motion; getting up to go visit friends, sitting down to order his food and drink, getting up again to visit other friends, sitting down again to eat his meal, getting up again and disappearing from my sight.

"Whatja doin Squirt?" said David as he returned to our booth, seeing me turned sideways looking towards the rear.

Startled, I mumbled, "Nothing...Just looking around."

"Yeah, so I see," he chortled spying who I was looking at. Instead of sitting down David walked back to where Chris was now sitting with the blonde-haired girl. For probably the next fifteen minutes or so, I sat alone in the booth, trying not to look back at David, Chris or the girl. What a stinking, lousy birthday this is turning out to be!

"Well, Punk," Chris exclaimed as he walked by the booth, "It's time to go."

I looked up, seeing Chris, David and the blonde-haired girl walk past me towards the front door. "Cissy," Chris yelled over his shoulder as he walked past me, "This is my kid-brother, Jack... As I told you...we're treating him to lunch on his birthday."

"How old are you, Jack," Cissy cooed softly. "Your brothers tell me you are six years old, but I can see that you aren't that young."

"I'm eleven," I said blushing. Cissy was tall, slender and quite pretty close-up; she also smelled good. I now understood why Chris spent so much time talking with her.

"We are going for that drive I promised you," Chris said, "We are driving Cissy to her home in Northwood Hills."

"Do we have enough time?" asked David. "That's quite a drive... Can we make it back in time to pick up Mother at three?"

"I'll worry about that," Chris retorted.

The ride to Cissy's house was long – longer than I think Chris had planned. The sun was still shining, but there were more, darker clouds in the sky than before.

"Cissy is quite the girl," exclaimed Chris as he reentered the Buick after walking Cissy to her front door. David and I had been standing in front of Cissy's one-story house in a neighborhood of similar bungalows, with the Buick's motor running for ten minutes or more.

"She is a looker," replied David, but without much enthusiasm getting back into the Buick. David inquired nervously, "Did you notice what time it is? Are we going to be able to pick up Mom at three o'clock?"

"Of course...you asshole! Just leave it to me and Big Red." Chris replied angrily, placing another cigarette between his lips and punching the Buick's cigarette lighter.

The maroon Buick sped along suburban streets, urban boulevards, and ever-widening roadways in pursuit of Chris' promised timely rendezvous with Mom. The darkening clouds began to thicken, and the sun disappeared behind tall cumulus shafts.

"I think we're going to make it in time," Chris opined in a less-than-certain tone, as the Buick encountered increasingly heavy city traffic.

I began to doubt that Chris would be able to pull it off. The Buick was just turning onto a crowded thoroughfare, with streetcar tracks imbedded in the brick-paved traffic lanes, when the clouds, which were turning an ugly green, quickly began to change daylight into night-time. It was if a green curtain was being drawn across the sky, and the Buick was desperately trying to outrun its shadow. The rain was now falling in big drops, accompanied by sheet-lightning and swirling winds. I slid over to the driver's side of the Buick, rolling up the rear window.

Just as I started sliding back to roll up the other window, I heard the continuous "plunk, plink, plunk" sound – like the noise marbles make upon hitting a metal garbage-can lid being used as a shield in a back-yard game of war. I saw the large white balls bouncing off of the windshield and hood of the Buick. "My God!" cried Chris and David – almost in unison, "Its hailing!"

In a matter of just a few seconds a huge downpour of quarter-size hail covered the brick pavement with ice-balls. The Buick continued to hurtle down the ice-slickened roadway. Chris struggled with the steering-wheel, trying to keep the vehicle moving in a straight line. Despite Chris' efforts, I felt the rear of the Buick starting to weave from side-to-side on the icy pavement. In an instant, the Buick's right-side tires lifted off of the pavement, tipping the doomed vehicle to its left side.

I thought I heard a voice exclaim: *Get down on the floor Jack! Curl up on the floor! Hang on to whatever you can get a hold of! Jack... the Buick is rolling over! We're going to be crushed!*

FRITZ, AT MY request, added these thoughts: *Jack, who was rendered unconscious by the force of the accident and the trauma he expe-*

rienced, asked me to add my thoughts to his recollections to how the accident happened. For me everything went blank after I told Jack to curl up on the floor of the Buick. All I could think of was that I was facing another life and death crisis with Jack! I believed that Jack was still alive. Otherwise I don't think that I would have been capable of composing these thoughts, nor would I have been aware of Jack's efforts to reach me. The fact that Jack couldn't feel, see or comprehend what was happening to him suggested that he had, as I feared was going to happen, suffered a devastating trauma in the Buick's roll-over accident. Because I was reliant upon Jack's senses in order to see, hear and feel what is happening, I was reduced at that time to mere speculation as to what took place when the Buick started tipping over.

Even if Jack were conscious, I was not certain that he could remember what happened. He may have had a serious head injury causing parts of his brain and nervous system to be malfunctioning; or Jack may have suffered such serious and extensive injuries to his body that he had been given a very powerful sedative to block the pain. I had seen this often when pilots crash their aircraft. The issue was whether Jack would ever regain consciousness; and, if so, would he be crippled to the extent that he would not be able to function fully as a man? I was torn – worrying about Jack and worrying about my own needs. But it was not a question of putting my needs before those of Jack's needs; because our needs were one and the same.

Obviously, much of what I believed must be done to accomplish my mission depended upon the extent of Jack's injuries and the degree of his recovery. Until Jack hopefully regained consciousness and some level of mental competency, I was stuck fretting about things over which I had absolutely no control.

CHAPTER 15

BIG CHIEF TABLET FOURTEEN | JACK

"Jack...Jack...Jack!" I heard the voice calling me from a distance.

"Jack! Get up! We have things to do."

"I'm up!" I lied. My eyes were still closed with my face buried in my pillow.

A few minutes later, the voice renewed its plea; "Jack, please get up. It's almost ten o'clock."

This time I lifted my head from the pillow and actually opened my eyes. "I'll be down in a minute," I replied groggily.

The brightness of the room caused me to squint through my sleep-encrusted eyes as I pushed myself stiffly up off of the soft mattress. Through the open window next to my bed, I heard the sounds of birds chirping in the tall trees that towered over the house, and Betsy — the milk cow — mooing somewhere nearby. The pleasant, country-side smells of freshly-mowed grass and grazing animals wafted in on the warm summer breeze. With some difficulty, I pulled myself up into a sitting position and swung my legs off the bed.

"Do you need help, Jack, with getting up, or with the shower?"

"No, thank you," I replied in as strong a voice as I could muster. Getting into a standing position was still hard to do, but it was getting easier now that the full-cast had been removed from my right leg. With the assistance of a wooden cane, I made my way slowly into the bathroom, a short distance down the hall. Taking a shower was also becoming an easier chore, although it was still difficult for me to avoid water striking the two spots on my scalp where they had drilled holes into my skull. This was a real problem when I washed my hair; which thankfully was not often because my hair was just starting to grow back.

The trip down the stairway to the first floor was slow, as I had to take it a step at a time, using the heavy wooden railing and my cane for support. Once I navigated the turn at the landing — half-way down — I saw Lady sitting quietly at the foot of the stairs, watching my every labored step. Lady waited until I had reached the first floor before approaching me from her sitting position, her tail wagging; greeting me with a toothy grin and licking my outstretched hand. Somehow, Lady knew that our former, carefree, romping relationship was now different; she had become watchful and careful, acting as an ever-present guide-dog, as I struggled around on my healing leg.

"How are you doing this morning?" Aunt Rita inquired from her seat at the kitchen table. Her head and upper-torso were framed in the kitchen window behind her, casting a dark-shadow across the yellow table cloth. With the light from outdoors shinning directly behind her, it was difficult for me to tell whether Aunt Rita was smiling or frowning at me. Aunt Rita was still having a rough-time with this. I don't think she was prepared for healing to take so long. Thank God, I can at least now get up and down the stairs...and on my own.

"Did you have any bad dreams last night?" Aunt Rita inquired solemnly. "If you did we need to write each of them down, so you can tell the doctor about them."

"No bad dreams...No headaches either," I reported.

"That's good," Aunt Rita said cheerfully. "How many nights now have you been bad-dream free?"

"Just a couple of nights," I replied. Oh, how I hate having these bad, sometimes terrifying, dreams — nightmares really; along with occasional headaches. I started having them shortly after I regained consciousness. The doctors attributed them to my head injury and the strong sedatives they gave me for my pain. They think I may have the nightmares and headaches for several more months.

"At least it is a start," Aunt Rita observed. "What would you like me to fix you for breakfast? It has to be a quick meal...We have an appointment at the University clinic in Columbia at one o'clock...For your leg this time...They want to see how the bone is mending...It's been over four months since it was last operated on."

It's been a struggle for me to figure out each day how today relates to yesterday, or to six months ago. It's as if I have walked into a movie that is already playing; I don't know how much I have missed, and I have to figure out what I have missed by watching the rest of the movie. But then there are parts of what I am seeing now that I think I've seen before; which makes me think that I should know what happened in the first part of the movie...the part I may have missed – or maybe not. I feel so terribly lost and confused; there are portions of my life which seem to jump backwards and forwards. Like right now...I know that I am with Aunt Rita and Lady at Fairways, but I can't remember why I am here; I feel like I should be somewhere else. In fact, is this real-time, or am I still asleep; is this only a dream? Will I even remember these thoughts...this dream...when I wake up? I am crying...Why am I crying?

"Jack! Jack! Are you all right? Why are you crying? We are only going for a check-up." Aunt Rita was talking to me in a voice intended to be reassuring and non-threatening. I did not see her get up from where she was sitting, but I saw her walking towards me with her arms open wide to embrace me. I moved unsteadily towards her, and melted into her arms. Aunt Rita held me tenderly, but firmly, and I sobbed uncontrollably with my face buried in her neck and shoulder, drawing in with each breath the wonderful fresh-scent of her soft hair. I love you Aunt Rita like I have never loved anyone else!

"JACK, I SPOKE to your mother today on the telephone," Aunt

Rita said in that tone indicating she had something important to tell me. We were sitting in our rocking chairs on the front porch after dinner. The sun was creeping down behind the house casting long shadows down the front lawn. The only sounds were those of the cattle lowing in the pasture at the crest of the hill on the other side of the barn, located just on the other side of the graveled county road. Lady was lying in her usual spot at the top of the porch steps, occasionally raising her head in reaction to a sound only she could hear. I remember this scene, but wasn't the landscape all covered with snow?

"I didn't hear the phone ring," I said quizzically.

"It didn't ring...I called her while you were napping upstairs... in your room." *I was right...She does have something important to tell me...Why else would she call my mother...And why call her while I was asleep? She obviously didn't want me to hear what she was telling Mom.*

"Why did you call Mom?" I asked; knowing full-well that this is the question Aunt Rita was anticipating.

"Well, we haven't talked in a while and I thought she would want to know how you are doing."

"And how am I doing?"

"You are doing much better, Jack, and I told her so."

I am not well though...Not by a long shot! But am I well enough to go to school in a month? At Mass on Sunday the priest announced the start of school at the parish school in mid-September.

"Am I well enough that I can I go back to school?"

"That was one of the things I wanted to talk to her about. We will need a transcript of your grades from St. Agatha's, before St. Benedict's will accept you, or to figure out in which grade to place you. With all the school you missed after the accident, you will most likely have to repeat sixth grade. You were too young for sixth grade anyway. You need to be in a grade with kids your own age. But, Jack, what I really wanted to talk to your mother about is that I am not sure you are ready to go back to school just yet."

"What are you saying?" I asked. "I feel much better, and I can walk without the cane...well, most of the time... And I am reading all of those books the clinic recommended I read."

"I know, Jack...But I am concerned about the headaches and the...a...nightmares. I want to take you to some specialists in Kansas...I would like for them to check you out. Uncle Ollie recommends them. He told me they have done a lot of work with pilots and other military who suffered serious head injuries during the war."

But the war is what most of my nightmares are about...Nightmares I don't fully understand...It's like I am someone else...caught in terrifying situations...bombs and flames...a woman...and a baby...and airplanes...and being shot at. These nightmares are so real...just like I was there. How can that be? How can I tell these specialists about these dreams...They will think I am crazy!

"Will these specialists ask me about my dreams?" I inquired.

"I would certainly hope so...As much as you complain about how the nightmares affect you...The shouting out in the night... The sweaty pajamas...The blank looks during the day. You don't tell me what the nightmares are about, but I know how badly you feel the next day. I want to find some way to make them stop...to make them go away. I want you to be my happy boy again – just like you were last summer!"

What about last summer? Yes, last summer! Of course I remember it. How could I ever forget last summer? It was the first time I ever felt loved; really, truly, unconditionally loved...loved by Aunt Rita in a way that I have never felt loved by even my own mother. How wonderfully my life changed last summer. And here we are again together; even more deeply into our "mother/son" relationship. Maybe this time it will last forever.

The sun-cast shadows were now fading into the oncoming night. The sounds of lowing cattle and the daytime birds – settling for the night – were being replaced with the sounds of the awakening night creatures; serenading us with their high-pitched chirps and bass-baritone grunts. Even the daredevil swifts and martins were bringing their aerial acrobatics to a close. The twinkling evening stars were being replicated by the twinkling lightning bugs filling the lawn, plants and trees. Aunt Rita and I continued to rock away – silently staring out into the gathering darkness – trying to recapture the joy of last summer's pleasant, revealing evenings when we first discovered our love for each other.

"What a beautiful evening to be together," Aunt Rita remarked, breaking the silence. "It reminds me so much of our evenings together last summer."

"Oh, yes!" I replied enthusiastically, trying to rekindle some of the warmth of last summer's incredibly close feelings. "Do you feel like talking about things?"

"What things?"

"Oh, you know, things about you and me...Like how long have you been taking care of me?"

"Since you got out of the hospital...which was sometime in March."

"Didn't I spend some time at home before I came here?"

"No. I picked you up at the hospital...and I brought you directly here to live with me."

"But, why...Why didn't I just go home and live with Mom and Dad?"

"There are a number of reasons...but the most important reason was that your injuries were going to take a long time to heal, and your mother didn't..."

"Want me!"

"No, Jack. Don't think like that. Your mother loves you... in her own way, perhaps, but she does love you...and she wants the best for you. With her working every day, and all...she felt that I could give you better care than she could."

"How badly was I hurt?"

"The doctors told me you had cracked your skull, suffered a massive concussion, fractured a vertebra in your neck, broke several ribs, and your right leg was broken in several places. The first time I saw you...a few days after the accident you were in a full-body cast with these ice tong-like things sticking out of your skull, with weights attached to them. You were unconscious, remaining unconscious for almost a week. They told me you were lucky to be alive. Apparently, they found you rolled up into a ball on the rear floor, jammed partly under the Buick's front seat. They think you were in this position at the time that the Buick tipped over...which kept you from being thrown about inside the automobile as it rolled over and over, before being struck head-on by a truck. Why you were in the position you were in laying on the floor of the Buick at the time of the accident remains a mystery."

"Maybe I was looking for something that had fallen on the floor?" *Or maybe I had a warning...but who would have given me a warning? Was it Chris or David?*

"Well, whatever it was, being on the floor of the Buick, and in that position, saved your life."

"What about Chris and David? Are they okay?" I asked, fearing the worst.

After a long hesitation, Aunt Rita struggled to say, "No, Jack... They both died in the crash."

"Oh," was all I could say. *No wonder I hadn't heard any mention of their names.* "Why hasn't someone told me they were dead until now?"

"I'm sorry you weren't told sooner. Your Mom and Dad were the ones who should have told you, but I guess they felt it was best not to tell you about Chris and David until you asked about them...You had enough pain to deal with. I shouldn't have been left with the responsibility to tell you, but I am sure you are now strong enough to handle it."

"I don't know why Mom and Dad felt I couldn't handle it. Mom still wants to treat me like a little kid. Well, I'm not a little kid anymore; and I resent being treated that way...especially when it involves my own brothers. I am very sorry Chris and David are dead; but I am even sorrier that I did not think to ask about them sooner.

"Jack, I can't answer for them. But maybe they felt that since you were lucky not to have been killed in the accident that you might feel guilty for living, when your brothers were not so lucky... dying in the crash. They may have wanted to spare you that feeling of guilt...Although that kind of absurd thinking requires that you would never learn about Chris and David's deaths."

I don't feel guilty about me living and them dying. I received a warning before the accident happened, and I obeyed that warning. Maybe they received a similar warning, but chose to ignore it.

"What if I don't feel guilty about them dying...and me living?"

"Then that's as it should be. It was an accident; and who lives and who dies is not your responsibility. It wasn't your time to die. God still has plans for you."

Aunt Rita got up from her rocking chair and stepped behind mine. She reached both arms around the back of my chair placing her hands lightly on my shoulders and began rubbing them. "It is getting late, Jack. We have covered a lot of ground this evening. I am sorry that Chris and David died...and I am sorry for your loss. But I am also so happy that you are alive...that you are living here with me....and for as long as you want to stay with me. We need to talk more about that...and about the trip to the Menninger Clinic in Kansas...but that will keep until tomorrow. You need a good night's sleep. I love you Jack, and I am going to do everything I can to make you well." Leaning over she kissed me tenderly on the top of my head. Then, removing her hands from my shoulders she said to Lady, "Come on girl, do your duty...we're going to bed."

———————

GOING TO SLEEP after an evening like that was difficult. My brain was filled with visions of the accident and thoughts of Chris and David. There were so many questions about how and why I escaped the death that ended Chris and David's lives. I missed David; he was trying to be a good older brother. And then there was my mother.

Why has my mother abandoned me? What have I done that makes Mom not want to see me anymore? What have I ever done that caused Mom to treat me the way she has? Still, I am so much better off being here with Aunt Rita. It is like a dream – a dream come true! Or is it just a dream...like the awful nightmares? Maybe Aunt Rita is right in thinking that I may need the help of spe-

cialists. *Am I going crazy? Am I already crazy? Please...Please, somebody help me! Please, dear God...Please, help me...I need you! I need you so much!*

Just as I was about to fall asleep, I was struck by a new thought: *Was it my guardian angel who warned me to get on the floor of the Buick just before it tipped over?* Immediately, I received a response to this thought, but in a different voice; a voice that I have heard before...a voice with a German accent: *No Jack...It was me...Fritz!* Suddenly, as if a curtain in my mind had been lifted, the memories on the other side of that curtain came running towards me, overwhelming me. In an instant, the dreams — the nightmares — began to make sense; they were Fritz's memories — memories so potent that they seeped into my inactive mind when I was sleeping — appearing to me as bad dreams. *Thank you God! Thank you God! You have answered my prayers.*

And Fritz added: *Yes, Jack. God has answered your prayers! You are surrounded by those who love you! Now go to sleep...for tomorrow we have much work to do! And you shouldn't be troubled with my nightmares any more.*

As I drifted off to sleep I was thinking: *Boy, won't Aunt Rita be pleased to know that it was only Fritz's memories causing my nightmares! Or will she? How can I tell her about Fritz?*

IN THE MORNING, after a dream- free night, I awoke earlier than I had in months, anxious to tell Aunt Rita about last-night's wonderful revelation. Before I could even begin the process of extricating myself from the soft bed, Fritz barged into my partially-awake mind sounding like some movie-version British sergeant-major bellowing out the day's orders: *I trust that you slept well last night. I am pleased that you did. You should share that fact with Aunt Rita, but I don't believe it would be wise for you to say anything about me, or the source of your nightmares, just yet. Trying to explain my presence in your body to your Aunt Rita will require some careful planning; and that may take some time, luck.*

Making my way down the steps with less pain than I could manage previously, the aroma of Aunt Rita's delicious bran muffins filled the stairwell. Lady was waiting to greet me, cheerfully as usual. This time I bent down to rub her bony head and kiss her muzzle. In the kitchen, Aunt Rita was pulling the tin of muffins from the oven. She looked my way with a big smile, her dark eyes bright and shining.

"I thought you would be up earlier today than you have been getting up," she said, placing the muffin tin on the top of the stove. "In case you didn't get up, I was going to send Lady upstairs to wake you. But then I heard the water running in the bathroom, and I knew you were up. Lady misses getting to wake you in the mornings like she did last summer. I only let her get as far as the bottom of the stairs...where she waits so patiently."

"Yes, she's my pal...Please let her come get me again."

"Are you sure...Do you think you are really ready for that?"

"I think so...I didn't have any bad dreams last night...In fact, I slept better than I have...forever."

"Oh, that's great Jack! I was so afraid that our talk last evening might have been too much for you to handle...I guess I was wrong."

"Actually, what you told me about the accident ...even about Chris and David's death...about how I escaped being killed...even about my injuries and being here with you, maybe explains some things...like why Mom has sent me away."

"How do you feel about being here instead of with your Mom and Dad?"

How do I answer this question? I've never had to answer a question about "feelings" before. If Aunt Rita had asked me whether I miss my Dad, or if I am glad to be here...I could answer both those questions with a "Yes;" but I don't know how to explain my "feelings" towards my mother. Can I tell Aunt Rita that I think my mother doesn't love me...has never loved me...and now wishes I that I had died in the accident?

Seeing the puzzled look on my face, Aunt Rita said, "Jack, I didn't mean to put you on the spot...about being here and...all."

"Oh, I love being here with you...There is no place I'd rather be...now and forever...It's just that while I miss Dad...I'm not sure that I miss Mom...but it's more than that...and I don't know how to say it."

"Jack, please sit down...We have a lot to talk about," Aunt Rita said.

I hung the cane on the back of my chair, and I sat down; my eyes brimming with tears. *What is happening? This day started out so happy, and now I am dealing with "feelings" that I don't understand; except that whatever they are, they are making me "feel" so sad that I am crying. I don't think this is going to be a pleasant conversation.*

"Jack, I can only guess at what you are struggling with, but let me take a stab at putting these feelings into words...You don't think your mother loves you...indeed you probably think that she wishes that you had died in the accident instead of Chris and David...And you feel anger towards your mother for not loving you, and guilt towards yourself for feeling anger towards your mother. These are very complex feelings, and I want you to think about them for a few minutes. While you are thinking about them, I want you to eat some of these bran muffins you love so much while they are still warm. I'll get you some butter and strawberry preserves, and a glass of fresh milk."

I have been thinking about these "feelings." Does "complex" mean that by thinking about these "feelings" that I will "feel" sad? Well, then I know that "sad" is a "feeling." And, I guess "anger" and "guilt" are "feelings" as well? But, what is so "complex" about that? And why do I still "feel" so sad?

Now sitting across from me at the table, Aunt Rita smoothed away a wrinkle in the table cloth with a sweep of her hand, took a sip from her cup of coffee, looked at me in a way which told me how much she loved me — that sweet-smile, the crinkles at the edge of her eyes — took a deep breath, and began: "Words, like 'love,' 'anger,' 'guilt,' 'hate,' 'fear,' 'hunger,' 'joy,' are the names we have given to 'feelings.' And 'feelings' are part of our very nature, our very physical make-up. 'Feelings' are neither good nor bad; they are just feelings — we can't control them. How we might react to these feelings, or how we let feelings affect our behavior, is where control comes in; but the feelings themselves we have no control over. 'Feelings' are the mind's reactions to things which the body's senses perceive are impacting, or might impact, the person. Sometimes, these perceptions are 'right-on,' and other times, these perceptions are 'flat-wrong.' It takes experience, it takes discipline, it takes a clear mind, and it takes a value-system, to discern whether the perception is real or it is false."

"For example, let's say you have a gun in your hand under the table, and we are talking just like we are right now. Suddenly, and with no provocation, you pull the gun from under the table at point it right at me, saying, 'I'm going to kill you!' My mind receives the sights and sounds from my eyes and ears, immediately perceiving danger, sending out the 'fear' response to my body to do something. Chemicals are released from glands, electrical charges race around the brain, and I am preparing to fight or to run away. At the same time, the mind is also analyzing the information still being transmitted from the senses, weighing that information against stuff stored in the brain to test the accuracy of the perceived threat. All of this takes but an instant.

"The mind observes that the look in your eyes and the smile on your face are inconsistent with the eyes and the face of a killer. The mind also remembers that you are my loving nephew – more like my son, in fact – and that the threat 'I'm going to kill you!' is totally inconsistent with your previous behavior towards me. On the basis of this analysis, instead of trying to fight you or trying to run away, my mind would conclude that this is just a practical joke; and I would smile and laugh at the joke. I would then expect you to lower the gun, and to laugh along with me. But, you could, instead, shoot me dead...because you are, in fact, a mentally deranged killer."

My God! Aunt Rita thinks I might be mentally deranged! That's why she wants to take me to that mental hospital in Kansas. She thinks I'm crazy...a killer! If she thinks that about me now, how can I ever tell her about Fritz?

Seeing the startled look on my face, the tears forming in my eyes, Aunt Rita cried out, "Oh, Jack, I'm sorry, Jack! I'm so sorry!

That was a bad example...a poor attempt at humor...I didn't mean anything by it. I was just trying to be funny...to make you smile... Of course I don't think you are crazy...or demented...or a killer!"

Then I heard Fritz say: *Jack! Jack! Don't overreact! Aunt Rita is telling you the truth...she's not telling you she thinks you are crazy...She made a mistake...She didn't realize how fragile your self-esteem is right now...You need to tell her it's okay...That you understand. You need to keep Aunt Rita talking about "feelings," and about your mother. These are issues we will need to deal with before you go to see the doctors in Kansas.*

"It's okay," I said, wiping the tears from my eyes with my napkin. "I understand now...I see the joke. Why would you say anything like that to someone who you truly believe is crazy? The fact that you said it to me, just means that you knew it wasn't true. I didn't understand it like that at first. Perhaps I'm still too upset with Mother...and how I am feeling about her right now."

"Are you sure, Jack? I didn't mean to upset you...Maybe we need to leave any further discussions about your feelings towards you mother to another time...As a matter of fact, I'm not sure I'm ready to deal with Nell...your mother...right now. Would you be too upset with me if we waited until this evening to continue this conversation?"

"Sure, that's fine," I responded.

"Good. Then, this evening it is. How would you like your eggs cooked this morning? The eggs are fresh out of the nest."

Nell...Nell. I like the sound of calling my mother...Nell. Chris and David would occasionally call her Nell behind her back...especially when they were angry with her, or she with them. Sometimes they would even say "Nell" to her face to see her reaction; but she would ignore it. Mom was not about to give them the satisfaction of a reaction. Dad also called her Nell; but usually he would call her "Lover" whenever he was asking for permission to do something, or whenever he was trying to calm her down for something he had done or not done. Since my 'mother' no longer wants to be my mother, maybe I should instead start calling her Nell!

FOR THE NEXT SEVERAL WEEKS, Aunt Rita and I avoided discussions about the accident, my injuries or my mother. I spent
my days either working on repairing my body's muscle-tone, or
restoring my mind's thinking process. The 'repairing' part now
included repeated leg exercises (now that the doctors have concluded that my leg is mending properly), added to the regimen
of arm and neck exercises that I had been doing since my arrival
at Fairways. After this, I spent several hours 'restoring' my mental
capacity by reading books geared towards sixth graders. In addition to this required reading, Aunt Rita had supplied me with
novels; mainly ones dealing with an historical theme – like *Last
of the Mohicans, Mutiny on the Bounty, Beau Geste.* For lighter-
reading she supplied me with stories of cowboys in the American
West.

 After lunch, I would usually nap for an hour on the sofa in
the book-filled den. When I got up, Lady and I would take a
leisurely stroll down the long, white-gravel driveway to retrieve
mail which had been placed by the rural mail carrier in the large,
white-painted, metal mailbox planted at the end of the driveway.
The mailbox, with its black lettering, announced to everyone
passing along the country road that the beautiful farm-land on
both sides of the road, for a mile or more, was named "Fairways."

 Seldom were there any letters for me, but there was always
yesterday's daily newspaper – The Evening Star – which had
wonderful cartoons that I glanced at as Lady and I made the
long trip back up the driveway.   One day, upon refolding the
newspaper I noticed an article on the front-page which spoke
about the current polio epidemic sweeping the country, naming
the local kids who had been struck down with the disease. This
made me think about my own injuries, and while they are severe,
I had it much better than these polio kids who were condemned
to spending long-periods of time in an "iron-lung" and years of
painful therapy. I remembered the prayer to St. Margret Mary
which we would say daily at St. Agatha's for my class-mate Bill
who got polio last summer, and I mumbled the words of the
prayer for the latest batch of victims.

 Putting the folded newspaper back with the rest of the mail

in my hand, I observed two envelopes I had missed seeing when I first retrieved the mail from the box; one was from the Menninger Clinic – addressed to Aunt Rita, and the other was addressed to me – with no return address, but I recognized the handwriting as my Dad's. I was hesitant to know what was in either envelope, though I had been hoping to hear from Dad.

Laying the rest of the mail on the kitchen table, I headed into the den, flopping down in my favorite chair. Tearing open the envelope from Dad with my finger, I slipped out the contents. There were two folded pages of handwriting on lined school-tablet paper. Unfolding the pages, a twenty-dollar bill was paper-clipped to the first page along with a newspaper clipping. Removing the paper-clipped items, I began to read the attached letter:

Jack,

I'm sorry it's taken me so long to write to you. I've started so many letters which I never could finish.

There really is no good way to start this letter, except to tell you how much I love you and miss you. The house is so empty without you. I don't even come home for lunch anymore. It hurts too much not having you here to share a lunch.

You are much better off where you are with Aunt Rita. She can look after you and give you the attention you need while you heal. How are you feeling? Is the leg doing any better? I would love to see you walking again. Actually, I would love to see you even if you can't walk.

It's a miracle that you survived the accident. The attached newspaper clipping describes how bad the accident was. The Buick was so badly crushed that the firemen had to cut you out of it.

I am sure that Aunt Rita already told you about Chris and David being killed in the accident. They were both good boys. Please remember them in your prayers. I pray for you every day.

Your mother is doing a little better. She took the accident pretty hard, especially the funeral. She went back to work right away, just so she had something to do to keep her mind off of what happened. It's hard for me to get her to say two words when we are here together.

I keep trying to get your mother to come see you or just call you, but she just looks away and cries whenever I bring the subject up. Maybe I'll just come see you on my own. I'll come by train.

If you get a chance, please write me a note and let me know how you are doing. Aunt Rita calls your mother occasionally to let her know what is happening, but she never tells me much. If you do write, please send it to my office.

I've also sent you a little money. You can always use a little cash to buy stuff in town.

I love you so much Jack. Please don't forget about me. And pray for your mother and me.

Love, Dad

Oh, how I miss you too, Dad. I'll never forget you. I love you so much! And I want to see you. We'll have lunch together here at the farm. I'll talk to Aunt Rita about getting you to come see me, soon.

I refolded the letter, putting it back in the torn envelope, together with the twenty-dollar bill and the newspaper-clipping.

Just glancing at the clipping I knew that I didn't want to read it, just yet.

Maybe I ought to let Aunt Rita see Dad's note and the news-paper-clipping. She can tell me what to do about writing to him, and about whether I should read the newspaper clipping.

After dinner, on the porch, in our rockers, while it was still light enough to see, I handed Aunt Rita Dad's letter. Watching her face as she read the note, and then studying the newspaper-clipping, I could see that she was seriously thinking about the contents of what was in her hands. Placing the note and clipping in her lap, and turning to look at me, Aunt Rita asked,

"How do you feel about what's in your Dad's note?"

"His note makes me feel very sad...especially for him...I didn't read the newspaper-clipping about the accident...I wanted you to read it first...and let me know if it will upset me too much."

"The note makes me feel sad, too. As to the newspaper-clipping, I am sure your Dad meant well in sending it to you, but I don't think you need to read it...you know all you really need to know about what happened...It was a very bad accident, you were seriously hurt, and Chris and David died. End of story...But, I have another question...How do feel towards your mother?"

"I'm not really sure how I feel about her right now. I guess I feel both sorry for her...for losing Chris and David...but angry at how she is reacting to Dad and me...I mean, why is she giving us the cold-shoulder...the silent treatment? Don't we count for something? She makes it so hard for me to love her!"

Seeing me starting to cry, Aunt Rita reached over, lightly stroking my forearm. "Jack. I know just how difficult it is for you to love your mother. Sometimes I think she does what she does to us just to keep us from loving her. It's almost as if she doesn't want our love: preferring our pity instead. I'm not sure she even knows what love is, or how to love or how to show love."

Right now, I am not sure what love is either, or how to love, or how to show love. Is it hugging and kissing? What is it? Can we love someone without showing it through physical contact? How do I answer Aunt Rita...if at all?

Perhaps reading my mind, Aunt Rita asked, "Do you think you

love your mother, despite how she treats you?"

"Probably...but I'm not sure," I answered, while wiping away the tears collecting on my cheeks.

"Do you think your mother loves you, despite how she treats you?"

"I don't know...I'm confused...I've tried so hard to make her love me...I try to be good...But no matter how hard I try to make her love me, I never feel that I am loved by her...I'm not sure I even know what love is."

"Jack, I'm quite sure that you know what love is. Doesn't your Dad love you?"

"Yes."

"Well how do you know that he loves you if you say you don't know what love is?"

Because he treats me as if he cares for me; he wants me. It's not just one thing; it's everything he does for me, and what he doesn't do to me. I feel cared for.

"Is caring for someone...You know, doing good things for someone...Is that loving someone?" I asked.

"Yes. Very definitely...caring for someone is a crucial element of love."

"Then Dad loves me. It's how he treated me. It's the way he acted around me. It's his smile...his hugs...his kisses. But it's more than that...It's his gentleness. I feel comfortable around him...Just like how I feel when I am with you...And I know how much you love me...I can feel it!"

"Thank you, Jack, for noticing," she said – her facing beaming.

"You don't need to ask," I quickly added. "I love you, too, so much!"

"Well this brings us to another subject...Our trip to see the doctors at the Menninger Clinic."

"I saw the envelope in the mail today," I said.

"I figured that you had seen it...Thus, we need to talk about it...which will it be, now or tomorrow?"

"Tonight will be fine."

"We have an appointment at Menninger's in two weeks, to

see a Dr. Glassberg, a clinical psychologist. He will interview you, maybe administer a test or two, and then make a recommendation as to whether any further treatment will be required, and of what type of treatment, if any. This initial interview should take just a couple of hours...And should be painless."

Why is my stomach churning if it is going to be 'painless'?

"It's too far to Topeka to make the trip from here in one day, especially with the morning appointment time...So I thought we could go spend the night at a hotel, probably the Muehlbach in Kansas City. And, on the way back home, it might be fun to spend a couple of days in Kansas City with Jon's folks...the Kaufmans...I'd like for them to meet you and to get to know you."

"Will they need to know why we are going to be in Topeka?"

"Of, course...they're family...You're family...And they were instrumental in getting you such a quick appointment at Menninger's."

Talking about 'family'...What more could Aunt Rita have to tell me about my mother this evening?

"You indicated that there might be something more we had to discuss about my mother," I said in an effort to jog Aunt Rita's memory.

"Oh. Yes. Just this...Don't be so hard on yourself about how you feel about your mother just now...Your Dad's letter...and our discussion about 'love' and 'caring'...has stirred up some pretty strong feelings and memories about your mother. It is going to take some time... thinking and talking further about these feelings and memories...before you can deal with them and your mother...And, for whatever it is worth: I don't think you are crazy!"

Standing up from her rocker, Aunt Rita moved before me on the now dark porch. Even in the dark I could see her radiant smile. "You've made a lot of progress this evening Jack, in fact, all day...If you're as drained as I am, you need to turn in." Turning away from me, towards the front-door, I heard her say, "Come on Lady, let's do your thing...we're going to bed."

CHAPTER 16

BIG CHIEF TABLET FIFTEEN | JACK

Going to sleep that night was difficult; with all the many thoughts, memories and emotions swirling through my mind. Remembering my promise to Dad, I offered some silent prayers, asking God to take care of Dad and my mother, and to let Chris and David rest in peace.

Before I fell asleep, Fritz chimed in with, *It has, indeed, been a very auspicious day. Although you have experienced much discomfort in having to deal with your intense feelings and memories, the end-result has been well worth the suffering...You are making remarkable progress Jack – both with confronting the bitterness in your relationship with your mother, and with developing an excellent, special relationship with Aunt Rita. We are both so lucky to have such a remarkable person as your Aunt Rita, providing amazingly thoughtful guidance. And may you have as tranquil a night's sleep as I am planning for myself to have.*

THE TRIP TO Topeka was filled with anticipation, as well as anxiety. Aunt Rita's comforting words – that she does not view me as 'crazy' – helped immeasurably whenever my mind drifted to the upcoming meeting with Dr. Glassberg. Still, I was troubled by my memories of my mother and my feelings towards her. I was not quite sure what Aunt Rita meant when she said, it would 'take time – thinking and talking about these feelings and memories – before you can deal with them and your mother'. Not a day went by that I did not think about these feelings and memories, but they never seemed to change, get better, or go away. Perhaps it was the 'talking' part that was the more important, missing step. On several evenings before our trip to Topeka, I tried to get Aunt Rita to talk about my 'feelings and memories' during our nightly talks on the front-porch, but she wouldn't talk about them.

During the several hours drive to Kansas City, I thought that this might be a good time to talk with Aunt Rita about my memories and feelings. "Can we talk about my mother?" I asked in a louder than usual tone because of the road noise.

"Sure," replied Aunt Rita in a similarly louder voice. She was wearing aviator-style sun glasses, with her hair tucked under a bandana. Her left-arm was propped on the window frame, her right-hand casually gripping the steering-wheel. "What would you like to talk about?"

"Well, I've been thinking a lot about my memories and about how I feel about my mother, just like you said I would need to do...But I just keep having the same memories and the same feelings...And you said I would need to talk about these memories and feelings...So I hoped that we could talk now...together."

"Jack, I know that I said that, but I've been thinking some more about what I said...and I am not sure it is a good idea to talk about your memories and feelings...especially your feelings about your mother...until you have had your interview with Dr. Glassberg. He's the professional...and maybe we ought to let him take the lead on how you should deal with the feelings."

"But what about the memories...how do I deal with them?"

"Again, that may be something we also need to let Dr. Glassberg decide. But, it seems to me that memories are just that... they are memories of life's experiences. Hopefully, the bad ones will fade overtime, and the good ones will not...but they will always be there. It's not the memories that are the problem...the problem is in how we deal with the feelings brought about by those experiences...those memories.

"Now, I am about to get in over my head talking about this psychology stuff ...and that's why we really need to defer to Dr.

Glassberg. But the real source of psychological problems comes, I believe, when a person tries to repress feelings caused by bad memories...and sometimes the memories themselves...But, Jack, I really don't think that you are repressing your feelings...or your memories...In fact, right now, you may be over-thinking your memories and feelings...Still, we need to let Dr. Glassberg decide about that."

"What does 'repress' mean?" I asked.

"I just knew that I shouldn't try to play psychologist...Trying to tell you what 'repress' means requires some basic knowledge of psychology...like what they teach in a basic college course on psychology...And that's the extent of my knowledge of psychology...a basic college course. As I best I can recall...In simple terms 'repress' means pushing the memory of a particularly awful experience out of your mind because just thinking about it causes you so much pain...But here is the tricky part...a person's mind is made up of a 'conscious' mind and a 'subconscious' mind. You can push the bad memory or bad feeling out of your 'conscious' mind, but it can wind up in your 'subconscious' mind...where it can show up in the form of nightmares, stranger-behavior, or other psychological problems...Does that help?"

I'm not sure that I understand what 'conscious' and 'subconscious' mean, but I'm not going to ask Aunt Rita...This is not helping me...I thought my nightmares were caused by Fritz's thoughts, but were they? I'll just work with Fritz on figuring this out...Maybe I have the 'conscious' mind and Fritz has the 'subconscious' mind. But whatever Aunt Rita is saying about this 'repress' thing, I'm not aware of any memory or feeling that I've tried to 'push out' of my mind. I'm ready to move on to something more pleasant — and simple — to talk about.

"I think I understand some of it, but I guess Dr. Glassberg can tell me if I'm having any psychological problems...But, thanks for trying to help me understand all of this."

"You're welcome...You just need to remember that you are so loved and accepted. There is nothing you need to do to earn my love...you have it now, you'll have it forever. Also, we are all damaged with bad memories, bad feelings...It just takes time to learn how to deal with them...I'll be here to help you deal with yours."

"How much longer, until we get to Kansas City?" I asked.

"It shouldn't be too much longer...Why do you ask?"

"I'm getting hungry."

AFTER SPENDING A pleasant night at the Muehlebach Hotel in downtown Kansas City, we traveled on to the Menninger Clinic in Topeka in the morning. The Clinic was located in an open area just to the west of the downtown section of Topeka. There were number of white buildings — some looking like barns — and a tall colonial-style brick building with a fancy cupola perched in the center of the high-pitched roof's ridge-line located in a park-like setting. It was this tall structure to which we were directed by the guard at the entry-gate.

Aunt Rita provided our names to the receptionist standing behind a marble-topped counter in the middle of a large open area. The receptionist studied a thick book on the ledge below the counter and pointed us in the direction of the hallway running off to her left. Midway down this spacious hallway a name-plate over one of the many doorways announced Dr. Glassberg's office. An attractive woman in a dark-blue dress took our names, motioning us to take a seat on the comfortable-looking leather upholstered sofa. The low table in front of the sofa was neatly stacked with popular magazines, like *Life, Collier's* and *Look*.

The cover of the *Life* magazine had a photo of General Douglas MacArthur, together with a caption stating "General MacArthur heads U.N. troops battling North Korean Invaders."

"Will this new war in Korea impact Uncle Ollie?" I asked.

"I suppose so...President Truman is sending every soldier and sailor he can lay his hands on to Korea immediately. I understand he is also calling up the National Guard Reserves and lots of veterans from the Second World War. I saw your friend Buzz in town the other day...He tells me he may have to go, as well as his pilot friend — Pete Roberts — who you wanted to meet."

I then heard Fritz: *That is not good news, Jack. This Pete Roberts may be the pilot I met in the Stalag in Poland. If he is the right pilot, then he has important information that would be helpful to us in solving the riddle of my death.*

"How long will Pete Roberts be gone?" I inquired.

"I really have no way of knowing that...He could be gone for several years."

"Well, do you think if we asked Uncle Ollie, he would be able to tell us how long?"

"Jack. I'm sure that nobody knows how long this war in Korea will last...not even President Truman...But, why is Pete Roberts so important to you?" Aunt Rita asked, somewhat irritated.

"Because...a...a...I...need to talk to him," I stammered. Oh, oh! How am I going to get out of this?

"But why do you need to talk to this Pete Roberts? You don't even know him."

"Well," I managed. "Buzz says I need to talk to Pete Roberts about P-38s."

"I'm sure that any conversations about P-38s will just have to keep until this Pete Roberts gets back from Korea."

Again I heard Fritz: *Jack! Let the subject drop! We are getting close to bringing Aunt Rita into our plans to spook her at this point. Your focus needs to be on convincing Dr. Glassberg that you are not crazy...And Aunt Rita is your biggest supporter right now. You could lose her support if you let her know about me before you get a clean bill of health from Dr. Glassberg.*

A short time later we were ushered into Dr. Glassberg's simply appointed office, smelling faintly of incense. Dr. Glassberg was a tall, thin, balding man, with a well-trimmed goatee, wearing a long, white coat. I couldn't see his eyes too well — they were hidden behind black-rimmed glasses with thick lenses. His graying hair and goatee made him look to me to be much older than Aunt Rita. In a soft voice, Dr. Glassberg greeted us warmly, including shaking my hand as well as Aunt Rita's.

"I have read your letter about Jack, Mrs. Kaufmann...and I believe it sets out your concerns rather concisely...Nevertheless, I will want to talk to you further about Jack...And while we are doing that, I am going to ask Jack to step back outside to my reception room...My assistant, Dr. Nelson will come get you Jack in just a bit to take you to his office where he will administer a few tests...so we can better evaluate your condition... After that, Jack, he will bring you back here. I'll want to review the test results with Dr. Nelson, and then talk to you so that I can get to know you better."

Dr. Nelson, who retrieved me from Dr. Glassberg's reception room, looked to be much younger than Dr. Glassberg — maybe even younger looking than Aunt Rita. His hair was long and very curly, but he was beardless. A bright smile caused his twinkling, light-blue eyes to crinkle at the corners. He wore a long, white coat; just like the one worn by Dr. Glassberg.

"Jack? I'm Dr. Nelson. I am so pleased to meet you. I'll be taking you to my office...where we can visit for a bit...and then I'll be administering a few tests...so we can develop a psychological profile."

In Dr. Nelson's office — which was dimly-lit, and even plainer-looking than Dr. Glassberg's office — Dr. Nelson had me sit in a chair made out of shiny metal tubes and green, leather-like cushions. I faced the desk behind which Dr. Nelson sat.
"Jack. I am sure that you are probably anxious and uncomfortable. But there is nothing to be afraid of. The tests I am going to administer are painless...and there are no wrong answers."

Fritz said: *He's putting you at ease Jack...That's fine...He's right, there is nothing to be afraid of...Just talk to him as if he is your friend...I'll let you know if there is anything that you need to be cautious about.*

Dr. Nelson was very friendly, smiling a lot as he asked me questions about where I lived, my interests, my injuries, Aunt Rita, my family. He let me know when he started the tests, which took about an hour. Most of the tests consisted of simple questions, but one required me to tell him what I thought certain blots meant to me. And another test involved Dr. Nelson saying a word, and I had to tell him whatever came to my mind.

"Well, that's it," Dr. Nelson said pleasantly. "It wasn't so bad, was it?"

I didn't know what to say to him, so I just shrugged my shoulders.

Again I heard Fritz say: *You did just fine, Jack. But I sure don't know what all those ink-blots were supposed to represent. I usually thought it meant something different from what you thought it meant.*

WHEN DR. NELSON brought me back to Dr. Glassberg's office, I found Aunt Rita waiting in the reception room.

"How did it go?" Aunt Rita asked with a concerned look.

"Fine, I guess. What happens now?"

"I think we are supposed to go to lunch...That should please you...since you're always so hungry," she said with a laugh. "Then we come back to see Dr. Glassberg at two-thirty. That's when he wants to visit with you."

WE WERE BACK in Dr. Glassberg's reception room before two-thirty. At three o'clock, Dr. Glassberg invited me to come into his office, alone.

Fritz said to me as I entered the office: *Don't be scared, Jack. Just answer his questions as frankly and fully as you answered Dr. Nelson. If I sense any problem questions, I'll let you know how to answer a problem question.*

Instead of sitting behind his desk, Dr. Glassberg moved towards a group of comfortable looking chairs, motioning me to sit where ever I wanted. I picked out my chair and he sat in the chair directly opposite to mine, looking directly at me. There were some papers on a clip-board in his hand. Smiling at me he asked,

"Jack, do you know why you are here with us today?"

"I guess it's because Aunt Rita is concerned about the bad dreams I was having."

"You are not having bad dreams anymore?"

"No."

"How long has it been since you last had a bad dream?"

"It's been about a month or so."

"Do you have any idea as to why the bad dreams stopped?"

Fritz: *Just tell him no, Jack.*

"No, I don't."

"When did you start having these bad dreams?"

"Some time after the accident; while I was still in the hospital, I think."

"Jack, I understand that you had a serious head injury in the accident...Do you understand that serious head injuries can lead to nightmares...bad dreams?"

"Not really."

"What kind of dreams were you having – these bad dreams, I mean?"

"They are hard to describe."

"Well, do your best, if you can."

"There were people that I have never seen before...in places that I have never been...and there was fire and loud noises... Those kind of dreams."

"Did you ever hear any of the people talking in these bad dreams...Could you understand what they were saying?"

Fritz: *Be careful, Jack.*

"I don't recall ever hearing any one talk to me in the bad dreams."

"When did the bad dreams start? Was it before, or after, the automobile accident?"

"I thought I told you that I'm pretty sure the bad dreams started after the accident."

"Oh, yes. You did say that. Are your brothers...either one of them...in these bad dreams?"

"I don't think so...I can't remember them being in the bad dreams."

"Jack, when you had these bad dreams...Did you ever cry out or scream?"

"I'm not sure, but I may have."

"Do you ever talk in your sleep, Jack...I mean at any time...Not just during the bad dreams, but any time?"

"I don't know."

"Has Aunt Rita ever told you that you were talking in your sleep?"

"No."

"Has any one, other than Aunt Rita...Say someone in the hospital...or one of your parents...joked about you talking in your sleep?"

"No."

"So you have no recollection of talking in your sleep since you have been living with Aunt Rita."

"No sir."

"Jack. Do you speak any foreign languages...like Dutch or German?"

"Oh. No sir."

Fritz: *Jack. Be attentive to his next questions. But just say no.*

"Jack. If your Aunt Rita told me that she thought she heard you speaking German in your sleep...with one of your bad dreams...do you have any idea why that might have happened?"

"No."

"Jack. To speak another language in your dreams, especially when you have never spoken that language, is unusual...Have you ever spoken another language...a language you have never learned or heard before...when you have been awake...maybe while playing one of your games?"

"No."

"Now, your Aunt Rita also tells me that right after the automobile accident the rescue team found you curled up in a ball on the floor of the car, partially lodged up under the front seat...and that this might have saved your life. Do you know how you assumed this ball position? Did either of your brothers direct you to take this position? Did you hear some voice prompting you to take cover in this fashion?"

Fritz: *Jack. Just tell him that you don't know; it all happened so quickly.*

"I don't know...It all happened so quickly...I don't remember anything about the accident."

"When you are awake, Jack...Do you hear voices or do you talk to some person that no one else can see, or hear?"

Once again Fritz says: *Just say, No!!! I'll explain this to you later.*

"No."

"How do you feel about that accident...Do you blame your

brothers?"

"No, I don't blame my brothers for the accident."

"Jack, how do you feel about your brother's dying in the accident?"

"I feel sad."

"How do you feel about the fact that your brothers died, but you survived the accident?"

"I've never really thought about it...I guess I feel that I was lucky...and they weren't."

"Do you blame yourself for your brothers' deaths?"

"Do you mean...Do I blame myself for the accident...that I caused the accident?"

"Well do you?"

"No...I was just along for the ride...It was my birthday."

"Well, who do you blame for the accident?"

"Nobody, really...There was a terrible storm...the street was covered with hail stones...the Buick started sliding...It was tipping over."

"Is that when you got down on the floor?"

"Yes."

"Jack, I understand from your Aunt Rita that you are a Catholic...Is that correct?"

"Yes."

"Do you believe in guardian angels?"

"Yes, I think so."

"Do you think your guardian angel warned you to get down on the floor of the Buick tucked into a ball?"

"Maybe...I really don't remember."

"Okay...Let's talk about your mother...Your Aunt Rita tells me that your mother is a difficult person...Can you describe your relationship with your mother?"

"I'm not sure what you are asking...Do you want me to tell you how I feel about my mother?"

"Yes, in a sense...But what I am really looking for is your description of how you and your mother act towards one another... Does that make sense to you?"

"I think so. I did everything I could to make my mother love me, but no matter how hard I tried, I never felt that she even cared for me...Nothing I did seemed to please her...She never hugged me, or kissed me...like my Dad does...and she never said anything nice to me...And sometimes she whipped me with a belt...I'm scared of my mother."

"How do you feel about your mother?"

"Do you mean...more than feeling scared? Are you asking whether I hate her? No, I don't think so...But I guess maybe I do in a way. I know I am supposed to love her...but it's hard to love her...the way she treats me...I don't think she loves me."

"And how does that make you feel?"

"It makes me feel sad, unhappy, even angry...Why doesn't my mother love me? Am I so bad? Why can't I figure out what I need to do to make her love me? Is it my fault that my mother doesn't love me?"

"Jack, in light of what you have told me, I am not surprised that you would describe how you feel about your mother as being 'hate'. There is nothing wrong with that feeling...We all have feelings of hate...That's not abnormal at all...It is very normal to hate someone who hurts you, either physically or mentally. Do you understand what I am talking about?"

"Oh, yes. Aunt Rita and I have talked about feelings. She told me that feelings are neither good nor bad...It's all about how we deal with these feelings...and bad memories."

"How are you dealing with your feelings about your mother?"

"I am trying to not let them upset me...or make me feel angry...Now that I have Aunt Rita...who I believe does love me...I don't care if my mother doesn't love me. You had asked me earlier how I feel about the accident...I guess it makes me feel happy...Because the accident has made it possible for me to live with Aunt Rita. And I love her so much!"

"Hmm!" uttered Dr. Glassberg, stroking his goatee. "Do you think that maybe your discussions with your Aunt Rita about your feelings towards you mother could explain why the bad dreams stopped?"

"I don't know...I think the bad dreams may have stopped before we started talking about feelings."

"Do you feel the same about your father as you do your mother?"

"No. I love my father, and he loves me."

"But hasn't you father failed to protect you from your mother?"

"Yes, and that makes me feel sad, both for him and for me... but I know how much he cares for me."

"Jack, I don't have any more questions. I don't think that there is anything else we need to talk about. I've enjoyed our conversation. You are a bright boy. You are also very fortunate to have a lady as competent as your Aunt Rita to help guide you through these difficult issues. Hopefully, I can talk to you further...when you are a little older...to see if your strange dreams reoccur. Can you go out now to the waiting area and ask your Aunt Rita to join us, so we can wrap this up?"

BY THE TIME that Aunt Rita and I reentered his office, Dr. Glassberg had reseated himself behind his desk, motioning us to sit in the chairs facing his desk. Looking from one of us to the other, as he polished his eye-glasses in his hands with a cloth, Dr. Glassberg studied our faces. After a few moments, Dr. Glassberg replaced his eye-glasses on the bridge of his nose carefully, methodically tucking the temples behind each ear. Looking first down at the papers on his desk, clearing his throat, Dr. Glassberg looked up at Aunt Rita, then me, and with a slight smile, said:

"Normally, I don't give an oral report of my professional opinions and conclusions following an examination of a patient, especially of a young patient like Jack...But under the circumstances... given the nature of the patient's perceived condition, and the rather unambiguous results of both the clinical tests and the one-on-one interviews...I believe that an oral report is warranted and appropriate.

"It is my professional opinion that you, Jack...are a stable, surprisingly well-adjusted, bright boy, exhibiting no clinically-notable psychological disease, abnormality or phobia. This is not to say that the serious trauma suffered in the automobile accident...

both from a physical as well as a psychical perspective…has not impacted Jack's psyche…I am quite sure that it has caused Jack both short-term and, as time passes, may impose long-term emotional anxieties, especially as he enters pubescence. But I have discerned no pathologically significant conscious or sub-conscious aberrations…certainly none that can't be dealt with in a stable, loving environment.

"I am, however, perplexed by the strange phenomena associated with Jack's miraculous escape from exceptional injury…even death…during the tragic automobile accident, and the amazing content of his bad dreams…including the unconscious vocalization of a foreign language.   Although I am personally puzzled by Jack's baffling escape and bad-dream experiences, I attribute them to the profound, deep trauma he suffered in the automobile accident.

"Finally, Jack, there are your feelings associated with your less-than-stellar relationship with your mother. As you have so appropriately stated…quoting your Aunt Rita, I believe…there are no good or bad feelings…just feelings. What you feel towards your mother is perfectly rational, perfectly acceptable, given her behavior towards you. These are very conscious feelings, and I have detected no subconscious feelings…feelings that you may have repressed into your subconscious, along with memories that may have authored such repressed feelings. The fact that you have such a loving…though weak…father clearly indicates that you perceive and discern the difference between love and rejection. Jack, you are not responsible for your mother's rejection.

"You told me earlier that you felt anger; but you never told me to whom your anger was directed. It is my opinion that you are directing that anger towards yourself, because you blame yourself for your mother's lack of love and affection. Based upon what Aunt Rita has told me about your mother…and what you confirmed in our conversation…your mother's behavior towards you is the result of her own psyche, her own demons. It is not your fault…So you can stop feeling angry at yourself… And if you now start having feelings of anger…or even feelings of hate...towards your mother, you do not need to feel guilty about any such feelings of anger or hate. If you do have any of these feelings towards your mother...or towards yourself, I would hope that you will talk to someone about them...don't repress them."

Rising from his chair, Dr. Glassberg reached out his hand to Aunt Rita saying, "Thank you for bringing me this extraordinary boy and his baffling bad dreams. I am so pleased that we have found nothing pathologically psychopathic. Based upon the possibility that Jack may be hearing voices, I was fearful that we would find that Jack was suffering with a schizophrenic personality. But I am now convinced that Jack is perfectly normal...You should be receiving my written report in a couple of weeks... Please have a safe trip home."

A VERY HAPPY Fritz said: *Well done, Jack! Now all we have to do is convince Aunt Rita that I am a bodiless, but real, person living in your body!*

I responded: *How in the world are we going to convince Aunt Rita of that without her sending me back to Dr. Glassberg? She will think that I have a 'schizoprentic" personality for sure. And what are we going to do about Aunt Rita hearing me...you... speaking German in my sleep?*

Fritz: *It's "schizophrenic" personality, Jack...And just leave Aunt Rita to me! Don't say anything to her right now about anyone speaking German.*

Why not? I want to know why she never told me that she heard me...you...speaking German in my sleep. And then she told Dr. Glassberg about it.

Fritz: *She probably assumed that you were not aware that you spoke German in your sleep...And she did not want to frighten you. But that is not what is important. Right now, what is important is that Aunt Rita needs to believe that this whole psychological episode is behind the both of you. So just don't bring up anything associated with your trip to see Dr. Glassberg. Go back to acting like an eleven year old boy acts.*

CHAPTER 17

BIG CHIEF TABLET SIXTEEN | JACK

The big Ford station wagon gobbled up the miles to Kansas City, to visit with Aunt Rita's in-laws – the Kaufmans. Yet, inside the vehicle, Aunt Rita and I were lost in our own thoughts, silently watching the passing scenery. Following Fritz's suggestion not to bring up anything about the visit to Dr. Glassberg, I struggled to come up with a safe subject to talk about. As if sensing my struggle, Aunt Rita broke the silence by asking,

"Have I told you anything about Jon's parents?"

"I think you told me something about them last summer, but I don't remember what you told me."

"Well, in that case let me tell you what I think you should know about them. I don't want you to feel awkward around them. I've told them quite a bit about you; and they are looking forward to meeting you. Jon's father, Dr. Stanley Kaufman, and Jon's mother, Gabrielle, are wonderful, thoughtful, loving peo-ple...qualities they instilled in all of their children, including Jon. I love them dearly. They are both in their early sixties, though you wouldn't know it by looking at them. Dr. K...as I, and most of his friends, call him...is tall, trim, with curly salt and pepper hair. He plays golf, tennis and handball regularly.

"Gabby...as Jon's mother is called...is an attractive lady, who also plays tennis. She is noted for all of the civic, social and cul-tural organizations to which she belongs. They are both patrons of the arts. Her greatest accomplishment...in addition to being a wonderful wife and mother...is her bridge-playing skill. I don't know which is worse in a bridge game...to have Gabby as your opponent or as your partner...she is that intimidating! But as a friend, she is warm and gracious.

"As you will soon see for yourself, the Dr. K and Gabby live rather comfortably in a beautiful Spanish-style home in an elegant part of Kansas City...known as the Country Club District. They have their own swimming pool, tennis court, and guest house. Jon and I lived in the guest house when we moved to Kansas City for Jon to complete his medical training...I lived there after Jon's death and before buying the farm.

"It goes without saying, but Dr. K has a very successful medical practice. He grew up in Pittsburgh...where his father was a successful surgeon...was educated at Harvard, including Medical school, and trained at Johns-Hopkins Hospital in Baltimore. I'm not sure why Dr. K came to Kansas City to practice medicine. As I may have told you ...when we were talking last summer about how Jon met Uncle Ollie...Dr. K also has a clinic he operates in rural South America, outside of Bogota, Columbia.

"Gabby is a Kansas City native. Her mother died when she was quite young. Her father, Aaron Silberman, owned a hardware store, and never remarried. Gabby was raised by her maternal aunt, who was married to Ed Jacobson. Mr. Jacobson was President Truman's army buddy and business partner in a men's store they ran in downtown Kansas City for a short while after the First World War. The Kaufmans are very close to the President. Gabby met Dr. K in Kansas City at a dance...It was love at first-sight."

IT WAS CLOSE to dinner-time when Aunt Rita brought the Ford station wagon to a stop on the circular drive in front of the Kaufmans' yellow stucco house...which is everything I envisioned it to be based on Aunt Rita's description of it. I knew it was close to dinner-time because I was hungry; more so than usual because I had little appetite at lunch-time. Now that the experience at Menninger's was behind me my appetite was in full revival.

A large black woman in a white dress answered the front door, who upon immediately recognizing Aunt Rita, said, "Oh, Miss Rita, you are a sight for sore eyes."

"Nadine," responded Aunt Rita, "Thank you. And I've missed you...and your wonderful meals."

We were quickly escorted to the rear of the bright, cheerfully decorated house, through French-doors onto a brick-paved area shaded by an enormous yellow and white striped canopy. The sunlight defused by the canopy bathed the area in a soft yellow color. Seated on matching chaise-lounge chairs were Dr. K and Gabby. Gabby was casually dressed in a colorful sundress. Dr. K – wearing an open-collar shirt and light-colored pants – immediately stood and moved towards Aunt Rita. They warmly embraced. Gabby extended her hand to me, giving me a very tender smile as I helped her from her chaise-lounge. Almost in unison, Dr. K and Gabby greeted us, saying,

"Welcome...Welcome to our home!"

"Thank you so much...Everything is still as elegant as I remember it...And neither of you has changed, not even a bit...How do you manage to stay so healthy-looking?" Aunt Rita gushed.

"You should talk," retorted Gabby. "Rita, you, too, look wonderful...maybe having a handsome boy around has restored your spirits. I have not seen you looking this beautiful since...since... Well, you know what I mean."

"Yes," echoed Dr. K. "You do look radiant...even after your long and trying trip to Menninger's...I'll bet you – both of you – could use a cold drink...Forgive my manners."

"And how are you, Jack?" Gabby inquired warmly, continuing to hold my hand.

"I'm fine, thank you...Especially now that the trip to Menninger's is behind me."

"I'll bet," said Dr. K. "You'll need to tell us how it went."

"We can cover all of that during dinner...I'll be you both are famished," said Gabby. "We thought we would take dinner out here if you don't mind...It is such a beautiful evening...Nadine has cooked up some of her famous shrimp gumbo."

"That would be wonderful," said Aunt Rita.

"But before we eat, I'll bet you both would like to freshen up... And perhaps Jack would like a quick dip in the pool. Albert has surely brought in your luggage...Rita, you'll take Sarah's room... and Jack, we're putting you in Jon's bedroom...Nadine will show you the way," said Gabby.

Waiting for us on the glass-topped white wrought iron table there were four placemats; each covered with a large bowl filled with shrimp gumbo. I'd never had shrimp gumbo before; it was spicy and delicious. Most of the conversation during the meal dealt with talk of friends and families. Occasionally I was drawn into the conversation out of politeness; and to let me know they knew something about me, but not really for information — like "How are you enjoying Fairways...I always love that name...it so reminds me of a golf course?" "Are you looking forward to getting back into school?"

After Albert — a thin black man with graying hair and a pencil-thin mustache — had cleared away the dishes from the glass-top table, Gabby, looking at me with sad eyes, said, "Jack, Rita has told us of the terrible accident...and of the loss of your brothers... We are so sorry for your loss...and for your injuries."

"Thank you," I replied softly, nodding my head.

"Rita has been quite worried about you...You know she loves you very much," said Dr. K.

Smiling directly at Aunt Rita, I responded, "Oh, yes. She is being a very loving...a...mother to me."

"That is so sweet," said Gabby, with tears welling up in her eyes.

The talk turned to the visit to the Menninger Clinic, and of how it turned out. I let Aunt Rita tell them about Dr. Glassberg's opinion.

Then Aunt Rita said, "Dr. K, I appreciate all that you did in helping us get the appointment with Dr. Glassberg...he is certainly a fine pediatric psychiatrist."

"Yes, he is the best around."

"I don't think that without your assistance that he would have seen Jack."

"Well, why not? Jack's problems are a perfect case for psychological examination."

"Well, it wasn't that...It was because I am just Jack's aunt... Not his parent or guardian. I spent quite a while convincing him that I am the appropriate person to seek help for Jack. After I explained how Nell sent Jack to me...because she didn't want to care for him...and I showed him a letter Jack's Dad wrote to Jack...and because I believed that it was an emergency...I think he relented. But, I think also that he performed the examination because of our relationship...yours and mine...and because you were involved in initiating the process. At one point he was insisting that Jack's parents be present...and, in lieu of that, that I have a court ordered guardianship for Jack. I had set up the application for the examination in my name, but Dr. Glassberg insisted that I provide him with Paul and Nell's name and address. It became quite stressful for a time."

"That's very unfortunate...Is there anything that I need to do now?"

"I don't think so...I'm praying that he doesn't contact Jack's folks...especially not Nell...since I never told them that I was having Jack examined by a psychiatrist."

"Yes," observed Dr. K. "That could be a problem, if Jack's mother makes it an issue...but why should she? Hasn't she effectively abandoned Jack to your care?"

"Yes, but I sense that there could be legal problems if Nell wants to cause me problems about keeping Jack...and... make no mistake...I fully intend to keep Jack living with me...permanently."

"Rita," interjected Gabby. "If you have Jack living permanently with you, I think you need some help with taking care of Jack and simultaneously running the farm...don't you?"

"I hadn't really noticed that I need any help...Jack is pretty easy to take care of now. At first, there were problems when his leg was still in a cast and he was wearing the neck-brace. But now that he can do things for himself, I think I can handle it on my own...But thank you for inquiring."

"I didn't intend to inquire just to be polite...I think you know me better than that...Frankly, I have a favor to ask of you...and it also involves getting you some help."

"I'll do you whatever favor you might ask...But I don't understand how 'getting me some help' could possibly be considered doing you a favor."

"I think you will when I tell what I am asking you to do to get that help. As you know I am involved in a number of Jewish Relief organizations. Right now I am working with the National Council of Jewish Women to resettle postwar refugees here in America. There are thousands of Jewish women, survivors of the Holocaust in Europe, who are coming to the States to make a new life for themselves and their families. Some of these women refugees have no families...either in Europe or here...and are looking for a home.

"We are currently resettling thousands of single young women throughout the country, trying to find them families and homes which are compatible with their backgrounds. Normally, we are looking for Jewish families to take in these refugees on a temporary basis...until the woman finds a permanent situation through marriage or career. Unfortunately, there are some young women who have issues or problems that make their placement problematic.

"Do you think that you might be interested in someone like that," asked Gabby. "You know...despite what you have said...I think you really could use the help."

"You certainly know how to pique someone's interest! If I didn't know you so well...and trust you so much, I'd swear I was being set up to buy the Brooklyn Bridge," Aunt Rita said laughingly.

Then I heard Fritz say: *Jack. If you are asked, you need to encourage Aunt Rita not to bring someone new to the farm...Having another woman...a complete stranger...at the farm could be a stumbling block to our ability to have Aunt Rita learn about my presence...without thinking that you are having psychological problems.*

"But, what do you think, Jack," Aunt Rita inquired. "Will the presence of another woman...a stranger...in our lives be a threat... or a problem...for you?"

"I'm not sure that it would work out," I responded. "With Aunt

Rita and me...I mean...I know that what I am saying may sound selfish, but I am still healing. I'm not sure how having a stranger around will help me...or Aunt Rita."

"Thank you, Jack, for being so candid," stated Aunt Rita. "Really, Gabby, I need to talk to Jack more about how the presence of another woman...especially a woman who might have serious needs...in the house will impact my ability to give Jack the kind of attention that I have come to believe he truly needs. I might even want to talk to Dr. Glassberg about this...not just for Jack's sake, but for mine as well. Do I have the background and stamina for helping two people at the same time?"

"That is a very real concern, I am sure," interjected Dr. K who, until this point, had stayed out of the discussion. "But, I think you may be viewing having a woman with maybe some needs in the wrong light. Despite their problems, we can be sure that whoever is placed with you is not an invalid. She may be even less a burden to you than Jack maybe has been...The whole point is that such a woman could be a real help to you...you'll see the difference she will make in your life. Gabby and I are not trying to palm off a problem on you."

"I understand what you are saying...I appreciate what you are trying to do for me...and for Jack. You both have done so much for me...and I would like nothing more than to be able to return the favor...But I really do need to think about it. Right now I need to focus all of my energies on getting Jack healed...physically and psychologically. Can you give me a week or two to get back to you about your offer?"

"Of, course," Gabby responded. "Take whatever time you need...We understand how you feel about Jack...And you know that we feel the same about him, too."

"Rita, let me apologize for putting you in this awkward position," interjected Dr. K. "We certainly didn't mean to drop this on you in this fashion...Especially, with all you have just gone through with the visit to Menninger...and with Dr. Glassberg. And you may be correct...the timing is just not right."

IT HAD BEEN several weeks since our return to Fairways; and Aunt Rita still had not made a decision about agreeing to bring a displaced Jewish woman into our home. There had been several letters from Gabby pleading for an answer; one enclosing a poor-quality, black and white photo of an ordinary-looking woman – with vacant eyes – valiantly trying to smile.

There had been no letter from Dr. Glassberg. Aunt Rita and I had concluded that Dr. Glassberg would also send a copy of his report to my parents. Every time I retrieved the mail, and there was an absence of a letter from the Menninger Clinic, I breathed a sigh of relief.

At least, until we get our copy of the report, Mom hasn't received hers.

Our evening visits in the front-porch rockers were getting shorter as the sunsets came earlier, depriving us of the warmth of the southward shifting sun-light. It had become sweater weather. The cattle, the birds, and even the night-time insects were terminating their evening symphonies more quickly. In no time at all, Aunt Rita insisted that we abandon these outdoor soirees, moving our evening discussions inside.

Our evenings on the front-porch are just another reason why I did not want a strange, needy woman to live with us. I am afraid that her presence will inhibit having Aunt Rita all to myself, especially for our evening talks. I am not so sure that I even want to share Aunt Rita with Fritz when that day arrives.

"I begin school next week at St. Benedict's," I reminded Aunt Rita. "It shouldn't be much different from St. Agatha's...the Parish school back at home."

"How do you feel about repeating sixth grade?" Aunt Rita inquired.

The thought of repeating sixth grade at a new school was an exciting one; I'll finally be the same age as the other kids, and I will have learned at least some of the subjects I expect to be covered in the new sixth grade. Also, I hoped to have help from Aunt Rita – and Fritz – with my homework; something I never had from my parents.

"I am actually looking forward to getting back into school... Though I'll miss the times we have had together each day."

"You remember the conversation with the Kaufmans...about bringing a displaced woman to live with us?" Aunt Rita asked, changing the subject.

"Yes, I do...Have you heard anything further about that?" I asked.

"Not since we received the letter with the unflattering photo of some candidate...But I have been thinking more about what Gabby has proposed...and of maybe how it could work if some-one were to come live with us...Especially now that you will be in school most of the day...which would give me the time to get to know the woman during the day while you're in school...without cutting into our time together."

"But...Won't she be living with us full-time?" I asked.

"Why would that matter?" she asked.

"I guess...I thought...I would have you all to myself after I get home from school...and on the weekends...but then a strange woman would be here too," I responded.

"Yes, that's right...But I am sure we can work something out so we will have some time together...Besides...in the next couple of years...I'm hoping that you won't need me the way you do now...In fact, you'll probably find my constant attention to be an-noying and embarrassing...It won't be too long before you'll be a teenager, looking for your privacy," Aunt Rita scoffed good-naturedly.

LATER THAT EVENING, as I was lying in bed, thinking of how blessed I was to have Aunt Rita, Fritz interrupted my thoughts with this conversation: *Jack, sorry to interrupt your pleasant thoughts about Aunt Rita, but we need to address a growing concern of mine...I am beginning to get the sense that Aunt Rita is weakening in her resolve not to bring a total stranger into our tight-knit little family. Your conversa-tion this evening demonstrates that she is now advancing reasons for... rather than against...bringing in a helper. You know what that will do to your growing relationship with Aunt Rita...not to mention the uncertainty the strange woman's presence will cast over our ability to bring Aunt Rita into my...our plans to get me back to Germany...and out of your life.*

But, Fritz, what can I do...what can I say...that I haven't already said...to persuade Aunt Rita not to bring someone new here? I am as much against that happening as you are.

In the short-term, Jack, you need to keep saying what you have been saying; you need to keep Aunt Rita focused on your current need for her undivided love and attention. She has great concern over how your health is progressing, and of how essential her restorative attention is to combat the effects of your mother's lack of love. But what do we do if Aunt Rita concludes that she can handle both you and a stranger, or that you are sufficiently on the mend that you don't need her attention quite so much anymore. Based upon what I heard this evening...regardless of which of her conclusions wins out...I believe that a stranger in our midst is inevitable.

So, what do we do then?

Jack, we can't wait until the interloper is here...We need to act now!

By doing what?

By telling Aunt Rita about me before the stranger arrives on our doorstep...Or at least begin the process of figuring out how to tell her about me...I estimate that we only have about six-months to tell Aunt Rita about me...and to get her comfortable with my presence. Fortunately, I think it will take that long before someone could get here even if Aunt Rita were to give Gabby her consent immediately.

Fritz...I just don't know if I am ready to tell Aunt Rita about you...It's just too soon after our trip to Menninger...And we haven't even received Dr. Glassberg's report yet. I can't even begin to think of what I can say to Aunt Rita that will be convincing...and without scaring her.

Don't worry, Jack...I'll be here to help you...We'll probably tell her together...Just as soon as it is practicable...after Dr. Glassberg's report arrives.

I think that that may still be too soon.

CHAPTER 18

BIG CHIEF TABLET SEVENTEEN | JACK

On our way home from my third day of school at St. Benedict's, Aunt Rita stopped the Ford station wagon at the foot of the driveway for me to retrieve the mail. Among the pile of stuff that I removed from the mailbox was the much-anticipated envelope: "Menninger Clinic" said the return address. Oh, crap! How soon do I have to tell Aunt Rita about Fritz? How soon will we hear from my mother?

"If you want to read Dr. Glassberg's report, I left it on the desk in the den," Aunt Rita advised me after dinner. "It's full of hard-to-understand psychological jargon...so it's not light reading...and bottom-line, the report is pretty-much verbatim what he told us in Topeka...Dr. Glassberg's cover letter indicates that a copy of his report was sent to your Mom and Dad."

"What do you think she will do about it?" I asked solemnly in response to the stomach-churning news. "Do you think she will contact Dr. Glassberg?"

"We can only hope that she does contact him...and for that very reason she probably won't...His report is too damning of her parenting. No, I think she will contact me...and probably by letter...She's too cheap to call me long-distance. I expect that we will receive her letter soon enough,"

Fritz, this is not a good time to tell Aunt Rita about you; she is much too anxious about how my mother might react to Dr. Glassberg's report. For that matter, so am I.

I wouldn't be too anxious about what your mother might do, replied Fritz. I have absolute faith in Aunt Rita's abilities to fend off whatever your mother has in mind. Aunt Rita is a very brave, capable woman. But, I do agree that we should wait to see what she does have in mind before moving ahead with our plans for you to disclose my presence to Aunt Rita.

FOR THE NEXT several days, I was filled with concern, worry and uncertainty. Even my school-days suffered from distracting, disturbing thoughts, resulting in a lack of concentration, participation, performance.

"Are you not well today, Jack?" Sister Saint Helena inquired solicitously in the hallway, after class — knowing of my accident and injuries.

"I'm fine, Sister," I responded.

"Well," she continued; clearly unconvinced, "Then, why do you appear to be so distracted? Is the work we are doing too hard...too easy?"

"Oh, no, Sister," I proclaimed. "I am enjoying school so very much...It's just that...a...I'm worried about a...a...family matter; about my mother."

"Is she ill?"

"Not really...I just can't talk about it right now."

"Well, is there something I...we...can do to help her...or you?"

"Yes, Sister...Can you pray for us?"

"Of course, I can, Jack...I'll be sure to pray for you...and for your mother...I'm sure the Lord knows what is best...Just put your trust in Him...He'll have the answer...You'll see."

Oh, I hope so!

EVERY TRIP I made to the mailbox was filled with fear. My stomach was tied in knots as I opened the lid to remove the mail — as if, lurking in the shadowy recesses, a rattlesnake is coiled to strike my hand...just like the unsuspecting victim in a scary movie. On the Saturday that the letter from my mother arrived, I put it — along with the other mail — under my poncho to protect it from the pouring rain while I trudged my way back up the middle of the driveway, avoiding the rivulets of water running down the tire tracks. Removing my wet poncho on the back porch, I carried the mail into the dark kitchen, calling out to Aunt Rita,

"It's here...my mother's letter is here...Where are you?"

"I'm coming," I heard Aunt Rita say from the doorway to the den.

I lifted the letter from the stack of mail now sitting on the kitchen table, handing it to Aunt Rita as if it was laced with poison. Taking the letter from my outstretched hand in the same manner as I had offered it to her, Aunt Rita gave me a look mixed one-part dread, one-part relief.

"Maybe I'd better read it first...alone," she said warily, walking back into the den.

Sitting on the staircase just outside the den, I spent the next twenty-minutes, or so, anxiously pondering my fate; experiencing a roller-coaster ride of emotions. I was hurled one-way and then another-way, listening to Aunt Rita commenting to herself on my mother's letter. After a long period of silence, Aunt Rita opened the door, giving me a scornful look.

"The bitch! The fucking bitch! I hate her...I hate her...I hate her!" she exclaimed, shoving a jumble of several handwritten pages at me, adding "Who the fuck does she think she is? No one talks to me like that, especially not her!"

My shock was beyond belief. *I'd never heard anyone speak like this before! What anger! What language! My Aunt Rita was really pissed! Look out Mom! I can't wait to read your letter... Although...whatever you have said in the letter may frighten and scare me.*

Trying to reassemble the handwritten pages into their original order, I carefully approached Aunt Rita with the intention of trying to calm her down by holding her in my arms; but she pushed me away, saying, "I can't right now...Please understand... It's not you...I love you...I just need to get out of here for a bit...I need to take a walk...Just read the letter...But don't let her scare you!"

I watched Aunt Rita grab my wet poncho as she exited the

backdoor. I hope she's okay! Fearfully, I made my way into the den, plopped down in my chair, and placed the reassembled letter in my lap. I picked up the first page to read the attached letter:

Rita,

This letter should come as no surprise; unlike the letter and report I received from that Jew doctor at that crazy place in Kansas. It's bad enough that you married a Jew doctor — who by the grace of God is no longer with us — but to now subject my only living son to those godless Jew shrinks, is reprehensible and inexcusable. What is also inexcusable is that you took Jack to a bunch of doctors dabbling in questionable medical practices without either telling me or asking me for permission. I pray that our poor mother — bless her soul — stuck in that awful nursing home; when she should be enjoying her last days in that house of yours, purchased with the Jew's money — should never learn of what you have done. It would simply kill her.

Letting my poor, injured Jack come live with you was a mistake. I should have known that you would turn him against me, teaching him to love you instead. You could never have a child of your own, so you have plotted and planned to snatch one of mine away from me. God has cursed your womb for marrying that Jew. And God has seen to it that you can't have my other two boys. He should have taken Jack, too.

You have always hated me. What did I do to have you hate me so much that you have taken Jack away from me? I was in no position to give up my job to take care of Jack, with all of his serious injuries. I was looking to you to help me in my hour of need and suffering, but you have stabbed me in the back instead. Even when we were young you turned Father against me. When he left us, then you did everything in your power to make Doddy love you more than me. And how many times did you try to lure my Paul into your clutches; with all of your sweet-talk and pretty smiles. But what you are now doing with Jack is the last straw.

I want you — no, I demand you — to return Jack to me, immediately. You have no right to have Jack in your home — where God-knows what is going on with you and your Jewish family and friends. I gave you only temporary custody of Jack. You are not — nor will you ever be — his guardian. I'll see to it that that never happens. In fact, if you do not bring Jack back to me in ten days, I will go to the police, and have them arrest you for kidnapping. I'll see to it that you are thrown in prison, where you will rot away until you die. And then you can go rot in Hell!

Nell

By the time I had finished reading "Nell's" letter, I was close to tears. But instead of crying, I reached out to Fritz, which resulted in the following conversation:

Oh, Fritz, what am I going to do...Mom...No, that bitch Nell wants to tear me away from Aunt Rita, denying me the only happiness I have ever known? This can't happen...We can't let it happen! Even a fool can see that she doesn't love me...She wanted me dead, for Christ's-sake! She is insisting to bring me back home just so she can punish Aunt Rita, and to make my life more miserable than before. As much as I want to love Nell...I just can't do it...From this moment on I no longer consider her to be my mother...she is simply Nell...the "Bitch" Nell!

Jack! Jack! You have every right to feel anger and frustration. Nell's letter is an abomination. But right now we must think coolly and clearly, as if we have been attacked by enemy aircraft diving down on us out of the sun! Panic in these circumstances would prove to be our worst enemy. We must think calmly, using all of the resources we have at our disposal, including the enemy's own strengths and weaknesses. Nell may think she has the advantage in this engagement because she believes she comes to the fray clothed with the sanctity of "Motherhood." But in her case, what she fails to grasp, is that "Motherhood" is her vulnerability, her fatal weakness. We need only to expose her lack of any genuine "mother-love" to win the day. We need only use her abusive, hate-filled letter against her; bolstered with Dr. Glassberg's report. As additional support, it may be time for your father to show his love; taking a stand on your behalf.

But what does Aunt Rita need to do to 'win the day' as you call it?

Aunt Rita is quite distraught right now, and may not be thinking clearly. The first thing you need to do is to try to settle her down; get her to relax. My thought right now is for you to show concern, getting Aunt Rita to talk about all the ugly stuff that Nell has included in the letter. Aunt Rita needs to voice her anger, but she also needs to explain the truth to you. Once Aunt Rita gets her anger towards Nell under control and out of the way, we can begin to deal with Nell's threats: the threat to take you back; and the threat to punish Aunt Rita...I just love the "rot in prison...rot in Hell" hyperbole.

IT WAS STILL raining, and turning dark, when Aunt Rita returned from her walk. I heard her stomp her feet on the back porch, shaking the water from the black poncho before hanging it on the coat-hook by the back door. By the time I reached the kitchen, Aunt Rita was standing at the sink — with her back to me, drying her face and hands with the kitchen towel. After she hung up the towel, she still just stood there with her back to me, her arms stiff, her hands tightly clutching the edge of the sink, her head hanging down. Hearing my approach, she said softly, firmly, "Don't...Please don't...It's hard enough as it is."

"What do you mean...I don't understand?"

"What I have to tell you...I've given it a great deal of thought, Jack. I don't want you here anymore...It's simply too hard...It simply won't work...I'm sending you back to your mother."

"You can't mean that...You can't do that!" I shouted, beginning to tremble.

"I can...And I will!" she said harshly, with her back still facing me.

"But I need you...I love you...What will I do without you?"

To which Fritz said: *Remember what I just told you, Jack...Don't panic...Don't cause Aunt Rita to panic! You've said the right things. Now give her the time to think about it...Leave her alone...Let her come back to you...when she is ready.*

Turning around at last, facing me, tears streaming down her face, Aunt Rita — her voice choking with concern — sobbed, "And, Jack, I love you, too...Please, please understand!"

Aunt Rita walked past me, out of the kitchen, up the staircase, into her bedroom, closing the door. I remained standing in the kitchen, crying.

THE FOLLOWING DAYS were the hardest days of my life. Except when necessary, Aunt Rita and I avoided talking to each other, avoided looking at each other, and avoided even being in the same place together. Lady — being the faithful dog she is — had chosen sides; sensing the turmoil, she remained close to Aunt Rita, providing her needed solace. There were times — late at night — when I would hear Aunt Rita moving about in the house as if searching for a solution; as if one would magically appear in the kitchen pantry. We were becoming like strangers; is *this her way of preparing me for a permanent separation?* Whatever it was to be, it was taking a toll on me; I couldn't sleep, I couldn't eat, and I certainly couldn't keep up with my schoolwork. I was sleepy; I was hungry; and I was sure that Sister Saint Helena was now spending more hours on her knees praying for my mother — when she should have been praying for Aunt Rita...and me.

Fritz and I had the following conversation: *Fritz, are you sure that your strategy is working? I'm beginning to think that Aunt Rita really is planning to send me home...back to Mom. Isn't there something we need to do...now?*

You must have faith, young Jack.

Have faith in whom?

Have faith in me. I believe that there may be something that you can do to help bring your mother to her senses.

What can I do?

You can write your father that letter we talked about; asking him to tell your mother that she is wrong about Aunt Rita, and that she is foolish to demand your return.

I don't know what to say; can you help me write the letter? Do you want me to show it to Aunt Rita?

Of course I'll help you write the letter, but I don't think it would be wise to let Aunt Rita see it — she'll learn about it in due time.

This is the letter which Fritz and I wrote to Dad:

DEAR DAD,

THANK YOU FOR WRITING ME. I MISS YOU VERY MUCH! AUNT RITA IS SO WONDERFUL, AND I AM SO HAPPY BEING HERE WITH HER. SHE TAKES SUCH GOOD CARE OF ME. I AM GETTING TALLER AND STRONGER, AND I AM BACK IN SCHOOL.

I HOPE YOU CAN COME AND SEE HOW WELL I AM DOING. MY LEG IS BETTER, AND MY HEADACHES AND BAD DREAMS ARE GONE. AUNT RITA TOOK ME TO SEE SOME DOCTORS AT A CLINIC IN KANSAS TO CHECK ME OUT FOR THE BAD DREAMS AND HEADACHES. I TOLD THEM ABOUT THE ACCIDENT AND HOW I FEEL ABOUT CHRIS AND DAVID. I ALSO TOLD THEM ABOUT HOW MOTHER TREATS ME AND HOW I FEEL ABOUT HER. WELL, YOU KNOW HOW MOM TREATS ME SO YOU KNOW THAT I TOLD THE DOCTORS THAT I DON'T THINK MOM LOVES ME, BUT THAT AUNT RITA DOES.

IN CASE MOTHER NEVER TOLD YOU, THE DOCTORS SENT A COPY OF THEIR REPORT TO YOU AND MOM. THERE MUST HAVE BEEN THINGS IN THAT REPORT THAT HAVE UPSET MOM, BE-CAUSE SHE HAS SENT AN AWFUL LETTER TO AUNT RITA, TELL-ING AUNT RITA TO SEND ME BACK HOME, AND THAT SHE IS GOING TO HAVE AUNT RITA PUT IN PRISON. I THINK THAT MOM'S LETTER HAS SCARED AUNT RITA, AND I AM AFRAID THAT SHE IS GOING TO SEND ME BACK. I HAVE READ MOM'S LETTER AND IT SCARES ME REAL BAD, TOO.

I JUST CAN'T GO BACK TO LIVING WITH MOM. I WOULD LOVE TO BE WITH YOU, BECAUSE I KNOW HOW MUCH YOU LOVE ME AND CARE FOR ME. I THINK YOU KNOW HOW MOM WOULD TREAT ME IF I HAVE TO GO BACK HOME, ESPECIALLY SINCE SHE WISHES I WAS DEAD. I'VE NEVER BEEN HAPPIER IN MY WHOLE LIFE LIVING HERE WITH AUNT RITA. I DON'T THINK I CAN LIVE WITHOUT HER. SHE LOVES ME SO.

I NEED YOUR HELP DAD. PLEASE TALK TO MOM AND TELL HER JUST HOW IMPORTANT IT IS FOR ME TO STAY HERE WITH AUNT RITA, WHERE I AM LOVED AND TAKEN CARE OF. JUST LIKE WHAT YOU WOULD LIKE TO DO FOR ME; IF IT WAS JUST YOU AND ME. MOM'S LETTER SAYS TERRIBLE, HORRIBLE THINGS. I AM WORRIED ABOUT MOM AND WHAT SHE MIGHT

DO. PLEASE TRY TO STOP HER!
LOVE, JACK

I posted the letter – addressed to Dad's office – from the Principal's office at St. Benedict's.

Do you think the letter will work, Fritz?

Jack, we can only hope that your Dad will see how important living with Aunt Rita is to your future. If he does, I believe that he will do the right thing. His love for you will overcome his fear of your mother; finally acting like a father...putting your mother in her place.

FOR THE NEXT several weeks, the tension at Fairways continued to grow. The weather was turning cooler, the leaves were turning colors; there was change in the air. I sensed a change in my life as well: I was frightened as to what direction it would take.

THEN IT HAPPENED. Picking me up from St. Benedict's, Aunt Rita, instead of sitting in the Ford – as she usually did – surprised me by standing next to the Ford wagon, with a smile that was as bright as the sun. Before I could even get to the car, she ran up to me, throwing her arms around me – like a happy school-girl, shouting jubilantly, "Oh, Jack! I have such wonderful news! You are going to be living with me...forever. Your mother has even agreed that I can adopt you."

Thank God! Thank you, God! Sister Saint Helena's prayers have worked a miracle!

"How can that be?" I asked. "After all that my mother said about you in that horrible letter...what happened? What changed?"

"Jack, don't worry about that now...Let's just be happy...I'm so excited...Aren't you?"

"But of course! It's wonderful...I just didn't expect it."

Fritz! The letter to Dad must have worked! I can't believe it. It is a miracle!

Jack, I am sure that your letter to your Dad played a role in your mother's change of heart...But I would like to know more from Aunt Rita...

I think she has played a more active role than she was telling you. But don't push things...Give her time to tell you what she knows...what she did...about her response to your mother's threats.

"Do you have much homework tonight, Jack," asked Aunt Rita. "I sure hope not, because I want us to go to dinner at the Country Club...We need to celebrate this awesome...victory...this achievement...God's loving blessing! I am so happy!" Aunt Rita exclaimed.

I don't know what I should be more happy about: Getting to be Aunt Rita's son; or seeing my mother fail with her threats; or knowing that Dad stood up to Mom on my behalf? Why can't I just be happy? Why can't I just be happy for Aunt Rita? Isn't this what we both have wanted for so long? What's wrong: Why do I feel like I have lost something...lost something very special... something very special in my life? It's as if I have walked out of a room — a room filled with all different kinds of memories, experiences, feelings — slamming the door closed behind me; locking it... knowing that I am never again going back into that room...ever. I miss my Dad, so much! When will I ever see him again?

CHAPTER 19

JUST AS I EXPECTED, NELL EXPRESSED TO HERSELF
in exasperation, as she tossed the just-read tablet on the growing pile of tablets at the side of her chair. *The three of them have ganged up on me; but it's that damn Rita who is at the bottom of it, as usual. She's been after me ever since we were young girls: just because I was prettier, smarter, our father's pet.*

Nell's mind drifted back to a time shortly after the Indian Territory had become a state, to life on the cattle ranch; the seventeen hundred acre spread in southwestern Oklahoma, where they all lived together as a family – the five of them: Edmund Douglas – their father, Doddy, Rita, Nell, and Trafton – their older half-brother, (Ollie was still to come). The ranch was so large, so isolated from Apache – the nearest community – that it warranted its own spur on the 'Katy' line (MKT - the Missouri-Kansas-Texas Railroad); serving as their lifeline to civilization – providing them with everything they needed for their everyday existence at the ranch. There were frequent sightings of native-Indians – poor, bedraggled creatures who would appear at the cookhouse door, begging for a handout, for scraps of food. Life in rural Oklahoma was still so primitive that Doddy was required to travel by train back to her family home in northeast Missouri for the delivery of Nell, then Rita, as she would later make the trip – her last trip home – to deliver Ollie.

Edmund Douglas was not a rancher either by training or by ability; he was a Chicago businessman who had thrown away a successful career in the tea-importing business to gamble on a risky cattle raising venture. It was not until years later – after everything had been lost – that Nell learned that her father was a luckless gambler, along with his many other faults. Edmund was not particularly tall or robust. He had a kind, pleasant face, remarkable blue eyes, fine, thinning blond hair, and a prominent handle-bar mustache, so common to the era, which he waxed and curled at the ends. To the other ranchers, and to their ranch-hands – he was considered to be a dandy.

To Nell – at least while they were all living together on the ranch – her father was the kindest, the sweetest, the most handsome man in the world; and she loved him dearly. Even though Doddy was the ever-loving mother, her father's displays of love, his affection, were more demonstrative, becoming Nell's very life-blood; and she would do everything she could to keep it flowing towards her. Nell suffered bouts of anxiety that her father's love and affection would be withdrawn from her; to be bestowed on another. So acute was her fear that she had fits of jealousy towards her siblings at the slightest sign of her father's attention directed at them; with her younger sister Rita being the principal target.

It was only later – after Trafton had left the ranch to live with his mother's family in Montana – that Nell realized that Rita had not been her rival for their father's love after all, but by then it was too late; life's course between the two had already been plotted – they would always be adversaries. It was also too late for Nell to garner her father's total attention; for by then her father was a broken man, distant, incapable of loving anyone.

Until Trafton was gone, Nell knew little about him: She did not even know that he was her half-brother – her father's son born of his first wife; a six-year old boy who came to live with her parents when they married. Nell was four-years old when Trafton left, and, as far as she knew, he was just another kid around the ranch – although a particularly favorite kid. She had no reason to know, to even suspect, that Trafton – not her, or not Rita – was the apple of her father's eye.

Nell was sixteen-years old when she learned the horrible truth: Not only that her father loved someone more than her, but that her 'good' Catholic mother had been married to a divorced man – a marriage not recognized by the Church; making Nell a 'bastard' in her mind. What news could be more devastating to a Catholic convent-raised teenager suffering from an acute case of nun-induced religious scruples? The fact that Nell had learned the truth from Rita – who had been told by Doddy while Nell was away visiting cousins – simply drove a deeper wedge between Nell and Rita; and caused a serious rift in her relationship with Doddy

The catalyst for these relationship-altering disclosures was a letter that Doddy received from Trafton, informing her of her husband's death; a death brought about by drink and depression. Nell had been aware of some changes in her father's behavior when he returned home alone from his trip to Montana, without Trafton – like his long absences from the ranch, his dissolute appearance, his inattention, his loss of the ranch. It was not, however, until Rita revealed to Nell the contents of Trafton's letter and the subsequent conversations with Doddy, that she comprehended the cause, and the extent of the changes in her father's mental state.

"What made you do it…Why did you marry Father…a divorced man," Nell demanded of Doddy, at the first opportunity to confront her mother. The confrontation took place at the kitchen table of the small two-story house on a tree-lined street in Waymore – a tiny town in northeast Missouri where Doddy had grown up, and now had resettled to restart her life with her children, now including Oliver, but without her father who had abandoned Doddy and his family.

"I don't believe that I have any obligation to explain my decisions…my actions to you."

"Oh, but you do," retorted the un-mollified, undeterred Nell, "Especially when your actions place my legitimacy at stake."

"What are you talking about? Your legitimacy has never been at stake. I was married to your father when you were born."

"But not in the eyes of the Church…which makes me a bastard."

"I think those nuns have been telling you things that they ought not to have…and without full information. Besides, how do you know…how do they know…that your father's first marriage was not annulled?"

"Was it," Nell asked, hopefully.

"No…but that's beside the point; the nun's have no right to infect your mind with such nonsense. In the eyes of the law, you are not a bastard. Whatever issues my marriage to a divorced man might have created, those are matters between me and my God."

"But if I'm not a bastard, why did Father love Trafton more than he loved me?"

"What in the world gave you that impression?"

"Well, if Father loved me as much as he loved Trafton, then why did he stop loving me when Trafton went away?"

"Your father never stopped loving you...he just lost the ability to show how much he loved you...or any of us. That sometimes happens to a parent who suffers the loss of a child."

"But Trafton is not dead."

"As far as your father was concerned, Trafton was forever lost...Trafton might as well have been dead. It killed something in your father...Which is the risk a parent takes in loving a child as much as your father loved Trafton...as much as he loved you...as much as he loved each of his children."

"What happened...How did Father lose Trafton?"

"Before I tell you that...let me just tell you that what happened to your father when he lost Trafton would have happened to him if he had lost you...or Rita, or Ollie. So don't take it too personally as to how he reacted to you after Trafton was taken from him: Don't be too angry with him... don't hate his memory."

"I'll try."

"Maybe what I am going tell you about what happened will be helpful."

"What can you possibly tell me that will change the fact that you married a divorced man...a divorced man who already had a family...with a son who you took into your home...treating him as your own child?"

"Stop it, Nell...You are acting like a petulant child...You are making it difficult for me to treat you like a young lady. You have made your point... But this childish behavior is unacceptable. You can't change the facts just because they do not fit your distorted sense of morality. If what I did was wrong, then I will have to answer to God for it...but I don't have to answer to you. If you insist on being obstinate...if you refuse to hear what I have to say...to accept the truth...then I have nothing more to say to you."

Stunned by her mother's outburst, her scolding, Nell began to cry. Nell was accustomed to being chastised by the nuns for bullying her classmates and being ill-tempered, but never by her mother. The tears, however, failed to move her mother as they often did the nuns who were usually all bark and no bite. "Don't give me your tears...they won't do you any good...You need to give me your apology if you want me to go on."

After some hesitation, while contemplating her dilemma – 'do I show remorse or continued defiance?'– Nell mumbled, but without much sincerity, "I'm sorry."

"I'm not sure that you really mean it, but I'll accept it for the time being…But if I hear any further criticism from you I'll treat you like the child you are acting like and send you to your room…Do you understand me?"

"Yes, Mother."

"Good. Now where was I? Oh, yes, I was about to tell you how your father came to lose Trafton. Now, you have to understand to begin with that I have to talk about certain things that may upset you…like your father's first wife, about how much your father loved Trafton, how much I loved your father, and how much I love Trafton. These are the facts…your bitterness notwithstanding. So I will expect no outburst, no criticism, from you. Do I have your complete agreement…understanding?"

"Yes."

"Trafton's mother, Olivia," began Doddy – warily eyeing Nell, "was from a very wealthy family, the McGonagles – an Irish immigrant Montana mining family. She met your father in Boston while she was attending a girls' school where her family had sent her to smooth over her rough western edges…to make her into a lady. Olivia was pretty, headstrong and passionate…given to making quick decisions based upon her feelings…her heart…not on reason…not on careful reflection.

"As things often happen, Olivia met your father at a reception in Boston – where girls like Olivia were expected to meet eligible young bachelors like Edmund Douglas, the handsome, well-educated, successful son of a prominent, old Virginia family. Just like me a decade later, Olivia was swept off her feet by this charming, urbane young man. Your father had that effect on both women and men; so much so, that he had risen quickly in the tea business firm owned by a British peer, Sir William Upton, who made Edmund Douglas his principal representative in North America.

"Your father was attracted to Olivia because she was outspoken, determined, pretty, and…above all…rich, very rich. While Edmund was successful at business, it was another man's business, and it would not make him wealthy. Edmund wanted to be his own boss, to be independent – an independence that only wealth can provide. Even though your father was just the kind of man Olivia's parents had sent her east to find...a man with a fine pedigree...they were not prepared to lose their daughter so quickly.

"In just a few months after they had met, Olivia dragged Edmund back home to Helena, Montana to meet her parents. Mrs. McGonagle was immediately charmed by Edmund, but Olivia's father – Roscoe, a hard-bitten, self-made mining-man – initially thought that Edmund Douglas was too much of a dandy, someone who had not worked a hard day in his life. But Edmund could ride a horse with the best of them, could shoot a rifle with uncanny accuracy, and could drink copious amounts of alcohol. These qualities, in addition to Olivia's insistence that Edmund should be her husband, won over Olivia's father...And, of equal importance, won the approval of her three older brothers who were as rough as their father, and doted on their baby sister. The nuptials were performed before a part-time judge as quickly as propriety would permit.

"Time would prove that Edmund and Olivia's marriage was not one made in heaven. Within months of the new couple's arrival in Chicago – where Edmund had been assigned by Sir William in connection with the Columbian Exposition – fractures began to appear in the marriage. Despite all of the festivities, celebrations, activities, and parties to which the attractive young couple attended, Olivia soon became bored with the City, with the Exposition, with her responsibilities of being a wife, a hostess, a lady. She felt more comfortable in the company of the men than she did with the women with whom she and Edmund interacted.

"Even when Olivia discovered she was going to have a child, her attitude towards her marriage, her husband, her life in Chicago did not change. She yearned for her freedom, to return to the life she loved in the Rockies, in the mining towns, being with her rough-neck brothers. After Trafton was born, Edmund hoped that their marriage would now improve with a happy, healthy son to fill Olivia's days. But it was not to be. Instead of taking charge of Trafton's infancy, Olivia abandoned the infant boy to nannies, and to Edmund. Edmund absolutely doted on Trafton, attempting to replace the love his mother refused to bestow on their beautiful son.

"Trafton was barely two-years old when Olivia packed up and moved back home to Montana, leaving Trafton and his father alone in Chicago.

Olivia sued for divorce in Montana as soon as legally possible. In order to gain your father's agreement to the divorce, Olivia agreed to pay your father a large sum of money – enough money for Edmund to have the independence he so pined for – and to give your father sole custody of Trafton… with the stipulation that when Trafton turned ten-years old he would come to live with his mother in Montana for a year. Needless to say, your father agreed to these terms, and the divorce was granted.

"Some three years after his divorce, your father met me in Chicago through mutual friends. As I indicated earlier, Edmund Douglas swept me off of my feet, and we were married. I, of course, knew of his previous union with Olivia and of the existence of Trafton – who was being cared for by a spinster aunt of Edmund's in Evanston, Illinois. Trafton was a handsome young boy of six when your father and I were married in the Episcopal Church…and I agreed, after having met and spent time with the boy, that Trafton would live with us, and I would accept him as my son… treating him as if he were my own flesh and blood.

"Shortly after our marriage, Edmund took the divorce settlement money and purchased the seventeen hundred acre ranch in southwest Oklahoma where we were living at the time you were born. Those first years on the ranch were very special: Your father was so happy there, even though he was not cut out to be a rancher; Trafton grew and blossomed, providing his father and me with a great deal of joy; and when you and Rita first became cognizant of ranch-life…with its ebbs and flows driven by the seasons… you followed Trafton around like chicks to a mother hen. And then everything changed…Trafton turned ten-years old, and in keeping with the divorce settlement, his father took him by railroad to Montana, leaving him there for a year with his mother.

"When your father returned home from Montana, he was all smiles, bringing each of us presents…acting as if nothing had changed. But I could tell that he was worried about Trafton…How he would adapt to a more robust, strenuous environment where might-makes-right. As the year went on Edmund became more distracted, less involved in the day-to-day operations of the ranch, leaving more of the decision-making to me and his foreman. Your father even took out a subscription to the Helena newspaper, reading cover-to-cover each copy that arrived at the ranch by the evening train...experiencing vicariously all that he could about Trafton's adventure. I, too, missed Trafton...for I had come to love him as if he were my own son.

"With the year almost up, your father re-engaged himself in the ranch...getting everything ready for Trafton's return. Seeing him off at our little train-station, on his way to retrieve Trafton, I could feel your father's anticipation of seeing Trafton again...But I could also sense a measure of anxiety, uncertainty in his goodbye kiss.

"My first indication that there might be a problem was the telegram I received from Edmund showing Bozeman...not Helena, as I would have expected...as the location from where the telegram was sent. Bozeman is the last big town east of Helena on the railroad line. The telegram simply said: 'I am headed back home. See you soon.' There was no mention of Trafton. And why had Edmund not sent it from Helena...the train station where he was to meet Trafton?

"Then there was another telegram from your father...sent from Kansas City...but it only gave the date and time of the arrival of your father's train at our little station. When the train arrived, it took some time for your father to appear at the passenger-car door. While the porter stood at the bottom step adjusting the portable step, your father was assisted down the steps by the conductor who held your father tightly around the chest to keep him from stumbling, from falling...Your father was drunk...He was mumbling incoherently...crying: 'They have taken my Trafton from me!'

"Several days passed before your father would tell me what happened... I had hidden all of the whisky, rum and brandy that I could find on the ranch...And I was forced to lure him into conversation with promises of strong drink. Even then, he would give me only partial, disjointed accounts of what had transpired. As best I could put the story together...when the train carrying your father to Helena arrived at the Helena train station, a group of some ten or twelve heavily armed men – mostly thugs – but also Olivia's father, brothers and uncles, were standing on the platform prepared to deny Edmund departure from the passenger car. When Edmund appeared in the doorway to the passenger car, his former father-in-law pointed his shot-gun at Edmund, advising him that he would shoot him, would blow his head off, if he put one foot on the platform. Your father protested that Olivia had agreed that she would have Trafton for just one year, to which Roscoe McGonagle scoffed, 'Well, she's changed her mind... You've done such a good job at raising that boy so's that she now wants him around her...'cause she's afraid you'll turn him into a dandy like you'. 'But her agreement is included in a court order', implored your father. 'So what,' replied McGonagle, 'we're the law out here...we'll decide what court orders are enforced, and which ain't.'

"Seeing that he was making no headway with the McGonagle clan, your father requested that he at least be able to see Trafton, to tell him goodbye. Even this modest request was rebuffed. 'You best get your dandified ass back on that train and head on back east before you get hurt... Maybe in ten years you can ask Trafton himself if he wants to see you...but you ain't seei'n him now'.

"Your father was certainly no coward...and he was a lot tougher than he looks, but he was also no fool either. Taking stock of the bunch of rough characters standing there armed to the teeth, your father chose discretion over valor, and went back into the passenger car, retook his seat. With the conductor's assistance and the stationmaster's cooperation, your father was smuggled off of that train and onto the next eastbound passenger train. In Bozeman, your father de-boarded the train long enough to send the telegram and to purchase the first of many bottles of whiskey...And you know the rest of the story."

"Yes," replied a clearly unmoved Nell. "He drank away the ranch, the rest of his family, and even his life over the loss of that boy...when he had three other children who needed his love...and would have loved him as much as that boy...if only he had given us the chance."

NELL SAT THERE, back in the present, for a long time; trying to forget about the hurt, the pain, her father had imposed on her. As she had promised herself so many times, she would never let anyone hurt her like that again. Reaching over the side of her chair, Nell picked up the next tablet.

CHAPTER 20

BIG CHIEF TABLET EIGHTEEN | JACK

Aunt Rita's enthusiasm about our future together was infectious; she filled our time together talking about how our lives had changed, and what plans we could now make that would otherwise have been subject to my mother's whims. Despite my sudden, unsettled feelings of complete abandonment by my immediate family – or what was left of it – I was drawn into fantasizing about the opportunities now placed in my path by being Aunt Rita's son. Yet, whenever I tried to find out from Aunt Rita about how – and why – things had turned out the way they had; what she may have done to get Nell to change her mind...she would simply say, "We have more cheerful subjects to talk about."

It was my impression that Aunt Rita was more interested in talking about the result, rather than about the process; she was more interested in running the victory lap – than in talking about how she was able to have such a victory. *Was Mom's surrender the real prize – the real source of Aunt Rita's joy – the defeat of a life-long, bitter foe? Am I just the trophy to be shown-off?*

Our trips to the Country Club for Sunday-night dinner – and now Saturday lunch in the Grille – became more frequent, as were shopping trips to town, and family gatherings with the Kaufmans in Kansas City; any opportunity to let the world – her world – see me in her company. But her biggest thrill was the trip to the local attorney to initiate adoption proceedings. I was made to sit quietly by while Aunt Rita and Mr. Trane, her attorney, discussed the details and the process of my adoption – even my new name, Jack Douglas Kaufman. Now that the necessary papers had been signed by my parents, the petition for adoption could be filed and a court date set for the hearing.

"Jack, now that we are about to be mother and son — at least legally — we need to decide how you will address me...I will continue to call you Jack — at least in public — and Jackie — in private, depending on my mood...and your behavior. I certainly don't want to be called 'Mother' or 'Mommy', or 'Mumby' at any time. After all, I am none of those persons...and such childish names are especially inappropriate for a boy your age. Perhaps a simple 'Mom' or 'Aunt Rita' will do in public.

"I will address you however you wish, Mom," I answered.

"That's my good boy, Jack...You are adapting quickly to your new role."

I HAD BARELY begun to digest my new circumstances, my new role, when, quickly enough, Fritz renewed his campaign to have me reveal his presence to 'Rita' with the following conversation:

Jack, I believe it is time that we begin the process of bringing Aunt Rita into our plans.

But Fritz, don't we have to wait until after I'm adopted?

I've given that some thought. It may be more risky to make Aunt Rita aware of my presence after she adopts you than before she adopts you. If, for instance, we are unsuccessful in convincing Aunt Rita that I am a benign presence, and my mission is noble — then Aunt Rita's response before adoption would be to send you home to your parents as damaged goods — despite what the folks at the Menninger Clinic have said about you; but after adoption you have become her problem and, if she thinks you are crazy, she will send you to the folks at the Menninger Clinic — or have you committed to an institution. She is not likely to admit she has been fooled by a mere boy; especially in front of her arch-enemy, your mother. I am sure that you can see just how dreadful that would be for the both of us. Also, we must keep in mind the possibility that Aunt Rita may eventually succumb to Gabby Kaufman's insistence that she bring Hannah into your new home. Knowing of my presence may keep Aunt Rita from succumbing to Gabby's entreaties...at least for a time.

But if I am sent home to my parents, won't my mother put me away?

Possibly, but based upon her current relationship with Aunt Rita she would probably dismiss anything Aunt Rita were to tell her about you as being sour-grapes. And, even if she were to believe Aunt Rita — also thinking that you might be crazy — based upon what I know about your mother, she is too cheap and too unconcerned to get you professional care — except maybe seeking an exorcism.

What's an exorcism?

It is some Roman Catholic mumbo-jumbo where a priest tries to drive an evil spirit out of a person's body. It is an old-fashioned ritual that was used when a crazy person was thought to be possessed by a devil or a demonic spirit. For all intents and purposes, it has been scientifically repudiated; replaced with psychiatry and medication. I doubt that exorcism has been used for centuries. But, it may be something only your mother would think of pursuing if she were to conclude that my presence in your body amounts to a possession. It's a risk — indeed a very small risk — that I would be willing to take as opposed to institutionalization at the hands of Aunt Rita. All may be lost if you are placed in an insane asylum.

Have you given any thought as to how I am supposed to tell Aunt Rita about your presence...without causing her to think that I am crazy? I don't know how to do it, and I am scared.

Don't worry, Jack. I'm working on it.

THE FRIDAY EVENING sky showed signs of fall. I observed that the wood-fire that I had started earlier, at Aunt Rita's request, was beginning to show signs of neglect. Opening the wire-mesh screen, I stirred the embers with a brass-handled poker, restoring some of their glow, and placed a set of three logs on the glowing embers. The fresh fuel immediately leapt into flame, crackling and hissing — not unlike the sound made by bacon frying in a hot pan. After watching the fire for a few moments, I turned towards my chair facing the fireplace.

I was just about to settle down into my wing chair when Aunt Rita — fresh from her evening bath — entered the den through the hallway door, stepping gingerly over the prostrate Lady who had taken up her sentry position in the doorway. Covered up in a white terry-cloth robe, wrapped tightly around her, bound by the matching terry-cloth belt, Aunt Rita smelled sweetly of high-quality soap and rich creams, her hair still glistening wet, holding a bath-towel in her right hand. She stood before the fireplace for a few minutes bending her head towards the heat, briskly rubbing her hair with the towel.

Turning her back to the fire, while still rubbing her hair with the towel, as if it would never come dry, she looked towards me, smiling as she asked, "What have you planned for our entertainment this dark, cold and gloomy evening, or shall we just read our books, basking in the warmth of the fire and each other's company?"

"If it is alright with you, I'd like to talk about things...like we did when we used to sit out on the porch in warmer weather...I miss those talks...talking about our lives."

"I do too, but I'm afraid that it would quickly become boring. I've already told you everything important in my life, and I certainly know everything important about your life...So what is there to talk about?"

Looking straight ahead at the turbulent fire, avoiding Aunt Rita's probing gaze, I said softly, almost inaudibly, "A lot."

"What do you mean...a lot? A lot, about what?" she inquired incredulously. "I don't think you need to tell me about private things...Like touching your boy thingy; if that's what you had in mind."

After a long pause, again avoiding looking at Aunt Rita, I began to tell her what Fritz and I have rehearsed over the last several weeks; "Remember when you heard me talking in my sleep? Talking in a language that you did not understand?"

"Yes, but that's all over. That was settled when we saw Dr. Glassberg at the clinic. I don't understand."

"The language that you heard while I was talking in my sleep was German, and I wasn't speaking it...I don't know enough German to speak it."

"Then who was speaking the German if it wasn't you?" she

asked impatiently. "And more importantly, how did I hear it? I thought you told Dr. Glassberg that you weren't hearing voices."

"That's the point I am trying to make. I don't hear spoken voices...At least not like when you thought you heard me speaking German in my sleep."

"I don't understand any of what you are saying," she remarked angrily, as she began to stand up. "And what's more, I don't want to get back into this 'Jack is crazy thing'."

"Please, let me explain. I can show you that I am not crazy."

"I doubt it...I doubt it very much. I can't believe that you have lied to me, and lied to Dr. Glassberg...when all we were trying to do was help you. Why have you lied to me Jack?"

"Please trust me." I pleaded. "I haven't lied to you or anyone, I promise. I promise. Just let me tell you about what I know has been happening to me. I can prove that I am not crazy...and that I am not a liar."

"Go on. I am all ears," she stated with a note of sarcasm, settling back down into her wing chair, staring into the fire, as if searching for an answer to what has just jeopardized all of her grand plans; visualizing them going up in smoke.

"I don't know how it happened, or even why it happened, but on the day that the Second World War ended in Europe... with Germany's surrender...I was struck in the head by a practice bomb attached to the end of a rope swing designed and created by my brother Chris. The blow to my head was severe enough to render me unconscious...or perhaps even dead...for hours. It must have been during this time that the spirit of a German soldier, who died on that very same day, entered my body. But it was several years before I first became aware of his presence. I started having these most unusual dreams...In one of these dreams a large wolf that had been pursuing me, began helping me to escape from a frightful situation. He then told me that he was a German officer, and said his name was Fritz.

"In a subsequent dream I witnessed a situation in which Fritz was shot in the back, not being able to see who shot him. It was after that dream that Fritz began to relate events from his life to prove that he was real...events containing real persons that

I looked up in history books and magazines. In time, Fritz saw the unhappy conditions at home with my mother and the rest of my family, and of how these conditions were turning me into a failure, destined for a very troubled, dreadful life. In an effort to improve my character, to improve my chances of becoming a well-functioning adult, Fritz began instructing me on how I could improve my lot at home, become a better student, and to make friends. He was most encouraged that I could escape the effects of Mom's destructive actions when he saw just how much you loved me, and of how you sought to protect me from my mother.

"Eventually, he told me how he needed me...and you...to get him back to Germany to find out who it was that had shot him in the back, and for what reasons. As you are aware, there have been a couple of incidents where my life has been in serious danger...One that comes to mind is the terrible car accident that killed my brothers...the other was when David took me swimming and I almost drowned. In the accident with the Buick, it was Fritz that warned me that the Buick was top-heavy, and it was Fritz who warned me that the Buick was tipping over, and for me to get down on the floor, to wedge myself under the front seat. In the drowning episode, it was Fritz who kept me afloat...by urging me to keep reaching for the surface...until the lifeguard spotted me and pulled me to safety.

"And it was Fritz who you heard talking in my sleep...and it was Fritz's bad memories of the war that were causing my nightmares. Fritz's personality is much stronger than mine, allowing it to leak over into my mind when I am asleep or in danger. Once Fritz and I determined that my nightmares were really just his memories seeping through into my sleeping brain...which was still being affected by the drugs I was given to ease the pain of my car-wreck injuries...the nightmares happily ended. I am sure you will remember when the bad dreams went away, together with the headaches.

"I know what you are thinking: Jack is not crazy. He is possessed! I've thought a great deal about that possibility, researching 'possessions' in the school library. Although 'possessions' are mentioned in the Bible...especially in the New Testament, there hasn't been a report of a 'possession' since the Dark Ages. Even then, the person alleged to be possessed, was supposedly 'possessed by an evil spirit'...In fact, that's the dictionary's definition of 'possessed'."

"I have no reason to suspect that Fritz is an evil spirit, a demon, or the devil. Look how he has saved my life, and provided me with advice on how to deal with my mother. I am sure you can tell what a better boy I am now than I was when I first started spending summers with you. Without your incredible, unconditional love and support, even Fritz's efforts to show me how to be a better boy would have come to nothing.

"Even if Fritz's motives for strengthening my character are self-driven...that is...to get him back to Germany, that does not mean he is evil or that I am controlled by Fritz. At worst, our spirits share the same body...but without my own spirit controlling my own body, Fritz's spirit is lost. In other words, I'm driving the bus and he is just a passenger. And with your continued love, acceptance and support, I have no reason to fear that Fritz would take over either my spirit or my body."

Now looking at me quizzically, Aunt Rita inquired, "Is Fritz with you right now?"

"Yes, his spirit is with me right now."

"Has Fritz been the one talking to me, or is it you, alone?"

"I alone have been talking to you, although Fritz and I spent long hours working on what I should say to you."

"How do you converse with each other? Does Fritz speak to you in your ear, in English or in German?"

"I really don't know how we converse, but I don't hear him with my ears...Just with my brain. It is my body, my brain, and my senses. Everything that Fritz hears, sees, feels, smells, or tastes comes through me. Fritz communicates with me in English. At first, when I was not aware of his presence, I think Fritz knew no English. He has told me that he learned English by hearing what I hear and seeing what I read, and by learning what I learned, both at home and at school."

"Are you and Fritz communicating at this very moment?

I heard Fritz say: *Jack. Tell her yes. Also, please tell her that I hope to be able to speak directly to her – through you, of course – whenever she feels comfortable to do so.*

"Yes. And Fritz asked me to tell you that he hopes to speak with you directly – through me – whenever you feel comfortable in doing so."

"How will I know it really is this Fritz, and not just you pretending to be Fritz?"

Again Fritz: *That's simple enough. I will tell her things which you are incapable of knowing anything about – which she can verify by speaking with people who were there – like the P-38 pilot Pete Roberts.*

"Fritz says that he will tell you things that I know nothing about – and am incapable of knowing about on my own. And that you can verify these things by talking to people who were there, like the P-38 pilot Pete Roberts."

Aunt Rita looked at me imploringly, like she wanted to believe me, but just can't take the step. She then looked away into the fireplace – where the blazing logs had devolved into glowing embers – like a gypsy starring into her crystal ball searching for the right answer. Not finding what she was looking for, Aunt Rita turned her gaze again on me, stating, "Jack, I don't know what to think, or what to do about what you have told me this evening. Right now I am wrestling with the unsavory dilemma that you have presented to me: Is Jack crazy, or is he possessed? And which is the least attractive alternative? Or is there any difference between them?"

On this note of uncertainty, Aunt Rita rose up out of her wing chair, drew the sash of her terry-cloth robe tightly around her waist, and walked out of the den without our usual night-time kiss and hug. I was left alone to bank the fire, to let Lady out the front door to do her duty, to let her back in, to lock the door, to turn out the lights, to climb the stairs, to walk past Aunt Rita's bedroom door from which no light was visible, to close my bedroom door, to fall tearfully onto my bed; all the time pondering: Is it back to Mother, or will it be to the insane asylum?

Fritz said: *Don't despair, Jack. I think things went as well as we could have hoped. The fact that Aunt Rita is thinking about whether to accept my presence as reality is a good sign. It was a smart move to let her know that she can listen to what I have to say, and then verify that what you are telling her on my behalf is true. I think that when she checks my tale with Pete Roberts, she will be convinced beyond a doubt.*

NORMALLY, I WOULD sleep late on Saturday mornings, but on that Saturday morning I awoke early, still troubled by the events of the evening before; Aunt Rita's reaction, her uncertainty, what she might do.

Everything was going along so well between Aunt Rita and me. Will things ever be the same again: Most probably, not. Aunt Rita is correct, I am either crazy, or I am possessed. There is no other choice. In her eyes, I am no longer the boy she thought I was, the boy she was just about to adopt. I am damaged goods. Oh, why has God let this happen to me? I should have ignored Fritz's advice to get down on the floor of the Buick, letting the car-wreck take my life too. And why should I have to screw up my life just to help some Nazis get back to Germany? How do I even know that what Fritz has been telling me is even the truth?

Fritz said: *Because, Jack, you have already verified that much of what I have told you is the truth. And, like you told Aunt Rita yesterday, you can ask Pete Roberts about me, and he will confirm that I am who I say I am, and that what I have told you is the truth, including the facts of my untimely death.*

I slipped out from under the covers, searched blindly in the still dark room for my slippers on the floor, for my bathrobe on the footboard; noting how much cooler the bedroom had become with the passage of the cold front during the night, with its gusty winds whistling through the trees, driving sheets of cold rain noisily against the exposed window panes. The room smelled strongly of heated metal as the radiators clinked and rattled, resisting the surge of hot water from the coal-fired furnace in the basement; just the first-round in an endless winter-time battle between cold metal and hot water.

Feeling my way to the bedroom door, I heard noises of movement elsewhere in the house; perhaps more radiators doing battle with the furnace. Upon opening the door, the upstairs hall was still dark, with no light emerging from Aunt Rita's bedroom, the door to which appeared to be open. But I did see light reflecting on the stair-case wall, evidence of some form of illumination present on the first floor. Lady was nowhere in sight, neither in my bedroom — where she regularly spent the night — nor in the upstairs hall, at the top of the stairs. *Have I been abandoned by both of the women I love…the two women upon whom I depend upon for their unconditional love and acceptance?*

I traced the source of illumination to the kitchen, the glare of the ceiling light revealing the real objects of my search — Aunt Rita, who was seated in her kitchen chair holding a cup in her hand, and Lady, laying at her feet; both looking at me with their sad, questioning eyes: *Who is this boy? Where is the boy we thought we knew so well? Can we love this boy just the same, just as well?* Not an encouraging setting, certainly not a very warm greeting; but what did I really expect given last-night's troubling revelations?

Clearing her throat, placing the cup on the table in front of her, looking at me with red-rimmed eyes, just the glimmer of a smile creeping across her face, Aunt Rita whispered hoarsely, "I see that you also have had trouble sleeping. Would you like me to fix you a cup of tea?"

"Yes. Please. Thank you," I answered haltingly, not knowing whether to read too much into either the content or the tone of Aunt Rita's offer. *Is she just being polite?*

Aunt Rita got up from her chair, walked towards the electric range, motioning me to take my chair at the kitchen table, and placed the tea kettle on a burner. Turning towards me she stated in a commanding voice, "I need to talk to you and the Kraut… Is he there with you now?"

"I don't know…I haven't had any contact with him so far this morning," I replied.

"What do you mean?" she inquired with a note of puzzlement, pouring hot water into the teapot. "Isn't he always sharing your body…can he leave your body?"

"I don't know whether he ever leaves my body. I just know

that there are times when I don't feel his presence; like he is unplugged from me...I picture him to be like a telephone switchboard operator who plugs into my brain whenever he needs to contact me or to view the world through my senses. He tells me that we each have our own minds. Fritz says that if he ever had to see what's in my mind that he would go crazy...He thinks that my mind is too full of silly, unimportant thoughts. So that is why he unplugs from my brain most of the time."

"Well, how do you get him to plug into your brain when you want to converse with him? Is that the right word...converse?" she inquired, pouring hot tea into a tea cup.

"I don't think so; we don't have conversations...we exchange mind thoughts when Fritz wants to. When I want to exchange thoughts with Fritz, I keep thinking his name. Sometimes he responds immediately, and other times he doesn't answer me for hours, or for days."

"So, this Fritz may not be hearing this conversation," she remarked with a slight smile, placing the steaming tea cup in front of me on the table.

"I think so...I mean he may not be listening to what we are saying right now, but I'd be quite surprised if he isn't listening in... He says he is always interested in you; in how you look, in what you are saying, in how you touch and hold me."

"So Fritz has taken an interest in me, has he?" Aunt Rita observed with a slight smile.

"Oh, yes. Sometimes I think he enjoys our close moments together as much as I do."

"I'll have to keep that in mind," she stated with raised eyebrows. "So," she continued, "This Fritz may be plugged into your brain...observing everything we do...but you may not even know it?"

"I guess so...but based upon how we have related over the last couple of years, I think I can sense when he is plugged in. His mind is so powerful, that his thoughts, his memories, tend to leak over into my mind whenever he is plugged into my brain," I told her, carefully holding the hot, still steaming tea cup, blowing on the hot liquid.

"Well, if his mind is so powerful, aren't you afraid that he can take over your brain, your mind, your body?"

"Yes. Fritz and I have exchanged thoughts on that possibility. He assures me that, even if he could take control of my brain or my mind, or even my body, he would never do that...He has no intention of doing so...He says that would not be the Christian thing to do. He thinks that God has a hand in what has happened to him, with him sharing my body...being given a chance to find out how and why he was killed. Fritz also thinks that as long as my self-esteem continues to develop...and I continue to have your love, affection, and acceptance...my mind...my spirit... will continue to grow...to the point where I will be strong enough to withstand any attempt by him to overwhelm my being," I said, glancing up at Aunt Rita over the teacup at my lips, taking a small sip carefully from the cup, placing the cup back on the table.

"Do you trust him...that he won't try to take control of your being...your mind...your spirit?" Aunt Rita asked skeptically.

"Yes...I think so...Besides, what could I do to stop him if he tried to take over?"

"I guess you're right...you...we...don't have much control over Fritz right now. Can you try getting in touch with him? I would like for you to let him know that I'm willing to listen to his story."

I heard Fritz say: *Well done, Jack....I think you may have convinced Aunt Rita that I am real. But let's wait a while before you let her know that I have responded to your efforts to contact me. I don't want her to know that I was listening to most of what you both were talking about. I like her thinking that I am not always 'plugged into your brain' – like a telephone operator. That, Jack, was a clever analogy. In the end, I believe that the story I am going to tell her will bring Aunt Rita fully into our plan; especially when she, I hope, can confirm major parts of that story with Pete Roberts. Now, tell her that you are trying to contact me.*

"I'll keep trying to reach Fritz," I told Aunt Rita, focusing on the tea cup once again before my lips; avoiding eye contact with her. *Why doesn't this feel right to me...Fritz's manipulation... his dishonesty?*

CHAPTER 21

DINNER WAS PREPARED, WAITING TO BE SERVED when Nell returned home from her office. Paul had removed his apron and was sitting at the already set kitchen table listening to the evening news on the radio while reading the evening newspaper. The early fall weather was warm; the backdoor onto the screened porch was open. When he heard the back gate close, Paul glanced up at the electric wall-clock, noting that Nell was home on time. Putting down the evening paper, Paul got up, moved to the stove, where he removed the lid on the well-worn pot of mashed potatoes, giving them a stir. Nell entered the kitchen without a word, without a glance at Paul, walked through the kitchen into the dining room; where she placed her purse on the table, removed her gloves and hat. Coming back into the kitchen, Nell paused to observe what was cooking on the stove, took her seat at her end of the table, unfolded her napkin, and placed it on her lap.

"How was your day," asked Paul, trying to break the ice.

"Ssh…I'm listening to the news," is what he got for his effort.

Chastised, Paul commenced placing food on the plates, placed Nell's plate in front of her first; then putting a plate on the table at his spot. Before sitting he asked shyly, quickly, lest incurring further rebuke, "Would you like a glass of sherry to go with your glass of water?"

"No. You know full-well that I wait until I've finished eating my food before I have my sherry."

The only sound heard in the kitchen during the remainder of

the meal was the sound of silverware touching china plates, plus the modulated tones of the newscaster dispensing the latest news from 'around-the-world': the war in Korea, the problems in the Middle-East – Israelis versus the Arabs – and the latest voter polls for the upcoming presidential election between Ike and Adlai Stevenson.

When the meal was completed, the news broadcast at its end, and Paul began removing the dishes from the kitchen table to the sink for washing, he tried one more time to begin a conversation with Nell, who had poured herself a small tumbler of sherry.

"If you don't want to talk to me about Jack…If you don't want to help me find Jack…Will you at least share with me whatever it is you found at Fairways…whatever it is you have closeted yourself for days in your bedroom reading…or examining…that would give me some clues as to what has happened to Jack…From what you said the other night…about knowing things that I would be surprised you know… I am sure that you are hiding things from me…important things… things that could help me find Jack, even to save Jack's life."

"How dare accuse me of hiding things from you! How many times have you learned things about Jack from my mean-spirited sister Rita that you withheld from me? I'll bet there have been plenty of times when you were privy to important information about Jack that you knew I would want to know – like his possible possession by a demon – but you wouldn't share it with me. I would have arranged for an exorcism had I known about that…And, we wouldn't be in fear for Jack right now."

"Whether Jack is possessed by a demon, and qualified for an exorcism, is questionable. But we are unquestionably in fear for Jack right now…Why are you withholding information that might save him… just because you are angry with me?"

Without responding to Paul's query, Nell rose from her chair, walked out of the kitchen, and stepped into the dining room. Paul then heard her climbing the front stairs to the second floor as he returned to washing the dinner dishes and cooking utensils. He was almost finished drying the frying pan when he heard Nell descend the front stairs. Turning away from the sink, and drying his hands off on the front of his stained apron, expecting Nell to return to the kitchen, Paul instead heard Nell open and close the front door.

No doubt Nell is off to church to pray…But to pray for what?

But Nell walked the two blocks to the priest house at Saint Agatha's, not to the church; carrying the book-bag containing a selection of Jack's writings. Nell was hoping that the pastor, Monsignor Francis Xavier Thornton, would see her; and that she could convince the good Monsignor to agree that Jack was an appropriate candidate for an exorcism. Nell had painstakingly removed any of the tablets which she believed contained criticisms of her treatment of Jack; especially the ones covering Jack's visit to Dr. Glassberg.

In response to Nell's ringing the doorbell, the rectory's heavy front door was opened by an elderly, unsmiling, white haired woman. Giving her name and telling the housekeeper that she wished to see the Monsignor, Nell was waved into the dimly-lit front hall, which served as the rectory's vestibule. The housekeeper inquired as to whether the Monsignor was expecting her.

Nell said, "No, but I'm sure the Monsignor will see me."

"I'll inquire…Please wait here."

The housekeeper opened one side of the sliding doors leading into a brightly-lit dining room from which drifted the aroma of roasted meat and fresh coffee. She stepped into the dining-room, and quickly closed the door behind her. Nell strained to hear the conversation on the other side of the heavy oak doors, but heard only muffled voices.

"What can I do for you Mrs. Johanson," said a heavyset, balding priest, with thick jowls, wearing a black cassock, as he moved from the dining room into the vestibule, the housekeeper right behind him. "I'm Father Stephens, Monsignor Thornton's assistant pastor. The Monsignor is unavailable this evening…Perhaps I can be of assistance."

The disappointment clearly showed in Nell's eyes, "I was so hoping to see the Monsignor…We've been such good friends for years."

"I'm certain that if you will leave your name and telephone number with Mrs. Bryan, she will have the Monsignor's secretary call you tomorrow to set up an appointment to meet with the Monsignor."

"But I need to speak with Monsignor Thornton tonight…Tomorrow may be too late."

"That's impossible. The Monsignor is traveling with the Archbishop…They are on their way to a convocation in Washington, D.C. As I said before, I'm sure that I can help you if you'll just tell me what it is that needs such immediate attention."

"I really don't think you can help me," replied a clearly distraught Nell, turning towards the rectory's front door, reaching for the doorknob. She paused before turning the knob, and while still staring at the closed door, asked, "What do you know about 'possession' and 'exorcisms'?"

"Not much, really," replied the priest hurriedly. "Neither does anyone else in the priesthood, as far as I know…With the advent of modern science – like psychology, psychiatry, and associated medications – there has been little need to treat mental illness as 'demon possession'. I dare say that there has not been an exorcism in the Catholic Church in American for the last fifty years…And I think that if you were to ask Monsignor Thornton about it, he would say the same thing."

"What would someone have to show to prove that someone was 'possessed' and not 'mentally ill'; that is, not 'crazy'."

"I'm sure that there is a high standard of proof required that the person really is 'possessed' by the devil…or one of his demons…before the archdiocese would authorize an 'exorcism'. You'd really have to speak with someone in the archdiocesan office about what would be required; but I'm sure it would take un-refuted and tested testimony from highly regarded professionals, known to and trusted by the archdiocesan officials, who have examined the allegedly 'possessed' person over a considerable period of time, as well as his or her family members."

"Oh," said Nell, dejectedly. *There is no way I am going to subject Jack, or myself, to the scrutiny of shrinks.*

"I'm so sorry," said the priest touching Nell's shoulder. "The person you are inquiring on behalf of must be very close to you. But I think you had better get that person some help from a mental health professional before you even begin to contemplate church intervention.

I can give you the name of some very fine psychologists that I have come to trust, if you would like."

"Thank you, but no thank you. I think I now know what I need to do now. And don't bother to have the Monsignor's secretary call me. Good night."

"And God bless you, and may He help you and your loved one, Mrs. Johanson."

On the walk back home, Nell thought of only one thing: *Jack's possession must be a part of God's plan to give a wicked soul an opportunity to seek redemption. I have no right to interfere in the Lord's plan. Does this mean that I should destroy Jack's writings, and let history take its current course unimpeded?*

DESPITE HER MISGIVINGS, Nell, upon returning home, climbed the stairs to her bedroom without seeing or speaking to Paul, resumed her reading of the next of the remaining tablets in the hope of finding something, anything that might provide some clue about the nature of Jack's 'spirit'. But unfortunately, too much time had passed, too many miles had been traveled, too many bridges had been crossed, and too many lives had been altered to ever permit Jack to live a normal life – 'good spirit' or 'bad spirit'. Whatever God's ultimate purpose for Jack and 'the spirit' might be, Jack's destiny was now out of Nell and Paul's hands. It made no difference whether 'the spirit' was evil or not; Jack and 'the spirit' were inextricably linked together in the eyes of those who were in charge of Jack.

CHAPTER 22

BIG CHIEF TABLET NINETEEN | FRITZ

Jack has done about all that he can to bring Aunt Rita to the point where I can, hopefully, convince her that I am the lost spirit of a real person stuck sharing Jack's body; that my motives are pure, and that my mission, in trying to return to Germany, is noble. Time is now – more than ever before – of the essence. If I fail quickly to convince Aunt Rita of any one of these elements of my story, then all may be lost.

Sensing Jack's sudden reluctance to mislead Aunt Rita about me, or my whereabouts, I purposely refrained from making my thoughts known to him. To Jack, I have 'unplugged' from his brain. The risk, of course, is that I was isolated from knowing about anything that is occurring in Jack's world. I was effectively cut off from my only contact with the real world.

I let Jack know that he should advise Aunt Rita of my willingness to explain why it is necessary for me to return to Germany, to resolve the mystery of my untimely death.

Jack, before you let Aunt Rita know that I am ready to tell her of my adventures, I need you to tell me what has transpired between you and Aunt Rita during this time that we have been unplugged, which might impact what I have to tell her.

Jack said: I'm not sure what you are asking about. If you mean, "Have we talked about you?" the answer is no. I have been in school during the days, and after school we haven't been talking as much as we used to. I think she is still struggling with how to deal with what I have told her about your presence. Oh, the adoption hearing has been scheduled for next Thursday morning. And Aunt Rita has sent a note to the school asking that I be excused for the day. I think she is having the Kaufmans and some friends come to the house after the court hearing for a party or something. She seems to be quite excited that the adoption is about to happen. This probably means that she is not sending me back to Mother. So that is some good news. I think that is all...Oh, yeah, and I heard her talking on the phone to Buzz – she was asking him to get Pete Robert's mailing address. Is that good news?

It certainly could be...Only time would tell. I thanked Jack for the briefing...that was helpful information. "Jack," I said, "Why don't you tell Aunt Rita that maybe we ought to wait until after the adoption proceeding has taken place before I proceed to tell her all about me and my quest, explaining that there are too many distractions right now, and that I need her undivided attention."

THE ADOPTION HEARING was a simple formality involving just the judge and Aunt Rita's attorney, who introduced certain documents which the judge received into evidence. Jack was called by the attorney to the witness seat, placed under oath by the clerk, and asked by the judge whether he understood what was taking place, whether he consented to the adoption, and whether he agreed to the name change. After Jack had answered affirmatively to each of the judge's questions, the judge read from a lengthy document stating that the court was approving and ordering the adoption.

The reception at Fairways was pleasant, but certainly not a jubilant affair – Aunt Rita having expended most of her happy excitement during the period immediately following her learning that Nell had capitulated; receding from her threatened actions against Aunt Rita, abandoning her natural claims to Jack.

The only excitement at the reception was caused by Aunt Rita's surprise announcement that she and Jack were spending the Christmas holidays with the Kaufmans at a resort in Acapulco, and that in January, Jack would complete his elementary schooling at a nearby young men's military academy as a boarder. The Acapulco trip was a gift to Aunt Rita from the Kaufmans; the military boarding school for Jack was intended to provide him with a better education than he had been receiving at St. Benedict's parish school. For me, the announced Acapulco trip was a pleasant surprise; but her announcement of sending Jack to the military boarding school was a brutal shock – Aunt Rita had smelled a rat; she was isolating herself from Jack, effectively limiting his ability – and my ability –to convince her to get me back to Germany. Aunt Rita was making this much more difficult than I had envisioned.

CHAPTER 23

BIG CHIEF TABLET TWENTY | JACK

Christmas, like my birthdays, had always been a big disappoint-ment, a huge let-down from all the buildup. The traditional holi-day cheer displayed in department store windows, promoted in Christmas cards, was felt throughout the land, but not at my house. The Christmas following my adoption, however, was quite different; for my many years of disappointment and let-down were replaced with joy, cheer, and a happiness that had — for so long — been only a dream far out of my reach.

Aunt Rita, Lady, and all our luggage and boxes of presents were waiting for me in the Ford station wagon outside Saint Benedict's parish school the moment my classes ended for the Christmas holidays; I was being swept away to Kansas City, to spend Christmas with the Kaufmans, to fly on to Acapulco for a week in a tropical paradise.

The entire holiday period in Kansas City was filled with laugh-ter, merriment, joy; the kind that I had only previously experi-enced watching other kids in the movies. Arriving downstairs at the Kaufmans on Christmas morning, seeing the enormous, heavily decorated fir-tree filling the large room with its scent, its multicolored lights projecting many hues around the room, its base surrounded by stacks of gaily-wrapped presents, I was stunned by the moment. *Why have I been so blessed? What have I done to deserve all of this? This really can't be happening to me!* In the midst of this splendor, I was thrust back in time to Christmases past; reliving the disappointment of a small, sparsely

decorated tree, with only a few presents, but with much bickering and acrimony. *What are Mother and Dad doing this morning,
alone and childless?*

"Merry Christmas, Jack," I heard whispered in my ear as I was
drawn backwards into Aunt Rita's firm embrace.

I responded to her Christmas greeting with as much enthusiasm that I could muster, "Oh yes. It is a very merry Christmas!
Thank you...Thank you so very much!"

"I hope it is not too much, though. I kept telling Gabby that
she was over-doing everything...That you may not be able to
handle it all. But being Jewish – and not having had much experience with the American-Christian approach to Christmas – she
just remembered the Christmas mornings that she has seen in
the movies, and has tried to replicate what she thinks will make
you happy. You are, after all, her grandchild now."

I was instantly reminded of my earlier trip to Country Club
Plaza with Gabby – she told me that that is the name I should call
her – on Christmas Eve to pick out a present for Rita – as Gabby
insists I call my new mother. I had a few dollars to spend; money
that I had saved from my allowance. When I told Gabby that I
didn't have much to spend, she stated that I had a good line of
credit with her and that I should select a present that had special
meaning to Rita – "I'll make up the difference in the cost." Gabby
– dressed in a fur coat – paraded me through store after store,
examining purses, scarves, watches, and fancy jewelry; leaving
me bewildered. I knew that Aunt Rita would use all the stuff that
I had been shown, but none of it struck me as having a special
meaning.

About to give up looking further, turning the choice over
to Gabby, she dragged me into a stationary store; where there
were, in addition to the many varieties of writing paper and envelopes, a large selection of writing pens and pencils, and fancy
desk sets. At last, I was enthusiastic about selecting a gift with
a 'special meaning' to Rita. After some time spent in handling
pens, pencils – feeling the weight and balance – my eyes settled
on a leather desk-set containing matching silver pen and pencil,
and a particularly attractive onyx-handled letter opener – with

its long, thin silver blade revealed when I withdrew it from its scabbard — feeling like a dagger in my hand. Without giving it further thought, this was the gift that I picked out as my Christmas present for Rita. *I hope that Mom/Rita will be as thrilled with receiving this desk-set, as I am in giving it to her. But, will it have a 'special meaning' for her?*

"Are you sure, Jackie dear," Gabby inquired in her high, sweet voice, "that this is what you really want to give to Rita for her only Christmas present? It is a beautiful desk set...and I am sure it is something she can use often...but it seems so...cold...so...impersonal...perhaps (looking at the letter opener), even lethal. I think that something she can wear...something that is close to her heart...would be more appropriate...more special...Like a single pearl on a gold chain." Handing the desk set to the sales clerk, Gabby instructed her to gift-wrap it and to, "Put it on my account." "Now," she stated, taking my arm, marching me out of the store, "we are going back to Goldman's, where we will pick out that 'special' gift for your 'special' Rita.

INTERRUPTING MY THOUGHTS of my shopping trip with Gabby, returning to the present, Aunt Rita said, "If it is not too difficult to wait for just a bit I would like the Kaufmans to be down here when you start opening your presents...especially because a fair number of the presents came from them. They are, unfortunately, late risers. Maybe you would like something to eat while we wait for them?"

In the large, expensively out-fitted kitchen, Aunt Rita looked at me, standing across from me at the large center island, her hands clutching the edge tightly. "We have not been as close these last few weeks," she complained; "ever since your startling announcement. I wish we could go back to those earlier times when we were so close...when we shared our deepest thoughts. It is not that I have changed my feelings towards you...I still love you so very much! But, now I am reluctant to share my feelings with you...when whoever is sharing your body may be listening. It is awkward, it is scary to know that someone else is listening in, hearing everything we say. I so hoped that this would be your best Christmas ever…and I don't want to spoil it for you."

I was just about to tell Aunt Rita that, as far as I was concerned, she had been wonderful, when Gabby and Dr. K walked into the kitchen, looking as if they have been up for hours; smiling, laughing, looking at us like we had forgotten it was Christmas morning. "Come on…come on, kids," Gabby commanded in her most effervescent voice, "we have so many presents to open… and a plane to Mexico to catch!"

The rest of the morning was so exciting, with presents, boxes, wrapping-paper, ribbons thrown everywhere, with each of us moving about handing out presents, receiving presents, looking at and admiring each others' presents, finally collapsing in our chairs exhausted – but smiling – amidst all of the loot and clutter; looking like a band of brigands who have successfully raided the camel caravan from the Orient. I was totally overwhelmed by the out-pouring – the bicycle, the wallet stuffed with five one-hundred dollar bills, the ice skates, the sled, the camera, the microscope, the pocket-knife – things that every red-blooded, almost twelve-year old American boy dreams about possessing.

There was so much stuff heaped on me, that I didn't know when or how I was going to use it all, or how I could ever thank these wonderful people, especially the Kaufmans – who I hadn't even met until six-months ago; suddenly feeling very guilty that I had not even thought to give them a present. *Maybe I can find something in Mexico to give to them? I also need to thank Gabby for helping me pick out the presents for Rita, especially the pearl necklace – she liked it so much…much more so than the desk-set.* Gabby, Dr. K and Rita exchanged presents which consisted mainly of clothes – including resort clothes for the trip to Acapulco – jewelry, and other grownup stuff; although Gabby gave Dr. K a new 16mm movie camera and a portable tape recorder.

CHAPTER 24

BIG CHIEF TABLET TWENTY-ONE | FRITZ

Several months have passed since the superabundant Christmas at the Kaufmans, followed by the trip to Acapulco's tropical paradise. While I tended to 'unplug' from Jack during the cold winter months in Missouri – thereby escaping the numbing cold Jack is exposed to – I quickly found the climate in Acapulco to be delightful. Besides, the sights and sounds of Mexico were an experience not to be ignored. The resort, nestled in the hills, overlooking the rocky shores of the blue Pacific Ocean, was breathtaking, as were the beautiful women lounging around the pool, many of whom were Europeans, speaking languages so familiar to my ears, evoking feelings of homesickness. I encouraged Jack to spend as much time by the pool as he could without raising eyebrows.

Jack had then been shipped off to boarding school, making the only time that Jack had access to his Aunt Rita was on those weekends that he was allowed to go home. Jack was once again lonely and perplexed; struggling with the idea that Rita had rejected him. Being tossed into military school in the middle of the year would be particularly difficult for any young man; but it was worse for Jack who was suffering through another major upheaval in his life. With my military background I was able to assist Jack to adapt to the military regime and discipline he was experiencing for the first time in his life. I could also prepare Jack for dealing with the difficulties of living with other young men at close quarters – the night-time taunting, rough-housing, licentious groping – that are the hallmarks of military life; as well as distinguishing between which boys are the good-guys and which are the bullies, the troublemakers.

All-in-all, Jack adapted quite well to these interpersonal aspects of the academy. He also adapted to the academics – where he was actually better prepared than Rita feared he would be with his parochial-school back ground. It was with Jack's perception of Rita's feeling towards him that I was of no help, since I too, sensed a significant change in Rita's attitude toward, and her treatment of, Jack. I came to the conclusion that this change in Rita was traceable back to Jack's disclosure of my presence. My conclusion – indeed, my concern – was verified one weekend in early May which Jack was spending at home.

It was a lovely spring Saturday morning; the sun was pouring in through the dining-room's opened casement windows, the birds were chirping happily, and the animal smells of the farm filled the dining room with a pungent aroma. Jack was sitting in his usual spot telling Rita about cadet life, and I was daydreaming about my youthful days in the German countryside, oblivious to the conversation taking place between Rita and Jack, seated at opposite ends of the long, spacious dining room table. I was wrested away from my thoughts when Jack interrupted my reverie: Fritz! Fritz!

Yes, Jack.

Jack said: *Aunt Rita wants to speak with you...I think she is ready to listen to your story.*

Okay. How much time do I have?

Jack replied: *I think she wants to tell you that herself.*

Fine...I'm ready whenever she is.

"Fritz – whatever-your-last-name-is," Rita began in a commanding tone of voice, "I assume that you are 'plugged-in', and that you are listening to what I am saying to you."

Wearing a plain white blouse, Rita was seated in her usual arm chair at the head of the table, with her back to the open windows; the backlight of sunlight making it difficult for me to discern clearly her features and expressions. On the highly-polished table were stacks of books and periodicals within arms-reach. Immediately in front of her was a thick tablet of lined paper, a container filled with various writing implements, and a pitcher of water and a drinking glass. I was immediately puzzled and alarmed by the scene in front of me. *Is this to be an interview, or is it an interrogation?*

"Although I am not inclined," she continued caustically ...looking and acting like an angry school-teacher, "to believe anything that comes from the mouth of a Nazi officer...particularly from one who has been shot under questionable circumstances...I am prepared to listen to your story, but only on the following conditions. My preference is that you...not Jack...will be speaking to me, using your own voice, rather than in Jack's voice. Second, I expect to interrupt your narration with occasional questions...requests for clarification. Third, you will provide specific information concerning your family...including, names, dates, places...that I can use for verification purposes. Finally, I am giving you twelve hours...six hours today and six hours tomorrow...to convince me that you really are who you say you are, and that the events you are attempting to describe to me are true...justifying my further consideration of your situation.

"In all fairness to you, I am skeptical...I am distrustful...and I am doubtful that you will be able to convince me that your quest for closure is genuine. You may have been able to convince a young boy...an impressionable, love starved boy...searching for acceptance...that you are some-kind of a hero searching for your killer, but I can assure you that I come from a totally different background: I am the widow of a Jewish doctor murdered by Nazis artillery in Italy while he was tending to wounded American soldiers fighting to free Europe from Hitler's tyranny. How do I know that you aren't personally responsible for the death of American soldiers, or Jews in the Holocaust? Until you can convince me otherwise, you are just another Nazi thug...deserving justice...certainly not mercy!"

Jack. If I am going to meet your Aunt Rita's conditions, I will have to take control of your voice – and that means that I will have to try to take control of your brain and your body, at least for a while. Just because I can hear through your ears and see through your eyes – when I am "plugged-in," that does not necessarily indicate that I can talk with your voice. Hearing and seeing are passive activities...and do not require that I can control or interfere with what you see and hear...while speaking requires some action on my part which may or may not impact the quality of your voice. Even if I can take control of your voice, the voice Rita hears may still sound just like you. If I am not be able to talk to her in my voice you will have to explain to Rita that I have failed to comply with her condition...and ask her if there is an acceptable alternative. If I am successful, and as soon as I have finished my story to Rita's satisfaction, I will return control entirely to you. I would like your permission to proceed.

Jack said: *Fritz, I don't know what to do. I'm scared. What if something goes wrong...and I can't be in control again? What happens then? Am I lost...forever?*

I can't imagine what can go wrong, Jack. As soon as I have satisfied Aunt Rita's concerns, I'll simply "unplug" and you will be back in charge.

Jack questioned: *But what if you decide not to "unplug"...What happens then?*

Jack. Jack. Please – I have given you my promise that I would never take control of your body...So why would I go back on that promise now?

Jack stated: *But that's what you want to do right now...You want to break that promise. Why is it all right now to take control of my body? If I let you take control of my body today, what assurances do I have that you won't take control in the future – with or without my permission?*

Jack! Don't you trust me? Have I ever given you a reason not to trust me? Haven't I taken care of you...Haven't I saved your life?

Jack argued: *Yes, you have, but you have had reasons of your own to keep me alive...Without me...Without my body, you would be lost...You would be trapped here in America. Besides, I've only heard your side of the story. Maybe I ought to be more skeptical – like Rita is skeptical. How do I know you aren't a "Nazi thug?"*

If I were a "Nazi thug" why would we even be having this discussion... Why would I have even bothered to ask your permission to take control of your body? I would have simply "taken-over." But I don't want to "take-over" your body permanently...only for a short while. So, will you help me, please?

"WITWE KAUFMAN. ICH entschulidge mich fur Sprechen-Deutschen. Let me begin again: I apologize for speaking to you in German; it is an old habit. Widow Kaufman, my name is Frederick von Bruckner, but my family and friends call me "Fritz." I agree to each of your conditions, including speaking directly to you in what I hope is my own voice...it is difficult to control the vocal chords of a young boy...so I hope you can tell that it is me...and not Jack...who you are hearing.

"I am willing to concede that the voice that I am hearing sounds different from Jack's voice," the widow Kaufman acknowledged unenthusiastically. "I do want to commend you for not addressing me as 'Aunt Rita'. I am not your 'Aunt Rita'."

Yes, Witwe Kaufman, I understand that. May I continue to address you as Witwe Kaufman, or would you prefer that I address you in another manner?

"Mrs. Kaufman will do just fine. I see no need for you to keep reminding me of my Jon's untimely, unnecessary death."

"Forgive me. I did not intend to be so callous. I very much appreciate you giving me this opportunity to tell my story of who I am, and of the events leading up to my unexpected, untimely death. I know that you are skeptical of what you have learned about me through Jack...including the fact that Jack and I occupy the same body. I don't know of any way that I can address your skepticism except by telling you the truth about myself and about what has happened to me. It is as much a mystery to me as it is to you as to how, and why, I came to co-occupy Jack's body. I can only attribute my being here to being an act of God.

"I can understand your skepticism. I believe that I have demonstrated to you that I am real, that I am sharing Jack's body by virtue of the fact that I am talking to you now in my own voice. I also believe that I can convince you that I am not a 'Nazi thug' by telling you verifiable information about me that is the antithesis of being a 'Nazi thug'. Indeed, my mission is to locate and – if possible – deal with the 'Nazi thug' who I believe took my life when I had identified his role in the systematic murder of Jews and the good German people trying to shield them from extermination. In this regard, I am sorry for the death of your husband...Herr Doktor Kaufman... and of all those poor Jewish people who were exterminated during the awful Holocaust. I can assure you that I never killed any American during the war, and that my family and I were personally involved in efforts to shield...and to help to escape...hundreds...perhaps thousands...of Jews. But, all of that will be covered in the story that I will tell you, much of which can be verified by the American P38 pilot...Pete Roberts.

"Are you currently in total control of Jack's mind and body?" Mrs. Kaufman interjected with a concerned look.

No, and yes. I am currently in control of Jack's brain and body, but not his mind.

"Well, then, where is Jack right now?" she demanded with a frown.

As far as I know, he is simply "unplugged" from his brain, like he is in a coma.

"How long can he survive being in a coma...'unplugged' as you de-scribe it?"

I believe he can remain in his current state indefinitely...just like I can when I am "unplugged."

"If you can plug into Jack's brain whenever you want to, why can't Jack just plug back in right now?" Mrs. Kaufman asked insistently.

My mind, my spirit, my personality, is stronger, more robust than Jack's. He can't keep me "unplugged," but I once I have "plugged-in," Jack simply does not have the power to over-ride my presence.

"But, aren't there times when you both are plugged into Jack's brain... How, then, can that happen?" she observed incredulously.

"Only because I let that happen."

"Oh!" Mrs. Kaufman stated, as if suddenly realizing the full measure of my presence; the true extent of my power over Jack. Then, as if she has had another thought, she inquired, "If you are in complete control, what you are seeing right now."

"I am looking directly at you...staring at your face, your eyes. Because the light is shining brightly behind you, I am having trouble discerning your handsome face's finer features. As best I can tell, you are frowning, your jaw is clenched, your lips are tightly closed...and your usually bright, smiling eyes, are giving me a cold, hostile look...a look that I have never observed when you look at your beloved Jack."

"Let me speak to Jack...Right now!" she commanded.

Jack...Your Aunt Rita wants to speak to you.

Jack responded: *"Yes, Aunt Rita, what do you want?"*

"Jack. I want to know if you are okay," she inquired anxiously.

"I think that I am scared...I don't know what is going on...I've been "unplugged," and I can't seem to get "plugged" back in... It's like I'm in a dark hole where I can't see, hear, smell, or feel anything...I don't know whether I am alive or dead."

"We can't have this happen," Rita complained somberly. "You've made your point, Herr von Bruckner. You have convinced me that you are a real spirit occupying Jack's body...having the power to completely take control of Jack's brain and body, rendering him isolated and terrified...If we are to proceed any further, you...Herr Kraut...are going to have to find a way to keep Jack 'plugged-in'."

"But Frau Kaufman, Jack gave me his permission to take control of his body...so that I could talk to you in my own voice – which was one of your conditions...So that you would know that I am real...To convince you that what you are hearing coming from Jack's mouth is not just something that Jack has made up. I told Jack that I have no intention of keeping control of his body...or his brain...beyond the time it takes for me to tell you my story. I am truly sorry if I have alarmed you...and frightened Jack...I am sure that we can figure out a way to allow me to tell my story in my own voice...without excluding Jack entirely from the process."

"Since I have now heard what you are saying in a voice that is not Jack's ...and in a voice you claim to be yours, I have no need to have to listen to you in a voice other than Jack's voice...Besides, I am not sure I like to listen to your voice...if indeed it is your voice that I am hearing...and I certainly don't like the idea that you are looking at me with what have become your own eyes...making judgments about me based upon my facial expressions. So why don't you just communicate to Jack what you want me to listen to, and then Jack...in his own voice...can tell me what he thinks I need to know. You can communicate with Jack without taking total control of Jack, can't you?"

"Yes, of course I can Frau Kaufman, but believe me, there are things that you need to know about me that are better heard coming directly from me, rather than second-hand through Jack. Please let me at least begin my story directly in my own voice about things that I have already told Jack. Then, if you and Jack are still uncomfortable with my taking control of Jack's brain and body...for even just that amount of time, we can adopt your approach."

"As I said earlier, you have made your main point; that you are a real person...or 'the spirit' of a real person...now co-occupying Jack's body in some way. Right now, I'm not sure that there is anything more I need to know about you. All I need to know about you is your presence, and of the risk that you pose to Jack...and to me...a grown man living in a young man's body, able to take control of that body whenever it pleases you. But let see how it goes for today...Let's see if you can tell your story in your own voice without 'unplugging' Jack, without putting Jack into a coma...Is that all right with you, Jack?"

"Yes, I guess so...But how will you know if I am 'unplugged?'"

"I'll let Herr Fritz talk to me about himself for a short-while, and then I will ask again to speak with you. If you tell me that you are able to see and hear as you normally do, then I'll let Fritz continue talking to me in his own voice. But, if you tell me you have been totally 'unplugged' then I'll stop this approach and we will revert to my suggested approach...After all, we are not in any rush to accommodate Herr Nazi's perceived schedule. Any problem with that Herr...who did you state you were?"

"I am Fritz von Bruckner, Frau Kaufman, and what you have suggested is fine with me. I was born in Potsdam, Germany on March 21, 1910. My parents are...excuse me, were...Kurt Baron von Bruckner and the Countess Ursala von Poppenhaus. I am the middle-child of five children: Marta, Wolfgang, me, Ernst and Maria. My formative years were spent at my parent's...actually, my mother's family – estate just outside of Potsdam, which is itself just outside of Berlin. My parents were both Catholic, and my brothers and sisters attended Catholic primary and secondary schools.

"When I was eighteen...and had successfully passed the Abitur, which is an examination that is used to determine if the candidate is qualified to pursue higher education, my father...the Baron...enrolled me in the Technische Universitat Carolo-Wilhelmina zu Braunschweig...the oldest, most prestigious school of technology in Germany. The Baron was a prominent builder of civilian aircraft, and he wanted me to follow in his footsteps... both as an engineer and as a pilot.

"In the First War, the Baron had been a pilot, but quickly demonstrated his ability to understand the fledgling technology of designing and building military aircraft, especially fighter aircraft. He was responsible for the development of many improvements to the maneuverability and safety of the aircraft, becoming friends with many of the more outstanding pilots... especially Baron von Richthofen, Ernst Udet, and Herman Goering.

"Because of the political power and reputation he acquired through his role in the development and procurement of new fighter aircraft, as well as the retrofitting of existing aircraft, the Baron accumulated important friendships...as well as some important enemies...within the aircraft industry. During the years following the First War, the Baron achieved considerable success designing and manufacturing precision equipment incorporated into aircraft built by the major aircraft firms.

"At the time that I graduated from the Institute, the Baron's firm was still designing and manufacturing sophisticated, precision aircraft parts, and building a few of his own radical design aircraft for civilian use. At this time...the early 1930s...Germany was still prohibited by the Versailles Treaty from building or using military aircraft...consequently all aircraft being built in Germany were civilian aircraft...to be used by civilian pilots in civilian-pilot clubs. In fact, I first learned to fly an airplane in just such a club.

"The political climate in Germany was quite unstable, with the upstart National Socialists, and their upstart leader...Adolf Hitler...embarking on plans to take over the government...the Weimar Republic...and to dismantle the much despised Versailles Treaty. The Baron foresaw an upswing in aircraft manufacturing...especially military aircraft...once the Versailles Treaty was unilaterally repudiated by the new German government.

"Like many industrialists, the Baron had little love for Herr Hitler, but thinking that once Hitler had come to power, he could be controlled by the industrialists and the military. In the Baron's view, Hitler's role would be limited, and when von Hindenburg died, the monarchy would be restored. Fortunately, the Baron kept these views to himself...at least for several years. Unfortunately, the Baron's belief that Hitler could be controlled was...as history has demonstrated...dead wrong.

"The Baron...and my mother the Countess...believed that they owed an obligation to the Fatherland to do what they could to prevent Germany from becoming embroiled in any further wars, or from engaging in social programs that pitted one class of Germans against other classes. Each of us children was instructed in the benefits of peace and prosperity for all Germans...and we were encouraged to do whatever we could in our chosen professions and careers to promote these ideals.

"This, of course, involved making some unsavory choices, and incurring some considerable personal risks. For example, the Baron renewed his friendships with a number of Nazi super-luminaries, like Herman Goering...who he quickly identified as a person of enormous power and influence within Hitler's close circle...in order for the Baron to have access to critical information about Germany's destiny under Hitler and his Nazi cronies. This necessitated that the Baron 'hold his nose' and join the Nazi party.

"It was through his contacts and friendships with the Nazi powerful that the Baron was able to place my brothers and me in positions within the government and the military where we could, hopefully, be able to influence and direct critical decisions. My older brother, Wolfgang, a trained economist, became the aide to Dr. Hjalmar Schacht, the President of the Reichsbank, who worked the miracle of saving Germany from bankruptcy. Ernst, my younger brother, went to the military academy where he excelled academically, finding a billet in military intelligence...ultimately working directly with Admiral Canariss, the head of the German intelligence service.

"Through his contacts in the *Luftwaffe*, the Baron was able to place me in a civilian job with the fledgling Air Ministry...where, through my exemplary work on the Stuka dive bomber, and the fact that I was the Baron's son, I came to the attention of Generals Erhard Milch and Ernst Udet, and Reichsminister Goering. I was ordered commissioned as a *Hauptmann* (Captain) in the *Luftwaffe*, and assigned to work with General Udet on a special new aircraft...an aircraft so advanced in design and propulsion, which if properly developed and manufactured, would guarantee that the skies over Germany would be impregnable to enemy aircraft.

"Like you, Mrs. Kaufman, I, too, have lost my one, true love. My beautiful young bride, Elise, or Lisa...as I called her...was killed in a night-time bombing raid on Potsdam by English aircraft in late 1944. Lisa and I were married at Christmas in 1937, after a brief courtship, spending an idyllic honeymoon in the Austrian Alps, never dreaming that in less than a few months time Herr Hitler would start us on the path to war and destruction. My first inkling that Germany was headed for conflict came about when Lisa and I returned from our honeymoon trip. It arrived in the form of a summons from my superior, General Ernst Udet, to meet with him immediately at the Air Ministry, bringing with me all of my materials on the production forecasts for the most current version, as well as for any future planned versions, of the Stuka dive bomber.

"Excuse me, Herr von Bruckner," Frau Kaufman interrupted. "I hate to interrupt your flow of thought, but I need to check with Jack, as we agreed, to determine whether he has been 'plugged in', whether he has been hearing what you have been telling me."

"Frau Kaufman, I am afraid that I have been unable to keep Jack 'plugged in'. He has not been participating in the telling of my story... he has not heard what you have heard. I apologize...but may I continue, please?"

"Of course not," Frau Kaufman exclaimed brusquely. "You know what I told you...if Jack is not participating then you may not continue. I see no reason to change my mind on this."

"But, Frau Kaufman..."

"There are no 'buts'," she quickly interjected, the color rising in her cheeks. "We had a deal, and you have not been able to carry out your end of the deal...And since you have failed to keep your end of the bargain, I will not enter into a dialogue with you. I will listen to your tale...and maybe it's only a fairy-tale...from Jack's lips, in Jack's voice. So if you want me to listen to your story, you will have to tell it to Jack first. That may take longer, but as I said before, we have lots of time to sort this out, including finding ways to verify your story. And one of the people you have identified as being able to verify your story...Pete Roberts...is still battling another band of thugs in Korea...and may not be back in the

States for several years. So just cool your heels Kraut-boy!"

"Is that why you have sent Jack away to a boarding school?"

"It is none of your business what I do with Jack. I love Jack more than you can ever know. All I want is for Jack to be happy...and to be safe... And from what I have now heard from your mouth...what you are capable of doing to Jack, I know that I must find some way to get you out of Jack's body, quickly...and permanently. Right now, though, I want you to 'unplug' yourself from Jack, putting him back in control of his brain and body...and I never want to learn that you have ever taken control of his body again. And don't you dare do anything to harm Jack. If you do, I'll know; and you will pay...pay dearly. You don't want to fuck with me on this! I hold all of the cards."

Don't be so sure about that! You really don't know who you are dealing with.

CHAPTER 25

BIG CHIEF TABLET TWENTY-TWO | JACK

I was suddenly snapped back into the present, as if awakening from a deep sleep, not certain of where I was or of how long I had been absent, shocked to see Aunt Rita still sitting at the other end of the shiny dining table, looking at me with angry eyes, her mouth opening.

"Do you understand?" she shouted at me angrily.

"Do I understand what?" I asked in a startled voice, puzzled as to what was happening.

"Is that you, Jack?" her voice now more quizzical than angry.

"Yes," I responded hesitantly; not certain as to what has just transpired that would cause her to ask me such a question.

"Jack, I have to be sure that it is really you."

"Why?" I asked, now even more puzzled.

"Because," she responded, with obvious frustration, "that devious Kraut bastard has made me so angry...that I ordered him to get 'unplugged' and to stay 'unplugged'. I don't trust him that he will do what I have ordered him to do. So I have to know that it is really you, Jack, who is in control...and it is with you who I am having this conversation."

"It is really me...I don't feel that Fritz is even 'plugged-in' right now. I feel alone."

"I guess I'll just have to trust that it really is just you, Jack. I wish there was some kind of signal that just you and I know about that proves it is you. Otherwise, I'll have to be always on my guard whenever you are around."

This is awful! What has Fritz done to make Aunt Rita so angry that she doesn't trust him? I have trusted Fritz. Should I not trust him? What is going to happen to my relationship with Aunt Rita?

"I am so scared!" I blurted out, suddenly realizing what was happening. "I need you so much...I need your love and affection so much...I couldn't stand it if you started treating me like a stranger. I'd rather be dead!" I sobbed, feeling the rising panic, feeling the tears running down my cheeks.

"My God, Jack!" Aunt Rita cried out, pushing up out of her chair, knocking it over in her rush to get to me. I was too shocked to arise from my chair, leaving Aunt Rita with no choice but to enfold just my head from behind, forcing her to lean her face over my head, kissing me on my forehead.

Pulling back, Aunt Rita exclaimed, "Jack! Jack! Don't say that. Don't be so foolish! You are my wonderful boy...My delightful son! I love you...I will always love you. I will never treat you like a stranger. We will find a way to deal with having that fucking Fritz in our lives, without destroying all that we have become...I promise!"

With these last words from Aunt Rita, I disentangled from her arms, pushed myself up out of my chair; standing, taking her into my arms daring not to speak, not knowing what to say. *Where do we go on from here? What is going to happen to us? I owe this wonderful woman so much...my life! How will I ever be able to repay her for all that she has done for me?*

BEING THRUST INTO barracks-life immediately after the Christmas holidays had been a difficult, scary experience. There was no welcoming committee when Aunt Rita dumped me off on the sidewalk on a cold winter's afternoon. As a new cadet, I was placed in a barracks already crowded with other young cadets, given a war-surplus metal-frame bed with a used mattress, well-worn sheets and a smelly blanket. The other boys in the barracks had already formed their friendships, they had a history.

Being a second-semester arrival, it was immediately assumed by the other cadets that I had been expelled from another school for disciplinary or academic problems; in other words, a reject to be viewed as just another dreaded cadet 'leper' – one of those cadets who by his behavior, from booger-eating, to bed wetting, to cowardice, has earned the dislike of some or all of the other cadets. I had a small window of opportunity to demonstrate that I was not a 'leper'; I had to quickly earn my way into acceptability: "Guilty until proven innocent," being the first law of the barracks. During those early days, having Fritz within me was a blessing; he was able to instill confidence, guiding me on making friends, avoiding devastating mistakes, and providing me with wisdom on military decorum available only to one who had experienced barracks-life first-hand.

Fritz told me: *You must be patient, Jack, you must be thorough; there are no short-cuts in life, especially in a military environment. You must be disciplined, you must not act rashly...Military life is harsh and unfair. You must expect to be hazed, criticized and punished...even when there is no justification, no reason, or no explanation. Do not cry, do not pout, do not give up...you must show that you are not a coward, or a quitter. Don't expect to be liked by everyone...you will have rivals, you will make enemies. You must be careful who you make your enemy...and you must be very selective in who you choose as your friends. Too many of your fellow cadets have serious problems with truth, honesty, and sexuality...that is why they are probably attending a military academy in the first place... they are discipline problems, and these are the very cadets who will prey upon you...pretending to be your friend...especially if they think that you are lonely, afraid, rejected.*

Throwing myself into cadet life with a good-humored approach, conducting myself like a seasoned cadet, good things began to happen to me. Within a month or so, I found myself accepted by most of my peers, even admired by some, and viewed as a rival by a few of the cadet leaders. There were, of course, a handful of bullies who tried to make my life miserable; I really needed to put on some weight and build up my physique over the summer if I ever hoped to deal adequately with that bunch.

In the mean time, I never backed-down from a bully's challenge, but I always gave him an opportunity to go peacefully on his way.

A group of sixth-grade cadets in my barracks, guided by Drake Powell, a born leader from Iowa, whose cheerful, bright, studious, demeanor had attracted my eye, extended me an invitation to join his friends in an after-school study group. The other members of the group exhibited similar interests and academic accomplishments, including a strong desire for studying hard, playing hard, and watching each other's back. Gaining a reputation as clever, resourceful pranksters, the group came under the watchful scrutiny of the cadet leadership, providing the incentive for the pranksters to engage in more inventive, riskier; but essentially juvenile, harmless adventures.

DURING THE WEEK before the blow-up between Fritz and Aunt Rita that I have reported in another tablet, while things at the academy were still recovering from the Easter break, the pranksters hatched a new plot. Sitting together in the commissary, at their regular table, out of sight under the mezzanine balcony running along three walls, George Franklin, a pink-faced boy with large ears, proposed that we put a small goat in the bell tower on Saturday-night, attaching the bell pull round the goat's neck — so that each time the goat tried to get lose from the rope, it would ring the bell in a random pattern; thereby hopefully disrupting the headmaster's — Colonel Wiggins' — sleep. The loose description of the plan raised a number of questions.

"Who is getting the goat," inquired Wally Blount, a tall, thin, likeable boy from Chillicothe, with a ready smile.

"Where are we going to find a goat?" inquired a nervous Billy Brownwaite, a city boy from somewhere in northern Ohio.

"Even if we find a goat nearby, how are we going to get it here without being spotted?" I inquired, realizing I was the only local member of the gang; the one most likely to be assigned the duty of finding the goat.

"Jack," interjected Drake, pointing at me. "Since you live just on the other side of town, and get to go home for the weekend, you are responsible for getting the goat to us during the day on Saturday. That way, you will not be around when the deed is done."

"But we don't have goats at Fairways," I complained. "Maybe, given a day or two, I'll think of where, between the academy and Fairways, there might be some goats. If I do, then I'm going to need some help bringing the goat here...we'll have to snatch it away without being seen. I don't relish the idea of getting caught stealing a goat. It would help if one of you could get a weekend pass to spend Friday night with me. It would be a hike from Fairways to find a goat, and bring it here, but we could get the goat here on foot. Then it's up to you guys to get the goat up into the bell tower. "

At this point, Fritz raised his concerns: *I applaud your enthusiasm, Jack, but I am concerned about your planning for this risky mission. In fact, I am not sure the hoped-for outcome is commensurate with the effort. I doubt that a young goat wandering about in a belfry will accomplish much in the way of bell ringing. Do you really want to risk possible arrest and expulsion for the theft of a goat, when there will be so little to show for the risk? You really need to think through this project a bit more...you need more, and better, planning.*

"The more I think about this plan...and the risks it imposes," I stated, "I believe that we had better look a little closer at what is being proposed here."

Over the next twenty-minutes, I explained what I saw as the weak-points, the risks of the prank. It took a bit of analytic effort and careful salesmanship, but I was able to persuade my new-found friends, especially Drake – who can, on occasion, be headstrong – that the proposed prank lacked sufficient impact to warrant the peril. It was decided that, in the future, we would use our military learning, cast about for a project with a more impressive, dependable outcome, while incurring minimal risk. *Another time! Better planning! A better result! A bigger BANG!* More importantly, I was able to increase my standing with the group without causing anyone to lose face. The credit for this rise in my popularity – as well as the increase in my self-esteem

– belonged to Fritz. He continued to watch after me, providing me with wise, dependable counsel.

IT WAS, THEREFORE, with ambivalent feelings towards Fritz that I anxiously returned to the barracks that Sunday evening, not knowing whether Aunt Rita's warnings to Fritz – that he must leave me alone – would affect his feelings towards me. I never found out, directly. During the following few weeks – the last weeks of the school year – I had no contact from Fritz during my waking hours. Occasionally, however, at night, just as I was about to fall asleep, I sensed Fritz's presence in my conscious-ness, prowling around in my mind, probing into my thoughts, my memories, searching for a retained vision of my day's activities. These invasions of my mind seemed to last for only a moment or two; perhaps it was because he found – or didn't find – what he was looking for, or maybe I just fell asleep.

I was now worried that Fritz would take control of my body while I was asleep, when I would be unable to know that I was not in control; that he might do something while controlling my body that raised questions among the cadets – questions that I would be unable either to understand or to answer.

———————

WHEN AUNT RITA arrived to pick me up at my dorm on the last day of school, I saw that she was not alone in the big Ford station wagon when it pulled up to where I was standing in the hot sun with my belongings, wishing several of my barracks pals farewell. There was a plain looking woman seated in the front passenger seat I did not recognize. It was only when she stepped out of the station wagon, and Aunt Rita proudly announced her name – Hannah – that I figured out who she might be; she was Gabby's project, the displaced person, the Jewish refugee.

"Hannah has come to live with us. She is going to help me run the farm...to be my companion," Aunt Rita announced cheer-fully, a bright smile on her face – her eyes hidden behind stylish, tortoise-shell sunglasses — an arm draped casually around Hannah's narrow shoulders. *So this is how Aunt Rita plans to handle the problem of ever having to be alone with me and Fritz; she won't ever have to be alone — she will have Hannah with her. But of what help can Hannah be at farm work or how can she be expected to provide anyone with protection? She doesn't look strong enough even to flush the toilet.*

Standing awkwardly in the bright sunlight, clinging to the partially-open station wagon door with one hand, shielding her eyes with her other hand at her brow, this peasant-looking young woman in a formless, plain cotton dress, with dull brown hair, was squinting at me through bespectacled eyes of indeterminate color, offering me a forced, pale-lipped, cheerless smile.

When I approach Aunt Rita to receive my much-anticipated kiss, Hannah quickly pulled away from Aunt Rita, darting back behind the still-open car door. *I only hope that my shock and surprise at seeing Hannah here is not as obvious as is her displeasure at meeting me. What has Aunt Rita told Hannah about me... and about Fritz? Hannah is reacting to my presence here, as if she is looking at the devil himself. What a great summer-vacation this promises to be.*

"Hannah. This is Jack," Aunt Rita stated, trying to pull a reluctant Hannah from behind the car door. "Oh, dear," Aunt Rita muttered as our eyes met, "this is not going as I had planned. Now I have a love-starved pre-adolescent on my hands...plus two war-refugees...a damaged Jewish farm-girl, and an arrogant Kraut spirit."

Watching Aunt Rita's sunny smile fade into a dark frown, I stepped backwards, giving Hannah some additional space, hopefully reducing my apparent threat to Hannah. An approving nod, a knowing smile crossed Aunt Rita's lips; so I returned to the sidewalk, retrieved my luggage, boxes of books, a canvas duffle bag, and lugged them to the rear of the station wagon, heaving them one-at-a-time over the lowered tailgate — into the back of the station wagon; like throwing hay bales onto a farm wagon.

Is this how I am going to spend my summer vacation — finding field work to stay out of the way of Hannah and Aunt Rita?

Maybe I ought to revert to thinking of her as Rita. Well, at least doing farm work will help me build up my muscles. On the ride home to Fairways, I was relegated to the back-seat, providing further evidence of my new status in Rita's life.

Later in the day, while Rita and I were momentarily alone in the kitchen, I asked her, "Why is Hannah here?"

"You know why she is here," she replied tartly.

"Do you really think that this farm-girl Hannah would be any match for Fritz if he decided to take over my body?" I asked.

"Be careful, Jack...you shouldn't judge a book by its cover. You may be surprised by what 'farm-girl' Hannah is capable of doing to a young boy like you."

"But why didn't you tell me...warn me...that you were bringing Hannah into our home?"

"You know damn well why!" Rita said, giving me a fierce, questioning look, her head cocked to one side.

"Oh," I replied dully after a long-minute's pause. *Of course!*

Realizing that any further conversation on this topic would be fruitless, I called for Lady to follow me. Hearing the back-porch screen door slamming with a thud behind me as we reached the bottom of the steps, Lady and I loped off towards the stable, pulling my cap down firmly on my head, bent on adventure. In the past, I would have expected to hear from Fritz by now with some question, some comment, but on that day I heard nothing. *Keeping your head down, Fritz old man? I think I'll do the same!*

THE BEAUTIFUL SPRING weather, with warm breezes making outdoor exploring a day-long priority, and cool nights demanding long-hours of sleep with the windows open, helped me to fulfill my promise to stay out from underfoot. I wolfed-down my bowl of cereal alone in the kitchen, and ate my lunch on the run munching on a well-aged, waxpaper-wrapped peanut butter sandwich pulled from the back-pocket of my blue-jeans. Not really being "country-folk," the evening dinner was the main, big meal.

By my keeping away from the house, Rita resorted to ringing

the dinner bell — a large cast-iron bell, like the one on a steam locomotive — to summon me home to dinner. The meal, prepared by Rita — with assistance from her apprentice, Hannah — was served at the kitchen table, usually consisting of a meat, a vegetable, some form of potatoes, and a substantial desert; all food designed to build bodies and restore good health — mine and Hannah's. After dinner, I helped clean the table, dried the dishes, fed Lady, and took out the garbage — which was thrown over the fence into the chicken yard.

One evening, a few weeks after Hannah's arrival, by the time I finished my chores and re-entered the house, Rita and Hannah had moved from the kitchen into the study, with Hannah now sitting in what had been my wing chair, paging through an aging Life magazine. I grabbed a newer Saturday Evening Post from the stack on the table as Lady and I passed through the room, out the screen-door, onto the front porch, pulling my rocker closer to the porch rail, dropping down into the rocker, placing my feet on the top of the porch rail, Lady circling to find just the right spot to lie down at my side. The slightly warm evening air was filled with Martins and Swifts, circling, diving, calling out, devouring the flying insects, like P38s attacking, destroying Me 109s. *Where is Pete Roberts? When is he coming home? When will Rita receive her verification of Fritz's tale, so we can get him back to Germany, and out of my life?*

My thoughts were interrupted by the squeak of the screen door opening, causing me to look back, over my shoulder, in that direction, to where I saw Rita stepping out onto the porch, a bowl in her hand, Hannah trailing closely behind.

"I hope we're not interrupting anything, but I thought you might like a bowl of freshly churned chocolate ice cream," she remarked cheerfully.

"Sure," I grunted with all the enthusiasm I could muster, dropping my feet to the floor, pulling myself up out of my rocker.

"I showed Hannah how to prepare and churn the mixture...I think she did a really good job...You need to try it," Rita stated matter-of-factly, handing me the bowl, which I received looking at it skeptically.

I suppose that this is some kind of a peace offering: What do I do, what do I say, if the ice cream is awful?

Taking a small spoonful of the chocolate ice cream — which is my favorite — holding it in my mouth, savoring the flavor, I was pleasantly surprised at how good it tasted. *This ice cream tastes really good! But do I dare compliment Hannah? Why am I reluctant to praise Hannah? Is it just because I am unhappy that she is here stealing away Rita's affections? Am I afraid that I will be under some obligation to Hannah if I say how much I enjoy the ice cream? But it sure is good ice cream.*

Taking another spoonful of the delicious ice cream, I concluded that maybe I ought to give Hannah the benefit of the doubt. "This is very good ice cream, Hannah," I expressed as I swallowed the delicious delight, giving Hannah my biggest, brightest smile. This earned me an especially glowing smile — and a telling wink — from Rita, and a cautious smile from a blushing Hannah.

"May we sit with you while you finish the ice cream?" Rita inquired sweetly, motioning me — when I moved towards the porch-rail — to sit down again in my rocker, while taking her place in the rocking-chair next to mine, directing Hannah to sit on the broad porch-railing facing us. *What does this mean — me in the rocking-chair, Hannah on the porch rail? Is this another peace offering?*

"Jack," Rita stated when I have finished scraping the last bit of melting ice cream from the bowl, "We have all been so busy over the last several days...with you reacquainting yourself with Lady and Fairways, and with me showing Hannah what it takes to keep Fairways going...that we have not had the chance to let you and Hannah to get to know one another. We are going to be sharing a lot of space and time together, and it just makes sense that you learn all you can about Hannah.

"I'm afraid that I have told Hannah a great deal about you, but you know precious-little about Hannah. Hannah has told me some things about herself, but I know that there is still much more to tell. So, if you are not too busy doing something else this evening, I will ask Hannah to begin to tell you about her experiences in the War, and about the Germans and the Jews.

"I know," Rita continued, "that Fritz has told you some things about his experiences in Germany, the War, and the Jews...but I believe that you would profit from hearing about those things from a person who is here, in her own skin and bones...talking with us face-to-face...with a different perspective. I am not saying that Hannah's story is reliable, and that Fritz's story is not. Only time...and further verification...will tell us who we can safely rely upon. Hopefully, both versions are reliable...and, if so, then we can all work together to solve how to get Fritz back home, and how to get him out of your body."

"How long will it take for Hannah to tell me her story," I asked politely. "It took Fritz a long time...over several years...to tell me his story."

"I am sure that what Hannah has to tell us will take several weeks...but not years, I hope," Aunt Rita observed somewhat cautiously.

"Yes, Jack," Hannah interjected in her broken English, "I veal try to tell you my story fast, but wary complete. I vaunt you to know all about me. Then maybe veal can be goot friends. Please forgive my poor use of the English. I veal try warry hard to make mine self understood."

This should be interesting. I wonder what Fritz will think about all of this?

As if reading my mind, Rita remarked, "Since Fritz has, if I remember correctly, only told us about things that happened to him before the War began, I think it only fair that before Hannah tells us her entire story...most of the relevant parts taking place after the War began...that Fritz tell us the remainder of his story... the part that takes place after the war began. I think Fritz's story will put a lot of what happened to Hannah during the war into context. Now that we have the whole summer-vacation before us, this should give Fritz plenty of time to provide us with his version of what happened to the Germans, the Poles, the Russians, and the Jews after 1939. It will also give us plenty of time to digest what he has to say."

"Can you tell me Jack," Rita continued, "whether Fritz is listening in, or whether you need to contact him?"

"I don't think Fritz is listening in...I haven't felt his presence during the daytime...at least not since you last spoke to him. *I also have not recently felt him prowling around in my mind as I nod off to sleep.* Have you told Hannah about Fritz?"

"No more than what you...and the Kraut...have told me about who he is, and of how he can take control of your body...just enough to scare Hannah, just enough to make her wary to be around you alone. So you had better get in touch with Fritz, letting him know that he needs to tell you his story, so you can tell Hannah and me. Remember, I don't want him taking control of your body. If he can tell his story directly to Hannah and me without taking over your body, that's fine...and we will listen to him. But if he can't do it that way, then you will have to relay his story to us...just like your St. Louis Cardinals broadcast the play-by-play of their away-from-home baseball games using some-one reading from a ticker-tape."

"I'll see what I can do," I said.

"In the meantime, Jack, as long as we are all together, and Fritz is not tuned in, I want Hannah to tell you a little bit about herself, so that you can see that Hannah is a friend...not a threat."

She may be your friend, and that makes her a threat to me — as long as she is the recipient of your affections; the affections that used to be mine alone.

Sensing my lingering jealously towards Hannah — perhaps by observing the set of my jaw in the dwindling twilight — Rita reached her hand across the space between our rocking chairs, and gently, but firmly, placed her long fingers on the back of my hand, carefully interlacing her fingers with mine, just like she used to do during our close-moments together here on the porch, but now causing a new, pleasurable sensation in the pit of my stomach. *I sure hope that this funny feeling doesn't arouse Fritz's interest into what is going on here. The last thing I need right now is to have Fritz grilling me about my confused feelings, my sexual arousal.* But I did nothing to extricate my fingers from Rita's; letting the thrill block out my concerns about how Fritz might react.

With the darkening sky — dotted here and there with faint

starlight — serving as her backdrop, Hannah began her narrative, her thin voice barely competing with the growing volume of cricket and frog noises filling the night-time air.

"I AM NOT sure where to begin, so I will tell you who I am now. I am a Jewish refugee, a displaced person who made it through the War in Europe, avoiding the German death camps, the only known survivor of my family. Although I was born and raised in Poland, I was found by American soldiers in what was to become the Russian sector of Germany at the end of the War. One of the nuns from the convent that was run by some German Catholic nuns who were hiding me from the SS, a special group of German military who ran the death camps, and I escaped from Posen and reached the American soldiers before we were about to be captured by the Russian soldiers. I was fifteen years old, though I looked much younger. I was placed in a displaced persons camp somewhere in West Germany, where I lived for several years while different groups tried to locate any living relatives that might have survived the Holocaust.

"The area of Poland where my family had lived for generations, Silesia, was dotted with small villages, some populated almost entirely by Jews, which did not even show up on maps, and no longer exist. No remnants of my family were ever found. So I was given the choice to either relocate to somewhere else in Poland, or to move to the new state of Israel in Palestine, or to find a sponsor in America. Fortunately for me there were Jewish women in America...like Gabby Kaufman...who offered to help me find a new home in the United States. It took a while... sometimes it felt like forever...for these kind women to find me a place where I could make a new life, putting the terrors of the past behind me. That is why I am here with your Aunt Rita now, with someone who is willing to talk with me, to help me adapt to the new world, to turn my nightmares into dreams."

"Jack," stated Rita in her most solicitous tone, still gripping my fingers, "You are, and you shall always be, the apple of my eye. I love you dearly, and you are the everlasting object of my affection. But right now, as you can now tell from even the briefest telling of her story, Hannah needs our love and affection. You have suffered at the hands of your mother, and for this I am bound...as your new mother...to shower you with the love and affection that you were so cruelly denied. As badly as you have suffered, Hannah has suffered terribly at the hands of vicious, horrible people. You have heard only a portion of what happened to Hannah. In time, you will learn...as I have...just how difficult her journey was."

Rita continued, "Jack, I need your help, Hannah needs your help...we need your understanding, your willingness to share some of the love and affection that I have showered on you. If nothing else, please be patient with me, with Hannah. Can you think of Hannah as your sister; the sister you never had... the sister who has been treated by your mother in the same way you were treated...the sister who is in pain...the sister who has been starved for love and affection as you were...the sister who needs the brotherly love you wished you had received from your brothers? Can you do that for me, Jack...for Hannah? Will you think about it?"

"Oh, yes. But I don't know what it is that I can do to help," I said.

"Don't worry, Jack...Hannah and I will guide you. Thank you!"

Then I heard Fritz: *Yes, Jack, we'll all help you.*

Oh, damn. How much did you hear?

Fritz said: *Enough, Jack. Yes, just enough.*

CHAPTER 26

BIG CHIEF TABLET TWENTY-THREE | FRITZ

The worst thing about arriving late at a gathering is not having heard what others have said about you before you arrive. That's how I felt when some unusual nerve impulses leaped across from Jack's brain to mine, causing me to hook into Jack's consciousness at the tail-end of an emotional outburst from the widow Kaufman. I heard just enough to comprehend that she was assuring Jack that she still loved him, and would assist him in accepting the pitiful, damaged Hannah as his sister. *What rubbish! What contemptible, shabby behavior; to use Jack in such a wretched manner, cleverly milking his naïve good nature with such obvious Jew-loving Schwachsinn!*

But then I concluded that the widow Kaufman's tact with Jack was more than Jew versus German outrage; it was sexual manipulation. Upon further reflection, I recognized that the unusual nerve activity I received from Jack's brain was actually sexual arousal brought about by the widow Kaufman's amorous hand-holding. *The widow Kaufman is one cold, calculating, clever Miststuck; using one of the oldest tricks in the book, bending Jack to her will through his libido! Poor Jack, he is just so ripe for picking.* As much as I would like to save him from being taken advantage of in such a shameless fashion, I couldn't risk alienating myself from the widow Kaufman any more than I already had.

The best thing for me to do was to hold my own feelings in check, letting Jack work out on his own how he responded to Hannah's exaggerated plight. I am sorry that I did not hear all of what Hannah was telling Jack about what had occurred during the War that requires such special handling of Hannah. There was something about Hannah, and her developing relationship with the widow Kaufman, that I needed to learn more about. It was becoming clear to me that Hannah's presence here had less to do with healing Hannah's alleged problems, and more to do with my presence in Jack's body.

It was also clear to me that if I was to prove my theory correct, I would need to hear more details about Hannah's odyssey; I was convinced that there was much information that the widow Kaufman was withholding from Jack and, therefore, from me. I supposed that if I was going to learn what was going on, I must complete my tale first — giving the widow Kaufman my version of how well-meaning Germans tried in vain to stop the horrors of the Nazi regime — before she will grant me access to Hannah's information.

EACH EVENING, OVER the next several weeks, Jack began the process of presenting the balance of my story of deception, treason and failure in Germany — the period from January 1938 until my untimely death in May 1945; my Germany, a proud Germany which plunged from invincibility to utter ruin at the hands of corrupt, evil, deranged leaders. Rather than try to tell the tale in my own voice — running the risk of "unplugging" Jack and incurring an expansion of the widow Kaufman's already obvious dislike — I delivered the narrative through Jack. It was a difficult task — requiring me to carefully flood Jack's mind with small batches of pertinent memories, relying upon Jack to assimilate them into his consciousness; and in some cases reading what I had written down and expressing them as his own. From my standpoint, the end-product had little of the immediacy and impact that I would have preferred.

Because Jack had to concentrate, focusing on reading what he had recorded of my memories or what I had written, he could not look at his audience, thereby denying me the opportunity to observe, through Jack's eyes, the facial reactions of the widow Kaufman and Hannah as they listened to what Jack was relaying to them. Even more disturbing; they sat there in stone-silence, making no comments, asking no questions. The following are my memories of those tumultuous times, those world-changing events, and those shattered dreams, as told by Jack to the widow Kaufman and the Jewess Hannah.

THE WEATHER WAS cold and bleak in Potsdam on that January day in 1938, with a smell of snow in the air, when Lisa and I arrived home from our winter honeymoon in the Austrian Alps; a small foretaste of what awaited me at the Air Ministry. There was little else to indicate what was in store for me, for us; the trains and the stations were packed with happy-faced travelers, as were the avenues, boulevards and the stores and restaurants that received and discharged cheery, vocal customers and patrons. I had never seen Potsdam or Berlin so vibrant, so filled with enthusiasm and Gemutlichkeit; it was as if the volks had decided to celebrate Christmas for an extra month that year.

Even in Lisa's mother, Helga's, cozy home, where things had been tight and Spartan for as long as I had known Lisa, there existed a relaxed atmosphere of modest prosperity, persistent hope. Helga arranged a small dinner-party, consisting mainly of my family and a few close friends from Lisa's school, to welcome us home. It was a nice touch, reflecting Helga's close attachment to Lisa and her acceptance of me and my family into her world. Although exhausted from our long journey home, Lisa and I managed to fulfill our roles as honored guests – even though we would be living in Helga's home until I learned where my next *Luftwaffe* assignment might take me – spreading ourselves cheerfully among the clutches of well-wishers. Inevitably, the conversations turned towards inquiries about Austria, war-preparations, and the Jewish-question.

"Well, Fritz, what do you think," asked Poppa, as we moved from the dining room, where the servants were clearing the remains of the sumptuous dinner, into a paneled room across the hall. "Are the Austrians anxious? Are they preparing for war with Germany, if Hitler proceeds with his plans to annex Austria?"

"Have you heard the rumors that Hitler has designs on both Austria and Czechoslovakia, and is willing to go to war with Britain and France to achieve his goal of Lebensraum [living space]?" Ernst interjected before I could respond, much to Poppa's surprise, displeasure.

"Perhaps we ought to have this conversation at another time," Poppa indicated to me, proceeding to light an impressive looking cigar, "After you have had your meeting with General Udet."

"Actually, Poppa," I calmly stated, "I need all of the intelligence... whether rumor or iron-clad fact...that is available as to what Hitler is planning before I meet with General Udet. If Hitler is willing to go to war with Germany's old enemies, Britain and France, over Austria and Czechoslovakia, then that means the pace of rearmament must be quickened. Germany is currently grossly deficient in war materiel and woefully mismatched in fighting capability compared with Britain and France.

"Hitler's generals have been telling him this for months...so something must have occurred that has convinced Hitler that he can acquire Austria and Czechoslovakia without a fight, but if he has to fight a war he will have to make do with what we have militarily now or in the immediate future. Right now, General Udet is very cautious about the strength of the *Luftwaffe*, and about getting cross-wise with Field Marshal Goering on its offensive capabilities. Ernst's rumor is an important ingredient on how I need to respond to General Udet if he inquires as to the status of the Stuka's availability, and in what numbers."

"Does the availability of the Stuka really make any difference as to whether Hitler will or will not continue his plans to annex Austria and Czechoslovakia...if he is simply bluffing, and I am convinced that he is?" inquired Poppa, shaking his head in disbelief, his eyes closed as if he was viewing a nightmare scenario of impending Armageddon.

"If Hitler is willing to go to war, then war there will be...unless the general's, the general staff, call his bluff by refusing to go along with his plans. But General Udet is correct to be cautious. There are rumors that Hitler is preparing a purge of the top generals who he believes are not willing to do his bidding. The worst possible scenario is for the generals to let Hitler go forth with his plans for Austria and Czechoslovakia, and then for Britain and France to back down and not threaten retaliation. If that happens, then Hitler will be unstoppable."

"Are there no plans...are steps not being taken...to prevent Hitler from catapulting Germany into another war?" I asked with a note of deep concern.

After a long pause, during which Poppa struggled to re-light his cigar, he opined in a hushed voice, "At the risk of being charged with treason, there are, I believe, concerned Germans who are engaged in efforts to force Hitler to abandon his plans. However, it will take the timely intervention of the officer corps to underpin any such efforts...and therein suffers the weakness of any civilian-initiated effort. Hitler knows...and so do his generals...that there is a plethora of ambitious, qualified young officers just waiting to replace the current batch of top generals should any of them stumble in their allegiance to Hitler and the Nazi party. Even though the Versailles Treaty prohibited a standing German army, the Treaty did not disband the officer corps or prevent the training of new officers. As a result there are more young officers available than there are soldiers-in-arms to be commanded. But this is neither the place nor the time to be engaged in such highly dangerous conversations."

In short order, the three of us disbanded our impromptu chat, moved out of the paneled room, each seeking another cluster of guests, hopefully engaged in less seditious talk. For my part, it was to no avail. Joining Lisa, her mother and Momma, gathered at the end of the now cleared dining table, sitting close to the warmth of the handsomely decorated ceramic-tile heat stove, I was quickly dragged into a tirade against the Nazis' anti-Jewish pogroms. Having recently been subjected to Lisa's persistent bewailing of how several of our Jewish friends had been dismissed from their jobs, including jurists, teachers, and other professionals, I should have been forewarned.

The persecution of the Jews was being carried out by the Gestapo and the *Schutzstaffel* [the dreaded S.S.], under the direction of the feared, despised Heinrich Himmler. Any efforts by sympathetic Germans to protect, speak-out on behalf of, or hide Jews were viewed as treasonous activities, coming within the purview of the Gestapo and the S.S.; leading to relentless investigation, persecution, ending in sure imprisonment and/or death. Again I found myself immersed in seditious conversations.

Just the thought of what disaster would befall my happy family should the Gestapo learn of our sentiments towards Hitler, the Nazis and their callous disregard of the fate of millions of Germans, not to mention the Jews, turned an evening of joy and celebration into a nightmare of fear, mistrust, and despair. All it would take is a denouncement by one disgruntled servant or the coerced betrayal by a friend to bring an ignominious end to my proud family.

Seeing my pained expression, sensing my discomfort, Lisa rose from her chair, saying to no one in particular, "We have had a long day and I am tired. So if you will excuse me, I am going to bed." Looking directly at me across the table, she added, "Will you join me, Fritz?" This was her cue, to me at least, that the party was over.

IN THE MORNING, in the dark, I reluctantly left the comfort of the down-filled bed, the warmth of my beloved Lisa, struggled into my *Hauptman's* uniform, and, exiting my mother-in-law's cozy home, worked my way along the now snow-covered streets towards the railway station, where I purchased a cup of coffee, bought a newspaper, and boarded a train headed to Berlin.

The over-heated, second-class carriage was crowded with passengers, stuffy with tobacco smoke and the odor of heavy winter clothing, its windows fogged over. I was forced to share a seat with a large, grey-haired, rosy-cheeked woman who proceeded to spend the entire trip rummaging through the threadbare sacks she balanced upon her ample, heavily-bundled lap and thighs, looking for something she never seemed to find. Her constant motion reminded me of a frantic sow working her way around the pig-pen rooting for a tasty, elusive morsel; the distraction prevented me from ever being able to concentrate on reading the newspaper.

Giving up on my reading, I began to think about just how perilous the life of most Germans – like this grandmother sitting next to me – would become if Hitler had his way, and Germany became embroiled in another prolonged, devastating war. Maybe if Germany became strong enough militarily, none of our enemies would dare to attack us; and Hitler would gain his *Lebensraum* without dragging us into a war. But how strong did

Germany have to become, and how long would that take, and how much Lebensraum might be enough to satisfy Herr Hitler? Depending on how these issues might be resolved, I was in a dilemma on how to proceed with my responsibilities: *Do I help to make Germany stronger militarily, or do I take steps to hamper Hitler's ability to make war? Maybe I can get some insight into how I need to proceed when I meet with General Udet.*

Anticipating the Air Ministry to be a virtual bee-hive of activity, I was immediately struck by how quiet it was, with no visible sign of hustle and bustle. Even when I entered my general work-area, there was little evidence of people frantically preparing the *Luftwaffe* for potential warfare. Perhaps the rumors I have been hearing about Austria are all wrong, or maybe Hitler is so confident in annexing Austria without a struggle that he has not called for all out preparations.

In any case, I spent considerable time in my cramped, cluttered office reviewing all the reports on the progress of the Stuka production so that when I met with General Udet I would be prepared to answer any questions he may have. At this time, about 200 of the Ju-87A versions of the Stuka were being built, while the Ju-87B version – with its much more powerful engine – was beginning its initial production at the Wesser Flug-zeugbau facility located at Berlin's Templehof airport, near Poppa's aircraft fabrication plant. Three of the Ju-87A craft were already in service in Spain, with five early-production Ju-87B aircraft scheduled for delivery to Spain in the spring. All of these aircraft were being flown solely by German pilots; both to give German pilots real-time combat experience with the Stuka, and to keep the aircraft from falling into the wrong hands.

Once I felt adequately armed to discuss the Stuka project with the General, I advised his aide of my availability to meet with him. In turn, I was advised that the General was currently meeting with Herr Goering, and that I would be informed when the General became available. Several hours passed before I was summoned to General Udet's office, where I found him alone, seated tunic-less behind his spacious desk looking downcast, appearing even smaller than he actually was – just under five-feet, four-inches tall.

Without a word of greeting, or his usual smile, he waved me to take my seat in one of the leather arm-chairs facing his desk. Picking up one of the many folders stacked in random piles on his desk, he opened it, scanned its contents, and, when he has finished looking at it, looked at me, a slight smile crossing his lips, brightening his warm blue eyes. "How are you, Fritz?" he began good-naturedly. "How was your trip to Austria? Restful, I hope?" he added, with a knowing wink.

"Very restful, my General," I replied with equal joviality.

"Are you ready to go back to work *Hauptmann* von Bruckner?" he asked with more formality, indicating that the conversation was about to take a more serious turn.

"Jawohl, General," I replied formally.

"Good! We have an extensive agenda, and a very tight timeframe," he remarked seriously, again consulting the folder in his hand. "Let me begin with a quick overview of the current political situation. As you no doubt are aware, the Fuehrer has cast designs on Austria, the home of his birth, wishing to make it a part of Germany."

As he spoke to me about the political, economic and military value to Germany of having Austria as a part of Germany, the General scratched a penciled note on a slip of paper; sliding it towards me across the desk, beckoning me with a movement of his head to look at it, and with a finger to his lips, signaled me not to comment on what I read: **Others are listening!** When I acknowledged the note's warning with a nod of my head, the General withdrew the slip of paper, and nimbly placed it in his mouth. While he was silently chewing the piece of paper, I related to the General what Lisa and I had observed about the Austrians' demeanor during our visit to Austria.

Having completed my report, the General said, "The *Luftwaffe* must do its part to see that the Austrian annexation proceeds peacefully, quickly, smoothly. This includes developing sufficient military aircraft and manpower capabilities to dissuade other possibly interested nations from interfering in the process. To this end, we must make certain that the Stuka project...of which you are an integral part...continues to develop improved versions, and to build these aircraft at an accelerated pace."

After I explained where the Stuka project stood in its development and production, General Udet continued. "Good. Now that the Stuka project is moving ahead so well, I think it is time to put you to work on an even more spectacular concept...turbojet propulsion...which, if practical, will revolutionize aircraft development. There is serious engineering work underway at several different academic laboratories, with some prototype engines being tested by Ernst Heinkel.

"I believe that this 'turbojet' program is sufficiently robust for the *Luftwaffe* to give it a well-informed look. Therefore, I want you to learn all you can about 'turbojet' propulsion, take a look at what is happening in the laboratories and in the real-life design area, and give me your analysis and recommendations. I am hoping that you will approach this assignment with your usual high-degree of skepticism and vision. This 'turbojet' propulsion could change the face of aerial warfare...and the German *Luftwaffe* must be the leader in its development and implementation."

"Thank you, General, both for the opportunity to serve the *Luftwaffe* in pursuing the feasibility of such a world-changing development, and for your high level of confidence in my abilities. I am looking forward to tackling this assignment. When do I start?"

"That depends on how quickly you can complete one last phase of your work on the Stuka project. As you know, there are currently several Stuka aircraft serving with our Kondor legion in the Spanish Civil War, and serving well. A batch of five of the newer version of the Stuka which are being sent to Spain also need pilots...and I want you to be one of those pilots. I know that you have flown several different versions of the Stuka, as well as the Ju-87B, but none of them in combat.

"I want you to experience air combat...real air combat. Nothing can beat real-life combat for knowing the strengths and weaknesses of a military aircraft. With your burgeoning responsibilities for developing the most advanced fighter aircraft, this Stuka experience will be invaluable to you over the next several years. I am sure your father, the Baron, can tell you how valuable his fighter aircraft experience in the last war was to his duties in the aircraft procurement process."

My God! The General is all but telling me outright that Herr Hitler is planning to take Germany into war...maybe not over Austria, but sometime in the near future. Of course, if you are planning to annex a country, you will need to be prepared to invade that country, or fight off those nations opposed to such an annexation.

"I know," continued the General, "that the Stuka is not a conventional fighter aircraft...and so the characteristics of air combat may not be the same...but the experience of handling an aircraft in the heat of combat... even if most of the enemy fire is from the ground...will give you a taste of how an aircraft...and its pilot...must be responsive to attack."

"Again, my General, thank you. I am excited by the prospect of real-time combat flying with the Stuka," I prevaricated.

Obviously, the General believes there to be little risk of my not returning from this assignment in Spain, or he would not also have given me the subsequent, more important assignment of determining the prospects of producing a "turbojet" aircraft. But does that not also mean that he is preparing me to fly a "turbojet" aircraft in combat, at sometime? And couldn't that "turbojet" aircraft be a "bomber-type" aircraft, just as easily as it could be a fighter aircraft; even a "dive bomber," like the Stuka...only a more advanced, more destructive, an offensive weapon? I am not sure I like where this is going. I need to talk to Poppa, soon...but somewhere in private, a place where "others are not listening"!

SEVERAL DAYS LATER, after using Lisa and Momma as our go-between, Poppa and I met at the flower shop in the village near the train station that Momma usually ordered her flower arrangements. It was not unusual for Poppa to stop there on his chauffeured ride home from work, picking up Momma's flowers; and now that I was married, I, too, could be expected to stop at the shop after my train-ride home from the Air Ministry, bringing flowers home to my Lisa. My intention was to have a brief conversation with Poppa at the flower shop – it was just a safe spot to meet without raising suspicion – where I could quickly explain to Poppa why we needed to talk privately about some serious matters.

"Gutten Abend, Poppa," I said in greeting as I entered the flower shop where he was standing by the counter, handing the clerk several large denomination marks for the bouquet of beautiful long-stemmed red roses, Momma's winter-time favorites, clutched in his other hand.

"Dankeschoen, Fritz," Poppa replied, giving me a broad smile. "I see that we are carrying out our husbandly duties. I wish that I had known that you were coming here...you should have let me know you would be here...We could have driven here together."

"Of course, that would have been the wiser thing to do...But I didn't know when I was going to be able to get away from the Air Ministry this evening. Perhaps another evening would be better?"

"As a matter of fact," Poppa remarked, "if it would not be too inconvenient, I would like for you to stop by the plant tomorrow evening on your way home...say about 1800 hours, at the old hangar. I need to show you some changes that I want to make to your old airplane."

And so began our series of covert meetings to discuss political and military matters setting a course of unbridled conspiracy against the Nazi regime. At first, Poppa resisted my insistence on absolute privacy. But after I tell him of the scribbled note General Udet had shown to me – and then consumed – Poppa acknowledged the soundness of my concerns. There were several different secret, secluded meeting places where I felt we could speak to each other at length without fear of detection, or of being observed. Sometimes, when we had matters which required only a brief exchange, we would meet at venues crowded with people, noisy, and where my *Luftwaffe* uniform did not stand out; where we shared a word or two, or surreptitiously passed a note.

Over the course of several meetings during early 1938, prior to my departure to Spain, Poppa expressed his deep concern for the fate of Austria, and of his good friend, Doctor Kurt von Schuschnigg, who tried valiantly – as Austria's Chancellor – to save Austria from being annexed by Germany. Poppa had a particularly warm spot for von Schuschnigg; they were both Catholic, Jesuit trained intellectuals who were horrified by war, and would do most anything to avoid bloodshed. It was this shared background of pacifism that troubled Poppa most about von Schuschnigg; that he would ultimately yield to Hitler's threats of invasion rather than risk Austrian deaths and destruction.

He also believed that von Schuschnigg stood alone against Hitler; neither his own countrymen nor other countries - like England and France – had the will to fight, to save Austria. He had learned through Ernst that Hitler would invade Austria if necessary – there was even a plan, "Special Case Otto"– which detailed the terms of invasion. Indeed, Hitler had already decided – at a secret meeting of his generals in November 1937 – that Germany would go to war, if necessary, to carry out his plans for Lebensraum.

Several of his generals protested these plans – primarily on the basis that Germany was ill-prepared to fight a war – but Hitler put these generals on notice that their "heads were on the block." This was not an idle-threat; he had already started purging the ranks of his ministers – like Dr. Schacht, the world-renowned architect of the economic plan that rescued Germany from bankruptcy, providing the basis for the current robust economy; replacing him with Walter Funk, a Hitler toady, an alcoholic, inept in financial matters, rumored to be a homosexual, and currently my brother Wolfie's boss.

Poppa was also concerned about his good friend, first war comrade, and now my boss, Generaloberst Ernst Udet. In addition to Udet's own concerns about his office being monitored, Poppa was concerned that General Udet did not sufficiently appreciate the political environment in which he must function. At heart, Udet was just a fighter pilot, an ace with over sixty confirmed "kills", but not an administrator, unhappy in his *Luftwaffe* relationship with his superior officers, Milch and Goering; and under tremendous pressure to build the *Luftwaffe* into a war-ready component of Hitler's military machine.

As much as Poppa liked and respected Udet as a military-man, Poppa – as a devout Catholic – found Udet to lack moral fiber, especially as a "ladies' man," a "womanizer," and an addict to alcohol. When I tried to defend Udet – after all, he had plotted a very attractive course for my career – Poppa argued that I would be better off working elsewhere than at the Air Ministry.

The most troubling topic we discussed was how Hitler was turning Germany into a police-state, with spies everywhere; with people of every rank being sent off to the ever-growing nests of concentration camps and prisons because of what they thought or said – no matter how serious or how trivial – about Hitler and his Nazi minions.

"You were wise, Fritz," Poppa admitted one day at one of our private meeting places, just before I left for Spain, "to demand that we hold our conversations about these topics in private. God knows where we would be right now if we had not. We already have too many enemies...people jealous of our success, our position, and our connections. If any of them learned of what we talk about, how we feel, and what we might be planning, the 'knock on the door in the middle of the night' would come sooner rather than later. The bad thing about bad enemies is that they never go away.

"Do you remember Otto Muenster and his equally obnoxious nephew Dietrich? As enemies go we could not wish for worse enemies. Unfortunately, Otto has parlayed his relationship with some of the worst of Hitler's inner-group into achieving greater wealth and power for himself... and a powerful position for Dietrich working as an aide to Heinrich Himmler, with the rank of *Oberst* in the S.S. Can you imagine what would become of us, our families, if Dietrich Muenster and his S.S. squad were to set their sights on us? It is not like we are beyond suspicion and reproach. Who knows, we could be under surveillance right now...and not know it."

The specter of Dietrich Muenster at the head of a phalanx of S.S. troopers banging on the front door in the middle of the night caused my stomach to turn and go sour. The vision of Lisa being dragged from her bed by some black-uniformed thugs in leather trench coats, to be subjected to unspeakable horrors and abominations, haunted me while I was away in Spain. All of the efforts being undertaken by Lisa, Momma, and my sisters, Marta and Maria, to assist the Jews were hard to conceal. Providing Jews with false papers, hiding Jews in attics and cellars, bribing ship's captains to smuggle Jews out of Germany, were activities that were sure to attract attention, to lead to unearthing; just as surely as the tantalizing scent of a subterranean truffle leads the rooting pig to search for and to dig it out.

IN MARCH, JUST as the fate of Austria had been sealed, with German troops storming into Austria in support of the newly-formed Austrian government – von Schuschnigg having capitulated to Hitler's ultimatum to surrender Austria, presented to him at Hitler's mountain retreat at Berchtesgaden – I traveled to Spain to join the Kondor Legion's squad of five new Ju-87B-1 Berthas. During the first several months, I received training on the earlier version of the Stuka – known as the Pig, because of the shape of its nose assembly – until I became proficient in dive-bombing techniques. We moved around a great deal – from airfield to airfield – as the Nationalist troops we were supporting in the field of battle clashed with the Republican troops.

By the time I was qualified to fly the Bertha, the Nationalists had gained control of much of the air space, making my baptism in battle less stressful from fighter attack; defeating at least one of the purposes of my assignment to Spain. On the other hand, I experienced, first hand, the awesome performance of the Stuka's dive-bombing characteristics and capabilities – including its incredible bombing accuracy – in support of ground troops; thus vindicating General Udet's decision to proceed with the Stuka program in the face of General von Richthoven's earlier adamant opposition to the Stuka. I sent my glowing report on the Stuka to General Udet at the end of July, and by the middle of August I received my orders to return to Germany, to begin the next phase of my career – turbojet engines; my love affair with the Stuka apparently at an end.

MUCH HAD CHANGED in Germany upon my reappearance in Potsdam. Hitler had absorbed Austria into his growing empire, and Poppa's good friend, von Schuschnigg had been arrested and was incarcerated in the Gestapo headquarters in Vienna. Now energized by his success in Austria – where had achieved a painless, warless victory – Hitler was now rumored to make Czechoslovakia his next victim, again creating the risk of armed conflict. As expected, Hitler had consolidated his power by removing several top generals who had opposed his designs on Austria, replacing them with more malleable officers. The presence of military equipment and personnel in Berlin and elsewhere was more evident than when I left for Spain.

At our first private meeting, Poppa was beside himself about Hitler, and what Hitler was doing to Germany; declaiming Hitler as that "little Austrian corporal." The stress of living under the Nazi rule was beginning to show on Poppa; he had aged considerably during the time I was in Spain – his thinning hair was whiter, his face was gaunt, his eyes were puffy and less brilliant, his carriage was less upright, and I noticed a slight trembling in his right hand. But most distressing was the darkness of his outlook, the lassitude in his voice.

When I inquired about Momma and my siblings, Poppa responded without enthusiasm, avoiding eye-contact, saying only that, "They are fine." When I tried to elicit more information by asking about them individually, by name, I gained little additional information; other than that my baby sister, Maria (who has always been Poppa's favorite) was about to take her vows as a nun in a Catholic order noted for its work with orphans. Even when I attempted to cheer him up with talk about Lisa's pregnancy (the birth of the baby was scheduled for January), he responded with little more than the perfunctory: "congratulations," "hope all goes well," type chatter.

"Is there something you want to share with me, Poppa?" I asked, finally.

"No. What makes you think I have anything that I have not shared with you," he responded angrily; rising from the box he had been sitting on in the abandoned aircraft hangar at the edge of an unused runway, heading towards the door, leaving without so much as a "goodbye." *There is something very wrong here. This is not like Poppa at all! He is frightened; frightened to death. Poppa is hiding something terrible; something so terrible that he will not tell even me – not even in private!*

At home, inviting Lisa to join me out in the garden – on the pretext of experiencing some of the wonderful, late summer weather – I shared with her my growing concerns about Poppa, his state-of-mind, his health, and the fact that I was sure that he was hiding something of significance from us. Lisa, too, had noticed the decline in Poppa's appearance, his haggard features, the trembling hand, his worried attitude; but she had been afraid to speak to Momma or my sisters – or even to me – about it – at least until I had returned from Spain. Poppa had never been one to withhold information – good or bad – from Momma, so there was a chance Momma knew something about what was causing Poppa's mental and physical decline.

Lisa suggested that she call Momma on the pretext of being a first-time mother, seeking Momma's counsel on how to be prepared in the event that I would be unavailable at critical times during the pregnancy. The plan was for the two of us to meet with Momma at some location in Potsdam where we could speak privately. Momma seemed to be flattered, but surprised that Lisa would seek her counsel rather than that of Lisa's own mother. Lisa can be quite convincing in a low-key manner, and she managed to have Momma agree to meet with us in a bustling coffee shop in a nearby village. I remained quiet, but attentive, during the course of Lisa's opening discussions with Momma about pregnancies and new babies. As the baby talk wound down, Lisa mentioned to Momma her concerns about Poppa's well-being.

"What has Poppa's health got to do with pregnancies and babies?" Momma declared in an uncharacteristically sharp tone. "Please, take me home, immediately."

"Please, Momma," I implored, placing my hand firmly on her arm as she began to rise from her chair. "We really need to talk about Poppa."

"Let me go," she complained, with real hostility in her voice. "I have nothing more to say!"

During the drive back to my parent's home, Momma remained silent in the back seat, staring out the window. The old mansion looked as beautiful, as tidy, as always. There was nothing to suggest that Poppa's business had fallen on hard times, or that my folks have had to let go of any of the domestic help. By the time that I had climbed out of the driver's side door and walked around the sedan to the rear door, Momma had already exited the car, walking resolutely across the gravel driveway the short distance to the front doorway. She never looked back, leaving me dumfounded as she opened the massive front door, slamming it loudly behind her. When I turned back to the automobile, I saw Lisa, her face buried in her hands, sobbing.

Over the next several days, I contacted my brothers and sister, one-by-one, in the hope that one of them knew, and could tell me, what was wrong with Poppa, and why Momma was acting so defensively. It was to no avail; not one of my siblings could offer me anything more than theories and speculation. "It could be cancer," suggested Wolfie; while Ernst tried, "The trembling might mean a stroke;" with Marta offering, "I think he is too worried about the family's political, criminal exposure."

Poor Maria, living in a convent, now more isolated from the family than ever, advised me in a brief note that, "Poppa's symptoms suggest a 'loss of faith';" promising to, "flood heaven with prayers on Poppa's behalf." We each agreed that, if anyone gained any specific information about Poppa, it was to be shared among us as quickly as possible. Hoping to repair some of the damaged feelings with Momma, Lisa and Marta worked out a schedule for visiting Momma at least once a week. There was no solution to the mystery of Poppa's health, despite all of our efforts over the next month or two to ferret out what was ailing him. Our efforts were handicapped by Poppa's constant refusals to meet with me – in private or elsewhere – or with any of my siblings; Momma acting as his vigilant, Schnauzer-tough guardian, intercepting any attempt to pry into Poppa's well-being – which, for the moment, appeared to have stabilized.

THERE WAS MUCH more of my story to be told, but Jack has been put to work by the widow Kaufman – work that, for Jack, is quite strenuous; leaving him exhausted at day's end, too tired in the evenings to do much more than eat his supper and go to bed for the night. It is just as well; the widow Kaufman and Hannah appear to have lost even further interest in listening to my tale; and it is pointless to my purpose if they were not moved to help me by what they had been hearing. Perhaps, my story will receive a better reception at a later time, when Jack is able to tell my story with more enthusiasm.

CHAPTER 27

BIG CHIEF TABLET TWENTY-FOUR | JACK

My first impression of Billy Lewis, when I saw him standing next to his daddy's flat-bed Ford, was of how small he was; his skinny, shirtless frame swimming in his bib overalls, the tattered, faded brown baseball cap pushing his ears out, its bill casting his face in shadow. *He can't be more than eight years old.* Dennis, his daddy, had been hired by Aunt Rita to build a wire fence around a new pasture, and to repair some fences that were in a sorry state.

At Rita's insistence that, "You need to experience some manual labor," I had been assisting Dennis for the past week on some of the fence repairs, by clearing the under-brush, fetching staples, handing him hammers, locating the ever-elusive wire-cutters, and helping him replace rotten fence posts and install-ing new woven wire where needed. She was correct; building fences was hard, dirty work, especially in the hot summer sun where there were few shade trees.

Dennis and I had finished the fence repair work, and were about to construct the new fence. Billy was supposed to be lending us a hand, but upon first sight of him I doubted that he could keep up with us. Yet, there he was opening the heavy wooden gate without any difficulty, waving his daddy to drive the noisy, rickety truck — loaded with rolls of wire fencing, spools of smooth and barbed wire, and a stack of cedar fence poles — for-ward into the barn-yard.

It was fun working with Dennis; he was easy-going, had

friendly eyes, loved to joke around, laughed easily, and didn't work too fast. He was tall, had broad shoulders with well-muscled, deeply-tanned arms, and huge hands. It seemed like nothing for him to toss an eight-foot cedar fence-post around like a match stick. I was amazed, then, that skinny, little Billy was his son. Even if Billy was Dennis' son, and he was able to carry his weight, I didn't want him to be 'lending us a hand'; I feared that his presence would interfere with my growing friendship with Dennis. *What if Billy's presence keeps Dennis from entertaining me with his tales of fighting Japs in hand-to-hand combat in some Pacific island jungle?*

I entered the barn-yard through the open gate, with Lady racing ahead to greet Dennis and Billy. Dennis was already out of the truck, climbing onto the flat-bed, preparing to transfer the materials onto the tractor wagon parked at its side. Billy was watching his father, paying no attention to my arrival, though he stooped down to receive Lady's lavish licks, stroking her silky red head in return. Eventually, Lady ran towards the open barn door and into the dark barn, in hopes of scaring up some careless critter; and Billy glanced in my direction, a slight smile crossing his lips, his dark eyes brightening. *Is he just reacting to Lady's kisses? Or, is he signaling that he wants us to be friends? Damn! Billy is making it hard for me. How can he and I be friends when I want to exclude him from my friendship with his daddy?*

"Hey, you must be Jack...I'm Billy," he stated quite matter-of-factly. "Daddy thinks you might need an extra set of hands when you get to setting the first corner."

Setting the 'first what'? "Yeah," I responded coldly, not at all sure as to what a "first corner" was. "I guess we can use your help for that." *Let's hope that that's all he will be doing...and that 'setting the first corner' won't take too long.*

"Daddy says that the first corner is the hardest, most important part of constructing a new fence, and that it can take a lot of time," Billy observed as he lifted a contraption consisting of handles, bars and hooks down from the truck.

"What's that," I asked.

"It's a fence stretcher...Ain't you never seen one of these before?"

"No," I replied shaking my head — both in response to his question and to my lack of familiarity with what must be basic farming equipment. *He must think I'm really stupid.*

"Then, I guess you ain't never built a woven wire fence before," Billy observed, adding, "You are in for a real experience, using this here fence stretcher...I'll show you how it works when the time comes to use it."

"Thanks," was all I could think to say in reply — both in response to Billy's offer of help, and for his passing on the opportunity to say how stupid I was. *Maybe Billy can be my friend after all.*

The rest of the day was taken up with transporting the fence-building stuff to the spot where the 'first corner' of the new fence was to be erected. There was more stuff than can be carried in one or two trips of the Farmall Cub tractor and wagon. Billy took the first turn driving the tractor pulling the loaded wagon slowly over the rolling hills from the barn-yard to the fence-building site at the far-end of the property. The Farmall Cub was simple to operate — once it was put into gear, it went forward at a steady speed; there was nothing to do but to steer it.

When my turn came, I followed Billy's instructions; thrilled that I, too, could drive a tractor — overly impressed with my rather-simple accomplishment. Surprisingly, Billy had no further interest in driving the rig, content to have me drive, him riding along standing on the hitch-bar behind me. I guess driving a tractor doesn't excite Billy any more. Each trip, back and forth, took about an hour, including loading time. During this time together, Billy was quick to point out things of interest along the route to the building site; the different types of trees, the grass, the birds, the animals. When he ran out of nature things to talk about, the conversation turned more personal.

"Daddy says that you waz adopted by Miz Kaufman. That you're really her nephew."

"Yeah, that's right."

"Are your folks dead?"

"No."

"Then why have you been adopted by Miz Kaufman?"

"After my brothers got killed, my mother didn't want me anymore...and my dad thought I'd be better off living with my Aunt Rita."

"Wow! Did your brothers get killed because of you?"

"No. They died in an auto accident."

"So, why didn't your mother want you anymore?"

"I don't know...I don't think she ever wanted me. At least that's how she treated me."

"That's awful! What did she do to you?"

"I'd rather not talk about it."

"I'm sorry. It's just that my mom sometimes treats me like I'm still a little kid, giving me anything I want...and hugging me, kissing me, telling me how much she loves me. It makes me feel loved and wanted...sometimes more than I can stand. I guess I'm just lucky."

"Yeah, you are lucky all right. And I'm lucky, too. Having Aunt Rita, I mean. She has been so wonderful...a lot like your mom is to you, I guess. Do you have any brothers or sisters?"

"Nah. It's just me. Mom and Dad wanted more kids, but something happened to Mom when I was born...something that keeps her from having any more kids."

"Aunt Rita says that your dad is the son of one of her neighbors...Mr. Lewis...who lives just up the road. Where do you live?"

"We live in a small house on my Grandpa's property...it's a tenant house actually. Dad works for my Grandpa, and we get to stay in the house as part of Dad's pay."

"How old are you, Billy? I am sure you are older than you look."

"Yeah, I'm a lot older than I look. What's your guess as to how old I am?'

"Well, you look about ten years old, but I'd guess...just seeing how you work and hearing how you talk...that you're probably more like twelve or thirteen."

"Good guess. I'm twelve. How about you? I'd say...as tall as you are...that you're twelve or thirteen. You're kinda skinny though...just like me."

"Well your guess was as good as mine. I'm twelve. Aunt Rita was hoping that this job with your Dad will give me some muscles...fill me out a bit so I can hold my own against the older boys at school."

"Why do you call Miz Kaufman, 'Aunt Rita', if she's now your mother?"

"That's what we decided I'd call her in public, since it is less complicated. In private, I call her 'Rita' rather than 'Mom' or 'Mother', because it just doesn't seem appropriate to call her 'Mom'." *If Billy thinks this is confusing wait until I tell him about Hannah...or Fritz — if ever.*

ERECTING THE 'FIRST CORNER' indeed consumed several days. Just clearing the area of under-brush and saplings seemed to take forever. The summer heat increased daily. We looked forward for every bit of shade, grateful for even just the shadow of a passing cloud; like the Foreign Legionnaires in *Beau Geste* manning their posts in the Sahara, struggling to repulse the relentless Arab onslaught. During our breaks from clearing brush, laying out the fence-line, measuring the 20 foot line-post spacing, starting the post holes with the hand operated post-hole digger, as well as during our frequent trips with the tractor/wagon rig back to the barn-yard to replenish supplies, Billy and I jabbered on about war and western movies, comic books, radio programs — just about anything that entered a curious boy's mind.

When I mentioned to Billy about the war-stories his daddy had been telling me, Billy just laughed, "I've heard them all...several times...though they seem to change with each telling."

"Are they true?" I asked.

"I'm beginning to think that maybe they are only partly true," he said.

On other occasions, when Billy brought his well-worn Daisy BB gun with him, we engaged in longer breaks from fence building — taking Lady with us — to hunt the wily rabbit and the elusive squirrel among the trees and brush that bordered the new fence-line. We seldom had any success in raising a rabbit or getting off a well-aimed shot at a treed squirrel. My brother, Chris had a pump BB gun that was too hard for me to handle, and he wouldn't let me near it, anyway. Even though the Daisy BB gun had a more manageable lever action, I was a poor shot. Billy observed that I needed to practice shooting the BB gun at tin cans and such. During subsequent break-times Billy taught me the art of pinging at any available targets.

When we finally tired of firing the BB gun, Billy produced a long-blade knife — together with its scabbard — which he claimed his daddy used in the War.

"Is this really the knife that you used in the War?" I inquired of Dennis, handing him the weapon, seeking affirmation of Billy's claim.

"If it ain't my trench fighting knife, then it's one damn near like it," Dennis replied, sliding the knife out of its scabbard, examining it closely, wiping the shinny blade on the leg of his faded, dirty, denim work-pants, carefully pricking the tip of his index finger with its sharp, tapered point, then sliding the blade back into the scabbard.

"Why don't you tell Jack how you used that trench knife on them Japs," Billy said, drawing his forefinger across his throat as if it were a knife.

"Which one...there were so many?" Dennis retorted, pushing up the brim of his sweat-stained Stetson with the tip of the sheathed trench knife.

"Do you have any that I ain't heard before?" suggested Billy.

"Probably not," Dennis stated bluntly. "But let's try this one: Me and my troop of Marines had waded ashore at Peleliu Island in September '44 to secure the god-forsaken place as an airbase for McArthur's invasion of the Philippines. Even though the whole island had received a helluva shellacking from the Navy, the Japs were still there, dug-in in pillboxes and hiding in caves, just waiting for our arrival. It wasn't until we were on the beach that the Japs surprised us by raking us with machine gun fire, mortars; giving us everything they had. We was pinned down there getting the crap beat out us for days. Every time we took a little bit of land they would counter-attack and push us back towards the sea.

"It was especially bad at night when the Jap bastards would come out of the jungle, try sneaking into our fox holes, and stabbing us in our sleep — so we'd sleep two guys to the hole with one awake at all times. One night, while I was awake on look-out, this Jap tried to infiltrate our fox hole carrying a rifle with a bayonet. I just jumped up, and he lunged at me. I side-stepped him and swung at his head as he went by with this here trench knife. I knew I had cut his throat, but he just laughed, turned around, and says, 'You missed, G.I.'! So, in the Jap tradition, I bowed to him. Then he, in the same tradition, bowed back...and when he did his head falls off!"

I had been listening to this story with rapt attention, absolutely immersed in the scene Dennis had painted so vividly; actually bowing my head and shoulders as Dennis had pantomimed. When I had completed my mimicking bow, I noticed that Dennis had been watching my body contortions, staring at the shocked look on my face; he had this great big grin, which quickly transformed into an enormous chest and shoulder-shaking laugh. Beginning to blush I caught Billy showing me a weak smile, shaking his head, saying, "Sorry, sucker — I fell for it, too...the first time he told me that tall tale."

"Don't be so quick to label that story as a 'tall tale' Billy," Dennis cautioned, the laughter ended, the smile gone from his face. "There are parts of it that are very true...true enough that I still have nightmares about what happened to me and my buddies out in that jungle hell-hole, fighting them dirty Jap soldiers. There was more than just that time that this here trench knife saved my life, protecting me and my buddies from some Jap mischief. I ain't told no one about some of what I done with this knife. I don't even like to think about those things...and see'n that knife is bringing back some really bad memories...So why don't you two just quit playing with it, and put it up in the truck where I don't have to look at it. Besides, we got lots of work to do here before dark. So quit screw'n around and give me a hand with building this here fence!"

Over the next several weeks Billy and I became real fence-builders, working like we had not worked before, viewing the job — and Dennis — in a whole new light. Dennis became my hero; a real, honest-to-God hero — not some comic book hero, not some Hollywood version of a hero. He had actually lived through the horrors of war, protected his buddies, and did what he had to, to stay alive...And I had the privilege of working for him, with him, doing man-type work.

It also brought Billy and me closer together — sharing the work assigned to us as a team; while we still competed to see who was stronger, faster; always seeking new ways of keeping Dennis happy. We still laughed at and with each other, trying our best to make the job enjoyable despite the heat, the sweat, the flies, the aches, the pains, the blisters. We worked shirtless, turning brown as berries in the intense summer sun-light.

Each time we reached the end of the pasture and made a right-turn, we were faced with the chore of building another corner, placing another corner-post and brace assembly, string-ing, stretching and stapling more fence wire. Stapling was par-ticularly tricky, dangerous work; driving 11/2 inch galvanized steel staples into seasoned cedar fence posts with a heavy claw ham-mer. Even wearing raw-hide leather gloves, I smashed my thumb or fingers on many occasions trying to hammer the staple. Prop-er procedures required the staple to be driven far enough into the post that it would not come out, but not so far in as to keep the wire from moving freely — that is; the wire needed to be able to move without moving the fence post, to compensate for ex-pansion and contraction. The process of stretching the woven-wire fence had its own set of problems, not the least of which was coordinating the placement of the hooks on the stretcher, and then applying the tension evenly to all points on the fence post. Essentially, we had to work together as a team, with just one leader, shouting out the orders to: 'prop the fence', 'place the hooks', 'attach the stretcher', 'puuull', 'align', then 'fasten'! Dennis clearly enjoyed reprising his Marine Corps master ser-geant role. "Aye, aye sergeant!" we replied in unison to his com-mands.

In some ways, attaching the woven-wire fence on the fence

posts turned out to be easier than setting the fence posts in the earth. Using a hand post-hole digger in the heavy clay soil to dig a post hole three to five feet deep for a corner-post was an option, but it was back-breaking and slow. Dennis employed the threat of hand-digging a post-hole to keep Billy and me in line. Thankfully, we had a powered earth-auger, a heavy piece of equipment that Dennis had borrowed from a friend, attached to the drive-train extension mounted at the rear of the Farmall Cub. Often temperamental to operate – the auger incorporated a large, long steel-bit that, when turned by the mechanism, bored down into the ground pulling out the soil and rocks, leaving a clean post-hole behind; just like a drill bit bores through a piece of wood.

"God!" Dennis proclaimed one day, standing at the rear of the little tractor – ready to move the levers that engaged the drive-train and lowered the auger bit – while Billy maneuvered the Cub into position, "I sure wish we had something like this in the Marines to dig all those blasted fox-holes." My assignment was watching out for large bits of rocks and tree roots appearing in the earth being extracted by the auger, with my shovel at the ready to move them aside quickly before they might damage the auger.

All the while, I yearned for the opportunity to operate the tractor or the auger. Even though I knew that Dennis and Billy had worked together for years – they were father and son after-all – I couldn't help feeling a bit jealous of Billy. I was also feeling again an outsider; someone to be impressed – but only to underscore their achievements; someone to be tolerated as the boss' son – but never to be accepted as an equal. I liked Billy – and Dennis – very much; and longed for their acceptance, if only for the summer. But, who was I kidding? I had little to offer in the way of sharing anything with them, especially about fencing or farming or hunting; the very things that made up their lives, making them who they were.

I was the proverbial city-boy trying to adapt to the ways of country-boy living. I had learned so much from Dennis and Billy; and I awoke each morning excited with the thought of spending another day with them; to share hard-work with them, to hear them talk about their lives, to eat lunch with them — me with my peanut butter sandwich or ham sandwich and a thermos of fresh milk prepared each morning by Hannah, and them with their baloney sandwiches and a gallon-sized cider jug filled with homemade iced-tea. Yet, for me this was a summertime adventure; while for them, it was employment, their livelihood — a way to earn their daily bread.

We usually worked on the fence all day, Monday through Friday and until noon on Saturday; although there were some days when I didn't show up for work at all on those days, or perhaps for even a weekend — when Rita, Hannah and I made trips to Kansas City to visit with the Kaufmans. One time, when I asked Billy what he was planning to do with his upcoming free-time on Saturday afternoon and Sunday, he informed me that he would probably play baseball or go fishing or go hunting or go to a movie or just hang out with his friends. I was surprised with his reply; thinking that Billy, like me, was a loner, having no other friends.

"Where do your friends live?" I asked, challenging Billy's statement.

"All around here," he replied with a sweep of his arm in all directions. "They are farm kids just like me."

"How do you know them?"

"From school," he answered with a puzzled look. "How else do you think I would know them?"

"Is your school in town?"

"Nope, it's just back up the road about a mile or so," he responded, pointing his arm in the direction away from town and up the road that runs in front of Fairway, towards where I thought he lived. "It's just a small, two-room schoolhouse. Ain't you never seen it when you've gone up this road?"

"Nope," I confessed. "How many kids go to your school?"

"There are about fifteen kids in the lower four grades in the one room, and maybe a dozen in the upper four grades in the other."

Not ever remembering seeing any school buses passing

on the road, I asked, "How do you and your friends get to this school?"

"Well, I can walk to the school, and some of my friends do to, but the other kids either ride their bikes, or their horses, or they come with their neighbors in one of their daddy's trucks, I guess. I don't think I done ever giv'd it much thought a'fore now."

"How come I never see any of your friends...you know, playing together after school...or on summer vacation?"

"We're farm boys," he responded, laughing. "We've got chores to do after school, everyday. And we ain't got no summer vacation like you do...We've got farming to do with our daddies, again, everyday, including most weekends, especially when there's harvesting to be done. We ain't lucky enough to have what you have. "

As Billy explained the life of a farm-boy, I was thinking about how incredibly different his life was from mine; whether living here at Fairways, or going to school at St. Agatha's back in the city, or St. Benedicts here in town, or at the military academy. *No wonder I'm not accepted. I truly am an outsider.*

Seeing my down-cast face – sensing my feelings of rejection, Billy interjected, "Say, if you ain't doin' nuthin' this Saturday afternoon, maybe you'd like to go with me and some of my friends to see a movie in town and then hang out, and I can maybe show you my school."

"Sure," I responded enthusiastically. "I don't think Aunt Rita has anything planned for me."

"Great!" Billy remarked, with similar enthusiasm. "I'll pick you up on our way to town. I think there's a good western movie... *Winchester '73*, with Jimmy Stewart...it's about a lever action rifle like my old BB gun...It's playing at the Rialto."

EACH EVENING I would drag my tired, aching, exhausted body away from the fence-building project, after locking the barnyard gate behind Dennis and Billy, trudge up the driveway with an equally dog-tired Lady trekking along at my side, covered with the residue of her romp in the fields and woods. Waiting for me on the wooden cover of the cistern, placed under the hand pump spigot, was a galvanized washtub of sun-warmed water, a sponge, a bar of soap, and a nearby towel; ready for me to scrub away the accumulated dirt and sweat of the day's work.

Depositing my filthy T-shirt and the empty lunch box on the edge of the cistern, I would then remove the dirt-caked work boots, strip off my dirt-covered khaki work pants, letting them fall to the concrete walkway in a heap. Standing in my jockey shorts – without a qualm – I applied the soap and sponge to my filthy body in an effort to make myself presentable to Rita and Hannah, thoroughly rinsing away the suds, wrapping up in the towel, gingerly removing the wet, soiled underwear, and letting them lay where they fell in the puddle of dirty water. Hannah would pick them up later.

Making my way quickly onto the back porch where my clean clothes were hanging on hooks next to a small mirror – of which I had no need thanks to my military-style haircut – I commenced posing; admiring my sun-tanned body, my newly developing muscles, my growing manhood.

"Get your clothes on Jack," the voice of a clearly agitated Rita erupted from the kitchen, filling my ears. "We are waiting for you, so we can eat our dinner together for a change." *She's sounding more like a mother every day.*

"Yes, ma'm," I replied cheerlessly; quickly pulling on my clean clothes. *Now that she's got Hannah for companionship, I'm no longer her 'darling Jack'. I'm just a farm-hand; not even a hired farm-hand at that!*

Glum-faced, I stomped into the kitchen without giving any greeting, plopping down on the chair that I had managed to drag noisily out from under the table, thumping it on the linoleum-covered floor as I drew myself up to the table.

"Had a hard day, Jackie-boy?" Rita cooed mockingly, placing a bowl of home-made potato salad on the table in front of me. *How do I answer this clearly 'loaded-question'? If I answer, 'Yes', then it will sound like I'm a wimp; but if I answer 'No', then she'll want to know why I am acting so grumpy – and then what do I say? I can't tell her that I feel like I am an outsider, a misfit, and not getting enough attention any more. This will just get her mad at me, and I can't get her mad at me if I want her to let me go to the movies on Saturday with Billy.*

"Not really...I guess I was just thinking of how Billy gets to drive the tractor when Dennis is working the power auger, and I am bigger and stronger than he is." *Maybe this explanation will do: True enough, but not the real reason for my down in the dumps attitude.*

"So it appears," Rita commented with a knowing smile. "But, Jack, remember that Billy has been working with his dad for years — they are a kind of a team — and Dennis needs an experienced helper at that point. I'm sure that before the job is over, Dennis will have the same confidence in you as he has in Billy. Besides, you needn't be jealous of Billy."

"Why not," I inquired, but without thinking.

"Well..." began Rita, pausing to gather her thoughts, her expression indicating uncertainty — as if regretting what she has just said about Billy, what she may have just started, and not knowing exactly how to end any discussion of Billy on a happy note. Following a deep breath, she said, "Remember how just you and Dennis were working on repairing the old fences...and Billy didn't work with you then?"

"Yes. That was fun." I replied, with a little more enthusiasm than I intended.

"I am sure it was fun...Dennis is a very charming fellow. He probably entertained you with all of his stories about himself."

"Oh, yes! He is full of good stories."

"We can talk more about Dennis some other time, but right now I need to tell you why Billy was absent for the first couple of weeks of the job I hired Dennis...and Billy...to do."

So I am just along for the ride after all.

"Billy," she continued, "was with his mother and his grandparents...the Lewises...having some tests run at the Mayo Clinic in Minnesota. As you can tell, Billy is quite small for his age, and his folks and his doctors here are trying to find out why. Billy is their only child, and he is the apple of his daddy and granddad's eye. They will do anything in the world for him, including treating him like he is as normal physically as you are. But you mustn't let on that you know any of this."

"Did the doctors at that clinic figure out what's wrong with Billy?"

"Unfortunately, no they didn't," she remarked, carefully avoiding making eye contact. "Billy will probably need to undergo more tests, perhaps in the fall."

She knows something but she is afraid to tell me what she knows.

"Is Billy able to do things other than helping his Dad," I asked. *Like, can he and I go to the movies and hang out with his friends?*

"I think so, but why do you ask?"

"Because Billy has asked me to go to see a movie in town... and to hang out with his friends...this Saturday afternoon...after we get off working on the fence."

"I don't see why not. I mean he asked you...I'm sure he knows what his parents will and won't let him do. Do you want to go to the movie with Billy and his friends?"

"Oh, yes, ma'm, I sure do."

"How are you going to get to town? It's an awful long bike ride, and I'm sure it will be too dark when the movie is over to ride your bikes back along this narrow country road."

"Don't worry, ma'm. Billy says he and his folks will pick me up on the way to town," I responded, brightly.

"What's this 'ma'm' business? What's happened to 'Aunt Rita' or 'Rita'?"

"Well, I use 'Aunt Rita' when I'm talking to other folks about you, but calling you 'Rita' makes me feel funny. It just doesn't sound right calling you a name that makes it sound like you're my girlfriend or something like that. Until we come up with something else to call you when were at home, can I just call you 'Ma'm'?"

"I understand. But I don't like you calling me 'Ma'm' either. So why don't we just move on to plain-old 'Mom'. I think enough time has passed that calling me Mom won't dredge up old memories of your mother."

"Sure. That's probably best." *Now that you have Hannah to*

be your 'companion' instead of me, and as long as you are now treating me like a 'plain-old' son, I may as well as treat you like a 'plain-old' mother, and call you 'plain-old' "Mom'. "So, Mom, can I go to the movies with Billy and his friends on Saturday afternoon?"

"Who are these 'friends' that Billy is including in this trip to town? Do you know any of them?"

She really is becoming a plain-old pain-in-the-ass mother! "They are just some of his school friends who live on the farms around here. I don't think I have met any of them before, but I may have seen some of them in town. The only time Billy can be with them during the summer is on weekend afternoons...The rest of the week they are working on their folks' farms. If they're friends of Billy, I guess they're okay."

"I guess that Dennis and Milly will be going to town with you," Mom asserted with some hesitation, like she was debating whether she thinks that is a comforting fact or not.

"I guess so, if we are going in his dad's truck," I answered not knowing that for a fact.

"Anything is possible with those folks," she observed, shaking her head in bewilderment. "Where are you going to ride in that old heap if there's already three people in the cab? I don't like the idea of you riding on the back of that flat-bed truck with nothing around you to hold you in, let alone with nothing for you to hold onto. And just be careful on the ride home if Dennis is driving. In fact, if you think he has been drinking too much, just call, and I'll come pick you up."

"Drinking too much what?" I questioned.

"Oh, you know, booze – liquor, beer, stuff like that."

"How would I know about that stuff," I asked.

"If you see him staggering around when he tries to walk, or if there's a strong smell of alcohol in the truck or on his breath, those would be the signs. Look, I've never seen Dennis drunk, but there are stories, lots of stories, about Dennis' problems with John Barleycorn. It's been a problem for Dennis ever since he came home from the War. That's why he and Milly and Billy have to live in his father's tenant house, and not in a big farmhouse of

QUESTION OF POSSESSION | 301

their own. That's why, when I hired him to build the fences, I re-quired that he have Billy and you working with him. He wouldn't dare drink around Billy, or you. He loves that boy so much, and he is too scared of what I would do to him if I ever found out that he was drinking on the job...and I'm sure that he is convinced that you would tell me if you saw him drinking."

"Well," I chimed in, "don't you think Billy and me being there Saturday night will keep him from drinking, drinking too much? And, where would he do his drinking?"

"Maybe yes, but maybe no. There's an old roadhouse right at the corner of the highway going into town and our road... it's where the farmhands gather on Saturday afternoon to drink and complain...to complain about the farmers they work for, and about life itself. If conditions are right, and the conversation turns black, there is no telling what Dennis might or might not do."

"What about Milly...Isn't she Billy's mom...won't she see to it that Dennis doesn't get drunk?"

"You would think so, but Milly has her own problems. And if she and Dennis get to dwelling on these problems...including Billy's health...then they start to drink to forget."

"Rita," interrupted Hannah, "do you really think you ought to be telling Jack...after all, he's still just a boy...about these...these... these unpleasant things about Billy's mother and father? Won't it make it difficult for Jack to be around Dennis and Milly...let alone to work side-by-side with Dennis...and Billy?"

"You're right, Hannah. Jack doesn't need to know all of the gory details. All you need to know at this point is that Dennis and Milly love Billy dearly, but that they have serious emotional issues which can be intensified with stress and alcohol. I believe that Billy knows how to deal with his parents' problems, so all you need to do is to back him up...and be there for moral support. He needs the help of steady friends."

Oh yeah! You think I can be a steady friend? Have you forgotten that I am the kid who is inhabited with the spirit of a German Fliegerin who can, at will, take charge of my brain and body?

AT THREE O'CLOCK, Saturday afternoon, scrubbed clean, wearing a pull-over collared shirt, khaki pants, standing at the foot of the driveway with my Schwinn bicycle at my side, I heard in the distance the distinctive sounds of the decrepit Ford flat-bed truck, chugging and banging its way down the potholed gravel road. Earlier in the day it was decided that we would take our bikes with us, be dropped off at the County Fairgrounds — where we would meet Billy's friends with their bikes — ride our bikes into town, do 'whatever', grab a burger at Marvin's Diner, catch the early-showing of *Winchester '73*, and — assuming there is still some daylight — ride our bikes back to Billy's house. If it became too dark, the plan was to go to the Roadhouse, determine the condition of Billy's parents, and based on that determination, either ride home with them or call my mom, formerly known as Aunt Rita, and she would pick us up.

I was watching the truck as it came jerking towards me down the rough road, kicking up dust the texture of an old lady's face powder, shuddering to a sudden, crunching stop. Expecting to see Billy's skinny, tanned arm propped on the passenger-side window frame, I was surprised to see Dennis' brawny arm instead. With the sun's glare and the dust on the windshield, I couldn't see who else was sitting in the front seat. *Milly must be driving and I'll bet that Billy is scrunched down on the truck bed just behind the cab.*

Just as I was about to lift my bike onto the truck bed, at the opening in the slats, I noticed that Billy was not seated where I thought he would be — only his rusty, old bike. *Oh, he must be sitting between Dennis and Milly.* Not until I climbed up onto the truck bed, seated myself where I had expected to find Billy sitting, and peered into the cab's back window — did I see Billy sitting behind the steering-wheel — well towards the front part of the seat, his right hand clutching the knob atop the floor-mounted stick shift. *He must be propped up on something to see out of the front window, but how do his feet reach the pedals?*

Dennis called out over the sound of gears grinding as the truck lurched forward, belching black exhaust; "Better hold on tight! There's a bumpy ride ahead."

Dennis' warning was prophetic — a rough ride indeed! There were times where I fully expected to be thrown off of the truck as I clung with one hand on my bike, and my other hand hanging onto the hand-hold at the back of the cab for dear-life. There were other times when I would swing from side to side, like a clock pendulum, as the truck careened around the many S-curves along the old country road.

With each movement of the truck, I was also in danger of being crushed by Billy's bike which slid around the truck bed on its side, like a deer on ice trying to right itself. The worst part was that I couldn't see anything in front of the truck, just what whizzed-by the side of the truck. The dust and exhaust smoke was so heavy that even the world behind me was invisible. *Where are we? Where are we going? Why did I agree to go to town with Billy? Why is Billy driving so fast? Are Dennis and Milly already drunk? Why do I feel so scared? Just let me off, and I'll ride my bike to town.*

And then the teeth-rattling journey ended with the screeching sound of brakes, the grinding of gears, the clatter of metal parts being twisted and jerked about; with the cloud of dust and smoke — which had been in hot-pursuit — overtaking and engulfing the stationary, silent vehicle. Several minutes passed before the cloud dissipated, and before I was able to open my eyes, to see where we had come to rest; and several minutes more for me to loosen my grip on the hand-hold. *Is it really over? Or will it start again? Please, dear God, let this be the end of my torture! I'm getting off of this death machine before it moves again.*

Struggling to get into a standing position, still clutching my bike, I observed Dennis' grinning face looking at me over the top of the wooden slats. "Quite a ride, huh, kid," he remarked, his smile fading. "You okay? You look a little wobbly, boy."

"I'm fine," I lied.

"Well, then hop down. This is where you get off."

Thank God!

Dennis relieved me of my bike, placing it on the gravel parking area of what I thought was the 'roadhouse', and then as he took Billy's bike which I handed to him I asked, "Was Billy really driving?"

"Couldn't you tell," Dennis responded laughing.

"How do his feet reach the pedals," I inquired.

"That's simple...we found him these magic legs. Come on over to the driver's side...I'll show you."

The driver's side door was open, with Billy sitting facing out the door, his legs dangling down, feet in the strangest-looking work boots I'd ever seen — even stranger than clown-shoes in the circus. The tops were just like normal lace-top boots, but the soles must have been six or seven inches thick; made up of a dozen, or so it appeared, of pieces of leather — of different thicknesses and shades of brown — all glued or sewn together.

It sure is lucky that Billy has strong legs — those boots must weigh a ton. I don't know much about driving — just using the brake and clutch pedals and the gear shift on the Farmall Cub — but how in the world does he lift his feet? How does he have the strength and coordination to move his right foot from the gas pedal to the brake pedal? And what about working the clutch pedal? No wonder there was so much grinding of gears and the truck lurching forward as Billy was shifting gears. This is crazy!

"I know what you are probably thinking," Billy asserted, as I stared at his strange pair of boots. "Yes, it is hard driving this here truck with them boots. And we'd be in a big pickle if the cops stopped us, and find me behind the wheel in these contraptions. My Granddaddy had them made for me, so I could help Dad with the farming by reaching the brake and clutch pedals on the big John Deere tractor. I don't think he ever expected that I'd be using these boots to be driving this truck out on the county road. Did I scare you?"

"Naw," I lied. There were just a couple of times when I thought the truck was going pretty fast, especially in some of those quick turns." *I think I need to take a pee!*

"Are you sure? Well, he sure scared the shit outa me," complained an unfamiliar voice behind me. When I turned around to see who had spoken, I was faced with a woman with curly auburn hair, freckles and a toothy smile. *This must be Billy's mom, Milly — they have the same hair color, freckles, facial features, in-*

cluding that dazzling smile. She was dressed in an old-fashioned peasant blouse which displayed her ample cleavage. *Don't stare, Jack!* Her blue-denim skirt was quite short – showing trim legs. Holding a cigarette between the fingers of one hand, she was holding Dennis' arm with the other.

"Someone needs to help Billy get out of those silly damn boots," she commanded, looking straight at me with emerald-green eyes. *How could I possibly refuse this pretty woman anything she might ask of me?*

"Yes, ma'm! I'll do it," I responded, moving towards Billy, whose feet were dangling over the side of the front seat.

"Thanks, sweetie. But be careful with them fruity-looking ol' boots as you take them off. You don't wanna drop 'em."

I was puzzled by Milly's statement. *Those boots look indestructible!* Billy had already started unlacing the boots. When I reached out to pull off the first one, it fell weightlessly into my hands. *What the hell is this? It's no heavier than the Keds I'm wearing!* I heard laughter behind me as I examined the object in my hands, trying to figure out why it felt so light, what it was made of.

"It's molded plastic...shaped and painted to make it look like a real leather boot, only with a much thicker sole. Billy's grandpa had them made for him." Dennis explained cheerfully.

These folks are sure full of surprises! What's next?

Five minutes later – Billy wearing his regular sneakers – we were on our bikes headed out of the roadhouse parking lot, on our way to meet up with Billy's friends. Glancing back towards the roadhouse I observed Dennis and Milly stepping up onto the roadhouse front porch, clutching each other, smiling and happy, like two young lovers out for a night of fun.

They sure make being married look like real fun. My parents never acted like that; and I never saw any of my old friends' parents act like that either. Why? Why are Billy's parents different? Maybe it's kind of like how being Mom's son is so different from being my mother's son. Maybe it's love and acceptance? Maybe Billy's parents love and accept each other, where my parents didn't, and don't, love and accept each other. But I sure miss my Dad!

WAVING OUR GOODBYES, Billy and I rode our bikes away from the "roadhouse" parking lot headed to the County Fairgrounds. Billy's friends, who were standing around their bikes when we arrived at the empty Fairgrounds, consisted of an assortment of sizes, builds and ages; not unlike the variety of guys that inhabited the academy – but a bit less refined, undisciplined, somewhat ragtag. *What did you expect? They are just farm boys, for god's sake! Don't judge a book by its cover – look how wrong you were about Billy.*

"Hey," called out Billy to his friends. "This here's Jack. He's the new guy I've told you about. His mom...Miz Kaufman...owns the big spread where my dad and I are working this summer building fences. Jack's been helping out."

"Hi," I weakly acknowledged to the group; not thrilled with Billy's indifferent introduction. I received a few nods in return, but no verbal acknowledgements. Billy did not even bother to tell me the names of his friends. *Here I am again, just the outsider.*

Despite the uncertain start, it turned out to be a good time by farm-boy standards; mostly rough housing in the movie theatre, and barnyard humor and explicit conversations over burgers and fries afterwards at Marvin's, the town-square burger shop...conversations littered with references to tits, pussies, cocks and asses (especially brought on by speculation about whether Jimmy Stewart is fucking his co-star Shelley Winters – "Great titties").

Such conversations were familiar territory given my brief time as a student cadet living in a barracks. Yet, there was something decidedly different about these conversations – a sense of more reality, less fantasy. *These guys talk like they've done it, not just fantasized about it like I am sure my cadet buddies and I have. Then the talk turned more specific, with the bigger boys talking about "hard on," "coming" – or is it "cumming?", "jerking-off", and "circle-jerks." I know something about "hard on,""coming" (but not how to spell it), and "jerking off," but nothing about "circle jerks."*

"Hey, Jack," interjected Wesley, one of the older, bigger boys, looking directly at me. His hair was close-cut, accentuating his ears which were large and stuck out, but it was his almost black eyes close set above a pig like nose that made him look fierce and ugly. "Have you ever jacked-off?" There was an immediate outburst of coarse laughter among the group catching the play on the words "Jack" and "off."

The question immediately brought back the memory of my late-night erections and masturbation. I felt the warmth rise in my cheeks, and I knew that I was blushing. There was no point in answering the question; my blushing had said it all. *If I don't say anything, however, I'll have earned myself an unwanted nickname – the dreaded, "Jack O."*

"What's it to you anyway? Who here hasn't," I responded with as much bravado as I could muster.

"You tell him, Jack," chimed in Billy, glaring at Wesley.

Not stopped by my response, or Billy's show of support, Wesley pressed the matter further, "I'll bet you and your cadet buddies do more than circle-jerk...I'll bet you spend time on your knees sucking each other's cocks...you pansies!" *Oh, dear. There is no easy way out of this taunt...this is a challenge. I know where this is going.*

Jumping to my feet – feeling my heart pumping, sensing the new-found strength from a summer of building fences increasing my courage – I shouted at the still-seated Wesley, "I'll show you who's a pansy...you fagot!"

Again, Billy displayed his support by jumping to his feet, also facing off at Wesley. "You have no call for what you've just said Wesley...Take it back! If you don't, you'll have to deal with the both of us!" Hearing Billy's threat to join in with me in any scuffle with Wesley, seemed to neutralize the other boys, who started to sit back down in their chairs; to move away from Wesley – who was still seated at the table, breaking eye-contact, staring down at the unfinished hamburger on the plate in front of him.

"I guess you two jerk-offs think you can beat me with that military jujitsu stuff that you – now pointing a table-knife at me – learned at that candy-ass military school you go to, or that you – now gesturing at Billy – got taught by your drun...your old man...Marine-hero Dennis. You two don't scare me one bit. In fact, neither one of you is worth the effort of wiping the floor with your asses."

Raising the palms of his hands in a gesture of yielding, Wesley continued, "But I'm willing to let this pass for now. Someday, though, I'm going whip your asses. Nobody calls me a fagot, and gets away with it." *I just did! You've missed your only chance. We've called your bluff.*

CHAPTER 28

BIG CHIEF TABLET TWENTY-FIVE | JACK

The bike-ride back to the roadhouse was quite a trip. Billy and I were both filled with excitement, still feeling the effects of the high from having scored a bloodless victory over the bully Wesley. We whooped, we hollered, we raced as fast as we could, filling the fading daylight with excited laughter. I couldn't wait to see Dennis, to see his face when we told him about our confrontation with the bully Wesley. *Won't he be proud of us!*

The parking lot surrounding the roadhouse was packed with all kinds of vehicles, with some still circling around to find a parking spot. Even the porch was jammed with people, talking, drinking from bottles, glasses and cans, streaming in and out of the open front door, through which the loud sounds of country music and singing were heard.

Scanning the crowd on the front porch and the vehicles in the parking lot for Dennis, Milly and the old Ford flat-bed truck, we saw no indication that they were still there. We even retraced our steps to where we thought the truck was when we rode away on our bikes; again nothing. If we couldn't find them, if they were gone, we were faced with a difficult bike ride – to at least my house – in the dark, over a rutted, twisty road.

While Billy looked for friends of his parents in the crowd on and about the porch – in hopes of finding someone who knew where his folks might be, I made one last sweep on my bike of the parking area, including the remote areas in the rear of the roadhouse. In the darkest corner of the property, partially hidden by the trunk of a large oak tree, I spotted the familiar Ford truck's cab; it appeared to be empty. *Dennis and Milly must still be inside the roadhouse. Maybe Billy has similar information from their friends.* Without giving any thought to taking a closer look at the truck, turning away I pedaled furiously around to the front of the roadhouse, to where I had last seen Billy.

"Billy! Billy," I shouted, seeing him talking to someone at the bottom of the porch steps in the glare of the floodlights that had just been turned on. "The truck's still here...out in the back...in the dark...hard to see it."

"They ain't inside according to the folks I talked to. No one has seen them here for the last hour or so. They says Daddy was pretty drunk and Milly was trying to get him to stop drinking, to leave, to get him somewhere to sleep it off."

"Do you think maybe he's in the truck...and I just didn't see em?"

"Could be...But that don't change nothing for us...We are still going to have to ride our bikes in the dark to your house...where maybe Miz Kaufman can give me a lift home."

"Can't you drive the truck back home?"

"Are you nuts? If you thought it was a rough ride coming here in the daylight, it would be pure suicide me trying to get this truck up that old road in the dark."

I'm not sure I like either choice. I'm not prepared to die either way.

"In that case, then, sure...Mom can drive you home. Or you can stay with me tonight if you like. Shouldn't we check on your folks first before we leave here?"

"Yeh, but I know what we'll find...and it ain't going to be pretty...So just be prepared for seeing some real ugly shit."

What does Billy mean...'be prepared'...'ugly shit'?

Leading the way on my bike to where I found the truck was a chore. There were no floodlights at the back of the roadhouse, so it was difficult to see the truck until we were almost on top of it, parked behind the tree. Getting off of our bikes, Billy put his on its side, mine I propped up on its kick-stand.

I couldn't see anyone in the cab, even when Billy pulled open the driver's side door. But on the flat-bed I thought I could see some shape or form; like a tarp thrown over a duffle bag. Billy had reached into the truck, pulled out a flashlight which he shined at the lump lying there on the flatbed. The lump stirred, an ashen-white face, with blinking green eyes, suddenly appeared in the flashlight's beam. "Go away you fuckers!" the face shouted angrily. "Leave us alone...We ain't hurt'n no body...Can't you see we's try'n to sleep?"

"It's okay Mom," Billy said calmly in a low voice. "It's just me ...and Jack. Go back to sleep...Me and Jack are going to ride our bikes to his house...where I'll spend the night."

"Come here and give me a goodnight kiss," Milly commanded in a slurred voice, raising herself up off the truck bed with one arm, letting the cover fall away from her. In that instant, the flashlight revealed her two large, milk-white breasts with raspberry-red nipples. A large suntanned hand and arm reached around her body searching for a breast. Milly slapped at the grappling hand with her free hand.

"Leave me be for a moment...we got company," she directed at the person who was attached to the hand and arm. "Hmph!" was all I heard from the hidden person; the hand and arm quickly disappearing under the cover. *I sure hope that was Dennis!*

"Mom! For Christ's sake! Cover yourself. You're showing your tits to Jack!"

"Well, I'm sure Jack don't mind...do ya, Jack?"

"Well, I mind, and I'm sure you are embarrassing Jack...ain't she, Jack?"

My eyes were riveted on the first naked breasts I had ever seen. They are were beautiful! Yes, I'm embarrassed! But it's because I'm getting a hard on. And it's Billy's mom, for Christ's sake! Please, Billy, don't do this to me.

"Just turn off the flashlight, Billy! The show's over!" a gravelly voice coming from under the tarpaulin cover mumbled gruffly. "Go home with Jack...We'll pick you up at Jack's sometime in the morning. And, Jack, you'd better call your mom to come get you. Otherwise, she's apt to skin us all alive!"

Making my way back in the dark to the front of the road-house, I located a payphone booth on the opposite corner of the porch. Pushing open the folding doors, I dialed zero for the operator, gave her the number and prayed that Mom — and not someone else on the party line — answered.

After several of the three rings assigned to our phone I heard a pleasant voice say, "Hello. I hope that's you, Jack."

"Yes, ma'm," I responded, with a sigh of relief.

"Where are you?"

"Billy and I are at the roadhouse down at the corner of the gravel road and the paved highway going into town."

"Well it's about time...I was beginning to get worried...it being too dark for you to ride home on your bikes. I guess the truck isn't operable right now, and you and Billy are looking for a ride home?" She knows exactly what's happened.

"Yes, ma'm. And can Billy spend the night? I don't think his folks will make it home tonight."

"Sure...I half expected that that would be the case. Another paycheck...another Saturday night! We'll be there in a few minutes."

Exiting the phone booth, I noticed Billy talking to some of the grownups on the porch. He was shaking his head, his lips set in a grimace; I could only imagine what he was saying to these people. How embarrassing for Billy. He loves his mom and dad so much. What makes them do this? Don't they know how much this hurts Billy? What can I say to Billy? How is he going to face me?

"My mom's coming to pick us up," I reported to Billy when he broke away from the people on the porch, joining me by the phone booth, his bike by his side.

"Thanks," he said, both of us avoiding eye-contact. *This is going to be an interesting ride home. What in the world am I going to be able to tell Mom about tonight when she asks about what we did...what we saw?*

Standing in silence, in the glare of the floodlights, waiting for Mom to show up, Billy and I watched the boisterous crowd of Saturday-night revelers ebbing and flowing on the roadhouse's porch — some standing in groups, some sitting on the porch-rail — others meandering — some staggering — in and out of its front door. For me it was an unpleasant time; dreading a possible re-appearance of Billy's folks; hoping, instead, for the quick arrival of the big Ford station wagon to spirit us away from this troubling, yet exciting, place.

ONCE BILLY AND I had stored our bikes in the station wagon's cargo area, we slid into the back seat, grateful for the darkness, hoping for silence. I introduced Billy to Hannah — explaining that she was a war-refugee now living with us. She only gave a weak, "Hi." Then all was quiet...for a while. Half-way home, Mom in-quired in her 'mom' way, "What's troubling you boys...you are awfully quiet? Didn't you have a good time?"

"Yeah, sure...*Boy, if you only knew what happened to me to-night!* Billy and I are just tired," I managed in response, hoping that this response would end any further questions.

"Okay," Mom responded half-heartedly. "I've made up the twin bed in your room for Billy...if you don't mind sleeping in the same room."

"No, that's great," Billy responded. "That sounds like fun." *What are we going to do that's going to be "fun"...talk about your mom's big, bare tits?*

Refusing Mom's offer of something to eat, Billy and I climbed the stairs, used the toilet, entered my bedroom; me pointing out which bed was to be Billy's for the night. We both stripped down to our underwear, climbed into our beds with just a sheet to cover us. I turned off the lamp on the night-table between the two beds. The room was instantly pitch-black, filled with the noise of the crickets, cicadas and frogs serenading us through the open windows. My mind was not ready for sleep; it was filled with visions of the evening's events...mostly the arousing effect of naked breasts...full breasts...breasts with bright-red nipples. I want to hold my arousal in my hand, to stroke it, to satisfy its craving.

"Jack," Billy whispered quietly. "I'm sorry about tonight; you know...about my mom. You're not the only boy she's showed her tits to...She only does it when she's had too much to drink, and only to get some guy aroused...but nothing more...She's what Dad calls a 'prick teaser'...Was that your first bare tits?"

"Yes," I responded.

"Well, I'll make sure they ain't your last. Jake Summerfeld... one of the guys you met in town...has a cousin...Martha Ann... who has tits bigger than my Mom's...she'll not only show 'em to you, she'll let you touch them...even suck the nipples...for a quarter."

How in the hell am I ever going to get to sleep now...with this hard on.

"Thanks,"

"No problem...Always glad to help out a friend. And you better take care of that hard on, or you'll never get to sleep. I'm almost done with mine...Stewart's co-star really did a job on me."

How did he know that? How did he do that without me knowing what he was doing?

SUNDAY ARRIVED QUICKLY, but Billy was gone by the time I woke up. I neither heard Billy leave his bed nor did I hear the noisy old truck arrive to take him home. I had so much to talk about with Billy, but it would have to wait. The day crept by slowly, standing between the memories of Saturday night and the possibilities of Monday. I was buried in the memories, and overcome by what might take place when Billy, Dennis and I returned to work. It was not a day that I wanted to spend around Mom and Hannah.

As soon as we arrived home from my guilt-filled 9:30 AM Mass at St. Benedicts, I began a long walk into the fields behind the house, with Lady always close by. After walking through the fields lost in thought, I arrived at the small apple orchard near the stable, where I stood looking out over the gently rolling, peaceful landscape, hoping that Fritz would plug in, join me, provide me with some much needed male input; but I heard nothing from him.

"You seem to be troubled Jack," Mom's pleasant, gentle voice interrupted my thoughts. "Did something bad happen last night? Do you want to talk about it?".

What can I tell her? How do I tell her?

"Look, Jack...it doesn't take too much imagination to figure out that Dennis and Milly were too drunk to drive you and Billy home. As I told you earlier, most everyone knows that Dennis and Milly have problems, mostly drinking related. But I can't see that them being too drunk to drive you home was enough to put you in such a gloomy frame of mind. It has to be something more, something else. Do you want to share what it is with me? Or do you want me to guess what it is? You know I don't live in a convent...I know what goes on in town...especially with that crowd at that roadhouse...on Saturday nights. And I'm not easily shocked...So don't be embarrassed to tell me what happened at the roadhouse last night that's got you so upset."

Here goes nothing! "When we got back to the roadhouse on our bikes after the movie...after dinner...we couldn't find Billy's folks, or the truck, where we thought they...and it...would be. It was getting dark, so I went looking in back of the roadhouse...out towards the woods in back. And I spotted what looked like the truck, but I couldn't see anyone in the cab...So I go get Billy, who is talking to some of his folk's friends to see if they know what's happened to Dennis and Milly...but they haven't seen them for a while.

"When I tell Billy what I think I've seen, we go back to the truck. The first thing Billy does is open the door to the truck, but there is no one in the cab. I spot a pile of something on the back of the truck – the flat bed – and Billy shines the flashlight he got out of the cab on the pile. I see a face looking at us...which starts cursing at us. We knew immediately that it was Milly. When Billy tells her who we are, she says she wants to give Billy a kiss...and when she raises up...her top gets uncovered...and she is naked... her breasts are bare...even the nipples. When Billy tells her that I'm there...she just says asks me if I'm embarrassed by seeing her...she says 'tits'. Before I can answer, Billy's dad...who's also under the cover...tells him to turn off the flashlight...'the show is over' he said...and then tells me to call you to come get us."

"Okay...So you saw Dennis and Milly drunk...and you saw Milly's bare breasts...But, she's always showing her 'tits'."

"That's what Billy told me later, but I didn't know it at the time...And it was Billy's mom."

"Did you get aroused? Is that it?"

"Yeah, I guess...but it's his mom."

"So what...At your age any naked breasts are sure to get you aroused...Even the Sears' catalogue lingerie ads will do it...And don't think I haven't noticed your interest in that catalogue...and taking it into the bathroom. But I won't ask you the obvious question."

By then I was blushing. *This is the kind of conversation that I had hoped to avoid by taking my walk. Oh, well!*

"The important thing is that life is full of these awkward, unexpected, embarrassing situations. You will learn from them, hopefully. You are not alone...we all have things like that happen to us. It helps if you have someone to talk to...honestly...about how they affect you...Hasn't our talk helped?"

"Yes...But, I'm also upset about Dennis...about why he has such problems that make him drink too much...and about how do I face him tomorrow morning when we have to work together again."

"Okay. Let's start with how you think Billy feels about what happened. Isn't he's the one most affected by his mom and dad's behavior?"

"I think Billy has already gotten over his mom's behavior...He was upset for me...but I guess he's use to it...he said his dad calls her a 'prick-teaser. But I don't know how Billy feels about his dad...he's never said anything about it to me. Last night was the first time I ever saw his dad drunk...and actually I didn't see him drunk...I just assumed...since he was lying under a cover on the back of the truck...that he was so drunk that he had passed out... like it happens in the movies."

"I don't know the reasons why either, although folks say that before the War Dennis was as sober as a judge, but when he got back he was a different man...a drunk. I don't know what happened to him in the War to change him. He was some kind of

hero...he got lots of medals for bravery. So there must be a connection there, but I just don't know what it is."

After a lengthy pause, Mom said, "My best advice for you is to
act as if nothing happened Saturday night...just go to work with
Dennis...and Billy...just like you have worked with them every
other day. If they want to share anything with you, then that's
their decision...and be very gracious...don't be crude or ugly...be
the young gentleman you have been taught to be. Now come
here so I can give you a hug...a mother's hug!"

ON MONDAY MORNING, Billy and Dennis arrived in the old Ford
truck at the barnyard gate, as Lady and I were crossing the dusty,
uneven gravel road, ready to face another day's hard work building the fence. This was to be our last week of working together
on that blasted fence. I was having mixed feelings about the
work coming to an end. The work had been hard, but working
with Dennis and Billy had been great fun, a great experience. I
knew that I would miss the friendship that had developed, the
team work that had been required by the nature of the job. In
keeping with my previous conversation with Mom, I vowed that I
would not let the events of that Saturday night destroy what we
had accomplished.

The day was hot and humid, with dark clouds beginning to
gather quickly in the southwest. The last stretch of fence had
been laid out, the location of the post-holes staked, moving
along the crest of a grassy hill-slope. We were near the end of
the project; about a hundred-fifty feet from the spot where the
new fence was to tie-in to the southeast corner of the existing
fence around the barnyard where there would be a gate.

The conversation that morning had been brief, pleasant, directed mainly towards the work at hand. Shirtless, the sweat
glistening on my tanned upper torso, I was struggling with a
role of barbed wire – my hands sheathed in heavy leather work
gloves – my army-style work boots clawing at the hard-packed
clay ground seeking traction – when the first bolt of lightning
flashed brightly across the darkening sky, followed almost imme-

diately by a loud clap of thunder.

The next thing I heard was the command from Dennis, "Drop and run! Drop everything and run!" Dennis' usually placid face was lined with tension, like someone who saw danger. Immediately responding to his command, dropping whatever it was we were holding onto, we ran towards the barn as fast as we could – with Dennis in the lead – while more lightning strikes struck around us. It felt like we were under attack by Mother Nature – or in Dennis' case, maybe under attack by the Japanese.

Making it into the barn through a sliding door, just as the first sheets of rain began to lash our backs, pelting the ground, turning the dust into splashes of mud, I breathed a sigh of relief. The air, which outside had been refreshed with a pleasant, electrical smell, was immediately replaced with the heavy odor of cow dung, straw dust, hay and animal feed. Even within the safety of the sturdy barn, Dennis' face was still etched with a look of terror, his body shaking with each flash of lightning. *Have I just seen the answer to my question as to what happened to Dennis in the War? Maybe what demons haunt him?*

"Wow! We made it in here safely...Without a second to spare!" I commented encouragingly, hoping to break the fear that had taken hold of Dennis.

Seeing me looking at Dennis, observing my look of concern, Billy commented – just loud enough to be heard above the noise of the storm, "Don't worry...Storms scare Dennis...He'll be fine as soon as it passes." But the pounding of the rain – and perhaps some hail – on the barn's corrugated metal roof, the booming, rolling thunder shaking the big wooden building, rattling doors, windows, any loose fitting, made it seem that we were caught in the end of the world.

Maybe so! But Dennis doesn't strike me as someone who would normally be terrified by a thunder storm. It must trigger some awful memories. Just like thunder and lightning, and gunfire, terrorizes poor Lady – who experienced warfare on Guam as a puppy.

The storm raged in waves for over thirty minutes, the rain and hail continuing to beat on the barn roof, the lightning and thunder moving away more rapidly. While Billy and I stood some ways into the barn, keeping an eye on the progress of the storm, relishing the cool breezes stirred up by the storm, my occasional glances towards Dennis revealed that Dennis' normally dark-brown skin was ashen white, his face covered in beads of perspiration, his hands still trembling. He remained crouched in one of the empty horse-stalls, his eyes darting from side-to-side as if looking for something, or someone. It was not until the lightning flashes stopped and the thunder ended that Dennis began to show signs of an inner calm, again standing.

"Are you okay Dad," Billy asked.

"I tink so," Dennis responded in a weak, shaky voice.

"Can I get you some water," I inquired.

"Yeh. Tanks. Tha sounz dood," he answered, slurring his words.

The jug of water that we had carried to the work-site that morning was still where we were working when the storm struck. Not wanting to fetch the jug, I hurried to the water trough, turned on the electrical switch to activate the pump to the deep-well that fed the water trough — happy to find that the electric power was not knocked out by the storm — waiting until there was the familiar flow of clear, cold water. Instead of waiting for me to bring him a dipper of the fresh water, Dennis had walked — somewhat unsteadily — to the trough, stuck his head into the stream of water coming out of the pipe, letting the stream douse the back of his head, neck and shoulders with numbing cold water, allowing it to cascade down his torso for several minutes. Removing his head, putting his hands under the water, using his cupped hands, Dennis splashed the cold water onto his face, filled his mouth with refreshing gulps. Without a towel, Dennis used his hands to scrape some of the water from his face, letting the rest remain on his body.

"There, that's much better," he reported as he turned away from the trough, the color returning to his face. "That was one bitch of a storm." Looking out the small door towards the fields in the distance, he added, "It may be several hours before it is dry enough for us to go back to work."

"While we are waiting," Billy asked, "don't you want to rest a bit? You must be tired from the storm. I've never seen you so upset before."

"It was one of the tougher ones," Dennis responded, looking off into the distance.

"Do you wanna talk about it? You know it usually helps."

Looking at me for several seconds, Dennis said to Billy, "Do you think it will bother Jack?"

"After what Jack saw Saturday night, I don't think it will bother him. In fact, it might help Jack understand what happened on Saturday night."

"Oh, shit! Yeah, Saturday night. Jack, I bet you seen things Saturday night that you ain't never seen before, didn't ya? Well, I'm sorry if what you saw upset you...we didn't mean for you...or Billy...to see us like that. You two was supposed to go on home without finding us back there in the woods, in the back of that roadhouse, or on the back of the truck. As far as what happened today, I'm sorry you had to see me like this. Let's just say that thunderstorms trigger bad memories from the war. I don't wanna talk about it today...or maybe ever...or with anyone but Milly. I appreciate your concern Billy, but all I wanna do right now is to get back to work.

CHAPTER 29

THE 8 1/2 X 11 SIZE MANILA ENVELOPE WAS SITTING on Paul's desk when he returned to his office after lunch. Even from a distance, Paul recognized the markings on the envelope, causing the remnants of his lunch to churn in his stomach. *What is this from the Adams County Sheriff's Department; what news are they sending; why didn't they just phone me with the news?* As he extracted the contents of the envelope, Paul felt his emotions swing from one of fear to one of anticipation. There was a single-page typed letter on Sheriff's Department stationary, to which were attached two poor-quality photos and pages of lined tablet paper filled with what appeared to be Jack's hand-writing. Putting the attachments to the side, Paul read the typed letter, dated September 28, 1952:

```
Dear Mr. Johanson,

Enclosed are some copies of materials that
we discovered at Fairways on a return visit.
We were looking for photos or other materi-
als that might help us to identify the miss-
ing people. We could only find a photo of a
woman and a photo of a boy, which were tucked
in the back of a drawer. Can you please tell
us if you recognize the woman and the boy,
and their names?
```

Also, we found the attached pages of writing tablet paper in the same drawer that mentions this Jack and widow Kaufman person. Are these two of the people we are looking for?

There was only a single mention of the Hannah lady, and there were some other names, like Fritz and a Dr.Glassberg. Do any of these names ring a bell?

If you have any other information, please call me.

Sincerely,
Deputy Roger Grace

Having read the letter, Paul picked up the snapshots of Rita and Jack. It was difficult to determine exactly the age of the snapshots, but they both looked to have been taken at the same time, probably in the last six months.

Picking up the lined writing tablet pages, Paul immediately recognized the handwriting as Jack's scrawl, something written in a hurry. With a sense of foreboding, Paul began to read:

Last night as I was going to sleep, my mind was filled with Fritz's thoughts. I don't know whether Fritz wanted me to experience what he was thinking, or whether he thought that I was already asleep and he had plugged into my mind to do his usual mind wandering too early. Here is what I can remember about what Fritz was thinking:

"I am still trying to figure out what the widow Kaufman has been doing behind Jack's back. This latest revelation that she and Hannah are recording Jack telling my story concerns me. I am familiar with the Gestapo, the S.S., using tape recorders to record interviews of witnesses. Is the widow Kaufman sharing these recordings with that Dr. Glassberg on the pretext that Jack is now exhibiting some psychological abnormality necessitating institutionalization? Or is she sharing my story with others in the hopes of discovering inconsistencies in the story Jack is telling? Everything that I have instructed Jack to report to the widow Kaufman about my past and about the von Bruckner family is, as best I can now recall, historically accurate.

"Then it must be that the widow Kaufman has become concerned with the possibility that I might take control of Jack, and she wants to have evidence of my power to do that. Could it be that she actually believes that while I am in control of Jack that I will cause her physical harm? But why would I do such a short-sighted thing like that? Without the widow Kaufman's involvement in my plans, there is little hope of Jack alone being able to carry out my mission. Besides, any harm inflicted on the widow Kaufman would surely be blamed on Jack; potentially resulting in Jack's incarceration or institutionalization; and, again, that would be something that hardly serves my purposes.

"In light of my concerns, I am determined to remain plugged into Jack's brain whenever he is at Fairways or around the widow Kaufman and her side-kick Hannah. But I will provide no further writings to Jack, and I plan to locate all of my previous writings and destroy them."

Something is not right. I think that Fritz is going to take some steps to protect himself from Aunt Rita. What can I do....

At this point Jack's writing ended. *What in the world is going on? Why has Jack been writing in these ratty, cheap Big Chief school-tablets? I'll bet anything that Nell found some of these writings at Fairways, and that she is spending her evenings reading what Jack and this Fritz fellow have written. I've got to find them.*

After calling Deputy Grace in Greenville, letting him know that the snapshots are of Rita and Jack, and that he thinks he recognizes the writings as being Jack's, and that he also recognizes some of the names set out in Jack's writing, but has no specific information as to how they might be involved with Rita, Jack and Hannah's disappearance, Paul left the office for home, determined to locate the rest of Jack and Fritz's writings, if any.

WHEN PAUL RETURNED home from work he attempted to enter Nell's bedroom before she returned home from work. He found the bedroom door locked; providing Paul with additional evidence that Nell was hiding something from him. It was an old-fashioned door-lock, which Paul easily unlocked with a similar key from a similar lock. The only illumination in Nell's bedroom was the diffused light coming in through a north-facing window. A slight scent of expensive perfume lingered in the air; a reminder of when he and Nell both occupied this bedroom. Careful not to disturb anything, Paul surveyed the room, not certain of what he was supposed to be looking for, or where to find it. *It can't be very big, or I would have seen her carrying it out of the Fairway's house, or have seen it in the Ford sedan, or have seen it when Nell carried it into the house and up to this bedroom.*

Paul looked in all the obvious places; dresser drawers, closet shelves, even under the bed, but he found no trace of the writings that he was convinced were in that room. Remembering Nell's past behavior in hiding things from him, from the boys, Paul concluded that she had taken the writings with her to her place of work – where they would surely be safe from prying eyes. With one last look around the bedroom, Paul exited the room and relocked the door.

In fact, Nell had not taken the "secret writings" with her to her place of work; the innocuous-looking book-bag in which they were kept was hanging on a hook in the back of her closet. But even if Paul had discovered the bag and the writings it contained, they would have been of little help in finding the missing Jack, Rita and Hannah, although they contained important clues as to what had happened to take them away from Fairways.

CHAPTER 30

BIG CHIEF TABLET TWENTY-SIX | FRITZ

Jack was getting quite an education at the hands of the uninhibited Lewises. Portions of his mental process to which I had access were a pulsating collage of vivid images, dazzling emotions, dark musings that kept bringing me back for more. It was difficult for me not to stay plugged in – even more difficult for me to remain just an observer, to not intrude myself into Jack's stimulating involvement with the Lewises; the risk being that, in the course of simply providing helpful input or counsel, I might get carried away, wresting control from Jack – thereby disrupting, ruining the precious learning experience. As much as I hated to admit it, the widow Kaufman, too, had been prudent in not over-protecting Jack, not preventing him from seeing, experiencing this coarser side of life; helping him to sort out his resulting confused feelings, his burgeoning lust, in a pragmatic, non-judgmental fashion. We may make a man of Jack, yet.

It was time, though, for me to turn Jack's attention away from the Lewises and back to the important task of completing the telling of my journey through the windings and turnings of Nazi Germany, compounded by its ill-conceived designs at world conquest. Without hearing my entire history, I was concerned that the widow Kaufman would not appreciate, or would not be compelled to accept and act upon, my ever increasing need to return to Germany. For it was being back in Germany that I can bring my odyssey, my torment, to its conclusion; when I would no longer need Jack.

Jack. Before you go to sleep and start to dream, I need to interrupt your thoughts. First, I want to commend you on how you have handled the recent experiences with the Lewises, especially the episodes at the roadhouse and the thunderstorm.

Jack responded: *You saw what happened?*

Yes, I was plugged-in. You know how sensitive I am to strong brain and nerve impulses. It was difficult to ignore your feelings of terror on the wild truck ride; you clinging on for your life to the back of Billy's truck. Or your feelings of anger and elation as you and Billy faced down the bully, Wesley. I was particularly aware of your emotions, your feelings of arousal and confusion when Billy's mom, Milly, revealed her attractive naked breasts. And it was hard to ignore your emotions of fear and concern brought on by the violent thunderstorm and Dennis' extraordinary reaction. So, yes, I experienced what you experienced, felt what you felt; and I was aware of how you struggled with understanding how these experiences and feelings color and shape your reactions to people and their behavior.

Jack said: *I think I understand better what Milly did — that she wants attention, but I would like to know more about what happened to Dennis during the thunderstorm. You were in the War... can you tell me why he reacted the way he did to the lightning and thunder? Mom says Lady is shell-shocked because of what she saw and heard during the fighting on Guam. Is that what's wrong with Dennis?*

Perhaps, but I would have to know more about what was happening to Dennis during the fighting. It is not just hearing the noise of battle that induces the trauma — the "shell-shock" — but the intensity of the fighting actually involving the soldier. Was he in hand-to-hand combat with enemy? Did he witness a particularly gruesome injury to a close comrade? Most such trauma is of a short duration, and the soldier can return to the front within days. There are other cases where the soldier does not exhibit any of the symptoms of trauma — such as appearing dazed or excessively anxious — and continues to fulfill his soldierly duties with little diminution of effectiveness, only to later suffer from nightmares and occasional strange behavior. This may be what afflicts Dennis, and thunderstorms may trigger the behavior that you witnessed during the thunderstorm. His binge drinking and lusty partying may be a symptom of his trying to escape what he calls his "bad memories."

In the German military, there are different approaches to dealing with battle-traumatized combatants during the conflict; from treating them as wounded, to giving them a short rest and sending them back into battle. This was what was happening during the Russian, North African and Italian campaigns; as well as following the Allied Invasion in France. I am, of course...since I was dead prior to the War ending, unaware of any long-term care for, or even about, the traumatized combatant once the war was over; unless the combatant had also received serious injuries — like the loss of sight, loss of limbs, or severe burns. At least that was my experience from seeing so many crippled veterans littering the streets of German cities after the first War, many of whom were incoherent — either with drink or suffering mental problems — both obviously the result of the impact of warfare.

Now, Jack, that is enough about Dennis. I have been patient during the time you have been working so hard on the fence-building job not to press you on continuing the telling of my story. You were just too tired in the evenings to manage corralling the widow Kaufman and Hannah together to continue the narrative. But now that the fence job is about to end, I would like for you to remind them of their agreement to hear me out, and to set a time when you can resume the story.

———————

"WHEN WE LAST spoke on this subject of Fritz's saga," Jack began, in his own voice, reading from the notes that I had prepared for him; speaking to the widow Kaufman and Hannah sitting in their rockers, staring out into the distance: "Fritz's father was acting strangely, with no explanation forthcoming from his father or his mother. We pick up Fritz's story with Fritz working in his office in the Air Ministry in Berlin, preparing himself for the assignment from General Udet to oversee the development of a jet propelled aircraft, winding down his involvement in the production of the Ju-87 Stuka dive bomber."

"The year was 1939. Germany had again annexed adjacent territory – this time Czechoslovakia – without spilling any German blood, by diplomatically outmaneuvering the British and the French governments, by promising no further territorial acquisitions. Hitler would keep no such promise. By accurately predicting that Britain and France – though both were much stronger militarily than Germany at the time – would not come to Czechoslovakia's aid, Hitler had proven once again that he had a better grasp of political and military matters than did the General Staff and the officer corps. He used this opportunity to overwhelm and purge the military leaders, leaving around no army leaders with any power or public support to effectively oppose his supremacy over Germany's fate. Hitler immediately turned his attention to Poland, to capturing and annexing its territory and peoples; to expanding the new German empire in Europe.

"It was also a time of intensified persecution of Jews in Germany – a foretaste of a deeper, more vicious, campaign against Jews living throughout the territories that were to come under German domination in the next few years. At that time, the campaign was directed at taking away Jews' rights of citizenship – including their possessions, their livelihood, their access to basic services and protections – best exemplified in the terror and horror of Kristallnacht, a night in November, 1938, distinguished by government-sanctioned murder of Jews, and untold destruction of Jewish property through arson and broken window glass. It was now too late for the Jews who had chosen to remain in Germany – even when so many had already fled to France, England, the United States in the face of Hitler's initial attacks on Jews – to escape their suppression, their agony, their fate, unless they had the financial resources to buy freedom.

"There were, of course, many Germans who were appalled at how Jews were being treated by the Nazis, but few would risk the dangers of speaking out on behalf of Jews. Those who did were quickly silenced by sending them to one of the many concentration camps springing up throughout Germany...originally constructed to imprison the Nazis' political opponents. This left those who wished to help Jews to do so in secret. The von Bruckners were among those who continued to risk exposure, relentless interrogation, and cruel incarceration by assisting Jews in whatever form...be it food, concealment or escape.

"It is against this backdrop of iron rule, inevitable military conflict and human destruction," Jack concluded, "that I resume reading to you Fritz's narrative, using the notes Fritz has prepared for this purpose."

IT HAD BECOME extremely difficult to remain in open contact with my brothers, Ernst and Wolfgang. There were indications that the SS and the Gestapo were monitoring our written correspondence, our telephone conversations, even our face-to-face meetings. It was rumored that there were personnel within the organizations for which we worked – the Abwehr (Ernst) and the Air Ministry (me) – or with whom we have had close relationships – Dr. Schacht (Wolfgang) – who had been engaged in a conspiracy to overthrow Hitler. Even though we held rather unimportant posts, and should have been beyond suspicion, we may have been targeted because of Poppa's outspoken criticisms of the Nazis – their attacks on the Catholic Church and the Jews – and because of his well-known ties to those men who were the natural subjects of suspicion, including my superior, General Udet.

Indeed, on one cold afternoon in late-February, 1939, the telephone on my desk rang. When I picked up the handset, giving my usual greeting, "*Hauptman* von Bruckner," there was no response, just static on the line. "Hello," I repeated several times, again without a response. I was just about to hang up, when a scratchy voice...in a low whisper...said, "Expect a visitor...Be prepared!" Then I heard a "click" and the line went dead. I pressed the switch hook several times hoping to reestablish the connection, but all I heard was a dial tone. *Who was that...One of my brothers? Who else would call me with such a message? What does this message mean? 'Be prepared' is clearly a warning, but 'be prepared' for what? Will I know this 'visitor'? Where will I meet this 'visitor'? When will I meet this 'visitor'? I have lots of 'visitors' in my job...How will I know which 'visitor' I need to be prepared for?" I guess I'll just have to wait to find out.*

Several days later, there was a knock at my office door. "Hereinkommen!" I responded, not looking up from the jet propulsion schematic that I was studying.

"*Hauptman* von Bruckner? Fritz von Bruckner?" queried a tall, handsome officer in the uniform and markings of the Schutzstaffel (S.S.), with the rank insignia of an *Oberst*, standing in the doorway. I immediately jumped to my feet, reaching for my tunic which was draped across the back of my chair.

"Ya. Herr *Oberst*," I replied, trying to put on my tunic – searching my mind trying to place a name with this familiar face. *Is this my visitor? If I can only recall his name, I will know if he is the one for whom I need to be prepared.*

"My name is Dietrich Muenster...I believe we have met before."

Of course we have! At the Nazi rally years ago. How can I ever forget that night? Your Uncle Otto – Poppa's sworn enemy – humiliated me and Poppa in front of that group of Nazis. You are my enemy! You must be my 'visitor'. Scheisse! This is beyond awful! This is a catastrophe!

"Yes, Herr *Oberst*...In Braunschwieg...while I was at the University...At a political rally."

"Those were interesting times," he observed, looking right at me with piercing black eyes, a sneer curling his lips in a make-believe smile.

Oh, this is the Devil himself!

"Take your seat!" he demanded, moving towards the chair next to my desk, placing his attaché case on the desk.

"Would you care for a cup of coffee," I enquired as *Oberst* Muenster opened his attaché case and extracted a thick folder.

"No thank you...I don't usually take coffee this late in the day...It interferes with my sleep."

I'll bet it does...Along with what you are carrying on your conscience Herr SS Oberst!

"But I would like an ashtray. A dreadful habit, I know. I see you don't smoke."

I sat there patiently, nervously watching Herr Muenster carefully insert a cigarette into a its black holder, light it with a few puffs, then clinching it in his teeth while he opened the folder, rifling through its contents, pausing to examine certain sheets, and then moving backwards and forwards in his search, finally settling on what appeared to be a single sheet of paper. Looking up from this sheet of paper, again directly at me, and after clearing his throat as he removed the cigarette holder from his mouth, Herr *Oberst* inquired, "Are there any Jews in your family von Bruckner?"

"Not that I am aware of," I replied without hesitation. Is this what this 'visit' is all about?

"Then why are your father...and other members of your family...engaging in potential treason by helping...protecting...Jews?"

How do I answer? Is this a 'fishing expedition', or does Herr Muenster have solid evidence of illegal activity?

"My family has many friends who are in need of help and protection. It may be that some of these friends are Jewish. But as good Christians...as good Catholics...we believe that we have an obligation to feed, clothe, comfort, and protect those less fortunate than we are...regardless of whether these people are our friends or our enemies."

"But you are aware, are you not, of the laws applicable to Jews...laws enacted by the Reichstag to restrain the Jews ability to undermine and upset the social order...the social fabric?"

"Yes, Herr *Oberst*."

"Why then do you disobey these duly enacted laws?"

"It is certainly not our intention to violate any duly enacted law...Nor do we believe we are disobeying any law by helping people in need...We are simply following our religious belief that we must help those who need help...regardless of the source of their suffering. The Bible says we are to visit those in prison...The Bible does not qualify that requirement to say that we are to visit only those who are in prison that did not break a law...Besides, the only law that these people appear to have broken is to have been born with Jewish blood."

"Be very careful, von Bruckner, you are engaging in sophistry...using the art of semantics to weave an argument that borders on reckless behavior. You know very well that the letter and intent of the laws is to strip the Jews of German citizenship, and to render them unqualified to receive humane treatment. What your family is doing....in the guise of Christian morality...is providing care and comfort to enemies of the state...and that is treason...treason, plain and simple. Your own words condemn you."

"But, Herr *Oberst*," I began to protest.

Raising his hand to silence me, *Oberst* Muenster asserted, "No more...
We are finished with that subject...Your treasonous behavior is not why I
am here." Studiously ejecting the stub of the cigarette from its holder, he
continued, "While it is true I am here to warn you that you and your family
are in serious danger because of your pro-Jewish behavior...which can result in being sent to a concentration camp, my real reason is to solicit your
assistance in a much more serious matter...a treasonous matter resulting
in summary execution."

Placing a new cigarette into the holder, Herr Muenster continued, "Let
me say that your defense of your family's pro-Jewish behavior is commendable, if only because you chose to defend it rather than to deny it."
After lighting the cigarette, exhaling a puff of smoke from the corner of
his mouth, and closing the silver lighter, he turned to his folder, extracting
a sheaf of papers.

Waving the papers in front of me, he added, "We have irrefutable evidence of several incidences where your family has engaged in hiding Jews,
and in helping Jews escape from Germany. There is proof enough here
to send you, your family, to the camps for years...where your father can
join his friend von Schuschnigg. Why do you think your father has been
acting so strangely? Reichsminister Himmler...my superior...as a favor to
Reichsminister Goering, has warned your father of the evidence against
him and others in your family...which your father continues to ignore. But
if you will now provide me with the assistance I am about to explain to
you...and if your family will cease helping Jews...then maybe I think we
can ignore the deplorable acts you have been committing, at least for the
time being."

"How can I possibly assist you, Herr *Oberst*? I don't have any..."

Again cutting me off with a wave of his hand, before I can complete
my statement, *Oberst* Muenster stated, "Before you try my patience with
your feeble protestations of ignorance and feigned innocence, just listen
to what I have to tell you. Your father thinks that he has been so clever
in his clandestine actions against the Reich, but he has been a fool. From
the very beginning...yes, that episode in Braunschweig in 1931 was not
by accident...your father, his family, and his kind are marked men. Why
do you think this folder, this dossier, is so thick? We have been gathering

evidence on your family's illegal, treasonous activities for years. So, as I said before, listen carefully: Your life and that of your attractive young wife and your infant son will depend upon it. Life in the concentration camps can be brutal and hard."

"Yawhol, mine *Oberst!*"

"Good. I thought you would understand. Now, all of what I have told you about the evidence we have collected on your family, and especially what I am about to tell you, is top secret. No one outside of a few high-ranked members of the S.S. and the Gestapo, have access to this information...and no one other than Reichsminister Himmler knows why I am meeting with you. Therefore, before I can tell you anything more about why I am here, I must have your agreement to do all that I will request of you, down to the tiniest detail. If you will not agree to work with me... or if you do, but later disclose any of what I will tell you about your assignment...you and each adult male member of your family will be executed immediately and in a manner that will not attract attention...and the women and children will be separated and placed in concentration camps. Do you understand? Do I have your unconditional agreement?"

What choice do I really have? I'm not afraid to die; and I am sure that Poppa, Wolfgang and Ernst would willingly give their lives as well, rather than sell their souls to Oberst Muenster and the S.S. But I cannot allow Momma, my sisters, Marta and Maria, my beautiful Lisa, my son, Kurt, or any of the other children, to endure the unspeakable horrors of the brutal, barbarous concentration camps.

"Ya, *Oberst* Muenster!"

"Fine, then here is what I want you to do. We believe that investigators in the S.S. and the Gestapo have already identified the majority of the *Wermacht* and *Luftwaffe* officers who have been plotting the overthrow of the Third Reich. However, there may be one or two high-ranking officers in the *Luftwaffe* who are engaged in the treasonous activity, but who have so far avoided detection, or who have not yet acted overtly. It will be your job to identify these traitors, and provide evidence of their complicity. We have our suspicions as to how many traitors there are, and who they may be; but I will not share that information with you...for obvious reasons. Once you have gathered enough evidence to bring these officers to justice, you will bring that information only to me...or my designee... and I will proceed from there.

"Under no circumstances are you to provide an officer you have targeted with any indication that he is under suspicion, nor are you to take any steps to protect him. The temptation to do so will be great...Most likely, these will be officers with whom you are friends or officers who you highly respect...But if you succumb to the temptation you will be discovered, and you and your family will be summarily and harshly dealt with."

General Udet must be one of the officers under suspicion...or he would not have found it necessary to warn me earlier about his fear that conversations in his office are being monitored. But who are the others? How will I be able to discover their 'complicity'?

Sensing my concerns about the difficulty of the task, *Oberst* Muenster continued, "You are in a unique position to ferret out the identity of the criminals. You have earned the trust and respect of most of the *Luftwaffe* high-command by virtue of your family background, by the manner in which you have handled each duty assigned to you, and by virtue of your current assignment...which places you in contact with a variety of officers at many different levels and responsibilities. I am expecting you to use your position to identify potential targets, and to gain the confidence of these targets so that they will reveal their involvement in treason. You do have an added advantage...you can reveal what you know about the conspiracy because your father is a conspirator...and the targets will trust you because if they are, in fact, conspirators they will most surely know of your father's involvement."

"Finally," Dietrich Muenster remarked, "In anticipation that you would see the importance of the assignment I have just given to you, and the difficult position in which your family's activities have placed you, I have had a document prepared for your signature. It simply outlines the terms of your agreement to serve the Third Reich in the manner I have outlined, as well as detailing the crimes you and your family have committed by assisting Jews in contravention of the laws proscribing such assistance. You will now sign the document, and then I can be on my way."

If I sign this document I will be signing mine and my family's death warrant. But what alternative is there?

After a cursory reading of the densely typed five pages, to assure myself that the document was consistent with *Oberst* Muenster's spoken version, I inquired, "How do I know that you will not use this document immediately to arrest, prosecute and condemn me and my family? What assurances can you give me that that will not happen?"

"I can assure you as a German officer that this document will not be used against you or your family as long as you carry out your end of the agreement...Namely, bringing me the names of the traitor *Luftwaffe* officers and the proof of their treachery."

"How quickly must I carry out this assignment? There is no mention of a time-frame in the document."

"The sooner we can end this conspiracy, the safer the Third Reich will be...although we have no real fear that any attempt to bring down the Thousand Year Reich will be successful. What we really want is the quick removal of the traitors from the Reich. Therefore, I will expect you to bring me the first name within six months, or give me good reasons why not...You know, von Bruckner, I can be very patient...as I have exhibited by waiting all these years to bring you and your family to its well-deserved downfall.

"Your arrogant, old-world father tried to destroy my uncle Otto during the First War because he was not an aristocrat, and then you and your unruly, unrepentant brothers destroyed Uncle Otto's prized rooster for typical aristocratic sport. Your family has represented everything evil and oppressive about the old aristocracy. Germany...the Third Reich... will be better off without you! But I think we can wait a bit longer to see that day."

It sounds as if the best I can achieve is a delaying action. Ultimately, we are doomed; unless I am able to work a miracle, find a way to keep Herr Muenster at bay.

With significant misgivings I signed the odious document, knowing that my family and I were now inescapably linked to *Oberst* Muenster; completely at his mercy, dependent upon him honoring his promise. He placed the signed document in his attaché case, snuffed out his umpteenth cigarette, leaving the expended butt in the overflowing ashtray, placed the officer's cap with the death head emblem on his head, uttered the required "Heil Hitler," and exited my office, slamming the door with a loud bang behind him. I was left staring at the door.

What in the world have I done? What have I gotten myself into? How can I possibly identify the officers he is looking for? Everyone in the building surely heard his grand exit; and putting two and two together they will conclude that I am damaged goods — and will have nothing to do with me. The presence of a high-ranking S.S. officer in my office means either my neck is in the noose or I have a confidential relationship with a member of the most feared organization in the Reich. In either case, I will henceforth be viewed as a pariah, a dangerous person! This assignment is preordained for failure from the very beginning. How can I have been so naïve? I need to alert my family as to what has transpired with Dietrich Muenster, and of the danger that confronts us; but how can I contact any of them without drawing in the S.S. who are sure to be watching my every move.

THE BALANCE OF my story revolves around my largely unsuccessful efforts to find the traitors in the *Luftwaffe's* upper-echelons, and to keep my family out of the clutches of Dietrich Muenster. The fact that I managed to survive to the end of the War and the collapse of the Third Reich was a miracle! I cannot say the same for the rest of my family — although I believed that my younger, sister Maria, a nun, was still alive and possibly still in danger.

By the time the six-month time limit imposed by *Obertst* Muenster for my initial performance arrived, Germany had invaded Poland on 1 September 1939...and all attention was quickly focused on all-out warfare... England and France immediately declared war on Germany. During this time period I had been completely immersed in assuring the production and availability of sufficient numbers of Ju-87 Stukas needed to spearhead a new concept of warfare which came to be known as the *'Blitzkrieg'* — Lightning War...so I had little opportunity for interaction with my fellow *Luftwaffe* officers, let alone with the higher-echelon officers. I suspected that *Oberst* Muenster was also similarly preoccupied with more important matters.

Once those portions of Poland overrun by Germany had been subdued (In July, 1939, Germany and Russia entered into a non-aggression
pact that included Russia having rights to certain portions of Poland), I
was working full time on the jet propulsion aircraft design, spending my
time with the design team at the Junker's plant which had been awarded
a contract by the Air Ministry to produce a production-ready, axial-flow
engine utilizing a compressor that employed rings of blades driving air
directly into the combustion chambers. BMW and Heinkel were also developing their own versions of a turbojet-engine.

Ultimately, the Air Ministry looked to Willy Messerschmitt to produce
a jet propelled aircraft, awarding a contract in July, 1940 for three prototypes. This aircraft – designated Me-262 – was an interceptor fighter to
be powered by twin turbojet engines mounted in pods under the wings.
I spent most of my time traveling between the Messerschmitt plant in
Augsburg – where the airframe was being built – and the Junker and
BMW plants – where the turbojet engines were still being developed.
The technical problems associated with such a radical new engine design
plagued the engineers, causing much delay in bringing the project to fruition.

It was not until late 1941 that there was a major breakthrough in turbojet engine design, thereby increasing thrust and reliability, bringing the
possibility of a turbojet powered fighter aircraft closer to reality. I informed the Air Ministry of this accomplishment, the news of which was
received with much relief. The Allied forces had commenced using much
larger, more powerful bombers in their bombing runs over Germany, necessitating that we retaliate with more powerful, faster interceptor aircraft.

FOLLOWING MY ANNOUNCEMENT of the break-through, I received a
message that *Generaloberst* Udet wanted to see me, to travel from Augsburg to Berlin. I had not been back in Berlin in months. The place for the
meeting in Berlin was undisclosed. I was informed only that his driver
would pick me up at the *Luftwaffe* terminal at Templehof airfield. I was

excited about the trip; hoping that I could extend it into a short furlough. These were tough months; being away from Lisa and Kurt who I missed terribly. I was looking forward to having an opportunity to see the love of my life and my handsome young son, even if for only an hour in the crowded, dingy military waiting room at Tempelhof airfield upon my unscheduled arrival; before my meeting with the General.

"I was so afraid that you did not receive my message in time," I murmured to Lisa, clutching her tightly to me, "I just learned late yesterday that I was coming to Berlin to meet General Udet today." Lisa was still so lovely, though much thinner than she was when I last left her bidding me goodbye in this same cheerless waiting room some six months ago. And Kurt, barely walking was standing, hanging onto her leg, looking at me like he would any strange man. His blond hair, his piercing blue eyes reminded me of what I must have looked like to Poppa coming home on leave – back when Germany was in the First War.

"Actually, General Udet's adjutant called me yesterday to let me know that you were coming home on business...and suggested that I might take the opportunity to meet you here for quick visit."

"That was very kind of him. But it also means that I will be here for only a short time...with no chance of even a three-day leave."

"Whatever the purpose, it must be important...The adjutant...whose name I do not know...said he would pick you up here at noon sharp...and to please be waiting outside...at the main door. He will flash the vehicle's lights to let you know it is him...and you are to enter the back seat as if it were empty."

It was already 11:35 AM, giving us just a short time to find a secluded spot to talk, to gaze at one another, to share a bit of intimacy, a furtive kiss. There were but a few women mixed in with this teeming mass of warriors scuttling from one place to another in the waiting area, but just enough people to give us some cover from snooping onlookers. Ever since my visit from *Oberst* Muenster, I was convinced that my movements were constantly monitored. Young Kurt being here with his mother did provide some rationale for our huddling together – just another young family suffering the agonies of separation. It quickly came time for us to part, and for me to make my way to the rendezvous with the General's adjutant. I held Kurt in my arms hugging him tightly while I kissed Lisa long and passionately, as if this was our last goodbye.

At exactly 12 Noon, as I was standing at the curb, an approaching drab-colored, unmarked sedan blinked its headlights twice, indicating that this was the vehicle I expected. The sedan had barely come to a stop when the rear passenger door opened – with the passenger remaining out of sight. I quickly slipped into the sedan, which immediately accelerated before I was fully seated. Even in the dark interior I observed that the other passenger occupying the rear seat was the diminutive Generaloberst Udet. Other than the driver, we were alone. I was surprised by the General's presence, and by the fact he was traveling in such a simple motor vehicle – so uncharacteristic of the type of vehicle usually used to convey such an important personage. *Is he traveling in cognito? Why is he avoiding attention? Are his activities being monitored?*

"Welcome to Berlin, *Hauptman* von Bruckner," General Udet greeted me pleasantly. "I hope your visit with Lisa and your son Kurt was pleasant...though unfortunately too brief I am sure."

"Yes, mine General, pleasant but all too brief. But thank you for making it possible."

"Think nothing of it. Even though I have no family of my own, I fully appreciate the importance of the love of a desirable wife and adoring children. I wish your visit could be longer...But we have some very important business to attend to which will necessitate your immediate return to Augsburg...I think you will be pleased, though, that we will be meeting with the Baron...your father...We are meeting him at one of his plant's outlying fabrication hangars, where he has been working, at my request, on a special project...

"But before we get into that, tell me what you think of the turbojet fighter aircraft...As you know I am not in favor of developing the turbojet aircraft. I see it as a great waste of time and resources. Unless I can be convinced that it will save the Third Reich, I will not support any request for its production. Will it save the Reich?"

"A very incisive question," I replied. "I think that the turbojet powered aircraft is the greatest technological development of the War...And that if it is used properly, it could definitely change the outcome of the War."

"How so," he asked.

"Using the Messerschmitt 262 airframe as the platform and the Junker's Jumo-004 as the power plant, this fighter aircraft has several characteristics that leave the piston engine fighter far behind. Theoretically, the turbojet fighter has greater speed, better climbing capability, a higher service ceiling, can burn any fuel...from kerosene to cooking oil...and can carry more fire power. Obviously, until we can get a prototype in the air for test flights, we can only speculate...But I am convinced that the turbojet fighter can be more than a match for any Allied fighter and bomber aircraft...The real unknown is the reliability of the turbojet engine. The turbine blades are critical...requiring high-strength metals and alloys that can withstand incredible stress without causing distortion or disintegration. And that is why the break-through reported to the Air Ministry is so important...We have fabricated a turbine blade using titanium, which is lighter and stronger than using conventional steel. Unfortunately, the supplies of titanium are scarce and the sources are unreliable."

"But is the new turbojet so superior that it will save the Reich?"

"It might not, by itself, save the Reich Herr General, but if it receives the full support of the Air Ministry, and gets into full production within the next year, the turbojet fighter could definitely give the *Luftwaffe* control of the air for years to come."

"In your opinion, *Hauptman*, will turbojet aircraft ever be capable of use as an offensive weapon, such as bomber aircraft? Most of Germany's bombers were destroyed in the bungled bombing attacks against Britain... Would a turbojet bomber be a better weapon for Germany if the Reich hopes to win the War, now that the Fuehrer has invaded Russia? Unless we are able quickly to defeat the Russians, I anticipate that there will be lengthy, debilitating conflict...which will necessitate that we be able to destroy the Russians' ability to manufacture war materials...And only bombers will give us that capability."

"Turning the currently planned fighter aircraft into a turbojet bomber will require major redesign of the airframe. Moreover, I am not sure the current turbojet engine design would provide enough thrust to power a larger airframe. It would take months to make the necessary alterations and modifications, and even then we would just be at the prototype stage, with months of additional testing ahead before we will know if we have a viable turbojet bomber. And I don't know if we have the necessary resources to pursue both projects at the same time."

"So, Fritz, if the Air Ministry should elect to pursue a turbojet bomber instead of a turbojet fighter, it could be years before the Reich would have any turbojet aircraft in its arsenal of weapons?"

"Yes, unless instead of choosing a pure bomber over of a fighter aircraft, we could find a way to modify an existing turbojet fighter aircraft to function as a turbojet fighter-bomber...like the Ju-87 Stuka. Then we could have both a fighter and a bomber...of sorts. Of course the bomb-carrying capacity of the fighter-bomber would not be as great as a pure bomber would provide...but it would be better than nothing."

"I like your suggestion, Fritz. It may be the very option that the Air Ministry can propose if forced to choose between a turbojet fighter and a turbojet bomber. Thank you. I am much encouraged that we will have aircraft that will help us...maybe not enough to win this unfortunate war, but at least to let us achieve an honorable surrender. Hopefully, the Baron will provide us with equally encouraging news."

POPPA WAS STANDING alone outside of the aircraft hangar on a remote portion of his plant's property when General Udet and I arrived in the non-descript military vehicle. The hangar's big doors were closed, and there was no evidence of ongoing activity as one would expect to see at a fabrication plant. *What is this special project?* There was a look of consternation on Poppa's face when I stepped out of the vehicle. His face brightened, though, when his old friend, Ernst Udet appeared from the other side of the vehicle.

The two old comrades embraced warmly, the physical contrast could not be more extreme; the Baron was tall, austere – hatless, dressed in a dark suit and tie – and the General was short (barely coming up to Poppa's shoulder), dapper – resplendent in his sky-blue and cream uniform and jauntily placed officer's cap, with the Iron Cross and Pour le Merite decorations hanging at his neck. After an exchange of pleasantries, Poppa escorted the General into the brightly lit hangar, pausing just long enough to ask me in a whisper, "What are you doing here? Don't you know how dangerous this is?"

"I had no choice," I replied.

Crammed into the hangar was a large, strange-looking three-engine aircraft – an engine built into each wing, with the third engine coming out of the nose of the aircraft. I had never seen such an aircraft like it before, nor had I heard anything at the Air Ministry about the existence of such an aircraft. It appeared to be a sleek, fantasy version of the more recognizable boxy Ju 52/3m tri-motor aircraft long operated by Lufthansa for passenger service. The aircraft was painted black, and appeared to be of metal construction, with a series of rectangular windows down each side, but no evidence of armament. Perhaps it was just a prototype of some new transport-type aircraft, and Poppa was participating in its fabrication.

"Is this it," inquired General Udet.

"Yes," replied Poppa.

"How soon will it be ready for use?"

"Whenever you tell me you need it."

"The cargo is being assembled now. How about 1 November?"

"That will be fine. Where will the cargo be delivered?"

"I'll need to let you know that just before departure."

Looking at me, Poppa remarked, "I am sorry that you have seen this aircraft. Just knowing that it exists puts you in severe danger." Turning to the General, Poppa asked bitterly, "Why did you bring him here with you?"

"I just assumed that Fritz was involved with the project, like the rest of your family," the General replied irascibly.

"He was earlier, but he hasn't been involved for a while...ever since he was visited by that snake, *Oberst* Dietrich Muenster of the S.S."

How did Poppa learn about that? Who else knows?

"That's unfortunate," commented the General. "But there is nothing we can do about it now...Hopefully, we are not being watched today...And if we are, we have long known the consequences of our actions...Obviously, then, the sooner we get this over, the better...And the sooner we get Fritz out of town, the less chance there is for his being drawn into this."

"I think it will be better," observed Poppa, "if I have one of my employees take Fritz over to the Junker's plant — where he is known and would have reason for being there. From there Fritz can get a ride to the air terminal later today. Has anyone else seen you here in Berlin?"

"Yes. The General was kind enough to let Lisa know that I was arriving this morning...She and Kurt met me at the terminal where we had a brief visit before the General picked me up."

"Did you tell her why you were here," Poppa inquired with deep concern marking his face.

"Only that I was here to meet with the General."

"Good. The fewer people who know you are here and why you are here, the better for all of us," Poppa stated curtly. "What about your driver, General?"

"He has been involved with me for years...He can be trusted."

"Even those we trust can be broken," observed Poppa. Then turning towards me he added — a pained expression crossing his face, "Even my own son, I'm afraid."

"Poppa," I began; only to be cut off from saying anything further by Poppa turning his back on me.

"Yes, Fritz, I know about your meeting with Herr Muenster...And of your bargain with that devil! Why do you think that you have been sent off on assignments...off to places...where you are not likely to complete that bargain...and why your family...except your sweet wife, Lisa...has shunned your very presence? I am sure you thought...in your naïve way... that you were trying to save us...but all you have done is provide a confession of the family's guilt...signing all of our death warrants. Don't you realize that your family is willing to die for its beliefs rather than to live in this madhouse...to serve these madmen...to make a bargain with the devil?

"Yet," Poppa continued, "all that you have accomplished by your 'noble' gesture is to prolong the agony that is sure to befall each one of us. You have, unfortunately, done nothing to improve the chances of ridding Germany of this evil regime that is taking us headlong into an appalling disaster. I am sorry that the General has brought you here today. I would have preferred never to lay eyes on you again. And, while I must as a father and as a Christian to forgive you, I never want to see you again."

"But, Poppa, please," I pleaded, "don't turn your back on me...I was willing to give my life right then and there...as I knew that you and my brothers would...I wasn't thinking about the men...I was only trying to protect Momma, Lisa, my sisters, the children, my son. It was never my intention to do any more harm than I thought had already been done... Actually, I was hoping to buy the family some time...some time to find a way to get out of Germany...just like you have been doings for the Jews... and carry the fight for saving Germany to a safer place...for the time being...until a realistic opportunity for success presents itself. The world cannot long ignore what is transpiring here...We need to provide the outside world with evidence of the Nazis' inhumane treatment of the Jews... and those of us who are trying to protect them. You...with your contacts and reputation...could do much to make the rest of the world accept the evidence...to react against the Nazis."

"Silence," Poppa shouted. "Haven't you retained any of what your mama and I have taught you about love and loyalty to the family...to the Fatherland? We would never run away from our duty to God and to the Fatherland! You are worse than a traitor...you are a fool!"

"But, Baron," interjected General Udet, "Fritz is, in my humble estimation, putting family before the Nazi Reich...and I would think that you would be proud of that...Moreover, you don't know what he has been doing to protect me and others who he could have turned over to the S.S. Doesn't that count for something? Doesn't that demonstrate that he was not acting foolishly? He is trying to keep people alive who can help bring down the Third Reich as quickly as possible...people who gain nothing by sacrificing their lives on the altar of old-fashioned honor. Times are changing, with certain beliefs taking precedence over others.

"We need valiant, honorable people...in and out of the military...to fight for the Fatherland by undermining the Third Reich...by bringing the Nazis to a quick end. This requires choices that may run against beliefs in some cases...like the choices Fritz has made, is making. No one has a crystal ball that tells whether one choice is any better...any more effective...than another...just as long as the choice is grounded on the belief that the Third Reich, the Nazi Party, Herr Hitler and his cronies, must be destroyed. We...I mean all of the right-minded citizens of this once honorable nation...may not be strong enough alone to bring about the collapse of the current government, but we must work every day to use our positions...however great or small...to weaken the government and its ability to win the war it has started...giving a better chance for success to those people, those nations who are stronger than we are, to finish the job."

Poppa started to interrupt the General, but the General indicated he would not tolerate an interruption, continuing his thoughts by saying, "And Fritz's suggestion that you and the Baroness escape Nazi Germany with the Jews, going to Britain or the United States where your position and family background could do much to publicize the plight of the Jews, is an excellent suggestion...Your title, your impeccable family background, even your accomplishments in the First War, now mean nothing here in Nazi Germany...not even to the industrialists and the burghers who previously were your supporters. In fact, you and your fellow aristocrats have become targets, viewed as reactionaries, deserving of eradication. So your leaving Germany is a sound option.

"And as for Fritz," observed the General, "I was going to ask him to help me in the job he is currently doing...and doing quite well, I might add...to find ways of lessening, and certainly delaying, the potential impact of a new, potent technology...the turbojet...which, if perfected, might just possibly win...and certainly would prolong this War and the Nazis' reign of terror. So let's try to work together now. There are so few of us who have the dedication, the talent, the opportunity to make a difference."

Moving towards the door we had earlier entered, General Udet stepped between us, grabbed Poppa and me by the elbows, dragged us along with him, saying as we walked together, "I really must get back to the Air Ministry before certain people realize I am not there...As Fritz so aptly pointed out we are all being observed, we are all subjects of suspicion. We are also grown men, dealing the best we can with a horrible situation, with dangerous consequences. I need the both of you to work together...in whatever way you can...to help me carry out increasingly more difficult projects."

Looking directly at me, the General declared, "Fritz, I want you to get back to Augsburg as quickly as you can, by whatever means of conveyance works best, and attracts the least attention...That also goes for how you leave the Baron's plant...I will travel back to Berlin directly and alone. You know what needs to be done, and I am sure you will discern a way to accomplish the task...Now leave us, Fritz, while I confer with the Baron — there are things we will discuss that need you not, and should not, have any familiarity...for your sake as well as ours."

"Fritz," Poppa implored, looking at me with tear-filled eyes, "I am sorry that I did not grasp the true meaning of what you are trying to accomplish...The way things are developing here, we may never see each other again — in this life. Please forgive me for labeling you a 'Fool'. You are, as the General has pointed out, a very perceptive, brave young man. I am so proud of you! May God bless you and protect you."

With tears welling in my eyes, I clasped Poppa to my chest, whispered in his ear, "Ach du Poppa...May flights of angels guide you to your rest. Please give Momma my love. And if you can, please take care of Lisa and little Kurt."

Releasing my grip on Poppa, I turned to General Udet, saluted him, asserting, "Thank you my, General, for your support...I will do all that you expect of me. Fur der Vaterland!"

CHAPTER 31

BIG CHIEF TABLET TWENTY-SEVEN | FRITZ

The trip back to Augsburg was long, circuitous, painful, and full of uncertainty. I exercised unaccustomed caution, being careful about not attracting attention – even resisting the strong temptation to telephone Lisa from a railroad station serving a small town on the outskirts of Berlin, where I boarded a southbound train to Augsburg late at night. Yet I was certain that I was still being watched, my every move scrutinized by the S.S., the Gestapo. My attempts at sleeping in the darkened, nearly empty train car were interrupted by frequent stops at other small towns and villages, and when the slower train moved onto a siding to allow an express train to pass by.

The events of the afternoon with Poppa and General Udet flowed through my mind like a surreal dream, causing me to reassess my role as husband, father, son, aviator, engineer, potential saboteur. *Am I a patriot, or am I a traitor? Am I to serve the Reich, or am I to serve der Vaterland; to serve my God?* Looking to Poppa and the General as my exemplars, I knew that there was no other choice but to employ my talents and my assignment to deny – or at least substantially delay – the development of turbojet aircraft; confident that General Udet would sustain and assist my efforts.

BACK AT WORK at the Messerschmitt plant in Augsburg, I spent the following days analyzing how best to accomplish my goals of denial and delay. Clearly, the most advantageous use of the turbojet at that stage of the War was as the power-plant in an interceptor fighter – where it might provide the Reich with needed air-superiority against Allied bombing attacks, fighter cover and invasion.

To prevent the Reich from achieving air-superiority, the further development of the turbojet engine had to be stopped or curtailed, or, at the very least, the end-product turbojet had to be rendered unreliable and inefficient. In addition, the airframe being designed to incorporate the turbojet had to be compromised: Should it be an interceptor fighter or should it be a bomber? I reasoned that the longer it took to resolve this controversy, the more likely it became that a turbojet aircraft of questionable quality would become operational too late, and in insufficient numbers, to have a positive impact on the outcome of this ill-advised, disastrous war.

BY MID-NOVEMBER, 1941, the invasion of Russia was moving rapidly; with German tanks and infantry within a hundred miles of Moscow – Hitler's goal-line for victory. German casualties, however, were disastrously high – over several hundred thousand officers and men – and an early winter was settling in – with heavy snow and below zero temperatures by the first week of November. With my new commitment to bring the Third Reich to a quick, complete end, I prayed that the Russian campaign ended in a defeat for Germany – even though I despised the godless Communist dictatorship, and even though I knew that a German defeat would mean the death of millions of valiant German soldiers captured, slaughtered in retreat.

At my desk in the Messerschmitt factory, I concentrated on outlining plans to eviscerate the Third Reich's turbojet aircraft project – doing my part to assist in the Third Reich's quick demise. At some point I needed to share my plans with General Udet so that he would not inadvertently countermand or reject actions that I may have orchestrated.

I was in the process of preparing a cryptic message for General Udet's eyes only – trying to make it the converse of what I was really planning –

when Ludwig Hurst, one of the Messerschmitt lead engineers on the Me-262 project with whom I have been working closely, approached my desk handing me a document, saying, "I thought you might want to see this. It just came in over the telex."

```
        For Immediate Distribution
        General Forces Headquarters
              17 November 1941


The Generalluftzeugmeister of the Luftwaffe,
Generaloberst Ernst Udet had a fatal crash this
morning while testing a new type of plane. The
Fuehrer has ordered a state funeral.
```

My God! General Udet, my protector, my friend, is dead! This can't be! A plane crash! An experimental plane! Was it the plane I saw at Poppa's plant? Who else was on the plane? Was Poppa on the plane? Was Momma on the plane? Did they die? Was it an accident? Where did it happen? If Poppa and Momma were on the plane, the Gestapo will surely cover it up. But why would General Udet be on that plane? I was sure it was going to be a one-way trip to smuggle Jews out of the country, to safety. And the General gave no indication that he would run away, that he would abandon the fight to destroy the Nazis! There has to be some better explanation. How do I find out what really happened?

"Fritz! Fritz! Are you alright," I heard Ludwig saying, breaking into my thoughts. "Did you know the General well?"

"Yes! Yes! I knew him very well...He was a close friend and a First War comrade of my father...He was instrumental in bringing me into the *Luftwaffe*, guiding my career to the turbojet development. I just can't believe he is dead...I just..." I quickly caught myself before I completed my thought − *"saw him recently." I must be very careful. If my paranoia of being spied upon is actually real, then I could be in considerable danger now...If the General's death is anything but accidental...And if I am linked, in any way, to events surrounding the General's death.*

"Then accept my deepest condolences," Ludwig offered with some emotion.

"Thank you...And if you see or hear anything further about the accident, please let me know."

Over the next several days, there were numerous newspaper articles extolling General Udet's many accomplishments, his achievements, describing the details of the state funeral and procession, but there were no details about the fatal accident. No mention about other deaths related to the airplane accident appeared in any publication. There were no phone calls, no letters, or no cablegrams from my family about my parents' death, which is what I would have expected if they had died in the crash – unless their deaths were now a state secret.

This lack of confirmation was most distressing; and I had no way of directly inquiring of those who might know the facts without creating more problems – each of our telephones was tapped, every piece of mail – coming and going – was intercepted, read by the Gestapo, the S.S. Even indirect efforts of contact were perilous and unreliable. *But if General Udet's death is related to the flight of the aircraft I saw in Poppa's hangar, then rest of my family would surely have been arrested if Poppa and Momma were on that same aircraft when it crashed. But if that were the case, why haven't I also been arrested?*

I was constantly on the lookout for the enemy. Each time an unknown person appeared on the floor of the Messerschmitt factory where my desk was located I broke into a cold sweat, thinking that perhaps it was the S.S. or the Gestapo coming to arrest me, or at least to interrogate me. Even at night, when I was locked in my tiny furnished apartment, hearing strange noises in the building or on the street outside, I was gripped with panic, again wondering if there would be a knock on my door signaling the arrival of the police. Trips to the market for bread and wurst (when they were available), or to a café for a light evening meal, was constantly an anxious time. I frequently alternated my routes – whether driving my small motorcar or when walking – and my clothing – *Luftwaffe* uniform during the day and civilian clothes after dark.

In my heart I knew that these precautions were silly – my *Luftwaffe* billet was widely known within the Air Ministry, and, I am sure, my location was known to the S.S., *Oberst* Muenster, and the Gestapo; they were after all intercepting my mail, listening to my telephone conversations – but I did not want to be nabbed unawares, unprepared. Dreading the thought of lengthy interrogation, fearing cruel, painful torture, I often considered whether it would be better for me to use my Walther P-38 side-arm, taking my own life, rather than being taken alive when they came to arrest me. *I'll make that decision if, and when, the time comes.*

Not surprisingly, these concerns affected my work on the Messerschmitt M-262 turbojet fighter; keeping me from focusing on how to compromise the airframe and diminish the quality of the turbojet engine – as I promised General Udet I would, his death notwithstanding. Additionally, my plans were dependent on assistance from others; and with General Udet's absence I had to look to others in the Me-262 project – someone who, like me, was knowledgeable about the airframe and engine, but I was skeptical about whom I could trust to help me.

I knew that it would take some time for me to develop the kind of relationships with people that I worked with that would allow me to ascertain who shared my sympathies; who was willing to put a life on the line. The perfect candidate was Ludwig Hurst, the lead engineer, the fellow who brought me the telex announcing General Udet's fatal aircraft accident. That was not, I thought, a random act of kindness: Hurst and I spent a great-deal of time together searching for advanced design techniques to assure that the airframe would withstand the demands imposed by a turbojet engine. We respected each other's intelligence and scientific approach. But I needed to get to know Ludwig better. I needed to ascertain his political views.

"Ludwig, have you heard anything more about General Udet's fatal aircraft accident," I asked one morning – several weeks after he had handed me the telex announcement – with the primary intention of cultivating Ludwig as a friend, but also hoping to learn something about the lethal accident.

"Nothing official, I'm afraid. But there are rumors that the announcement of an aircraft accident is a cover up...General Udet may have committed suicide...I figured that you already knew this. I'm surprised that you did not hear about it from your friends at the Air Ministry. Didn't you work with officers there who would have better knowledge about what is true and what might just be a rumor?"

"You would think so, wouldn't you? But there are very few officers at the Air Ministry with whom I have a close working relationship...Both this project, and my previous project...the Ju-87 Stuka, were assignments made directly by General Udet. I reported directly to him. So I can't just call anyone at the Air Ministry who I would feel confident to provide me with the real truth of the General's death...But, can you tell me anything more about this suicide rumor...anything about a motive?"

"Remember that whatever I tell you came from people at Messerschmitt, so I can't vouch for its accuracy, reliability. What I have heard is that the pressure of the job just got to him. It is said that the invasion of Russia, coupled with the tremendous loss of planes in the bombing of Britain, caused the General to become depressed and to start drinking heavily. But, you worked for him, you knew him better than most officers. Do you think there is any basis to such a rumor?"

This rumor can't be true! I never saw him depressed or drunk. I'm sure that if the General had become so distraught Poppa would have known, would have said something, and he definitely would not have been involved as he was with the General in whatever adventure involved the secret aircraft I saw in the hangar at Poppa's factory!

"Do the people who have told you these rumors say how the General killed himself? Was it an airplane crash?"

"They now say it was not an airplane crash. What I have heard was that he shot himself. The question I have is: 'Which story is the true story?' I mean...What are they trying to hide?"

Yes, Ludwig...I have the same questions? But, unlike you, I think I know the true answer!

Instead of sharing those exact thoughts, I opined, "From my considerable contact with the General, I would never conclude that he was suffering from depression or using alcohol as a crutch...Quite to the contrary, he always struck me as being optimistic and positive towards his responsibilities. He may have expressed some concerns about the direction of the War..." *(Here I added, hoping to draw Ludwig into my conspiracy)* "But who hasn't from time-to-time questioned whether Germany is moving too quickly for its available resources?"

Ludwig, the consummate scientist, did not take the bait, did not express his feelings, but instead inquired, "What do you think the military is trying to hide?"

Sensing a new opening to explore Ludwig's political views, I asked, "Why do you think it is the military that is behind trying to hide the reason for the General's death? If it wasn't an accident, and if it wasn't suicide, then it can only mean that the General died of natural causes...or was killed. They certainly have no reason to hide the reason for his death if it was from natural causes...They would have plenty of reasons to hide the nature of his death if the General had been killed, executed, assassinated."

"But who would kill the General? Everyone I know in the aircraft industry who had anything to do with the General always spoke so highly of him. And the *Luftwaffe* pilots considered him their friend for all that he did in the First War and for what he was doing to make sure they have the best aircraft possible to fight this War...as hard to do as that has become."

'as hard to do as that has become!' So maybe Herr Hurst does have some private political views that I can work on. But I must not pursue this opening for the time being.

"Do you think," I continued, "that the Air Ministry will pursue the development of a turbojet fighter aircraft more enthusiastically than did General Udet? The design of a turbojet fighter is already requiring a considerable expenditure of time, money and resources...and it is still not a sure thing. If General Udet's successor or his boss, General Milch, were to ask you, as Messerschmitt's chief design engineer, whether the pursuit of such an aircraft is really worth the effort, what would you tell them?"

"You are putting me on the spot...especially since you work for the Air Ministry...for the very same men who would be asking that question."

"Forget that I am working for the Air Ministry. Just assume that I am a friend...someone with no vested interest in the turbojet aircraft project in general or in the Me-262, in particular. How would you answer?"

"Well, there certainly are a number of current technical problems – mostly associated with the development of a reliable turbojet engine – for which, I might add, Messerschmitt has no ongoing responsibility... but the theoretical advantages of such a turbojet aircraft over any other operational, piston-engine aircraft makes the gamble, in terms of time, money and material resources, worth it."

"Is the turbojet aircraft capable of changing the outcome of the War? Will it assure Germany's victory over its enemies?"

"Perhaps, but only if the United States does not enter the War on the side of Britain and the U.S.S.R. any time soon."

"Why would the United States entry into the war...being Germany's enemy...change the outcome?"

"Because the United States has access to the necessary material resources to build whatever is needed to fight a large-scale war; and because it is currently immune from bomber attack, unlike Germany, whose manufacturing capabilities and resources are already being subjected to periodic attack. If the United States should enter the War it can build more and better aircraft than Germany currently has...So even if Germany quickly fills the skies with turbojet aircraft, it may not be enough to overcome whatever military might the United States will be able to mount against the best that Germany has. It is simply a matter of men and resources; which is something that the Nazis failed adequately to consider when they started this War!"

Well, at least Herr Hurst is not a true-believer. But is he willing to make it easier for Third Reich to lose this war, and to lose it more quickly?

IN JUST A few days following our conversation, at the beginning of the second week of December, Ludwig and I received the answer as to what role the United States would play in the Third Reich's ongoing War. On Sunday, 7 December 1941, warplanes from aircraft carriers flying the flag of Imperial Japan attacked the United States' Pacific Fleet anchored at Pearl Harbor. Four days later, on 11 December 1941, Germany declared war on the United States. It would, of course, take some time before we saw the effects of the United States' full commitment of its men and resources to the war effort. *Will Herr Hurst's predictions come true...and how quickly? How long will it take before he sees the futility of the Nazi war efforts, so that he will join me in my efforts to undermine the efforts to produce an effective, reliable turbojet fighter aircraft?*

Even without any mischief on my part, the development of the turbojet fighter was further delayed by airframe issues and engine failures – both the BMW 003 and the Junkers Jumo 004 continued to be undependable. I couldn't have been happier. Even when at long-last a reliable turbojet engine was finally produced, there were problems with accommodating the new, larger engine into the wing-mounted nacelles. Moreover, the aircraft then experienced incessant handling problems, especially at takeoff. Both issues required extensive airframe redesign efforts.

The program experienced an additional setback when, in July 1942, seeking to have the advantages of a paved runway to overcome the temperamental prototype turbojet aircraft's takeoff problems, the entire assembly facility was moved from Augsberg to Leipheim. I, of course, made the move to Leiphiem, but Ludwig Hurst – my hoped for co-conspirator – stayed behind in Augsburg to save an already troubled marriage. It was just as well, because by October 1942, the entire turbojet program was again relocated, this time to the experimental station located at Lechfeld, an austere outpost near Augsburg. But Herr Hurst was close by once again.

By that time, the United States' presence in the War was being felt, as was the failure of the Third Reich to defeat the Russians quickly. The situation for the Third Reich became even more difficult over the next several months. Almost daily Germany was subject to saturation bombing; the American bombers during the day and the British bombers at night. And still the turbojet fighter aircraft was just in the prototype stage, with no formal requisition by the Air Ministry.

It was not until spring, 1943 that the V-4 prototype Me-262 performed sufficiently to impress General Adolf Galland, the head of fighter aircraft pilots. After his test-flight of the Me-262, General Galland raved about the aircraft. He was so impressed with the aircraft that he attempted to persuade Herr Goering to cancel all contracts with Messerschmitt producing piston engine fighter aircraft, and to concentrate solely on the production of turbojet fighters.

I realized that I could no longer rely on chance alone to keep the turbojet fighter out of the *Luftwaffe's* arsenal of warplanes. I had to come upon a way to keep General Milch from adopting General Galland's enthusiasm for the Me-262 fighter. The best place to start, I concluded, was to convince Messerschmitt that, while the Me-262 was a promising aircraft, it was still experimental, and that until Herr Hitler had placed his stamp of approval on using the turbojet exclusively in a fighter aircraft, Messerschmitt would risk its long-term survival as a primary airframe manufacturer. *Is this the appropriate time to test Ludwig Hurst's interest in further delaying the production of the Me-262 turbojet fighter? Can he help me convince Messerschmitt to apply pressure on General Milch to resist General Gallard's production plans for the Me-262?*

PLEASE FORGIVE ME, but I have rushed ahead in my story, failing to fill you in on my efforts to ascertain the fate of my family members following the news of General Udet's untimely death. Because of the suspicious nature of the General's death, perhaps also involving my parents, I was reluctant to contact any of my family members for fear that whatever contacts I might have with them would be intercepted, and whatever was communicated between us could tie my family to potentially criminal activities. After much prayer, I put the matter in God's hands.

Shortly thereafter – right before Christmas, 1942 – I received a letter from my younger sister, Maria, the nun, telling me that she had been invited by Poppa and Momma to spend Christmas with them in Potsdam, and she wanted to know if I would be there, too. Assuming that Maria's letter was intercepted and read by security police, I now had the perfect pretext to request a Christmas pass, to contact my parents, Lisa and my other siblings by mail in order to at least elicit an innocuous reply, without unduly raising suspicions. Any reply would provide affirmation that they were still alive and free. During the course of the next week, I received my pass and, more importantly, I received letters from Lisa, Momma, and the others, expressing excitement about a Christmas family reunion. *Perhaps the rumors of General Udet's suicide are true after all. Whatever the facts are, his death is not tied to my family, or so it would appear.*

My only hope to arrive in Potsdam by Christmas day was dependent on my ability to catch a plane ride on a *Luftwaffe* plane from Lechfeld, a chancy endeavor – Lechfeld being an experimental station with no regular air service to Berlin. After waiting around the base terminal for hours, I was offered a ride on the prototype of a new military transport aircraft under development by Junkers which, miraculously, was headed for Berlin. Even though the sky was dark when I hiked the quarter mile to where I was told the plane would be waiting – its engines running, ready for take-off – I recognized the silhouette, the tri-motor layout. As I approached the plane it struck me as being the same aircraft that I had seen that day with General Udet in Poppa's hangar.

The co-pilot was waiting for me at the foot of the steps leading up into the strange-but-familiar aircraft, urging me to hurry along, "If you plan on making Midnight Mass."

"What is this aircraft," I inquired of my seat-mate, a young *Leutnant*, while the aircraft began to taxi to the main runway.

"As best I can tell, it is some type of new military transport. It is being built by Junkers, and has the Ju-262 V1designation. It had its first flight only in October, so I hope all of the problems have been worked out."

"I could swear that I saw a very similar version of this aircraft in a hangar at Templehof in October. I wonder if this is the same aircraft?"

"It might have been there at that time, but I rather doubt it. I know that the Air Ministry is very interested in this aircraft...even more than Luftansa...and is keeping it under close wraps. In whose hangar was it, where do you think you saw the similar plane?"

"I can't answer that," I lied. "For security reasons...You understand."

"Oh, yes. I understand. Please forgive me for intruding...but I thought since you mentioned it that it was permissible to speak of it."

"No apology is required...You are absolutely correct...I raised the issue...and should have known better. Please forgive me."

What were Poppa and General Udet planning to do with this new aircraft? Do I dare ask him when I see him?

As long as the *Leutnant* was so talkative, I pressed him on the issue of General Udet's death: "The report of General Udet's death mentioned that he died in the crash of an experimental plane...Do you know what type of plane it was," I asked – fully aware of the rumors of his suicide – but again treading on dangerous ground.

"I'm not sure what aircraft...and I'm not sure he died in an aircraft accident...Some are saying he might have taken his own life...that he shot himself...Quite frankly I don't know what to believe. But whatever the cause, the General's death is a terrible tragedy, a serious blow to the fortunes of the *Luftwaffe*."

"I couldn't agree more. The effects of his loss are going to be felt at all levels – especially in the production of aircraft and the development of new warplanes." *I hope the General's replacement doesn't support the development of the turbojet fighter aircraft.*

"Are you stationed at Lechfeld," the young *Leutnant* inquired; confident enough to again question me in an area of some sensitivity.

"Yes, I am. And you, *Leutnant*?"

"No. I am stationed at Regensburg, flying Me-109s. I am headed to Berlin, and like you I was able to board this plane in Regensberg. And what is your assignment, *Hauptman*," he asked – even more boldly.

"I have been assigned by General...by the Air Ministry...to work with Messerschmitt on the development of the Me-262 turbojet fighter. Are you familiar with the aircraft?"

"Oh, yes! What a marvelous aircraft. We fighter pilots can't wait to fly it. How soon do you think it will be available?"

It will be never...if I have anything to do about it. I thought to myself, but, I replied, "As soon as we are able to solve some technical problems... Which I hope won't take too long. Its availability will have a significant impact on who achieves air superiority." And it won't be the Third Reich, if I can help it!

THE CHRISTMAS VISIT with my family turned out to be a most joyous occasion; but sadly too brief. Everyone was alive and well. Even Poppa was his old-self again; curious, dogmatic and cautiously enthusiastic, now that the United States had been brought into the War. When I related to him my flight to Berlin in the new Junkers tri-motor military transport – in the hopes that he would confirm that it was the same aircraft that I had seen in his hangar – he simply smiled enigmatically, inquiring, "Was it a comfortable flight?" While I had so many questions I would have liked to ask Poppa, his cool response to my story informed me that I was unlikely to receive a straight answer to whatever I asked. Still, just the fact that he was there — both physically and mentally — was more than I had hoped for.

My only meaningful discussion with any of my family members — other than Lisa, of course — occurred late one evening out in the same apple orchard where my brothers, Wolfgang and Ernst and I were involved in throwing apples at a rooster so many years ago, setting in motion the infamous incident involving the death of Herr Otto Muenster's obnoxious rooster, Barbarosa. We were bundled warmly against the frigid cold, smoking the last of Poppa's best cigars, drinking the last of the good Cognac, reminiscing about pre-Nazi Germany, speculating about how soon the Third Reich would crumble and fall, but avoiding the topic of how and when the three of us might be eliminated by the S.S. or the Gestapo; it was just a matter of time we all agreed. That discussion directed us to a brief discussion of General Udet's death; including the why and the how — especially whether Poppa might be in any way implicated, and the role of the mysterious aircraft I saw in Poppa's hangar. It was decided that only Poppa knew the truth, and that he was not going to talk about it.

Maria, the person that brought us all together that Christmas with her letter to me, announced that she was being assigned to an orphanage in Posen, formerly Poznan, in the now German-occupied Polish Territory, to assist with the growing influx of Polish war orphans. It was assumed, but unsaid, that she would also be assisting in the care of Polish-Jew refugees as well. The family's commitment to helping Jews escape the Reich's ever more harsh treatment remained undiminished, despite the efforts of the S.S. and the Gestapo to infiltrate, to quell such ventures. We were convinced that it was just a matter of time before the S.S. and the Gestapo achieved success, and we would suffer extermination. I was surprised that *Oberst* Muenster — with as much as he knew about our clandestine enterprises — had not swept down on us already, terminating our crusade. *What is he waiting for? Why haven't I heard from him?* Perhaps Maria's assignment to the orphanage in the Polish Territory might allow her to escape the oncoming Armageddon. We exchanged tearful farewells, as if this was the last time that we would all be together.

CHAPTER 32

BIG CHIEF TABLET TWENTY-EIGHT | FRITZ

Back again in Lechfeld, again at my task of trying to keep the Air Ministry from adopting General Gallard's plan to have Messerschmitt concentrate solely on the production of the Me-262 fighter, which now appeared to be ready for full production, I had many things to accomplish. My plan was simple in concept, but more complicated in execution: I had to convince General Erhard Milch, who was the Air Inspector General (in charge of the production of aircraft), or Herr Goering – the Commander-in-chief of the *Luftwaffe* – or Herr Hitler himself, that although the turbojet engine had proved to be reliable, the best use of the turbojet engine was not the Me-262 fighter aircraft, but the best use of the turbojet engine was to power an offensive weapon; a multi-engine, turbojet bomber aircraft.

The argument I proposed to put forward to the Reich's policy-makers was this: The turbojet fighter is a defensive aircraft; it can only intercept the enemies' offensive weapon – the bomber aircraft – once the bomber aircraft is already in the air, flying over Reich territory. What the Reich needs is its own offensive weapon; a Multi-engine turbojet bomber that flies higher and faster than the enemies' piston engine interceptor fighters, a bomber that can reach the enemies' sources of war materiel and resources – especially its bomber airfields – destroying them before they can be used against the Reich. If the Reich hopes to win this War, it must take offensive steps to bring the War to the enemy. If the Reich had had such a multi-engine turbojet bomber aircraft at the start of the War, it would have quickly crushed Britain from the air; and Russia would by now be subdued by the same weapon. The opportunity to have such an effective offensive weapon is now; before the Americans can bring their unlimited resources to bases in Britain and elsewhere where they can be used against the Reich.

I knew that this argument might resonate with the Fuehrer; Herr Hitler was always demanding that the Reich take the offensive. But before I could present my argument to the Fuehrer, I had to convince General Milch and Reichsmarschall Goering that the multi-engine turbojet bomber was the most efficient use of turbojet technology. What I needed was a major shift in direction; it must be a large multi-engine bomber aircraft, capable of carrying a large bomb load over long distances; not just a fighter-bomber like the Ju-87 Stuka, which was used so ineffectively in the Battle of Britain. Converting the Me-262 into a fighter-bomber would not be a large enough change to guarantee the scuttling of the fighter aircraft, since fighter-aircraft production could run parallel with the fighter-bomber conversion. Of course, I worried that my argument might be too persuasive, and the Third Reich could wind up having a practically invincible multi-engine turbojet bomber, capable of delivering a large, lethal load of bombs; plus having the air supremacy benefits of a lethal Me-262 turbojet fighter.

Once again Providence smiled graciously on my efforts to undermine the production of turbojet fighters. Even though, based on General Galland's high praise of the Me-262, the Air Ministry ordered the production of one hundred Me-262s, there were still opportunities for me to convince the top command to turn the turbojet engine in a different direction. As quickly as possible, I prepared a dispatch for General Milch, advising him of my enthusiasm for the now operational turbojet engine, but suggested that it could provide a much better return if it were associated with a long-range, multi-engine bomber. To that dispatch I appended a copy of my rationale for such an approach.

Without belaboring the point, I received an order from General Milch to meet with him and Reichsmarschall Goering at the Air Ministry at my earliest convenience. During that meeting, which began with the usual inquiries about their First War comrade, the Baron — neither Milch nor

Goering giving any indication that Poppa was a target of the S.S. or Gestapo – my proposal was thoroughly analyzed and critiqued. Thanking me for my thoughtful, provocative proposal, Herr Goering suggested that I not share my recommendation with anyone else; that he was going to present it to the Fuehrer in the near future. General Milch was much less enthusiastic about snatching the turbojets away from the Me-262, in favor of a currently non-existent bomber aircraft. It was clear to me that General Milch had become a disciple of General Gallard in his support of the Me-262: In time, his support would cost General Milch his job.

It did not appear that my proposal to create a turbojet bomber in place of the Me-262 was bearing fruit, despite Herr Goering's support for it. Production of the Me-262 as a pure fighter aircraft continued throughout the summer and into the fall of 1943, despite the problems of having the production facilities relocated from Regensburg to the Bavarian town of Oberammergau following a particularly damaging Allied bombing raid. But then, on 2 November 1943, at a meeting with Willy Messerschmitt at the Augsburg plant, where I was in attendance as the onsite representative of the Air Ministry, Reichsmarschall Goering raised questions about the future of the Me-262 as a pure fighter aircraft. Herr Goering inquired as to how far the Me-262 could carry one or two bombs, acting as a fighter-bomber; explaining that the Fuehrer was now interested in giving the Wermacht another weapon to be used in the event of an Anglo-American invasion. I overheard General Galland mumble to himself that the best defense against invasion was having air superiority, which the Me-262, as a pure fighter, would have given the Reich.

So, General Galland understands what I have been trying to accomplish. And, it appears that my proposal – while not being embraced in its entirety – is bearing some fruit. I'll support any steps that prevent the Me-262 from being used to provide air superiority. And without air superiority, not only will the Reich be unable to repulse an invasion, it will also be unable to prevent the bombing of the factories that build and assemble the marvelous Me-262.

Willy Messerschmitt, for his part, tried to answer Herr Goering's inquiry like an engineer, opining: "Of course, it is possible to equip the Me-262 with bomb-carrying fixtures, but any such reconfiguration of a fighter to carry bombs would create a significant loss of performance, which any decision to reconfigure the Me-262 must take into account."

In typical bureaucratic fashion, my divisive actions un-explicably resulted in my promotion to *Major.*

Several weeks later, I inquired of my friend, Ludwig Hurst – one of the Messerschmitt lead engineers on the Me-262 project, who I had been trying to co-opt into my scheme – as to whether he had heard of any further discussions about reconfiguring the Me-262 into a fighter bomber.

"Oh, yes!" he exclaimed. "The Fuehrer himself has now weighed into the matter, confirming what Herr Goering had stated at the meeting in Augsburg. At a meeting held at the aviation center at Insterburg, located near the Fuehrer's headquarters in East Prussia, the superior flying characteristics of the Me-262 were demonstrated to Herr Hitler, who was astonished by its excellence. It is said that he inquired of Herr Goering whether the aircraft can carry bombs. Based upon what Willy Messerschmitt had told Goering at the Augsburg meeting, Herr Goering told the Fuehrer, "Yes, theoretically, it can carry bombs weighing 500 kilos (1,000 pounds), perhaps even 1,000 kilos (2000 pounds)." Then, so I have been told, the Fuehrer complained that for years he had been demanding a 'speed bomber' which can reach its target in spite of enemy fighter defenses, and that the Me-262 fighter aircraft he had just seen will serve as his 'speed bomber.' He wanted the Me-262 converted into a fighter-bomber, 'So that I can repel any invasion when it is at its weakest phase – the recently landed troops and material'."

How wonderful! Even the Fuehrer has now fallen victim to my scheme to prevent the Me-262 from being used as a pure fighter, to be used as it should be, and can be, to gain air superiority. Soon it will be too late for the Me-262 to serve either role – pure fighter or fighter-bomber – with any hope of saving the Third Reich.

"Unfortunately," Ludwig continued, "The Me-262 will never be effective as a fighter-bomber. The flying properties and safety features of the Me-262 are unsuited for aimed-bombing attacks; and diving or gliding will not work because the aircraft will fly too fast and become uncontrollable. Low level bombing attacks will consume too much fuel so as to unduly limit its operating range; and high-altitude bombing attacks will be ineffective because such small bomb loads are unlikely to hit small targets – like an invasion beach-head." *This is even better news than I had hoped for. I should have anticipated this information based on my work with the Ju-87 Stuka dive-bomber. Is this the effective demise of the marvelous Me-262, the closing of the last chapter on the Reich's ability to achieve air superiority?*

DESPITE THE FUEHRER'S clear, unequivocal demands for the conversion of the Me-262 into a fighter bomber, work continued on perfecting the aircraft as a fighter-interceptor. Somehow Generals Milch and Gallard managed to convince Willy Messerschmitt to disregard the Fuehrer's orders. I can only speculate that they saw, as I did, that the Me-262 was the one weapon – perhaps the only weapon – the Third Reich had that was capable of achieving and maintaining air superiority for the foreseeable future; the key to crippling, perhaps ending the increasingly devastating Allied bombing raids on Germany's heartland. Maybe, with satisfactory results of the Me-262 fighter-interceptor against the Allied bombers, they thought they could persuade Hitler to change his mind.

When it became clear to me that the general's strategy of disregarding the Fuehrer's instructions might be working, I pondered what course of action to take; settling on bringing the deception to the Fuehrer's attention. Being just an unknown *Luftwaffe Major* with little likelihood of being taken seriously, I did the unthinkable: I decided to contact my old nemesis, *Oberst* Dietrich Muenster in the hope that I could convince him to investigate the allegations; thereby bring the matter directly to the Fuehrer.

It was my belief that Herr Muenster would at least verify that the Fuehrer had issued an order to turn the Me-282 into a fighter-bomber, requiring him to contact the Fuehrer's staff for that purpose. Hitler's Staff would certainly want to know the purpose of the inquiry. If Herr Munster disclosed that he had heard from a reliable source within the Air Ministry that an order of the Fuehrer was not being adhered to, Staff would make its own inquiries and, regardless of what the Staff did with the information, the generals would be alerted to the inquiry from Herr Hitler's Staff;

leading the generals to reverse course, obeying the Fuehrer's decision — which is all I really wanted to happen.

In order to entice *Oberst* Muenster to listen to me, I had to provide the proper bait: "That I have identified certain traitors." *If Herr Muenster still wants the name of traitors in the Luftwaffe, I will give him the names of traitors; those Luftwaffe officers who are defying the Fuehrer's orders with impunity. Forget that they are actually trying to save the Third Reich; ignore their motives. Also overlook the fact that I am the real traitor to the Third Reich; one who perceives himself to be a true patriot trying to save the Fatherland from those who are systematically destroying its heart and soul.*

Oberst Muenster, it turned out, was difficult to contact. After some effort, I learned that he was stationed in Poland supervising the gathering and transporting of Jews from the urban ghettos to the death camps which were being constructed throughout rural Poland. Even when I was finally able to locate the *Oberst* in Warsaw, actually making contact with him was a bigger nightmare. I was passed from one S.S. office clerk to another, from one adjutant to another; each wanting to know more information about why I wanted to speak to the *Oberst*; wanting more information than I was willing to share. *The Oberst must be a very important man indeed.* The most I was able to achieve was to leave my name, my rank, and how I could be contacted. *Surely the Oberst will recall who I am and will be curious enough as to why I am calling him to call me back.*

After several months of not hearing from *Oberst* Muenster, I received a telephone call from an S.S. *Major* Wilhelm von Goeben in Berlin advising me that the *Oberst* had asked him to call me; that the *Oberst* was no longer involved in such "trivial" matters; that I was to give the *Major* any "relevant" information; and that, "The *Oberst* wanted me to remind you of your agreement with him, that you have not honored that agreement, that your family is still engaging in illegal activities, and that you and your family can expect to be dealt with harshly, and soon." *This was turning out worse than I had thought it could.*

Recognizing, from the nature of threat being conveyed to me by this unfamiliar *Major* von Goeben, that my opportunities to be a patriot were quickly diminishing, I elected to press forward with my initial plan. I began by only hinting at the rank and importance of the traitors, and the nature of their treasonous activity. The *Major*, however, pressed on – demanding more concise information about the treasonous activity, and the names of the conspirators. In the end, I outlined the chain of events, including the Fuehrer's explicit orders to convert the Me-262 turbojet fighter-interceptor into a fighter-bomber, and then I named Generals Milch and Galland as the principal conspirators. I could tell from the pauses after my answers to his questions that the *Major* was taking notes.

After a lengthy pause, *Major* von Goeben remarked in light-hearted manner, "You know, Herr von Bruckner, that under normal circumstances the activities which you have just described, and the participants that you have just named, would amount to nothing more than insubordination... to be dealt with through normal channels. But in light of the Fuehrer's explicit orders...and his personal involvement with the Me-262...I believe that I will pass your information on to Herr Himmler (Reichsfuehrer-S.S.), and let him deal with it as he sees fit. You can be sure that if this information is passed on to the Fuehrer he may view the activities you have described as treason...in which case the heads of these treasonous Generals will roll...just as happened to General Udet. *So my suspicions were correct – General Udet was murdered – probably by the S.S. – his death made to look like a suicide; but, on whose orders?*

"At the very least," *Major* Von Goeben asserted, "careers...including your own...will be ruined. I am sure *Oberst* Muenster will be pleased to hear of the role that you have played in exposing this treachery...at last you have done something positive for the benefit of the Fuehrer and the Third Reich. Heil Hitler!" *Nein! Ich sagen Heil das Vaterland!*

SEVERAL MORE MONTHS passed, and there was no sign that the Fuehrer's orders to convert the Me-262 into a fighter-bomber were being followed. I was again about to take a different approach to undermining the Me-262 fighter-interceptor program – by recommending the installation of reserve fuel tanks in the rear fuselage, ostensibly to give the aircraft greater pursuit range, but in fact to make it less maneuverable, more vulnerable – when my friend, Ludwig Hurst, the Messerschmitt chief engineer, handed me documents and drawings outlining the conversion of the Me-262 fighter-interceptor into a fighter-bomber; Hitler's 'Blitz bomber'!

"What has happened?" I asked incredulously, "Why is Messerschmitt suddenly going to build the Me-262 as a fighter-bomber?"

"I hear it is because the Fuehrer found out that his order to convert the Me-262 into a fighter-bomber was not being followed. I also heard that Hitler was furious that his order was being ignored...the blame being placed on General Milch who has been stripped of his command. And General Galland, who is also sharing the blame, has been sacked as General of the Fighter Arm. Given that Hitler has again ordered the conversion, this is what we are doing...although Hitler did consent that some Me262 aircraft could be built as fighter-interceptors, so long as they are readily capable of being quickly converted to fighter-bombers."

Was this the hand of the S.S., the answer to my prayers? Whatever the cause, this was wonderful news; especially the news that General Galland – the one officer that truly understands the importance of air supremacy – was no longer able to influence air defense policy.

"Will it take long for Messerschmitt to change over its operations... making fighter-bombers instead of fighter-interceptors?"

"If you will perform a close examination of the plans and schematics I've placed on your desk, I think you will see that the structural changes will be significant and time-consuming," Ludwig explained, with a wink of his eye. *So maybe I do have a co-conspirator; or maybe Ludwig has developed a nervous tic – the pressures of his job can do it.*

BUT THE ME-262 saga was far from over. Within weeks after receiving the news of Herr Hitler's furious reaction to the conscious efforts of his *Luftwaffe* high-command to disobey his explicit orders, I received orders from Herr Goering transferring me from the *Luftwaffe* and the Air Ministry – which was then held in some disrepute – to the Ministry of Armaments, serving as an aide to the Reich Minister of Armaments and War Production, Albert Speer; again working in Berlin, but now with the new rank of *Oberstleutnant*.

I was ecstatic: Not only did I get to be with my Lisa and my son, Kurt, again, I would be working with the one person in Hitler's inner-circle who was not a Nazi, not a professional militarist, not an industrialist, or not a politician; the one person who was able to save my Vaterland from the destruction that was becoming increasingly inevitable – especially now that the American and British forces had secured a beach-head in Normandy. It was reported that Herr Speer – an accomplished architect – had the ear of the Fuehrer, who thought of himself as being a fellow architect. Spear was not afraid to tell Hitler what he thought, but was politically astute enough not to embarrass the Fuehrer or to criticize the Fuehrer to others.

Before leaving the Messerschmitt experimental station at Lechfeld, I paid a last visit to Ludwig Hurst, letting him know of my new, expanded aircraft production responsibilities – including overseeing the production of the Me-262 as a fighter-bomber – and cautioning him that I needed to know if any efforts were being mounted to resume full-production of the fighter-interceptor version of the Me-262. With the few Me-262 fighter-bombers available being used ineffectively against the Allied invasion on the French coast, I anticipated that the fighter-interceptor version of the Me-262 would become a higher priority among the *Luftwaffe* elite.

The previously demoted General Galland, had put together a Me-262 fighter-interceptor squadron using the best of the fighter pilots, and was beginning to have considerable success against the American daylight bombers. Having learned that my new boss – Herr Spear – was present at the infamous meeting with the Fuehrer at which General Galland was demoted, and strongly supported the failed effort to convince Herr Hitler to build the Me-262 as a pure fighter-interceptor, I anticipated that Minister Speer would use the facts of the recent Me-262 fighter-interceptor successes in an attempt to have the Fuehrer retract his order.

In my first meeting with Minister Speer, my concerns about his favoring the fighter-interceptor version of the Me-262 were confirmed. Among his outline of my new duties was an assignment to travel to General Galland's Me-262 fighter-interceptor squadron, learn to fly the Me-262 fighter, and to fly it in combat situations against the Allied forces' fighter and bomber aircraft.

"I am aware of your familiarity with the Me-262 aircraft, but have you ever flown it, felt its surge of power, or its incredible speed?" he inquired.

"No, Herr Speer."

"Well I don't know how you can support one version of the Me-262 over the other, without experiencing the outstanding flying qualities of the pure fighter version. So I want you to have that experience. I think you will find it exhilarating...a far cry from the Ju-87 Stuka that you helped to develop and then fly in Spain."

"I, of course, will do as you ask Minister, but may I inquire as to what purpose it will serve...given that the Fuehrer has already made his decision that it is to be the fighter-bomber version?"

"Yes, he has, but I still believe that his decision is clearly now the wrong decision...and was the wrong decision from the very beginning. And you know it was...and is...the wrong decision. If it weren't for that damnable memo that you sent to General Milch and Reichsmarschall Goering recommending that the Me-262 be used as a bomber...an offensive weapon...I doubt that we would ever have had this interminable controversy over the role of the Me-262. Herr Goering...the toady that he is... couldn't wait to use your arguments with the Fuehrer, knowing that your position was what the Fuehrer wanted to hear...an offensive weapon is a positive position...a defensive weapon...like using the Me-262 as a fighter-interceptor...is a defeatist position.

"You are smart and clever, *Oberstleutnant* von Bruckner. I think you have known since the beginning of your involvement in the turbojet project that a fighter-interceptor was the better use of the technology, but you didn't want the Third Reich to gain air superiority and possibly win this War. So you embarked on a campaign to undermine the Me-262 project, to delay it, to compromise it. And you have succeeded by bringing delay and confusion...but you also managed to damage the careers of two fine generals...Milch and Galland...who knew the real value of the Me-262 fighter-interceptor...risking their careers...and possibly their lives...by disregarding the Fuehrer's misguided decision...a decision based entirely on your purposefully misguided recommendation. And you surely knew when you launched your scheme that the Arado Company was already working on a pure multi-engine turbojet bomber...the Ar-243...making your recommendation for the Me-262 a mere sham, a misdirection."

"Then, if you feel that way about my performance and question my motives, why have you given me a prominent position on your Staff?"

"Because I believe that you alone hold the key to changing the Fuehrer's mind about the fighter-interceptor role of the Me-262...thereby vindicating Milch and Gallard. This means that you have to learn to fly the Me-262, and experience it in combat against the Allied bombers and escort fighter-aircraft. Time is now of the essence. Although I believe that the War is lost, the Fuehrer will never accept that conclusion...leaving the Americans, the British and the Russians no choice but to destroy Germany's ability to fight on. This means more bombing of Germany's cities, its industrial areas, its bridges, its highways and railroads...leaving Germany totally prostrate in the rubble. I, and others, find this unacceptable.

"Our only option is to regain air superiority, making it too expensive, too painful for the Allies to continue the bombing of Germany's heartland. Hopefully, we can save something for the German survivors while at the same time giving the Allies a reason to accept something less than unconditional surrender."

"Aren't you taking a chance with relying on me...given your belief that my previous behavior was to prevent the Third Reich from achieving air superiority?"

"No, because what you will be doing has nothing to do with assisting the Third Reich in achieving air superiority in order to win this dreadful War...allowing it to carry out its evil plans. You, like me, want to save German lives, to protect the Fatherland from total annihilation. So we will be achieving air superiority for the German people...not the Nazis. I know from my research that you and your family are patriots...And I am convinced that you will now do whatever you can to leave a viable Germany to the survivors of the Nazi's war...which is what patriots are expected to do. This will be difficult to do, and not without serious risks to our person. The S.S. is closing in on enemies of the Third Reich...and what I am asking you to do will make you an enemy of the Third Reich...unless you are able to convince the Fuehrer to change his mind. Of course, even if you fail in that endeavor, we are going to again disregard his order...we are going to build the Me-262 as a fighter interceptor."

"Have no fear Herr Speer...I am already a target of the S.S. for activities against the Third Reich...so adding another treasonous activity to their dossier makes little difference to me. You are correct...I have always thought that the pure fighter version of the Me-262 is an incredible aircraft, capable of making a difference in protecting Germany. I also must agree with you that nothing now can win the War for the Third Reich...and that we must do whatever we can to protect the German people from the total destruction that will come from pervasive, massive bombings by the Allied air forces. I am prepared to follow your lead, and I will do anything you ask me to do. Thank you for your confidence in me."

INSTEAD OF SPENDING time in Potsdam with my family — especially Lisa and Kurt — I was once again at the Lechfeld experimental station, learning to fly the Me-262 fighter-interceptor. The station was bombed in July, and the damage was extensive, destroying several aircraft, setting back the forward progress of the Me-262 program severely. The talk around the station was of how the bombing by the Americans would not have happened if more of the fighter version of the Me-262 had been available. Besides the loss of aircraft there were civilian and military casualties as well, including my friend and confidant, Ludwig Hurst, who was my one sure source of reliable Me-262 information and station scuttlebutt.

My presence at the Lechfeld station was itself a source of rumors: What is Minister Speer's aide doing learning to fly the Me-262? Isn't von Bruckner the Air Ministry representative who recommended to Milch and Goering that the Me-262 ought to be used as a fighter-bomber? Has someone in the *Luftwaffe* set this up with Herr Speer to get rid of a personnel problem? How long will it be before *Major* von Bruckner is shot down or crashes?

I had the benefit of a veteran Me-262 fighter pilot as my trainer, my mentor. *Hauptman* Georg-Peter Weber, was one of the earliest *Luftwaffe* pilots to convert from piston-engine to turbojet aircraft. At the time that he was tutoring me Weber was still flying the Me-262 in combat; my training was just a side-line for him — resulting in a tailor-made training program that was rapid, intense and thorough. Being fully aware of my background in developing and flying the Stuka dive-bomber; Weber initially concluded that I was at Lechfeld to learn how to fly the fighter-bomber version of the Me-282.

Consequently, my first training exercises were with the fighter-bomber version. Once I had convinced *Hauptman* Weber that Minister Speer wanted me to focus on the fighter-interceptor version so that I could help to persuade Herr Hitler to retract his order, Weber became more than happy to train me on the fighter-interceptor version; getting me in the air as soon as he could certify that I was qualified. By early September, I was accompanying *Hauptman* Weber on sorties against Allied bombers; where I learned how to control the speedy Me-262, so as not to overshoot the lumbering American B-17 and B-24 bombers.

Once I had demonstrated to his satisfaction that I was proficient enough to survive the tricky take-offs and white-knuckle landings, and the other aspects of the aircraft, he turned me over to Me-262 fighter-interceptor 3. Staffel (squadron), Gruppe II (Group), based at Lechfeld, for some one-on-one combat experience. I knew that if I survived combat I would return to Berlin; trying to convince the Fuehrer that the better role for the Me-262 in gaining air supremacy was clearly as a fighter-interceptor, not as the fighter-bomber.

IT WAS DURING a one-on-one combat mission that I had my first encounter with the American pilot Peter Roberts; intercepting his F-5 Lightning – the reconnaissance version of the twin-engine P-38 – over the Adriatic Sea. I was waiting in the ready room when Flight Control alerted all bases in southern Germany to locate and destroy an F-5 that had been observed photographing unspecified facilities in southern Poland. The assumption was that the F-5 had been dispatched from an airbase in Allied-occupied southeastern Italy, and was attempting to return to its base. Believing that the photos were of significant value to the Americans, the call was directed to the Me-262 fighter squadrons because of the aircraft's climbing-rate, pursuit-speed and ceiling of operation.

The flight group to which I was assigned consisted of four Me-262 aircraft; our instructions were to proceed as quickly as possible to the area between Salzburg and Wein (Vienna), split into two pairs – one pair heading northeast towards Poland, and the other pair, consisting of my partner and me, flying south/southwesterly towards Italy – covering the presumed flight path of the F-5 Lightning 'recon' aircraft. Upon reaching our optimum cruising altitude – to conserve fuel, as this could prove to be a long chase – we concentrated on watching the sky below us, thinking that the F-5 would also be flying at its fuel conserving altitude which was below that of the Me-262.

The weather was clear, with scattered clouds, so visibility was not an issue. The north-bound pair of Me-262 aircraft first sighted what was believed to be the F-5 Lightning and its two P-51 Mustang fighter escorts. Breaking radio silence, the pair-leader advised my partner and me of the location, direction and altitude of the American aircraft. As we thought, the American aircraft were flying at about 6,000 meters (19,000 feet) in a southwesterly direction. It was agreed that the north-bound pair of Me-262 aircraft would reverse course, maintain their 10,000 meter altitude, and, when they again achieved contact with the American aircraft, attack the two P-51 fighters from the rear.

My partner and I were instructed to climb to a higher altitude, reduce air-speed, allowing the F-5 Lightning to catch up, to pass below us. In less than ten minutes the leader of the other pair of Me-262 fighters again broke radio silence; informing us that they were engaging the P-51 Mustangs, which had just dropped their auxiliary fuel tanks. While the P-51 aircraft were engaged in aerial combat with the Me-262 fighters, the F-5 Lightning was now unprotected; allowing my partner and me the opportunity to swoop down on the unarmed reconnaissance aircraft, which was jettisoning its auxiliary fuel tanks. My partner signaled me to maintain a position above and behind the F-5 aircraft, while he descended to the same altitude as the F-5, creeping up alongside the F-5, signaling the pilot to accompany us to an airstrip in German-occupied northern Italy.

The pilot of the F-5 indicated his refusal to comply with the order by putting his aircraft into a steep, turning dive away from my partner's aircraft. I immediately began pursuing the F-5, taking my aircraft into a turning dive, bringing the F-5 into my gun sight, firing several bursts from the Me-262's four nose-mounted 20mm cannons, striking the F-5 Lightning's port engine, producing an immediate trail of blue-black smoke, with the propeller ceasing to rotate a few moments later. The speed of the F-5 diminished rapidly as the aircraft veered to the right, being pulled in that direction from the torque provided by the still running starboard engine.

It was difficult for me to keep the now spiraling F-5 Lightning in my view; my aircraft would stall if I tried to fly as slow as the crippled, dying F-5. The bubble canopy of the Lightning popped open; the pilot emerged from the cockpit, and jumped from his spiraling aircraft. Making my turn to rejoin my partner I observed a parachute opening. I circled the area until I observed the F-5 Lightning spiral into the ground, breaking into pieces upon impact. There was no fire or explosion when the F-5 met its demise. Now running low on fuel, it was time for me to get the Me-262 back to the Lechfeld station. Giving no further thought as to what had happened to the F-5, I turned my thoughts to my debriefing, reporting my first kill, packing up my gear, making my goodbyes, traveling back to Berlin.

THE MOOD IN Berlin among both the military and the civilians reeked of gloom. In the west the British and American forces were now moving swiftly through France and into the low-countries, while in the east the Russian forces were pushing into East Prussia. Food and fuel had become scarce; incessant bombing had crippled all forms of transportation, and had brought death and destruction to the civilian population. Civilians were still being rounded up by the Gestapo and S.S., herded into camps, and executed by firing squads in retaliation for the failed attempt on the Fuehrer's life on 20 July 1944, at his bunker – "Wolf's Lair" – at Rastenburg in East Prussia. Although the time-bomb contained in a briefcase placed under the conference table at which Herr Hitler was seated detonated, killing many – Hitler, who was shielded from the blast by the stout oak table and its massive supports, escaped serious injury, death.

It was not surprising then that upon my return to Berlin I learned that among the civilians killed by bombs, either by bombs falling from enemy bomber aircraft, or perhaps as a result of the failed bomb assassination attempt on Herr Hitler, were many members of my family. Momma, Lisa's mother, my sister, Marta and her family – all staying with Momma to conserve dwindling resources, were victims of a bombing attack on Potsdam. Poppa, Wolfgang and Ernst were arrested for unspecified reasons after the failed revolution following the failed attempt to assassinate Herr Hitler, and later were executed by a firing squad.

I was stunned by the loss of my family members, saddened by the death of Lisa and Kurt; but with so much death and destruction around me I had to keep moving forward, knowing that I was just like the millions of others in Germany who were enduring the same grief, uncertainly, loss.

Given the conditions then existing in Germany, I was convinced that it would just be a matter of time before I would be arrested; suffering the same fate as my father and brothers. When I explained my fears to Herr Speer, he agreed that it would be foolish and fatalistic for me to meet with the Fuehrer, to explain my change of mind, and heart, regarding the use of the Me-262 as a fighter-interceptor. Instead, he had me draft a written report, supporting my new-found belief in the Me-262 pure-fighter version.

DESPITE VALIANT ATTEMPTS to manufacture the fighter-interceptor version of the Me-262, Allied bombers continued to destroy the Me-262 manufacturing facilities, and partially built aircraft, faster than German manufacturing could build and rebuild them. Even if we had been able to get Me-262 aircraft built, the turbojet engines we were getting from Junkers and BMW remained unreliable, under-powered, and required extensive maintenance; leaving the *Luftwaffe* with too few available aircraft to mount successful campaigns against the enemy bombers and their fighter escorts. We even resorted to hiding partially-built Me-262 fighter aircraft in forests and caves, rather than leave them at the manufacturing facilities, where the enemy bombers concentrated their attacks.

The rest of the armament industry was suffering similar, systematic destruction from day and night bombing attacks. With the failure of the last great offensive that the Reich was able to mount against the American and British troops in the Ardennes Forest (known by the Americans as the "Battle of the Bulge") at the end of 1944, it was clear to everyone but the Fuehrer that the War was lost. The best the German military could achieve against the Americans and the British in the west, and the Russians in the east, were rear-guard actions to slow the advance.

Once the Rhine River was crossed in the west and the Oder River in the east, it became a case of slow strangulation. The Fuehrer began preaching a "scorched-earth" policy requiring the destruction of all bridges, highways, railways, power plants, etc., leaving nothing of value for the victorious enemy, particularly the Russians. Such a policy also guaranteed that the surviving German people would be left destitute, broken, starving, and without the ability or the means to survive, to rebuild their lives. Minister Speer vehemently opposed such a policy; not only refusing to implement the required destruction, but also interfering with those who were trying to destroy the infrastructure that remained the German peoples' only hope for long-term survival. It was as if Hitler had decided that the German people had failed him, had failed to carry-out his plans for world domination; and they were, therefore, no longer worthy of surviving as a nation.

CHAPTER 33

BIG CHIEF TABLET TWENTY-NINE | FRITZ

But I have again gotten ahead of myself with my story. There was one last episode involving my antagonist, S.S. *Oberst* Dietrich Muenster, which I must describe; since it is crucial to my convincing you that I am who I say I am – and it involved the American F-5 (P38) Lightning pilot, Major Peter Roberts. You will recall that I shot down a reconnaissance aircraft – while I was pursuing that aircraft in a Me-262 fighter aircraft – over German-occupied Italy. I saw the pilot bail out of his aircraft, saw his parachute open, but I didn't know if he survived the crash.

In late October, 1944, while I was on one of my rare visits to my office at the Ministry in Berlin, I received a telephone call from a man identifying himself as an aide to S.S. *Oberst* Muenster, inquiring as to whether I would be available to visit with the *Oberst* at the S.S. Headquarters, on Prinz-Albrecht Strasse, the following day. Do I have the choice of refusing to meet the *Oberst:* Of course, not. When I inquired as to the purpose of my visit with the *Oberst*, I was firmly, but politely, advised that I would learn what it was about when I met with him. Foremost in my mind was whether this meeting was just a pretext to have me arrested in the confines of the S.S. building – from where I could be dispatched without a trace. With the way things were in Berlin following the failed assassination attempt on the Fuehrer, few people would have been surprised by my demise or disappearance; and there were few others still alive who would even notice my absence.

Oberst Muenster was standing to meet me as I entered his office at the direction of his adjutant. The office was dominated by a massive, highly polished desk – reminding me of his Uncle Otto's desk in the office over the stables on his estate outside of Potsdam.

"Good afternoon, *Oberstleutnant*," he greeted me with uncharacteristic warmth. The *Oberst's* dark hair was beginning to show signs of graying at the temples, but he otherwise looked youthful and trim. "I apologize for taking you away from your important duties at the Ministry, but I really need your help on a very important matter of state. I really should have come to your office, but when I sought Reichsminister Himmler's permission to speak with you he suggested it might attract less attention and speculation if you were to meet me here.

"Thank you, *Oberst*," I replied.

Oberst Muenster introduced the topic of why he needed my assistance – which turned out to be my locating the whereabouts of the cameras and film that were supposedly onboard the F-5 Lightning returning from a reconnaissance mission over Poland that I had recently shot down. After congratulating me on my successful attack on the reconnaissance aircraft, *Oberst* Muenster proceeded to describe events subsequent to the crash of the Lightning and the capture of the American pilot – a Major Peter Roberts – by German troops in the area.

When the crash of the F-5 Lightning was located – spread over a large area of mountainous terrain along the Adriatic coast of Italy – the cameras and film were not found with the wreckage or anywhere in the immediate area. Interrogation of Major Roberts at the *Dulag Luft* – the *Luftwaffe* Aircrew Interrogation Center – located near Frankfurt, proved to be fruitless; Major Roberts declined to provide any information to the interrogators other than his name, rank and serial number, as all American servicemen had been instructed to do; and he had now been transferred to a regular *Luftwaffe Stalag* in Poland.

"*Oberstleutnant* von Bruckner, are you sure that the American F-5 aircraft was the aircraft you were sent to intercept?"

"I have no way of knowing that for sure. The aircraft I shot down was first identified by another pair of pilots flying Me-262 aircraft in the opposite direction. My partner and I received directions indicating the speed, altitude and heading of the aircraft, with the added information that the F-5 aircraft was being escorted by P-51 fighters, which the other pair of pilots were going to handle. When the aircraft being flown by this Major Roberts appeared beneath me, I confirmed that it was a reconnaissance version of the P-38, and since it was being escorted by P-51 aircraft, I assumed that it was the aircraft on a reconnaissance mission that we were told to intercept...destroying it if necessary.

"Other than that, I can't help you. I suppose it is possible that the aircraft being flown by Major Roberts was a decoy luring us away from the actual reconnaissance aircraft. But if that was the case, then it would suggest that the purpose of the surveillance was more than filming a routine military target." *And since an S.S. Oberst – with Jewish 'resettlement' responsibilities was interrogating me – this reconnaissance flight must have involved locating "resettlement" camps in Poland – from which Jewish slave laborers were being selected to work in the factories and mines under the direction of Minister Speer.*

"That is a very perceptive observation, *Oberstleutnant*, but I am not at liberty to provide you with the nature of the target...I only want to know what facts you can provide to solve the mystery of the missing camera equipment and their film. Since you are the only *Luftwaffe* officer still available who was involved in the pursuit and attack on the American reconnaissance aircraft, I thought you might be able to shed some light on whether this was even the correct recon aircraft."

"I am sorry, *Oberst* Muenster, but I have told you everything I know about the matter, and I don't know how to help you further."

"That's what I would now like to talk to you about...I think that there may be something you can do to solve the mystery...It involves you visiting with Major Roberts at *Stalag Luft III* near Sagan, Poland. I am hopeful that as one pilot to another you can break through Major Robert's steely façade, giving him some reason to provide you with some clue as to where the camera and film can be located."

"I would like to help you, but if I make this trip to the *Stalag*, I must have more information about the supposed reconnaissance mission... what it is that Major Roberts was photographing...and does he know that the camera and film are missing? I mean, he could have jettisoned the camera and film when he concluded that his aircraft was mortally wounded...that it clearly would crash and fall into German hands."

"Let me put it this way...if Major Roberts will not divulge where the film of the target is to you, he will be compelled to provide what we need to know...by whatever means necessary. You can tell him for me that he is living on borrowed time...the Geneva Convention's prohibitions against the mistreatment of prisoners of war notwithstanding. Good luck, *Oberstleutnant* von Bruckner."

SO IT WAS that I came to meet the American prisoner of war, Major Peter Roberts face-to-face at *Stalag Luft III*. The *Stalag*, which was located a hundred or so miles east from Berlin, turned out to be a bleak, open, virtually treeless compound consisting of a dozen or so barracks-type one-story buildings; the entire compound encircled with double barbed wire fences. Located outside of the fenced compound were a number similar buildings housing the guards and support forces.

Upon my arrival at the *Stalag* I was escorted to the main building which served as the Commandant's headquarters. I had been expected, and the Commandant had Major Roberts waiting for me in an interior, windowless interrogation room furnished with three rustic chairs and a bare wooden table. Hoping to put Major Roberts at ease, I came dressed in my recently-pressed light-blue *Luftwaffe* officer's uniform – to distinguish me from the dreaded, black-uniformed S.S. officers – the badges on my tunic showing my *Oberstleutnant* rank and fighter-pilot's wings.

Major Roberts sat hatless, dressed in a uniform which maybe was his, but it was rumpled and torn. Attached to the tunic were insignia of the U.S. Army Air Corps, fighter-pilot wings, a Major's oak leaf, and a Twelfth Air Force patch. Major Peters was tall and slim, with light-colored hair; he had a pleasant face, and attractive blue-eyes. Also in the room was an older, plainly-dressed woman – presumably the interpreter. Before the door was closed and locked from the outside, I instructed the guard to bring us coffee and, if none was available, then some water.

"Major Roberts," I began in English. "My name is Fritz von Bruckner. I am a *Luftwaffe* fighter pilot. My English is limited, and if I lapse into

German, this lady will interpret it for you. Please forgive me if I don't understand your American-English. If I don't, the lady will also interpret what you say for me. This should not take long, but please be seated."

"Let me explain the purpose of my visit." I continued, "You, Major, and I have had a previous encounter, although we did not meet face-to-face. You were piloting an F-5 Lightning reconnaissance aircraft, and I was piloting a Me-262 turbojet fighter aircraft. In that encounter I fired my cannon at your aircraft, striking, and disabling the port engine, causing your aircraft to crash. I saw you climb out of the cockpit and jump off of your aircraft, the parachute opening normally. I was unable to tell at the time whether you survived the jump, but I am pleased to see that you did.

"My current assignment involves the production of the Me-262 turbojet aircraft as a fighter-interceptor, and at the time of our encounter, I was assigned to a fighter gruppe – I'm sorry, fighter group - to see first-hand the combat capabilities of the aircraft from a fighter-pilot's standpoint. Perhaps my engagement with the reconnaissance version of the P-38 Lightning you were flying could not be characterized as 'hand-to-hand' combat because your aircraft was unarmed...and for that I apologize... but you left us no alternative but to shoot at you since you refused my partner's order for you to land your aircraft. Let me say, your bravery is commendable...for you could have just as easily been killed, as was your aircraft. If I ever found myself in a similar situation, I would hope that I would make the same decision that you did."

During this introduction – my attempt to develop some rapport with Major Roberts – he remained stone-faced, staring blankly at the wall behind me, showing no apparent interest in what I was saying. *I might as well be talking to myself.* So, I tried a new tact, asking the Major, "What do you think of the Me-262...Did we surprise you by our sudden appearance?"

"My name is Peter J. Roberts...my rank is Major...my serial number is..."

"That's all right, Major," I interrupted before he could finish his prepared response. "Is it your intention to tell me nothing more than your name, rank, and military serial number?"

"Yes," he replied coldly, but politely, looking at me for the first time, his facial expression signaling firm intransigence.

"Look," I stated in my most friendly manner. "I am just a fighter-pilot like yourself, trying to get a fix on your opinion of the aircraft I was flying...with or without a comparison to the aircraft you were flying. I have always been impressed with the speed, the maneuverability, the versatility of the P-38...and since this was my first and only combat experience, I was hoping to learn something from a skilled fighter-pilot like yourself as to whether I really learned anything useful about the Me-262 from my encounter with you...other than, of course, that you are a brave pilot."

"I'm sorry, Colonel, but I simply cannot...and will not...help you. We may both be pilots, but we are also bitter enemies. You seem like a nice guy, but that doesn't cut it with me...you tried to kill me. And I won't tell you anything that might be used by you to enhance the chances of killing the next G. I. pilot you come up against!"

"Well, then...let me ask you something that surely would not involve aircraft and flying prowess. Did you jettison the cameras and film from your aircraft before it crashed?"

"My name is Peter J. Roberts...my rank is Major...Do I need to go on?"

"No. Of course not...but let me give you some friendly advice. I don't personally care what you were photographing...you could have been photographing ant-farms for all I care...or what you did with the cameras and film...if anything...but there are people who are quite anxious about learning the whereabouts of the cameras and film...And they will go to extreme-lengths to extract that information from you. I admire you, Major Roberts...for your bravery and resolve in the face of danger...and I would hate to have you experience the type of interrogation I believe you will face if you do not cooperate. I personally know how ruthless these people can be. It will be much easier for you if you will answer me one simple question: Did you jettison the camera and film from your aircraft before it crashed?"

After a long pause, Major Roberts responded, "My name is Peter J. Roberts...my rank is..."

"Thank you, Major. We are done here. I pray that you have not made a serious mistake by refusing my offer to talk, my advice to cooperate."

AND SO, I now come to the last chapter of my life in Germany; the events leading up to my untimely, mysterious death that brought me into Jack's body. I apologize for the length of this telling; I know that it may have been difficult at times to follow all of turns and twists in my life bringing you to this point, but I have tried to limit my story to the relevant facts, the high-points of my bodily life.

There is no point in retelling the gruesome details of the Third Reich's demise, which you already know from reading the abundance of World War II history books, magazine articles, and personal memoires that fill libraries, that line private book-shelves, and that are being made into movies – the types of movies that Jack likes so much.

It was for me the last few days of the War: Hitler was dead for four days, but fighting continued intermittently around Berlin, the last pocket of Third Reich resistance, and Herr Speer and I were spending every waking hour issuing countermands to the Fuehrer's scorched earth policy being carried out by misguided, but steadfast Nazis. We confronted the 'misguided' in person when necessary, explaining why it was necessary to leave critical infrastructure – like power plants – in place for the benefit of the German people.

The fighting for Berlin was getting closer – it was the Russian Army bringing tanks and artillery into the city itself, destroying everything in its path. The air was filled with heavy, acrid smoke; giving a sense of dusk, when it was really only the middle of the day. I was wearing civilian clothes, standing near a telephone central office, watching three men loading boxes of what appeared to be explosives in an excavation at the base of the building where the telephone cables entered the central office building – cables that connected that central office to the vast telecommunications network providing telephone service throughout Berlin and beyond. I shouted to the men to stop their work, to refrain from sabotaging this critical installation, but before the next words leave my mouth, "You must not do this...you are only hurting yourselves..." I experienced the pain of a severe blow to my back; excruciating pain, then darkness: My physical body was dead; my immortal spirit was freed of its mortal body.

The Ordeal is over. I hope that I have achieved my goal of explaining to the widow Kaufman and the Jewess Hannah of why I must return to Germany; to right the wrongs inflicted on my person; to find the remnants of my family. Jack has performed his task as my spokesperson admirably, giving a sense of immediacy and veracity to my story. He has even managed to present my antagonist, Oberst Dietrich Muenster, in a credible, balanced manner. I must remember to thank Jack when the appropriate opportunity presents itself; but for right now, I going into a much-earned hibernation.

During my hiatus I intend to figure out how the widow Kaufman has in fact received my story. She has left few clues as to whether she believes or questions Fritz's professed efforts to undermine the Nazis and the Third Reich's war efforts, and my family's endeavors to save Jews' lives at great personal risk. My task of discerning her reaction is complicated by the fact that she made no comments, or asked any question or expressed any opinion over the course of Jack's lengthy reading, covering several weeks of evenings. In the evening's failing light it was difficult for me to observe the widow Kaufman's facial expressions, her body language. Even when there was light sufficient enough for me to observe the widow Kaufman, her face remained impassive, her posture unrevealing. Unless I am able to discern something more, or different, from musing back through my limited observations, I am left with relying solely upon her previously expressed skepticism and disbelief towards my motives and veracity. To her I am just an untrustworthy Nazi; but why?

It would not surprise me if the widow Kaufman undertakes an independent verification of the truth and accuracy of Jack's version of Fritz von Bruckner's biography. I can only hope that what she has been told will stand up to careful scrutiny.

CHAPTER 34

BIG CHIEF TABLET THIRTY | JACK

Having finished my role in the telling of Fritz's wartime experiences — serving as his 'mouthpiece' — I was once again free to spend my evenings with Billy after he finishes his chores on his dad's farm. Riding my bike up the road to the Lewises' place at the first opportunity, I was struck by the thought that I had never said anything to Billy about Fritz. *What should I tell Billy if he asks about what I have been doing in the evenings for the last several weeks? Even if he doesn't ask, is it time for me to tell Billy about Fritz? And, what can I tell Billy — that I have this person... this German fighter-pilot...sharing my body, invading my mind, telling me about his life, performing at times as my own 'Jiminy Cricket'? If I do tell Billy about Fritz, will Billy believe me, or will he think I'm crazy...and stop being my friend?* By the time I reached Billy's house, I concluded that I was not ready to expose Billy to Fritz; there needed to be an incident or an occurrence that provided a credible reason for me to tell Billy about Fritz — or as Mom called him, the Nazi, the Kraut. That opportunity occurred sooner than I had expected

Summer was passing quickly; school would begin again shortly. In response to the oncoming end to our freedom, Billy and I were in constant search of adventure and mischief; and we didn't have to search too long or too far to find it. The billboards had been advertising the Adams County Fair for months; and it was now in full operation at the Fairgrounds: providing every kind of thrill and danger a twelve-year old boy could dream of, and just a bike-ride away – the exciting rides, the gaudy midway, the prize-winning livestock, the dazzling sideshows, the fascinating freaks. Friday night was known to be the best night to go to the Fair for having fun; it was the night when young people descended on the fly-by-night carnival, like swarms of locusts on a wheat field.

For weeks, Billy and I had been planning and saving our dimes and quarters in anticipation of our BIG Friday night at the Fair. It was the first thing we talked about when I arrived at Billy's house: We talked non-stop about what rides we'd ride; whether we'd try the 'shooting gallery' – where everyone knows the rifles are fixed – which of the 'freak shows' we'd attend – if they'd even let us in – when we'd get there, and when we'd come home. All of this 'big' talk assumed, of course, that Billy's mom and dad, and my mom would give us permission to go to the Fair; on our own, without adult supervision. After the unpleasant experiences surrounding our trip to the movies and the episode at the road-house, Billy and I were trying to keep knowledge of our activities solely to ourselves; even resorting to using a form of 'pig-Latin' – which we happened upon in an old *Archie* comic book – to disguise our 'important' conversations in the presence of others.

"Illybay illway ouyay omecay erehay," I'd say in asking: "Billy, will you come here?"

"Foay oursecay, Ackjay" he'd respond; meaning, "Of course, Jack."

It was a simple, but confusing, form of speech, taking us some time to get accustomed to reversing the first letter of a word to become the last letter of what was the actual word, and then adding "ay" to complete the disguised spoken word – for example, Billy became Illybay. Memorizing the more frequently used words and expressions, as well as repeated use, developed our abilities in using this strange language. I couldn't wait to introduce this form of speech to my pals in the barracks when I got back to military school in the fall. We were Illybay and Ackjay, which immediately drew stares and questioning looks from those within earshot of our greetings, or overhearing our conversations.

Permission was given – but not without expressions of concern – for Billy and me to attend the Fair unsupervised, but only so long as someone drove us to the Fairgrounds and someone picked us up at the Fairgrounds afterwards. Mom agreed to drive us to the Fairgrounds and, because it was felt that Dennis would know how to handle unruly, adventurous boys, he would be there at ten o'clock to pick us up. It was assumed that because Saturday was a workday Dennis would be sober. For us there was the lengthy list of do's and don'ts: no eating greasy food just before climbing on the more aggressive twisty, turning, bumpy rides; no games of chance – this did not including target shooting; no picking on the smaller boys; no hanging around with the older boys; and, most importantly, no fighting – with anyone – even if provoked.

THE SKY WAS just getting dark when Billy and I tumbled out of Mom's station wagon at the far end of the slowly filling parking lot – she had agreed not embarrass us by dropping us off directly at the Fairground's entrance gate. Walking through the gate, my eyes were immediately drawn to the sights and sounds of the brightly-lit Midway with all of its whirling attractions, including the Ferris wheel.

All slicked up and wearing our better casual shirts and blue jeans, Billy and I were determined to have a good time. After attacking a couple of the less challenging rides – just to get a few under our belt, to see what we could expect when we took on the bigger rides – we consumed hamburgers and french fries, topped off with funnel cakes handed to us in greasy newspaper pages; just what we had been instructed not to do. Billy and I then made the rounds of the games of chance, which were set up in the booths and stalls crowding the Midway.

Who could resist the chance to win a prize by simply throwing a ball at some wooden milk-bottles, or by tossing rings over prizes on a table, or by shooting a rifle at a moving target? Never mind the odds against winning anything, let alone winning that large stuffed-animal sure to brighten any girl's face; perhaps even earning the lucky guy a hug, a kiss. We stared in fascination and envy when we beheld a lucky guy receiving his reward from a happy, exuberant sweetheart clutching a fuzzy, stuffed-animal. We clearly lacked the skills to win a big prize; all we could hope to achieve was to walk away with a few cheap beads and a couple of worthless trinkets.

While we were waiting in line for a turn on the 'Whirl-A-Round' ride, we ran into some girls who Billy knew from the 4H Club. The ride is a nausea producing experience as the car spins around a flat surface, with unexpected swings, snapping from side-to-side, rotating without any warning. Billy's invitation to the girls, who he introduced as Marge and Jo, to join us in the ride was accepted, following giggles and whispers. At first I thought "Jo" was "Joe," but when I commented that "Joe" was a strange name for a girl, she corrected me: "It's J O, not J O E. It's short for Josephine, silly."

"Oh," I responded, "Jo sounds much better."

When our turn came, we climbed aboard with Billy and me occupying each end of the vinyl covered seat, with the two girls sitting between us; forced to squeeze together when the attendant lowered the safety bar across our laps. I was just beginning to enjoy the cozy contact with Jo as the 'Whirl-A-Round' began a slow, lazy circle; and then all hell broke loose as the car went into a series of violent thrusts, sudden pulls, quick reverses of direction, shaking twists and severe rotations. The air was filled with shrieks, screams, shouts – terrified riders clamoring to be released from this heart-pounding, stomach-churning, nerve-rattling experience. Instead of enjoying my closeness to Jo, I was suddenly clinging onto the safety bar for dear life, praying that I wouldn't throw up, embarrassing myself in front of the others. The ride seemed to be going on forever, my panic growing with each twist, turn, revolution.

Then Fritz said: *Jack! Where are we? Are we going to crash? What is happening to the aircraft?*

It's just a carnival ride, Fritz! But I think I'm going to barf if it doesn't end soon!

Fritz: *No, Jack! For God's sake, get a hold of yourself; you're not in any real danger. It's no worse than a rough ride in an airplane.*

Thankfully, the ride ended before I lost my lunch. The instant the attendant raised the safety bar, I leaped from the seat, raced to the edge of the platform, leaned over the railing and started retching. Behind me I heard sounds of laughter from Billy and the girls who were watching me suffer through my nausea. Stifling any further retching, and making our way off of the ride as new thrill seekers pushed us aside, filling the cars, I felt a hand on my shoulder, the pleasant voice of Jo was asking, "Jack, are you all right? Do you want some water...a soda? I know how you feel...I got sick my first time, too,"

Well, Jo, I only hope that you didn't vomit in front of someone you were trying to impress. What do they say about the importance of first impressions? Thank God that I didn't vomit directly on you, Jo.

Fritz again entered my thoughts: *Don't worry too much about it, Jack. You panicked once the ride got too scary for you...which is why I plugged in trying to determine what was happening to you...but you don't need to panic again about 'first impressions'. There is plenty of time for you to show her your strengths, and maybe not necessarily with this girl. There are many more girls for you to meet...and impress. What you need to do now is put this unfortunate incident behind you; maybe you shouldn't have eaten the food you did before taking that ride...but that's in hindsight. You can blame your eating habits for the problem, and just laugh it off. Show them that what happened has not upset you. Now that you have cleared your stomach of the greasy food, you might even want to try that ride again...just to prove it was not you, but the food. I actually found it to be quite exhilarating...and I would rather enjoy another go at it.*

Are you telling me, Fritz, that you didn't experience enough excitement flying the Stuka dive bomber and the Me262 fighter in combat, as you had me tell Mom and Hannah?

Fritz: *I'm not sure that I can compare my flying experiences with the gyrations of the 'Whirl-A-Round' ride.*

This exchange lasted only a moment, not much longer I am

sure than the blink of an eye, but when I looked at Billy he gave me a puzzled look; like "What's going on, Jack? Where have you been?" By then Jo was handing me a paper cup of water, allowing me to avoid Billy's gaze, to turn my attention to Jo, thanking her, taking a gulp of the refreshing water, letting it rinse my sour-tasting mouth. Once the unpleasant taste was gone, once I was sure that nausea had passed, I put on a brave face, saying to those standing around me, "That's what I get for eating that greasy crap...I'm ready for another try at this monster...Anyone else willing to join me?"

"I would...but I'm not sure I'd want to be in the same car with you," said Billy laughing, looking at the girls, trying to get them to laugh with him.

"Thanks, Billy...I really appreciate your support," I answered.

"I'll go with you, Jack," said a concerned Jo, lightly touching my forearm.

"You will," I asked with surprise and a hint of uncertainty.

"Sure, why wouldn't I? Everyone deserves a second chance... Besides, like my granny always says, 'If you get thrown off the horse you'd best get back on right away...at least if your neck isn't broken'."

Billy, Marge and Jo were laughing now, and I sensed that I should be laughing as well. I noticed that Jo had a pleasant laugh. I also noticed for the first time that she had a pretty face, dancing dark eyes, and an abundance of freckles.

"I like your grit, Jo," remarked a chuckling Billy, "But, I think we'd best walk around a bit before tackling that ride again...I ate the same greasy stuff that Jack did...and I don't think my stomach is up to it right now. We might not be as lucky this next time." *Yes, Jo, you sure do have ' grit'. And thank you, Billy, for delaying the trauma of another Whirl-A-Round ride...for a while.*

THE MIDWAY WAS in full-swing; with crowds of young people, boy and girls, waiting to get in the freak show, standing three and four deep at the games of chance, cheering on one another as the balls were thrown, the rings tossed, the air rifles fired, the prizes awarded. *Gosh, I would love to win a stuffed animal so I can pay back Jo for her kindness to me.* At the shooting gallery, we stood in line for forever, waiting our turn to get our hands on one of those rifles — knowing full-well that no matter how skilled we had become with our air-rifles, the barrels of these rifles were bent and the sights were misaligned, making slim our chances of hitting enough targets to win a prize.

We stood watching the guys standing at the counter already shooting the rifles; trying to determine which of the half-dozen rifles was not completely inaccurate, and how to compensate for their inaccuracies. Watching the guy in front of me, who I thought provided me with the best opportunity to see someone hit one of the moving rabbit targets, I watched his aim, calculated the path of the projectile, noting the actual direction of the missile, whether it hit or missed the target. When he fired the last of the six shots, the disgusted shooter angrily slammed the misaligned rifle down on the counter, and pushed his way through the crowd empty-handed.

Then it was my turn to show what I could do with the unreliable, sorry-ass rifle. *I can probably do just as well with this piece of junk by closing my eyes, and just aiming in the general direction of where I think the target might be.* Putting aside this unhelpful thought, I adjusted my aim at a moving rabbit, taking into account my earlier observations of where the shot might go; and holding the rifle as steady as I could, I squeezed the trigger, felt the slight recoil of the rifle, but did not hear the expected 'ping' of the pellet hitting the metal target. *Drats!* Taking aim again, making a slight adjustment in pointing the rifle at the target, giving it a little more of a lead in front of the rabbit, I squeezed the trigger, felt the recoil, heard the 'ping'. *Hurray! I've hit it!*

Behind me I heard the cheers, the yelps, of the girls, the 'Atta-boy' from Billy. Now filled with confidence and certainty that I had beaten the game, I took aim, made the same adjustment as before, squeezed off another shot; but there was no 'ping'. And so it went for three more shots. I had only two shots left; *I must make both of them if I am to win a decent prize for Jo.* Making a few more adjustments, taking a deep breath, clamping my elbows firmly on the counter, I aimed and pulled the trigger, 'PING'! *All I need is just one more!* But, there was no 'one more ping' sound; only silence, followed by groans of disappointment coming from Billy and the two girls.

"Nice try, kid," I heard the attendant say, pointing at the side-wall of the booth where all of the prizes were stacked. "You got two hits, so you can pick one of the prizes from row two." My survey of row two revealed nothing but paper fans, strings of cheap colored beads, plastic tiaras decorated with sparkly stuff, fake rubber knives, and other assorted trinkets. *None of this stuff is worthy of Jo. She deserves a stuffed animal, not this second-row junk.*

"Jack," I heard Jo say. "Nice shooting. Your mom might like the colored beads...Or if you have a little brother, he might like the rubber knife."

"But I was hoping to get you a stuffed animal, not any of this other stuff."

"Well, since you didn't win a stuffed animal, then I'll take the necklace...it looks like fun, and it will remind me of the Fair."

"But, I can keep trying to win the stuffed animal, if you'd like."

"No thanks, Jack...I'm fine with the necklace."

"Billy says he knows you from the 4H Club. Isn't that a club for farm kids?" I asked Jo as we walked away from the shooting gallery and along the Midway.

"That just shows how little you military school guys know about rural life. Besides, Greenville is not a city at all...it's just a small town. Except for the folks in town that don't depend on agriculture for their living – like the people that own and work for the fire-brick factory – or like your family who didn't grow up here, life in Greenville revolves around agriculture: the farms, the farmers, the crops, the cattle, the livestock, as well as the people who make their living selling to, buying from or caring for the farm folks. And 4H ties us farm community kids all together with educational opportunities, and not just in agriculture. We learn about other things related to the four Hs: Head, Heart, Health and Hands."

"I guess then, that even though I live – and maybe sometimes work — on my mom's farm, I've got a lot to learn about what goes on around here," I responded lamely not knowing what else to say.

Jo then asked, "What's military school like? Do you just learn army things, like, you know, marching, saluting, and firing guns... that kind of stuff?"

"Sure, we do some of that kind of stuff, but it's mostly regular school stuff; like going to any other school...just learning the three Rs."

"Then why do you go there rather than going to one of the schools in town?"

"I did go to St. Benedicts for a while, but Aunt Rita...I mean Mom...thinks I'll get a better education at the military school than I was getting at St. Benedicts...or anywhere else in town."

"Well, you are sure a lot different from most of the boys that I go to school with. I mean, you seem to be interested in things other than just sports and hunting and bragging about how strong they are."

I was just in the process of telling Jo something about my life at school, when I spotted a group of older, bigger boys coming straight towards us, so as to block our way. All the boys, except one, were unfamiliar to me. The one boy I recognized was Wesley; remembering him as the jerk, the bully, who tried to pick a fight with me when Billy and I went into town to see a movie with some of the guys from the neighboring farms.

"Well, looky who we have here," said Wesley in an angry way, glaring directly at me with his small, cruel eyes. "Ain't you the pansy that goes to that hoity-toity military school...learning all that jujitsu fighting stuff...but wouldn't fight me when I dared him to? Let's see if you'll try to run away again tonight."

"That ain't what I remember happened, Wesley," replied Billy, stepping directly between me and Wesley. "It was you who tried to pick the fight with Jack...and when he took your dare...it was you...not Jack...who backed down...just like the cowardly bully you've always been. Maybe...now that you've got some of your 'thug' pals with you...you think you got some balls...But I doubt it."

"Shut up, ya little runt," Wesley grumbled, advancing towards Billy menacingly.

I was about to say, "Pick on somebody your own size!" when Billy, squaring up his shoulders, said bravely, "Who're ya calling a 'little runt" ya big coward?"

"You," snarled Wesley, making a grab at Billy who backed away quickly, out of Wesley's reach. "You're such a little runt that the best part of ya musta run down your old man's leg," Wesley guffawed, looking around at his pals for support.

Taking his eyes off of Billy, even for just an instance, was Wesley's big mistake. Billy immediately lunged forward, his head lowered, attempting to ram his head into Wesley's stomach. At the last instant Wesley looked down at Billy's rapidly approaching form, took a step back, grabbed at the back of Billy's head and neck.

But, Billy was too quick, too strong, and like a powerful tackle going after the quarter-back, his head made contact with Wesley's stomach, knocking Wesley backward. Instead of falling down, however, Wesley kept his balance, using Billy's forward momentum to his advantage, pushing on Billy's back causing him to stumble, fall to his knees. As Billy tried to get up, Wesley swung a clenched fist at Billy's head.

"Uckday Illybay," I cried out.

When Billy ducked, Wesley's fist passed above the now crouched Billy, causing Wesley to lose his balance, collapsing over Billy's back. Before Wesley could regain his balance, I lunged at him, grabbing Wesley in my arms, twisting him away from Billy, pushing him to the ground, saying, "Now, pick on someone your own size, Wesley," as he struggled to climb back up.

Like the bull in the cartoons spying the red cape, Wesley charged at me with his right arm and fist cocked back, poised to strike me in the face. Remembering what Fritz had taught me years ago, I stood my ground, waiting for the exact moment when Wesley threw his fist at my head; then I ducked, stepped to my right, then swinging my right arm and clenched fist catching the now off-balanced Wesley on the left side of his head, just in front of his left ear. Wesley's fist totally missed me, but my blow to Wesley's head dropped him first to his knees, and then his body pitched forward, landing face-down in the dirt; where he laid still for several minutes.

Billy was at my side immediately, taking a wrestler's crouched pose, preparing for further battle as Wesley's pals moved toward us, encircling us. Rubbing my aching right hand... *God, it hurts so bad...* I hoped that these other guys really didn't want to help Wesley. But seeing the vengeance in their eyes I now was concerned that we would be no match for these guys if, as a group, they attacked us.

Fearing the worst, I looked around to determine if there was a way of escaping from these thugs. It was then that I saw Jo hurrying towards us, bringing a bunch of boys who looked to me every bit as tough as the bullies who were just about to pounce on us. Feeling at the moment like General Custer and his troops surrounded by the Indians at the Little Big Horn River, but with the cavalry coming to our rescue, I shouted, "Over here!"

Seeing that we had help arriving, Wesley's pals began to scatter, looking for their own ways of escaping, abandoning Wesley, who was now sitting up, rubbing at his dust-covered and tear-stained face, clasping the left-side of his face and ear — which was turning the color of a ripening plum.

Fritz then commented: *You were very brave, Jack. More brave than I would ever have thought you could be.*

It required just a moment for me to understand what had happened, to appreciate the danger, and to see the importance of having good, brave friends. Suddenly, I also became aware of where we were, noticing that except for Billy, Wesley, and the boys who Jo brought to help us, the area around us was empty of people — I heard no laughter, shouting or other sounds of enjoyment, just distant background noise. *Did the fight scare the folks away? Why are the vendors, the booth workers staring at us? Have they sent for the police? What will happen to us? I need to find and thank Jo for her help.*

I had just located Jo, standing with Marge, engaged in conversation, when from out of nowhere Dennis grabbed Billy and me by our wrists, tugging us towards one of the spaces between the booths. I tried to break free of Dennis' vise-like grip, saying, "No. Not yet. I've got to tell Jo thanks."

"Not now! Not here! I've got to get you out of here," Dennis growled angrily, dragging Billy and me down an open way between the booths leading towards an area behind the carnival, where it was dark, empty. Milly was just a few steps behind us.

"You boys are in a heap of trouble."

"But, Dad...It wasn't our fault...Those bullies attacked us."

"That don't matter to them roustabouts...them carnie folk. You all are troublemakers as far as they're concerned. And they hate troublemakers. We warned you all not to get into a fight, any fight...You just shoulda walked away when they started giving you trouble."

"I just couldn't help myself," Billy said. "They said something about me 'n you, Dad...someth'n that I couldn't let pass."

"I'm sure that anything they said bout me I heard before. Look boys I was watching you two for a while here, and I seen what happened...I know'd how it started. And while I'm proud of how you took care of that bully Wesley, we ain't too happy about you not obeying us. Unless your mom and me can get you and Jack outa here without being spotted by the enforcers...them carnie thugs...things could get rough...and I got no stomach for fighting with those thugs."

"Why," I asked, "are they so upset with us...we were just defending ourselves...Besides, we didn't break anything."

"To them you are troublemakers, an' troublemakers scare the regular folks, keep'n them away from the Midway, the games, the rides, the fun stuff...And that's where they make their money, it's their livelihood...And nobody fucks with their livelihood. I'm sure you saw how folks cleared out of the way, left the midway...they stopped playing the games of chance when the fighting started.

"You all just fucked with their livelihood...and they are gonna fuck with you, rough you up, make a show of throwing you out on your ass...just to teach you and the other troublemakers a lesson, a painful lesson so that you'll never want to cause any trouble again...I should know, I've been on the receiving end of their brutality too many times. I know what it means when one of those bastards hollers, 'Hey, Rube!' It means they's calling for all their buddies to come help beat the shit outs some poor guy. So we need to get you outa here, quickly, quietly...I think I know a way, but you've got to stay close to Milly and me."

"What about Jo and Marge," I asked, "What's going to happen to them...They were right there with us...Won't they be in trouble, too?"

"We can't worry about them right now...Besides, they was just bystanders...It'll be hard for the screws to tie them to you all if they'll just keep their mouths shut...When they hear what the screws are asking, they'll figure it out...they're smart girls...You'da dumped them if they weren't...And they'll fig're out quick enough why you two skedaddled."

With Dennis in the lead, and Milly bringing up the rear, we moved quickly through the dark passage-way leading to another area even farther away from the Midway. We came into a dimly-lit, open-air enclosure of several acres which appeared to be an exposition site that was closed for the night. It was crammed-full with farm equipment of all shapes and sizes, grouped together according to type and purpose. Behind us I heard the voices of several men talking loudly, in angry tones, shouting something like, "I think two of them boys went this way...They may be moving through the equipment exhibit...headed to the livestock sheds...If they make it into the livestock area, we'll have a helluva time finding them in there." There were occasional flashes of light reflecting off of the pieces of farm-equipment located all around us. *This is not looking good. They are onto us. They have flashlights. I hope that Dennis' plan to get us out of here will work.*

I heard Dennis whisper, "Keep on movin'...We need to distance ourselves from these guys behind us...I'll let you know when to stop...when we need to hide...where we need to hide. As long as they don't spot us we're okay."

In front of us I saw the outline of a closed gate, barring our way into the livestock area. Dennis unlatched the gate, swung it open, but he did not go through it. He quickly turned to the right, motioning us to follow him as he ran along the fence separating the livestock area from the farm equipment area. When that fence met with another fence, Dennis again turned to the right, following the next fence for about one-hundred feet. *We are doubling back to where we started...Why?* Then I saw why: All along this fence were parked dozens of trailers; some open, some enclosed. Dennis grabbed Billy, had him climb on the fence – directing him to pull himself onto the rigid top of an enclosed livestock trailer, to lie down, and to be absolutely still. Then he did the same with me. Once Billy and I were safely out-of-sight, Dennis and Milly moved away from the trailers, back out into the area where various pieces of farm equipment and wagons were displayed.

I couldn't see what Dennis and Milly were doing in the darkened area, but I could hear the men who were following us talking as they moved through the equipment exhibition area, and I could see the beams of their flashlights reflecting off of the equipment as they passed by. Suddenly, the men stopped moving, the beams of their flashlights showing on one spot. "Did you hear that?" a gruff voice asked.

"Yeah, I heard something...sounds like voices," a deeper voice answered.

"I think it is coming from the wagons over there," a third voice added, "I think someone's hiding in one of those wagons."

"Let's go take a look," the gruff voice commanded.

"I'll bet it's those two boys we're looking for," the deeper voice remarked, adding, "Barney, you take those hay wagons over there. Buddy, you take those over there...while I look through the ones here."

For a while it was quiet; then the gruff voice cried out, "What the hell! What have we got here?"

Again, the voices and flashlight beams showed on one spot.

"Whatcha got," the deeper voice asked.

"It's just some guy and his gal going at it," the third voice responded.

"What's you folks doin' in here? Don't youse know this area is closed? How long youse been here," the gruff voice asked.

"Not long," Dennis responded. "We just come here from the

Midway...not more than a few minutes ago."

"Oh, shit," growled the deeper voice angrily. "We've been following the wrong damn pair."

"Did youse see a couple of boys come through here...maybe just ahead of youse," asked the gruff voice.

"A couple of boys?" asked Dennis; his words sounding slightly slurred. "Whatja mean...a couple of boys? If we'd seen anyone else in here we'd never have come in here...We're just looking for some privacy."

"I still think they came through here...We're just waist'n time jabbering with these two love-birds, while them boys get away," said the gruff voice.

"Whatcha want to do with these two? They can't stay here," complained the deeper voice.

"We'll go," Dennis responded in a weak voice. We know when we ain't wanted."

"Fine, and don't youse come back in here again. If we catches youes two in here there'll be hell to pay...let me tell you," the gruff voice said.

"Thanks...You won't have any more trouble with us," Dennis offered.

"We'd better not. Okay guys...let's get down to the livestock area...But I want you, Barney, to go check the trailers over by the fence...those would be a good place for them kids to hide in." After a pause, the gruff voice added, "When you're finished doing that come on down to the livestock area, where Buddy and I'll be searching for them boys."

Oh, God! Now what are we supposed to do? Will he think to look on top of the trailers, not just in them? How is Dennis going to get us out of here? Will Billy and I have to spend the night on top of these damn trailers?

"Damn," I heard the voice which I guessed belonged to Barney say. "Why do I always have to do the shit job? Them boy's are long gone from here. I'd rather of had to escort that tipsy fellow and his big-titted girl friend outa here. Now that'd be interesting...seeing her big tits in the bright lights."

I could hear Barney scuffling around the trailers, opening and closing doors, and I could see the beam of his flashlight as it moved from trailer to trailer. When he reached the two trailers where Billy and I were quietly lying – hopefully out of sight – I heard Barney open each door and then close it, moving on to the next trailer. Just when I thought he'd finished his search, I heard Barney coming back up the line of trailers, stopping at each one, grunting, muttering to himself, "Why would they want to hide under these damn trailers?" After hearing him shamble off towards the other end, I heard him struggling to climb the fence.

Oh, no! He's now going to look on top of the enclosed trailers. We're doomed.

Now paralyzed with fear, my heart racing a million beats a minute, I could see Barney's cap, the large, long flashlight held in his right hand, appearing above a trailer with a canvass-top down the line. Just when I thought he was going to go back down, he turned the beam of his flashlight in my direction. Oh shit! He's seen me !

Then I heard him shout, "Hey, Rube! I done found one of them boys back up here…Hiding on the top of one of them closed trailers next to the fence. Come on back up here and help me before he and the other one gets away."

I couldn't believe what was happening. I had been so sure that Dennis' plan was working, and that we would escape the "carnie thugs." But now we were trapped on top of the trailers. I guessed that maybe we could try to jump off of the trailers, but in the pitch-black dark, it was likely that we would break a leg or worse when and where we landed.

"There's the other kid," I heard the Barney guy say as I saw Billy's white and scared face caught in the flashlight's beam.

"Jump, Billy," I shouted, hoping to distract Barney, who then looked like he was not sure who to go after first.

Billy started working his way towards the fence-side of the trailer, and I could see him begin to slide over the side, his feet trying to find the top of the fence. At the same time, I saw Barney's hand reaching towards me, grabbing at my legs. I kicked my feet at Barney's hands, but he managed to get hold of my right ankle, and started pulling me towards him, all the time hitting the calf of my leg with his big, long flashlight, using it like a billy-club. There was immediate pain in my leg, like he was breaking it, and he kept dragging me to the edge of the trailer-top. There was nothing I could find to grip onto to keep from being pulled closer to Barney where he could start beating the rest of my body with that big damn flashlight.

"Come here, you fucking little bastard, so's I can clip you good on the head with this here flashlight."

The last thing I remembered was the pain from the blows creeping up my body as the flashlight hit me in the stomach, the chest, the shoulder. Everything went blank, and the next thing I recalled was me kneeling on top of Barney, on his chest, beating his head with the same flashlight that he had been using on me. But it wasn't Barney lying under my knees yelling, twisting and screaming, "Stop. Stop. You's killing me!" It was one of the other thugs. As I paused hitting the fellow under me, I could see in the flashlight's beam, Barney lying on the ground next to the fence, not moving. I couldn't see the third guy, but I could hear him groaning and cursing, and Dennis yelling at him to, "stay down, or I'll have to kill you!"

I could hear, but I couldn't see, Milly and Billy urging Dennis on with, "Kick him in the balls...Break his head...just like he was trying to do to Jack!"

"Let's get the fuck outa here," Dennis hollered as I felt him grab me by the arm pulling me off of the guy I was kneeling on, still beating the guy on the head with the flashlight. "Enough, Jack...Enough! Drop the flashlight...You're going to kill him!"

I was in a kind of a daze, having no idea of what had happened, or even where I was, for sure. As I was trying to figure out what had taken place, how I came to have the big flashlight in my hand, I felt Dennis tear it out of my hand, and start dragging me along with him, headed for the Midway with Milly and Billy beside us.

We managed to slip between the closed, darkened booths, blending into the stream of fairgoers moving along the Midway, headed for the exits. Still unsure of what had happened, Milly slipped a baseball cap on my head and taking my hand we walked along like mother and son, acting as if nothing at all had just taken place.

Passing by the carnie workers standing on either side of the Midway, watching the crowd, looking for troublemakers, I kept smiling, my eyes searching for familiar faces, praying that the guys who we had just tangled with had not managed to catch up with us. I breathed a great sigh of relief when we passed through the front gate untouched, moving on towards the parking lot.

ON THE DRIVE home, I was lost in thought, still trying to understand how I had managed to get away from that Barney guy, to escape from what had become a terrible situation. I was sure, when Barney was beating on me with that awful big flashlight, that everything Dennis had warned us about the carnie workers was about to come true; a horrible beating, broken bones, a bloody nose, even arrest. And then, in a flash, it was me who was holding the flashlight, giving the beating, already having knocked Barney out. And then it was over; we had escaped, getting away from the thugs we had overpowered, leaving them lying in the dirt.

My thoughts were interrupted by Dennis saying, "You was really something back there, Jack. It was too dark for me to see exactly what happened...One minute I thought you was a gonner...and then I heard that fellow who was trying to drag you off of that trailer start yelling and screaming...like he's having his nuts yanked off. Hell, the next thing I know'd he was lying on the ground with you on top of his back hitting him with that big flashlight he'd been carrying.

"Then one of them other fellers came at you from behind, swinging at you with his big flashlight...And the next thing I hear'd was him crying out in pain, that his knee cap's been broken. By that time I jumped up there and got ahold of that guy from behind to keep him off of you...though you was doing fine without my help, or so it seemed. But that's when the third guy showed up...him charging at you too. In a flash, he too was on the ground, on his back, and you was on top of him clubbing him on the head with that long, heavy flashlight like you'd done to that other fella, like you was goin to kill him. That's when I decided you'd done enough damage...and it was time for us to skedaddle."

Milly asked, "Where'd you learn to fight like that...to handle guys twice...hell...three-times your size?"

It then came to me. I had been ignoring the obvious: It wasn't me at all; it had to have been Fritz. He had taken control of my body, using skills and strengths that I don't have. While I was glad it happened, I was still scared, now knowing just what kind of damage Fritz could do using my scrawny body.

"I don't know what came over me," was all that I could say.

"Yeah," said Dennis. "I've seen that happen a couple of times in the heat of battle. Some ordinary guy does things...some feat of heroism...something nobody thought he was capable of doing."

CHAPTER 35

NELL PICKED UP THE NEXT TABLET FROM THE
dwindling stack. But before she began reading, she thought back on
what she had just read in the last tablet. *Jack has every right to be
scared of Fritz…and so should Rita…Although that bitch deserves whatever might come her way.* Thinking then back to the day that she found
the tablets, she tried to remember what Paul had said about Rita being concerned that Jack was possessed by a "spirit," and that Rita was
scared of Jack. *Did Paul say that it was an "evil" spirit, or just a "spirit?"
Whatever, if Fritz's spirit can take over Jack's body, and something bad
happened, would it be Jack, or would it be the "spirit?"*

Turning her full-attention to the next tablet, Nell began to read,
but still thinking: *Where are Jack and Rita?*

BIG CHIEF TABLET THIRTY-ONE | JACK

I need to talk to Billy… I thought several weeks after the night at
the County Fair. *We need to talk about what happened that night
in the exhibit area, at the trailers, with the carnie thugs,*

I went to Mom's bedroom to ask her permission to spend
Saturday afternoon with Billy, at Billy's. *We can't talk here, not
where we could be heard by Mom.* I stood at the door to Mom's
bedroom enjoying the scene.

The morning sun was slanting in through the open French
doors leading from Mom's bedroom onto the second floor porch.
The late-summer air was filled with smell of newly cut alfalfa hay
laying in the fields waiting to be raked and baled, to be carted
into the hay-loft. Sitting at her writing desk, ledgers in front of
her, Mom was transferring amounts to an open ledger from the
scraps of paper littering her desk. She looked up from her work
as I entered her bedroom from the hallway, lightly tapping the
door frame as I did so. A distracted smile broke across her lips as

she placed the mechanical pencil in the crease of the open ledger. Standing in front of her desk, I toyed absently with the onyx desk-set that I had given to her as a Christmas present, slipping the dagger-like letter opener in and out of its leather scabbard. Staring at my fidgeting, Mom cleared her throat, prompting me to cease my playing with the dagger.

Thrusting the letter opener one last time into its scabbard, I inquired, "Do you ever use this stuff? I thought it would be a great present...but Gabby had other ideas...and that's why we got you the gold necklace as well. I still think the letter opener makes a swell dagger." I withdrew the opener from the scabbard with my right hand one more time, gripping it thumb first, making forward thrusts like I was poking it at something.

"Put that thing away before you stab me with it...You could put an eye out with that dagger!" she demanded angrily, putting up a hand as if to ward off a knife attack to her face.

"Sorry," I apologized, slipping the opener back in its leather case, putting it back down on Mom's desk.

"I hope you had something on your mind, other than blinding me, when you came in here. As you can see, I'm busy doing the accounts...So I don't have time right now to play games...This farm doesn't run itself. What do you want?"

"Well," I stammered. "I know its Saturday...and I have chores to do...But this is the first weekend I have been home from school in over two weeks...And I thought I could go see Billy...we had planned to do some hunting and stuff. But only if that's all right with you."

"Like I just said...this farm doesn't run itself. Fortunately, Hannah has taken over most of your chores anyway, so you've got a free pass to go and see Billy today."

"Gee, thanks. And thank Hannah for me, too."

"Will you be home for dinner? It's been a while since we've sat down to dinner together...and had one of our good chats."

"Probably, but what if Billy's folks ask me to stay for dinner, would you mind too terribly if I said yes? I haven't seen or talked to Billy's mom and dad since our trip to the County Fair. Billy's dad has some great stories he likes to tell."

"No, I'd really rather that you have dinner here. By the way, you never really told me much about the County Fair...other than you got sick from one of the rides because of what you had eaten beforehand...even after I had warned you that would happen. Any other excitement you want to tell me about? Did Billy's folks show up on time?"

If you only knew just how much excitement I had.

"Yeah, they were there in time. *If only you knew how 'just in time' their arrival was.* When you have more time I'll tell you all about how much fun we had. More like excitement...even terror... than fun!

"You really like Billy...and his folks...don't you? For all of his problems, Dennis is a good dad...isn't he?

"Sure. And he's a lot of fun, too. I've learned a lot from Dennis about...you know...doing man-type things that..."

"You miss your dad, don't you?"

"Sure...But if I had him, I wouldn't have you."

"That's very thoughtful of you to say so...Still I don't make a very good father...providing you with a father-figure in your life. Is that why you like to be around Billy and his dad?"

"Yeah, maybe...but it's more than that...Dennis is fun to be with...when he's not having one of his spells...He's done more stuff with Billy and me than my dad ever did."

"That's because Dennis is more like an overgrown boy than a man who – like your dad – has had all of the fun taken out of him...by life, by his wife. And remember, Jack, life is more than just having fun...it is about taking responsibility...being dependable...and your dad has those qualities; he is a very good man – just married to the wrong woman. I'm not sure that Dennis is quite as dependable...he could let you down in a tight situation... when he's acting more like a boy than a man."

"Yeah, I'll be careful...Don't you worry about me when I'm with Dennis."

"Well, have a good time then...And please telephone me to let me know when you'll be coming home for supper...Love you!"

"Me, too. I'll call."

DURING MY BIKE ride up the road to Billy's house, I reflected back on that night at the County Fair. I remembered that I still had not told Billy anything about Fritz. *Maybe if we get to talking about the fight with Wesley and those awful thugs at the Fair, I can tell Billy how I learned to fight like I did.* But then I realized that it was more than Fritz just teaching me how to box, remembering that it must have been Fritz – not me – who had fought with, and beat up, the carnie thugs. Fritz had actually taken over my body, used my scrawny body like it was the body of a well-trained athlete

When I arrived at Billy's house, I was greeted by Billy's two mongrel dogs on the gravel driveway, wagging their tails, happily prancing around my bike, following me into the yard, where I kick-stand my bike, and climbed onto the back porch. Through the open back door I could see Billy's mom standing at the kitchen-stove, turning toward the sound as I knocked at the screen door.

"Hi, Jack," Milly said cheerfully, walking towards the doorway. "Come on in. If you're looking for Billy, you just missed him. He and his dad are taking a load of hay over to his grandpa's place. But they should be back shortly." Motioning me to take a seat at the narrow kitchen table, she continued her chatter: "Sit down... take a rest. Can I get you a glass of iced tea? You look hot. Did you ride your bike up here? We haven't seen you for a while... since the night at the Fair. You back at the military school? How's miz Kaufman...your mom, I mean?

None of these statements, none of these questions, needed more than a one-word answer – like "yes," "no," "fine." Eventually, Milly pounced on what she really wanted to talk about.

"You know, Jack, we never got around to...you know that awful night at the Fair...to thanking you for what you did...you know when those mean boys started picking on Billy...you know how you stuck up for Billy...how you fought that bully Wesley. And then what you done with them carnie thugs...when Dennis and me thought you both was gonners. Boy, you really handled them like they was just punks...you put them on the ground...just like you knew what you were doing. Billy, Dennis and me thought that you was going to kill that one guy. You done real good, Jack. I'll bet your mom is real proud of what you done for Billy... for us."

"I haven't told Mom about that."

"Well, why not? You should tell her. If you won't, then I will."

"Oh, please don't. I'm not sure whether she would like that. She told me not to get into a fight...and then when I did, look what happened. If it hadn't been for you and Dennis...Damn, I don't know what would have happened to Billy and me. Mom would probably have had to come get me at the city's hoose-gow. God, she really would have been mad at me if that had happened. I'd probably still be in trouble with her...and not sitting here talking with you right now."

"Don't thank us...We didn't do much when it came to saving Billy...You done it all...and she would have been proud about how brave you was and everything...I know I am...and so is Dennis."

"Thanks...That means a lot."

"How did you learn to fight like that? Is that something you learned at your military school?"

"Yeah, it's some military training I picked up." *But not at my military school, and it wasn't me at all.*

"That's great...And it might have saved Billy's life. I don't know if you know it, but Billy's got some fairly serious health problems. The docs don't know exactly what it is, but he's not growing the way he should...it's something to do with muscle and bone stuff. And if he gets hurt, he don't heal too well...or very quickly. At first they thought it was some growth gland...but now they ain't too sure what it is. I mean he's a tough little critter, but he's never been real strong...and I'm afraid he's getting weaker...or so it seems to us."

Turning away from me, lifting the hem of her apron, wiping at her face, her eyes, Billy's mom remarked, "If something happens to Billy it will just break my heart in two...and it will destroy his Daddy...He just loves Billy like nothing else in this world. 'Cept for Billy...and me, of course...Dennis ain't got much to hang on to... The war took away most of his dreams...It done left him a broken man...Though he does his best...most of the time not to show it. I think you seen one of those times when he showed it."

This was all something new to me. I'd never seen such emotions before; the fear of loss, the grief of loss, the obvious pain. I started to say, "Miz Lewis," instead, I said, "Milly."

"You don't need to say nothing, Jack...I know how you feel about Billy...You showed it when you came to his defense... made his fight your fight. Some things you just don't need to talk about...just doin says it all. Now, doesn't the Bible say: 'No greater love does a man have than to lay down his life for his brother?' I think that says it all."

"But, I only wish I could do more for you, for Billy, and for Dennis."

"And, you can...you can just keep on being Billy's friend...I just wish I could have you around here all the time...being Billy's friend every day...He really likes you Jack...you're like a brother to him...You tell him things he ain't never heard about or seen... good things...important things...not just a bunch of stuff like his school friends talk about."

"That's not true...Billy has taught me things I'd never see or learn about if it weren't for him treating me like he does. I'd be lost out here in the country if it weren't for Billy...and Dennis... and you. I love my new mom dearly...she has saved me from a dreadful life with my real mom...but she's never had real kids of her own...and she doesn't know much about raising a boy like me...So, you all..."

"You don't want to go there, Jack...As you've seen, we ain't no great model family...Picking us as your family would turn out to be a bad bargain. What we provide in excitement and fun, we lack in providing stability, a long-term relationship. We're burning the candle at both ends...there's no telling where we'll be next week, let alone next year. No, we're here for you now, but you need to hang in there with Miz Kaufman as your mom...she's much better for you...She's the better choice...Just give her time to grow with you. Think about all that she has done for you already...in just a year."

And look at all that I have done for Mom in that same year...I

*have presented her with an impossible situation: Either I'm crazy
– with a make-believe Fritz – or I'm actually possessed – sharing
my body with the spirit of a dead German, who says his name is
Fritz. There is no third possibility. I am certainly not a normal
boy...a model boy. No wonder I feel so at home with Billy's family. So do I really want to present Billy with the same dilemma to
which I have subjected my Mom? If I do, will he stand by me as
Mom has?*

"Yeah, she has been great for me. I need to remember that
more than I do."

The rumbling sound of a tractor engine interrupted my
thoughts, bringing me back to the reality of having to deal with
my friendship with Billy, his family, and what impact my secret
might have on that friendship going forward.

"Hey! Jack," exclaimed an excited Billy throwing open the
kitchen screen door. "How long you been here?"

"Not too long," I replied, as I stood up. "I know your dad has
you helping him, but I thought I'd come by and see if you want
to do some hunting when you're done...Before it gets too late."

"Hell! It's never too late to go hunting, Jack...Just depends on
what you wanta go hunting for," he said giving me that grin; the
one that lights up his whole face, the whole room.

"Yeah," responded Billy's dad from where he was sitting on
the top of the porch steps pulling off his work boots. "A little
hunting this beautiful afternoon sounds like just the thing to do...
Would ya mind if an old codger joins you two youngsters? I'm
hankering for some squirrel and rabbit stew for my supper tonight."

"Sounds like fun," acknowledged Billy. "Jack and me we're
gonna use our Red Ryders. You gonna bring a real rifle?"

"Well, since it looks like you didn't bring that gun shy Irish
Setter...I'll bring along the Remington .22 pump-action. Besides,
we don't need no hunt'n dog to scare up squirrels and rabbits.
It's about time you boys get the feel of a real rifle. Billy's told me
about them miserable air rifles you had to shoot with at the Fair,
and how you got two of them moving targets...Not too bad a
shoot'n Jack...With them whacko rifles that was quite a feat."

It was indeed a beautiful Saturday afternoon; that first fall weekend. The sky was a soft blue, with strands of wind-whipped high clouds. To reach the woods where we expected to find our quarry we crossed through recently mowed and raked alfalfa hay fields, crunching along over the drying stubble. There had yet to be the first frost, but the leaves on the trees at the edges of the field were already beginning to show signs of losing their deep-green color. *Wouldn't my Dad love to be here enjoying the out-of-doors with us? Being an old Wisconsin farm-boy himself, I'm sure he'd fit right in with Dennis and Billy.*

Imitating Dennis, Billy and I tramped along with our Daisy BB guns resting on our shoulders, much like a soldier would. But if we had been cradling our trusty Red Ryder rifles in our arms, we wouldn't have missed shooting at a couple of rabbits that scampered away upon our approach. By the time we were able to swing the rifles off of our shoulders and into firing position, the rabbits were out of range.

In the woods that afternoon, our quarry was pretty much limited to squirrels. After a few missed shots with our air-rifles, Dennis said he would take the next shot using the Remington. The squirrels that had eluded our earlier errant shots were now scurrying in the higher branches of the trees, angrily barking and chattering at us — like a bunch of kids who think they are out of range of the water balloons, yelling "Nana, Nana, Nana," at their attackers. Pumping the Remington to insert a .22 round into the firing chamber, taking careful aim at the first squirrel, Dennis squeezed the trigger, dispatching the first squirrel. Dennis pumped again, aimed and squeezed off another round, bringing another squirrel to the ground.

"See, guys," Dennis said proudly, "that's the way it's done with a real rifle...Weren't that easy?"

"Can I have a try, now," asked Billy.

"Not quite yet," responded Dennis. "You need some train'n afore you can fire this here rifle. Shoot'n a air rifle ain't the same as fire'n a fire arm...You need some basic understanding of what you're usin before you get to use it."

"Aw, gee, Dad," Billy cried peevishly. "We ain't in the Marines here."

"Don't make no difference...Train'n is train'n! No train'n...No shoot'n. Now sit down here in this clearing...and I'll give you some lessons on this Remington."

While Billy and I were lowering ourselves to the ground, Dennis brushed away dead leaves and sticks that littered the ground, removed his jacket, placing it on the cleared ground in a spot where the daylight coming through the trees was at its brightest. This, as it turned out, was pretty basic training. We had expected Dennis to hand us the Remington, have us pump the action to load a bullet into the chamber, pick out a target, take aim, and pull the trigger. Instead, Dennis said, "You need to watch what I'm gonna do."

Dennis proceeded to unload the Remington, putting the bullets in his pants pocket, and took the rifle a part piece-by-piece, until it was entirely in pieces, down to the firing block. Carefully laying each piece on his jacket, Dennis took a cloth from his pants' pocket, and proceeded to pick up each part, clean it, and replace it on his jacket. Satisfied that all of the parts were ready for reassembly, Dennis picked up each part in its proper order and reassembled the Remington. Upon completion, but not putting bullet cartridges into the tube magazine, Dennis pumped the mechanism — which cocks the firing pin and would normally place a cartridge in the firing chamber — pointed the rifle towards a clearing between the trees, and pulled the trigger, fake firing the empty rifle at some unseen target. The only sound we heard was the click of the hammer striking the firing pin.

Handing the empty rifle to the still seated Billy, Dennis said, "Okay, Billy, I sure hope you was watch'n what I just did. Cause now let's see you strip down this rifle and reassemble it just like I did...It's gonna get dark soon, so you better work quickly if you wanna shoot this rifle today." The look on Billy's face was one of disappointment, surprise, frustration and anger; but he started breaking down the Remington as Dennis had directed.

"Now, Jack, at that military school you go to, did they teach you anything about handl'n a fire arm," Dennis asked as he watched Billy struggling with dismantling the Remington.

"Not so far...But I've been going there for only six months... They may have given the other boys in my class such training, but not while I've been there."

"So, do I need to have you do what Billy is doin?"

"Yes, sir."

"Hey, I like that 'Yes sir' stuff...Did you hear that Billy? Can I get you to answer me like Jack just did?"

"No, sir," Billy replied sarcastically.

"Now don't you go gett'n surly with me, boy! This here's no chicken shit exercise...Your rifle is your friend...You never know when you'll need that rifle...And it better be in tip top condition when you do...There was many a time in the Pacific when a guy got killed because his weapon jammed...and his weapon jammed because he didn't take care of it like he shoulda."

Seeing how Billy was struggling with his assignment, Dennis commanded, "You weren't pay'n no attention when I showed you what to do, and now you cain't do what I showed you."

"It's getting dark, Dad. I cain't see what I'm doin."

"Yeah, well that's just too bad. Darkness ain't no excuse...We had to learn how to disassemble and reassemble our weapons in the dark...use'n blindfolds when it wasn't dark, until we could."

"I'll bet having to do it blindfolded was hard," I said. "Being blind must be terrible."

"Nothin's worse," Dennis replied. "There were lots of guys in the Pacific who was blinded...shot in the head, or from shrapnel and other stuff. God, I'd felt so sorry for those guys...I'd rather have lost an arm or a leg than have been blinded. There ain't no way you can get around by yourself. It's like being in a black hole...a black hell hole. Some of my buddies, when we caught Jap soldiers...or when they surrendered to us, instead of killing themselves like they was trained to do...would go and poke the Jap's eyes out so they wouldn't have to guard them out there in the jungle."

"That's awful," I said.

"Yes, it was awful...and I still have nightmares about it...But remember we really had no choice. There was no place at the front to keep them Jap prisoners under lock and key...We was so short-handed in fight'n the Jap soldiers that we couldn't afford to take a Marine out of the line to watch over them...and they'd sneak away back into one their caves or bunkers at night anyway."

"How'd you poke their eyes out," asked Billy, who has given up trying to take apart the Remington, and was looking at his Dad.

"With a knife...Usually we used a bayonet or a trench knife... We'd use anything with a sharp point...like a dagger...something that would do it quickly."

"Why didn't you just blindfold them," I asked.

"We did that at first...But the bastards...even when we had their hands tied behind them would find a way to tear off the blindfold...That's when we discovered that they was getting away...back into the jungle...even when we had someone guarding them...We didn't have no trouble with them once we poked their eyes out...though we still had to tie them up. Then they just sat there...wishing they'd committed that hari-kari shit rather than surrender'n to us."

"Didn't anyone say anything about what you'd done to the Jap soldiers when someone came to get them," I asked.

"I don't know what happened after we left them where we'd captured them...cause we'd just move on...fight'n the next batch of fanatic, holed-up Jap soldiers. Listen, guys, I really don't want to talk any more about it...I'll probably have nightmares about that whole shit tonight as it is. Besides, if we want to get back to the house before we have to get there in the dark...groping along like a bunch of blind guys... then we need to skedaddle right now."

"Yeah, we don't want to have to stumble around in the dark trying to find our way to the old jungle cave with 'Jap-eyes'," I exclaimed.

"Jap-eyes! Jap-eyes! We don't want no Jap-eyes," Billy said in a sing-song fashion.

"That's enough of that, boys," Dennis commanded wearily. "Let's hope that your mother has fixed us some supper, 'cause I really don't think these two old squirrels I shot will be enough for stew tonight.

"Do ya think there will be enough food for Jack to stay for dinner," asked Billy. "Cause there's a couple of things I was hopin to talk with Jack about."

"Sure," Dennis said. "And if there ain't, I'm sure we can scrounge enough of something up to fill his belly...Can you stay with us for supper, Jack?"

Not wanting to put the Lewises out, I replied, "I'll have to check with my Mom...She'd said something about expecting me home for dinner tonight."

When we stepped up onto the porch, Billy's mom was waiting behind the screen-door watching us. "I was beginning to worry about you all...You're much later than I thought you'd be... Jack, your mother telephoned...she was also concerned since she hadn't heard from you about when you was going to get home to eat your supper. I done told her you could eat with us see'n that it's getting too dark for you to ride your bike back home. She said that she had fixed a big dinner...and said that she would come get you and Billy in the station wagon...And for Billy to spend the night...Would you like that, Billy?"

"Say yes, Billy," I said "Then we'll have all night for you to talk about whatever it is you want to talk to me about."

"Gee, that sounds great!"

OUR DINNER THAT evening was out-of-the-ordinary – consisting of some of our Hereford roast beef, mashed potatoes with gravy, green beans, and fresh baked apple pie – served in the dining room on good china plates. Billy and I were scrubbed clean, wearing fresh shirts and pants, seated in the fancy Queen Anne-style table chairs, waiting for Mom and Hannah to remove their aprons in the kitchen and join us.

Mom had been training Hannah in how to cook American-style meals, and how to bake pies and cakes. The evening's meal was the result of Hannah's first effort – thus explaining Mom's insistence on having me, and now Billy, home for dinner; if only to serve as the guinea-pigs. Despite Mom's best efforts to keep the focus away from Hannah's cooking asking about our after-noon hunt, Hannah nervously watched each bite we put in our mouths, watching our facial expressions. She needed not have been so nervous; the quality of her cooking was great — not that Billy and I qualified in any respect as food critics. After we each asked for second servings, Hannah's face beamed, her shoulders relaxed, and Mom smiled proudly.

Sitting cross-legged on the colorful Persian rug covering the center portion of the study's wood floor, carefully eating from bowls of apple pie and fresh-churned vanilla ice cream in front of the first wood fire of the season, while Mom and Hannah were busy with cleaning up the dishes, plates and eating utensils that Billy and I carried into the kitchen, Billy said, "I've been wonder-ing about that night at the Fair when we had the trouble with Wesley ...and then all the trouble with the those tough guys that came after us...Dad saw what you did...And him and me have been talk'n about how it looked like you knew what you was doin...How did you learn how to fight like that? Was it at the mili-tary school?"

"Not so loud," I whispered, nervously looking towards the door leading into the hallway. "I haven't told Mom about the fight...or much at all about what happened at the Fair." *And now, what am I going to tell Billy about what took place that evening at the Fair...How I think that Fritz took control of my body. Is this the time to tell Billy about Fritz? Mom and Hannah know all about Fritz, so they wouldn't be surprised by anything I tell Billy about Fritz. But would Mom want me to share Fritz with Billy? I need to ask Mom.*

"Billy," I said as I was getting up off of the floor, "I'm going to get some more pie and ice cream...would you like me to get you some too?"

"Sure...That's some great apple pie...And I'll have some more ice cream too."

"Hannah will be pleased to hear that you approve of her des-sert."

Carrying the empty bowls across the hall and into the kitchen, I was nervously thinking about what I was going to say to Mom about telling Billy about Fritz.

In the kitchen, Mom and Hannah were just finishing up wash-ing the dishes. The kitchen table was piled with washed and wiped dishes, pots, pans, kitchen knives, forks and spoons, as well as with stacks of clean plates, glasses and tableware. But the apple pie and ice cream were nowhere in sight.

"I'm back for some more of that wonderful pie and ice-cream for Billy and me, but it looks like I may be too late."

"No, you are not too late," responded Mom cheerfully. "I've just put the pie in the pantry and the ice cream is in the freezer... But I can get them out again for two hungry, growing boys."

"Thanks," I said, following Mom into the pantry. "I've got a question I need you to answer while Billy's not around...Can I... should I...tell Billy about Fritz?"

"You mean you haven't already told him about the Kraut? I'd have thought that with all that Marine, war-stuff Dennis has been telling you about, that you'd have told Billy about the Nazi's war experiences...flying all those airplanes and jets, and stuff. Sure, if you think Billy will believe you...go ahead and tell him whatever you like about your Kraut body-mate."

"But, if Billy says he doesn't believe me about Fritz, can I tell Billy that you know, and that he can ask you if I'm telling the truth?"

"I don't think that will happen...but, yes: I'll back you up...even as much as I hate to admit it that that Kraut bastard's spirit is lounging around somewhere inside of you, complicating your life...and damn sure complicating mine. Maybe Billy and Dennis can help you find a way to get rid of the lying Nazi shit."

"You don't believe him," I asked incredulously. "What has Fritz told us that now makes you think that he is lying about who he is, about what he's done?"

"I just don't trust the bastard...and neither should you. I don't trust any Kraut whose soul won't go to hell when it's supposed to...or maybe to heaven...but I doubt that."

Walking out of the pantry with the bowls of apple pie and ice cream, I was more confused about Fritz, my Mom and me than ever. I knew that Mom had problems with dealing with Fritz; but

I'd never realized that she did not believe that he was who he said he was. *What does Mom know about Fritz that I don't know about him...or that she doesn't want to tell me? What would she think if I told her how Fritz took control of my body that night at the County Fair?*

Handing Billy the now refilled bowl of apple pie and ice cream, I said, "Billy, I'm going to tell you how I learned to fight like I did at the County Fair...against Wesley...and against the thugs. But before I do, there are some things I need to tell you about what happened to me many years ago ...years before I came to live here at Fairways...back when I was living with my real parents. I've never told anyone but Aunt Rita...not even my real folks... about what I am going to tell you. She knows...because I felt she needed to know about it before she took the steps to adopt me... But I never told my real parents because they'd think I am crazy... And you may think I'm crazy, too."

Seeing the funny look on Billy's face, I knew that I had to just blurt it out. "Billy, I have the 'spirit' of a dead German pilot living somewhere here in my body, sharing my brain. He tells me his name is Fritz. He apparently came into my body on the day he was killed at the end of the War in Germany, which is the same day that I was hit in the head so severely that I may have been dead for a short period of time. Well, whatever happened, Fritz's spirit came into my body, and was in my body for years before I was even aware of his presence. I was probably about nine or ten years old when I first became aware of Fritz through the dreams I was having. I think he was entering my mind at night... giving me these dreams. Then one-night he came right out and told me who he was...That's when we started talking to each other in our minds.

"When Fritz wants to go beyond this mind-talk...to be in contact with the world I live in, he can plug into my brain...And when he does that, he knows what I am thinking, what I am saying, what I am seeing, hearing, feeling. His spirit has been stronger than mine, and he has been able to take over my brain when he feels it is necessary to do so. He has spoken to Mom in his own voice when he took over my brain to tell her his story. Mom was very upset that he could do that, and she has forbidden him to ever take over my brain again. She told him that she would do nothing to get him back to Germany if he ever did it again. I think he's really afraid of my Mom. As far as I know, Fritz did not break Mom's rule until that night at the County Fair.

"I've never felt as threatened by Fritz as Mom thinks I should be, or as I did that night at the Fair. Even though he has the power to take over my brain, he has promised me that he would never do that without my permission. Besides, he's always been helpful to me...giving me advice on how to make friends, be a better student, be braver, how to fight, and stuff like that. Yes, it was Fritz who taught me how to fight like I did that night at the Fair...against Wesley. And later that same night, when those thugs came after us, I am convinced that it was Fritz who did the fighting...Not me...I didn't learn that stuff from Fritz...He just took control of my body."

"Jack," interrupted Billy. "If Fritz didn't have your body to live in, what would happen to him? If you were to die now, where would he go?"

"I don't know. Like I said, I don't even know how he got into my body in the first place. I don't know what God's plan was when he let Fritz's spirit enter my body. Maybe Fritz get's just one more chance to be on this earth...and if I were to die now, I guess he'd go where the souls of all dead people go."

"Ackjay...Like my Dad always says: 'I'm just a dumb country boy'. But, I ain't so sure about this Fritz guy liv'n with you in your body. I want to believe you, and it seems to me that if what you're tell'n me is true, then this Fritz guy has every reason in the world to keep you alive...And the stuff you say he is tell'n you...teach'n you...the things he has been doin' using your body...is just stuff you need to know...to have...to stay alive."

"So, Illybay, do you think maybe Fritz is just fooling me? Or do you think I'm just dreaming all this stuff...That I'm just plain nuts?"

"Does your Mom believe that this guy Fritz is liv'n with you in your body?"

"Yeah, I think so...You can ask her yourself."

"Does your Mom trust this guy to be tellin' the truth?"

"I don't think Mom trusts Fritz, period. She calls him the Nazi Kraut bastard."

"Was he a good guy or a bad guy durin' the War?"

"He says he was a good guy...trying to keep the Nazis from winning the War...and helping Jews hide from the Nazis. I'm not sure Mom...or Hannah...believes that he was a good guy. Hannah is a Jew...she lived in Poland while the Germans occupied Poland...so she should have a pretty good idea of what the Nazi soldiers did to the Jews. I know she talks to Mom about those things...but whenever I'm around she clams up."

"What did Fritz do to help keep the Nazis from winnin' the War?"

"Well, you see, the Germans developed a neat new turbojet engine and built this really fast jet fighter, the Me-262, which could fly faster than any fighter the Americans had. If the Germans had had enough of these fighters, they could've had air supremacy over Europe, and the Americans would have had to stop bombing the German cities and factories, which would have given the Germans more stuff to fight the Americans with, keeping them from invading Germany. Fritz says he was responsible for the development of the Me-262, and he kept changing how the jet plane was to be used...to delay its use as a fighter. I know this sounds confusing...but you'd have to hear Fritz tell it."

"What about the Jews...What did Fritz do to save Jews?"

"Fritz has never explained to me what he did to save Jews... He just talks about what his parents did, what his family did... something about hiding them, helping them get out of Germany. He says the Jews were in lots of trouble with the Nazis...and some S.S. guys, but he never said what happened to his folks."

"Why haven't you told me about this Fritz guy before?"

"I didn't know you well enough until now...And I didn't think you would believe me...That I'd scare you away...And I wanted you to be my friend."

"Of course I'm your friend...And, I'm still here...ain't I? And if you're ly'n about this Fritz guy, you've sure got me fooled...That story has the makin's for a great movie."

CHAPTER 36

BIG CHIEF TABLET THIRTY-TWO | JACK

"Jack," I heard Mom calling to me from the down stair's hall. We're going to be late if you don't get a wiggle on. I am hoping that we can arrive at Dr. K and Gabby's house before dark, but we'll have to leave right now. Where's your suitcase? Hannah and I have already loaded our bags in the station wagon."

It was a late October Friday afternoon, and we were making a spur-of-the-moment trip to see Mom's in-laws, the Kaufmans, in Kansas City, normally a two hour jaunt. I first learned of our journey on Thursday evening when Mom called me at school to inform me that I'd need to be on time when she picked me up at the end of classes on Friday, and not to make any plans for the weekend.

I'd been back in school for about a month, adjusting to being in seventh grade, renewing my friendship with the gang, trying to resume good study habits, searching for ways to avoid de-merits. I had not, however, arrived at the stage where I'd regu-larly 'have plans for the weekend'- except for spending time with Mom, Hannah, and Lady at Fairways. Yet that weekend – one of my first weekends home since school resumed – I had hoped to visit with Billy, spending some time together, seeing if Billy had developed any misgivings about my revelations of Fritz, who had been noticeably quiet.

The reason offered for our visit to the Kaufmans – when I inquired – was for Mom, Hannah and me to replenish our winter wardrobes, the rationale being that: 'Jack has grown like a weed over the summer, and none of his clothes fit him properly'. It was true that I had grown taller and filled out in the chest and shoulders, but most of the time I was in uniform at school — an already new uniform — so I was convinced that my growth was just an excuse for Mom and Hannah to go clothes shopping at the fancy stores at Kansas City's Country Club Plaza.

The 'Plaza' is one of the country's first, and most impressive, shopping malls. This was the shopping area where Gabby and I purchased Mom's Christmas presents — the onyx desk set, with the dagger-like letter opener, and the gold necklace. Besides clothing stores, there were some terrific sporting goods stores and toy stores. While Mom and Hannah were spending time shopping for their clothes, I planned to visit the sporting goods and toy stores. *I wonder if I can talk Mom into buying me a Remington .22 pump-action rifle, if I can find one there.*

Never an early riser, Gabby did not make her appearance downstairs on Saturday morning until ten o'clock; announcing that to have awakened earlier would have been a waste of her time, 'since the better shops in the Plaza don't open until eleven o'clock'. Dr. K had already left for his Saturday morning golf game at the nearby Missouri Hills Country Club.

By lunch-time, Gabby, and her troops, including me, arrived at a ladies' fancy clothing shop — and I was granted permission to wander around the Plaza, searching on my own for a winter jacket; with the understanding that I'd meet Mom by the big water fountain at the Wornall and Ward Parkway entrance at two o'clock. From there she and I would go to lunch at a nearby sandwich shop, and, if I had been successful in my search for a jacket, then to return to the store to complete the purchase.

My first objective was to locate a sporting goods store where I could look at hunting rifles; specifically a Remington .22 pump-action rifle. Although it did not take me long to locate the store, the rifle, my request to hold and handle the weapon was rejected by a grumpy sales clerk because, "You're too young, son... You need your dad to be with you." I didn't have any better luck at any of the other sporting goods stores on the Plaza that carried the Remington rifle. *Maybe Mom is right; I do need to have a Dad — well, at least a father-figure. And to think I once had a Dad...I do miss my Dad. I know he loves me. Too bad that Dad and Rita aren't my parents.*

In my dejected, depressed frame of mind I began to search for the 'winter jacket', turning it into an unpleasant chore, rather than the opportunity to be free of the women-folk, to be on my own, which I was sure Mom meant it to be; the end-result for me being a long, empty-handed quest. Leaving a men's store that I had hoped to be the last of my searches for the 'winter jacket', I turned towards the fountain where I was to meet Mom, not paying any attention to the windows of the shops on my side of the street, or of the other pedestrians alongside or in front of me on the sidewalk.

Just as I was about to cross the plaza to the island where the big water fountain was located, I noticed a man walking away from the fountain, away from me — who from the back looked familiar — was it the gray fedora, the overcoat, his walk? Before I could get close enough to identify the man, he was swallowed up by the crowd of pedestrians moving to and fro around the fountain. Still looking for the figure, I saw Mom standing on the other-side of the fountain — at the same spot where I thought I'd first seen the man; she was waving her arm above her head at me.

"You look upset, Jack," Mom remarked as I approached, wearing an unhappy face. "What happened to you?"

"Nothing," I replied.

"Then let's get some lunch...and we can talk about it. I'm starved...I think you'll like the food here."

It better be good...I don't think I can handle any more disappointments today.

The sandwich shop was crowded; people standing several deep in front of a counter with a display case loaded with many different meats, and bowls heaped full of prepared foods. There were a few tables and chairs arranged in front of the large window which was plastered with fliers and announcements. The shop smelled wonderfully of spices, warm bread, and cooked meats. Standing in front of us in line was the man whose back looked so familiar. He was examining the sign-board hanging on the wall in back of the counter — 'Deli-Selections' — listing a bunch of different meats, cheeses, potato-chips, plus some other foods; but no hamburgers. *But I wanted a hamburger...not another disappointment.*

Most of the people who ordered food at the counter walked away with paper bags and exited the shop, maybe to eat their meal elsewhere. The instant the familiar-looking man turned around with a paper bag in his hand, I was shocked, the breath leaving my lungs: it was my Dad! *How could I have not recognized my own Dad...It hasn't been that long that we've been apart. Why is he here? Why didn't he tell me he'd be here? Did Mom know that Dad was here? Of course she did!*

"Dad," I cried out loudly, causing others in the deli to stop what they were doing, and stare at me.

"Jack," Dad responded, moving towards me, his arms wide-open, the paper bag holding his lunch clutched in his hand. There it was, the same handsome face, the twinkling blue eyes, the black hair slicked back — parted in the middle, the well-trimmed mustache, the warm smile.

"What in the world are you doing here, Dad," I asked as he wrapped me in his arms, crushing me to his chest.

"You've grown so much...Has it been that long?"

"Too long, Dad. Much too long! I've missed you so much!"

"Let's put in our order, Jack," Mom interrupted. "Then we can sit and visit with your Dad. Better yet, tell me what you want, and you can visit with him while I order the food and wait for it."

Once we sat down at a table in a corner, away from the crowd at the counter, I asked, "What are you doing here, Dad?"

"My team and I are in Kansas City for a bowling tournament. I got here yesterday."

"So did we. We're staying at the Kaufmans' house. Where are you staying?"

"I'm staying at a hotel near the bowling alleys, where the tournament is being held."

"Did Aunt Rita...I mean, Mom...know you were going to be here?

"Yes, she knew I was coming to Kansas City for the tournament. We have been staying in touch...about you...for several months...ever since you told her about this German guy who is sharing your body."

"Does my mother...Nell...know about this," I asked with great concern.

"No, Rita has been talking with me by telephone at the office... and I have not said anything to your mother about you...certainly nothing about your possession...it would serve no purpose to get her involved...she'd want to take charge of your life again... and find a priest...and have an exorcism performed."

"Oh, Dad...that would be awful. You don't think I'm possessed, do you?"

"Jack, I really don't know whether you are or you are not. But, I think it there is a question of possession...If what you have told Rita, and if what she has heard for herself...and told me...is true, then you definitely have a spirit living in your body...a spirit who can take control of your brain, your body. The question of possession, it seems to me, turns on whether this spirit is an evil spirit."

"How can we tell if he is an evil spirit...Fritz has never done anything bad to me...In fact, he has helped me...like saving me from getting killed during the car accident that killed Chris and David." *I can't tell him about the fracas at the County Fair when Fritz took control of my body...saving me from certain harm.*

Before my father could answer me, Rita arrived at our table carrying a paper bag and two drink containers, placing them in front of me. "Did I interrupt anything," she asked, taking her seat at the table. Before either of us could answer her, she remarked, "Jack, I know you probably had your heart set on a hamburger, but since they don't sell hamburgers here, I got you a roast beef on whole wheat bread sandwich...I think you'll like it."

"We were talking about Jack's questionable spirit," Dad stated, as I removed the waxed paper from my sandwich, lifted up a corner of the bread, examined the roast beef, smelled it, and, looking at Rita, made a sour face.

"Just try the sandwich, Jack...sometimes you just have to be flexible...try something new."

"Yes, ma'am."

"Good," Rita said. "Now let's talk about something more cheerful...We don't have a lot of time together."

It was difficult for me to think of a subject to talk about that would not drag us back into talking about either my mother or Fritz. Rita had no such trouble finding suitable conversation topics; babbling on about Fairways, the new bull pasture that I helped build with Dennis and Billy, my budding friendship with Billy, the progress I had been making at the military academy, and my good health and improved physical stature. Ugh! My father and I were provided no entrance into Rita's monologue — we just had to sit there finishing our sandwiches, while Rita chattered away, occasionally pausing to snatch a bite of her food.

Upon exhausting her agenda, Rita announced that, "I'll leave you two to catch up on whatever else needs catching up on while I drive Gabby and Hannah home. After that I'll come by and pick you both up at the fountain, and we'll go with your father to the bowling alley, to the bowling tournament. How much time do you have before you bowl?"

"A couple of hours," my father said, looking at his wrist watch. "We'll walk out with you Rita,....I need to stretch my legs a bit... Where'd you like to go, Jack?"

"You still need to pick out a winter jacket, Jack...maybe your father would like to help you...wouldn't you, Paul?"

"Yes, I'd like to do that...if it's okay with Jack."

"Yeah, that would be fine...I only hope I have better luck this time than before."

"I'm sure you will," Rita remarked mockingly; turning, walking down the street away from us.

After watching Rita disappear into the large crowd of coming and going shoppers, my father and I turned and started walking in the other direction, towards the Plaza's stores and shops.

"Where would you like to go first," my father asked.

"To the Mid-America Hunting Store, please. They have jackets and other stuff that I want to look at...It's just around the corner up there," I said pointing in the direction I hoped it was.

"How is my mother," I asked my father while walking towards the store; now that it was just the two of us.

"She's pretty much the same. I'd hoped that she would have accepted all that has happened by now, but she still appears dejected, unhappy...She is spending time in the morning before going to work, and again at lunchtime, in church...or praying her rosary at home...all evening...probably until she falls asleep in her own bed...to the point where she is wearing the silver off of the rosary beads. We rarely talk to each other...even at dinner-time when I have dinner waiting for her when she gets home from work."

"Does she ever ask if you have heard anything about me?"

"No...But I am sure she is praying for you."

This is too depressing. I want to spend some happy time with my father, but it isn't working. I'm sure he also wants this visit to be happier than it has become. Why did Rita leave us? Without her here, what is there for "Dad" and me to talk about?

Sensing a need to change the subject, my father observed, "That is quite a nice report that Rita gave about you and your activities, Jack...You seem to be getting on with your life at Fairways much better than even I had hoped. Especially your physical development...I was afraid the injuries from the accident would take longer to heal...especially the leg injury...that it would limit your activities."

Before I could respond – as if a response was necessary – we reached Mid-America Hunting Store. I proceeded my father up and down the aisles of jackets in the 'young men' department, occasionally pausing to examine a jacket here and there, then moving on; going through the motions, knowing that my real objective was the Remington .22 pump-action rifle in the 'hunting equipment' department. My father, however, was true to his commitment to Mom; he kept trailing behind, lifting jackets off of the racks, fingering and examining each one, as if he was getting it for himself.

"You know, Jack," he called out to me from the next aisle,

holding up a red and black plaid jacket with a black fur color, "I had a jacket like this when I was sixteen or seventeen years old... when I spent the winters in the North Woods lumber-jacking. It was a life-saver for me. Have I ever told you how cold it would get...and how deep the snow would drift...up there in Wisconsin's north woods in the winter? And, God, how hard and fast the snow would fall...if you laid your ax or saw flat on the ground and turned away for just a moment, when you turned back the ax, the saw, had disappeared, were buried in snow to where you couldn't find them...so we always stood the ax on end, and propped the saw up against a tree."

"So, you think I need that plaid jacket to keep me from freezing to death in the middle of Missouri," I asked cheekily. *Yes, 'Dad'. And I've heard the story about it being so cold up there that the lumberjacks would build two log cabins at the start of the lumberjacking season, so that when it had been so cold for so long...and the frost had come all of the way through the logs in the cabin you all had been living in for months...turning the log cabin into an ice box that not even the hottest fire in the stove could thaw out...that you would have to move into the second log cabin...hoping that winter would end before the same thing happened to that cabin too.*

"Maybe not...but I think it's a nice looking jacket," he responded, ignoring my impudence with a smile.

At 'Dad's' insistence I tried on the jacket; it fit me nicely, and after looking at myself in the mirror mounted on a nearby pillar, I conceded that it was what I was looking for. I located a clerk who agreed to put 'the jacket' on 'Will Call', in order to keep 'Dad' from spending his money – which I believed was still tight for him.

"Can we look at just one more thing before we go," I asked 'Dad'; after the clerk had written down Mrs. Kaufman's name on the slip he attached to the jacket while he walked towards the 'Will Call' department.

"Sure...What would you like to look at?"

"Just something in the 'Hunting' department...a rifle I'd like to look at...but they won't even let me hold it without 'my father being with me'."

From the look on his face, I could tell that 'Dad' was less than enthusiastic about what I had in mind.

"Jack, owning a rifle is a serious responsibility...I am sure that you are aware of that...that it's not a toy. Why do you want to have a rifle? Have you ever fired a real rifle?"

"No," I confessed, thinking I knew where this conversation was going. "But it's just a .22 rifle. Billy's dad has one, and he is teaching Billy and me how to take it apart, learn the pieces, and put it back together again...just like they'd do it in the Marines. Once we learn how to do that, he will teach us how to load it, handle it safely, and only then to fire it. I was hoping that when Dennis...Billy's dad...teaches us things about the .22, that I'd have my own .22 rifle to learn on."

"Jack, if the situation you're currently in were different...if you were a normal twelve year old boy...then what you're proposing would make sense...but as things are...with you being possessed by this Fritz guy...it would not be a good idea to have a rifle...even a .22 rifle...or any gun in your possession. Until we can make sure that this Fritz is the good guy he claims to be... we can't let you have any kind of firearm. Your Mom...Rita...and I think that since Fritz can control your body he might try to harm her if he is indeed a bad guy.

"Look, Jack, what I am about to say to you may upset you, but if you are possessed by an 'evil spirit', there is a good chance that he will take over your body permanently, and he might harm Rita. I want you to promise me that you will do everything you can to protect Rita, to keep her from being harmed by whoever this guy turns out to be."

"I think I understand what you are saying...And I will protect Mom from any harm...But can I at least show you the rifle...and can I hold it?"

LATER THAT EVENING, Dr. K suggested that we watch some shows on the TV in the study. Upon entering the room, the three walls of which were lined with bookshelves, crammed with books of all sorts, I noticed that the tape recorder was now standing in its assigned spot, while it was not there when we arrived on Friday evening. When I asked Dr. K where the tape recorder had been, he said, "I thought your Mom had it."

But it was not until on the drive home that I was able to ask Mom about why she had the tape recorder, to which she responded, "Hannah and I thought that it would be helpful if we could record the Nazi's narrative of his experiences, both in his own voice and yours...There was simply too much information for us to absorb as it was being conveyed to us. It was a wise thing that we did that." When I asked why, Mom said, "We are still analyzing some of the things the Nazi says he was involved in for accuracy."

I heard Fritz say: *It seems that the widow Kaufman is craftier than I even gave her credit for being. What has she found out about me...and my story?*

SO, THOUGHT NELL, *this is where Paul was that bowling weekend last fall; playing daddy with Jack, and maybe some hanky-panky with Rita. And this is where Paul learned about Rita's concerns about Fritz being able to take control of Jack...But he wouldn't tell me about it because I might want to pray for Jack...or maybe have an exorcism...Well, I've been down that road. Maybe if I knew then what I know now I maybe could have done something about it. It's too late now. Damn him! Damn her! Damn them all!*

CHAPTER 37

BIG CHIEF TABLET THIRTY-THREE | JACK

"Jack," Mom said as Billy and I were sitting in the kitchen. "I've had a telephone call from Buzz...you know...that fellow you met several years ago who has the race car with the airplane engine. He just wanted to let us know...you in particular...that his friend... the P 38 pilot you wanted to talk to...Pete Roberts is home from Korea. Buzz wanted to know when it would be a good time for us to meet with Colonel Roberts."

This led to an immediate reaction from Fritz: *This is great news, Jack. This is my long anticipated opportunity for the widow Kaufman to hear directly from Oberst – no, I mean Colonel – Roberts. He can personally verify that I am who I say I am. He can provide the very information I needed to convince the widow Kaufman that I was not a threat to Jack or to her; and that my mission to return to Germany is a noble quest.*

"Wow," I exclaimed. "Does Buzz still have his neat racer? Billy, this is the greatest car you'll ever see...It's powered by an old P38 airplane engine! Buzz said he'd let me see it race someday...Did Buzz say when he was going to race it?"

"I thought you were more interested in the P38 than Buzz's race car...That's why you wanted to talk to Pete Roberts," Mom said.

"Oh, yeah," Jack responded. "But that was before I learned from Fritz and Uncle Ollie about the Messerschmitt Me-262 turbo-jet fighter...It can run circles around the old P38...No wonder the P38's engines aren't used now for anything but powering race cars."

"So you don't want to talk with Pete Roberts any longer?"

"No. Not really," I said.

Fritz: *Jack, I'd like to hear what Colonel Roberts thinks about the Me-262 in comparison to the P38.*

"Unless," I continued, "if Colonel Roberts wants to talk about how the Me-262 shot down his P38...You know...maybe just how much faster and better the Me-262 was than the P38 he was flying?"

"Well, I don't really think that would be fair to Colonel Roberts...Buzz says the Colonel is quite proud of his flying record with the P38...And Buzz approached the Colonel about talking to you on the basis that you wanted to hear all about what a wonderful aircraft the P38 is...or was. I don't see how we can possibly ask the Colonel to take time away from his other pursuits only to criticize the P38...asking him to compare it to a German aircraft...indeed, the very aircraft that shot him down...that sent him to the horrors of a German prisoner of war camp."

Fritz: *Jack. I must have your mother talk with Pete Roberts...You must say whatever it takes to convince your Mom that it is important for you to talk with this Colonel Roberts...Even if it takes you saying that you still think that the P38 is the finest American fighter aircraft of the War; and that it would be an honor to hear from such a brave pilot.*

I said, "Mom, I didn't mean that I don't still think that the P38 fighter is a great aircraft...I only meant that the P38 isn't still the best fighter aircraft...And of course, I'd like to hear how Colonel Roberts still feels about flying the P38...So, please, see when we can talk to him...And see if Buzz will let me see his racing car again."

"We'll see...We'll see. I'll work with Buzz to see when there might be a mutually acceptable date. I'm in no hurry, if you aren't."

ON MEMORIAL DAY Mom, Hannah and I drove to Buzz folks' home for a picnic and for what Mom said was to be a surprise;

her only hint being that we needed to be at Buzz's place in time to listen to the radio broadcast of some car race. Upon arriving at the Carlson's, I immediately spied Buzz's fancy red and yellow race car with Billy sitting in the cockpit of the racer, his hands on the steering wheel, smiling like the guy who'd just stole his best friend's girl.

"What are you doing here," I asked. "Are your mom and dad here, too?"

"Yeah, the Carlson's asked us all to come. Hey, you was right about this car, it sure is neat."

"How's the race going," inquired Buzz, suddenly appearing from around the side of the building with the sliding doors. "What lap are we in? Is Bill Vukovich still leading?"

"Is he driving a race car like yours," asked Billy.

"No, he's driving a standard up-right Indy racer, with a standard type engine."

"Can you start up this car," I asked pointing at Buzz's racer.

"Can we drive it around," asked Billy.

"We can try," Buzz said as he tugged at something inside of the engine compartment. At first there was only a whining sound – an electric motor sound – growing in intensity and pitch. And then suddenly an enormous explosion of sound filled the air; a sound so loud that I instinctively covered my ears and started backing away from the race car that was belching smoke and flames from of its several exhaust pipes.

Buzz watched and listened to the engine, occasionally stepping to the engine compartment, touching and tinkering with this or that part of the engine, then moving to the cockpit, staring at the gauges lining the dashboard. Apparently satisfied that the engine was performing properly, Buzz closed the cowling, climbed into the cockpit, thumped gauges with his finger, wiggled some switches, and gripping the steering-wheel with one hand, shifted some levers with the other hand. The race car slowly moved forward, the noise of the engine increasing as the vehicle gathered speed. After about fifty feet the race car came to a sudden stop, the engine coughed and sputtered, and then there was silence, blessed silence. It was several moments, however, before I removed my hands from over my ears.

The unrelenting, thunderous noise had one positive effect: it brought the rest of the folks from wherever they were gathered, to assemble on the front lawn, to view the source of the racket. The voices calling out from the front lawn were shouting things, like: "Are you trying to scare us to death?" "Not one of the hens will lay an egg for a week!" "The neighbors are going to be finding escaped cattle on the roads for days." "You could at least have given us a warning you were going to fire up the racer!" But there was one voice that announced a different reaction: "It's been years since I've heard that awesome roar – the distinctive sound of an Allison V-12 at full throttle, without its supercharger!" This could only be the voice of Colonel Peter Roberts.

"Was the engine this temperamental when you were relying up on it to keep you in the air," asked Buzz.

"There were lots of reasons why we lost P38s, but an unreliable engine was not one of them...And I was blessed, I guess... 'cause I never had an engine let me down...unless it was shot up."

Once the race car had cooled down enough, the men pushed the vehicle back to the building with the sliding doors. This time, instead of parking the racer on the pavement in front of the building, Buzz steered the racer into an empty space inside the brightly lighted building. Once the race car was placed in the building, Buzz and Billy's father, together with Colonel Roberts, left the building, heading back to the patio. Billy and I wandered into the building, not certain of what to do.

"Sorry, boys...I'm afraid the 'beast' is done for the day...its race is over...and no checkered flag," Buzz said dejectedly as he wiped his oil-stained fingers on a cotton rag – like the one the gas station attendant uses to wipe off the engine's oil dip stick. "You are welcome to stay here with me to listen to the end of the Indy race, or you can go to the patio where your folks are visiting...Maybe they've got some food and drinks for you...Or maybe Pete Roberts is ready to tell you about his adventures with the old P38."

The offer of food and drink was too much for Billy and me to resist. We made our 'thanks' and said our 'goodbyes' to Buzz, and headed in the direction of the patio which was located in a tree shaded area at the rear of the Carlson's big house.

AFTER BILLY AND I had our fill of sandwiches, iced-tea and cookies, and had taken our seats on the patio, Pete Roberts began talking after Mom's introduction. This is what I remember of what Colonel Roberts told us:

"I suppose that the place to begin is to tell you something about the P38, and then tell you of my more notable experiences in flying that marvelous machine. You heard the terrible racket earlier coming from an engine that powered a P38; but the P38 was never that noisy...In fact it was a very quite aircraft, even with two of those powerful engines...And that is because the superchargers that were driven by the exhaust from the engines muffled the sounds of the engine, just like the muffler on your folks' cars muffles the sound of the engine. Have you ever heard the sound of an un-muffled car engine...or a big tractor?

"I understand, Jack, that you are a big fan of the P38, holding the belief that it is one of the great World War Two warplanes; but as compared with the German's Messerschmitt 262 turbo-jet fighter, you no longer think it is the greatest warplane. As one of the few living pilots having had the opportunity to see both aircraft in action, I would have to agree with your assessment, but only in one respect; the Me-262 was a tremendous technological leap forward...it completely changed the course of aircraft design and propulsion...and it was accomplished under the most adverse conditions imaginable. Although the airframe design, incorporating turbojet propulsion, was superb...allowing it to fly faster than anything else in the air...the Me-262 turbojet was actually underpowered and unreliable.

"The P38, on the other hand, was powerful, versatile, reliable, and had an extensive range, and, in its prime, was the toughest fighter aircraft in the air. Some would agree with me that the Germans were forced to bring the Me-262 into production as fast as they did in order to combat the effectiveness of the P38 Lightning...which the German *Luftwaffe* called *'der Gabel-*

schwanzteufel'...'Forked-Tail Devil'. I acknowledge that the P38 was not without its faults, and not without its detractors, but what aircraft has ever been perfect?

"I flew my first P38 in late 1942, after graduation from the University and then the Army Air Force basic flight school. At first I was not interested in flying the P38...it had the reputation of being hard to fly...and dangerous to fly...especially if there was an engine failure on take-off. I took a chance, giving the big plane an opportunity to convince me that we were a match...and it was a chance well worth taking...we fit together like a hand in a glove. After mastering the techniques for flying the P38, I was assigned to a combat wing within the 14th Fighter Group of the 12th Air Force in North Africa in early 1943. Most of my flying and combat experience took place in the Mediterranean theatre of operations. Throughout the summer and fall, I was involved in hundreds of sorties where the P38 was used to protect bombers and to attack German and Italian ground forces.

"I am sure that you boys would like for me to tell you some tales of heroic air combat...dogfights...in which I was involved, but I really don't want to talk about those things. It took quite an effort on Miz Kaufman's part just to get me to tell you anything about my flying the P38 in the War. I'm just a farm boy at heart...I am not a killer by nature, nor do I enjoy seeing people killed...friend or foe. And I saw my share of both during the War. I think Dennis knows what I'm talking about...his experiences as a Marine in the jungles of the South Pacific islands are the stuff of nightmares. Like Dennis, I have tried to shut those memories out of my mind...So, I'm afraid you will have to do with just what I have told you.

"Now having said that, I will...again after much urging from Miz Kaufman...tell you some things about what happened to me in unarmed combat with the German Me-262, and of my experiences as a prisoner of war. Again, I am going to leave out some details which are still too unpleasant to me to this day.

"In 1944, I was transferred from a combat role to flying the reconnaissance version of the P38, the F-4, and then the F-5. It was while I was flying the F-5 on a top secret reconnaissance mission that my aircraft was attacked by a pair of Me-262 fighter aircraft as I was crossing over the Adriatic Sea heading to my airbase in the Foggia area of southeastern Italy...an area the Allied forces had earlier captured from the Germans. The two German fighters attacked me from the rear, strafing my aircraft in an effort to get me to land in German-held territory. When I refused their invitation, one of the jets zoomed past me while the other jet swung around and attacked me in a flanking attack, firing its nose canons directly at my port engine and radiator intake, severing the rear rudder control cables, effectively causing fatal damage to the aircraft. It was too late for me to try to ditch the F-5 in the Adriatic, let alone try to make it back to the airbase. I was forced to bail out of the crippled F-5, parachuting safely to earth in German held Italian countryside, within eye-sight of the Adriatic.

"I was initially assisted by Italian partisans who hid me for several days until German soldiers stormed the rustic stone building in which I was hiding, killing some Italians and roughing me up. The local German soldiers transported me by truck to Verona where German officers interrogated me for several days...claiming that I had taken films of secret German installations...and that the cameras and film were missing from the wreckage of the F-5.

"The German officers who submitted me to round-the-clock interrogations were convinced that I jettisoned the cameras and film prior to bailing out of the doomed aircraft, and that I told the Italian partisans where to find the camera and film in the hopes that the partisans would get the film through German lines and into the hands of the Allied troops advancing northward through Italy. The last thing I wanted to have happen, was to let the cameras and film fall into the hands of the Germans, or for the Germans to learn from me what happened to the incriminating photos."

"Can you tell us what happened with the cameras and the film," asked Hannah in her broken English.

"I cannot...The mission was top secret...and as far as I know it is still classified as top secret. I am still bound by my oath as an officer not to divulge any information about the mission to anyone without specific executive-level clearance...meaning some-one at the level of a cabinet officer or higher. All of which made it very easy, but very dangerous, for me during enemy interro-gation."

"He means, it would take a clearance from the President of the United States," Mom said.

"Must have been some important shit," said Dennis.

"Yes, you can conclude that it was indeed 'some important shit'...why else would the intensity of my interrogation escalate at each stopover in the chain of my confinement as a prisoner of war. But, again, as I cautioned you earlier, I don't like to talk about those things...and, as far as I know, this is the first time I have told anyone of my experiences as a P.O.W.

"Verona was clearly ill-equipped to carry out such a demand-ing inquiry, and my captors were instructed to deliver me as soon as possible to Munich where more sophisticated forms of inter-rogation were available. But even in Munich, they were unable to extract anything more from me than my name, rank and se-rial number. So, I was shipped up the chain of interrogation to the main entry point for captured Army Air Force person-nel, the infamous *Dulag Luft*. That is the abbreviated name for *Durchgangslager der Luftwaffe* (Transit Camp – Air Force). The camp was located near Frankfurt-am-Main, with the Interroga-tion Center located at Oberursel.

"For the first week or so I was held in solitary confinement and subjected to periodic interrogation by a crew of different German officers. Each interrogation was carefully conducted by German officers who spoke perfect English, attempting to develop a relationship of familiarity and ease, lulling me into a sense of relaxation with casual conversations about schooling, girl friends, flight-training, plying me with American cigarettes, etc. When that approach failed to produce any information be-yond my name, rank and serial number, other, more aggressive techniques were employed...basically threats of torture and de-pravation.

"After about two weeks of solitary confinement and inces-sant, but ineffective, interrogation, I was sent with a group of other Army Air Force officers to *Stalag Luft III*, a permanent camp located at Sagan, Poland, somewhere southeast of Berlin, deep in a pine forest. This was a large camp of over 10,000 Allied air officers, more than half being American air officers, divided into several separate compounds, with each compound having maybe fifteen buildings. The groups of one-story buildings in each compound were surrounded by tall wire fences, and were monitored by guards in strategically located towers.

"The building in the compound to which I was assigned was carved up into several barracks crammed with five triple-decked bunks in each room. The other fourteen guys in my barracks were American air officers; which, as I was to learn, was the composition of the other barracks and buildings in this compound. This was the newest compound in the Stalag...and most of the guys were from bombers shot down and captured during the time of the Normandy invasion, meaning that they had been there for only a few months,

"At first, the other guys pretty-well avoided talking with me, even isolating me from conversations among themselves. I later learned that this was a safety mechanism they imposed on all new P.O.W's until someone could verify that the new P.O.W. was in fact a bona fide American air officer. It seems that *Stalag Luft III* was a hot bed of escape attempts, and the Germans had resorted to slipping a phony American P.O.W. into the compounds to learn about, and report on, planned escapes. Because I had been based in southeastern Italy, far from the Air Force bases in England...and the bases now cropping up in France...it took a while before another Army Air Force officer could be found who could vouch for me. It was actually a P38 combat pilot who I served with in the Mediterranean who had been transferred to a combat unit in England, and was shot down in France a few weeks after the invasion, who vouched for me.

"Life in the camp was routine, the food was inadequate, maggoty and unappetizing. Without the red-cross packages and packages from home, starvation would have been a daily experience. As it was most of the food in those packages was pilfered by the guards who themselves were near starvation. The only clothes I had were the clothes I was wearing on the day I was shot down, minus the leather flying jacket which was taken from me by the Italian partisans. With winter approaching I was able to scrounge a cloth jacket from the piles of clothes gathered from the remains of P.O.W.'s who were no longer among us. Like many of my buddies, I resorted to wrapping myself in my bed blanket during the coldest days.

"This difficult routine was broken by two episodes that made me wish for the 'routine' to have continued. The first occurred shortly after I had settled into the camp's daily monotony. Early one morning in November, 1944, I was rousted out of my warm bed by two *Luftwaffe* guards who half-dragged me out of the barracks, the compound, and into the commandant's building, where I was transferred to the care of a burly *Feldwebel* (sergeant) who placed my wrists in shackles, then escorted me into a small, windowless room with a rough plank table and three unmatched, wooden, straight-back chairs, where I was instructed to remain standing.

After hours of standing, the pain in my feet, legs and back, was equal to the pain of needing to relieve myself. Just as I was about to wet myself, the sergeant opened the locked door and handed me a bucket. When I had finished relieving myself in his presence, he instructed me to carry the bucket out of the room and follow him to a latrine where I emptied the contents of the bucket into a toilet. This humiliation was just the prelude to what was to follow."

Mom, seeing that Colonel Roberts was in pain said, "Would you like to take a break Pete...perhaps a glass of cola or iced-tea...a smoke?"

"Just a smoke...Do you have one? I've already smoked a whole pack. I'd rather not stop...I'm not sure that if I did stop that I'd have the courage to continue...to articulate what follows."

"Thanks, Pete. I am sorry that I have asked you to do this...I could never have imagined how painful this must be for you. I am feeling your pain right now...And you can stop right now if you want to."

"Thank you, but no. I've come this far...and the memories

have already been dredged up, so there is no point in not letting them out now. It may even be a good thing...to get them out in the open. So I'll just keep on talkin'...and keep on smokin' while I do.

"Let's see, where was I? Oh, yeah...I was taken back to the small room where the door was again locked and I was left standing alone for what seems to be several more hours. Just as I was about to collapse from lack of food and water...I had nothing to eat or drink since the last evening...the sergeant again unlocked the door and entered, carrying a metal tray on which were sitting...and I kid you not...a glass pitcher of water, two glasses and a plate with two slices of dark bread and pieces of sausage and cheese. He placed the tray on the table, left, locked the door, and I was left to stand there, my eyes glued to the feast sitting there in front of me.

"Before I had reached the point where I could no longer resist the urge to eat and drink what was before me, the door was once again unlocked...but this time it was not the sergeant who entered the room. Instead, it was a tall, dark-haired officer in the sky-blue uniform of a *Luftwaffe Oberstleutnant*, followed by a short stocky blond man in the black uniform of an S.S. *Leutnant* carrying a briefcase in one hand and a folder in the other. When the *Oberstleutnant* removed his cap, placing it on the table, I became aware of his most striking feature: his eyes...they were black as coal, and as cruel and cold-looking as a snake's. His demeanor, his grooming, suggested power, authority, upbringing and impeccability...yet his uniform looked like something else... ill-fitting, un-pressed.

"He began the interrogation by instructing me to sit in the straight-backed chair across the table from him. Once I took the seat, he poured water into two glasses, taking a big gulp from one of them, leaving the other on the table just out of my reach. He then drew the plate of bread, sausage and meat towards him, picking at the sausage, putting a chunk of cheese in his mouth. After watching me for several moments, savoring the obvious pain of hunger on my face, the *Oberstleutnant*, barked at the *S.S. Leutnant*, "Hand me the folder." Rummaging through the folder, the *Oberstleutnant* settled on a page which he extracted from the folder, examined it closely, then said,

'Major Roberts (I was still a Major at the time), we have met before, only not face-to-face. I was piloting the Messerschmitt 262 fighter that you encountered in September over Austria...I believe it was...and when you failed our polite invitation to land...I was forced to shoot down your F-5 reconnaissance aircraft. I want to tell you that it grieves me terribly that you had to endure capture and detainment...but that is what happens in wartime. As a fellow pilot, I am hoping that you will be cooperative in the inquiry that I am going to conduct.'

"Continuing in this non-confrontational manner, the *Oberstleutnant* said: 'It appears that during your nosing around in southern Poland you stumbled upon some very important German facilities...or was your journey from southern Italy to purposely observe and photograph these facilities? At any rate, whatever you saw, whatever you photographed, whatever you filmed, it was important enough that someone in Berlin thought it necessary to intercept and capture you and your photos.' I said nothing...I just kept staring at the food and water.

"In impeccable English, the *Oberstleutnant* asked sarcastically, 'Are you perhaps hungry, thirsty, Herr Major? If you will just answer my few questions, then you can have all that you see in front of you...although it is not very good, by Berlin standards'.

"'My name is Peter Roberts. I am a Major in the United States Army Air Force. My serial number is 298346525,' I responded as I was required to do."

'And my name is Fritz von Bruckner. I am an *Oberstleutnant* in the *Luftwaffe* of the Third Reich. And you apparently are still not hungry or thirsty enough to answer my simple questions... We have all day to deal with your bodily needs...and we have other means to deal with your refusal to cooperate. Now what did you film, what did you photograph...And what did you do with the camera equipment and the film in the cameras?'

"'My name is Peter Roberts. I am a Major in the United States Army Air Force. My serial number is 298346525,' I repeated."

"And so it went on, hour after hour, question after question, with me not budging, not giving any answer but the standard 'name, rank and serial number'. At one point, the *Oberstleutnant* became so exasperated that he un-holstered his side arm...a Walther P38 pistol...placed it on the table with the muzzle facing me, threatening to use the weapon on me. I don't think he saw the irony of his threat...using a P38 pistol to force me to divulge the contents of the F-5, nee P38, aircraft's cameras.

"In the end, the threats of bodily harm producing no information from me, the *Oberstleutnant* leapt up from his chair, threw the glass of water in my face, shouting, 'I am not finished with you, Major Roberts, but when I am finished you will regret that you were ever born!' He stormed out of the room, instructing the *S.S. Leutnant*, who had remained stationary in his chair, to get up, to do something, anything, to get me to talk.

"In the meantime, I was gratefully licking the water running down may face and on the table as quickly as I could, before it moved out of tongue-reach. The shocked, befuddled *S.S. Leutnant* un-holstered his Walther P38 pistol, and struck me as hard as he could across the face with the barrel of the weapon, breaking the bridge of my nose, before he, too, exited the room."

Fritz, who must have been following Colonel Robert's story closely said to me: *This is a far different version of Colonel Robert's interrogation than what I remember taking place, and I was there. Although I didn't see the S.S. Leutnant hit the Colonel with his pistol.*

"It was reported to the American P.O.W. camp leadership that I had tripped and fallen, striking my face on the edge of a table, breaking my nose. After a brief visit to the camp infirmary, where my nose was packed and bandaged, I was returned to my barracks, back to the monotonous routine and the ever-present starvation. Despite his clear threats of further mistreatment, I was never visited again by the *Oberstleutnant*, but I am convinced that I did see him again."

Fritz: *What is this man talking about? I never ever saw him again. Where would he possibly have seen me again? He must be mistaken.*

"It was during the second of the breaks in camp routine that I experienced my second sighting of the *Luftwaffe Oberstleutnant*;

which occurred in late January, 1945. Without warning or preparation, all the barracks in my compound were instructed to assemble in the dead of night at the front gate. It was wintery cold; the snow was deep, it was pitch-black. Blessedly, I had grabbed the blanket from my top bunk when ordered to assemble outside. With the piercing sounds of the guards' whistles we were marched out of *Stalag Luft III*...destination unknown. The rumor quickly spread through our ranks that the Russian Army had reached the Oder River, less than twenty miles east of Sagan.

"This was a forced march, not a leisurely stroll through the dark country-side. It was a nightmarish experience, running as fast as we could along snow-covered roads in the dark, not being able to see anything around us, stumbling over fallen comrades who were too starved, too sick, too tired, to go on any further. Even when daylight appeared through thick clouds, the nightmare continued. When we arrived at crossroads there were few cars in sight, just hundreds...perhaps thousands...of poorly dressed men all trying to go in one direction...running as fast as they could towards the west...driven by armed guards using their bayoneted rifles to prod on the upright, to stab the fallen, leaving their bleeding bodies to stain and expire on the snow-packed ground. I lost many fellow P.O.W.s on that forced march...some who I considered close friends.

"At a town called 'Spremberg', the march was halted...We were forced to wait in the freezing cold for days...for the arrival of the locomotives and boxcars that were supposed to transport the remnants of the compound to Bavaria. Besides us P.O.W.s, I observed that a short distance away there were large groups of rag tag men...and some women...dressed in stripped uniforms huddled together for warmth...also waiting for something. To me these wretched masses appeared to be Jewish inmates from the many concentration camps that I knew first-hand were located in southeastern Poland, east of Sagan.

"They were being guarded by soldiers dressed in the black uniforms bearing the 'death skull' insignia of the S.S. One of our 'friendly' camp guards...who were *Luftwaffe*, and not S.S.... and on the whole not bad guys...confirmed my suspicions...The Germans were trying to move as many of the healthy Jews as they could to the west...ahead of the Russians...to be used as slave labor. He also told me that we were being moved out of Poland for fear that if the Russians were to over-run and free us from *Stalag Luft III*, we'd be back in airplanes in weeks, back to bombing Germany again.

"On the second day...or maybe it was the third day...of our wait in Spremberg...I just know that the sun was shining brightly for a change...a convoy of trucks...filled with more S.S. troops... preceded by a large black Mercedes sedan...pulled up in the town square...not fifty feet from where I was standing in the sun. The Mercedes stopped in front of a multi-story building displaying several German flags, the massive front entrance guarded by S.S. soldiers. My first thought was that the S.S. troops were here to now guard us...replacing the more docile *Luftwaffe* guards. But my fears temporarily vanished as I watched the S.S. soldiers leave their trucks, and take up positions among the groups of Jews.

"Until now, I had paid no particular attention to the black Mercedes sedan, but my attention was drawn in that direction when a very attractive blond woman, dressed in a fur coat, exited the building's front entrance, and walked towards the Mercedes and the tall S.S. officer standing at the rear of the vehicle. The officer was dressed in the traditional black uniform of the S.S. with rank insignia designating him to be an *Oberst*, and when he doffed his cap to greet the woman, I immediately thought that I recognized his profile. After kissing the blond woman on the cheek, the *S.S. Oberst*, turned in my direction...looking straight at me with those cruel black eyes...There was a moment's hesitation...I detected a flicker of recognition...a blink of those snake-like eyes. There was no longer any question...I did know this man...It was my brutal interrogator from *Stalag Luft III*...the *Luftwaffe Oberstleutnant* von Bruckner...But how could that be? The *S.S. Oberst* quickly broke eye-contact, turned back to the woman, grabbing her by the arm, smartly hustling her into the Mercedes, which then sped away, quickly disappearing out-of-sight.

"During the week-long, difficult journey to the next camp,

somewhere in Bavaria...fifty or so of us packed into boxcars, with no way to even sit down...I was haunted by what I had observed in Spremberg...trying to figure out whether it was an hallucination brought on by lack of food, water, sleep...or whether I did in fact recognize the man in the *S.S. Oberst* uniform as my interrogator. When I went back over the facts: including the purpose of my secret reconnaissance mission...the purpose of the interrogation – 'what I saw, what I did with the incriminating photos'...the presence of the *S.S. Leutnant*...the P-38 pistol...the brutality of my interrogator...the ill-fitting *Luftwaffe Oberstleutnant* uniform...and nothing pointing to this interrogation as being a matter of interest to the *Luftwaffe*...Everything pointed to my interrogation at *Stalag Luft III* as just a charade...it was actually conducted by the S.S., with the *Luftwaffe* uniform being a part of the ruse. Maybe there was a *Luftwaffe Oberstleutnant* named von Bruckner...but my interrogator certainly was not that man... or maybe my interrogator's name was von Bruckner...but he was not a *Luftwaffe Oberstleutnant*. My interrogator at the camp in Sagan was a *S.S. Oberst*...the very same man I saw in Spremberg.

"For the next three months, I endured all the horrors and monotony of *Stalag Luft VIIA*, located near Moosburg, Bavaria. Gone were the benign *Luftwaffe* guards...replaced by brutal, heartless S.S. guards. Food was scarce, with death from starvation, disease, illness and brutality daily stalking the camp. I suffered through many sleepless nights, kept awake by the noises from my own starving stomach, and the cries and whimpers of my barracks-mates who were in the process of dying from malnutrition and disease.

"It was not until the end of April, 1945, that I was liberated... together with tens of thousands of other P.O.W.s... from this dreadful place by U. S. troops from General Patton's 14th Armored Division. Living in close proximity with the obnoxious S.S. guards...seeing the lengths to which they went to torture and humiliate the P.O.W.s, I was absolutely convinced that my interrogator at *Stalag Luft III* was an *S.S. Oberst*. A day did not go by that I did not fear that the *Oberst* would track me down, find me there, and carry out his earlier threats of torture and deprivation.

"I hope that what I've told you about my war and P.O.W. experiences will in some way help you to find an answer to your dilemma...I pray now, as I did daily in the camp, that I never ever again have to be faced with an evil spirit like the one that possessed the *S.S. Oberst*."

AFTER A LONG, clearly painful silence, in which Colonel Roberts, stared vacantly at the ground in front of him, fumbling through the crumpled cigarette pack, looking for one more smoke, Mom broke the dreadful silence by asking: "Pete, you have been most gracious to provide us with such a detailed account of what for you, I am sure, has been a most harrowing experience. I never knew how horrible it was...and if I had I probably would not have asked you to resurrect such nightmarish memories. I am so sorry for what you went through and what you have just put yourself through...I hate to ask...but I really need to know one more thing...Do you think you would recognize this *S.S. Oberst* if you ever saw him again, or perhaps saw a photo of him?"

"I suppose I would...he's not a character that one can ever forget his face...like the face of the bully who beat you up in the school yard when you were in fifth grade."

"Actually, Pete, I have two photos for you to look at if you are up to it."

"Sure...go ahead."

Fritz again complained: *What is going on here? What are these photos? Where did the bitch get these photos? Jack, I need to see these photos!*

Hannah handed Mom two eight by ten black and white photographs. She, in turn, handed one of the photographs to the Colonel. After carefully reviewing the one photograph for some time, the Colonel handed it back to Mom with the comment that, "The man in the photograph you have just shown me, I do not recognize. He may be wearing a *Luftwaffe* uniform, but I have never seen that man before."

Mom then handed the Colonel the next photograph, asking:

"Do you recognize the man in this photo?"

Without a moment's hesitation, the Colonel said, "That's him... That's the *S.S. Oberst*...There is no question about it...it's in the eyes...those snake-like eyes. Is he the von Bruckner fellow?"

"No." responded Mom. "The man in that photo was *S.S. Oberst* Dietrich Muenster! We have un-controvertible evidence that this Muenster fellow was responsible for the extermination of thousands of innocent Jewish men, women and children. He also ordered the execution of the entire von Bruckner family, including the man in the first photo you reviewed...and save for the young nun, Maria...in August, 1944. And it is the same evil spirit who inhabited Dietrich Muenster's body until his death on May 6, 1945, when, instead of receiving a one-way ticket to hell, was allowed − and only God knows why − to take up residence in the body of my son, Jack. I hope you are hearing this, Herr Muenster, you fucking Nazi bastard! I want you to out of Jack's body today...now...immediately!

"Thanks to you, Colonel Roberts, and your identification of *Oberst* Muenster's photograph," Mom continued, "we know for sure that for several years now, this demonic 'spirit' has pretended to be Fritz von Bruckner, the very person he stalked and then had killed; fabricating a fascinating, heroic tale designed to deceive and win over an impressionable boy. Hannah and I believe that Muenster fashioned his 'Fritz' impersonation on his review of the transcripts of the S.S.'s interrogation of Fritz and some of the other von Bruckner family members as ordered by *Oberst* Muenster prior to their executions − a copy of which was found among Muenster's personal belongings seized after his death; together with the interviews and surveillance reports of the Gestapo and S.S. of the entire von Bruckner family.

"In addition to Hannah reviewing these transcripts, we have been granted access to other Muenster-related documents which were accumulated by the staffs of the various groups responsible for identifying, locating and prosecuting the Nazi war criminals − including the *Nuremberg International Military Tribunal*. Some of the documents reviewed by Hannah and her cohorts in the Jewish community include interviews with eye-witnesses to *Oberst* Muenster's activities — like Fritz's sister, Maria.

"These first-hand accounts confirm Herr Muenster's long history of persecutions, torture and executions of Jews, and of patriotic Germans who tried to assist the Jews. We have even been able to confirm the time of Dietrich Muenster's death at the hand of his mistress...while trying to make his escape from Allied troops in May, 1945. It just so happens, that Herr Muenster's death coincides with what Jack and his father, Paul, have pinpointed as the day on which Jack suffered his momentarily fatal head injury."

FRITZ ANGRILY SAID: *I've heard enough of this Schwachsinn! The widow Kaufman is trying her best to provoke me...hoping that I will confirm her outlandish disclosures about my true persona...by taking command of Jack's body, by lashing out in my own voice. But I won't fall for her taunting. In due time, however, I'll fix the Miststueck!*

Fritz then added: *So now I know what had been going on with the Jewess Hannah...and what they had been pursuing behind your back, Jack. I was not totally certain as to how much of what the widow Kaufman said about me that you either heard or understood. The only thing that matters to me is my mission to resurrect the most important program established by the Nazis — the extermination of God's chosen people, the Jews. I just need a human carrier — and it doesn't need to be you at this point — just someone who can take me to where I might reunite with other Nazis, disciples who are patiently waiting for the reappearance of a Fuehrer.*

CHAPTER 38

BIG CHIEF TABLET THIRTY-FOUR | JACK

During the drive back to Fairways from the picnic at the Carlson's house I was riding alone in the back-seat of the big Ford Station Wagon, lost in my thoughts about what had occurred at the conclusion of Colonel Roberts' war stories. *Did I correctly understand what Colonel Roberts' told us? Did he identify the photograph of Dietrich Muenster – not the one of Fritz – as his interrogator? Did Colonel Roberts tell us that the S.S. Colonel who he saw with blond lady in that town in Poland was the same man who had questioned him at the P.O.W. camp in Poland? And what about Mom's statement that Fritz was killed months before the spirit who shares my body and mind was killed? Does that mean that 'the spirit" cannot be Fritz's spirit, but that 'the spirit' is the 'evil' spirit of Dietrich Muenster who has just been pretending to be Fritz? Is Mom right? But how could that happen? I really believed...trusted...Fritz. Why did this have to happen to me? Why did God let it happen to me? Am I really 'possessed' by an 'evil spirit'...a demon?* The more I thought about how I might be possessed by an 'evil spirit', the more scared I became. *I'm really scared. What's going to happen to me now? Are Mom and Hannah in any danger? Please, dear God...Please help me...Please get rid of this demon in me.*

I also began to think about whether Billy heard and understood what Colonel Roberts and Mom said about Fritz not being Fritz; and that I was inhabited by an 'evil spirit'. What will Billy, and his folks, think about me now? Billy's mom and dad didn't seem to be too shocked about what Colonel Roberts and Mom said about the spirit of Dietrich Muenster having just been pretending to be the spirit of Fritz. Perhaps Mom had already told them what she and Hannah knew about this Dietrich Muenster, and the Lewises were there to hear if Colonel Roberts would confirm that Fritz was really Muenster – the 'monster'. In that case, then maybe Billy and his folks could be in danger...really in danger if the 'monster's' spirit takes over my mind and body! I have to find out from Billy if he has told his parents about how I am sure that 'the spirit' – whoever he is – took control of my body that night at the County Fair, and that it was 'the spirit', and not me who inflicted all of the damage on the carnie thugs.

"Jack, were you asleep," I heard Mom ask

"No," I replied.

"We need to talk about what happened this afternoon...You know...the discussion about who Fritz really is. Did that upset you?"

Of course it did, but I'm not going to let her know that it did. "I don't know, maybe."

"Sure," Mom continued. "I understand. You have come to think of Fritz as your friend...a friendly spirit...who has provided you with some good advice to make you a stronger, better, more intelligent person. I am sure that you trusted Fritz...and that you would find it difficult to accept any criticisms of Fritz...even from your 'old' Mom. The truth is, Jack, I couldn't think of a different, or better, way of telling you that Fritz is not Fritz...other than the way you found that out this afternoon. Have you heard from your 'spirit' during or since Colonel Roberts and I told you who we believe...we are convinced...that the 'spirit' is?"

"Yes, but only briefly...at the end... and he seemed to be quite upset about what you said. But I did sense his presence...that he was 'plugged-in' for much of what Colonel Roberts said...and since then I have felt his absence ...like I do when he 'unplugs' from my brain."

"Well, I'm not surprised...But I am sure you will hear from him again at some point in time. And before that happens, I want you to hear from Hannah.

"You know, Jack, from the moment when you first told me about Fritz...that the spirit of a dead German was residing in your body...I have been working with Gabby and Dr. K, and as well as many others here in America and Europe, to find out the truth of your situation. It was not by accident that the Kaufmans found out about Hannah...or that she came to live with us. With the information that 'Fritz' provided to you, and you passed on to me, we were able to locate people in Europe and Israel who could verify the existence of the real 'Fritz', and the time and circumstances of his death. They could also identify certain discrepancies in the tale the 'spirit' was telling you. Those people, in turn, put us in touch with Hannah who, it turns out is both a Jewish displaced person and, because of her intelligence and unique experiences, has been working with a Jewish organization tracking down certain Nazis who had been identified as being intimately involved with the 'Final Solution', but who had disappeared at the end of the War, thus escaping prosecution.

"Hannah was present in Poland and Germany at the end of the War...and she has first-hand information about the von Bruckner's and *Oberst* Dietrich Muenster...This is information that goes beyond what Colonel Roberts confirmed this afternoon. Hannah was personally acquainted with the nun, Maria von Bruckner, and with the lady who Colonel Roberts says he saw with the *Oberst* on that January day in 1945, in Spremberg, Poland...and who is the very same lady who was with the *Oberst* when he was shot and killed on May 7, 1945, which is the day the 'evil spirit' departed the dead *Oberst*, taking up residence in your body!

"There were rumors circulating at the end of the War of a particularly evil member of the dreaded S.S. who was believed to have gone underground and would, in time, reappear...with the goal of reassembling groups of Nazis who had strong sympathies towards continuing the 'Final Solution', pursuing that evil program of exterminating Jews. We believe that this evil person was Dietrich Muenster, whose 'spirit' now resides in your body. He may be planning to make his way back to Germany ...or perhaps to Brazil, to South America, where many Nazis escaped to after the War. He now has the perfect disguise...your body...the body of a young American boy in which to hide until the time is ripe for his reappearance.

"Having now established the probability that the 'evil spirit' present in you is the one on whom thousands of former Nazis are waiting, Hannah's charge from the Jewish organizations is to prevent the 'spirit' from executing any such plan...And, Jack, it is our job to help Hannah, even though it may at times become risky and dangerous.

"I know that there were times when you were upset that I was keeping you away from us...like sending you away to military school...But we were fearful that if your 'spirit' was who we thought he might be, there was a chance that he would find out what we were doing...and either use you to immediately make his escape, or he would somehow discover who Hannah really is...and maybe harm her."

"You know that your name, Jack, is a very strong name," interrupted Hannah. "...And over the last year, Jack, you have become a strong young man...both in your physical self and your mental self. We are going to have to keep you mentally strong if we are going to prevent the 'evil spirit' in you from achieving his goals. And you are going to have to trust us...your mother and me...when we ask you to do certain things, including not letting the 'evil spirit' convince you that he is not evil...or not letting him take control of your mind and body if he tries. You must always let one of us know if he is attempting to convince you to do something that you know might be wrong...or if he tries to take control of your body and mind. There may even be times when we will need to restrain you if we discover that you are under his control."

Is this the time to tell Mom and Hannah about what happened at the County Fair; of the damage the 'spirit' did to those carnie workers when he took control of my body? If I do, won't they want to restrain me right now?

"We are not trying to scare you, Jack," Mom said. "But now that the 'spirit' knows that we are onto him, he will no longer be the 'good old' Fritz you have been accustomed to. He has no reason now to be your buddy...He is now a known enemy...

someone who has demonstrated that he can inflict harm...to you, as well as to Hannah, me, and even Billy. So it is for your safety and our peace of mind that we are concerned about how we can protect you from the awful things this 'evil spirit' is capable of doing."

"Are you saying that the 'spirit' is a demon, like the devil," I asked.

"Yes," replied Mom.

"Precisely," interjected Hannah.

"So, are you saying that I am possessed by the devil?"

"Let's just say that it is 'a question of possession'...but we don't know if it is the devil himself. But, whoever the 'evil spirit' might be, you can't blame yourself...it's not your fault! It may even be that God...in His eternal wisdom...has selected you to be the one to hold this demon captive...to keep him from doing further harm to the Jews...and maybe to the rest of mankind. You are very, very special, Jack! Ever since I became convinced that the 'spirit' in you is evil...I have been praying that God will give you the strength and courage to deal with this 'spirit', and that He will intercede and render the 'evil spirit' harmless, powerless."

What a rotten Memorial Day picnic this had turned out to be. The "Dream Racer" wouldn't work...I never got a turn or a ride in it... And Pete Roberts' story about the P38 Lightning didn't tell me a thing about what a good warplane it was...and what he told Mom and Hannah about Fritz means that I'm not possessed by Fritz, but that I'm holding some 'evil spirit' captive. Why has this happened to me?

CHAPTER 39

BIG CHIEF TABLET THIRTY-FIVE | JACK

I am trying to record, as best I can, what Hannah said about how she came to have so much information about Fritz – or should I now say – about Dietrich Muenster.

HANNAH'S STORY

"Jack," Hannah began the following afternoon, speaking with a curiously Slavic/British accent, "your mother thinks it might be a good idea to let you hear directly from me what I know about the 'spirit' present in your body...and I am sure that you are curious about my role in trying to identify the 'spirit' who inhabits your body. Your mother's concern about you, of course, is the main reason why I am here...but as I mentioned to you after the meeting with Colonel Roberts, there are others who care very much about who that 'evil spirit' might be.

"I have access to some very important information about Fritz, and about *Oberst* Dietrich Muenster...information that has been of incalculable assistance in identifying the 'spirit'...information that came into my possession as the result of a very long and complex journey. What I am about to tell you is an abbreviated version of that journey...a journey that I was forced to take by reason of my being a Jew...a Jew living in the country of Poland, a country with a troubled past located just to the east of Germany...actually Nazi Germany at the time my journey began.

I am shortening the story because you don't need to hear all of the details at this time...just those facts that relate to identifying your 'spirit'. And, quite frankly, I don't want to detract from the seriousness of your situation by getting you swept up into the details of my own adventures. If later, you are still interested in hearing more about my life, my experiences during a most thrilling, hair-raising journey, I'll be happy to give you the expanded 'Memoir' version when we have more time.

"By way of some necessary background: Centuries ago, before the Nazis instituted their diabolical plan for the extermination of the Jewish race, Jews...God's chosen people...were forced out of their Biblical homeland in Palestine by other kingdoms and empires, were left to wander the earth from one location to another, always reviled and persecuted...but never tolerated. From European ghettos to Czarist pogroms, from Christian nations to Muslim domains, Jews were under constant harassment for their religious beliefs and customs. It is difficult for Americans to appreciate the plight of the Jews in other parts of the world, particularly in certain European, Asian and the Middle-Eastern countries. Jews in the United States are generally accepted as full participants in the American dream, and it is only in rare cases that Jews are excluded from activities or functions...but they are never publicly persecuted or ostracized like they have been in other parts of the world.

"My Jewish ancestors are a good example of how Jews have had to flee from one home to another to escape unfair laws and treatment. Because of the events of the Nazi take-over of Poland and my separation from my parents, I never learned the full history of my family. As best I can now recall, my father's family...I don't know what the family name was at that time... was forced out of Holland in the 17th century, where they were craftsmen and artists...and fled to an area called Silesia in what is now western Poland...adopting the Wolkowitz family name... actually pronounced Volkovitz. Jews were tolerated in this area of Poland which was mainly rural and impoverished, because the Polish leaders and landowners needed workers and farmers. Even though my ancestors agreed to move to Poland, they soon learned that there was no work for craftsmen and artists, so my father's family was forced to become farmers and tradesmen.

In the small, nameless village located south and east of Poznan, where my father, Eli, and my mother, Sara, settled, my father was the butcher, and my mother was a seamstress. Besides me, in my family there were two other daughters...Ruth and Marian... and two sons...Aaron and Solomon. We were poor, but Mama and Papa saw to it that we were well-fed, nicely dressed and received some schooling...each of us could read and write...both Hebrew and Polish...and some German.

"My sister, Ruth, the oldest, was always the smartest, the most ambitious, and the most beautiful. As I was growing up in her shadow...I was the middle child...her talents, her blond hair and sparkling blue-eyes, her figure, her poise...well, most everything about her...left me envious, feeling inferior and inadequate. Life in a small, poor village caused Ruth to yearn for something better, something bigger, and always something more exciting. Our infrequent trips to Poznan, the nearest big city, usually thrilled Ruth, except that depression quickly replaced joy once she found herself back at home facing the same dull existence.

"Both of my brothers...Aaron older than me...and Solomon the next in line...were bright, curious, and steadfast. Although they, like Ruth, were ambitious, they were not intrigued with city-life, or with the compromises they would have to make in their much cherished Jewish heritage and traditions should they move away to a more cosmopolitan environment. They were much devoted to Mama and Papa, and looked upon Marian...the youngest...and me as if we were their own children...requiring constant supervision and protection.

"While neither Marian nor I were as attractive as Ruth, my brothers often commented that the local boys had their eyes on us as second-best choice if they could not have Ruth...And, of course, Ruth was unavailable to such 'dolts'. She would have nothing to do with any local male...Jew or Gentile...since...in her view...by still living in this rural back-water...they 'have demonstrated the lack of sufficient wisdom, sophistication, or ambition to warrant my interest'. My brothers found Ruth's extraordinary beauty and difficult behavior to be dangerous...believing that her presence, her Aryan features, her arrogance simply drew too much unwelcomed attention to our otherwise unexceptional, innocuous family. In time, Aaron and Solomon's fears about Ruth proved to be warranted...although by then Ruth was living her dream, and our nightmare was just beginning.

"The nightmare, of course, was the German invasion of western-Poland in September, 1939, and all that transpired thereafter...most notably the horrors of the Nazis 'Final Solution' for eliminating undesirable persons...the main focus of which was the extermination of all Jews found in Germany and Nazi-occupied countries. But the Nazis' plans for extermination of 'undesirable' persons also applied to Polish landowners, intellectuals and professionals...thereby intending to leave the Polish workers and farmers leaderless, more susceptible to being reduced to slave labor status. Obviously, extermination was also in store for members of Catholic religious orders and lay persons who attempted to aid and protect Jews, and other undesirable persons.

"Within months after the defeat of Polish military forces, our small village was ransacked by Nazi S.S. and Gestapo thugs, carting off all valuables and foodstuffs, moving 'undesirables' to concentration camps for extermination, shipping the healthy workers and farmers to factories and mines as slave laborers. Mama and Papa had placed blond-hair, blue-eyes Marian and me with two different Catholic families in a nearby town, to be raised as their own children. Solomon, who was a soldier in the defeated Polish Army managed to escape capture, joining a group of Polish partisans living off the land, hiding in the pine forests and hills of West Prussia. Ruth, as mentioned, had left home prior to the invasion...and as I was later to learn, was living in Poznan using her Aryan features and her 'other' physical attributes to escape detection as a Jew. I never learned what precisely happened to Mama, Papa or Aaron...I can only assume, since I never heard from or about them again, that they were some of the millions of Polish Jews that perished in the Nazi death camps.

'The father of the family with whom I had been placed was also a butcher named, Ivan, who Papa had known for years, and had become close friends. This was a devout Catholic family, Ivan and his wife Suzanne, and their four children, with me becoming the fifth child...the ruse remaining undetected for several years. As the tide of the war in the East turned against Germany, as the Russian front began to collapse, life in Poland also began to worsen...with food and fuel disappearing from Poland to feed the German soldiers and their families in Germany, with squads of S.S. goons scouring the Polish cities, towns and country-side looking for able-bodied workers.

"Inevitably, I became a liability to Ivan and his family, a liability that they could no longer afford...so I was shipped off to an orphanage run by an order of German nuns in Poznan...or Posen in German...where I was taken in, accepted as a gentile. Although I was deeply hurt by being forced to leave a family who I had learned to love deeply, my abandonment was a God-send in retrospect...it was at the orphanage that I met and fell under the care of the German nun, Maria von Bruckner, and by being at the orphanage I miraculously escaped the unfortunate fate that befell Ivan and Suzanne and their children...I later learned that they were separated from one another and shipped into forced labor, a slow but sure death from starvation, overwork, exposure, and disease. I never learned what happened to my younger sister, Marian and the family with whom she was living, which means that she, too, probably suffered the same fate as did Ivan's family.

"Life in the orphanage was generally pleasant, but we too suffered from the growing shortages of food, fuel, clothing, and medicines. At maximum there were maybe forty-five or fifty orphans of both sexes being cared for by six or seven nuns, but by the time the Russians had pushed back the Germans, reaching Poznan, there were fewer than twenty orphans and three nuns still alive. It was during these end-days that the German nun, Sister Maria told me of what had happened to her family...the von Bruckners...at the hands of the dreaded S.S. in Germany...I guess she was preparing me for what might happen to the nuns and their wards at the hands of the retreating Nazi S.S. death squads, but surely at the hands of the barbarous, advancing Russian army.

"It was during Sister Maria's tale of woe that I first heard the name of her family's oppressor, *S.S. Oberst* Dietrich Muenster. Besides having crossed his uncle Otto decades earlier, the von Bruckners had committed the unforgiveable crime of protecting, hiding, and helping Jews to escape from the horrors of the Nazi imposed anti-Jewish laws. It was only later, after I heard the 'Fritz' story...a story we now know was concocted by the 'evil spirit' of *Oberst* Muenster... that I became aware that *Oberst* Muenster had been holding the von Bruckner family hostage in hopes of landing some more important traitors to the Reich. Obviously, when more important traitors were exposed by the failed assassination attempt on Hitler, followed by the unsuccessful usurpation of power in July 1944, the von Bruckners' crimes against the Reich no longer warranted being ignored. It was during this period – probably in August 1944 – that Fritz, his father, his brothers, and his brother-in-law, were summarily tried, convicted and executed by a Gestapo firing squad. The von Bruckner women and children disappeared into the concentration camps...with their ultimate fate still unknown.

"As for Sister Maria von Bruckner, she and I escaped both the S.S and the Russians in Poznan... being rescued at the last moment by a squad of Polish partisans led by my brother Solomon. The timing of our rescue was critical...it had to occur precisely at a point in time during which the Nazis were retreating in disarray and the Russians were not present in full strength. Thanks to intelligence being supplied by someone who had access to secret S.S. reports, Solomon was able to sweep us away out of Poznan and into the country-side under partisan control under the very noses of the two combating forces. As the Germans retreated and the Russians advanced towards Germany, the well-armed partisans...with Sister Maria and me in tow...slipped along in the no-man's land created by the retreating Germans and the attacking Russians, killing Germans and Russians alike when necessary to make our escape. With God's help, we finally reached, and crossed the Elbe River, somewhere between Dresden and Leipzig, making contact with members of the U.S. 1st Army.

"After many hours and days of interviews and interrogation by the American military intelligence officers, Solomon and I were able to convince the Americans that we were Polish refugees who did not wish to be repatriated to Poland. Sister Maria, however, because she was a German, was treated differently, subjected to more intense scrutiny. Ultimately, after several anxious months, Sister Maria was able to obtain confirmation from her Order of her status, and she was allowed to return to her Order at a location in the Western zone of Germany...where she continued her work with the orphans...those displaced children who were quickly filling the relief camps throughout the Western zone of Germany. I was crushed to see Sister Maria, a true saint, leave us, but I knew that she and I had important work to do, just in different places.

"Solomon was a prized internee, having a wealth of information about Nazi atrocities and the names of high-ranking S.S. officers – including *Oberst* Muenster – involved with the Jewish exterminations. He also was able to reveal the name of the source of secret information about the S.S., the same person who helped us escape the S.S. and Russian troops in Poznan: It was our sister, Ruth. The Allied authorities assisted us in trying to find Ruth...but the chore was complicated by the fact that there were no records of a Ruth Wolkovitz having ever been present in Germany...and the records in Poland were then in Russian hands, and unavailable.

"After several months of fruitless search for Ruth, just when we are about to give up hope of her being found alive, one of the many Jewish relief organizations with whom Solomon and I had been pestering for information received word that Ruth was alive, having been shuttled from one Jewish agency in Germany to another. Once U.S. Military Intelligence learned of her existence, and ascertained her 'phony' name...thereby connecting her to S.S. *Oberst* Dietrich Muenster, she was interviewed, and placed in the hands of a Jewish group investigating the whereabouts of notorious members of the S.S. S.D. (Death Squads) who had escaped capture by the Allied military police.

"Once considered by her siblings to be 'vain Ruth', 'arrogant Ruth', 'beautiful Ruth', Ruth was now a celebrated Jewish heroine...the story circulating of how she had managed to infiltrate the S.S., gathering critical, secret information relating to the conduct of the Nazis' Final Solution of the Jewish Question. Ruth was now living in Nuremberg, under the guard and care of the U.S. military police, being protected from possible harm at the hands of former Nazi officials and S.S. officers who wished to remain unidentified and in hiding. Only after we had endured endless days of scrutiny, even with the approval from the Jewish intelligence groups with whom we were working, we were finally granted access to the woman we believed to be our sister, Ruth.

"The woman to whom we were granted access was living in a drab, non-descript building in a military enclave located deep in a rural area of Bavaria. The woman to whom we were escorted to see appeared to be smaller, frailer than I remembered Ruth to be...perhaps time and strain had greatly diminished her storied beauty, her vitality, her charm. Ruth, however, retained a goodly portion of her former arrogance, wearing her 'heroine' status proudly, excitedly telling us of her daring, bold exploits, worming her way into the very heart of the S.S. operations. At first, she told us, the Western military police were reluctant to accord her information any reliability, viewing her as just another Jewess collaborator, a traitor, a prostitute, who used her beauty to save her attractive 'ass' from incarceration, incineration in a Nazi death camp.

"Ruth told us that at the time of the German invasion of Poland, she was living in Poznan, working as a fashion model...using the name Ingrid Faust...being supported by a prominent attorney, who, like Ruth, was secretly a Jew, but with significant ties to the Nazis. After the Polish government capitulated, 'Ingrid' and her paramour became prominent at parties and functions welcoming the new German masters. Within a short time of wining and dining with Nazi dignitaries and high-ranking German officers, Ingrid was accepted as a part of the German establishment, giving her access to goods, services and facilities denied to most other Poles. At some point after it became clear that Ingrid had successfully passed as a non-Jew, agents of the burgeoning Jewish underground approached Ingrid, requesting that she use her position to aid Jewish efforts by gaining access to Nazi plans to 'resettle' Polish Jews. At first, Ingrid resisted such efforts, fearing that she had neither the talent nor the chutzpa to be a successful spy...but she ultimately agreed to give it a try on the condition that she would chose the time, the source, the nature of the information.

"These three conditions coalesced in the form of a darkly-handsome *S.S. Oberst* recently assigned to the Posen district for Jewish 'resettlement purposes...our friend...Dietrich Muenster. Yes, the same Dietrich Muenster who Sister Maria claimed was responsible for the execution of her brother, Fritz, and the rest of her von Bruckner relations. Although Ruth/Ingrid was initially put-off by the *Oberst's* manner, especially his piercing, cruel snake-like eyes...doing her best to play coy, to keep the *Oberst* at arm's-length...but still interested. Dietrich Muenster pursued Ruth/Ingrid like a bull pursues a heifer, and with the same purpose in mind. The details of the pursuit, the conquest, are too lengthy and too sordid to repeat here, suffice it to say, that Ruth/Ingrid played the *Oberst* like a spider plays the fly into her web.

"From the point in time that Ruth/Ingrid became the *Oberst's* companion until the last days of the War, Ruth/Ingrid was constantly at his side, having access to some of the most important S.S., Nazi, and German military and political information imaginable. She passed on what information of immediate importance she could to her contacts in the ever-shrinking Jewish underground, and she retained in her marvelous memory the very most important names, places, dates, facts. When we asked Ruth about the information she sent to Solomon, that allowed us to escape both the retreating Germans and the advancing Russians, she revealed that she was long aware of my presence in the orphanage in Poznan and of the care I was receiving at the hands of the German nun, Sister Maria. There were, Ruth said, many times when food and clothing were delivered to the orphanage late at night from an anonymous friend.

"Ruth was shocked, but not surprised, when I told her about what Sister Maria told me about *Oberst* Muenster being responsible for the deaths of the rest of the von Bruckner family members. 'Remember,' Ruth said, 'I knew Dietrich was a bastard from the moment I met him, and nothing he ever did thereafter surprised me or changed my opinion of him. I never loved him in the least, and would have killed him in his sleep many times, except that through him I had access to the very best Nazi intelligence. He died being a bastard to the very last.'

"When I then asked Ruth what she meant by 'remaining with *Oberst* Muenster until the very last', she said that she did her best to never let the *Oberst* out of her sight for very long. 'He had invaluable information, which changed from moment to moment towards the end, and, besides, he was about as faithful as a flea.'

"'If you were with *Oberst* Muenster at the end, did you see him die," I asked Ruth'.

'Yes, I was there.'

"'I then asked Ruth the obvious question: 'Can you tell us how he died...and when...and where'?

"'Yes, I can,' replied Ruth, in a calm, even voice. "'I shot the son-of-a-bitch with his Walther P-38 pistol...several times...in the back!'"

"'Why," I asked incredulously.'

"'Because the bastard had it coming to him...and if I didn't kill him then and there, there was a good chance that he would have escaped from Germany, the pursuing U.S. Military Police, and the punishment he so richly deserved...The bastard was trying to get away with some of his cohorts...they were dressed in stolen U.S. Army uniforms...they were headed for Switzerland, and then to South America. They had crates of gold and secret documents that they were loading onto stolen U.S. Army military trucks. I couldn't let him get away...I couldn't let him survive, to later return, to resume killing Jews. He was as evil as they come. At times I felt as if the man I was living with was Satan himself.'

"'When and where," I asked her again. "The date is more important than the place."'

'It was on May 6 or 7, 1945, the last days of the War...somewhere in southern Bavaria...near Berchtesgaden. I buried him in a shallow grave in a clearing in a nearby stand of trees after his cowardly band of thieves drove away...leaving him there to die... They were more interested in saving the load of gold, than in saving their dying leader. Even though I told the U.S. Military Police where I buried the *Oberst's* body, no one has found it to date... and as far as I know his cronies were never apprehended. These two facts...no dead-body and no accomplices...has created an uncertainty that I really did kill the *Oberst*...perhaps forming the basis to rumors that Dietrich Muenster is alive somewhere and is preparing for an eventual return to Germany, to pick up where he left off killing Jews.'

"In 1949," continued Hannah, "the new Israeli government created a secret intelligence service, the Mossad, which was given the responsibility to track down and capture known enemies of the Israeli state, including former Nazis with ties to the 'Final Solution'. Because of our extensive experience and success in Germany from the end of the War in assisting local Jewish organizations in finding missing Nazi S.S. S.D members, Solomon and I were recruited by the Mossad to expand our efforts...to make them more global in scope. There were a number of notorious S.S. S.D. members still unaccounted for...like Dietrich Muenster, Klaus Barbie and Adolf Eichmann. No lead was too obscure, too preposterous, or too thin for the Mossad to pursue.

"And so, when the Kaufmans of Kansas City, Missouri, U.S.A. began making inquiries through the traditional Jewish organizations for assistance in verifying the contentions of an eleven year old American boy that the 'spirit' of a dead German soldier...said to be Fritz von Bruckner...was sharing his body, Mossad became interested...and I was asked to look into the matter. I became particularly interested in the matter when I learned that the alleged date of the 'spirit' entering the young boy's body...around 7 May 1945...coincided with the date that my sister Ruth claimed she had shot and killed Dietrich Muenster.

"Moreover, I knew from what Sister Maria von Bruckner had earlier told me...that there was a critical link between the von Bruckners and Dietrich Muenster. I also knew...from several sources...that the time-frame in which Fritz von Bruckner was executed...in August, 1944...made it impossible for 'the Fritz spirit' to have been the 'spirit' that entered your body. On these facts I believed that there might be something here worth looking into. The tape recordings that your Mom made of the 'spirit' speaking in his own voice was reviewed by Ruth...and she confirmed that the voice was too much like that of the *Oberst* not to be his voice...even taking into account the fact that the voice came through the voice box of an eleven year old American boy.

"After gathering all the information that was available in Germany about Fritz and Dietrich, I agreed to travel to the United States, to Missouri, to pursue the possibility that the 'spirit' of the evil Dietrich Muenster had somehow been transported to Missouri, and had taken up residence in your body. But because of U.S. immigration requirements, it was necessary that I acquire status as a displaced person to enter the U.S., to be placed with an American family, to travel to Missouri, and to live with your Mom as my sponsor.

"Now that I have had the opportunity to hear Colonel Roberts say that the man in the photo of *Oberst* Dietrich Muenster is the same man who claimed to be Fritz von Bruckner, but is also the same man Colonel Roberts saw in Spremberg, Germany, wearing the uniform of an S.S. *Oberst*...and putting that information together with what the nun, Sister Maria von Bruckner, and my own sister, Ruth, have told me...I am convinced that the 'spirit' who is sharing your body, Jack, is the 'evil spirit' of Dietrich Muenster. The question now becomes: What are we going to do about that?"

CHAPTER 40

BIG CHIEF TABLET THIRTY-SIX | JACK

If Mom and Hannah expected me to take any comfort from what Hannah told me, the truth was that I was more frightened than I was when I first learned that I was being haunted by the 'spirit' of a dead German. At least at that earlier time I believed that the 'spirit' was my friend, a good 'spirit'; the 'spirit' who was who he said he was. *Maybe I should have suspected that I was in trouble when Fritz told me not to tell Dr. Glassberg that I heard voices... Maybe if I had told the truth then, I wouldn't be where I am now... a prisoner of some 'evil spirit' who can take control of my mind and body...an 'evil spirit' who can do evil things...and I will be the one who will be blamed for the outcome of his evil actions, blamed for his evil behavior. Now that I know what damage 'the spirit' can inflict using my body, I am really scared for Mom, Hannah, and anyone else who tries to get in 'the spirit's' way. What a fine summer...indeed, what a fine life...this is going to be!*

"Mom," I asked, "What am I going to do this summer? Will I be able to play with Billy, be with my friends...or am I going to have to spend all of my summer vacation locked up here in the house?"

"It does seem that we have a problem with what you will be able to do this summer, and I am afraid that there will have to be limitations placed on who you will be able to be with, and under what circumstances. As long as Hannah and I are with you either when you are here at Fairways or in town with your friends, or if Dennis and Milly are with you when you are with Billy, I think that you can pretty well do whatever you please."

"Oh, Mom," I replied, angrily. "You've got to be kidding...What kind of summer vacation will that be?"

"I know it's not a perfect situation, but unless we can come up with some other less restrictive, but still a safe, approach, it will have to do."

"But just think about it, Mom...What can possibly happen if I'm alone with Billy...or my friends? Even if 'the Muenster' were to take control of my mind and body, what can he possibly do to them, or to me, that could help him? I mean, Billy knows all about the 'old Muenster'...and he'll know what to do."

"Let Hannah and me think about it...It's just that the 'old Muenster' is a particularly crafty, evil demon...and maybe when he gains control of your mind and body, he can give you strength that you normally wouldn't have...to go along with a devious intellect that is beyond human comprehension. We just can't take that chance."

I was about to suggest that I was just a thirteen year-old boy, and what harm could I do, when I remembered what had happened at the County Fair...how the 'spirit' had taken control of my body and had beaten those carnie thugs to a bloody pulp, and would have killed at least one of them if Dennis hadn't interfered. *I can't make that argument...It's not true...And besides I've never told Mom about that night. But do the Lewises, who witnessed the beatings of the carnie thugs, now know the truth... having heard what took place at the Memorial Day picnic...how Colonel Roberts identified a photo of 'the Muenster' as being the 'evil spirit'? Have they told Mom about what happened at the County Fair?*

"I know it isn't fair, but it is what it is, and we need to deal with it as best we can. I hear what you are saying...and maybe there's another way we can see to it that you have a good summer vacation. I've been thinking that a trip out West...to see the Rockies...to go to a dude ranch...might work. I know it means that you won't get to be with your friends for most of this summer, but I think such a trip will be loads of fun."

FOR THE NEXT several weeks, now that school had let out for summer vacation, but my freedom of movement had been curtailed, I moped around the house trying to read books that fail to capture my attention; my thoughts always returning to how much my life had changed now that my "friendly spirit" has been revealed to be an "evil spirit," a monster.

Billy, too, had been out of school, but he had been too busy helping his dad on their farm or working with him at various odd-jobs around the county, to spend much time with me. And when we did get together on Saturday afternoons, Billy was well-aware of the controls under which I must live, and he knew that our times together would always be under the watchful eye of my Mom, Hannah, or his folks; leaving our activities monitored, curtailed, our usually intriguing conversations reduced to talking about normal stuff. No more spur-of-the-moment bike-rides around the country-side or into town; no more un-chaperoned hunting trips in the fields and woods pursuing the wily scurrying creatures with our air rifles; no more conversations about girls and their body-parts. I began to sense that our meetings had quickly become as much a disappointment for Billy as they had for me.

"Jack," Billy began on the third of our Saturday afternoon visits, sitting with me on the broad front steps at Fairways. "I can't stay long today...I'm going to town this afternoon to see a movie and have a burger with some of the other guys. Can you come along?"

"Do you think that Jo might be there, too," I asked hopefully, in a whisper; remembering the girl who I met at the County Fair last fall, the girl Billy knows from the 4H Club, the girl who went for help when Billy and I were set upon by the bully Wesley and his rough friends, the girl who often fills my mind with pleasant thoughts.

"Maybe," Billy responded.

"Mom, can I go with Billy," I asked knowing full-well the answer I would receive.

"Of course you can, Jack...as long as either Hannah or I, or Billy's folks, are with you."

"But, what could possibly happen, that Billy and the other guys can't handle," I lied, knowing how the 'evil spirit' could turn my scrawny body into a killer.

"We've been over this too many times now, Jack, for you to argue with me about what needs to be done...what you know must be done. Either Hannah or I go with you, or you don't go."

"This isn't fair...I might as well have no friends...Who'd want to be my friend if they have to be watched over by some old people...I'm sure Billy doesn't want me to go to town with him if you two have to come along with us. His friends will shun him for sure."

"Jack, I think you're over-reacting."

"Well, I think you're being unreasonable...If you or Hannah insist on coming along every time I want to go somewhere, don't you think that people are going to wonder why? What do we tell them if they ask? I sure don't want to tell them...I don't want everyone in the county to start knowing about my 'evil spirit', my possession...Do you?"

"Of course not...And, that's all the more reason for us to get away for the summer...To take our trip to see the West."

"That's fine for this summer, but what are we going to do this fall...when I have to go back to school?"

"We'll cross that bridge when we get to it...And, hopefully, the problem will be solved by then."

"What are you planning to do while we're on the trip...find an Indian witch doctor to cast out my demon...or are you planning to lock me up somewhere out there, where no one will ever find me?"

"Jack, that's cruel and unfair of you to even joke about such things. You know how I feel about you...We only want to do what is best for you."

"And doing what's best for all those Jewish organizations who want me to be the 'Muenster's' keeper...his jailer."

"You're talking nonsense now...You're just upset...You're making me upset...And you are certainly not going to town with Billy today with that attitude...I'm afraid that you would just tell Billy's pal Joe about your situation just to spite me."

"Jo's not a pal...Jo's a girl...And she's the last person on earth who I'd tell about my 'situation'... or who I would want to know about my 'situation'. Besides, I've already sworn Billy to secrecy about the 'Muenster'."

"That's not the issue...The issue is that the 'Muenster' might take control of your mind and body...That he might harm some-one...others."

"But, why has that suddenly become a concern? Up until Me-morial Day, you didn't seem concerned...and I had total freedom to come and go as I pleased."

"We weren't sure until then that the 'spirit' was the 'Muen-ster'."

"But, 'the spirit' certainly knew before then that he was the 'Muenster'." And look what he did when he found it necessary to protect me...and, really, his self."

"True...But he didn't know until then that we knew who he was...Now that he knows that we know who he is, he'll see that there is no point in keeping his promise to me not to take control of your mind and body...And he is sure to be mad at Hannah and me...And if we're not watching you all of the time, he'll use that opportunity to take over your body, and find something that he can use to harm us...Just like the letter opener that is part of the 'desk-set' that you gave me for Christmas...Remember the start you gave me when you kept jabbing that dagger at me?"

"But, I got you that present...And Gabby was with me the whole time."

"That's not my point...I know that you bought me the 'desk-set'...My point is that things have changed. We can no longer as-sume that the 'spirit' means no harm. Based on his track record in Germany and Poland, the 'Muenster' is a diabolical monster...a mass murderer! Why should we assume that he is now a re-formed 'spirit'...someone who we can trust with our lives? Until he proves to us that he is no longer a demon, I am going to as-sume the worst about him...And I won't let you out of my sight."

EACH NIGHT, AS I tossed and turned in my bed, waiting for sleep to come, my soul cried out: *Fritz! Fritz! Are you there? I need to talk to you.* I need your help. And all I received in return was silence; not even a feeling that the 'spirit' – whoever he is, was plugged-in, was listening to me. In quiet desperation, one night, instead of trying to contact the 'spirit', I prayed to God to listen to me, to help me; something I've never done before: *What have I done God to deserve this? I'm just a boy. What do I need to do to get rid of this 'spirit'? Will you help me, God, please?* I supposed I really didn't expect to hear God's voice or to see a sign that He was listening to me; and so I wasn't disappointed when I didn't hear anything.

But, I did hear from the 'spirit' a few nights later: *Jack, Fritz isn't here...He's never been here...You have had only me...Dietrich...for all these years. I know that you considered Fritz to be your friend, and that, for now, we are not friends. But, I'd like to be your friend. If we are to become friends, I know that I have to show you that I'm not an 'evil spirit'... that I'm no longer a monster. While I'm doing that, can I ask that you please address me as 'Dietrich', and not the 'Muenster'? I know that you use the name 'the Muenster' to address me because it sounds like the word 'monster'...because that's what you think I am...because that is what your mother and Hannah have told you that I am. They are, of course, both correct...that I was a monster, an evil person...but I've changed. So while I'm trying to show you that I am no longer a monster...a monster to be reviled...to be feared...would you please call me by my given name 'Dietrich'?*

I don't think so...After all the lies you have told me, why should I believe what you are telling me now? Yes, I liked Fritz...He was a good guy...and you killed him...and then pretended to be him... just so that I'd like you. Why did you lie to me?

Fritz: *Because I couldn't tell you the truth...I needed you to like me... to be my friend...to trust me...to grow up...to be strong. But, if I had told you the truth about me, and I knew that you were too young and too fragile to handle the truth, you were not ever going to be able to help me complete my true mission. Most of what I told you about Fritz is true. I chose him because I knew from my meeting with him, my interrogations of Fritz and his family, the interviews, the surveillance reports, and because I knew that he was a good man...a man I actually admired. But, you are correct...A great-deal of what I told you about Fritz was not true; certainly everything after August 1944 was pure fabrication...since Fritz was dead by then.*

So you weren't really trying to be my friend...you were just telling me lies...using me for your own evil purposes...So how do I know that what you are saying now is not just more of the same thing?

Fritz: *You don't...at least not right now...But I hope to convince you that I am a different person...or spirit...different from who I was then.*

What could you possibly tell me that would convince me that you are a good guy...like Fritz...that I should trust you? I can't believe anything you say...your words are just words...and I'm from Missouri...you need to show me...and since you don't have a body...how can you possibly show me that you are now a good guy?

Fritz: *Jack, you have every reason not to trust me, but I can assure you that I have no reason to cause you any harm...I still need you, if only for my own well-being. But I can't say the same about others: You need to be wary of Hannah, the Jew bitch...she has an agenda that does not have your best interest at heart. I am her enemy, and she wants to control me at all costs...even if it means harming you, harming others – innocent others – to accomplish her objective, her mission.*

IT NOW HAS been a couple of weeks since I last had contact with the 'Muenster'. I have been going through the tablets that I thought that 'Fritz', the 'spirit', had written, as well as reviewing my tablets to see if there was anything that the 'spirit' had thought or said that would help me understand why things have turned out the way they have. I'm now afraid that the 'Muenster' will try to find and destroy my tablets if he takes control of my body. I don't trust the 'Muenster', not one bit. I must find a place to hide the tablets so he can't find or destroy them.

I think that Mom and Hannah are becoming more concerned about what to do about me, and what they can do to make sure that the 'Muenster' does not take control of me. I know, from what happened at the County Fair, that there is nothing that can be done to keep the 'Muenster' from taking control of my body. If he should take control of my body, I don't know what they can do to stop him from using his strength to overpower them, to hurt them...like he did to those carnie thugs. *Please, dear God, don't let that happen!*

CHAPTER 41

NELL CLOSED THE LAST TABLET. IT HAD TAKEN HER
the better-part of a week's worth of evenings closeted in her bedroom
to wade through the trove of writings she was now convinced were
Jack's handiwork. The floor around the chintz-covered upholstered
chair was littered with some three dozen writing tablets thrown in
haphazard piles. Nell had tossed the final tablet – the one with the
last reported conversation between Jack and the 'spirit' – on the floor,
turned off the floor lamp, her head thrown back, her eyes closed; exhausted from the marathon reading sessions she had endured pouring
through Jack's supposed writings. Besides physical exhaustion, Nell's
psyche was wracked with the bitter taste of anger, humiliation, and
disappointment.

The more Nell thought about what she had just read, the angrier,
more confused and more despondent she became; the pain behind
her eyes growing in intensity, spreading to her temples, to the base of
her skull. Letting her mind race away, Nell conjured up a vision of the
'spirit' who had allegedly taken up residence in Jack's body, and had the
ability to take control of Jack's mind, and body. As she was reading
the writings attributable to Fritz, Nell was drawn to that character; but
now that she has finished the saga she envisioned the 'spirit' as being
the 'evil spirit', Dietrich – an 'evil' character to be sure; a character she
must surely revile. There was, nevertheless, a nagging thought that
neither version of the dead German was authentic. *Can Jack really be
possessed by the spirit of a dead German, or is Jack's claim of possession just
a nightmare, a fantasy – the result of a damaged brain traced to the blow*

to Jack's head when he was six-years old, compounded by the trauma he received in the horrible automobile accident?

Getting undressed in the dark Nell heard a knock on her closed and locked bedroom door, and the muffled, tremulous question, "Nell, are you still awake?

"Go away, Paul...I don't want to talk to you now...And I certainly don't want to see you."

"But, Nell, we need to talk...to talk about Jack...about finding him."

"Go find him yourself...Right now I have no desire to ever lay eyes on him. He clearly has no desire to ever see me again."

"What are you talking about? What gave you that impression?"

"You know damn well how that ungrateful brat feels about me..."

"I'm sure he loves you."

"Bull crap! Then you must have forgotten what Jack told that Jew shrink in Kansas how he feels about me...Or what Jack told you in that letter he wrote to you soliciting your help in getting me to give up my rights, so that he could go live with my bitch of a sister? I'll bet you didn't know that I know about that letter...Well the joke is on you and Jack...Rita really didn't want Jack to be her son...she just wanted to take him away from me."

Paul, his head bent forward, his forehead pressed tightly against the bedroom door, mumbled, "That's pure speculation, Nell...Remember, I've seen them together...They couldn't be more like mother and son."

"Yes, Paul, I most certainly know how you have been sneaking around behind my back to be with that home-wrecker...and with your gullible ex-son Jack...ogling them being all lovey-dovey. But I know what Jack thinks about Rita, and how...once I had agreed to relinquish Jack to her, began to treat Jack just like she treats me...Jack is nothing to her but a trophy...a constant reminder of her victory over me! A victory she should never have won except for your role...you Quisling! Now leave me alone...I'm exhausted."

Only after Nell had heard Paul use the bathroom, then close his bedroom door, did she resume her night-time rituals of creaming her face, putting her hair up in curlers, saying her prayers, climbing into bed; all in the dark. That night her prayers were different, more anguished; seeking an answer from God as to why all these terrible things were happening to her: *What have I done to deserve this unhappiness? Don't I go to Mass and take Holy Communion everyday…say dozens of rosary decades…keep all of the Commandments…send money to the missionaries? I'm not a bad person, not an immoral person. What more do you want from me, what more can you expect of me? I don't deserve having a son who is possessed. Don't you love me God? Please tell me what I need to do differently to earn your love.*

In the other bedroom, Paul was still awake, trying to remember what Nell has just said about Jack and Rita; something about having seen Jack's letter, something about knowing how Jack feels about Rita, and she about him. Nell did find something, or things, in the house, something among Jack's stuff that she is not sharing with me. I'm going to call the Kaufmans…they certainly must know something, or heard something by now. Please, dear God, help us to find Jack.

PAUL – WHO HAD taken Nell at her word; that she would not help find Jack – contacted directory assistance in Kansas City, requesting the telephone number for Dr. Stanley Kaufman, preferably his home phone number, and was provided with both Dr. Kaufman's residential and business phone numbers. During the afternoon, while his assistant was on her afternoon break, Paul asked the switchboard operator to please place a call to the Kaufmans' residence. When the operator had Mrs. Kaufman on the line she rang Paul's office line, and when Paul answered she told him, "I have Mrs. Kaufman on the line."

"Mrs. Kaufman," Paul began, "This is Paul Johanson in Saint Louis…I'm Jack's father."

"Of course, Paul, I know who you are," responded Gabby Kaufman in her most saccharine voice. "How are you and your wife…Nell isn't it?"

"I wish I could say that we are fine, but actually I am worried about Jack and Rita. Nell and I have been to Fairways recently to see if there is a problem…Rita's telephone service has been disconnected…but no one was there...and it looks as if no one has been there for some amount of time...Have you seen them recently...Do you know where they might be?"

"I'm not sure what you are saying...what you are concerned about," responded Gabby, the sound of her voice turning noticeably chilly.
"I really can't say if something has happened to Jack and Rita...But last fall, Rita told me that she was convinced that Jack was possessed by an 'evil spirit', and she was fearful that the 'evil spirit' would take control of Jack...She was concerned that the 'possessed' Jack might harm her."

"Yes, Rita told my husband and me of her concerns...But she also told us that as long as Jack was being watched by Hannah and her, there should be no problem. That was also one of the reasons Rita enrolled Jack in that military boarding school...where he would be away from her, and be supervised. Have you checked to see if Jack is back at the military school? You know, Rita and Hannah may just be away on a trip...Rita said something about showing Hannah something of the American West."

"No, I haven't, not yet...But I will...Right away. Still, that doesn't explain the non-payment of bills...like her mother's nursing home care, and the utility bills...and the disheveled, unkempt appearance of Fairways, which she always kept immaculate. We've even been to see the Adams County Sheriff...and filed a missing persons report, since there was no evidence of foul-play to warrant a criminal investigation."

"So, why are you calling us? What do you expect us to do to help you?"

"I just thought that you might know where Jack and Rita have gone...Or maybe that you have heard from them."

"And why should I tell you, even if I know? Jack's no longer your son, anyway...Why should I care what has happened to him?"

"Please. I don't understand your attitude...Jack's still my flesh and blood...I still love and care for him...It was my love for Jack that persuaded me that Jack would be better off with Rita."

"Yes, I'm sure that you have convinced yourself that that was your motive...But in reality, you were passing off damaged goods to Rita...

So Rita...and not you and your treacherous wife...would have to deal with the possessed...or crazy...Jack!"

"I think you are being unfair to Jack. Nell and I may have made some mistakes, but why should Jack...and even Rita...now suffer? As I recall, you love Rita...you treated her as a daughter. Please, for her sake, if you have any information, please help me."

"You know, Rita was just a daughter-in-law...she was not family... she was never really one of us. I've given you all the help that you deserve...Why don't you go ask Jack's friend, Billy Lewis what he knows has happened! Goodbye!" Click!

What is happening? Why was Gabby Kaufman so insensitive, so unhelpful? You would think that even if she hates Nell and me...and Jack, too...that she would still have affection for Rita...at least be concerned for Rita's safety. What does she mean by: 'Never really one of us'?

CHAPTER 42

PAUL REMEMBERED GABBY KAUFMAN HAVING
mentioned Jack's friend, Billy Lewis, but he did not have Billy's parents' names, only that they were neighbors. In the guise of inquiring as to whether the Adams County Sheriff's Department had come into possession of any information on the missing Rita Kaufman and her son, Jack Douglas Kaufman, Paul inquired of the Deputy who took his call about how to contact Jack's neighbor and friend, the young Billy Lewis, who might have some relevant information. Fortunately, because of Billy's parent's frequent run-ins with the law over drunken behavior, the Deputy was able to link Billy Lewis' name with that of his folks, Dennis and Milly Lewis; plus a telephone number.

After his several telephone calls to the Lewises over a period of several days went unanswered, Paul again called the Adams County Sheriff's Department in the hopes that he would reach the same Deputy, and that he would have some further information on how to reach the Lewises. After searching the Dennis Lewis file, the helpful Deputy supplied the name of Dennis' parents, Richard and Elsie Lewis, plus their telephone number.

On Paul's first try, the telephone was answered by Dennis' mother, Elsie. After explaining the purpose of his quest for information, Billy's grandmother tearfully responded that, "Billy is in the hospital…He is seriously ill…He is not doing well…I thought your call was from his grandfather, telling me how he is doing."

"I'm sorry to hear that Billy is ill…so I won't keep you long…I was hoping to talk with Billy, but I can understand that that may not be possible. But maybe Billy's folks might know something about Jack's whereabouts. Do you think that Dennis or Milly might be able to give me a call sometime in the next couple of days…Or do you think if I came to Greenville, they might find the time to talk with me? I'm afraid that time is becoming critical if I am to find Jack."

"I know that Dennis and Milly are quite fond of Jack…He and Billy have become such good friends…But Billy is at the Mayo Clinic in Rochester, Minnesota, as are his parents and his grandpa. I've been too ill myself to make the trip, but I hope to go there to see Billy next week if it's not too late…So you see, I can't guarantee that Dennis or Milly will be able to call you anytime soon, but if you'll give me your phone number, I'll let them know you need to talk with them about Jack. All I know is that Jack's dog showed up at Dennis' house a month or so ago, and when Dennis took her back to Fairways, the place was deserted. Dennis began looking after Mrs. Kaufman's cattle…that is, until Billy took sick a week or so ago. I've got our hired-hand looking after them now."

"That's very kind of you…especially under the circumstances. Had Billy been sick for long?"

"Yes, Billy has had an unexplained neurological condition for several years, but we thought he was getting better…Then about the time Jack's hungry, scared dog showed up at Dennis' place, Billy began to feel poorly…but I think maybe Milly can explain it better to you than I can."

"Thank you. I look forward to hearing from Dennis or Milly… whenever they can find the time to call me. My office number here in Saint Louis is CAbany 3414…I'm here every day but Sunday, and I come back here most evenings. I'll be praying for Billy and for you all. Hopefully you'll hear some good news about Billy, soon. Goodbye."

None of what I've learned from Billy's grandmother is good news… either for Billy or for Jack. There is no way that Jack or Rita would have left the dog, Lady, alone, on her own, unless something tragic had happened, something that required an instant departure from Fairways. But what could that possibly have been? It has to have something to do with Jack's 'evil spirit.' I'm sure that Nell has some information on this that she is withholding from me.

ONE EVENING, WEEKS later, after dinner, back at his office, Paul received the telephone call that he had been expecting, hoping for, but also dreading. The days had grown shorter, and the evenings had grown cooler as the evening sun quickly dipped below the tops of the apartment buildings that stood on the western edge of the parking lot across from Paul's ground-floor office window.

"Hello," Paul said when he answered the telephone on the second ring.

"Hi! Is this Jack's dad," asked a somewhat tipsy voice on the other end.

"Yes, it is."

"Well this is Milly…Milly Lewis…Billy's mom."

"Yes, I know who you are…I've been waiting for your call."

"I'm sorry it has taken so long to call you…But ya see, we've been goin' through a lot out here…with Billy…and all. I guess ya ain't heard, but we done lost Billy a couple of weeks ago. It's been so sad. He struggled so hard…the poor little guy."

"You have my deepest sympathy for your loss…Jack always had such wonderful things to say about Billy…I dare say he loved Billy like a brother. Jack also said how much he thought of you and Dennis. How is Dennis doing…How is he taking Billy's death?"

"Very hard. Yes, very hard. I think Billy's dad loved Billy more than anyone else in this whole wide world…including me. I don't think Dennis has drawn a sober breath since the day we buried Billy. He done pretty good up 'til then…and then it done hit him…it hit him so hard. I done started drinking myself, just to keep Dennis company…There we are, just the two of us cryin' and drinkin'…sit'n there stare'n at Billy's picture for hours on end…Like if'n we was to try hard enough, we'd bring him back ta life."

"I think maybe I can understand how you're feeling right now… me not knowing where Jack is…whether he's alive or dead."

"Oh, yeah, Jack…Ain't you heard nothing about him yet?"

"No. And the worst of it is we don't know where to even begin to look for Jack…It's like he's dropped off of the face of the earth…I hate to impose on you and Dennis at this time of your grief, but can you tell me anything about what you think might have happened…Why Jack and Rita left so quickly…even leaving Lady behind…and bills unpaid?"

"Sure…We love Jack so much…he's such a special boy…so kind to Billy. I would hate to think what it'll do to Jack when he hears that Billy's dead…they was a special pair…always into adventures and mischief. But then maybe you don't want to hear about all that…you just want to know what might have happened to Jack and Rita, right?

"I guess it all started on Memorial Day, when me, Dennis and Billy went to this here picnic, along with Jack, his mom…I guess Rita to you…and this strange lady named Hannah…I think. Well, anyways, the picnic was at some folks named Carlson where they had this big old racing car…and we were listening to a retired flyboy colonel named Peters…or maybe it was Roberts…but any way, he was telling us about some of his adventures flying a P-38 airplane during World War II…and how he was shot down by some Germans flying jet planes. It seemed like he was captured by the Germans and put in somewhere called a Stalag where a German officer who was pretending to be someone else grilled him for information about some pictures this American Colonel had taken…it was all hush-hush stuff.

"Rita and this other woman showed the Colonel some photos of two different men…I think one was named Fritz and the other guy was named Dietrich…ain't that a funny name? Well, the Colonel picked the photo of the man who grilled him as the same man…as the man who he saw in a town in Poland, or maybe it was Germany. Anyways, that was while the Colonel was waiting with other American prisoners to be taken somewheres else by a train that hadn't show'd up.

"Well, when the flyboy Colonel identified the photo as being this Dietrich guy, Jack's mom…Rita…and this other lady…I think her name may have been Hannah…started claiming that the dead soldier who was sharing Jack's body was not the person who he claimed to be…and was the bad guy instead. Oh, I forgot to tell you that Rita had already told Dennis and me that Jack claimed he had the 'spirit' of a dead German sharing his body…Jack had also told Billy the same thing. But you knew that didn't you?"

"Yes, I did…But go on with your story."

"After that day at the picnic, Jack's mom and this other lady wouldn't let Jack out of their sights…Billy said when he would go by Fairways to see Jack, Jack could'n go anywheres with Billy…or any of his other friends…without Rita and this Hannah tag'n along. Try as he might, Jack was unable to persuade his mom to let him leave the house…even to run in the fields, or play in the barn…without one or both of them ladies be'in with him.

"Then one day Jack's mom called me to find out if I'd ever seen Jack act funny…I mean strange…like he wasn't hisself…like he was stronger than he should be…be'n he was so skinny. I done told her that something happened at the County Fair, and I asked her if Jack hadn't told her what took place. But she said, 'No'…so I done told her about how some carnie thugs were after Jack and Billy, and Jack done beat the crap out of three of them…big guys they were.

"After that, Jack's mom clamped down even harder on Jack. This went on for what seemed like a month…Billy going by to see Jack, but Jack couldn't talk his mom and that Hannah lady into let'n him go anywheres without them ladies tag'n along. Then one Saturday afternoon Jack showed up at our house on his bike…with only Lady… his dog…tag'n along. Billy was still doing right fine at the time…and he'n Jack they head out into the woods with Billy carri'n someth'n in a sack…well I later come ta find out it's Dennis' .22 caliber rifle that he'd been teach'n Billy and Jack to shoot.

"So's the two boys were gone for hours…durin which times I could hear the occasional 'pop' sound that the .22 rifle makes. Lady, of course, ain't movin off that porch see'n them boys leave with the rifle, and hear'n them rifle shots. When the boys come back, they ain't laugh'n and a smile'n like they usually does…they was more sad and silent. Billy stands on the porch watch'n Jack ride off on his bike with Lady racing ahead down the road back to Fairways. Billy never seen or heard from Jack again…and we didn't know that Jack and his mom had left Fairways until poor old Lady shows up here...she's at Dennis' folks now."

"Can I ask you about the .22 rifle...Did Jack take it with him when he went back home?"

"I don't think so...Billy woulda caught holy hell from his dad if done let Jack take that rifle...Billy knew the rules...Even if Jack was his best friend...But I really don't know for sure."

"Thanks...Could I ask that you or Dennis check around to make sure...If Jack had taken the .22 rifle back to Fairways then we might be looking at some possible foul play."

"Sure. Yeah, I hadn't thought about that. Can I call you back on that?"

"Thanks. That will be fine. One more thing, can you tell me anything at all about this lady you said was with Jack's mom – was it Hannah? I don't remember Jack, or Rita, ever telling me anything about her."

"I can't say I know much about Hannah...I just seen her that one time. She weren't a looker...kind of plain and mousy...though she coulda looked better when she was a bit younger...though she couldn't be much more than thirty. She talked kinda funny, with an accent. I think I heard Rita say she was a Jew from Poland...and that she had this important-like information about these Germans who'd been killing the Jews. That's how they was able to get photos of the two German soldiers. I just know that Rita sure hung on every word that came out of that Hannah's mouth.

"According to Billy, it was 'cause of Hannah that Jack couldn't be allowed to go around by hisself. Hannah was so sure that the 'evil spirit' in Jack was going to take control of Jack...and then kill both Rita and herself. Billy thought that maybe Hannah was going to do something about the 'evil spirit' that involved Jack. That's why I was so surprised that afternoon when Jack showed up at our house by hisself...He'd either done a lot of fancy talkin' to get them to let him go... or he'd just up and went without them knowing he was gone. If he done what I think he done, then that Hannah would have been madder than a wet hen when Jack showed up back home. Do ya think maybe the 'spirit' done figured out what Hannah might do to him… and Jack…and done ran away with Jack?"

"I don't know. Did Jack say anything to Billy that you may have overheard…Anything to indicate why he and Bill were out shooting the .22 rifle?"

"The only thing I remembered Jack saying to Billy was that he needed to be careful…something bad might happen…and something about 'Jap-eyes…Jap-eyes'.

"Do you know what that 'Jap-eyes' meant? Was it some kind of code-language.?"

"No. They had their own code language, but 'Jap-eyes' weren't no part of it…I think it had something to do with one of them Dennis' stories he would tell them boys about his adventures in the Pacific… something about the Marines blinding the Jap prisoners by poking their eyes out with a sharp knife so they couldn't escape…couldn't see to do harm to the guys guarding them."

After a long pause, when Paul began to think that Milly had hung up on him, Paul said, " Milly, that's really helpful," and then added, "I just realized that you are paying for this long distance phone call…and we've been talking for quite a while. So I'm going to let you go. But, I want to thank you so much for talking with me…and for the help-ful information. I also want to again tell you how sorry I am for your loss…Please, take care of Billy's dad, Dennis…and tell him that I un-derstand some of his agony. Some time I'd like to sit down with both of you and have a drink or two together…to grieve together about our two boys."

"Yeah, Dennis and me would sure like that. I hope you find Jack… soon and well."

CHAPTER 43

PAUL AND NELL WERE STILL BARELY TALKING TO each other. At times, when he was particularly melancholy about Jack, Paul was tempted to tell Nell what he had learned about Jack during his telephone conversation with Milly; especially the part about how the 'spirit' had taken over Jack's body at the County Fair, and of how dangerous Jack had become. He thought about telling her of his alarming vision of Jack overpowering Rita and Hannah, leading him to consider calling the Adams County Sheriff to urge a more serious investigation, a thorough search of the house and out-buildings at Fairways; and his thoughts about calling Dr. Kaufman, asking him about this Hannah person. But he resisted the temptation; he kept his thoughts to himself.

Nell, too, had many thoughts about Jack despite her best efforts to push any thoughts of Jack from her mind. She continued to dwell on the possibility of Jack's possession as detailed in the writings she had found. With Jack missing, her only proof of Jack's possession by an 'evil spirit' was contained in those writings; and she was adamant that no one else would examine the writings, in whole or in part: there were simply too many passages that implicated her role in Jack's possession and/or his aberrant fantasies. She tried to assuage her feelings of guilt by convincing herself that she was just 'doing the best I can'.

———

WHEN PAUL DID not, as he feared would happen, hear from Milly after a week following their telephone conversation about the .22 rifle, Paul made his call to the Adams County Sheriff's Department. In his call he outlined to Deputy Clark – the Deputy who had sent Paul the note, photos and snippets of some kind of writing – what Milly has told him about the .22 rifle, the restrictions on Jack's being alone, and reminded the Deputy of the possible role of the lady named Hannah, and his growing concerns about foul play. Deputy Clark was at once skeptical, but intrigued. But before he could authorize a further search of Fairways, he told Paul that he would need an authorization from the owner to do so. Paul knew that Rita and her brother Oliver purchased the property for their mother, Doddy; but he did not recall in whose name the property was titled. With Rita now missing, and Doddy deep into senility, Paul told the Deputy that he would need to obtain the ownership information from his brother-in-law, Captain Oliver Douglas.

It took some time, and it took some doing, before Paul was successful in tracking down Captain Oliver Joseph Douglas, USNR. That quest was not nearly as difficult as was Paul's effort in formulating what he was going to tell Ollie once they made contact. *How do you explain to someone who is unfamiliar with what has been happening for several years that his sister, Rita, is missing; that Fairways has been uninhabited for months; that his nephew Jack is either possessed or insane; that Rita, a lady named Hannah, and even Jack, may have been harmed or, worse yet, killed, perhaps at the hand of Jack; and why no one has bothered to tell him about these events for almost six months?* Paul elected to take the most difficult course; he would tell Ollie everything he knew that had happened, everything he suspected had happened, everything that he believed still needed to be done, and be prepared to take a tongue lashing for waiting so long before telling such an improbable tale.

After concluding the usual pleasantries, Paul said, "Ollie, I think we may have a serious problem involving Rita and Jack," and then Paul proceeded to detail all of the facts, suspicions, speculations, concluding with what he needed from Ollie. Ollie listened patiently, quietly, throughout Paul's lengthy discourse, occasionally muttering various 'sailor-type' obscenities.

When Paul concluded his explanation, Ollie – reverting to his naval rank and training – remarked, "Thanks for that report Paul. I thought I'd heard everything until this...It's the most incredible story I have ever heard...and I've heard some cockamamie stories in my time... But I've got to believe you...You're not the type to tell tall tales...and this story is really too bizarre not to be true. I can certainly understand why you haven't contacted me sooner...It takes some guts to tell such an improbable story. But like I said...I believe you.

"Now, what can I do to help find out what the hell really happened...and what can you tell me about Doddy...is she okay...I know you said that she's in that nursing home...but when's the last time Nell bothered to go see her? And are the cattle being tended to? And I think you told me that Lady is all right.

"Doddy is still being taken care of at the nursing home, but I haven't taken Nell to see her since we got the call about the unpaid bill...that's my fault and I'll see that Nell sees her soon. The elder Mr. Lewis is having someone tend to the cattle, and he has taken Lady into his home. His son Dennis...and his wife Milly...probably have more attachment to Lady...but they're so messed up right now with the death of their son Billy...that I wouldn't want to leave Lady in their care."

"So, I guess that leaves talking to the Sheriff about searching the place as the next topic on our agenda...Or is there something else that you want some help on?"

"Well, Ollie, in addition to getting the Sheriff to search Fairways... which may be a waste of time...We need to track down this Hannah person...to find out who she is, where she really comes from and what she has to do with Jack and Rita's disappearance. The Kaufmans, well at least Gabby Kaufman...who is the one that talked Rita into bringing Hannah into her home...have 'clamed-up'...acting like she has no interest in...or responsibility for... what has happened. I thought about calling Dr. Kaufman directly, but I don't know if he'll be any more helpful."

"You say this Hannah person is a Polish Jew refugee from the War...and that she has some connection with intelligence concerning

Germans that committed the atrocities on the Jews?"

"Yes…But remember that I heard that from Milly Lewis…who right now may not be the most reliable source for such information."

"I understand…but it's the only lead we have. Look, Paul, here's what I propose to do: First, I'll call the Adams County Sheriff and, as the co-owner of Fairways, will instruct him…authorize him…to make a thorough search of every inch of Fairways…and send me a copy of his report…which I will share with you. Next, I'll try to find out something about this Hannah person…Do you have a last name? If not, then I'll have someone I know in the Immigration Service call the Kaufmans, and get it from them – they'll have to talk to the Immigration folks. Once I have her full name, I'll turn it over to my friends in Naval Intelligence.

"The Navy has some pretty important stuff going on with Israel… providing them with fighter aircraft and stuff…and my guys work closely with the Israeli Intelligence Agency…the Mossad. I'll bet those Israeli intelligence guys will be more than happy to tell us who she is, and all other particulars about her, just to stay on our good side. I have the feeling that if the Israelis really think that Jack is harboring the spirit of a dead German Officer who was involved in eradicating Jews, their intelligence folks will want to look into that possibility. This Hannah may be their agent on this…If so, we might get some actual leads on Rita and Jack's fate.

"But, Paul," Ollie continued, "here's the thing…I believe you…I believe everything you've told me. But frankly, I've got to be able to convince my Naval Intelligence types that there may be a real connection with the Israelis. We need some corroborating evidence…someone, or something that can back up your story, your suspicions. I'm with you…I don't think that the Lewises make reliable witnesses. But what about that Air Force Colonel you mentioned who picked out the bad Kraut from the good Kraut…You know the fellow from the Memorial Day picnic who said which guy was the *Luftwaffe* officer and which guy was the *S.S. Oberst.* "

"Yes, I think his name was Peter Roberts…or maybe it was Robert Peters…but Milly Lewis wasn't too clear on that. I don't even know if the picnic was at his place or whether he was a guest."

"Ollie," Paul interjected, "I hadn't mentioned this sooner, principally because it is pure speculation, but also because it involves Nell…I believe that Nell found something important at Fairways on the day we first went there trying to figure out why Rita and Jack were missing. While I was outside with the Deputy looking around the outbuildings Nell was alone inside the house looking around. I have asked her if she found anything, but she would never tell me yes or no. But for about ten nights after we returned home Nell locked herself in her bedroom and the light was on until one or two in the morning each night. I was convinced that she had something she was reading… and my suspicions were further raised…when I received a package from the Sheriff containing some snap-shots of Rita and Jack, as well as some pages from a school tablet that Jack had written on. Before Nell came home from work that evening, I found a key to unlock the bedroom door. I searched around trying not to disturb anything, but I found nothing. I still think she has something…She mentioned a couple of events…even something that Jack wrote to me…that she would have had no knowledge of unless she had found something that recorded those things."

"Do you have any idea why Nell would not share whatever it is she found with you?"

"I think that there may be something in what Nell's hiding that she thinks is not very flattering to her. Nell is convinced that Jack hates her…and he probably has good reason to hate her…She never wanted Jack, even as a baby…and she has always treated him pretty badly… Rita was really outspoken about Nell's parenting skills…or her lack thereof."

"I'll see what I can do to make Nell cough up whatever she found, whatever she is hiding. She's always been scared of me…so I think if I bully her hard enough she'll come clean…But if you are correct…that she might feel that she'll be embarrassed by something in what she is hiding, she's likely to destroy it…whatever it is. While I would love to see what it is that she's hiding, we just have to assume for the time being that we'll have to move on ahead without it. As for this Air Force

Colonel…I don't think it will be too hard for the Naval Intelligence guys to find a World War II P-38 pilot named Peters or Roberts that was in a Stalag in Poland. His testimony could be most useful."

"Thanks, Ollie, for all that you are doing…I'm at wits end…I can't turn up anything that makes me feel like we'll ever find Jack or Rita."

"No problem, Paul…We're family."

CHAPTER 44

SOME TIME EARLIER, PROBABLY IN LATE-AUGUST,
before Paul and Nell had discovered that Jack and Rita were missing, on a sun-baked stretch of back-road somewhere east of Mexico City, a dusty, wood-sided Ford station wagon wound its way east towards the port-city of Veracruz. The driver was a female: with her in the front-seat was a teenage boy wearing sunglasses, his head drooping forward, his wrists tied in front of him; a bundle of something wrapped in a canvas tarpaulin lay on the back seat. A few small duffle-type bags and an army-surplus trenching shovel were placed haphazardly in the cargo area.

Nestled next to the driver was a leather satchel containing a Walther P-38 9mm semi-automatic pistol with three spare clips, a dagger with a nine-inch blade covered by a leather-sheath, a detailed road-map of Mexico, several bundles of U.S. $100 bills, a list of Greek-registered cargo ships arriving and leaving from the seaport at Veracruz – with names of those ships known to make stops at the Israeli port of Haifa circled in red, and two Israeli passports – one issued to a Hannah Wolkowitz, born in Poznan, Poland, and the other issued to a Jack Kaufman, born in Saint Louis, Missouri.

When the driver was convinced that the road was deserted in both directions, that the area was desolate, she pulled the Ford station wagon off onto a dusty set of tire tracks leading away from the road back into the foot-hills. At a spot where the road was securely out of sight, the driver brought the vehicle to a halt. After checking to see that the teenager's restraints were secure, and that he was adequately sedated, the driver opened her door, exited the vehicle, stretching her arms and legs as she did so, shaking the dust that had blown in the car window from her arms, wiping the dust from her face and neck.

Scanning the area dotted with mesquite, cactus, and scrub plants, the driver walked stiffly towards the rear of the vehicle, lifted the rear-hatch, lowered the tail-gate, and extracted the trenching shovel. Returning to the driver's-side of the Ford station wagon, opening the rear passenger door, the driver reached in, pulled the tarpaulin-wrapped bundle – the size and shape of a medium-sized person – out of the vehicle, dumping it on the barren ground. In a nearby grove of bushes and small trees, the driver excavated a shallow grave with the trenching shovel, dragged the bundle to the grave, and placed the bundle in it, covering it with the dirt and any available rocks and stones. Having completed her task, the driver returned to the station wagon, replaced the tools in the cargo area, closed the tail-gate and hatch, and then moved towards the driver's door, closing the rear passenger door as she passed by. She climbed into the driver's seat, started the engine and quickly drove away.

I'm so sorry, Rita, that it has had to end like this. I admired you, Rita... You were a good, brave, loving woman. But your valiant defense of your son, Jack – when I elected to render him ineffective – left me with no other alternative but to kill you. If I hadn't, I knew that you would, at some point, try again to prevent me from carrying out my mission. And you knew from the beginning Rita that my instructions were to bring Dietrich Muenster to the justice he so richly deserves...that I would have to bring him to Israel in any way that I am able...And blinding Jack was the only way that I could be sure that Dietrich Muenster would be unable to overpower me if he took control of Jack's body, and tried to escape...And killing you is what some might call an "unavoidable consequence."

Pulling the Ford station wagon back onto the main road, Hannah reflected back on all that had happened to her, to Rita, to Jack, to have brought them to this point. It seemed like months had passed since the Memorial Day picnic when Dietrich Muenster had been unmasked; shown to be the "monster," the "evil spirit" that he was. Hannah knew then that she would have to get Dietrich Muenster to

Israel in Jack's body. She just didn't know – she certainly didn't plan – that she would have to eliminate Rita in the process. Jack's life, of course, was a different issue; she had to keep him alive at all costs. This was more difficult than she had imagined; how was she to prevent the "evil spirit" from taking control of Jack's body...or more to the point... how was she going to keep the "evil spirit" from overpowering her and Rita once he had taken control of Jack's body? What could she do to handicap Jack in some way that even if the "evil spirit" were to take control of Jack's body he could not use Jack's body to hurt, harm or overpower them?

It was in early August when matters came to a head. Despite their best efforts to keep Jack under strict, constant surveillance, Jack managed to slip away one Saturday afternoon. He was gone for several hours. Up until that time Jack remained unfettered, just locked in his bedroom where he spent most of his time writing away in those cheap school tablets that Rita had purchased for him in town.

Jack had been confined to his bedroom – under lock and key – after Hannah, who was searching for possible weapons, had discovered one of Jack's writings – the one in which he described the violent altercation at the County Fair with the carnival workers, in which the three thugs were overpowered, with one of them being almost killed. This episode was confirmed by Jack's friend Billy's mom, Milly, who had seen what Jack done to the most seriously beaten thug. For Hannah and Rita the episode presented the clearest evidence yet that not only could and would Muenster take control of Jack's body – which he had been doing occasionally for years – but that when Muenster took control, he imparted such strength and skill into Jack's body that Jack became a lethal weapon, a dangerous threat. Hannah had confronted Jack with his writing, but he only reiterated what he had described there: he could not explain how it happened.

"Do you think," asked Hannah, "that it was Muenster who did it... that he had control of your body?"

"I don't know...But, probably...I have never asked him about it... I've been afraid to ask him...I didn't really want to know for sure. When I told him that I was now scared of him...being the 'evil spirit'...he said he understood...him lying to me, and all...but that he is a changed 'spirit' and he wants to be my friend."

"Do you believe that he has changed...and that he can be your friend?"

'I don't know...I am so confused...I just want to be free of all this...I want to go back to where it was before you told me who the 'spirit' really is. I liked Fritz...I trusted him...He was my friend."

"That is simply not going to happen," said Hannah. "In fact, based upon what happened at the County Fair...what Muenster...using your body...did to those carnival workers, I'm afraid that your freedom will need to be further restricted."

"Mom," Jack implored, "Isn't there something you can do to help me?"

"Jack, I'd love to help you...But we're all in danger here. Please indulge us...We can't let you wander around free."

IT WAS AGAINST this background that Jack returned to Fairways following his surreptitious visit to Billy Lewis. Hannah was livid with anger; while Rita was fearful – knowing that it would now take more than simply locking Jack in his bedroom at night – and concerned for Jack – not knowing what Hannah would insist be done to render Jack harmless even if Muenster did take control of his body.

"Who is responsible for your escape," demanded Hannah. "Was it you...or was it the Muenster...Did he take control of your body?"

"No. No, it was me. I just had to get away from here...I needed to see Billy. I've missed him so. He makes me laugh...I don't get to laugh anymore."

"Did you get anything at Billy's...A knife, a gun ...Anything that the Muenster could use to harm us with?" Hannah asked in a low, almost whisper-like voice...as if she thought Muenster might not hear what she was asking if he was 'plugged-in', listening.

"He says he wants to be called 'Dietrich', not 'the Muenster'...He says that 'the Muenster' sounds too much like 'Monster'...and he says he's not a 'Monster' anymore."

After Hannah had stopped laughing, she asked again, "Did you get any weapons?"

"No...Not that I'm aware of ...But I am certain that I was in control the whole time. If Dietrich was in control, I'd know it...and so would Billy."

"Don't call him Dietrich," Hannah commanded sternly. "Don't ever try to personalize him...He's not your friend...Despite what he is telling you, he is a 'monster'. Do you hear me? I never want to hear you use his first name again...Only call him Muenster...or better, yet...'the Monster'...like you did when you first learned that he had lied to you...that he had killed Fritz and all of his family...and all of those innocent Jews."

"Hannah, please," said Rita. "You are scaring Jack...It is not necessary. Jack's not the one at fault here...He's as innocent as those poor Jews you are so concerned about. We can't be punishing Jack for what the 'evil spirit' inside of him has done...what Muenster did."

"Bullshit!" exclaimed Hannah. "Jack's body is also Muenster's body...You'll have to admit that in the blink of an eye Muenster can take total control of that sweet-faced boy standing in front of us... turning him into a killer...turning him into the monster that is inside of him...A monster too strong, too clever, too evil for us to restrain or subdue him if he wants to...if he feels sufficiently threatened to defend himself...just like he did at the County Fair."

"Then why go about threatening his alter-ego Jack as you are doing right now...How do you know that he isn't listening to all of this?"

"You're right...We'll talk about this later. But for now...since the Muenster may be listening...I want Jack bound hand and foot...and locked in his bedroom until we can figure out a better way to keep Muenster...and Jack...under our power."

LATER, WHEN JACK was securely tied and locked in his bedroom, Rita and Hannah resumed their conversation about Jack and his 'evil' spirit.

"Are you sure that Jack can't get out of his locked bedroom...I can see Muenster breaking down the door, or jumping out of a window," said Hannah.

"The door is quite substantial...stout white oak as I recall...and the windows are some fifteen feet above the ground, making it perilous for someone attempting to jump without the use of their hands."

"Well, I don't like the idea of staying here...trying to baby-sit a monster. This has to be considered a temporary arrangement," Hannah observed, sipping from her cup of strong-brewed coffee, then adding, "We can't keep Jack and the Muenster here for long...It just won't work...Eventually...actually sooner than later...we will need to find somewhere where Jack can roam about without fear that even if the Muenster takes control, he can't escape or harm anyone."

"That sounds like he'll either have to be placed in a mental hospital or in a prison," Rita remarked sourly. "I can't do that to Jack."

"I agree...So that leaves placing Jack with folks that are accustomed to handling situations like this...at places in remote locations...even overseas."

"But it has to be somewhere where I can live with Jack or at least visit him on a regular basis...I can't just abandon him."

"I don't know that we have such an option."

"I'm beginning to think," Rita said, "that you already have some place in mind. Someplace that will take care of your needs...and the needs of your superiors...while sacrificing my needs...and Jack's freedom...forever. I don't like it."

"Well, then you tell me...what choices do we have? I didn't come all this way to find the 'evil Muenster'...and then just to let him escape because we can't control Jack or him. I can't let him get away to continue his evil program of exterminating my race. I am under strict orders, and I have sworn an oath, to bring the Muenster to justice... even if it means sacrificing Jack's freedom in process."

Rita wanted to scream out in protest, but was speechless. She knew that what she had so long been refusing to accept as a possibility was now a reality; that Jack was lost, and that there was nothing she could do to give back either his freedom or a normal existence. *If only*

I can do what I can to keep him alive.

AT DINNER A few days later, Rita was feeding Jack – his hands still tied together, lying useless in his lap – as if he were a small boy; the baby Rita never had. Despite Rita's best efforts to keep the atmosphere light and cheery, Jack was sullen, refusing to speak, avoiding eye-contact with Rita; reserving his most hateful glares for Hannah who, whenever she spoke to Rita, acted as if Jack was not even in the room.

"While you do the dishes," Hannah said, "I'll be out in the tack room getting some stuff together that we'll need for the trip."

In the tack room Hannah located the trenching shovel, several lengths of heavy twine rope, and a couple of canvas tarpaulins, carrying them into the garage, placing them in cargo section of the Ford station wagon. From the back-seat of the station wagon, Hannah removed a large, paper-wrapped shipping box – a box she had picked up at the Greenville post office that morning – and carried it into the house.

"What's in the box?" Rita asked from the sink.

"Oh, just something I ordered," Hannah replied, adding, "Just something for the trip."

CHAPTER 45

AS EXPECTED, THE ADAMS COUNTY SHERIFF'S Department's 'by-the-book' investigation of Fairways – having already discovered the snapshots of Rita and Jack, and the few pages of handwriting on the lined school-tablets on an earlier return visit – uncovered nothing else of note, certainly nothing to suggest criminal activity; only things that they already knew or suspected: that the inhabitants had left in a hurry, as demonstrated by the lack of arranging for the ongoing care of the property, its animals and the pet dog, Lady. There were no signs revealing why the three inhabitants left in a hurry; no indications pointing to where they were going. Even the few brochures for resorts and dude ranches found in Jack's bedroom were empty leads. The only thing missing was the Ford station wagon; but a nationwide search conducted by state police turned up nothing there either. There was not even any indication that they took much in the way of clothing with them; other than what they maybe were wearing.

The interviews with neighbors and friends in Greenville, other than with the Lewises – both the elder and the younger – yielded no clues. The investigators were baffled by the strange tales of 'evil spirits', 'possession', the mysterious Hannah; especially as told by the slightly inebriated Dennis and Milly Lewis. In the end, the report prepared by the Adams County Sheriff's Department, a copy of which was sent to Captain Douglas, concluded that there was no evidence of a crime committed at Fairways.

When Ollie received the Sheriff Department's report of its investigation, he read the conclusion first, scanned the previous four pages without much interest. Instead of sending Paul a copy of the report, Ollie picked up his telephone, called Paul at his office.

"I got the report from the Sheriff's Department," Ollie began, "and bottom-line, as we anticipated, it finds no evidence of foul play at Fairways, although it confirms your theory that Rita and Jack left in a hurry. The only mention of Hannah is contained in the report of the Sheriff's interview with the Dennis and Milly, which as you would expect is a rambling, drunken tale of 'evil spirits' and of dead German soldiers, real and imagined. Speaking of Hannah, my intelligence guys are making some head-way with the Israelis on who she is, what she's up to, etcetera. But until we can get a better fix on where Hannah is right now, they're not giving us much hope on finding Jack and Rita."

"How in the hell are we going to find that out, when we have no clues on where to look...I think those folks in Israeli intelligence service are giving us the run-around...I think I'd have better luck getting information out of Nell. By-the-way, have you ever called Nell? We're off to see Doddy next weekend. This might be a good time for you to use your powers of persuasion on Nell to soften her up so that I can use the long drive to get her to talk about what she is hiding."

"Do you really think that there is something out there that we haven't already considered? We know about Jack's German 'spirit'... we know that the German 'spirit' is the 'evil spirit'...we know that the 'evil spirit' can take control of Jack...we know that Hannah is a Jew who is interested in the 'evil spirit', and may have an Israeli intelligence connection. What we don't know is whether the 'evil spirit' has taken full possession of Jack...thereby endangering Rita and Hannah, or whether Hannah has taken control of Jack, and thereby controlling the 'evil spirit', and is taking Jack to where the Israelis can dispose of the 'evil spirit'. Have I missed anything?"

"Yes. Where does Rita fit into all of this? Isn't it likely that under either scenario, Rita's life is in danger? And isn't Jack's life likely to be forfeited?"

"Sure. You're correct, but what can we do about it...except to find Jack, Rita, or Hannah. And I can't imagine that Nell found anything that will help us there. I'll put my money on Hannah being the key to finding Jack and Rita. If Hannah is a Mossad 'katsas', then we are up against one tough, ruthless bitch."

"You've mentioned this Mossad before, and I meant to ask then, 'What is this 'Mossad'," asked Paul. "What is a 'katsas'?"

"The 'Mossad' is the Israeli equivalent to our Central Intelligence Agency...the C.I.A. The word 'Mossad' is short for a Hebrew phrase: something like 'HaMossad, something, something', which translates as the 'Institute for Intelligence and Special Operations'. It is Israeli Prime Minister David Ben-Gurion's personal intelligence gathering agency. Its motto is: 'For by wise guidance you can wage war'. And a 'katsas' is a Mossad 'field intelligence officer'. These Mossad agents are ruthless, and they are authorized to capture, kill or assassinate Israeli enemies anywhere in the world they can find them."

WITHIN A WEEK of that telephone conversation, Ollie telephoned Paul to update him on what Naval Intelligence had learned through their locating and interviewing the Air Force Colonel, Peter 'Pete' Roberts. According to what was reported to Captain Douglas, Pete Roberts not only confirmed the story that Milly Lewis had told Paul – that he identified the two German officers – Colonel Roberts went on to tell the interviewers what he knew about the two Germans, including their identities: the *S.S. Oberst* is Dietrich Muenster; and the *Luftwaffe* officer is Fritz von Bruckner. Muenster was the one who interviewed Pete Roberts at the Stalag, pretending to be von Bruckner. Muenster was also the *S.S. Oberst* that Pete Roberts observed in Spremberg accompanied by a beautiful blond woman who may have been Hannah's sister.

"In Pete Robert's opinion," Captain Douglas reported, "*S.S. Oberst* Dietrich Muenster was not, and cannot possibly be, a figment of Jack's imagination. Colonel Robert's opinion was borne out through a thorough review of records maintained by the U.S. Military, the West German government, and the Jewish organizations charged with tracking down Germans responsible for the extermination of the Jews during the Nazi regime. The official records reported that Dietrich Muenster was allegedly shot and killed by his mistress on or about the day the Germans surrendered, but that his body has never been located…she claimed she buried him in a shallow grave in a grove of trees.

"The records also report that on the day Muenster is supposed to have been killed, an airplane filled with gold and silver jewelry and bullion, and several of Muenster's known associates, left the spot where Muenster was allegedly assassinated, but crashed and burned while trying to fly over the Bavarian Alps into Switzerland. Muenster's body was not among the bodies of the dead escapees that were recovered. This absence of Muenster's body has fostered a rumor that Muenster is still alive, in hiding, and waiting for an appropriate opportunity to make his return to carry out the *Fuehrer's* master plan for exterminating the Jews.

"So, Paul," Ollie continued, "we may now have to conclude that this Dietrich Muenster is in charge…that he has taken control of Jack's body…that disguised in the body of a teenage American boy, he is trying to make it to where ever he can profitably resume his infamous behavior against the Jews…and that Rita and Hannah are now his captives, or that he may have already killed them. Hannah may not, after-all, be the villain in this piece.

"Oh, and get this," Ollie continued, "the mistress/assassin, whose German papers said she was Ingrid Faust, is actually a Polish Jew, named Ruth Wolkowitz. She not only turns out to have been a spy for the Polish underground and the Jewish partisans during the German occupation…she has the same last name as Hannah's.

504 | **JOHN FONS**

CHAPTER 46

AFTER THE DINNER DISHES HAD BEEN ATTENDED
to, Rita and Hannah escorted the bound Jack upstairs to Rita's bedroom. Preparing Jack for bed was a complex chore. Given that Jack's
hands and feet were bound together, getting Jack undressed, getting
him into his pajamas, just putting him into his bed required coordination. Over the past weeks Hannah and Rita had developed a routine
which had worked successfully: After removing his trousers, and putting on his pajama bottoms, Rita would bind Jack's legs together at
the ankles. Upon completion of this step, Rita would stand and take
hold of Jack's right arm while Hannah untied Jack's hands and remove
Jack's left arm from his shirt that had already been unbuttoned. She
would then place Jack's left arm into the sleeve of his pajamas. They
would then change places and do the right arm; always making certain that Jack's free arm was held firmly. Once his pajama-top was on,
Hannah would tie Jack's hands together. Then they would help him
hop into his bedroom, and lift him into his bed.

They were at the point where Hannah was inserting Jack's left arm
into the pajama top when the Muenster took control of Jack's body,
screaming in his own voice: "I will not let this happen! I must complete my mission! I will kill you both."

As he was screaming this message, Muenster yanked his left hand
out of Hannah's grasp, striking her on the side of the head with what
was only a glancing blow; but strong enough to knock Hannah backwards, causing her to collide with Rita's desk. In his next movement,
Muenster ripped his right arm out of Rita's grip, and began grappling
with a frightened, paralyzed Rita, managing to capture her head and

neck in the crook of his right arm, while managing to keep his balance. Only dazed by the blow to the side of her head, Hannah lunged at Muenster, grabbing at his left arm in the hope of knocking him off balance. But Muenster avoided Hannah's grasp and countered with a backhand slap at her face. Hannah managed to duck under the slap and, seeing that his swing at her had thrown Muenster off balance, took a step back and kicked out with her right foot, hitting Muenster in his groin. This had the intended effect of causing Muenster to let go of Rita's head, to instinctively to pitch forward reaching for his painful groin area.

In that same instant, Hannah reached for the desk set and removed the dagger-like letter opener from its scabbard. With the dagger in her right hand, Hannah grabbed a handful of Muenster's hair with her left hand, and pulled Muenster's head up to where his face was almost upright. She then quickly, but carefully slipped the point of the letter opener into Muenster's left eye, just far enough to pierce the eye, but not enough to enter his brain. Muenster screamed in pain and letting loose of his groin area brought both of hands to his face, covering both eyes.

Seeing what had just occurred, seeing only Jack and not the 'evil Muenster', Rita started screaming, "No! No! Please, no! Don't kill Jack! Don't blind him!"

"Don't you worry," replied a panting Hannah, "I won't kill him... but I have to render him harmless."

Releasing her handful of Muenster's hair, Hannah stepped back, letting Muenster pitch forward onto the floor, blood streaming down his face from the area of his damaged left eye and eye-lid. Then handing Rita the letter opener with the onyx handle – Jack's cursed Christmas gift – Hannah said to Rita, "Here take this...Watch him carefully...Stab him if he tries to get up...but just enough to hurt him. I need to get the 'box'. There are some things in it that we can use to subdue the Muenster."

Returning to Rita's bedroom with the box, Hannah set it on Rita's desk and started picking through it, lifting out a syringe and several vials from which she selected one, filled the syringe, and injected the still prostrate Muenster in the side of his neck.

"There...I've sedated him...He should remain unconscious for a while."

Turning to look at Rita, who was clearly in shock, her eyes looking longingly at her boy, Jack, Hannah said, "Rita, for god's sake, you saw what just happened...Jack is gone...the Muenster has taken over...he has taken control of Jack. In retrospect, I should have seen this coming...I should have sedated Jack before we started preparing him for bed...I had thought about doing it, but I knew you would resist it...So, now see what has happened...But believe me, this is not what I wanted to happen...We're just lucky he didn't kill us.

"For our purposes, Jack is now gone...His body may still be here, but it is no longer Jack's body...It belongs to the Muenster. You can no longer look at that body and think that it is Jack lying there. It is not Jack...it is a monster...A monster who will do whatever it can to escape...to escape from me. The Muenster knows why I am here. He hates me...And he will kill me if he can...And you if he has to...If killing you will accomplish his escape."

"But what are we going to do," asked a thoroughly upset Rita. "We can't stay here...Won't Jack die if we don't get him medical help?"

"How many times do I have to tell you...that body is no longer Jack's body...It is Dietrich Muenster. And the Muenster will not die...We are going to get him medical help."

"Where? Surely, not in town...How will we explain what happened to...Jack."

"Of course not here, Rita," responded Hannah ignoring Rita's use of Jack's name..."in Kansas City."

"But why in Kansas City?"

"Because that's where Dr. Kaufman lives...that's where our trip begins...Now start putting some things in a bag, including some of Jack's things."

"We can't just get up and leave...What about Lady...the cattle...the horses...the milk cow...the farm?"

"They'll just have to take care of themselves...Lady will find Billy soon enough...Now get packing while I tidy up here, clean up the blood…and get my stuff together."

"I won't do it," said a clearly angry, unhappy Rita. "I can't just walk out of here…it's my life…And what about Doddy…what'll she do?"

"Okay, here's how it is…You can stay here…and never see Jack again…or you can come with me now!"

"You mean what's left of him…He's just a boy…and now a half-blind one at that…I'm surprised that you didn't poke his other eye out while you were at it."

"It crossed my mind once he was sedated…But I decided to teach him…and you…a lesson. Unless you both cooperate…and do what I tell you to do…without hesitation…I will poke out his good eye…Let that be my warning to you!"

IT WAS WELL past midnight by the time Hannah had assured herself that everything was tidy and neat…with no evidence of a struggle…or of her ever being there. Rita had packed a bag containing only those things Hannah had approved of…some of her things, some of Jack's things. Hannah had put the bags in the station wagon, together with a satchel containing the contents of the 'box'. It took both of them to carry the body of the still unconscious and bound teenage boy to the car and place it on the back-seat, covering the body with one of the tarpaulins.

Rita made sure that all of the lights were turned off, the doors and windows were locked and latched, and that Lady had plenty of food and water in a covered area by the tack room. Leaning down she gave Lady a kiss on her black nose and a pat on the head saying, "You take care of things, Lady…and if we don't come back soon, you go on to Billy's house…he and Milly will take care of you."

Hannah was already in the driver's seat of the big Ford station wagon when Rita climbed in and closed the door. Even in the dark, Hannah knew that Rita was crying…a low mournful sound. *Have a good cry Rita…for Lady, for Fairways, for 'lost' Jack, and for yourself…for your life that will never be the same again.*

CHAPTER 47

DAWN WAS BREAKING WHEN THE BIG FORD wagon pulled to a stop on the circular driveway fronting the Kaufmans' stately home. Even at this early-hour, the occupants of the station wagon were expected; Hannah having called ahead before leaving Fairways. The still heavily-sedated Muenster was carried into the house and placed in a first-floor spare bedroom where his damaged left eye and eye-lid were attended to by Dr. Kaufman by administering antibiotics to the eye – which was beyond repair, and by applying a few stitches to close the wound to the eye-lid. After another injection of a powerful sedative, Hannah restrained Muenster's feet and hands. Rita was supplied a sleeping pill which Dr. Kaufman assured her was just to help her relieve the anxiety, to get to sleep, and then was sent off to bed. Once Rita had fallen to sleep, Dr. Kaufman injected her with a strong sedative, and locked her bedroom door upon exiting.

When Hannah awoke from her cat-nap, she, Dr. Kaufman and Gabby gathered in his study to discuss the plans for "resettling" *Oberst* Muenster. These plans had been prepared by the Mossad after they were advised of the Muenster's unmasking, and were delivered to Hannah in the 'box'. Now that the Muenster – known as the 'package' to the Mossad – had made his move, acknowledging his true identity and mission, and was securely restrained, the plan identified specific steps for its delivery into the hands of the Mossad, including a final 'resettlement' destination, pre-arranged transiting points and time-frames, safe locations, and a courier – Hannah.

"We have been very fortunate," began Dr. Kaufman, "to have located the 'spirit' of the evil Muenster in Jack's body. You cannot fully appreciate, Hannah, the excitement, the joy...the absolute sense of re-lief when Gabby and I passed on your news to our friends when you informed us that you had exposed the 'spirit' in Jack's body as being *Oberst* Muenster. Our friends were beginning to believe the persistent rumors that your sister Ruth had not in fact killed Dietrich Muenster, and that he had escaped...leading to the belief that he was planning to make a return sometime in the future. They were ecstatic that they could now quash that rumor once-and-for-all.

"Just think of the harm, the damage, the evil that the bastard could have done to us Jews if he had been able to move about undetected in the body of a young American boy...well, a teenager...or even as an adult. The Muenster would have had a new lease on life...He would have gained twenty, thirty...hell, even fifty years to perfect his plans, to recruit disciples, to move around anywhere unhampered. Just think of the horrible impact he could have had on the new-state of Israel, the Jewish-settlers if he were to join forces with the Arabs in Palestine and throughout the Middle-East. He could have become the Nazi-version of 'Lawrence of Arabia'."

"Can I ask," said Gabby. "Where are you directed to deliver the 'package'?"

"I don't think that you really want to know...for your protection, our friends' protection, for my protection. In fact, I don't believe that I am at liberty to tell you, even if I thought it was necessary...That is why our friends sent the 'box' and the instructions in the 'box' to me. We don't want to put you in the awkward position of having to invent a lie in the event you are asked...probed about the matter."

"I assume," said Dr. Kaufman "that you have the 'box' with you... that you did not leave anything incriminating behind at Fairways."

"Better yet, I have transferred all of the materials and equipment in the 'box' to the satchel I have here at my side. I disposed of the 'box' somewhere between here and Greenville, in a fashion where it cannot be identified...or traced."

"Then there is nothing else for us to do here. As soon as you feel sufficiently rested, we'll get you on your way...I assume that you will take Rita with you...she can't stay here."

"Of course...I have passports for all of us, including Rita, if I need it."

"Good...The station wagon is in the garage where I parked it after I went and had it filled with gasoline, something I'm not used to do-ing...But under the circumstances, we have given the help the day off. When it becomes dark, we'll further sedate the Muenster and Rita, and then help you get them into the station wagon...sending you on your way.

CHAPTER 48

THE FIRST SOLID CLUE IN SOLVING THE MYSTERIOUS
disappearance of Jack, Rita and Hannah occurred when a concerned resident in a ramshackle neighborhood bordering the port area of Veracruz, Mexico, reported to the Mexican police the presence of an abandoned Ford Station wagon that had been languishing on a side-street for weeks. In time, the Mexican authorities contacted their U.S. counter-parts, tracing the vehicle through its Missouri license plates, finding it to be registered to a Henrietta Kaufman of Greenville, Missouri, who, in turn, had been reported as a missing person through a bulletin issued by the Adams County Sheriff's Department.

Within hours of his receipt of the report from the Sheriff's Department on finding Rita's station wagon in Veracruz, Mexico, Captain Oliver Joseph Douglas, USNR, had passed on this startling information to his contacts in Naval Intelligence, who had already been pursuing various leads, hoping to trace the disappearances of Rita and Jack to Israeli interests. Armed with this information, plus the full-name of the Jewish agent, Hannah Wolkowitz – which was the only information they were able to obtain from the Immigration Department's interview with Dr. Stanley Kaufman of Kansas City, Missouri – Naval Intelligence officers, working with Mexican authorities and the U.S. State Department – most likely covert C.I.A. operatives, commenced the laborious task of pursuing leads as to where the missing Rita, Jack, and Hannah may have proceeded from that ramshackle Veracruz neighborhood.

Beginning with the most obvious possibility – the Port of Veracruz, the investigators interviewed port personnel, shipping company and passenger line agents, and ships' officers and crews. The process was complicated by not having a specific destination port for the trio, and, depending on which suspect might be running the show, they could be headed for Europe, the Middle-East, or even South America. Ships leaving the Port of Veracruz, Mexico's busiest Atlantic seaport, were headed for destinations all over the world. The investigators failed to turn up any ship's manifest containing the names of the missing women or the teenage boy; which was not that surprising – for the right amount of cash, a 'tramp' cargo ship's skipper would carry any passengers willing to endure the cramped quarters, the lousy food, the rough seas, the loathsome crew, the protracted journey.

Through their interviews with persons known to hang around the seaport picking up odd jobs as stevedores and baggage-handlers, the investigators obtained several reports of a woman and a teenage boy seeking passage on, or boarding, a cargo ship; but there were no reports of seeing two women traveling with a teenage boy. Out of desperation, the investigators pursued the one woman, one teenage boy sightings; leading them to a jobber who remembered seeing a woman in her thirties escorting a youngish-looking teenage boy onto a 'tramp' cargo ship – a Greek-registered craft named the *Oedipus* – leaving for the Mediterranean. Reviewing the Port Director's log, the investigators learned that the *Oedipus* had identified destinations all along the Mediterranean Sea from Valencia, Spain, on the northern coast, to Haifa, Israel, at the eastern end, to Tunis, Alger, and Tangiers on the southern coast.

CHAPTER 49

AFTER THREE DAYS OF DIFFICULT DRIVING, MAINLY traveling on back-roads, following the map provided in the 'box' of materials, spending nights in seedy motor courts, Hannah arrived at the Rio Grande River, on the dusty outskirts of Laredo, Texas, late on a hot August day. In the front-seat next to her lounged a groggy Rita, her hands tied together resting in her lap. A fully-sedated, fully-bound Muenster lay on the back-seat of the Ford station wagon, covered with a canvas tarpaulin. This had been the same seating arrangement throughout the trip from the Kaufmans' home in Kansas City.

Because it was late in the afternoon, Hannah was faced with the decision of whether to cross the border into Nuevo Laredo, Mexico during the daylight, during the evening rush hour – made up mainly of Mexicans returning home from their jobs in Texas – or to spend the night at another out-of-the-way tourist court in Laredo, crossing the Rio Grande River early the next morning. Her decision was made for her when, as she approached the area of the bridge – the only border crossing for miles along the river – she observed the large number of cars, trucks, buses, and even horse-drawn and donkey-drawn wagons and carts in line, heading into Nuevo Laredo. Surely, with this amount of traffic, any surveillance of the station wagon by the Mexican authorities handling inbound traffic would be cursory at best. Besides, why would they pay any attention to two gringo touristas – one of whom was so tired that she was dozing – proceeding into Mexico at this hour? Certainly, the U.S. border authorities would pay no attention to the Ford station wagon leaving the United States.

Unless, thought Hannah, *the American and Mexican border authorities were warned by American police to be on the lookout for just such a Ford station wagon with 'Missouri' license-plates, carrying two women and a boy, one of whom might be a fugitive. But it has been less than a week since we left Fairways and, even if someone has noticed our absence, it would still be too soon for anyone to conclude that there has been foul-play so as to mount a manhunt, and certainly no one could have concluded – with no incriminating evidence left behind – that Mexico was our destination.*

Having made her decision to proceed into Nuevo Laredo with the evening traffic, but before she joined the line of traffic moving slowly towards the bridge and the crossing point, Hannah reached behind her and removed the tarpaulin covering Jack's sedated body. She then reached across to where Rita was dozing in the passenger side of the front-seat, untied her hands, and poked her finger into Rita's shoulder: "Don't say a word if we are stopped up here by the border guards…You are too tired and sleepy to talk…If you say anything…if you even let on like there is something wrong, I will shoot you and Jack…Do you understand?"

"Hmph," replied Rita, moving her head up and down.

As the station wagon crept along in the line moving evenly towards the international bridge, Hannah rehearsed in her mind what she would say if she were stopped by the authorities. She pulled the passports out of the satchel and tucked them under her buttocks. She also removed the Walther P-38 semiautomatic pistol and slid it in back of her, down into the space between the seat-bottom and the seat-back. In case bribery was available, or necessary, Hannah removed three one-hundred dollar bills from one of the packets of dollar bills, tucking the bills into the front of her blouse. What do they say, one bird with two stones?

The Mexican guard was waving the traffic in front of Hannah through the crossing point without hesitation until the big Ford station wagon with the Missouri license plate on the front-bumper, and the two attractive, unaccompanied women in the front-seat approached him. Giving a broad smile, he motioned for Hannah to bring the station wagon to a complete stop.

"Buenos dias, Senoritas" he said politely, as he scanned the passengers. "Are you traveling into Mexico for business or for pleasure?"

"We are tourists," Hannah responded, looking directly into the guard's eyes…giving him a bright smile. "We are looking for a good place in Nuevo Laredo to sleep for the night. As you can see my companion is quite tired…we have had a long day on the road. We have been driving around south Texas, and thought we might see some sights in your lovely country while we were down this way…But we didn't realize that it was getting so late. Can you recommend a good hotel – but not too expensive – for us to get a good meal and a good night's rest?"

"Welcome to our beautiful Mexico…Of course, I think we can help you find a nice spot to stay for the night. If you will just pull off up at the building over there they can help you with what you are looking for." Then he added, with an even more impressive smile, "If they can't help you lovely senoritas, you just come back and let me know…I've got a great place to recommend…but it may be hard to find…and I'll maybe need to show you the way."

As he started to move away from the station wagon he asked, "But may I inquire about the young hombre in the back-seat? Is he ill?"

"Not really," responded Hannah. "He may be a little car sick…I think all he needs is some time to get out and stretch his legs."

Hearing a horn honk from one of the vehicles in the line building up behind the Ford station wagon, the guard looked back at the line of vehicles, shook his fist, and said to Hannah, "Okay senorita…or is it senora?…you need to proceed on…I am sure that you will find what you need in the way of assistance just over there."

"Thank you…You have been most helpful," Hannah said as she put the big station wagon in gear, and pulled away from the guard. She drove, as instructed, to the building the guard had designated, got out of the station wagon, but did not go into the building. Seeing that the guard had lost interest in them, Hannah got back into the station wagon and drove away; headed for the next safe-house designated on the Mossad map.

That encounter could have gone either way, thought a clearly relieved

Hannah. *What if he had asked for Jack to sit up, to get out of the station wagon and stretch his legs right then and there? Thank God, the vehicles behind us showed their displeasure while our Lothario guard flirted with me.*

Moving back out into the traffic, Hannah calculated that she had at least four more days of hard driving on difficult, unpaved back-roads before she would reach her next destination, her final destination in Mexico – the Mexican port city of Veracruz. While they had been making good time so far, time was a precious commodity; and she could not afford to get delayed by an accident or break-down. Her rendezvous with the next mode of transportation was critical, and was only five days away, not giving her much leeway. Of equal concern was Hannah's realization that as each day passed the risk of becoming a wanted fugitive – and Rita and Jack becoming 'missing persons' – grew exponentially.

Hannah's other concerns were the boy's health and what to do with Rita. She knew that she could not leave the boy – as she now thought of the body in the back-seat – bound hand and foot, and heavily sedated, indefinitely. *At some point I will need to allow him some movement about if I hope to have him mobile enough to be able to walk, to climb steps, to eat on his own, to appear to be a normal young man traveling with his mother, or his guardian.* On the itinerary provided by 'our friends', there were no safe locations at which she could count on being able to accomplish this chore; she would just have to use her best judgment on the place, the time and the circumstances.

As to Rita, Hannah had no desire to take her with the boy to the final destination; but as long as Rita behaved herself – as it appeared she had at the border crossing into Mexico – Hannah would put aside thoughts of Rita's future. *In fact,* thought Hannah, *I will need Rita's assistance at such time as when I release the boy for his exercise.*

THE FIRST OPPORTUNITY for the boy to get some exercise presented itself the morning of the second day after Hannah and her 'wards' had crossed into Mexico. The small hacienda that had been identified on Hannah's itinerary as a place to spend the night turned out to be the perfect location for the boy to get some exercise – it was nestled in the foothills of the nearby mountains, part of the Sierra Madre Oriental chain, and was isolated from the narrow main road, surrounded with a tall stone and stucco wall. The evening before putting him to bed, Hannah did not renew the boy's sedative, but kept him secured, bound hand and foot with stout ropes. Rita was given only a sleeping pill, but her hands were bound together behind her with twine rope.

The boy and Rita were both awake and alert when dawn appeared, the early morning sun shining brightly into the simple bedroom they shared together. Removing the rope bindings from the boy's ankles, and with Rita's hands still bound behind her, Hannah – after assuring herself that it was safe to do so – led them both out into the empty courtyard. She had planned to let the boy – who was at first unsteady on his feet – have an hour's worth of walking about with Rita walking silently at his side. Hannah was always close to them, monitoring the boy's progress, making sure that there was no verbal or physical contact between them. At about thirty-minutes into the exercise the boy was walking more confidently.

Then it happened quite quickly; as if rehearsed and on some non-verbal cue that Hannah did not observe, taking her quite by surprise: the boy and Rita separated, each walking in a different direction, moving away from Hannah. "Run, Jack...Run for it," Rita shouted, as she started to run at Hannah to block Hannah's way when Hannah appeared to be going after the boy who was running as fast as he could toward a slightly opened gate. Before Rita could interfere with Hannah going after the boy, Hannah pulled the P-38 semi-automatic pistol from her skirt pocket and aimed it at Rita, yelling to the boy, "Stop! Take another step and I'll shoot Rita."

When the boy did not stop as ordered, Hannah swung the barrel of the P-38 pistol at Rita, striking her on the side of her head, the blow knocking Rita to the ground. One quick look told Hannah that Rita was down-for-the-count, and she took off running after the Muenster. Although the Muenster – no longer the 'boy' in Hannah's mind – was running as fast as he could, his out-of-shape legs were no match for the athletic Hannah, and was easily overtaken before he could reach the slightly ajar gate. Grabbing the Muenster's still bound hands, Hannah slipped one of her legs between his, tripping him, slamming him onto the ground on his back.

"What are you going to do to me, you fucking Jew bitch? You certainly aren't going to shoot me…kill me. Your ass-hole superiors wouldn't be very happy with you if you turned up empty handed, would they," the Muenster taunted.

"No, Muenster, I'm not going to shoot you…and I'm certainly not going to kill you, you arrogant bastard! But I am going to fix it so that you will never run away from me…or anyone else…again…or get even this far. I'm going to do something now that I should have done back at Fairways when I had the chance…when you revealed your true 'spirit'…you fucking 'monster'."

Pulling a dagger from the sheath strapped to her thigh, hidden beneath her skirt, Hannah leaned over Muenster's face and carefully inserted the point of the dagger into Muenster's good eye, making sure to twist it into the eye, to render him totally blind, and to induce as much pain as possible without damaging his brain.

While the Muenster lay writhing and twisting on the ground – not even able to bring his hands to his face – spewing German obscenities at Hannah's back, Hannah walked back to where Rita lay unconscious, face-down on the ground. Placing a silencer on the muzzle of the P-38 pistol, Hannah took aim and shot Rita in the head, just in front of her left ear.

It all happened so quickly that, despite the outburst from the blinded Muenster, no one else from the hacienda appeared in the courtyard, either during or after fracas. Unhampered, Hannah dragged the angry Muenster to his feet and pulled him back into their bedroom where she injected a sedative, bound his ankle with a rope, slapped a bandage over his newly stabbed eye, and threw him on the floor.

Grabbing a towel from the small bathroom, Hannah returned to the courtyard, wrapped Rita's head with the towel, and dragged her limp, dead body through the gate, placing it on the ground next to the station wagon. Returning to the bedroom, Hannah gathered all the clothing and other personal effects, threw them in the duffle bag, and then dragged the drugged and bound Muenster out to the station wagon, placing him face down in the back seat, throwing a tarpaulin over his limp body. The next item of business was retrieving the duffle bag and the satchel from the bedroom after making sure that the room bore no trace of their having even been in the room, save the missing towel.

After placing Rita's tarpaulin-wrapped body, with its towel-wrapped head, carefully and reverently into the station wagon's cargo area Hannah got behind the steering wheel.

Before leaving the hacienda, the scene of such a tragic morning, Hannah paused and thought, her hands tightly gripping the steering-wheel, her forehead pressed firmly against its rim: *Damn you, Rita. You just couldn't get it into your head...could you, Rita?...that the body was no longer Jack's...it was no longer your boy Jack's body...it is Muenster's body...and the rotten bastard used your love for Jack to deceive you into helping him try to escape...And your refusal to see that deception cost you your life. I never even got to tell you goodbye...or to tell you how much I loved you.*

CHAPTER 50

THE NEXT INFORMATION DEVELOPED BY THE investigators was helpful to the investigation, but it was devastating and heart-wrenching information for Ollie, Paul and Nell. The investigators had been provided an explanation for the one woman/one teenage boy scenario, but with that explanation they were now pursuing a murder/kidnapping investigation.

"Paul," began Ollie somberly, "I've got some rather troubling information...The Mexican police have discovered a body...a woman's body...It might be Rita's."

"Oh, my God! Where did they find it?"

"I don't know all of the details...But somewhere between Mexico City and Veracruz...buried in a remote area, in a shallow grave. One of us may have to go to Mexico City to identify the body, the remains...It's pretty gruesome they tell me...Wild animals had at the body. It may require using dental records to make a positive identification."

"I'll make the trip if it is necessary...Do the police have any idea who did it?"

"They haven't indicated that they have any leads...I think we both know two people who might have done it...but I'm not sure which one of them did it.

"If it turns out to be Rita's body," Ollie continued, "then we have a whole new ball-game...the authorities are no longer looking for some 'missing persons', they will be looking for someone who has committed murder, as well as kidnapping. This will give every police department, in every port where the *Oedipus* drops anchor, or ties up to a

A QUESTION OF POSSESSION | 521

dock, a reason to board her, searching her from bow to fantail. Let's just pray that the *Oedipus* has not already discharged its cargo…and that its cargo is more than just one person."

"If what I am thinking is now the case," opined Paul, "then Jack will be on that ship when it makes port…whether there are two people or just one. Hannah wants to turn Jack over to the Israelis…so she won't kill him en route. But if Dietrich Muenster has taken control of Jack, there is no longer any reason for him to need Hannah once they are at sea, and he can kill Hannah…dumping her body in the ocean, paying the skipper some more bribe money…then he leaves the ship as an innocent looking American teenager at any port along the way. Do you agree?"

"Yes," Ollie said, "I agree…But if you are correct, then what's gained if we are able to rescue Jack? He is either fingered as a murderer if he is alone, or he will forever be a prisoner either of the Israelis or, if we are able to get him back, held as an inmate in an American insane asylum. I know this is hard for you to accept, Paul…but Jack is a permanently damaged, dangerous boy."

While Paul was contemplating the import of what Ollie had just said about Jack, Ollie added, "What we have been talking about is this…what happens if only two people, or even one person alone is on the *Oedipus*? And aren't we faced with a similar dilemma if three people are on that ship? As long as Jack is possessed by the 'spirit', capable of being controlled by the 'spirit', he is a danger, unless, of course, the 'spirit' has given up his 'evil' ways, repents and asks for forgiveness… but are you willing to take the risk that such an 'evil spirit' will mend his ways? Well, I'm certainly not."

"So what are you suggesting we do?"

"I'm suggesting," Ollie said coldly, "that if the body they found is that of Rita, then we bury Rita, and mourn the loss of a wonderful, loving woman…and then we step out of the way, letting God, nature, and the authorities deal with Jack."

"But that's so cruel, so merciless," Paul complained.

"I certainly agree…But life is cruel, it is merciless…Just think about Rita. Isn't she just as innocent as Jack? Why did she have to die in such a cruel, dreadful way…and for what purpose…just so an 'evil spirit' might not escape justice…or maybe to prevent the 'evil spirit' from causing more evil? Obviously, God has a plan…a great big eternal plan…and we just need to trust Him…that He knows what He is doing."

CHAPTER 51

THE GREEK-REGISTERED CARGO SHIP, OEDIPUS

deposited its cargo at the Port of Haifa, Israel without interference or challenge. A later investigation of the custom agents on duty the day the *Oedipus* made port, denied any wrong-doing, even though there were witnesses who observed a woman escorting a blind teenage boy through customs on that very day: a woman and a teenage boy fitting the general description of the wanted fugitives. When confronted with this eye-witness testimony, the custom agent on duty defended his conduct - allowing the woman and boy entry into Israel - on the basis that the woman was carrying an Israeli Diplomatic passport, which guaranteed unencumbered passage into Israel for her and the boy. Despite all efforts to locate and apprehend the woman and the teenage boy, they were never found, simply disappearing into the ever-growing populace – fed by the Jewish refugees flooding Israel daily.

When Ollie passed on the information that Hannah and the now-blind Jack had made it into Israel without a challenge, slipping in through the chaos of new nation creation, simply disappearing, Paul philosophically observed, "This truly must be God' plan."

PAUL AND NELL, who had now lost Jack twice - or was it three times – agreed that they would never again mention Jack's name, although both vowed that they would continue to pray for him; asking God to give him the strength and courage to carry out what was clearly – at least to them – God's plan.

Both Paul and Nell attended Rita's memorial service at St. Bernard's Church in Greenville. Nell would have preferred a Mass, but because Rita's decomposed body was cremated the Church would not authorize a Mass when only ashes in an urn were available. After the service they accompanied Ollie and the urn to Rita's beloved Fairways, where the urn was buried in a small grove of red cedar trees containing an ancient, but unrelated family's, cemetery.   At the internment, Ollie gave a brief eulogy, praising Rita for her love for life, her love for Fairways, her love for Jack, her love for Lady – who lay quietly at Ollie's feet, feeling quite at home in the small grove where she had treed many a squirrel.

Dennis and Milly Lewis stood in the back of the large gathering silently watching the ceremony; at the end they started to walk away, but Paul intercepted them, asking them to stay for a moment, to allow Nell to meet them, to thank them for all they had done for Jack, to express condolences for the loss of their Billy, and to accept condolences for Jack's disappearance, and for the loss of Rita. Despite her best efforts to show grace and compassion towards the Lewises, Nell couldn't help but recall from Jack's writings that Milly Lewis was *the drunken slut who filled Jack with lustful thoughts, caused him to break the Sixth Commandment.* Nell's response to the Lewises' overtures was cool, perfunctory, and puzzling; causing Paul to be more effusive than usual, only increasing the awkwardness of the encounter.

IN MARCH, 1954, an envelope – with an Israeli stamp and postmark – was stuffed in the mail box next to the front door, along with the other mail. Paul did not discover the envelope until he had hung up his hat and overcoat on the hall clothes tree, and was walking back towards the kitchen, thumbing through the mail as was his custom. It took him a moment to comprehend what he was holding in his hand. He knew in his heart that it was a letter from Jack, even though the typed envelope lacked a return address. It took Paul everything in his power to resist the urge to open the envelope, even though it was addressed to him alone.

Turning on the kitchen light, Paul began the ritual of preparing dinner for Nell and him. It would be a simple meal; heating up left-over meat, mashed potatoes, some vegetable. The unopened envelope, hopefully containing a letter from Jack, lay propped up on Nell's dinner plate, waiting for her arrival from work. Coming into the kitchen through the back door, Nell immediately noticed the envelope on her plate; a clear break from their usual dinner routine. As Nell removed her gloves, overcoat and hat, she could not take her eyes off of the envelope, sensing, as Paul had, that it contained a letter from Jack. Unlike Paul, who was looking forward to a letter from Jack, Nell was filled with apprehension. *If it contains a letter from Jack, will it mention the writings... Will Jack say unflattering things about me? What can I tell Paul so that I can read any letter first, in private?*

"Well, Nell" Paul began, "aren't you going to open the envelope?"

"Why should I? It's addressed just to you."

"That's probably just a mistake... We don't know why we're getting this letter."

"Well, that may be. But still, shouldn't we wait until we've eaten... So we can read it without being so rushed?"

"We're only having leftovers... Who cares about when we get around to eating? Hopefully there's a letter from Jack to read."

Not wishing to push the issue, not wanting to appear too anxious about the contents of the envelope, Nell sat down, picked up the envelope and slit it open with her butter knife.

The envelope indeed contained a letter; there were several pages of very thin paper with lines of cramped typing on both sides, which Nell quickly shuffled through to see who signed the letter, as there was no indication on the first page as to who the letter was from. Nell's pulse quickened when she saw a scrawled, handwritten name which appears to be 'Jack'. With Paul standing behind her, where he could read over her shoulder, Nell turned back to the first page, took a deep breath, and began reading:

January, 1954

Dear Dad,

I hope you are well. I am sorry that I havent written you sooner. Im not allowed to write any letters. And it has been hard to find someone who knows enough English and can type a letter for me. I am blind. I need help to do almost everything. The person typing this letter says that because she feels sorry for me she will write the letter and smuggle it out of here and mail it to you. Yours is the only address I can remember.

I dont really know where I am, just somewhere in Israel. It is so sandy and rocky here. Most of the days are really hot. But it gets so cold at night. I only have short pants to wear. At night I have to wrap my legs in a blanket if I am outside. I am never alone. Someone is always here watching me.

I often hear gunshots and explosions, usually at night when I am trying to sleep. Sometimes I am grabbed and put in a small, smelly room filled with women and small children. I hear the men shouting. Sometimes I hear them scream in pain. It is scary.
The other people here mostly speak Hebrew, so I dont always know what they are saying, although I am beginning to learn some Hebrew.

The food is strange, and there is never enough meat for me to eat.

If you are wondering how I got here, I think it is because Hannah brought me here after she says she lost Mom somewhere in Mexico. I dont see Hannah often, and when I think she is here, she does not speak English, only speaking what I now know is Hebrew. I hope someone found Mom in Mexico and is she all right.

I guess you want to know what we were doing when Mom got lost in Mexico. One night Mom and Hannah had a big fight about the spirit taking control of me, with Hannah wanting to do something to me that Mom did not like. I dont know what

Hannah was worried about. The spirit told me he wasnt evil anymore. The next thing I remember was getting ready for bed at Fairways, and then waking up in the back of the station wagon. I couldnt see out of one eye. My eye was bandaged. Then one day I woke up and I couldnt see out of either eye.

When I called out for Mom, Hannah said she wasnt here. She said Mom got lost in Mexico and Hannah said she couldnt find her. When I told Hannah that we needed to keep looking for Mom, Hannah just kept giving me some awful tasting stuff to drink. She said it was for my eyes which really hurt a lot, but all the stuff she gave me did was make me sleepy. At some point on our trip Hannah put me in the front seat with her. I was glad to get out of the back seat. Something behind me was beginning to stink really bad.

The next thing I remember was Hannah helping me walk up some steps somewhere where it stank of dead fish, kinda like how it smelled in the car. Hannah put me in some smelly, noisy room and gave me more of the awful tasting stuff to drink. A couple of times I remember getting sick to my stomach and throwing up as the floor kept rocking.

Hannah stopped giving me the awful tasting stuff and let me walk around the stinking room and sometimes outside. I soon figured it out that I was on a boat and it was moving. I got fed the same terrible food everyday for weeks. But I stopped throwing up. Thank God.

When the boat stopped moving Hannah took me off of the boat. I could hear lots of people talking, shouting, and hollering. But I couldnt understand anything they said. They were all talking in languages I had never heard before.

After weeks of moving from one place to another every day, Hannah left me with some people who asked me a lot of questions in different languages about the spirit. The questions made no sense to me and I couldnt answer them. They

even asked me if I would have the spirit talk to them.   But I dont think he
ever did.   I have not heard from Hannah
for a while.

Then I was brought here.   I dont know
how long I am going to have to stay
here.   It is very lonely and strange,
even with all the people around me.
The only person I can talk to, other
than the person typing the letter, is
the spirit.   He and I have become kind
of friendly, but not like I was with
Fritz, now that we found out that he
is the bad spirit.   He has asked me to
call him Dietrich.   Sometimes some men
and women come here and ask Dietrich to
speak to them, but he never does, even
when they say things to him in I guess
it is German.

Several weeks ago, Dietrich told me to
tell the people who are in charge of
me that I was Catholic and I wanted
a priest to come to hear my confession.   But it was really Dietrich who
wanted the priest to hear his. When the
priest came to see me, I let Dietrich
take control of my body for a while.   I
guess he made his confession while he
was in control.   Afterwards, when he
unplugged, he thanked me.   And he told
me he was now at peace.   I wonder what
he told the priest.
I hate not being able to see.   If you
get to see Billy, tell him I miss him.
Also tell him that I have Jap-eyes, and
it is worse than Dennis said it was.

I would love to hear from you.   But they
wont tell me where I am.   So I cant give
you an address to send me any letters.
Ill try to write to you again if I can
get someone to help me.
Please pray for me.   Im praying for
you.
If you talk to my Mom, please tell her
that I love her, and that I miss her
and Lady so much.   Also tell Nell that
I love her, and I forgive her.

Love, JACK

After they both had finished reading the letter, Nell refolded it, put it back in its envelope, and handed it to Paul saying, "Please get this letter out of my sight...And if you ever get another letter from Jack, I don't want to read it, I don't want to even know that you got it, or what it says."

Paul took the envelope from Nell, walked out of the kitchen, put on his hat and coat, and left the house. At his office, at his desk, in just the light from a desk lamp, Paul reread the letter over and over; crying until there were no more tears. He did not go home that night; he could not face being in the house with Nell, and all of the bad memories; so he slept on the sofa in his office.

The next day, Paul had a photocopy made of the letter, and attached it to a letter he sent to Captain Oliver Joseph Douglas, USNR, asking Ollie to see if his contacts might be able to find Jack somewhere in Israel. He also suggested that since Hannah was the murderer, Jack's name should be removed from the bulletin asking for apprehension of Hannah and Jack as suspects in a murder/kidnapping. At some point later, Paul's letter to Ollie resulted in high-level talks between U.S and Israeli intelligence services, and a call from Ollie to Paul thanking him for sending him Jack's letter.

"Paul," Ollie began cautiously, "the Israelis diplomats know where Jack is being held, but Mossad refuses to disclose the location of the Kibbutz, though, given Jack's description of the night-time attacks, it is probably in some area that is being disputed by the Palestinians, the neighboring Arab countries, and Israel. Mossad also refuses to do anything about Hannah...even going so far as to claim she doesn't exist. I suggest that we will just have to wait this thing out...until we get something Mossad wants from us...and is willing to bargain for.

"Oh, and even though our guys were very careful not to reveal the source of our information, I wouldn't expect to get any more letters from Jack...The Mossad will have the security people at the Kibbutz watching Jack like a hawk. Jack is still considered a very special guest...needing very special treatment. Mossad has been convinced... probably by Hanna and her superiors...that Jack's 'spirit' is in fact the infamous *S.S. Oberst* Dietrich Muenster who was responsible for the deaths of so many Jews…as well as folks like the von Bruckners who tried to help Jews…They will take all steps necessary to keep Muenster right where he is…even if it means that we'll probably never see, or hear from, Jack again.

CHAPTER 52

FOR THE NEXT SEVERAL YEARS, PAUL - WHO would rather had been living in an apartment on his own, but stayed put in the house with Nell in the hopes of receiving another letter from Jack, despite what Ollie had said – received no further letters, and he heard nothing further from Ollie – except a note saying that he was retiring from the Navy and was moving to Fairways.

THEN, IN OCTOBER, 1958, Paul received a telephone call at his office from a man who identified himself as being a member of the U.S. State Department staff in Washington, D.C.

"Is this Mr. Paul Johanson," the staff person asked.

"Yes," Paul responded, his stomach rising in his throat.

"Are you the father of Jack Johanson, also known as Jack Kaufman?"

"Yes, I am."

"Mr. Johanson, I have been instructed by the Department of the Navy to inform you…in the absence of Captain Oliver Douglas, who has retired from the service…that we have received a cable from our Embassy in Tel Aviv, Israel, which states that Jack Johanson, residing in Israel, using an Israeli passport issued to a Jack Kaufman, has been killed…an apparent victim of a terrorist attack at the Kibbutz in Israel where Jack resided. You have our sincere condolences."

"Thank you," Paul said, tears filling his eyes.

"There may be some delay," the staff person continued, "in when Jack Johanson's body will be transported to the United States. First, Israeli security has demanded an autopsy of your son's body...which is a most irregular demand given the reported circumstances of your son's death. And second, your son was living in Israel on an Israeli passport with a different name – his adopted name I believe. The United States has no record of ever issuing Jack Johanson, or a Jack Kaufman, a passport. Once we receive verification that the information on the Israeli passport, stating that Jack was born in Saint Louis, Missouri, is correct, that technicality will be cured. Hopefully none of this will take too long. We will inform you when Jack Johanson's body will be transported to the United States for internment...so that you may make the necessary funeral arrangements."

"Again, thank you."

Hanging up the telephone Paul said softly to himself, the long-awaited tears now flowing down his cheeks, *God bless your soul, Jack Johanson. You are free at last. And thank God that I won't ever have to face losing you again.*

LATER THAT SAME day, in the glare of the front-porch light, Paul delivered the news of Jack's death in person to a tearless Nell while he stood nervously fingering the brim of the hat he held in his hand. Making no effort to enter the house – his house – Paul concluded his visit by telling Nell that he was leaving her, and that he would return later to gather his things.

As Paul turned to leave, placing the hat on his head, Nell said from the doorway where she had been standing, stoically receiving Paul's message, "Wait, I have something for you." Nell returned a few moments later carrying a brown book bag which she thrust into Paul's waiting hands, saying, "Here, I don't need these any longer...They're yours now...Take them with you."

Nell turned away, and without so much as a goodbye, closed the front door behind her, turned off the porch-light, leaving Paul standing in the gathering darkness with the book bag filled with what Paul immediately sensed were Jack's writings, what Nell had been withholding from him for all those years, clutched lovingly in his arms.

AFTER TWO YEARS of fruitless waiting, frequently prodding an unresponsive State Department, Paul abandoned any hope of ever receiving the promised body of his dead son, Jack, for a proper burial. *I don't even know if Jack is actually dead.* Periodically, Paul would re-read the three-dozen Big Chief tablets and the solitary letter that Jack had sent from the Israeli Kibbutz, determined to unearth something new, something helpful in these extraordinary, disturbing writings, anything that would provide some clue, provide some finality; but each time he came up empty-handed, left still wondering, still hoping. *Maybe I'll take a trip to Israel, locate the Kibbutz, track down Hannah, search for answers, maybe even find Jack; for all I know he may still be alive, waiting for me. Too bad I don't have Rita here to help me.*

ACKNOWLEDGEMENTS

TO ALL OF THOSE DEAR FRIENDS AND RELATIVES who assisted in the launch of this maiden novel-writing effort, and without whose help and encouragement, this product would have never made it out of the proverbial 'shipyard'. I am especially indebted to my daughter-in-law, Kersten Fons, whose generous efforts of plowing-through early drafts and librarian's-eye kept me at the task; my daughter Laura Granberry, who, with her sense of style and passion for clean design, is responsible for the awesome, clever presentation; my good-friend Betty Harrison, who, with her keen-eye for writing style and 'good-old-fashion' sense for punctuation and grammar, has raised the product to the level of readability; my tennis-buddy Bob Peters – an honest-to-God hero and denizen of the German Stalags, who helped me with his encouragement and eye for detail, earning him a place in the book as the American P-38 pilot, Colonel Pete Roberts; my friend and fellow avid reader, Jake Kraft, who shared his wisdom and Naval experience in reviewing the book's earliest efforts and providing kind, gentle suggestions; and my brother-in-law, Joe Reis, another avid reader, who likewise provided insightful suggestions.

BUT ABOVE ALL, I want to thank my loving wife, Kay, without whose patience, insight, encouragement, prayer and support, this book would have foundered on the shoals of indifference and despair. She has been a staunch supporter of my making the effort and taking the risk, never in doubt about how it would turn out.

SOURCES

Davidson, Eugene. *The Trial of the Germans.* New York: The Macmillan Company, 1966.

Eisenhower, Dwight D. *Crusade in Europe.* Garden City, N.Y.: Doubleday & Company, 1948.

Felty, Warren. *Life in Stalag Luft.* Northstar Gallery.

Foreman, John and Harvey, S. E. *The Messerschmitt Me262 Combat Diary.* Surrey, England: Air Research Publications, 1990.

Galland, Adolf. *The First and Last.* New York: Henry Holt and Company, Inc., 1954.

Phillips, Richard E. *Constructing Wire Fences.* Columbia, Mo.: University of Missouri Extension, 1993.

Shirer, William L. *The Rise and Fall of the Third Reich.* New York: Simon and Schuster, 1960.

Smith, J. Richard and Creek, Eddie J. *Me262, Volume Two.* Burgess Hill, England: Classic Publications, 1998.

Speer, Albert. *Inside the Third Reich.* New York: The Macmillan Company, 1970.